The Judas Codex

The Judas Codex

James Stevens

ATHENA PRESS
LONDON

THE JUDAS CODEX
Copyright © James Stevens 2008

ISBN 978 1 84748 324 9

First published 2008
ATHENA PRESS
Queen's House, 2 Holly Road
Twickenham TW1 4EG
United Kingdom

Printed for Athena Press

*This book is dedicated to the memory of my late brother.
Sorry it took so long, Rob, but wherever you are,
I hope you found it worth the wait.*

Acknowledgements

A vote of thanks goes out to Eleri King and Eirwyn Williams for their helpful comments in the formative stages of the manuscript, as well as to Gareth who kindly offered the use of his garage to hide in, should I suddenly become the Salman Rushdie of the Christian world! A special thank you, however, is extended to my two main proofreaders, Lawrence Jones and Geoff Rix. Not only did they spot myriads of stupid mistakes, but their constant patience and encouragement kept me going when I began to doubt my own ability. The final thank you is extended to my son Ashley, who it must be said spent ages sorting out the tangled mess I'd made of the manuscript due to my computer illiteracy.

My sincere thanks goes also to Athena Press, whose patient scrutiny and professionalism helped turn what was, at best, a raw manuscript into something readable.

Preface

This novel took embryonic form in the early seventies after I came across quite by accident, an incredible book called *The Passover Plot* by Hugh Schonfield. At the time I was the Head of Religious Studies in a local grammar school, and its contents completely transformed my way of thinking about the life of Jesus. Unfortunately, due to my teaching commitments, I was unable to do much more than outline my ideas until I retired several years ago.

Recently, there have been many other books calling into question the veracity of the traditional way of looking at the Jesus portrayed in the Gospels, not least the equally impressive *The Holy Blood and The Holy Grail*.

From the outset, I must make it clear that the central theory of the novel is not original. However, what I hope is original is the way in which I have interpreted the findings of years of research, involving countless textbooks, magazine articles, the Internet and the like, in order to produce what is essentially a work of pure fiction. That said, I would hope the more thoughtful reader, on completing it, might pose the question: but what if?

For the more discerning the clues are all there. The examples used are either taken from the Gospels, or the most recent archaeological discoveries. On that basis, the facts are indisputable; they are there for all to see. However, it is what we do with the information that is the issue.

Those of you who live in small country villages will soon realise that Raven's Hill is real, but with the name altered in order to protect its identity.

Strangely, many of the more bizarre snippets of information the book contains are true. For example, it is recorded fact that the Roman abbot, Dionysius Exegius, did make a mistake with our calendar, and consequently Jesus' birth is seven years out.

Finally, the theory about the Sicarii surviving the destruction of the temple in AD 70 and their resultant escape from Masada is my own, along with the wild ideas regarding Joseph. Both are simply flights of fancy on my part and so cannot be blamed on anyone else.

Abraham Lincoln once famously wrote:

You can fool all of the people some of the time and some of the people all of the time, but you can't fool all of the people all of the time.

I respectfully suggest that the central tenet of this novel might put his philosophy to the ultimate test!

Innocence is a state of mind. The more you become convinced of the validity of your action, the less likely you are to feel guilty about the subsequent outcome.

The Author

Prologue

STAGGERING UNDER THE WEIGHT OF HIS BURDEN, THE OLD MAN trudged wearily along the narrow path that wound its way through the forest. Desperately tired and hungry, each additional step only seemed to reinforce his belief that he was becoming hopelessly lost. Threading his way carefully through the tangled undergrowth, he'd long since ceased to admire the beauty of his surroundings. Instead, his focus was now centred on nothing but survival.

At every turn, dense foliage of a type he didn't recognise seemed to reach out in a determined effort to devour unprotected skin. On several occasions he was forced to clamber over giant boulders covered in slimy green moss, while tendrils of deep fluffy mist drifting through the trees gave the forest an eerie haunting atmosphere.

The going was made more difficult by the lack of natural light. Only the odd weak ray, filtering down like a beam from a failing torch, managed to pierce the gloom.

For the last mile a deep chill had settled into his old bones. Starting in his toes, it had spread like icy tentacles through every fibre of his being. Looking around nervously, he saw danger lurking everywhere. By now a feeling of supernatural dread had descended on him, the sense of unease almost overpowering. Almost tangible on occasions, it seemed to hang in the air like a cloak of dark brooding menace. Berating himself for what he regarded as irrational fear, he tried to shrug off the feeling of unease.

Suddenly, in a rare moment of lucidity, he realised it was nothing short of a miracle he'd survived when everyone else had perished. The details were still hazy, glimpses of buried memories returning from time to time in vivid flashes. He remembered the violent storm, the sudden bolt of lightning, the splitting of the mainsail, but then nothing. His last memory was of being tossed about by giant waves whipped into a savage frenzy by hurricane force winds.

Unbidden, a thought suddenly struck him. How long had he been travelling?

One day?

Two days?

Surely no more than that, he reasoned, for if that were the case he would never have managed to get this far.

Fingering the deep six-inch wound that ran down the left side of his face, it didn't take him long to work out that it was the probable cause of his disorientation. With that, he became increasingly frustrated at the black hole in his memory. All he really knew was that somehow, guided by some primeval instinct, he'd followed the course of the river, until for the last mile or so he'd been forced inland.

Bone weary and nearing the point of exhaustion, he realised he needed to rest. The decision made, he lowered the bag from his shoulder and placed it gently against a small stone at the edge of the path. Stretching one way and then the other, he was easing the pressure on his aching back when it happened. Without warning, a bolt of white-hot lightning shot through his brain. The pain was beyond belief, greater than anything he'd ever experienced. Dropping to his knees, he lay there for several minutes, whimpering like an animal.

Gradually, as his mind cleared, the pain began to ease, until miraculously, amid a confused kaleidoscope of flashing colours, his memory returned. Little by little, like pieces in a jigsaw the picture became clearer, until with one final blinding burst of clarity he remembered.

Dear God, he now knew who he was! He was a wealthy man, a person of substance, who as a dealer in precious metals often travelled the tin route from his beloved Holy Land to Cornwall. Putting two and two together, he knew the storm must have driven the ship wildly off course, before dumping him unceremoniously onto a remote shingle cove.

With that the enormity of what he was attempting hit him. It threatened to drown him in a wave of conflicting emotions, the greatest of which was fear. Turning things over in his mind, he remembered how it had all started: a well-intentioned act that had spun wildly out of control, and then before he knew it, it was too late; he'd unwittingly opened Pandora's box. Unleashed, the evil had spread like ripples in a pond, reaching out to contaminate everything it touched.

The decision for the chalice to be taken overseas was unanimous. The hope was that eventually a hiding place would be found, one so safe that the foul object would disappear for ever. Looking at the bag in horror, he knew now why he'd hung onto it so tenaciously.

On its own the package wasn't heavy; what made up most of the weight was the codex. Intended as a warning for anyone who found it, it outlined in detail the dangers of its contents. Unknown to the others, he'd made a last minute decision to include the details of Project Lazarus, something he reasoned that must remain secret at all costs.

Thinking about the responsibility of his sacred duty weighed heavily on his shoulders and it took a huge effort of will to force himself to his feet. For mile after mile he endured pain and hardship, his footsteps making no sound on the wet springy carpet of rotting vegetation. Suddenly when he thought he could go no further, he emerged into a small clearing. Eerily quiet, it had never struck him before that since he'd entered the forest he'd never heard a sound, not one; nor had he seen a single bird or animal, when reason dictated there should have been myriads. His imagination at fever pitch, he began to wonder if the chalice had been damaged, that little by little the evil had started to seep out.

Suddenly the courage he'd shown for the last few days deserted him.

Without a thought for personal safety he broke into a run. Hurling himself forward at breakneck speed, his only concern was to escape a forest, which by now he was convinced was haunted. Such was his panic, it was fifty yards or so before he came to an unscheduled stop. Tumbling head first through a wall of what had at first appeared to be impenetrable undergrowth, he found himself lying in an undignified heap. Shaken but amazingly unhurt, covered in blood from countless small scratches, he lay there trying to work out where he was.

Eventually he scrambled unsteadily to his feet, and on taking in his surroundings was astonished to see he was in some kind of narrow tunnel. Created naturally by gigantic ferns that folded in on themselves, it appeared to stretch far into the distance.

Looking around in amazement, the old man became excited, reasoning that as it was dark, the path might be invisible to anyone from the outside. After all he'd only found it by accident, hadn't he?

He'd gone no further than a hundred yards or so when the tunnel ended abruptly, its dark narrow confines giving way to an astonishing sight. Towering above him on either side were walls of granite and limestone that seemed to rise to a height of some eighty or ninety feet, the only vegetation small bushes that hung precariously over the void. Running between the walls of sheer rock was a small stream. Craning his neck in order to get a better look, he saw how it wound its way steeply upwards until eventually it disappeared into the mist at the top of the valley. Seeing it reminded him of just how thirsty he was, and so he knelt and cupped his hands in the crystal clear water before slaking his thirst greedily. After bathing his wounds he felt better, and on the spur of the moment made the decision to try and find the source of the stream. Despite the difficulty of the climb, one thought kept him going: perhaps he'd at last found a hiding place for the chalice.

Some ten minutes later he heard the sound of roaring water, and within a few more yards he stumbled across a majestic sight, a waterfall that seemed to literally tumble out of the sky. Looking closely, he saw how the falls seemed to cascade in a torrent from the midst of two steep granite banks. Tearing down the mountain, the cataract narrowed into a chute before crashing over several large boulders in its haste to reach the bottom.

Spellbound, he looked at it for several minutes before deciding to make his way back.

About to turn away, something caught his eye. A narrow beam of light appeared to shine directly onto the waterfall, suggesting that something lay behind it. Being careful not to slip on the wet stones, he scrambled up the steep base. Once there, he saw that his first impression had been correct. Hiding behind the cascading flow was a small cave. As a man of faith, he immediately interpreted the discovery as a miracle. In his mind the beam of light was a sign from God, a sign of approval for his sacred task. Being careful not to look down, and with the spray almost blinding him, he made his way tentatively behind the curtain of water.

Once the narrow opening had been safely negotiated, he found he'd been mistaken. What he'd taken to be a small cave was in fact the first in a network that seemed to burrow into the very heart of the mountain. Pressing forward with increasing excitement, he gazed in wonder at the maze of passageways with their long, curving galleries that lay either side of him. In several places narrow openings gave way to huge chambers, whose ceilings were wreathed in deep, dark shadows. As the old man made his way deeper and deeper into the damp gloomy labyrinth, often by touch alone, the silence was broken by the incessant echoes of dripping water, which at times was unnerving.

Without warning he was brought to a sudden halt.

Before him was a natural barrier, the like of which he'd never seen. As a boy he'd explored caves in his native Holy Land, but they'd been nothing like this. With reverential awe, he gazed in incomprehension at the huge subterranean lake that seemed to stretch into infinity. But that was not all; stalagmites of all shapes and sizes, some as big as houses, pointed upwards like accusing fingers, while stalactites of every hue looked down at him in lofty distain. The scale of what he was seeing left him breathless. So vast was the cavern it lent the scene a cathedral-like atmosphere.

It was several minutes before he could tear his eyes away from the beauty of his surroundings. Forcing his mind back to the present, it was some time before he found what he was looking for; a small ledge formed over the millennia by natural erosion seemed to provide the perfect hiding place. Placing his precious package onto the shelf above his head, he decided to rest for a while. His intention was to recover his strength before making his way back to civilisation, although he realised in his present state it might be beyond him. Not that it really mattered, he reminded himself; the secret would remain safe here.

With a heavy heart, he remembered how it had taken the life of his dearest friend to imprison the evil. How ironic, he told himself, that he'd saved his life once, only to see him forfeit it willingly decades later... The memory of his last words still haunted him, were still fresh in his mind, as the fatal heart attack struck.

A momentary crushing pain in his chest was all he felt, but for the old man it was immaterial. He'd achieved what he'd set out to do, he'd found the perfect hiding place. No one would ever find the poisoned chalice here, it was safe for all eternity... and he was almost right!

Chapter One

Central Paris, 6 March 1967

As gently as falling butterflies, the two men dropped soundlessly from their hiding place onto the balcony beneath. Dressed in matching roll-neck sweaters, black tracksuit bottoms and sneakers, their outlines were almost invisible against the inky blackness of the Paris skyline.

Using hand signals as a means of communication, the leader stepped aside as his colleague opened the French doors to the bedroom with a skeleton key. With a barely audible click, they slid open on well-oiled runners. Within seconds the men were inside.

Closing the heavy drape curtains, a precaution against any escaping light, one man switched on the small bedroom lamp, while the other was alert for any sign of danger.

Hearing nothing, they stepped cautiously into the corridor and headed quickly for the lift.

Having studied the blueprints provided by the Grand Master, they were familiar with the layout of the building. Inside information indicated they would be up against four armed guards and the information proved to be correct. Two were hidden at the end of the corridor, one on each corner, while the other two protected the entrance to the lift.

In order for the operation to have any chance of success, David Naami, the leader of the two assassins, realised that all four guards would have to be taken out simultaneously, a task considered by the owners of the house impossible. To them their home was impregnable, their safety precautions foolproof, and to all intents and purposes they were right. Unfortunately they'd reckoned without the genius of David Naami. At twenty years of age, his skill and cunning were already legendary within the Brotherhood. Such was his arrogance that a word like 'impossible' simply didn't feature in his vocabulary.

After several last minute adjustments, the assassins removed the razor sharp sicas from the protective leather pouches at the base of their necks, before inching forward silently.

Knowing the attack had to be timed to perfection, the margin for error nil, they turned the corner cautiously. Suddenly, in a blur of motion they exploded into action. With perfect coordination each covered the guards' mouths with one hand, while with the other they slashed their throats with practised ease. David Naami killed his target with his left, while the other man, code-named Hawk, standing on the other side of the corridor, took his out with his right.

At almost exactly the same moment as the first two guards were sliding soundlessly to the floor, bright red blood spouting from severed arteries, the other sicas were launched. At such a distance neither man could miss. There was precisely ten feet between the end of the corridor to the guards stationed either side of the lift. So swift was the twin strike they barely had time to register their surprise before they toppled forwards, a knife protruding from each of their throats.

The whole affair had taken less than ten seconds from start to finish, but knowing they had no time for self-congratulation, the men pushed on.

Punching in the correct four-figure code, they caused the lift doors to sigh open. Stepping inside and closing the metal gates behind them, it took the occupants only moments to reach the ground floor.

Although they expected no further resistance, they were too professional to take such a thing at face value. Stepping from the lift first, David Naami swivelled right and left, before indicating the coast was clear.

The room they were heading for was situated on the far right, the last one at the end of a long dark corridor. They were within a few feet of their objective, when they saw the door was already open several inches. The sound of muted conversation was clearly audible.

'Are you sure the evidence in these manuscripts will provide us with incontrovertible proof?' asked one.

'Oh, yes,' came the smug reply. 'I assure you everything you need is here. That's why the asking price is so high. The information these documents contain is so explosive they will make you a fortune. Believe me, gentlemen, you could recoup your original outlay in days. Used correctly, the secrets they contain would enable you to quadruple your initial investment in a very short time.'

With a sly smile he added, 'Knowing your legendary persuasive powers, the world would be your oyster. However, before we go any further I'd like to see the money, if you don't mind.'

About to make their move, the assassins suddenly froze as the shrill peal of a telephone cut through the hub of conversation like a klaxon. Within seconds it was followed by the sound of running footsteps, a clear indication that something had gone badly wrong.

Looking at each other in consternation, they decided to throw caution to the wind, and making an instant decision they burst into the room. Caught in the act of gathering papers into a brown leather briefcase, the three elderly men looked up in astonishment, unsure of what to do. The slight hesitation was all the assassins needed; within seconds the targets were rendered unconscious. Although they would be out for hours, nothing was taken for granted. Using the rope that hung from the thick curtains of the luxurious living room, they bound and gagged them.

It was then it struck David Naami that the fourth man was missing. Looking around the room frantically, David remembered that his instructions stated clearly there would be a fourth person; but not only that, the precious files would be in his possession. Strangely, the money was regarded as unimportant. The whole object of the exercise was to recover the documents, and then…

Holding his hand up for silence, he was sure he'd heard a noise.

Yes, there it was again, so he hadn't imagined it.

Suddenly everything fell into place – the phone call had been a warning.

But it didn't make any sense, only the Grand Master and the inner cadre had known about the raid. It was then alarm bells started ringing in his head. Acting on instinct, he headed for the only other door in the room, the one leading to the lounge. Knowing it would be locked, he wasted no time. Pirouetting on one leg, he delivered a devastating kick with the other. Against such brute force the lock offered little resistance and it flew open on shattered hinges.

Stepping into the room, David saw he was almost too late. The missing man, his back to him, was busy throwing documents onto a blazing log fire.

Knowing his orders were that initially everyone had to be taken alive, that later their deaths would be made to look like suicides, David reversed the sica in his fingers and in one deft motion hurled it with all the strength he could muster. Fractions of a second later, the bone handle of the knife struck the man in the back of the head and he dropped like a stone. Like the others, he too would be out for some time.

That part of his task complete, David rushed towards the fire. To his dismay he saw that some of the manuscripts were already beyond redemption, while others were burning fiercely. Taking hold of as many as he could, he dragged them free. Stamping down hard, he attempted to douse the flames with his feet, and seconds later, realising he was fighting a losing battle, he shouted for help. Between them, the two men saved as many as they could.

When David was certain there was no chance of them reigniting, he placed them carefully into a small suitcase he'd taken from one of the bedrooms at the opposite side of the corridor, along with the money.

That done, he returned his attention to the prostrate figure lying in front of the fireplace. Flipping him over with his foot, he gasped in amazement. *But it couldn't be*! was his immediate reaction; yet there was no denying the evidence of his own eyes.

Despite his amazement, in seconds he was fully in control of his emotions once more. Making an instant decision, he picked up the phone and, using the number he'd been given for an emergency, he dialled. He was rewarded with an answer on the third ring. When he was certain of who he was dealing with, he outlined the problem.

'Are you sure?' was the incredulous reply.

'Perfectly, Number One; there can be no mistake, I assure you. The phone call was a warning, somehow they were tipped off. As it was, I managed to save most of the files, but I'm afraid two are beyond redemption and a third damaged in several places.'

'Which two were destroyed?' came the inevitable question.

Almost afraid to answer, David eventually blurted out, 'The ones pertaining to *Le Serpent Rouge*.'

When it came, the Grand Master's reply was not the one he'd expected. Instead of a tirade of foul-mouthed invective, a long-drawn-out sigh was followed by a carefully controlled voice. 'Well, David, as strange as it seems, it may well be that in the long run it might turn out for the best.'

Several moments of stunned silence were followed by an incredulous response. 'But surely, Number One, it is the worst possible disaster! It means we no longer have the vital evidence.'

In measured tones, the Grand Master explained patiently, 'But you see, David, it doesn't really matter. Those in power have no idea we are no longer in possession of the originals. As long as they have the copies we sent them, they will accede to our every little request. Besides which, it ensures that from now on only the Grand Master will be in possession of the full facts.'

'Of course,' said David, recognition suddenly dawning, 'as far as they're concerned they're blissfully unaware of what has happened!' And with that he gave a deep-throated chuckle.

'However, David,' came the voice of the Grand Master again, 'we still have to rid ourselves of our little problem. As for the businessmen, I take it your colleague is capable of taking care of that side of things?'

'Perfectly,' was the response.

'In that case I'd like you to perform a delicate task for me, one only you and I will ever know about. Do it, and the rewards will be great.' And with that he explained exactly what he wanted done.

Hardly able to contain his excitement, David fought to control his racing heart, before measuring his reply carefully. 'The honour of carrying out such a sacred duty for the Brotherhood will be reward enough, Number One.'

'Admirable sentiments, David, but I mean what I say… and David, bear this in mind, I always keep my word.' With that he rang off.

David Naami was still trying to come to terms with the implications of how a single phone call had dramatically altered the course of his life, when the voice of the other assassin broke into his reverie.

'What do we do with the bodies, David?'

Holding his hand up he said, 'Before we do anything else, remember our instructions. They make it perfectly clear the bastards are to be made examples of. Two of the three in the next room,' he explained, gesturing with his outstretched arm, 'are to be taken care of here, while the third – the taller one – is to be removed to his own home and executed there.' Pulling a slip of paper from his pocket, David handed it to his colleague. 'Here, the address is on there.' Making sure his colleague realised the gravity of his sacred task, he added, 'Looking after those three will be your responsibility.'

Indicating the fourth body lying at his feet, he said, 'Taking care of this piece of shit will be mine.' About to turn away, he was stopped in mid-stride by another question.

'If I may be so bold, why *hanging*?' his colleague asked in bemusement.

Serious now, David said, 'Only one person alive knows the answer to that. All you need ever know is that we did our duty for the Brotherhood.'

Crouching low, his head almost brushing the roof of the tunnel, David Naami made his way forward by the light of the heavy-duty torch he carried in his right hand. Despite the slime that covered the worn stonework under his feet, he never once stumbled, even though the man slung over his left shoulder was unconscious. The stench was nauseating, the reason obvious. He was negotiating a labyrinth of deep dark tunnels that made up the primary sewage system running beneath the outskirts of Paris. Several hundred yards further on, he turned sharply right and entered another tunnel, this time a much bigger one. Immediately below him was a fast stream of human effluent.

Not in the least put off, he took hold of the rusted ring ladder and descended several feet until he was standing on a narrow ledge inches away from the raw sewage. At shoulder height on either side were further ledges, and even as he watched he saw a flash of tiny red eyes penetrate the darkness, accompanied by the telltale scurrying and occasional chatter of confrontation.

Smiling mirthlessly, he knew that rats held no fear for him. Most of his formative years had been spent in these sewers, and in those days the creatures had been his constant companions.

Suddenly he was there.

Standing in front of him was a large rusted iron door. Shifting the weight of the body on his shoulder, he pulled a key from his pocket and inserted it into a well-oiled lock. It opened easily. Replacing the key, he pushed the door gently and it opened with the minimum of fuss.

Moments later he was inside.

Reaching to his right he threw the switch. A few seconds' delay was followed by a crackling sound; suddenly the neon light sprang into life, bathing everything with an eerie fluorescent glow. Switching off the torch, David stepped into a room that had been decorated in an open-plan style.

Wanting for nothing, it even boasted a tiny kitchen and a rudimentary shower cubicle. Easing the body from his shoulder, he propped it against the wall for a moment, before removing his wellington boots and replacing them with a pair of soft slip-on shoes. What he was looking for was situated near the back of the room.

Hefting the body onto his shoulder once more, he made his way over to what looked suspiciously like a dentist's chair. Dumping the figure into it, he immediately secured the hands and feet by means of clamps. Tilting the head backwards, so that he was looking directly into the man's mouth, David proceeded to position it by means of a roll of industrial tape which he took from a nearby shelf.

The beauty of his little hiding place was that it had been abandoned decades ago. Apart from him, no one knew of its existence. He'd come across it quite by accident, during the early days when he was literally living in the sewer system. Then quite suddenly his life had been turned upside down. By some miracle, his skill with a knife had brought him to the attention of the Brotherhood. Having worked his way slowly through the fringes, it wasn't long before his cold-blooded ruthlessness ensured he'd made a name for himself. And the rest, as he liked to put it, was history.

Opening the briefcase, he rummaged through his little toys until he found what he was looking for. His only disappointment was that the object of his little game would be unconscious for the first few extractions. As it turned out he was wrong; it was while he was taking out the eighth tooth that the man's eyes suddenly flew open. Looking around in horror, it took him only seconds to realise the hopelessness of his predicament. With that he opened his ravaged mouth and, despite the agony, screamed in terror. Several minutes later he was dead. The pain and shock had simply been too much.

The next stage of the operation required the skill and dexterity of a surgeon. Removing a scalpel from a protective compartment at the top of the briefcase, David lifted it into the air, admiring its cruel beauty as the blade glistened under the flickering neon light.

He made the first shallow incision just below the jawline. Tracing it upwards, he followed a path inside the left ear, before stopping halfway along the forehead. Reversing his direction, he proceeded to do exactly the same thing on the other side of the face. Peeling the skin away a few inches at a time, he stopped every so often in order to ensure there was no snagging. After all, he reasoned, when the skin was finally removed it needed to be in perfect condition. As a perfectionist, the last thing he wanted was blemishes. That wouldn't do at all.

Twenty minutes later and he held his prize to the light – a perfect death mask!

Finally, using a meat cleaver, he cut off the victim's hands and feet. Such was his strength he needed only four blows to achieve his objective. Stepping back in order to give the blood time to drain away, he declared himself satisfied. Placing the body parts into a plastic bag, he decided to dispose of them later.

Staring at the face, he chuckled in delight.

Unlike the other bits and pieces, this wasn't to be disposed of. Oh, no, this would be presented to the Grand Master in person...

Chapter Two

Towards the end of the old millennium

IT WAS A FULL MOON, THE AIR CRISP AND CLEAR; ONE OF THOSE
nights when you felt you could reach out and touch the stars. Despite
the moon's clarity, several pools of inky blackness remained, the legacy
of shadows cast by some of the more prominent gravestones. Taking
full advantage of these, the five – Jared, Emma, Roger, Aled and Michael
– cast nervous glances over their shoulders as they made their way
towards the back door of the chapel. Jangled nerve ends bore testimony
to the fact that although each had made the journey on countless other
occasions, it had never been at this time of night.

Carmel chapel nestled snugly on a large hill commanding an imposing view over the village of Raven's Hill. Squat and ugly, it seemed to
glare down at the rest of the village, as if daring it to contest its position
of pre-eminence. To add to this, it was common knowledge it had a
troubled past. Legend suggested that it was extremely old, possibly one
of the oldest in the country. At any rate, it was certainly the oldest in the
area. Rumour had it that its foundations had been built on top of a
monastery that went back as far as the Dark Ages.

If you spoke to the right people, they'd have told you reluctantly at
first, and then with greater relish, that all kinds of unsavoury incidents
had taken place within its hallowed walls – things, they pointed out, that
had no rightful place in a house of God. They'd have told you for
instance that it had never felt right, that it harboured an offensive smell
which no amount of scrubbing could eradicate. Rumours were rife that the
bread for communion was often stale, when in fact the loaves had been
freshly purchased that morning. On other occasions, the congregation had
experienced an icy wind running through the building. When pressed,
several members would gladly have gone even further, relating incidents
which seemed at the very least to be wild exaggerations, flights of fancy.

They were already nervous, but on the spur of the moment Jared decided to add to the tension. Conscious that sound travels a long way at night, he whispered, 'Listen, you lot, did you know that in the old days it was fairly common to be buried alive?'

'How the hell do you know that?' exclaimed Roger.

'Shh! Keep your voice down for Christ's sake,' said Jared.

'Sorry,' said Roger sheepishly, 'but go on – how did you find that out?'

'Read it somewhere,' murmured Jared, before adding, 'remember, they didn't have the sophisticated ways of testing we have today.'

'So, how did they get round it?' asked Aled.

'The most practical way was to place a small mirror in front of the face. If there was no condensation you were pronounced dead.'

'Christ!' said Roger again. 'What if you were only in a coma or something?'

'Tough – you were buried alive. That's why until recently bodies in mortuaries had bells tied to their toes. If they woke up, they'd be heard and the burial cancelled.'

'Yeah, but that kind of thing was rare, wasn't it?' chipped in Emma.

''Fraid not, Em. Only the other day I read about a graveyard being dug up to make way for a new motorway. When the graves were emptied in order to transfer them to an alternative site, they found a high percentage had been buried alive.'

'Rubbish!' declared Emma. 'How would they have been able to tell?'

'Easy! When the coffins were opened there were scratch marks on the lids.'

Seeing their blank expressions, Jared said, 'They woke up, realised where they were, went berserk and tried to claw their way out. Get it?'

The looks on their faces showed they had, but wished they hadn't.

Enjoying himself now, Jared carried on, 'The worse case I came across was the one where a woman had not only been buried alive, but had given birth as well.'

'Oh, no way,' said Emma, 'this time you're definitely lying. You made that one up, didn't you?'

'Unfortunately, I didn't; like all the other stories its true. Imagine the scenario, though. If it happened to you, what would you do? You'd probably do the same thing. You're six foot under, remember, so the only avenue of escape would be to scratch away at the coffin lid till you've no nails left. If it was me, I'd hope to suffocate before I went completely mad.'

By the looks on their faces he knew he'd said enough.

'Anyway, to end on a lighter note, the story has a happy ending.'

'What, they found one person who hadn't been buried alive?' quipped Roger.

'No, you prat, they found something better,' said Jared. 'A solid gold coffin!'

With a soft whistle, Roger said, 'Now, that's more like it. Can you imagine what that little lot would be worth today?'

'That's the whole point, Rog, everyone did, and before long all hell broke loose. The Church said it belonged to them, seeing as it was in their graveyard, while the family claimed it was theirs, even though they didn't have a clue it was there. Finally the government tried to get in on the act, although how they thought they had a legitimate claim is anybody's guess.'

As usual it was Roger who had the last word. 'Nothing changes, then!'

With a burst of quiet laughter the mood lightened, although it didn't last long.

Until now they'd looked on what they were about to do as a joke, suddenly the gravity of the situation struck home.

Taking responsibility, Jared said, 'Look, so far we've done nothing wrong, crossed no boundaries. As it was my suggestion in the first place, don't think you have to go along for the ride because of me.'

Being sure to make eye contact, he said, 'I want you to think hard about this before we go any further. If anyone wants to walk away, do it now. I'm sure the rest of us won't think any the less of you, honestly.'

'Well, what do you think, do we go for it or not?'

Jared had never considered his grandparents wealthy, but on reflection he supposed they must have been, as they owned a large house on the outskirts of the village. He'd often thought of it as a rambling old mansion, but that was a description which did it an injustice. Although over a hundred years old, it was in excellent condition, both inside and out, kept that way by a small army of local workmen. Paid handsomely, they were always prepared to take on any task at the drop of a hat. Several years ago, the wooden windows, down pipes and troughs had been stripped away to be replaced by modern UPVC fittings. That was the only concession his gran had allowed to modernity, however, as the remainder of the wood, which virtually covered the whole upstairs section of the house, was original. Painted deliberately in black and white, the overall effect was that of a Tudor dwelling. The ground floor, on the other hand, was built of genuine dressed stone, purchased from the local quarry situated some five miles away.

Inside was a contradiction in terms, as the two sitting rooms placed on either side of the hallway were decorated in totally different fashions. One was minimalistic: light-blue emulsioned walls were complemented by a sumptuous royal-blue carpet, interspersed here and there with a pink flower pattern. Apart from that, a cream-coloured three-piece suite and two small watercolours above a television and built-in CD player, were the sum total of the contents.

The other room was full of Welsh flavour. Traditional hand-crafted furniture was complimented by oil paintings of nautical scenes. Most of the shelves displayed expensive china, the legacy of a lifetime's collecting by his gran. The floor still boasted its original oak planking. Burnished over the years lovingly by his grandmother, it had settled down to a beautiful light-brown colour, reminiscent of home-produced honey, Jared often thought. A study, toilet and bathroom and a large open-plan kitchen completed the downstairs setting. As Jared's grandmother had never been one for cooking, the kitchen was rather Spartan. Pine chairs and cupboards were the order of the day, while an old-fashioned coal-burning Rayburn took pride of place in the corner furthest from the back door.

Upstairs, there were five bedrooms: two on one side of the wide wooden staircase and one enormous bathroom and toilet; on the other side were the other three, two of which had recently been converted to en suites. The views from the bedrooms at the front of the house along with those from the bay windows downstairs created one panoramic prospect of the sweeping lawns and the row of stone cottages at the other side of the road. Until the planting of the conifers, that is.

The main drawback to the house was the steps. Sixteen in all, they led from the edge of the pavement flanking the main road to the top of the bank approaching the front door, which was itself a further twenty yards away. On each side of the shale path, rows of rhododendron bushes had been planted as a means of breaking up the artificial hues of the lawns running to either side.

The front door was a work of art: a combination of solid oak and stained glass. On either side stood granite lions; complete with short, stubby wings, they looked a ferocious sight as they guarded the short flight of steps leading to the door itself. Above it, in the style of those displayed at the side of old-fashioned hansom cabs, was a security light, painted gold and black.

Although Gran was nothing to write home about in terms of culinary expertise, she was a magician in the garden. The gently sloping lawns, both back and front, were a picture, kept in peak condition by tons of Feed and Weed. Regular cutting with her single-seater petrol mower had ensured she had drawn many an amused glance from visitors as she spun around in dizzying fashion. Despite the attributes of modern technology, there was one thing she was never without – a pair of old-fashioned garden shears. It was these she used for the fiddly jobs – the ones around the lawns and the flower beds; those which needed 'special care and attention', as she put it.

Then one day, completely out of the blue, she had decided to plant a row of conifers along the wall near the bottom of the steps. When Jared had pointed out that eventually, when the trees had grown to a height of ten or so feet, no one would be able to see the gardens she had spent so much time looking after, she had looked at him with a straight face and declared that it was exactly what she wanted. Seeing Jared's puzzled expression, she had explained patiently that the conifers ensured privacy for those days when she wanted to sunbathe in the nude – after ironing out all the wrinkles from her ageing skin, she'd added. Jared still wasn't sure whether or not she had been teasing him.

Behind the house, the expanse of lawns was even bigger, but equally well kept. The boundaries of the back garden were defined by a hedge of wicked thorn bushes on three sides, while the fourth – the one furthest from the house – was once again covered by a row of tall conifers. There was only one possible means of access to the property – a six-foot-tall wooden gate, bolted from the inside. Beyond the latch gate was a dense forest which, after only a few yards, rose steeply towards the mountain peaks in the distance. About a mile away and to the right-hand side of the garden, was the unmistakable outline of what the locals called the 'giant's mask'. On a cloudless day, the imprint of the huge face was clearly discernable.

On the left-hand side of the garden, in-between a beautiful silver birch and cherry tree, was a large wooden shed in the shape of a doll's house. Stained a reddish-brown with wood preserver, it was where Gran kept all her garden tools, including the single-seater mower.

At several carefully selected points in the lawn were rockeries which contained several species of alpine flowers, the bright purples of some complementing beautifully the red and blues of others. 'Expensive,' was the salesman's comment when his grandmother had enquired about them, but well worth it as they stay in bloom all the year round. She'd needed no second bidding and had bought them on the spot. The only other thing of note was a compost heap, tucked away near the opposite side of the garden to the gate, and a battered old wheelbarrow which she kept propped up against the hedge. She'd never seen the need to put that under lock and key, commenting that anyone who wanted an old thing like that could bloody well have it.

Although in her late fifties, his grandmother cut a sprightly figure, while his grandfather, a good deal younger, was still working. Quite what he did, Jared never knew; but of one thing he was certain, he was very well paid. Whatever it entailed it certainly involved a good deal of travelling. He was away from home most of the time, sometimes for weeks on end. He realised that his gran must have been happy with the situation, though, as he'd never once heard her complain. Although he called him 'Grandad' it felt strange, because he was Gran's second husband, her first having been killed the previous year in a bizarre hit-and-run incident that the police had never solved.

In hindsight, the visit to his grandparents on that fateful Sunday evening was prompted more by boredom than anything else.

Although his new grandfather was reluctant to talk about his own past, he was quite happy to speak at length about any other subject. In the last few months he'd become fascinated by a strange and enigmatic figure from Gran's side of the family called Thomas. It seemed that in the distant past, Thomas had run away from home at an early age. Penniless on leaving, he apparently returned some thirty years later as a ship's captain of some repute.

According to Grandad he was a man of dubious character, involved in all kinds of nefarious goings-on. One thing was certain: he was never forgiven for his early misdemeanours, because he was rarely if ever spoken about inside the family circle. It was as if they had blanked him from their memories, as if for them he'd never existed. He certainly looked the part; in the only picture Jared ever saw of him, he had long white hair and a black leather patch over his left eye.

Many people in the village felt Jared's present grandfather was strange. It had nothing to do with the fact he was an outsider, or that he had a strange accent, but had more to do with his nocturnal habits. As an avid historian, he could often be seen pottering around graveyards, making sketches and taking brass rubbings at all times of the day and night.

Both Jared's grandparents were fond of the odd glass of port, and as there was no chapel that evening, they'd started their tipple early. By the time he arrived, his grandmother was already in bed, and it was obvious grandad had consumed more than his usual quota.

What happened next could only be attributed to the drink, because he started to tell Jared a story he'd never heard before.

'It's true what they said about Thomas, you know; he returned from sea a wealthy man.' Pointing around the room, he commented, 'Where else do you think all this came from? To say he'd changed, though… don't know about that. What I do know – only rumours, mind,' he said, looking over at Jared, 'is that somewhere along the line he became obsessed with witchcraft, devil worship and that kind of stuff.'

'Surely not,' said Jared in amazement.

'Can't be sure; as I said, only rumours. Strong ones, mind you, but when you think about it, he had plenty of opportunity to get involved. All those different countries, all those different ports,' he said with a wink.

'Put like that, it does sound plausible,' was Jared's reply.

Continuing, Grandad said, 'Anyway, while staying in Scotland it seems he became mixed up with all kinds of strange characters, a rum lot if you ask me. Mind you,' he added pensively, 'Scotland… hardly a hotbed for such goings-on, you would have thought, eh?'

Sitting up straighter, his interest now piqued, Jared said, 'That's why he's never spoken about in the family then; regarded as the black sheep. It all makes sense now.'

'Suppose you're right,' said Grandad, 'but think of the problem it would have caused.'

'What do you mean?' asked Jared.

'Well, just remember, lad, in those days if you stepped out of line you were an outcast, excommunication and all that. To add to that, the family had always been so, well you know, righteous and all that. Pillars of the community, if you like. It would have been enough to break a lesser family.'

Knowing there was more to come, Jared waited, and within a few moments his patience was rewarded.

Lifting his eyes and staring at some remote point in the ceiling, his grandad said, 'That was only the beginning; it seems the next step was taking part in actual experiments.' Suddenly he lowered his voice as if someone might be listening, and in barely a whisper said, 'Holding séances at the dead of night, sacrificing animals and all that stuff.'

By now Jared was genuinely impressed, despite himself. 'He was in to it in a big way, then?'

'So it seems,' said Grandad, 'so it seems. It appears all the bad stuff began with his visit to Scotland.' Stopping suddenly, he said, 'Have I said that before? I'm sure I have, must be the drink, eh? Or perhaps old age finally catching up... What do you think?'

'Can't be the drink, Grandad,' said Jared with a straight face.

With a sly look he replied, 'Flattery will get you everywhere. I suppose this means you want to hear the rest of the story, then?'

Moving on as if nothing had happened, he said, 'Anyway, he seems to have stayed in a big mansion with some real weird buggers. The leader was, now let me think, some Alasdair – no that's not it, Aleister – yes, that's it, Aleister Crowley.'

In amazement Jared blurted out, 'Bloody hell, Grandad! Don't you know who he was?'

Rubbing his chin pensively, he thought for a moment before saying, 'Can't say I do, lad.'

Before he could say another word, Jared said reverentially, 'He was only the founder of the first group of satanists in Britain, that's all.'

'Impressive,' was grandad's only comment.

'Well, well, who would have imagined it,' said Jared. 'Old Thomas certainly moved in exalted company. How did it all end, then?'

'You sure you want to know? It's not a pretty story, I can tell you.'

Then smiling he said, 'Of course you do, everyone likes a grisly ending, don't they? Anyway, where was I? Oh, yes, the cleaning lady came in early one Sunday to find him sprawled across the altar table, quite dead! Blood all over the place, there was – on the table, the wall, everywhere. As I said, not a pretty sight.'

Putting a hand up to forestall any questions, he carried on, 'That's not the end of things, scattered around him were all kinds of weird paraphernalia. At the time, it was said they were to help conjure up spirits of the dead, but who knows?' he said with a shrug. 'No one knew much about that kind of thing then. Conducting experiments on the altar table! Bloody sacrilege, if you ask me.'

When he'd calmed down a little, he said, 'Oh, yes, I almost forgot, one of the things they found was a weird kind of board, no one could make head or tail of that.'

Hardly daring to believe what he was hearing, Jared said, 'Was the killer ever found?'

'Now that's the strange thing,' said Grandad, 'there seems to have been no witnesses.'

'Why wasn't the family hounded out of the village, then?' asked Jared.

With a wink Grandad said, 'Now that's where a bit of money and influence come in handy, don't they? The end result was that it was hushed up, swept under the carpet and all that. Course, they had to come up with some kind of a story, didn't they, so they said it was suicide. Most folks were only too ready to believe it. Remember, they thought he was mad anyway. As luck would have it, the cleaner was family too – paid handsomely, no doubt, to keep her mouth shut. There were rumours, of course, but nothing was proven, and so in the end things just died a death. Sorry – bad choice of words there,' he said with a little chuckle.

'What about the things that were found with him? Where did they end up?'

'Ah, now why did I think you'd get around to asking about those? The fact is they were dumped in his old sea chest, locked away and never seen again.'

'No one knows where they finished up, then?' enquired Jared almost breathlessly.

'Didn't say that, did I?' said Grandad. 'As a matter of fact the old chest and I presume its contents are up in the attic somewhere. To my knowledge it hasn't been touched since. Not surprising, since no one wanted anything to do with the bloody things.'

Before Jared was able to ask another question, his grandfather's head dropped onto his chest and he was suddenly fast asleep. Within minutes he was snoring loudly, and Jared realised he probably wouldn't wake until morning. He wondered if when he woke he'd even remember the conversation. He doubted it, considering how tipsy he'd seemed. Now he had time to think he went over the story in his mind. No wonder no one spoke about old Thomas. It was amazing.

Had the story been true, though?

Of one thing he was certain, drunk or not, his grandfather had appeared to believe it. Jared realised there was only one way to be certain, one way of finding out the truth, and that was to try and find the chest hidden somewhere in the attic. Glancing at his watch, he saw it was much too late to look now, but vowed there and then that as soon as he could find the time he would return.

Waiting outside the door of the chapel, the group were frozen. Rubbing their hands together vigorously, they attempted to restore some feeling to fingers that over the last few minutes had become increasingly numb. Jared remembered thinking vividly they were like fugitives, and in many ways he supposed they were. In a moment of silent contemplation, he wondered what would happen if they were caught. He felt somehow as if what they were about to do was a betrayal of old Eric Roberts' trust. One thing was certain, the consequences of being found didn't bear thinking about. They'd never be able to pass it off as a harmless prank. Even in these so-called enlightened times it was blasphemy of the worst kind.

While the others listened carefully for the slightest sound, Emma inserted the key into the lock. The door opened with an eerie creaking sound, but despite this, within moments they were all safely inside.

Hesitant to take the first step, they eventually made their way forward by the light of the moon which filtered in through the stained glass windows. Gazing up at them, Jared was suddenly reminded of their original intention. They'd been designed so that at certain times of day, light would be strategically thrown into the darker, more gloomy areas of the little chapel. He found it faintly amusing to think that at this time of night the windows seemed to be having the opposite effect. Many areas were bathed in murky shadows, allowing already fertile imaginations to conjure up all kinds of childhood fears.

Looking at the others, Jared saw that the expression on their faces showed clearly they were fighting the same demons as he was, trying just as unsuccessfully to suppress what experts labelled an unreasoned fear of the dark. From a personal point of view he wasn't so sure about the unreasoned bit. Recent paranormal studies showed clearly that behind many of the popular myths and legends lay an element of truth.

As they stepped through into the main body of the chapel, the going became a little easier.

Narrow shafts of light speared the gloom, and dust motes caught in the beams appeared like angry spirits furiously debating their fate. Shivering inwardly, Jared reflected on the fact that churches and chapels were supposed to be places of warmth and comfort, of sanctuary; but at that moment Carmel seemed to offer neither. Perhaps it was reminding them they were trespassers about to embark on something dangerous; something the old building viewed as far more than a harmless prank, though Jared ruefully.

The smell of mildew and decay seemed stronger the further into the chapel they got, and before long Jared's fevered imagination began to run riot. Even harmless electrical cables took on new meanings. In his mind they suddenly became giant tentacles from some long forgotten giant squid.

With difficulty he dragged himself back to the task in hand.

Whispering instructions to the others, he led them swiftly up the few short steps towards the altar table. Checking they were all there, it came as a surprise to find that for the last minute or so, he'd been holding his breath. Letting it out slowly, it hung before him like a cloud of cloying mist.

Finally he whispered, 'That's the easy bit; now for the hard part.'

Lifting the satchel he'd brought with him onto the table, he carefully removed the contents, placing them gently onto the altar's well-worn surface. First came the candles and pointer, followed by the paper and pencil and then finally the board. This was the first the others had seen of it, and he could tell by their expressions they were impressed.

Lighting the candles with a box of matches from his pocket, he placed each of the four at the corners of the table. The flickering flames seemed to bring the board to life, as it lay before them in magnificent splendour.

As if reading Jared's mind, Emma whispered, 'It's stunning, the workmanship is incredible.'

Then it was Roger's turn. 'It's certainly beautiful, but I don't know… there's something strange about it. I can't put it into words, but it seems to radiate a kind of malevolence, somehow. Anyone else feel the same way?'

'I can't speak for the others,' said Jared, 'but from my point of view you've summed it up perfectly. I can't help feeling there's something intrinsically evil about it.'

'It's almost as if it's watching us,' said Emma again.

'That's what worries me, Em. If it really is evil, do we dare use it?'

Unexpected and unwanted, the memory of how he'd obtained the board suddenly surfaced.

As it happened, it was almost a week before he was finally able to return to his grandparents' house. Timing was all important; it had to be when neither of them was at home. Letting himself in with his own key, he stood in the hallway for a minute making sure he was alone. Satisfied, he made his way quickly up to the second floor, and was scrambling up the ladder into the attic in record time.

His first reaction was one of dismay. How on earth was he going to find anything in the middle of this lot? Almost every corner seemed to be filled with something or other. Furniture was heaped on top of furniture, while old clothes lay scattered in untidy piles as far as the eye could see. Stuffed animals and birds vied with such odd curios as antler heads and an old German helmet for pride of place, while cobwebs hung everywhere like ghostly shrouds.

One particular item made his blood freeze. There, stuck away in a remote corner, its head flattened ready to strike, was a full-sized stuffed king cobra. It was so lifelike that for several moments Jared couldn't move. It was discoveries such as this that made him want to find the chest and get out of there as quickly as possible.

Some considerable time later, full of dust and filthy dirty, he conceded defeat. It was as he was making his way back towards the trapdoor that he quite literally stumbled on it. Hidden under a pile of old crates, it was made of solid oak and boasted a substantial brass lock. Fortunately for Jared, it was broken. Lifting the lid he could barely contain his excitement. He didn't know what he'd expected, but what he saw dampened his enthusiasm. Determined not to be put off, he ploughed through several sheaves of loose documents looking for evidence of Thomas's link to the occult. It was while leafing through these he came across the board.

His pulse quickened when he realised what he was looking at. In appearance it was very similar to a Monopoly board, although that's where the similarity ended. This one was covered with intricately carved figures of demons, gods, goddesses and the like, some of which he recognised and others he hadn't a clue about. Beautifully inlaid with gold leaf, lapis lazuli and other semi-precious stones, it had obviously been carved with loving care. Strangely, the letters were in English, twenty-six in all.

Peering more closely he noticed what appeared to be reddish brown stains in several places. With a feeling of dread he wondered if it could be Thomas's blood. Pushing aside such macabre thoughts, he put his hand further into the chest and came up with an ivory pointer that was obviously part of the same set. He assumed it was ivory, anyway, as the once brilliant white surface had been tarnished a dull yellow, similar in many ways to the keys on his gran's piano.

He supposed if he were really honest, it was at that moment the idea came to him. The occult had always fascinated him, but he'd never dabbled.

As soon as he gazed at the board everything changed.

Chapter Three

MAKING SURE HE WASN'T DRAWING ATTENTION TO HIMSELF, THE OLD man turned around slowly.

Without appearing to, he studied the faces of the passers-by with deep intensity. He checked faces and eyes, looking for any that might quickly turn away from his. Despite all his precautions he saw nothing suspicious. Reassured, he moved on. Suddenly he stopped and looked into the large glass frontage of a furniture shop, using the reflection from the window to double-check. His eyes moved restlessly from right to left while pretending to study the items for sale, but still he could spot nothing untoward.

For days he'd had the feeling he was being followed, but he knew that was highly unlikely, hidden away as he was deep in the country. Hardly seeing a soul from one week to the next, he'd become something of a recluse. But that had suited his purpose.

At times it had felt like the perfect cover, although as a realist he knew there was no such thing as perfect. One day they would finally trace his whereabouts and then they would hunt him down like an animal.

As the senior guardian his days were numbered. Another five years perhaps, but until then he had plenty of time in which to make his plans. Besides himself, only one other remained, but the mantle of leadership would not pass to him.

The ingenuity of his predecessors never failed to amaze him. But for them, the guardians would have ceased to exist centuries ago. However, the time had finally arrived to awaken the sleeper. Perhaps 'sleeper' was the wrong word, he thought to himself, as this one was different. For the safety and well-being of the organisation, he'd been kept totally in the dark as to who and what he really was; innocent of the burden he carried on his shoulders. With a feeling of profound sadness, he realised that once activated he would be the last, and so the ancient prophecy handed down through the centuries would never become a reality.

Casting aside such negative thoughts, he sensed that his immediate priority was to find a way of ensuring the sleeper inherited that which belonged to him; but more importantly, the legacy should be passed on without arousing suspicion.

While in such a positive mood he made a quick decision.

Now the guardians were on the verge of extinction, why not go on the offensive?

Yes, that was it; he must do something before it was too late. If he could only gather a detailed dossier about the Brotherhood, by the time the sleeper was activated he might be able to take the fight to them. He was in no doubt he was capable, both in terms of academic ability and courage. Over the years he'd studied him from afar, had seen him display admirable tenacity on more than one occasion. Yes, he would fit the bill perfectly.

The stumbling block was how he would react to being told who and what he really was, to the fact that until now his whole life had been nothing but a carefully orchestrated lie. Enough of that; he was getting ahead of himself, he told himself sternly. He would cross that bridge when the time came. Suddenly he had a flash of inspiration, and with that he knew exactly how to achieve his objective. The answer was so simple he wondered why he hadn't thought of it sooner.

Grant Kramer was a pro, his rate of success unprecedented. At five foot eight inches tall, and blessed with a slim athletic build, he was ideally suited to his profession. His work demanded the suppleness of an Olympic athlete and the dexterity of a skilled surgeon, but strangely his was not a noble profession, far from it. In fact Grant Kramer was a thief. Not just any thief though – he was the best!

During the last few years his reputation was such that he was able to select only those offers which he viewed as a challenge, or those which paid extremely well. As an already wealthy man, money had become relatively unimportant to him, and so lately he'd been toying with the idea of retirement. Indeed, he'd decided this was to be his last job. One final pay day and then he was out. He was getting out while the going was good and for the most basic of reasons: the one which warned him that deep down old Father Time was catching up. Common sense dictated that eventually his luck would run out. But this job was different. Apart from the fact he was being paid a king's ransom, he admitted to himself that this one he'd have done for nothing.

The headquarters of Chameleon Enterprises... the very thought brought goosebumps to his flesh. A fitting climax to a glittering career, he reasoned.

Over the years, much of his success was linked to his golden rule: never meet a client in person; that way no one ever knows what you look like. Not that it would have done anyone any good anyway, as one of Kramer's priceless assets was a face that was eminently forgettable, the kind that never drew a second glance.

Despite everything, he was under no illusion about the task facing him. He'd heard the rumours about David Naami. There was no doubt he was a cold-blooded killer, and the band of elite assassins he commanded frighteningly ruthless. Still, when it came to the rough stuff, Grant reflected, he was no slouch. As an ex-mercenary, he could look after himself, mix it with the best. Strangely, what he felt now was not fear, but excitement.

To be the best, you have to pit yourself against the best, he reminded himself with a chuckle.

In his line of work preparation was everything, and so he'd been studying the building for days, making plans and deciding on the best method of entry. With grudging admiration he'd been forced to concede that the job was a tricky one, the list of hurdles to overcome endlessly formidable.

He'd toyed with several means of gaining access to the building, but in frustration dismissed each one as impractical. The answer when it came was brilliant in its simplicity. If getting in from the outside was difficult, then why not look at it from a totally different perspective?

Posing as a businessman, he'd found gaining access to the top floor relatively simple.

It was while he was sitting there taking in his surroundings that the plan was formulated.

All he had to do was to hide in one of the air conditioning ducts built into the ceiling and stay there until he was ready. What he needed, he realised, was a distraction, and once again it was amazingly simple to contrive.

The following day he was ready.

As part of the next batch of high-powered visiting businessmen, he waited patiently while a break was announced. Hanging back while the others made their way into a large room where coffee and tea were being served, he suddenly made his move. Already sure the large waste-paper basket at the side of the door was full of combustible material, he looked around nonchalantly before dropping in a lighted cigarette.

Within seconds it began to smoulder.

Moving towards the door with practised ease, Grant made his way forward to join the others, who by now were deep in conversation. He was half-way through his cup of coffee when the first cry broke out.

Along with several others, he moved quickly towards the source of the disturbance, noticing with satisfaction that the fire had taken hold far more easily than expected. He knew that eventually water sprinklers would bring the blaze under control, but a few moments were all he needed.

Before anyone knew what was happening, he'd removed the air conditioning panel, clambered up, secured it by means of double-sided industrial tape and was lying face down in the narrow tunnel. His aluminium briefcase was clutched tightly to his chest. He'd gambled on the fire causing a distraction, doing just enough damage to necessitate the remainder of the seminar being cancelled. Furthermore, in the haste to get everyone down from the top floor he would not be missed, and he was right.

Displaying infinite patience, Grant lay in the dark narrow confines of the duct, amazed at how easy it had been. In the end, all those safety measures had counted for nothing. He didn't allow himself the luxury of dwelling on his success for too long, as he knew the job was only half complete.

The next stage would have been impossible but for the information he'd been supplied with by his client. How he'd managed to obtain it was a mystery. All he hoped was that it was accurate.

Listening carefully, Grant heard nothing, so he removed the covering to the duct and lowered himself down by his fingertips. Bracing himself, he dropped down lightly, the rubber soles of his shoes making no sound on the thick pile of the expensive carpet. Making sure to replace the covering, he then removed his outer garments, including his shoes, before placing everything into a black bag which he slid under one of the chairs in the boardroom. Clothed in a specially adapted black nylon catsuit, he was now unrecognisable compared with the figure that had walked into the building all those hours ago.

Drifting in and out of the deep shadows, he moved like a phantom, secure in the knowledge that unless the guards altered their routine, he would be safe. It never ceased to amaze him how even the best security measures often failed to take into account that they had to vary their time patterns in order to avoid predictability.

As if on cue, two guards suddenly appeared.

Moving stealthily, the beams of their torches traversed the room in a 360° sweep.

Careful bastards, he thought to himself.

Waiting a few moments until they'd disappeared, he pushed forward with greater confidence, knowing that if everything went according to plan they wouldn't be back for several hours.

Within moments he stood at the threshold of the outer door. Looking in, he saw how to the untrained eye all appeared deceptively benign, but he knew better. This was the most difficult part.

Placing the briefcase on the floor he opened it carefully, before removing what looked like a small metal detector. Switched on, a small green light sprang to life; then, holding it in front of him, he walked forward slowly, one step at a time. Almost immediately the light flashed red. Grinning, he allowed himself a mental pat on the back... pressure pads! Anyone attempting to walk across the room would have been caught in seconds.

Moving the detector a foot at a time, he made his way slowly towards the double doors, identifying each pressure pad as he came to it with a light sprinkling of white powder he'd brought along for the express purpose.

About ten minutes later he reached the doors, but before he took the last few steps he made a final check. Immediately he was glad he had, because a cursory examination showed the presence of two hidden infra-red beams. One was situated a foot from the floor, while the other was placed several feet higher.

Stepping over the first and under the second, he made it undetected.

Easing open the double doors, he stepped into the narrow corridor and made his way quickly towards the vault-like door in front of him. Approaching the touch pad, he keyed in the correct sequence of numbers from memory and was soon inside.

Walking along the narrow corridor, he didn't have time to appreciate the magnificence of his surroundings as he made his way quickly towards the inner sanctuary. The room was dark and gloomy and he had difficulty in seeing, so switching on the torch he'd brought with him, he directed the beam upwards.

He didn't know what he'd expected, but it certainly wasn't this.

Overcome with loathing, and unable to move a muscle, Grant gazed at the thing staring down at him with a mixture of horror and amazement. Certain he was seeing things, he moved closer to get a better look. Standing only feet away, he saw his first impression had been correct. There, looking down at him from the confines of a glass pyramid, was what appeared to be a bearded male head. Perfectly preserved, it seemed to gaze down at him in hypnotic malevolence. If he hadn't known better he would have sworn it was still alive.

Eventually, he managed to drag his eyes away from the repulsive sight, and turned to run. It was then he bumped into something hard. Convinced nothing worse could be in store, he shone the light over the obstacle. What he saw made him jump back in sheer terror.

Moving the beam around in a slow arc he was unable to believe his eyes. By now he was convinced he'd stepped into a madhouse, for there, as far as the eye could see, were scores of much smaller heads. Proudly displayed in glass cases on top of tall individual pillars, each one stared at him with dull lifeless eyes.

Managing to overcome his initial fear, he realised he'd made a mistake. What he'd instinctively taken to be the heads of small children were in fact those of fully grown humans! Shrunken to childlike proportions, they'd miraculously retained every nuance of their death throes.

Backing away in horror, he fought down his mounting panic.

With a supreme effort of will he reminded himself he was a professional, a professional with an important job to do. What was on display was beyond imagination, something no sane person should be allowed to see. Nevertheless, his pride would not allow him to back out now. Convinced what he was looking at was some kind of shrine, he was suddenly struck by another thought: if that was the case, what kind of inhuman monsters worshipped such abominations?

Taking several photographs of the gruesome spectacle, the whole scene was given an even grislier dimension as the darkness was punctured intermittently by the flash of his camera. As soon as he'd completed the onerous task, he headed straight for the vault, which he knew lay behind the thick black curtains.

Confidence in their impregnability was such that they hadn't bothered attempting to hide the exterior of the vault. The lock was state of the art, one of those given the highest security rating. Without a trace of arrogance, it amused Grant to think that such a rating had been given without a thought to anyone of his skill. In less than two minutes he was inside.

To his trained eye, there seemed little of monetary value, just shelf after shelf of meticulously arranged files, each one colour-coded. Working methodically, he photographed everything he saw. When he'd finished he re-placed everything as he'd found it. Then he relocked the safe and spun the tumbler to a random setting. He knew it was a futile exercise, as they would eventually realise someone had breached their security; but for him it was a matter of pride.

Getting out was easy, but again he took time to ensure everything was left as he'd found it. Finally satisfied, he retrieved the black bag and headed for the floor beneath.

Knowing the windows were alarmed, he'd already disarmed the one in the gents' toilet. Taking the length of strong nylon rope he'd carried in his briefcase, he let it out slowly before squeezing through the small opening in the toilet window. With the bag attached to his waist, he abseiled down. Within moments his feet hit the ground, and shortly after he made his escape into the night.

Despite the fact that at this hour of the morning there would be very few people about, Grant took no chances. It was another reason he'd stayed at the top for so long.

Within a hundred yards he'd reached the alley in which he'd hidden a change of clothing. Quickly donning a tracksuit and running shoes, he was now less conspicuous.

One of the conditions laid down by his client was that the rolls of film were to be posted immediately the job was completed. So, taking the small cardboard box he'd prepared the previous evening from his case, Grant popped them inside and sealed the lid.

Throwing the remainder of the stuff into the black bag, he tied it securely before placing it carefully at the bottom of the large bin, making sure it would not be discovered by covering it with several others.

Leaving the alley, he moved cautiously from street to street under cover of the early morning mist. Passing the post office he'd chosen the previous evening, he eased the small parcel through the narrow aperture cut into the door, nodding in satisfaction as it made a small thud at the bottom of the box.

Picking up his car from the 24-hour multi-storey car park, he was opening the door of his penthouse flat in London several hours later.

Stepping over the threshold, he congratulated himself on a final job well done.

'Jesus, but you're good, Kramer!' he shouted in triumph. No, not just good, he reflected – *the best!*

Chapter Four

STANDING AROUND THE BOARD, THE GROUP DECLARED THEMSELVES ready. The problem was that no one was sure what to do. Eventually it was Emma who came to the rescue.

'In this book I read, everyone just sat around in a circle, put their hands on a glass, and asked if anyone was there.'

'Did it work?' asked Aled.

'Course it did,' said Roger, butting in, 'it was a bloody book, wasn't it?' Then he added, 'Seriously, though, it can't be that simple, surely?'

'Only one way to find out,' said Aled.

'OK, OK,' said Roger, 'I take it back. But let's say we do get lucky, what then?'

'What do you mean?' asked Jared. 'What's bothering you?'

'I don't know… well, yes I do, but I'm not sure how to put it. What if we get through to something and we don't like the answers?'

'Good point,' said Jared thoughtfully, before turning to the others.

Emma joined in. 'Yes, but let's take it a step further. What happens if we contact something and it turns out to be, well, you know, nasty or something? There's no guarantee it'll be friendly, is there?'

'That's what I was trying to get at, Em,' said Roger, 'but you put it in a better way than me. Think about it this way. What if we call up something and find that it's evil? What if we can't get rid of it? What then?'

Holding his hand up, Jared said, 'Why do I suddenly get the feeling that now we've come to the crunch, some of us are starting to get cold feet? Remember what I said earlier – if anyone is having second thoughts, now's the time to pull out.'

It was obvious one or two of them had reservations, but despite this the vote to carry on was unanimous.

'Who's going to ask the first question?' someone asked.

Surprisingly, it was Michael who spoke up. In a faltering voice he said, 'I think you should, Jared, seeing as it was you who found the board.'

'I'm OK with that,' answered Jared, 'if the rest of you don't mind, that is… *Is anyone there?*'

For some reason as soon as he'd asked the question, Jared burst out laughing. After a moment of stunned silence the others joined in.

When everyone eventually settled down, he analysed his strange reaction. The only conclusion he came to was that it was a combination of two factors: feeling silly, and then not really expecting anything to happen anyway.

Contrite, he said, 'Do you think we might have blown it? What I mean is, if there is really anything there it might not bother answering now.'

'Only one way to find out,' said Aled, 'Try again!'

So he did.

'Is anyone there?'

This time there was a deathly silence, during which time none of them dared move a muscle. The moment was almost surreal. Jared was aware of nothing but the steady rise and fall of his chest. Time seemed to drag interminably, when it fact it had only been a minute or so. Just as he was about to suggest that someone else should have a go, it happened.

Suddenly and without warning the pointer moved.

With short jerky motions it spelled out, '*Y-E-S*'.

Jumping away from the table, they looked at each other in amazement.

'What the fuck!' said Roger, clearly shaken. Immediately embarrassed by his language he said, 'Sorry!' Then, realising he might have been set up, he started grinning.

'All right – who's the clever bugger who moved the pointer?'

Within seconds he had his answer; it was clear none of them had.

'My God, we've done it!' said Aled in amazement. 'We've actually bloody done it.'

Disappointment was etched clearly on her face as Emma said, 'Yes, but perhaps it's gone now; after all, we broke the connection, remember.'

'So let's try again,' said Aled imploringly. 'You never know, it might still be there.'

'If we do re-establish contact, what do you think we should ask?' said Jared.

'Make it simple,' said Roger. 'How about finding out how old it is? After all, if it's a bloody spirit then the odds are it must be ancient.'

'Do you think that might tempt it into making contact?' said someone else.

'Only one way to find out,' said Jared, and when the question was asked the answer wasn't long in coming.

'*Very old indeed... I was born over 2,000 years ago.*'

'Christ, I bet he's an ugly bugger then,' said Roger, ever the comedian.

'Ask it what its name is,' Emma said.

'*I was known as the man of Kerioth,*' came the almost instant reply.

Immediately, Jared looked up. 'For some reason that name rings a bell,' he said to the others.

'What did you do when you were alive?' was the next question.

'*That's interesting,*' it said. '*I looked after the finances for a group of people. As a matter of fact, their leader went on to become quite famous.*'

Before they could think of another question, the pointer moved of its own volition. '*Do you like surprises?*'

Looking over at Jared, Roger said, 'I'm not sure it's supposed to happen like this, is it?'

'Don't look at me, I haven't a clue,' said Jared in reply. 'Let's just go with the flow for a minute, see what happens.'

By now there was no need to take any notes. Everyone was watching the pointer in rapt fascination as it seemed to fly across the board.

'*Did you know there's a secret room under the altar table? It's very old and well hidden, and belonged to an ancient monastery which your chapel was built over.*'

In astonishment, Jared said to the others, 'Well, well, the old legend seems to be true after all.'

Knowing they were intrigued now, the spirit carried on.

'*It's a small room, but its contents are beyond price. An old skeleton and a beautiful black chalice. The chalice can be found hidden in a small recess directly behind the old man's head. Take it, it is a gift.*'

With that the writing stopped.

'I don't like this,' said Jared. 'How do we know we can trust it?'

'Seemed friendly enough to me,' Roger said, 'but it does sound too good to be true.'

'Ask it what it wants in return,' suggested Emma.

'*Nothing,*' came the reply, '*it is a gift. What you do with if after is your affair.*'

'Well,' said Jared, making eye contact with the others, 'what should we do?'

'I say we go for it,' said Aled.

Even though they knew it was there, the entrance to the secret room was so well hidden that it took them nearly ten minutes to find the trapdoor. Making their way down a short flight of steps, they found themselves in a room that was about fifteen feet by ten feet. The walls had been put together in dressed stone by a person of great skill. Ominously, from Jared's perspective, there appeared to be large brass crosses embedded in each of the four walls. Surprisingly, the interior was remarkably dry.

The skeleton dominated the centre of the small room, and once they'd brushed away the cobwebs, they found to their surprise it was wearing a ring.

It was certainly striking.

A strange symbol was engraved into the face, made up of what appeared to be the Star of David encircling a black chalice.

'Wait a minute,' said Jared, 'I've seen this before. I'm sure it's the same symbol old Eric Roberts found on that tombstone a short while ago. The one in the graveyard, remember? The one all the fuss was about.'

'Yes,' said Roger excitedly, 'you're right, but nothing came of it.'

'Not until now anyway,' said Emma quietly.

It didn't take long to find the chalice. Sitting proudly in a small niche near the skeleton's head, it was certainly beautiful, and yet the more they looked at it the more it reminded them of the board. It too seemed to exude an aura of brooding menace. Reaching out tentatively, Jared began to remove it from the recess when suddenly he felt as if he'd been hit by a bolt of electricity. At the same time he felt as if he was standing outside his body, looking down at something which was taking place in another time, another dimension. From his elevated position he saw a man hanging from the branch of a large tree, surrounded by a group of people. Swinging lazily in the light evening breeze, he was a pitiful sight. In death he looked like a broken puppet. Looking closely, he could see that the man had already started to change colour. The tongue, flopping from an open mouth, looked like a purple reptile squirming to escape the prison of its rapidly cooling body. Amazingly, Jared realised he could hear as well as see. Straining so as not to miss a word, he could tell from the tone of the voices that the people in the group were arguing fiercely.

Initially it seemed that none of those present had any thoughts of remorse, least of all sympathy when they'd dragged the man sobbing and begging for mercy from his home. Instead it was clear they'd harboured a deep sense of anger towards the victim. The hatred had been almost tangible, so close to the surface that it had burst out like pus from an aching boil. Now, looking up at the pathetic figure hanging above them, their anger began to cool. Perhaps revenge wasn't so sweet after all, one of the more level-headed of the group was saying. True, it had satisfied their blood lust for a while, but it wouldn't bring the Master back. In the cold light of day doubts began to emerge.

Suddenly Jared was jerked back into the present.

Shaking his head from side to side, he found it difficult to believe the experience had been real, so wisely he decided to say nothing to the others. Amazingly, they seemed to have noticed nothing amiss.

It was then Jared saw the small intricate symbols. Nine in total, they'd been beautifully engraved into the body of the chalice. As it was completely black, he guessed it had been crafted from solid obsidian.

Lifting it to his ear and shaking it, Jared said, 'I thought as much. I think there's something inside, but to find out what it is, we'll have to break it open, and I don't think that's a good idea somehow.'

Looking around at the others, he could see they agreed with him.

About to turn away, Aled noticed the recess seemed to be deeper than they'd first suspected. Shouting in triumph, he put his hand in and came out with what appeared to be a small scroll. With a theatrical flourish he handed it to Jared.

'Here, brains, you're the language expert – what does it say?'

Studying it by the dim light of the single candle they'd brought from upstairs, Jared could see it was in fairly good condition. It was a scroll, his initial guess had been correct; but surprisingly, whatever was on it had been written in an ancient form of Latin.

'Well,' they said in unison, 'can you read it?'

'It'll take a few minutes,' said Jared, 'but yes, my Latin should be up to it. It shouldn't pose too many problems.'

'Why don't we take it upstairs? The light's better up there,' said Emma.

'Good idea, Em,' said Jared, and so carefully, one step at a time, they made their way back.

With everyone pushing and shoving, Jared soon lost patience. Finally he'd had enough. Forcing them back, he said, 'OK, that's it! Give me some room, or I'll never be able to translate the bloody thing.'

When he finally managed to obtain some semblance of order he began.

'It seems to have been written by the founding father of the monastery that Carmel's built on, and it's badly faded in places, but here goes anyway.' He paused.

'Oh, shit! That's a bright start...'

'Why, what's the matter?' cried Roger in alarm.

'Well, it's a warning – and not a very subtle one at that.'

'Never mind that,' said Emma, 'just get on with it, will you! The suspense is killing me.'

And so he did.

' "Whoever finds the chalice, beware! For all that is holy, I implore you to leave it unopened. Found accidentally by two young boys, they have sworn never to reveal its source to anyone but us. Brought to our humble monastery along with a large codex, things soon began to change. Our once happy environment became polluted; brother quarrelled with brother and in some instances physical violence broke out. I can only thank the Lord we decided to leave the cursed object untouched until I had the opportunity to translate the codex."

'Hang on,' Jared said, stopping for a moment. 'What codex? There wasn't anything else hidden in the hole, was there, Al?'

'Nah, nothing – I checked,' said Aled.

'Never mind,' was Jared's comment before carrying on with the translation.

' "Written in some ancient form of Aramaic, our dear Lord's language, it took several weeks to work through. However, the horrors I discovered therein will haunt me for ever. I dare not reveal everything to the brothers, for fear of their very souls. There remains a single section to decipher, and although it appears quite detailed, I hope to complete it by tonight. Now that I am clear as to the deadly intent of the foul object imprisoned in the chalice, I have commissioned a small tomb, a secret room in which to bury it, in the hope that its power may be less effective. However, in truth I do not hold out too much expectation of success. Should anyone inadvertently find what we have hidden, the contents of this scroll will act as a warning, although I pray it will never be needed."

'That's strange,' said Jared, stopping suddenly and looking up at the others. 'The handwriting appears to be different here... it's almost as if someone else has taken over.' He continued reading.

'Ah, that explains it,' he said a moment later.

'Explains what?' asked Emma.

'My guess was right. Another guy has taken over the story – listen.

' "Dear God in heaven, disaster, our small community is in turmoil! Early this morning, we found the old father hanging in his cell. That it was suicide is beyond doubt, for he left instructions the secret room be completed as soon as possible. His death seems to have had something to do with the translation of the final section, for inscribed on the wall behind him was the symbol he'd puzzled so long over.

' "His final instruction was that I move heaven and earth to ensure the codex be returned to its original hiding place. Apart from the two young boys, I am now the only one who knows where the codex is hidden. That secret I will take to my grave, but for anyone who has the patience and skill I leave behind a clue.

' "Beneath the grave of the sleeping giant lies the valley of the haunted forest. Through the passageway of the gods, between the mountains that reach to the sky, lies the waterfall that tumbles from heaven. There behold the mouth of the demon. With crooked fangs and ocean wide, therein lays the hiding place of the codex."

'That's it,' said Jared glancing up at the others, 'that's all it says, I'm afraid.'

The silence was broken by Emma, who said, 'Well, where do we go from here? What do you think we should do with the chalice?'

'I'm for putting it back and forgetting all about it. Quit while we're ahead, I say,' said Jared.

'I'm with you there,' said Roger. 'Remember the old father was explicit: whatever's in that bloody chalice is pure evil. Come on, admit it, we all felt it when we handled the damn thing – a strange tingling sensation. It felt to me as if whatever was inside was trying to get out.'

None of them noticed Jared's startled expression.

As if speaking to herself, Emma said, 'Imagine how powerful it would be if it managed to escape. Despite all the old father's precautions, it still wasn't enough, was it?'

'What do you mean, Em?' asked Jared quizzically.

'It's obvious, isn't it? Carmel and the old legends – no wonder it feels so wrong.'

'Of course!' said Jared in excitement. 'You're right, how stupid of me not think of it! Its power must have been seeping out over the centuries – like radiation leaking from a nuclear power plant, if you like.'

It didn't take them long to replace the chalice, and then with one final lingering look they turned to leave.

Roger was poised at the first step when Jared, waving the scroll in the air, said, 'Forgotten something, have we?'

Stepping forward, Aled said, 'Want me to put it back? It won't take a minute.'

'No, thanks, Al, as a matter of fact I'm going to burn it.'

'What the hell do you want to do that for?' asked Roger in astonishment.

'Simple – I don't want anyone working out the riddle and stumbling on the codex. In the long run I think the secret its harbouring might turn out to be just as dangerous as the chalice. Remember, the old father gave his life to protect it.'

While Roger lit a match, Jared held the scroll upside down.

Starting at the bottom, they watched as the flames took hold. Slowly at first and then with greater speed they swiftly devoured the old material. When he couldn't hold on any longer, Jared let it drop to the floor. Within seconds all that remained was a small pile of ashes. Scattering them with his foot, he said a silent prayer that the old father's death hadn't been in vain.

Making sure they left no traces, they all trudged sombrely back to the altar.

As they were about to pack everything away, Michael spoke up. 'Do you think we should talk to the spirit again, let it know we've seen through its little plan?'

'I'm not sure that's wise,' said Emma. 'I wouldn't want to piss it off or anything.'

Thinking about it for a moment, Jared said, 'No, you're right, Michael. Let's let the devious bastard know we've seen through its little scheme.'

The reply, once they'd asked if it was still there, was instantaneous; it was almost as if the spirit had been waiting patiently for their return. Once they'd made contact however, all pretence of patience vanished.

'*Have you brought the chalice?*' it spelt out.

Smiling Jared spelt out, 'N-O'.

'But you did find it, didn't you?' it asked again.

'Oh, yes,' Jared wrote, 'but you forgot to mention the scroll, the warning. It was very explicit. Well, we've news for you, we're not prepared to be pawns in your sick little game.'

Although the conversation was taking place by means of a pointer, they could almost feel the waves of hatred emanating from the board.

The next time the pointer moved, the spirit took a completely different tack. It began pleading for its release. It explained in length how lonely it had been, imprisoned for all those centuries. Finally it promised them riches beyond their wildest dreams.

Putting an end to the charade, Jared explained they knew it was evil, had polluted both the monastery and chapel, and as far as they were concerned it could rot in hell!

The expected explosion of foul-mouthed rhetoric didn't materialise; instead what it spelt out was something far more disturbing.

'Fools, my patience is endless. Do you think I will be imprisoned for ever? The time is approaching rapidly when I will return. For you it would have been better had you not been born, for in those days I shall receive retribution. Those charlatans who stand as symbols of power in their pathetic sanctuaries will learn the truth. The houses of their God shall be brought crumbling down, their faith exposed as a worthless sham.'

Looking at the others, Jared said, 'That's strange, it's almost as if it's quoting chunks from the Bible.'

'Don't know about that; you're the expert on that kind of stuff,' said Roger. 'But if you ask me, it sounds as if it's bloody crackers.'

'No, Rog,' Jared replied in a serious tone. 'The stuff its spouting is too structured for that. I if I didn't know better I'd say it was taking chunks straight out of Revelations.'

Once again the pointer moved.

'For some reason, you, Jared, seem to be special. Perhaps even a worthy adversary. However it will do you no good. I will have my revenge. Heed my words, special one. Once I am free your entire village and your places of worship shall drip with blood. But for you I will reserve a special gift.'

For several seconds they stood there stunned, taken completely by surprise at the savage fury of the thing's hatred. Suddenly the pointer rose from the board, hovered in mid air and without warning buried itself in the pulpit directly behind Jared's head.

'Christ!' said Roger visibly shaken. 'That was bloody close – an inch either way and you'd have been talking to that thing in person!'

'That's not funny, Roger,' Emma said, 'he could have been killed.'

'It wasn't meant to be funny, Em. What I'm saying is we might have underestimated its power, that's all.'

'Shit!' said Aled. 'If that's the case, what other kind of nasty surprises has it got up its sleeve?'

Speaking quietly, Jared turned to the others and said, 'Aled and Roger could have a point, although I'm convinced that as long as this thing remains trapped in the main body of the chapel its powers are limited.'

'What about the biblical mumbo jumbo it was spouting before the pointer tried to decapitate you? Do you think it's capable of anything like that?' asked Michael.

'I'm sure if it could escape it would be, but as I said before, as long as we leave it where it is I think we'll be safe.'

'I agree with you,' said Michael, 'up to now its influence has been localised. Think about it; everything unpleasant that's taken place, has occurred inside the church. Nothing bad has happened outside these four walls, has it?'

'Not yet,' said Emma, so quietly that no one else heard the comment.

'Look, this is getting us nowhere,' said Jared. 'Let's pack up and go home. Perhaps a good night's sleep will do us the world of good. Things might seem a lot better in the morning.'

Glancing at his watch, Roger said, 'It's 1 a.m. now. If we don't go soon, were not going to get any bloody sleep.'

'How about meeting in Alec's café tomorrow – to talk things over, I mean? About seven suit everyone?' Looking at his own watch, he suddenly realised what Roger was talking about and, correcting himself, said, 'Sorry – tonight, I mean.'

They were nearly home when Jared said, 'The only thing that puzzles me is why on earth the thing thought I was special. I can't figure that one out.'

'No, it was odd, wasn't it?' said Emma in reply.

Chapter Five

DRESSED ENTIRELY IN BLACK, HIS FACE COVERED BY A TIGHT-FITTING ski mask, the man blended seamlessly into the dark shadows cast by the recess of the underpass. Suddenly, the inky blackness was pierced by two tiny pin-points of white as his eyes flickered towards his Rolex Submariner.

Shit – she was five minutes late…

With a sudden stab of unease, the thought came unbidden. What if she'd changed her routine? It had never happened before, he realised, but that was no guarantee of success, was it? Apprehension seeped from every pore, and with mounting panic he knew that if that were the case, at such short notice, he'd never find a suitable replacement. What made success more imperative was the sacred task had to be performed before midnight, otherwise… the remainder of the thought was left hanging in the air.

As a member of an elite group of assassins called the Brotherhood, failure was not an option. The very thought brought icy tentacles of fear coursing through his body, and without warning his chest tightened involuntarily.

Forcing himself to remain calm, he took several deep breaths until gradually the feeling of panic eased.

Just then, he heard the familiar sound of stiletto heels reverberating on the surface of the hard cobblestones at the entrance to the underpass. Seconds later she appeared out of the gloom, her silhouette barely visible against the backdrop of weak light produced by the only undamaged bulb in the tunnel. Breathing a sigh of relief, he was careful not to let the air escape his mouth for fear it would betray his position.

Removing one of the razor sharp sicas from its sheath, he was suddenly distracted. The sight of her wearing the by now familiar cheap rubber skirt and black fishnet stockings brought an instant hardening to his groin. Knowing it was not the time for such distractions, he fought hard to force the disturbing image back into his subconscious; back to where it could do the least damage.

Then he was ready.

Letting her get two paces ahead, he judged the moment to perfection. With the speed of a striking mamba, he covered her mouth with one hand, while with the other he angled her head sideways before slitting her throat from ear to ear. The blade was so sharp it not only cut through her windpipe, but severed sinews and cartilage as well. Experience had taught him that jetting blood gushing from slashed arteries would spray over a large area, and so he was careful not to allow any to splash over the pram and wake the sleeping infant. His task complete, he wiped the sica on his sleeve before replacing it with almost reverential care into its leather holder. Looking down, he was surprised to see the wound was so deep that the only thing holding the woman's head onto her shoulders were a few tattered remnants of tendon and skin.

With infinite care, he lowered her to the floor.

Ashamed now of his earlier fear, his abject terror at failing in his appointed task, he decided on the spur of the moment to break with protocol. As a punishment for making him feel foolish, he decided to have some fun with the body. Placing the woman in the pram, he positioned her torso so that her head was resting on her knees. Once he'd finished, he stepped back to admire his handiwork. Satisfied, he gave a little chuckle, as from a certain angle, the deep gaping wound gave the impression that she had two mouths.

Knowing he was taking a chance indulging in such fantasies, and that someone might appear at any moment, he wasted no more time. He hastily picked up the child and, hugging her to his chest, hurried off into the night.

Eric Roberts, the ageing minister of Carmel chapel, was suddenly brought out of his reverie by the interruption to the programme. Until then he hadn't realised he'd become so bored with the film that his mind had wandered. Suddenly he was back in the present, his mind alert and sharp.

'Good evening, this is Julie Owen and Martin Thomas speaking to you on behalf of BBC Wales. We are sorry to interrupt the programme, but the police have just issued the following newsflash. It seems an eighteen-month-old baby girl was abducted and the mother brutally murdered in the Cardiff Bay area at around 9 p.m. this evening. At present we have no further details. Meanwhile, we have been asked to make the following appeal on behalf of the police. They would like to hear from anyone who was in or around the area at that particular time. It might be that someone saw or heard something that at the time seemed inconsequential. However, in the hands of the police it may turn out to provide an invaluable clue to the kidnapping. Should that be the case, the number to contact will be given at the end of the programme.'

Far from being disturbed by the announcement, old Eric had been expecting it. Indeed he would have been surprised had it not been made. He wondered what the police would have made of the fact that from 1967 onwards, somewhere in Britain a young child had been abducted on exactly the same date every year. He was surprised that so far no enterprising journalist had picked up on the fact. The pattern was always the same, and he was convinced of one thing: whoever the perpetrators were, they were highly organised and extremely clever.

No clues had ever been discovered at any of the crime scenes, but more importantly until now, the organisation had been meticulous in ensuring they drew no undue attention to themselves. For that reason he was at a loss to explain why this kidnapping had involved the use of extreme violence. Reading between the lines, the murder of the young mother appeared to have been a particularly brutal one, and he wondered why. Why break one of their golden rules? he thought to himself. By now he was fairly certain in his own mind of the reasons for the kidnappings. It had all started with his obsession with the Knights Templar.

His interest had begun innocently enough, with some research material for a doctoral thesis. Unfortunately, the more he'd delved into the subject the more problems he'd unearthed. In the end he'd been forced to admit he'd come up with more questions than answers. From that time on he'd become hooked, and gradually it had taken over his life. Now, some thirty years later, he admitted in a modest way, he was probably one of the foremost experts in the country on the subject. What he'd unearthed had been incredible. His hypothesis was staggering, although he had to admit there still remained a few pieces of the jigsaw to be fitted in. One of those pieces had suddenly fallen into his lap quite by accident on 6 March 1967, or to be precise the 6th and 7th, with the deaths of three figures he'd become familiar with through his research. The story had caught the attention of the media simply because it was extremely unusual to have three hangings in a two-day period. For Eric, however, the deaths had been no coincidence – and certainly not suicides, as had been reported at the time. He was convinced the three had been deliberately silenced in order to stop further revelations pertaining to a publication entitled *Le Serpent Rouge*, or *The Red Serpent*. Of that much he was sure.

With a weary sigh, he suddenly switched off the television and made his way to the spare room. Over the years his collection of material had become so extensive that he'd had to convert one of the downstairs rooms into a makeshift library. Books, files and magazine articles of all kinds were scattered everywhere, while sitting on top of his battered fake antique desk stood the only article of high-tech equipment he owned: his prized computer. A Microstar with Intel Pentium 4, it was by no means the most expensive on offer when he'd bought it years ago, but surprisingly it had turned out to be far more powerful than many more glamorous and highly priced models. To a casual observer it might have escaped their attention that despite the amount of clutter, everything was neat and tidy, testimony to the fact Eric's records were meticulous.

Sitting in his favourite armchair, which he acknowledged had seen better days, he thought about the broadcast, and suddenly his mood turned to one of nostalgia. He remembered what he euphemistically termed as the 'good old days'.

On leaving theological college he'd been bursting with missionary zeal, confident in the knowledge his faith would sustain him, come what may. His choice of location had been a good one. Where else but in the Welsh valleys could you find so many places of worship squeezed into such a small area? He had to admit he'd found it amusing at first, to see each chapel clinging fanatically to its own denominational doctrine, while at the same time professing allegiance to the same God.

Despite everything, he'd found an instant rapport with the people. They, like him, were deeply religious and proudly patriotic. If he was honest he would have admitted that he did have serious misgivings when he'd been offered the position, wondering how a North Walian would be accepted in the heart of South Wales, but his fears had been groundless. He'd been accepted immediately. The people had been crying out for spiritual guidance, for spiritual nourishment, and he was only too willing to provide it.

So where had it all gone wrong?

In hindsight he realised it was probably the combination of several factors. The demise of the mining industry was one, but most of all the arrival of science. Science was the new religion, it had the answer to everything, and because of that God had become redundant. The new credo was simple: if you couldn't see it, touch it or weigh it, then it simply wasn't true.

Casting his mind back to the youngsters he'd taught over the last thirty years or so, he was forced to an unpleasant conclusion. The five who'd recently past through his hands might well be the last. Ticking them off in his mind, he attempted a brief mental summary of each.

First there was Jared Hunter, the natural leader of the five. A talented boy and extremely gifted, he was destined to follow in his uncle's footsteps when he took up his place at Oxford University next year.

Then there was Emma, Jared's lifelong girlfriend – if that's what you called them these days, he thought with wry amusement. She was a charming girl who always seemed to have time for others; nothing seemed to be too much trouble for her. A striking looking girl, she was totally unaware of her looks and the effect she had on the opposite sex. To add to that, she had the personality to charm Old Nick himself, he thought with a chuckle.

The third member of the group was Roger Carrington; just thinking about him brought a smile to Eric's face. He recalled with fondness how on several occasions he'd almost driven him to distraction. The joker in the pack undoubtedly, but unless he was mistaken, he'd find work, despite the fact he could hardly be described as an academic.

Aled, he mused... now he was something of an enigma, really. A solid, dependable type with a leaning towards the theatrical, but given the right break, he was sure he could make something of himself.

Finally there was Michael. His was a tragic story. His whole family had been wiped out in a car accident leaving him utterly alone. Since then he'd been brought up in the local homes. A shy boy, Jared had taken him under his wing, looked after him like a brother. His patience and understanding had worked wonders, however, as over the last few months he'd gradually come out of his shell.

Dragging himself back into the present, Eric was amazed that so far his little chapel had survived, when several of the others in the area had either closed or been left to rot. As a realist, however, he knew the writing was on the wall for Carmel too. It was only a matter of time. He supposed that's why the hierarchy had asked him to stay on for a while longer, despite his age.

Carmel had never been a happy place; he knew that only too well. He knew too the stories handed down about it over the years. The problem was he couldn't refute them. In all honesty there were other incidents, ones he'd kept to himself, for the simple reason he was afraid to mention them.

It was then the odd incident of a few years ago came back to him with startling clarity.

With a smile, he reflected that it was probably one of the most exciting things that had ever happened to him. It had even earned a mention in the national papers, if he remembered correctly. For a short while he'd been a minor celebrity.

Yes, it came back to him now; it was just after the storm. He'd gone into the graveyard to tidy up after the damage caused by the high winds, when he'd noticed two small bushes uprooted in a remote corner of the cemetery. Intending to burn them along with the other detritus, he'd stooped to pick them up, when suddenly he discovered what could only be described as a flat tombstone. Not big, about two foot square, it was embossed with a striking symbol. The Star of David he was sure about, but on the inside was something he'd never seen before – an enclosed black chalice. Lifting the stone had been beyond him, so he'd sent for one of his parishioners who lived at the bottom of the hill, an immensely strong man. It wasn't long before between them they'd prised it free.

To their disappointment there was nothing hidden underneath. In consternation, they'd even dug down a few feet just to make sure. In the end they'd put the stone back and forgotten all about it. And of course there had been the other thing, but the least said about that the better. That was his little secret.

A week later, Eric was browsing through his Sunday newspaper when a particular item caught his eye. It was related to the abduction of the infant and the murder of its young mother. Since then the full extent of her horrific injuries had become common knowledge, and the seemingly unwarranted viciousness of the attack had drawn a good deal of media attention. For reasons the police were unable to fathom, the body of a man dressed in black had been found hanging from the lamp post at the entrance to the underpass in which the young mother had been killed. What made the incident even stranger was that his tongue had been surgically altered. According to the reports it looked more like that of a serpent than a human being. Experts trying to explain the anomaly had hypothesised it had been done deliberately, that it had been carried out as some kind of ritualistic warning.

On finishing the article, Eric was in a pensive mood. One part of the puzzle had been cleared up. The murder of the young mother had been a mistake, a rush of blood to the head perhaps, or some reason that was beyond understanding. Whatever… having broken one of the cardinal rules of the organisation, the assassin had been made to pay with his own life.

The second part still bothered him. Just like the three men in Paris, he'd been hanged. So why was the organisation using such an archaic form of execution? He had no doubt that eventually the answer would come to him, but for the moment he had to admit he was baffled.

Chapter Six

'IF YOU WOULD JUST SIGN HERE, PLEASE, MR HUNTER,' SAID CARL Rivers, handing his client a solid gold Parker pen with a flourish. It never failed to amaze him how it was always the little things that impressed people. Even now, after all these years, he could still hear the old man's advice ringing in his ears. 'Rivers, if you want to succeed in this game then get the little things right. Do that and the other things will take care of themselves.'

How right he'd been, he realised, as he leaned across the desk to turn over the first page of the document. 'And then here, and finally here. Yes, that's it, sir, in those places marked in pencil with an X.'

Checking everything was in order he said, 'All done, sir.'

He'd certainly hit the jackpot with this one; the commission alone would pay for a Caribbean cruise for the wife and kids, get them out from under his feet for a while. Then he'd have time on his hands to complete some unfinished business with his new secretary, he thought with relish.

Rising from his leather chair, he leaned over to shake Edwin's hand, 'Congratulations, Mr Hunter, you're now the proud owner of Mendel Hall. I'm sure you'll be very happy there.'

On a more serious note, he added, 'But if I might be so bold, I can only admire how you obtained such a treasure at a fraction of its market value. A masterly piece of business, I must admit.'

Grasping the proffered hand, Edwin was surprised to feel that it was limp and damp... like a cold fish, was the analogy that sprung to mind. He was not about to explain to Carl Rivers that his purchase of the house had nothing at all to do with shrewd business acumen, but was in fact more the product of sheer dumb luck. In all honesty, he still couldn't believe how it had come about. Suddenly one morning, completely out the blue, a final year student had approached him offering the house and trappings for a song. In truth he hadn't needed much time to think about it, and so before he really knew what was happening the deal was done and dusted. Amazingly, by the time he'd sold his other house, which had doubled in value since he'd bought it years ago, he'd ended up with a mortgage that hadn't broken the bank. True, there was one downside to the deal: it meant that in future he would have to commute to Oxford several days a week in order to fulfil his obligations to the university, but that was small price to pay for such an acquisition. Besides, he told himself, it wasn't a particularly arduous journey anyway. Talking to the student afterwards he'd learned that his father, a rich diamond merchant, had bought the mansion for his only son to live in while he was studying. Now he'd finished his course, he was going back to South Africa to join his father's company.

'Be glad to see the sun again,' was his parting shot.

Why he'd decided to offer it to him he never knew. True, he'd helped him with some personal research, but no more than several others in that year. Despite this, the boy was adamant his father wanted to repay him for his kindness.

Looking back at his life, he saw that he'd been lucky, with a well-paid job, a mansion and a glowing reputation as one of the best scholars of his era. Not bad for someone who'd been dumped on a doorstep as a baby, he thought.

It had all started when he and his older brother had been found on the steps of a nursing home all those years ago. It had been a remarkable story. Two young boys, the eldest no more than eighteen months, were found squashed into a large basket along with enough money to last for a year. Wouldn't have worked out today, Edwin thought wryly; the two of us might have survived, but the money would have disappeared, that's for sure.

Despite weeks of searching, their real parents had never been found. Put up for adoption some time later, the two boys were eventually taken in by an elderly couple who turned out to be idyllic parents. When they finally passed away, the house became theirs. Deciding to sell, they were pleasantly surprised when the proceeds amounted to what was in those days a fairly substantial lump sum. Edwin didn't see as much of his brother as he liked, but whenever he thought about him it was always with mixed emotions. He felt fierce love and pride, tinged with a trace of sadness, but in particular guilt.

As far as brothers went, they couldn't have been more different. Edwin was dark and a shade over six foot tall, while Thomas Vivian, affectionately known as TV, was fair-haired and shorter. The differences didn't end there, either. Along with most other men in the village, Tommy became a coal miner, while Edwin graduated from Cardiff University with a first, and shortly after began teaching. With his qualifications he was destined for better though, and in time accepted a post at Oxford University lecturing in Semitic languages.

Yes, all in all he'd done well for himself.

Yet, he admitted with a heavy sigh, at times he felt there was something missing.

His busy work schedule ensured very little time was left for personal pleasure. Admittedly there'd been the odd romantic dalliance, but they'd come to nothing, as he knew they would. 'You're married to your job,' one of his more permanent encounters had informed him, before walking out of the door without a second glance. He supposed that in one way he envied his brother's family life, but it was too late for that now, far too late.

Telling himself he was in danger of spoiling the moment, he had a sudden thought: I know what you need, Hunter; it's a visit to your newly acquired stately home. The comment was made tongue in cheek, because in reality Edwin was totally unpretentious. Despite the trappings of wealth, he remained the same old Edwin he'd always been. Had he only known it, that's why he was so popular with students and colleagues alike.

Arriving in his X-type Jaguar saloon at the entrance to his new home, Edwin picked up the remote from the passenger seat and pressed the red button as he'd been shown. Almost immediately the large gates, operating electronically, swung smoothly inwards. Made of wrought iron and painted in black and gold, they were an impressive sight.

Cruising along in low gear, he opened the window in order to enjoy the scenery. On either side, well-manicured lawns slopped gently towards the drive. The strategically placed flower beds were a riot of colour at this time of year. Trees of all shapes and sizes, startling in their diversity, were spread out as far as the eye could see. The whole scene was so breathtaking that it appeared as if it had been borrowed from a painting by Constable. The beautiful burnished red of the copper beeches vied with the more subtle tones of the conifers and oaks in an outrageous display of horticultural vanity.

All this, he thought to himself in amazement, and there's still no sign of the house.

Suddenly, there it was.

Struggling with superlatives with which to describe it, he had great difficulty in believing it was really his.

Unable to contain his growing excitement, he parked the Jaguar in the gravel driveway and trotted up the short flight of stone steps to the large double doors which fronted the house. Opening them with the key the estate agent had given him was easier than expected, as in the end a gentle nudge was all that was required. Stepping into the hallway he was greeted by a magnificent wooden staircase that provided open plan access to the first and second floors. Built in semicircular fashion, it spread out like a rippling wave on either side.

If his memory served him correctly there were twenty bedrooms, ten to a floor, and each with its own en suite facilities. It took him nearly an hour to work his way through them all, noting with amazement how each had been decorated in its own individual style.

The ground floor was equally impressive. Jokingly, he chided himself that it was so spacious that unless he was careful, it would be quite easy to get lost.

The kitchen was a work of art. Tastefully furnished with a blend of high technology and old-world charm in mind, the designer had succeeded perfectly. The focal point was a huge open fireplace from which hung all kinds of pots and pans. Noting the stack of freshly cut logs, he imagined himself standing before it like a country squire on a cold winter's day. Above the fireplace was a flue of magnificent burnished copper, and although it was obviously a later addition, it complemented the rest of the room beautifully.

Cleverly, the ceiling had been lowered in order to give it a nineteenth-century effect. Meanwhile in order to complete the overall image, magnificent oak beams had been installed that ran the length of the entire room.

Amazing as the kitchen was, it was surpassed by the library, which quite simply took his breath away. Covered from floor to ceiling with every kind of book imaginable, it even boasted its own movable ladder. What at first looked like a novelty soon proved otherwise, however, as Edwin soon found it was the only practical way in which some of the more inaccessible shelves could be accessed. A brief survey showed that several of the books were very valuable first editions. Bound in leather, the titles had been overlaid in gold leaf.

With time running out, the last place he visited was the study. Sumptuously decorated in oak and mahogany, it boasted furniture that was worth a king's ransom. The smell told him long before he touched them that the settee and armchairs were of the highest quality leather. The floor, decked out in solid oak, was covered in several places by what appeared to be genuine Persian rugs.

Glancing at his watch, he saw that time was running out. There were several other rooms to explore, in particular the games room, which according to the brochure had a full-size snooker table; but that would have to wait for another time, he thought. Besides, he'd seen enough for one day. The enormity of what he'd acquired was beginning to dawn on him. This was wealth beyond his wildest dreams.

In joyful anticipation he wondered if Jared would visit; he would love this place, he was sure, especially the library. Despite an overwhelming feeling of elation, a nagging doubt still lingered. Could anyone be this lucky?

The following morning, awaking as if from a bad dream, Edwin opened one eye tentatively, looked around the room, then when he felt it was safe opened the other. Deciding to chance it, he sat up and threw back the covers.

'So far so good,' he mumbled to himself. It was then the headache hit him.

Christ, he felt like shit...

Not normally a big drinker, he'd gone over the top last night, but what the hell, he'd reasoned, it wasn't every day you acquired a mansion! In hindsight, he realised he remembered very little of the previous evening. Then it came back to him. Even taking it steadily it hadn't been long before he'd polished off the first bottle, but then like a bloody fool he'd started on the second, and then in no time at all that was gone too. Normally he treated red wine with respect for the simple reason he knew what a mess it could make of people, especially him. Yes, he thought wistfully, last night had been living proof of that. Still, it had been worth it, he admitted.

Forcing himself out of bed, he said, 'Come on, you lazy bugger, you've work to go to, hangover or not!'

Making his way to the bathroom, he rubbed his hand over his chin and felt the thick stubble. One of the curses of being so dark, he mused, was that he often had to shave twice a day. When he was younger he'd been able to get away with it, to pass it off as 'designer stubble', as his students fashionably called it. At his age, with the grey showing through in patches, he knew he simply looked scruffy.

Studying his face in the mirror, he realised that he looked dreadful. Still, nothing a couple of paracetamols and a cup of strong black coffee wouldn't cure, he told himself. And he was right. Several hours later, the drive to Oxford a blur, he was walking up the steps at the entrance to King's College; a new-found spring in his step.

Opening the door of the outer office, he was greeted by a cheery, 'Good morning, Edwin,' from his secretary. In her late sixties, Marlene had been eligible to retire several years ago, but for some reason had decided against it. For that, Edwin had been eternally grateful, openly admitting that without her he'd be lost. Hating any kind of formality, they'd been on first-name terms from day one, and their good-natured ribbing of each other was legendary within the department.

True to form, peering from behind her computer screen, she lifted her glasses. 'Oh, my, but you look like shit – if you don't mind me saying so, that is,' she said with a chuckle.

Sheepishly, Edwin said, 'It wouldn't make any difference if I did, and you know it, you old witch!'

With a burst of laughter Marlene returned to her work.

Before he could open the door of his private office, she called out, 'Oh, by the way, a parcel arrived for you this morning, so I took the liberty of putting it in your office,' adding, 'I suppose you could do with a cup of coffee. Strong and black too, by the look of you.'

'Yes, please!' shouted Edwin before moving into the office.

The package when he saw it took him by surprise. It wasn't what he'd expected at all. He'd had visions of a box or something similar. Instead what greeted him was a long thin cylindrical holder, the kind usually associated with rolled up posters or valuable maps. Inspecting it, he thought, That's odd, there doesn't seem to be a return address.

Sticking his head out of the door, he nearly collided with Marlene who was in the process of bringing him his coffee. A disaster averted, they both laughed before he asked, 'You didn't happen to notice who delivered this, did you? It's just that whoever sent it seems to have forgotten to add a return address.'

'Funny you should say that,' she replied, 'but it doesn't seem to have been delivered in the normal way. It was just sitting there propped up against the door when I came to work. Nothing the matter, is there?'

'No, no,' said Edwin, 'nothing like that. I'm just intrigued, that's all. Do me a favour, will you? Hold all my calls for the next hour or so; this could turn out to be interesting.'

Peering over his shoulder he could see she was trying her best to work out what it was, until with a grin he said, 'OK, that's enough, you nosey old bat! Back to work, if you please.'

Seeing her crestfallen face, he added, 'Don't worry, as soon as I've worked out what it is you'll be the first to know, I promise.'

Her dignity restored somewhat, she perked up visibly before moving out of the office and closing the door behind her.

Picking the parcel up gingerly, Edwin removed the top before looking inside. Whatever it was, it was some kind of document; that much he was sure of. Tipping it out carefully, he was amazed to see that it seemed to be a photocopy of a scroll. With the utmost care he unrolled it. Using paperweights to hold down the corners, he proceeded to study it through a magnifying glass, knowing that only a cursory appraisal would be possible in the limited time available to him; knowing too, that even if it had been the original, the only sure way to determine its age would have been by radiocarbon dating, and that would have taken time.

Disappointingly, it appeared at a glance that several portions were missing. On closer inspection he saw that the original must have been burnt. It was almost, he surmised, as if someone had attempted to destroy it and then had second thoughts, or perhaps had been physically restrained from completing the task. There were several other small areas which looked suspiciously like scorch marks too, he noted.

Anyway, first things first, he thought to himself, let's see what it says.

It was more difficult than he'd first anticipated, but as he began to translate, an incredible – and fanciful – story emerged. Surprisingly, it turned out to be written in what appeared to be a very early form of Aramaic, the kind that was used in and around the time of Jesus. That, he reasoned, boded well for its authenticity. The scroll didn't make clear who the author was, but the bulk of the story concerned an ancient ritual that was frightening in its implications.

According to the tale, a sinister secret society existed whose members were rumoured to be able to bring the dead to life. The story seemed to have originated with the brother of a man called Barabbas, who for some unknown reason was brutally killed in a mob hanging. Overcome with grief, Barabbas traced the sect to their hiding place, a skilfully concealed cave deep in a remote desert area between Egypt and Israel called the Negev. It appeared that for a substantial sum of money, his brother was brought back in order to exact revenge on those who had callously taken his life.

As he read on, Edwin noted with a growing sense of horror that in order for the ritual to work, the body had to be decapitated and preserved using a secret process handed down by the ancient Egyptians and further refined by the sect. What remained was then burned and the bones reduced to ashes. According to the scroll, once the ancient cabbalistic words of power had been used, the spirit of the dead person returned to life. Interestingly it seemed the sect had issued a warning to Barabbas. They had hinted that depending on the intensity of his brother's hatred, once brought back, he might well prove to be uncontrollable, even by him. Devastated by his brother's death, however, it seemed he was prepared to take the chance.

Towards the end, the scroll went on to describe how once the spirit had been activated, it embarked on a killing spree that no amount of blood seemed to be able to satisfy. Disgusted, but at the same time fascinated, Edwin read on until suddenly in mid-sentence the tale came to an abrupt end. In disappointment, he realised the damaged scroll would never reveal its final secret, and he was left wondering how, or indeed if, the horror was ever overcome.

Dragging his mind back to the present, he told himself the first thing to do was to find out who had sent it and why. True, he was acknowledged as one of the foremost experts in translating old documents, but when people wanted his advice they usually made an appointment.

In this case he had no idea who had sent the text.

Even more baffling, there was no return address…

Chapter Seven

STARING AT EACH OTHER ACROSS THE TABLE IN ALEC'S, THE GROUP looked a sorry sight. Bright-eyed and bushy-tailed they certainly weren't. Instead, the trademarks of a troubled night were there for all to see: haggard faces, dark rings under the eyes and swollen puffy cheeks bore ample testimony to lack of sleep.

To call Alec's a café was pretentious, as in fact it was a corrugated tin shed. True, it had been painted green in order to lend it an air of respectability, but it was a tin shed nevertheless. The inside was an anachronism. Stepping through the door gave you a feeling you'd been transported back to the early sixties. During the winter months an ancient coal-burning stove ensured the place was warm and cosy. In strategic places around the room sat several small wooden tables, the legacy no doubt of some local car boot sale. Brightly coloured plastic tablecloths and cruet sets of a garish design lent the place a warmth and cheerfulness that surprised many a visitor. But, along with everything else in the café, they were spotlessly clean. Behind the large wooden counter that ran almost the length of the room was a treasure trove of sweets, crisps and canned drinks. The last section, euphemistically dubbed 'Alec's kitchen', was hidden from view by a simple curtain and was strictly off limits to anyone but him. Directly opposite sat the pièce de résistance – the jukebox – complete with sixties music!

An amiable Welshman of Portuguese descent, Alec worked up to ten hours a day in the café and then was up very early the next morning to perform his duties as the village postman.

Pushing the chair back from the table, Jared made his way wearily over to the counter.

'A Diet Coke for Emma, please, Alec, and four Irn-Brus – no, sorry, better make it four Red Bulls – for the boys.' We bloody need it, he mused.

Looking at him quizzically, Alec said, 'Rough night, eh? And from the looks of the others they're no better. What's the matter – seen a ghost or something?'

Turning away to get the order, he missed Jared's reply. 'If only you knew, Alec, if only you knew.'

With the drinks on the table, Roger was the first to voice an opinion.

'Well, did we imagine all that stuff last night or what? In the cold light of day, I'm starting to have doubts about it all. Do you think it's possible it might have been mass hypnosis or something?'

'Seemed bloody real to me, anyway,' was Aled's caustic comment.

Backing him up, Jared said, 'Oh, it happened all right, Rog. I'm afraid denial is the easy way out. To me the real problem isn't so much about what we saw as what we do about it.'

In something like blind panic, Michael blurted out, 'Just what are we going to do?'

'Simple,' said Jared, 'we leave it where it is and forget about it.'

'It's easy for you to say that,' replied Michael, 'but I don't think I can.'

Feeling sorry for him, Jared said patiently, 'What's the alternative – to spend the rest of our lives looking over our shoulders? Waiting and wondering if something nasty is going to turn up? Well, I'm not prepared to do that, I'm afraid.' He got up and started walking out. Turning back at the door, he said with a confidence he hardly felt, 'Trust me, nothing is going to happen.'

If only he knew how bitterly he was to come to regret those words.

'Wait up, for Christ's sake!' shouted Emma, as Jared crossed the road.

Catching him up, she swung him round to face her. 'Did you mean what you said to the others back there? Can you just brush it under the carpet like that?'

Looking her in the eyes, he said, 'No, of course not. To be honest I'm rattled myself. But there was no point telling them that; you saw how they were. I just didn't want to make it worse, that's all. Christ, did you see Roger? He usually doesn't give a shit about anything, but he was wound up like a clock. If he's like that, think what the others are going through!'

'Never mind Roger,' Emma said quietly, 'I'm scared stiff myself. I'll never be able to pass Carmel again without thinking about what happened.'

'Here, give me your hand, silly,' said Jared. 'We'll take the short cut home.'

Already dark, it was almost pitch black by the time they were halfway along the narrow lane that ran behind the school toilets.

Stopping suddenly, Emma grabbed Jared's head between her hands and began kissing him fiercely. Within seconds he realised it was no ordinary kiss and, thinking it was because of her fear, he pulled away.

'Hey, you really are scared, aren't you?'

Feeling her breath coming in short ragged gasps, she said, 'Yes, but it's more than that stupid, I want you – now!'

Looking at her oddly, Jared said, 'We've been going out with each other all these years.'

'Twelve, as a matter of fact!' Emma blurted out.

'Yeah, OK, twelve... and I mean, well, you know, we've done everything else but that, and what I mean is,' he said stumbling over his words, 'you've... never said anything like that before.'

In exasperation, she said, 'Jared, how can I put this?' Knowing there was no easy way, she blurted it out before her courage failed, 'I've wanted to do it for years, but for some reason you've always stopped just short. Don't you realise how frustrating it is?'

In dismay, he cried out, 'But that's because I thought it's what you wanted! Oh, Christ!' he said, slamming his fist against the wall in exasperation. 'All those years, and Jesus, what did you think of me? Or perhaps I shouldn't ask,' he added.

With tears in her eyes, she said, 'To be honest it crossed my mind you might be seeing someone else.'

Lifting her head up and looking into her eyes he said, 'Em, look at me, please.' Kissing away her tears, he carried on, 'How can you even think that? I've never even thought about anyone else, never mind gone with them. I couldn't, even if I wanted to. I love you, always have and always will, for better or worse, as the saying goes.' He paused.

'What about you?' he asked on the spur of the moment, secretly dreading the answer. 'You ever been with anyone else, Em?'

'You bastard!' she said, exploding. Then, when her temper had cooled somewhat, she added, 'But if we don't do it tonight, Hunter, I might think about it!' She ran away from him playfully.

She'd barely managed a few yards before he caught her from behind and lifted her off her feet, swinging her around as he said, 'I tell you one thing, I don't want our first time to be here – behind the boys' bloody toilets – that's for sure!'

Laughing, Emma said slyly, 'Well, I'm not sure about this, but aren't both our parents away for the weekend?'

'Of course,' he said excitedly, 'I'd forgotten all about that.'

Suddenly it dawned on him. 'You devious little bugger, you've been thinking about this for a while, haven't you?'

With a deep-throated chuckle she said, 'What do you think?'

His recollections of what happened next were hazy.

Eventually he opened the door of his parents' house after dropping the key several times in excitement. Before either of them knew what was really happening, they were gazing shyly at each other across the bedroom. After she'd stripped down to her panties, he led her gently towards the bed, where she lay back stiffly.

Now the time had actually arrived, he could see she was beginning to panic. As if instinctively knowing what was required, Jared eased himself down besides her, stroking her hair and whispering softly. In moments he could feel her relaxing. Although they'd never gone all the way before, they'd explored each other's bodies, and so he knew just how to arouse her.

Kissing her gently behind her ear, he nibbled and teased the lobe until he gradually began to feel her respond. Tracing the slender curve of her neck with his tongue, he moved slowly downwards until, reaching her nipples, he began to lick around them in a circular motion. Popping them into his mouth one at a time, he sucked and teased until he could feel them growing hard between his teeth. By now Emma was groaning loudly, her breathing coming in short ragged gasps. Moving his head downwards, Jared nibbled at her stomach, which was by now taut with unreleased tension. Blonde wispy pubic hair peeked through her black lace panties in several places. Gazing down at himself, he saw he was harder than he'd ever been in his life.

With a superhuman effort of will, he forced himself to think of one thing – satisfying Emma – before he could allow himself the luxury of his own orgasm. Easing her legs apart he slid down until he was just below her knees. Moving upwards slowly, he licked and kissed the skin on the inside of her thighs which by now felt feverishly hot. Reaching the crotch of her panties, he ran his tongue over the outline lightly, noting with satisfaction how a thin layer of moisture suddenly sprang to the surface.

Gasping for breath, Emma reached out for him. Pushing her back down, he removed her panties, which by now were soaked with her own juices.

With a wracking sob, she cried, 'Please, Jared, don't tease! I don't think I can hold back much longer.'

Pulling her to the edge of the bed, he lifted her legs and, kneeling before her, placed them on his shoulders on either side of his head. The lips of her vulva were so swollen they appeared purple with engorged blood. Placing his hands either side of her mound, he parted her lips with his thumbs. Taking her clitoris gently in his teeth, he was nearly overpowered by the sweet, heady smell of musk. Suddenly without warning her vagina flooded with warm sticky moisture.

Looking up quickly, he saw that she was nearing orgasm, so he ran his tongue one last time from her anus to her clitoris, before thrusting it into her as deeply as he could.

With a cry, she shouted, 'Oh, God! No more, no more, please! Just fuck me.'

Knowing he couldn't hold back much longer, he stood up and, taking his aching penis in his hand, placed the tip between the lips of her vagina. Pushing gently there was a single moment of awkwardness, a feeling of slight friction, and then he was inside. By now her legs were wrapped around his waist, forcing him deeper and deeper into her. Thrashing about wildly, she threw her head from side to side as if in great pain until suddenly she screamed, 'Oh, God! Fuck me, Jared, fuck me!'

Unused to hearing such language from her, Jared was surprised, but for some reason it only served to excite him further. Suddenly, all thoughts of holding back disappeared as he lost himself in the deepest parts of her beautiful body. With each surging thrust he grew more frantic, forcing himself deeper and deeper inside her wet sticky slickness.

The feeling was beyond belief, beyond description, and for a fleeting moment he worried whether it was as good for her. He didn't have to wonder long, as suddenly she screamed again, 'It's gorgeous! Oh, please don't stop, I'm almost there!'

When Jared pulled out, she was caught completely by surprise.

Distraught, she shouted, 'Christ, not now – put it back in, please!'

Before she could protest any further he turned her onto her stomach, lifted her bottom into the air and took her from behind. From this position his prick felt as if it had been clamped by a steel trap with a velvet lining. Shouting in pleasure, she said, 'Oh, fuck, this is even better!' while thrusting back hard in order to benefit from every last inch.

The orgasm felt as if it was coming from his toes, and within seconds he shouted, 'Oh, shit, I'm coming!' Before the words were even out of his mouth, she exploded with an orgasm so fierce it rocked her to the core.

Collapsing in a heap, they held each other tightly, unable to comprehend the pleasure they'd brought each other. It hadn't finished though, as for nearly a minute afterwards they twitched rhythmically as the aftershock of their climaxes rippled through their bodies.

Eventually they pulled apart, content simply to look at each other.

Seeing a smile break out on Emma's face, he was intrigued, until following her gaze he looked down and with astonishment saw he was hard again. They made love several more times that night, until, exhausted, they were ready for sleep. Just as he was nodding off he suddenly remembered…

'Christ,' he said, sitting up in bed like a frightened rabbit.

'What the hell's the matter?' asked Emma.

'I don't know how to tell you this, but in the middle of all the excitement I forgot to use anything.'

A moment of sheer panic crossed Emma's face until suddenly she said, 'Who cares? I'm not bothered if you're not.' Then she leant over and kissed him gently on the forehead.

Within minutes they were asleep in each other's arms.

Turning his head to say something to his teenage son sitting in the back of the new Ford Focus, the driver never saw the other car until it was too late. The visitor, driving an old Volkswagen Beetle, had pulled out to overtake on a corner that had claimed the lives of many an unwary driver since the new slip road had been built four years ago. A notorious accident black spot, the innocuous looking corner was deceptive.

The driver of the old battered Beetle was almost alongside the other car when he knew he wasn't going to make it. With growing horror, he stared at the Focus coming straight for him. Realising there were now three cars crowded into a space designed to accommodate two, he froze.

Laughing at his son's reply, the driver of the Focus turned his attention back to the road and almost panicked – almost, but not quite. Instead, he made his decision instantly. Turning the steering wheel sharply to his left, he took a calculated gamble, one that might have worked had he not hit the kerb. As if in slow motion, the drivers of the other two cars watched in fascinated horror as the Focus took off. Clearing the barrier by several feet it soared into the air like a bird taking flight, until suddenly gravity took charge and flipped it onto its back.

Hitting the steep bank below, it tumbled over and over, bouncing off several large trees and demolishing several small bushes that tried manfully to halt its fateful slide into the swollen river some thirty feet below.

But they never stood a chance.

With one last graceful somersault, the Ford hit the swollen river with a bone-jarring impact, instantly destroying the car's central locking system. Unable to open the doors, the passengers were doomed. The mother and father, by now unconscious, were spared the fate that the grim reaper had in store for their unfortunate son. It was almost as if he'd prepared something special for him. Tumbling around in the back seat, the boy had been unable to see what had happened, but from the cries of his parents he knew they were in desperate trouble. Suddenly he felt a searing pain in his head before darkness enveloped him.

Shaking his head and coming instantly awake, he reasoned he must have been out for mere seconds.

Then in one terrifying flash of memory it came back to him.

A quick glance out of the window confirmed what he'd been afraid of. He could see just enough to establish that the car had settled at the bottom of the river, and from somewhere water was pouring in. Already up to his waist, it had been the shock of the cold water that had brought him round. Screaming in desperation, he beat frantically at the window, until, with hands bleeding, he realised the futility of what he was doing.

Within seconds the car was almost full. All that was left was a small pocket of air trapped in one corner of the roof. Craning his neck in order to take advantage of it, the boy filled his lungs in one final act of desperation. To his credit, he held his breath for almost two minutes, until, unable to hold it any longer, he was forced to open his mouth. After that the end came quickly, his struggles became weaker and weaker as his lungs filled with water. Finally his limp and lifeless body floated back towards the roof of the car, eyes open and staring into the void.

As if being dragged back from the end of a long dark tunnel, Jared came awake slowly.

'Wake up, wake up!' said Emma, shaking him vigorously while at the same time looking down at him in anxiety.

Unable to comprehend where he was, he shook his head several times in order to rid himself of the strange fuzzy feeling he was experiencing. Looking up at Emma's worried expression, he suddenly remembered where he was. Covered in perspiration and freezing cold, he said, 'Thank God for that! It was only a nightmare after all.'

'Must have been some nightmare,' she said worriedly. 'Want to talk about it?'

Sitting up, he said, 'It was so bloody real.'

And then he told her exactly what had happened.

'Do you remember any details?' she asked, 'like the faces of the people, for instance?'

'If I put my mind to it I can remember everything, but to answer your question, no. That's the funny thing, I saw the accident in every horrific detail; but the faces, no, they were blurred somehow. I don't know how to explain it, really, but it was almost as if I was looking at a photograph that hadn't been properly developed.'

Putting his head in his hands, he said quietly, 'What I can't get out of my mind is how that poor kid died! At least for the parents it was over quickly, but I dread to think about what that poor little bugger went through. What a way to die,' he added with a shudder.

At that moment the phone rang.

Turning to face Jared, Emma said coyly, 'You'd better get that in case it's your parents. It might look a bit suspicious if I answered at this time of the morning, don't you think?'

Smiling, he moved to the edge of the bed and picked up the phone. The call was short, but seeing the colour drain from his face, Emma knew immediately something was badly wrong. For several minutes Jared didn't move, then without a word he got up and made his way stiffly to the bathroom.

Following behind, Emma said, 'Talk to me, Jared, for Christ's sake! What the hell's the matter?'

As if coming out of a trance, he suddenly focused. He laid his hands on her shoulders and said, 'Sorry, I've just had some bad news, that's all.' Then he broke down.

Hugging him tightly, she felt his body tremble with the intensity of his sobbing, until several minutes later he eased himself away gently. Looking up at him, she saw the supreme effort he was making to regain his composure.

He said quietly, 'They're dead, Em. They're gone, all three of them.'

Moving back into the bedroom, he lowered himself to the edge of the bed. Then, staring blankly into space, he recounted in a voice eerily devoid of any emotion exactly what had happened.

'It was a car crash; an eyewitness said they didn't stand a chance. Wasn't their fault... some stupid bastard tried to overtake on a blind bend.'

Taking a few deep breaths, he carried on, 'Their car hit the curb, flew into the air and tumbled thirty feet down into the river. They all drowned, Em, they all drowned!'

Looking at her with something like madness in his eyes, he went on, 'But I knew that anyway! It happened just like in my nightmare. Dear God,' he said, breaking down again, 'that kid I told you about, the one who drowned. That wasn't just any kid, Em, that was my brother! And do you know what? The evil we brought to life – the spirit thing in the chalice – was right after all, wasn't it?'

'What do you mean?' she asked in puzzlement.

'Think back! What was one of the last things it said? "And for you I shall reserve a special gift." '

'But,' said Emma, spluttering in confusion, 'you can't think it had anything to do with the death of your family, surely? We all agreed its power was limited...'

As if in a daze he replied, 'Yes, but it seems we might have been wrong, doesn't it?'

The funeral took place a week later in Carmel chapel. All three were buried side by side, as Jared knew it was what they would have wanted. By the end of the proceedings, he'd almost managed to convince himself the evil lurking deep inside the confines of the chapel wasn't to blame for their deaths. Almost, that is, but not quite.

Looking around, he was gratified to see that the small graveyard was packed; everyone in the village it seemed had come to pay their last respects.

Finally, thank God, it was all over.

With a last lingering look, he left the graveyard. Clutching Emma's hand tightly, he gazed at her lovingly, knowing he'd never have made it through the week without her. She'd been a tower of strength. With a start, he suddenly realised the only family he had left were his grand-mother, grandfather and Uncle Edwin. They were all that remained.

As they made their way down the steps towards the main road, his grandmother said with tears in her eyes, 'Remember now, I'll take care of all the financial arrangements. By the time you return it will all be done and dusted. A few days with your Uncle Edwin, away from it all, will do you the world of good.'

Leaning over and kissing her on the cheek he said, 'Thanks, Gran.'

Turning to Emma, he said, 'You're sure you don't mind, love?'

'Of course not,' she replied, 'your grandmother's right; the break will do you the world of good.'

Chapter Eight

><

JARED CAUGHT THE 10 A.M. TRAIN FROM SWANSEA THAT SATURDAY
morning, which by some miracle was on time. His intention was to
return on the Wednesday, giving him five full days to relax, and he
looked forward to it with relish. Looking out of the window of his
second class carriage, he'd forgotten how much he loved travelling by
rail. Everything about it was so relaxing. The noise of the carriages as
they sped over the rails, clickety-clack, clickety-clack, clickety-clack,
always made him feel drowsy. As a confirmed insomniac he found it
quite puzzling.

Out of the corner of his eye, he suddenly noticed the last minute
dash of commuters hurrying to catch the train. It never ceased to amaze
him why so many people left it so late. For some strange reason the
sight brought to mind a documentary he'd seen recently about lem-
mings – how for no reason they would commit suicide by throwing
themselves wildly over a cliff. Yes, he chuckled to himself, they look just
like that.

Suddenly the train lurched forward violently.

Looking up in alarm, he was just in time to catch a small item of
hand luggage that toppled from the shelf above. Replacing it, he heard
loud groans of protest from wheels that sounded as if they'd never seen
a drop of oil or grease. The sounds lasted for several more minutes until
the train gradually picked up speed, and with a last shuddering screech
they were on their way. Within moments the buildings on either side
became a distant memory, the advertising boards a blur as the train
accelerated smoothly away from the station.

In such soothing surroundings, it wasn't long before his thoughts
turned to what had happened between him and Emma just over a
week ago. Was it that long ago? he thought wistfully; then to his
embarrassment he felt the first stirrings of an erection. Pushing it
down with his right hand, he looked around to see if anyone had
noticed. Feelings of guilt suddenly crowded in on him when he

realised his first thoughts had been of Emma, rather than the tragedy which had claimed his family.

Putting such negative feelings aside, he cast his mind back to the first time he'd seen her. With her mane of long golden curls shimmering in the summer sun, he though she was an angel. At such a young age he'd never thought about girls, but one look at Emma and he was smitten. And it had been that way ever since. For Emma, older than Jared by a year, it had been slightly different. If he was brutally honest he had made a complete nuisance of himself, pestering her mercilessly, showering her with affection, unwilling to even entertain the thought that she might not feel the same about him. At first Emma had merely tolerated him, at times amused by his feelings for her. For her, love had grown slowly, until eventually she knew to her astonishment that she too felt the same way about him. From that time on there had been no one else for either of them. Shaking his head in amazement at how two people could be so ideally suited to each other, it was then Jared noticed the discarded copy of the *Western Mail* on the empty seat alongside. Leaning over, he picked it up.

About to turn to the sports section first, a habit he'd picked up at a very young age, the photograph on the front page caught his attention. In itself it was a gruesome spectacle, but the story which accompanied it was even more horrific. It explained how the body of a man had been found in Cardiff Bay early yesterday morning. To date, the police had no clue as to the identity of the person, for the simple reason the body had no face. Apparently it had been peeled off, and the man's legs and arms hacked away. On top of that, every single tooth had been extracted. The only comment the police would make was that the injuries had been so specific it was almost as if they had been inflicted deliberately – perhaps in order to make identification impossible they conjectured.

Lost in thought over the story, he came out of his reverie just in time, as looking out of the window he noted with alarm he was almost at his journey's end. He'd almost missed it. The past two hours had flown by. Making sure it was the right station, he proceeded to lift the small holdall from above his head and make his way towards the door.

Stepping from the train, he saw that Uncle Edwin had been as good as his word. Rushing forward to meet him, Jared was always overwhelmed at how he always seemed so genuinely pleased to see him.

Shaking his hand vigorously, Edwin said, 'Made it all right, I see, and for once the bloody train was on time!' Then he added mischievously, 'Would that come under the heading of a modern miracle, do you think?'

He was such an easy-going character; everyone seemed to relax in his company.

The greetings over, Edwin bowed at the waist and with a gesture of his arm said, 'Your carriage awaits you, young sir.'

Staring in open-mouthed admiration, Jared gazed lovingly at the carriage, which turned out to be a black Jaguar saloon.

Laughing loudly, Edwin said, 'Close your mouth, before the flies get in.'

'But she's beautiful,' was all that his nephew could say.

'Yes, she is an impressive looking beast, isn't she?' he said, patting the bonnet affectionately. 'It's brand new, but isn't it strange how people always seem to describe a car as "she"? Although in this case I suppose it's because it's seen as a thing of beauty.' With a snort he carried on, 'With the amount of mileage I do, I might just as well have bought a Mini. I'd have saved myself a fortune on petrol, not to mention the cost of the car. What do you think?'

Jared was far from convinced and said, 'A Mini would never have been good enough for you, Uncle. You know how you love your big cars. Apart from that, it wouldn't have fitted your image of sophistication, somehow. Besides, from now on you're going to need a big car in order to commute to Oxford on a regular basis.'

Shaking his head in amusement, Edwin said, 'How stupid of me! I'd forgotten all about that.'

'The insurance must be costing a fortune, though,' commented Jared.

'Funnily enough, it isn't. Because I do less than 4,000 miles a year, it's much cheaper. It's a special deal, you see.' Realising what he'd said, he corrected himself. 'Or used to, anyway. That's another thing I'll have to do – inform the insurance company, I mean – so that they can get the wording on the policy altered.'

The car's interior was even more impressive than the outside. The upholstery was of the finest quality leather, while the dashboard and trimmings were made out of either mahogany or walnut, Jared wasn't sure which.

Seeing the look of delight on his nephew's face as he stroked the leather, Edwin commented, 'I'm afraid it's not very practical.'

Puzzled, Jared asked, 'Why on earth not?'

'In hot weather it can get sticky, especially if you're wearing shorts.'

'But that's what the air conditioning's for,' said Jared by now even more bemused.

Looking sheepish, Edwin said, 'Funny you should say that, I haven't managed to find the damned thing yet.'

'Here, let me have a look,' said Jared, laughing. In moments it was working.

Indicating, Edwin turned left out of the little station and accelerated smoothly through the gears until in no time the Jaguar was touching seventy miles per hour.

Pre-empting Jared's next question, Edwin said, 'About half an hour,' before adding, 'if it wasn't for these bloody lanes we'd do it in far less.'

The countryside leading to Edwin's home was breathtaking. Admiring the beautiful scenery, the gently rolling hills, green meadows and well-tended hedges, Jared found himself sinking further and further into the Jaguar's sumptuous leather upholstery. Unwinding completely, he allowed his mind to drift until the cares and horrors of the past week were forgotten, if only for a short while. Time passed so swiftly the journey seemed to be over all too soon. One minute they were travelling along narrow country lanes, the next they'd pulled up outside a pair of gigantic wrought iron gates.

Turning to his uncle, Jared said in half-jocular fashion, 'The only thing missing is a family crest.'

'I'm working on it,' was the reply.

Although the long curving driveway was impressive, it paled into insignificance besides the splendour of the actual house. When Jared finally managed to find his voice, he said, 'But this is a mansion, not a house! You must be one of the richest men in the country.'

Laughing, Edwin said, 'Far from it.'

'But how did you manage to afford such a place, and all this land as well?' asked Jared, at the same time making a sweeping gesture with his arm.

Without a trace of arrogance, Edwin said, 'Oh, there's much more behind. What you can see from here is only a small part of the estate. How I managed to get it is a story in itself, but it will keep for another time.'

Stepping into the house was like walking into another world.

'Before you ask,' Edwin said with a grin, 'the last time I counted there were twenty bedrooms, ten on each of the first and second floors. And by the way, most of the furniture came with the house. I'll show you around later, but for the moment you'd better familiarise yourself with the downstairs layout. If you're not careful you'll get lost.'

Looking at his face, Jared saw he was only half joking.

Ten minutes later, a by now shell-shocked Jared was led into the library.

'The look on your face is a picture!' said his uncle. 'If I was to try and describe it, it might go something like, "you've just died and been transported to heaven".'

Dragging Jared away with the greatest of difficulty, Edwin said, 'One more fleeting visit and then I'll get Mrs Daniels to rustle us up a cup of tea or something.'

Edwin had never married, and Jared had often wondered if perhaps it helped explain why he'd always taken so much of an interest in him. The son he never had, and all that, he thought to himself.

Once tea was out of the way, they moved into the study.

Covered from floor to ceiling in what appeared to be solid oak and mahogany, the overall effect was completed by the addition of Persian rugs, several of which he was assured were genuine. Hanging from the walls was a collection of large oil paintings, some of which he guessed were originals, but he couldn't be sure, while dotted here and there were some expensive pieces of porcelain. To his amazement, a pair of green Buddhist lions known as the 'Dogs of Fo' had been split up and placed on either side of the door to his uncle's study. Made originally as tomb guardians, they looked perfectly at home in their modern twentieth-century setting.

The really striking feature of the room was a large collection of bows that covered the entire length of one wall.

'Did these come with the house as well, Uncle?'

'No, funnily enough, they're mine, and there's an interesting story behind them if you want to hear it.'

'Of course,' said Jared, 'we've plenty of time.'

'Did you know for instance that we Welsh had the finest archers in the world at one time?'

'No,' said Jared, genuinely astonished.

'According to my research, the longbows they used were so powerful, that an arrow tipped with metal could penetrate a solid oak door up to a depth of three to four inches.'

'Bloody hell, that's impressive!' was Jared's comment.

Warming to his subject, Edwin went on, 'One of the favourite tricks of the archers was to pin the legs of the soldiers to their horses so they couldn't move. That way they made easy pickings.'

'Gross – but very clever!' exclaimed Jared.

'Damned effective too,' said Edwin.

Picking out a bow from one of the racks, he held it out to Jared.

'Here's a genuine longbow I picked up at auction several years ago. Try and bend it.'

Holding it in his left hand, Jared tried, but try as he may he could only move the string back a few inches.

Seeing the look of astonishment on his face, Edwin said, 'Now you know how strong the buggers were.'

Moving along the line Jared pointed to another piece. 'A crossbow, right?'

'Correct,' said Edwin, 'A truly frightening weapon. It had double the firepower of a longbow, but was far les effective in battle.'

Seeing the look of puzzlement on Jared's face he explained. 'Crossbows were accurate in those days up to about 350 feet while the bow went to about 200 feet. The big difference,' he said with a smile, 'was in the rate of firing. While skilled archers like the Welsh could loose an arrow every five seconds, the crossbow took much longer because it had to be loaded by means of a windlass and pulley system. Anyway, enough of that; let's move on.'

For the rest of the afternoon Jared was left to do what he wanted, but before they parted company, they arranged to meet for food at seven.

The evening spread was more a banquet than a meal, in Jared's initial estimation. For starters they dined on home-made broth called 'cawl', followed promptly by wild pheasant only recently shot on the estate.

When Jared declared he couldn't eat another thing, they congratulated Mrs Daniels on a fabulous meal and left the table.

When asked if they wanted coffee, Edwin said with a wink, 'No, thank you, I think we'll try something a little stronger, if you don't mind.'

Turning back to Jared, he said, 'If you like wine then I've got something to show you.' Leading the way, he moved into the hall, along the corridor and back towards the kitchen before making his way down a long flight of stone steps. Halfway down, he looked over his shoulder and shouted back, 'What's your preference, by the way – white or red?'

'Red,' replied Jared, 'as much as I know about wine.'

The cellar was enormous.

'Choose whatever you want. The whites are over there and the reds – my preference too, by the way – are here.' Edwin extended an arm and pointed to his side of the room. 'It all depends on your taste, of course, but at the moment I'm into Spanish reds, especially Riojas. This little beauty here, he said pulling one from the rack and holding it to the light, is my current favourite. It's a Faustino – Gran Reserva 1994, oak matured and bloody marvellous! Then with a wink he said, 'A friend of mine brought me back a dozen from Spain last year. Shall we try a bottle?' Before Jared could answer, he said, 'Good, right you are, then.'

Before Edwin had gone more than a few paces, he suddenly turned back, 'Best get another one just in case, eh? Never know, it might be a long night.'

Sitting in his high-backed antique leather armchair, a glass of wine in hand, Jared felt like royalty. Holding the glass up to the light, he rolled it around gently. The wine had an almost purple colour. It glistened like blood and contrasted sharply with the specks of foamy white froth that adhered here and there to the inside of the rim.

Knowing Jared didn't smoke, Edwin asked permission before lighting his pipe.

'Do you know its funny, Uncle, I detest the smell of cigarettes, matches even more; but the smell of cigars and pipe tobacco... now that's different, the aroma is wonderful.'

'Well said, lad,' commented Edwin. 'Right, let me light up first –' puff, puff – 'before we have a chat. Now, where was I?' Suddenly he was hesitant. 'I know you probably don't want to talk about it so soon, but how do you feel?'

Knowing his uncle was awkward with this kind of stuff, and wanting to put him at ease, Jared said, 'I'm coming to terms with it now. I don't suppose I'll ever really get over it, but they say time is a great healer, don't they?'

'I guess Emma's been a great help there,' observed Edwin.

'Yes, in all honesty I don't know what I would have done without her,' was Jared's honest reply.

'You two are very much in love, aren't you?'

'Is it that obvious?' said Jared, smiling, before describing how they'd met.

'That's a really touching story,' said Edwin with genuine feeling, before adding with a twinkle in his eye, 'of course, you realise what the next logical step is, don't you?'

Within moments he'd subtly changed the subject. 'Don't take this the wrong way, but after your traumatic experience, has your outlook on religion changed? Seeing as you've been brought up with a strict chapel background and all that, I mean.'

'It shouldn't have, Uncle, but the honest answer is yes. I'm afraid it has. It's not just the accident, though, it's more than that.'

'Want to talk about it?'

A moment's hesitation followed before Jared said, 'Yes, I do, I feel as if I want to get things off my chest.' The wine was beginning to have a relaxing effect, and so Jared began to explain himself.

'For some time now I've been struggling to come to terms with the more philosophical aspects of religion. I mean, when you're younger you accept everything the Bible says, don't you? But the more I studied, the more I began to question.'

'There's nothing wrong with questioning, lad,' said Edwin breaking in briefly, 'it's a sign of maturity; but go on, give me an example.'

'That's easy,' said Jared. 'Take the continual struggle between good and evil.'

'Ah,' said Edwin, 'the age old problem rearing its ugly head again.' Then he held his hands up and said, 'Sorry, didn't mean to interrupt, please go on.'

'Well, to me the problem just seems to get worse every year. The present century is rapidly becoming a cesspit of greed and immorality; it seems to me we have a new God, and its name is materialism.'

'You mean Mammon,' said Edwin, chuckling away to himself.

'Exactly,' said Jared, 'you've got it in one. But let's look at it from another angle. Take the suffering in the world. If God is all seeing, all powerful – omnipotent, if you like – if he's got the power to end things like that, then why doesn't he? It seems to me he's a cruel, heartless bastard if he doesn't. Correct me if I'm wrong, but isn't this the same God who's supposed to be caring and loving and all that?'

Holding his hand up to forestall any interruption, Jared carried on, 'I know all the trite answers, from this being the best of all worlds, to the free will argument, but to me they're bullshit,' he said slapping his knee with his hand.

'Well, well,' exclaimed Edwin. 'You really have thought about this, haven't you? Cool off a little, and I'll explain a few things to you – things you'll find interesting, I guarantee. First of all let me say I agree with everything you've said, but remember it's not a modern problem. Did you know for instance that it was the Pharisees who came up with the idea of heaven and hell? No? I thought not; not many people do.

'At the time, the Jews didn't think much about life after death, their only concern was to keep the commandments. Keep God – or Yahweh, as they call him – happy, they thought, and when the time comes he'll look after us. It was as simple as that. From their point of view, after death you went to a place called Sheol, or the underworld, where you lived a shadowy existence for a while and then gradually faded away.'

'So why did the Pharisees feel the need to invent such places as heaven and hell?' Jared broke in.

Knowing Jared had taken the bait, Edwin said, 'Because they were faced with the same problem as you: why should people suffer and die – especially young children? There was a ready made answer for older people; they were sinners. Remember your Sunday school lessons, they believed in the sins of the fathers coming back to visit the family. It was a cruel and heartless way of looking at things, but it provided an answer to a ticklish problem. For young children it was different, though.'

'In what way?' asked Jared.

'They didn't know the difference between right and wrong. They hadn't experienced life yet, so how could they be sinners?'

'Yes,' said Jared, the truth suddenly dawning on him. 'We Christians got around that one neatly by introducing original sin, didn't we.'

Pleased he'd grasped it, Edwin carried on. 'Thanks to Adam and Eve, who disobeyed God, everyone from that time on was born into sin. That's why Jesus' death and resurrection is so important to Christians. As the perfect sacrifice, his blood washed away the sins of mankind. Then by coming back from the dead, he gave everyone hope that as long as they believed in all that, they too could live again. Death wasn't the end any more, it was the beginning!'

'Let's see if I get this,' said Jared, 'you're saying the Pharisees invented heaven as a place where young children without sin went. A kind of better place, as they liked to think; and then of course there was hell, which was reserved for the other lot.'

'Got it in one,' said Edwin, 'but the interesting thing is that they also came up with the revolutionary idea that messengers could travel between these worlds.'

In excitement Jared suddenly shouted, 'Angels from heaven and demons from hell!' Stunned, he whispered, 'My God, but it's ingenious, Uncle. It explains so much. While we're still on the subject, am I right in assuming that in Jesus' time they were into evil spirits and demons in a big way?'

'Oh, yes, but it wasn't only the Jews; the Romans were even more obsessed. Those buggers had temples dedicated to all kinds of gods and goddesses. Sacrifice was the in thing in those days, but really all it was,' he said was a chuckle, 'was an early form of bribery. But then along came Jesus. Now, he was a character. Did you know he was the first exorcist?'

'Funnily enough, I did. It's an area I've been researching for a while,' replied Jared, omitting to tell his uncle that it was so he could conduct a seance on the altar of Carmel chapel.

Sitting upright and pointing his pipe towards his nephew, Edwin said, 'So you know there are several good examples of what we're talking about in the Gospels then? What do you make of it all, then, lad?'

'I know the Catholic Church takes it very seriously, but from what I gather they don't like to admit it.'

'I agree,' said Edwin, 'although I'm afraid it's not my only worry on that score. You see, I'm firmly of the belief it has deliberately withheld and suppressed documents that might paint a very different picture of Jesus to the one we have in the Gospels. It's common knowledge at the moment that there are several strange accounts in circulation which scholars refer to as the "Hidden Gospels". By that I mean Gospels which have never seen the light of day. Four in particular have come to our attention fairly recently: the Egerton Gospel, the Gospel of Thomas, the secret Gospel of Mark and the Gospel of Peter. They were discovered in 1886–87 in Akhmim in Egypt.'

'I'm totally in agreement with your concerns,' said Jared. 'Like you, I'm convinced there are literally scores of priceless treasures hidden deep in the archives of the Roman Catholic Church. Who knows what secrets are buried there destined never to be seen. What I'd like to know is, what's so frightening about some of them that they have to remain hidden? Over the centuries, many ancient documents have probably been destroyed simply because they were regarded as heretical or Gnostic. The problem is, whose to say those documents didn't contain the real truth and what we've been allowed to see is only what the early church has wanted us to see!'

Guessing it was a topic of conversation that could go on all night, Edwin decided to nip it in the bud for the time being and said, 'Right, that's enough for the moment. Besides I don't know whether you've noticed, but we've just finished the second bottle of Rioja. Anyway, it's the Sabbath tomorrow, and so I thought we might take it easy – if that meets with your approval, that is?'

'That's fine by me,' said Jared, 'but I never suspected you were religious… No work on the Sabbath and all that. Have you seen the light, or something?'

Laughing loudly, Edwin replied, 'I'm not particularly, but the folks around here are. They take their Sabbath seriously, and so as I'm a newcomer to the area, I don't want to rock the boat.'

Chapter Nine

GRANT KRAMER WOKE EARLY, TOSSED ASIDE THE DUVET AND ROLLED to the edge of the bed. He was about to put his foot on the floor when he suddenly stopped. Something was nagging at him. Something was different. Then it hit him. Collapsing back on the bed, he screamed with joy. It had been several weeks now since he'd retired, but he still couldn't get used to the freedom. No more early morning runs, no more punishing fitness regimes, he was through with all that. Savouring the moment yet again, he realised this was how it was going to be from now on.

In a while he got up anyway.

He'd found that over the past few weeks it was one habit he couldn't rid himself of. Within minutes he was dressed, ready to face the day and everything it could throw at him.

Then suddenly he grew pensive, recognising that now he'd made the decision to leave he was going to miss the old place. Dragging himself back into the present, he comforted himself with the thought it was only on lease anyway. He was sure of one thing, though; he wasn't going to miss the London weather.

Most of his wealth was tied up in a Swiss bank, in a numbered account which he knew was untraceable. The rest of his money, which he'd held in a building society account, he'd withdrawn several days ago. With a considerable amount of cash to hand, he was well prepared.

Glancing at his watch, he saw he had plenty of time to spare.

Travelling light, he took with him only a small leather holdall. The rest of his clothes were being kept in storage until he sent for them.

Lifting his jacket from the back of the chair, he checked the inside pocket, noting with satisfaction that his flight ticket and passport were exactly where he'd put them the previous night. Taking one last lingering look around, he headed for the door and a new life.

Travelling to the airport by taxi was expensive, but what the hell, Kramer, he told himself, you can afford it!

As it turned out he arrived early, and to kill time he browsed around the terminal shops. Indulging in a little nostalgia, he remembered the bad old days, when as a mercenary he'd come close to death on many occasions. And for what? He knew full well it had been for the buzz; the money had been shit. Living on the edge for all those years had really been something. Then suddenly one day he'd woken up and realised he didn't need it any longer. Finding something that had suited his special talents, as he'd liked to call them, had been difficult. It was strange, but all his life he'd been driven by one thought, that whatever he did, he had to be the best. Unfortunately, he'd always come up short. Then, quite by accident, he'd tried his hand at burglary. Starting off in a small way, he gradually became so proficient his skills were in constant demand. Soon, to his astonishment he'd found something he was not only good at, but in the words of his clients – the best!

Caught up in his own thoughts, he failed to notice two smartly dressed men who seemed to be taking an inordinate amount of interest in his movements. Normally he would have spotted them, been alert to the danger, but with so much on his mind his guard was down.

Keeping a room's width apart, the two men's understanding was almost telepathic.

Arriving early, they'd waited patiently for an opportunity to make their move.

Now it was presented to them on a plate, when quite unexpectedly their target made his way towards the men's room. Instantly alert, the smaller of the two killers followed him into the toilet. By the time Kramer was relieving himself, the man was standing next to him. While he attempted to make polite conversation, his colleague was keeping a careful check on the door. When he made his move, he was so quick that Grant Kramer knew nothing until the needle had punctured his left bicep. The drug took effect almost immediately, so Grant had no time to shout for help. Within seconds his legs gave way and he hit the floor with a resounding thud. Taking an arm each, the two assassins lifted the unconscious figure, and between them they carried him out of the rest room and into the corridor. As professionals they knew the hardest part was in front of them.

There was no way in which they could avoid looking conspicuous, and so they didn't try. Past experience had shown that the key to pulling it off was confidence; look as if you belong, was their credo. Within moments their theory was put to the test, when, on turning a corner, they were confronted by one of the airport security guards.

'Can I help you, gents?'

'No problem,' said the taller of the two assassins, 'our friend here's had a little too much to drink, that's all. Does it all the time... drinks because he's afraid of flying, then forgets that unless he sobers up he can't get on the plane.'

Looking at the slumped figure, the guard said, 'I'm afraid you're right, there's no way your friend's going to be allowed on any of our planes looking like that.'

'Oh, we know that! Don't worry, everything's in hand.'

Pretending to look at the flight information timetable on the display above the guard's head, the assassin said, 'Luckily we've got three hours to sober him up before he boards. As we said, it's a regular thing; we know how to handle him.'

With one last lingering look, the guard turned on his heel before calling over his shoulder, 'Rather you than me!'

When he was out of earshot he said, 'Pricks! The things people put themselves through just to get on a fucking plane. I don't know why they fucking bother!'

The remainder of the operation went without further mishap. Within moments, Grant's unconscious figure had been bundled into the back of a waiting van before being whisked off to a date with destiny.

Coming around slowly, Grant Kramer hadn't a clue where he was. Shaking his head in order to dispel the fogginess which seemed to cloud his mind, he gradually began to make sense of his predicament. Despite the fact that everything was still blurred and frayed around the edges, one thing was certain: he was in a small, cold, damp room.

Looking at the trickle of water running down the bare brick walls in front of him, he guessed he was somewhere deep underground. The smell of damp and mustiness helped reinforce the conclusion. Sitting in a rough wooden chair, hands and feet tied by what looked suspiciously like duct tape, he stared at the single bulb hanging precariously above his head. At that moment an absurd thought sprang to mind. Didn't they know it was dangerous to mix electricity and water? But in his present predicament it was probably the least of his worries.

Staring up at his two captors, their dull lifeless eyes confirmed what deep down he already knew: he was doomed. Whatever traumas he'd survived as a mercenary, whatever torture he'd endured would be of no use against such merciless killers. With that a cold, hard certainty washed over him in waves.

Surprisingly, they didn't resort to the conventional means of extracting information, going instead for drugs. The only reason he could think of was that they were working to a tight schedule.

The first one rolled up Grant's sleeve, while the other inserted the needle of the syringe into an ampoule. Extracting it, he held it up to the light and with a single flick of his finger checked to see there were no air bubbles. Satisfied, he took one long lingering look at his companion, before deftly jabbing the needle into his captive's arm.

Grant didn't know how long he'd been out, but when he woke he saw in dismay they'd got what they wanted. The look of savage triumph on the face of the shorter one told him clearly he'd told them everything.

In one last act of defiance, Grant said, 'Before you finish me off, tell me one thing: where did I go wrong?'

The two assassins looked at each other, until with an almost imperceptible nod the shorter one gave his consent. At that, the bigger of the two said, 'You stupid fuck – you thought you were so clever, but you weren't as good as you thought you were. You see, you missed the hidden camera in the ceiling. It took us a while, but eventually we tracked you down.' Without a trace of arrogance he added, 'Escape from the Brotherhood is impossible.'

The last thought that Kramer had, before his neck was broken, was that for an assassin the man had an extremely effeminate voice…

*

Jared woke early on the Monday morning and by 9 a.m. he'd settled down to a full breakfast prepared just the way he liked it, his eggs soft and his bacon crisp. He was just about to tuck in when Uncle Edwin walked in.

'Good morning, how are you feeling after your day of rest? I hope it wasn't too boring?'

Looking up, Jared replied, 'Not at all. To be honest it was just what the doctor ordered, really. I spent the whole morning exploring the forest behind the house, and I must admit it's incredible.'

In astonishment Edwin said, 'I hope you didn't go too far, it's like a jungle up there. I decided to take a look at it myself, last week. Mind you, when I say take a look; it was only a little stroll. Take it from me, I didn't get very far. Once I stepped off the little path that cuts into the mountains I went no further. Either side of that appears to be virgin forest, impenetrable at the very least. So how did you manage?'

'It's everything you described, and more,' said Jared. 'But I love exploring, and within the hour I'd found a little stream that runs down from the top of the mountain. It cuts through the middle of the forest. As you said, the undergrowth is so dense the stream was virtually invisible. I came across it by accident. Oh, and by the way if you'd followed that steep track you were on about, you'd have been disappointed; it's a dead end. And one other thing, if you ever decide to retrace your steps then take a tip: whatever you do, don't step off the trail or I'll guarantee you'll never find your way back.'

'Advice noted and taken,' was Edwin's reply. 'What did you do in the afternoon, then?' he added.

With what was obvious relish, Jared said, 'Something I've been dying to do since I got here. I gave the library the once-over.'

'Good, I was hoping you'd say something like that, because you needed the time to yourself.' Changing tack, he said, 'After you've had your breakfast – which I'm rudely interrupting, I might add – I thought we might try a spot of fishing.'

Speaking between mouthfuls of bacon and fried bread, Jared said, 'That sounds great, but I have a confession, I'm not much good. The last time I tried it I caught a few, but before I could pull them in they dropped off the line.'

'What was the problem?' asked Edwin.

'You'll never believe it. It took us ages to work it out, but in the end the answer was simple. I was casting the line back so far the hooks were de-barbing on the stones behind.'

'Ah, I see now,' said Edwin, understanding dawning. 'There was nothing to hold them on, was there?'

Chuckling to himself, he led Jared, who by now had finished, out of the room and into the hallway, where he pointed to an array of rods and reels lined up against the wall. Seeing the look of astonishment on Jared's face, he said, 'All these are new, so choose your weapon carefully and follow me.'

Amazingly, Edwin's own rod and reel looked as if they'd seen better days.

'Incidentally, do you want Mrs Daniels to rustle us up a few sandwiches, or are you up for some pub grub in the village afterwards?'

'I'll take the pub lunch, if you don't mind,' said Jared with a straight face.

'Thought you would, somehow,' said Edwin, deadpan.

Walking through the vast expanse of the estate, Jared asked the inevitable question, 'Is all this really yours?'

'Yes, I'm afraid it is, as far as the eye can see and more. It's a fair walk to my private stream, so do you mind if we chat a bit?'

'Not at all,' said Jared. 'Any particular topic in mind?'

'Seeing as you're interested in the occult, I thought I'd mention something I came across a few days ago. It's a book called *The Golden Bough*, by James Frazer. Have you read it?'

'No, but I've heard about it. A study in magic and religion, if I'm not mistaken.'

'In a way, yes, but that's only one of the sections, although I can see how for you it would be the most interesting. Anyway, see what you think about this idea. It offers the thesis that man progressed from magic, through religious belief, to scientific thought. It covers everything from fertility rites and human sacrifice to symbols and practices that influenced a whole generation of twentieth-century writers. One area fits in perfectly with what we were talking about last night – the expulsion of evil and the omnipresence of demons. It explains how down through the ages mankind has become conditioned to expect that if there is a force for good, then surely there must also be a force for evil. The philosophy behind the theory strips nature of its personality and reduces everything we don't understand to the intervention of evil spirits and demons. According to this way of looking at things, the world is teeming with unseen malevolent forces... and, frighteningly, they're just waiting for the slightest opportunity to break into our world.'

'It's similar to the way the Gospels interpret things, then, isn't it?' said Jared.

'Very, that's why I felt it worth a mention. But I must admit it took me by surprise, as I thought such ideas had died out centuries ago.'

'It doesn't surprise me in the least,' said Jared. 'You only have to look at the popularity of the horror genre to see that countless people still believe in the forces of evil. To take it a step further, many believe that demons and spirits lurk around every corner, especially at night, when they seize the opportunity to manifest themselves through bad dreams and nightmares.'

Suddenly an icy finger of fear ran up his spine as he remembered the vivid nightmare he'd had just before the fatal crash claimed his family.

Turning to Edwin, he said, 'Imagine the strain on people who lived like that. They must have been in constant fear, the pressure almost intolerable.'

'Exactly,' said Edwin, 'and it's the main reason why through the centuries those who lived in primitive outposts of civilisation resorted to physical expulsion. In desperation, they saw it as a last resort. It still goes on today you know in certain countries. Take Haiti, for example; the power of voodoo still retains an incredibly powerful hold over the people there. Without the witch doctor or shaman, whichever name you prefer to give them, they wouldn't survive. Anyway, Frazer's book says the most benign form of sacrifice involves an animal, where the blood of the creature represents its life force.'

'That's all very well,' said Jared, 'against what might be described as minor demons or spirits. But what if you were faced with a force so evil so powerful that none of those remedies were effective?'

'What kind of force had you in mind?' asked Edwin in surprise.

'I know this sounds rather fanciful, but let's just say an evil so ancient, it could never be defeated, only imprisoned or contained.'

'Well, I suppose I'd have to say human sacrifice, then; but in this case I guess it would have to be someone who would be prepared to give their lives unselfishly, say, a sacrifice performed out of love. Then of course there is the more obvious one, the sacrifice of someone who had lived a life of extreme devotion or piety... say, a saint.'

After thinking for a moment, Edwin carried on, 'Yes, in my considered opinion either of those might work.'

Suddenly striking the side of his head with the flat of his hand he said, 'Of course, how stupid of me! I've just remembered something which will be of interest to you. A short time ago I received a photocopy of a mysterious scroll. Parts of it were in poor condition, but I eventually managed to work it out. Written in a very ancient form of Aramaic, the story was too fantastic to be true. Nevertheless, it made for incredible reading.'

'So what did the scroll say?' said Jared, intrigued.

With a twinkle in his eye Edwin said, 'I was coming to that, just trying to drag it out a bit, that's all. It was supposed to be written by a group calling themselves the "sect of the dead". Astonishingly, they claimed to be able to bring people back from the grave.' For the next few minutes he explained in detail what he'd been able to transcribe. So intent was Edwin in explaining his story, that he didn't see the colour drain from Jared's face. It had to be more than a coincidence, he reasoned. Before he could give it more thought, he was jerked out of his stasis by his uncle.

Extending his arm in an expansive gesture, he said, 'Well, what do you think?'

The water in the river, for it was more of a river than a stream, was crystal clear. The fertile red soil reached out from gently sloping banks like fingers, creating shallow eddies that were perfect for fishing.

Jared's first impression was that if nothing else they certainly looked the part, especially Edwin with his trilby-style hat stuffed full of hooks and home-made flies.

'No need to use the rods, Uncle, I'm sure the fish will simply throw themselves at us.'

Several hours later, all their sweat and toil had produced the staggering total of two small brown trout.

'We shouldn't grumble, I suppose,' said Jared. 'With all the sound we've made, it's a miracle we've caught anything.'

'Perhaps they had a death wish,' was Edwin's witty reply.

'I'll second that!' said Jared, laughing. 'One thing's certain, there was no skill involved.'

Walking back, Edwin, who had surprised Jared with his constant source of dry humour, turned and said with a straight face, 'Lucky I didn't tell Mrs Daniels we'd be providing our own evening meal, isn't it?'

With that they both burst out laughing.

It didn't take them long to reach home, and after a quick shower and change of clothing they headed for the village. By now the two whales had been safely entrusted to Mrs Daniels' care.

It was one of the most picturesque villages Jared had ever seen. 'Little' was the operative word, because it consisted of the village green complete with obligatory ducks, two dozen houses, a tiny post office and shop combined, and of course the inevitable centrepiece – the pub.

The houses were like something found on a picture postcard, complete with thatched roofs and fences painted a uniform white. The gardens looked as if they'd come straight out of *Country Life* magazine. Although small, the village pond was deep enough to sustain several species of fish, prompting Jared to wonder how the locals managed to protect them from herons. The branches of the willow trees stooped so low they provided a safe haven for some of the miniscule balls of fluff waddling about masquerading as baby ducks.

'The Country Squire' – the name of the pub – was equally as impressive, and as soon as he stepped through the door Jared was caught in its spell. The atmosphere of warmth and friendliness was cleverly created by a combination of low ceilings, genuine oak beams and rough stone walls. Brasses of every sort hung from every spare inch of space. A nightmare to clean, was Jared's initial thought. The whole place was so full of old-world charm that even the landlord looked the part. Short and stout, the impression he gave was of someone who enjoyed his own food and ale. His silvery hair, worn on the long side, allied to his thick bushy eyebrows and bright red complexion, reminded Jared of Father Christmas. On closer inspection Jared wasn't too sure about the complexion. It looked suspiciously like blood pressure. The home-made shepherd's pie and chips were superb, as was the pint of real ale with which it was washed down.

The next hour or two was spent talking to the locals and watching them play cards and dominoes. Even though the stakes amounted to little more than a few pennies, the games were as fiercely contested as if a fortune was involved. As Jared had guessed, Edwin insisted on paying for everything, and no amount of arguing would persuade him otherwise.

Despite the wonderful afternoon, Edwin couldn't help but notice how Jared kept glancing at his watch from time to time. 'Phoning Emma when we get home are we?' was all he said with a glint in his eye.

'That obvious, is it? I don't mean to be rude. You know how much I've enjoyed these last few days; it's just that I miss her.' Then, as if talking to himself he went on, 'I don't know what we're going to do in the long run. You see, I've accepted a place at Oxford and Emma's set her heart on teacher training.'

'It's hardly as if you're going to be a million miles away from each other,' was Edwin's comment. 'Besides, life has a funny way of sorting things out somehow. Mind if I make a suggestion?'

'Not at all,' said Jared.

'Well, I think these last few days have done you the world of good. When you arrived you looked gaunt, shadows under your eyes and all that. Quite understandable, of course. However, as good as my company has been,' he said, smiling to show he was only teasing, 'I think it's time you went home to Emma. I won't deny I'll be disappointed, I've loved every minute of the last few days, but it would be selfish of me to keep you here any longer. It goes without saying you're welcome here anytime.' Then in a more serious tone he added, 'Never forget, Jared, that my home is your home.'

Looking at his uncle with affection, Jared said, 'Thank you. I'll never forget your kindness.'

'One other suggestion,' said Edwin. 'Why don't you surprise her? She won't be expecting you back so early. It might be worth it just to see her face. As soon as we get back, you can pack, and after a quiet night in front of the fire you can have a lie-in. Then after a late breakfast I can drive you to the station to catch the afternoon train.'

It was early evening on the Tuesday before a somewhat tired Jared arrived at his grandmother's house. A quick shower and change of clothing was followed by a hurried meal, after which he made his way down in the gathering gloom to Alec's shed.

Approaching the café, Jared was greeted by the deep driving sound of Steppenwolf's 'Born to be Wild'. The breeze carried the distinctive vocals clearly through the open window, even though the main door was closed. Guessing Emma would be with the others, he was disappointed when he looked through the window and found she was nowhere to be seen.

Opening the door, he shouted over to Roger, 'Seen Emma tonight?'

'No,' was the immediate reply. 'But I thought you were away until Wednesday. Missing her already?' Roger said with a smirk.

Embarrassed, Jared said, 'She's probably in the house. Like an idiot, I didn't think of looking there first. Catch you later,' he said, closing the door behind him.

Making his way along the side of the school past the small tuck shop, he hesitated for a moment, sure he'd seen something in the corner of the yard. It had only been a brief glimpse, so he looked again, this time more carefully.

What he saw made him want to crawl away and die.

There was Emma, his Emma with her arms around someone, holding him tightly. Suddenly he recognised who it was, and in a daze he moved towards them. As if sensing his presence, Emma lifted her head. Pulling away quickly, she opened her mouth to say something, but it was too late, much too late.

Turning on his heel, Jared ran. He didn't know where he was going; all he knew was that he had to get away. Stumbling blindly, he knew the tears of betrayal would come later, but for now there was only the numbness of shock.

It was hours later when he returned home.

As soon as he opened the front door he saw that his gran had waited up for him.

With his feelings now firmly under control, he listened quietly while she explained that he was to call Emma the moment he came in, no matter what time it was.

Seeing that he was upset, she left it at that and went to bed. She was halfway up the stairs when she had a sudden thought. Smiling to herself, she wondered if after all these years of being inseparable, Jared and Emma had just had their first falling out.

It was the following morning as she was making breakfast she saw the note. Instinctively she knew it was something bad, and so with trembling fingers she opened it.

Chapter Ten

Six years later

'NEVER THOUGHT I'D SEE THE DAY,' SAID CHARLIE TUCKER TO Albert, an expression of profound sadness on his face. Shaking his head, he said, 'Suppose it was inevitable, though, what with so many already gone. At least there's one consolation: old Carmel held out for longer than some of the others.'

'That's one way of looking at it,' said old Albert in reply. 'Sign of the times, I'm afraid. Next thing you know they'll be turning it into a bloody mosque or something.'

'Don't worry, Albert,' said Charlie turning to face him, 'the deacons would never have stood for that, take it from me. They made sure there was a clause in the contract stating it could only be sold as a private house.' Looking at the wire fencing surrounding the perimeter, he added, 'From what I can see their going to gut it first and then rebuild on the old foundations.'

'What's going to happen to the money?' asked Albert.

'I voted for it to go to the local hospital – God knows they need it – but true to form I was outvoted. The other buggers decided it should go to the remaining chapels in the area. Waste of bloody time, if you ask me, there's no depending how long they'll manage to keep going – and if they close, what then?'

'Probably go to the bloody council or something,' said Albert. 'Corrupt bastards the lot of them.' The comment brought a wry chuckle from Charlie, standing to the side of him.

The conversation was suddenly interrupted by the noise of a bulldozer starting up.

'Christ, look at the size of that!' said Albert. 'Never had them that big in our day.'

Glancing at him, Charlie said with a grin, 'They never *had* them in our day, you daft bugger.'

Looking sheepish at his mistake, Albert said, 'Suppose you're right, but they'd better hope the foundations are solid enough to carry the weight of that bloody thing.'

In order for the bulldozer to gain access to the main body of the old chapel, a large section of the front had already been demolished. At the same time, most of the pews had been removed, so the inside was virtually empty. Trundling slowly through the gaping hole, the heavy machine made its way towards the back of the chapel, to the spot where the altar table and pulpit still held pride of place. Suddenly, with a loud roar and a cloud of dust, the front end of the bulldozer disappeared from view.

Within moments the driver had scrambled desperately from the cabin and was looking at a hole in the ground that had appeared from no-where. Taking off his bright yellow safety helmet, he scratched his head in bemusement and then, looking at the two old men who by now were standing behind him, said, 'Christ, that was a close shave! Thought my end had come, I did.'

'If you want a bit of advice, lad,' said Charlie, 'cordon off the area and get your boss to have a look before you do anything else. Perhaps the dozer hasn't settled yet. For all you know, it could disappear completely while you're standing here looking at it.'

Replacing his helmet, he said, 'Bloody good idea, mate.' He stepped over the rubble and ran towards his works van. Within moments it was screaming down the road, leaving in its wake a cloud of exhaust fumes and burning rubber.

As soon as it had disappeared, Charlie said, 'Right, that should give us enough time to look around before he comes back with the cavalry.'

Laughing, Albert commented, 'You sly old bugger – you planned that, didn't you?'

Before Charlie could answer, the dozer began to settle even further into the hole, accompanied by more groaning noises and a billowing cloud of dust.

Peering down in fascination, Charlie said, 'What the hell do you think it is?'

Shaking his head, Albert replied, 'Haven't a clue, but whatever it is, it's not supposed to be there unless...' His voice trailed off suddenly.

'Unless what?'

Pensive now, Albert replied, 'Don't you remember the story about Carmel being built on top of an old monastery?'

'Yes, of course,' answered Charlie, 'but I didn't think there was anything to the rumours.' Then, looking around, he said, 'But I suppose there must have been.'

With a twinkle in his eye, Albert said, 'Let's have a look then, settle our curiosity and all that. Before you start making excuses, I think I've found a way down.' He pointed to a flight of stone steps on his right-hand side.

'OK, but we'd better be quick. If we're caught it could get nasty; remember, we're technically trespassing.'

'I'm more worried about the bloody dozer falling on top of us than the worker coming back,' said Albert. 'Although as long as we keep to this side, I think we should be safe enough.'

'*I think!*' said Charlie sarcastically. 'That might make a good epitaph on my tombstone, in case you're wrong!'

Within moments they were at the bottom of the steps, only to be greeted with a sight that frightened the life out of them. Looking closely, they saw an old skeleton covered in cobwebs.

Swallowing his fear, Charlie said, 'Do you think it's real?'

'Course its bloody real!' said Albert. 'Think it's a dummy or something? Listen, let me give you a bit of advice. It's not the dead you should be worrying about in this day and age, it's the living.'

'Whatever, but I'm not so sure we should go any further.'

'Shame on you, Charlie!' said Albert. 'You being an old miner, and all that.'

'Yeah, but don't forget I was getting paid to take risks in those days, wasn't I?'

At that moment Albert noticed something lying under some loose stones in the corner.

Making his way over, he found to his surprise it was some kind of strange black object. Clearing the dust away, he showed it to Charlie, who asked if it was damaged.

'I think so, but not too badly,' Albert replied.

Looking more closely, he said, 'From what I can see, it looks like the top bit is hanging on by a thread. Hold on, I'll just see if I can lift it off... There, that was easy,' he said, holding the lid in his hand.

As soon as the lid was removed, an audible sigh escaped from the body of the open chalice, and suddenly without warning the temperature in the little room plummeted.

'Here,' said Charlie, 'is it me, or has it just got colder?'

'No, it's like a bloody fridge all of a sudden. What the hell's going on?'

'Let's have a look at the thing,' said Charlie, snatching it from Albert's hand.

He was about to look inside, when black smoke like tendrils began to emerge from the body of the chalice, followed by a stench that was almost overpowering.

'Jesus Christ!' said Albert. 'What the fuck is that? It's revolting, smells as if something got trapped in there and died.'

Looking inside, Charlie saw what looked like a pile of ashes, before commenting, 'If this is what I think it is, we'd better leave well alone.'

'Why, what do you think it is?' said Albert.

'I'm not sure,' was Charlie's reply, 'but if I'm right it's some kind of fancy funeral urn. If that's the case, that black stuff is probably some poor bugger's ashes. All the same, they shouldn't smell like that, should they?' he said turning to Albert with a puzzled expression on his face. 'If you ask me, I think we'd better put if back where we found it… don't want to disturb the dead, do we.'

With a chuckle, Albert said, 'Never knew you were superstitious, Charlie.'

'I'm not,' said Charlie, defensively, 'except there's no point in pushing our luck, is there?'

'Suppose not,' said Albert.

He was about to give it back when something at the bottom caught his eye.

'Hang on, Albert,' said Charlie excitedly, 'I'm sure there's something else in this bloody urn.' At the same time he plunged his hand into the ashes. By now all thoughts of not disturbing the dead were forgotten. Within moments his hand encountered something metallic, and with a shout of triumph he held it up for inspection.

Intrigued, Albert shouted excitedly, 'What the hell have you found?'

Inspecting it more closely, Charlie said, 'Looks like some kind of coin.' He began rubbing it vigorously on the leg of his trousers. Within moments he found several others, until eventually he had a small pile in the palm of his hand.

Turning to Albert he said excitedly, 'Here, Alb, these are the strangest looking coins I've ever seen. Think they could be worth anything?'

'Haven't a clue. What do you think we should do with them?'

'Finders, keepers, I say,' said Charlie. By now, visions of wealth were dancing before his eyes. 'But let's see how many there are first.'

Counting the coins, he found there were twenty-nine, and looking up he said, 'That's awkward, Albert; there's twenty-nine, an odd bloody number.'

'Never mind! You found them, Charlie, so you take the fifteen, I'll have the rest.' Then he added, 'I've just had a thought: the next time we find ourselves in town we could have them valued.'

'Better still,' said Charlie, 'we could check up on the Internet, they'll probably give us a better deal.'

'What shall we do with the urn, then?' asked Albert urgently. 'Can't leave it here, can we, or someone might work out we've been here tampering with things. And don't forget, that bloody workman knows we were watching. He didn't come across as the sharpest pencil in the box, but I bet it won't take him long to put two and two together if he realises something's missing.'

Thoughtful now Charlie had an idea. 'Let's put it back exactly as we found it. Put the top on and hide it under those stones. Make it look as if no one was ever here.'

'Good idea,' said Albert.

In the excitement of the moment, neither of them noticed that a single coin had dropped from Charlie's hand before the counting begun. Rolling soundlessly across the dusty floor, it came to rest under one of the smaller stones which littered the bottom of the small room.

Meanwhile, in their haste to scramble up the steps, the two men completely missed the dark shadow in the opposite corner. Not that it mattered, for in seconds it had disappeared completely, leaving behind no trace of it ever having existed.

At 10 a.m. the following day, the fog rolled in over the village of Raven's Hill. Almost instantly it turned a beautifully clear morning into something that looked remarkably like a clip from a cheap horror movie. Within moments, people panicked, barely able to see their hands in front of their faces. It was the strangest thing, but it seemed to cover the boundaries of the village precisely. A few yards to either side and there was no sign of it. It was almost as if someone had built a wall around the village using fog instead of the usual bricks and mortar.

Sticking her head out of the front door, old Mrs Penrose took one look and decided it wasn't going to stop her daily stroll to the shops. She'd been allotted the title 'Old' for the simple reason it seemed she'd been around for ever. In fact, at seventy-eight years of age, she looked a good deal younger. In remarkably good health, she was fiercely independent. Refusing help of any kind, her routine included shopping for herself in the corner store situated about a mile away. It was a journey that could be halved if you were prepared to take the short cut that ran along a steep narrow path running past the side of her home and down across the stream. Difficult to negotiate at the best of times, the path was almost suicidal for a woman of her age in those conditions. Common sense dictated that no one should use it on such a morning, but as usual, Mrs Penrose stubbornly refused to take the long way round.

Despite her outward show of bravado, she was secretly afraid. Making her way tentatively down the steep slope a few feet at a time, she became increasingly nervous. In her heightened state of imagination, perfectly normal objects she'd passed countless times before took on new meanings. Looking around in apprehension, she imagined the trees lining the route to be alive. Each branch became the bony finger of a long dead skeleton, reaching out lovingly to enfold her in its death-like embrace. At the same time, the tendrils of white swirling mist that drifted around her ankles looked uncomfortably like the tattered remains of ghostly shrouds.

By now she was working hard to keep a lid on her fear, and she kept peering into the gloom in a vain attempt to persuade herself there really was nothing waiting to pounce on her and drag her off into the murk. Unbidden, a distant memory stirred and within seconds she had it; she remembered vividly a fleeting visit to London. The smog that day had been so thick her father had told her the story of Jack the Ripper. Realising the fog was similar in consistency to that which surrounded her now, the story came back to her in all its horrendous detail.

Admonishing herself for what she saw as irrational fear, she told herself, 'Get a grip, you old fool, you're too long in the tooth to worry about things that go bump in the night!' With that, she thrust her head back and tilting her chin upwards, forged ahead with a new-found sense of determination.

Shouting at the fog to bolster her courage, she said, 'I've been taking this short cut for forty years, so if you think you're going to stop me now you've another think coming!' Anyway, she thought to herself, as long as I'm careful I'll be fine.

Reaching the long narrow bridge across the stream – it was nothing more than two planks of wood placed side by side – she paused. At roughly twelve feet long and a foot wide, it was dangerous. Crossing it demanded a good deal of care, even in the best of conditions.

Stepping gingerly onto the bridge, she eased herself forward six inches at a time until she was roughly midway across. Suddenly she stopped dead in her tracks, and turning her head to one side she listened carefully. Sure she'd heard a loud squealing noise, her heart began to pump wildly. To her own ears the sound was so loud she was sure anyone within a hundred yards or so could hear it. Fighting to remain calm, she took deep breaths in order to stave of hyperventilation. After several moments she felt better, but suddenly there it was again, she hadn't imagined it after all. If she wasn't mistaken it was coming from directly in front of her. All at once, the noise seemed to rise in intensity, until without warning it was joined by several other high-pitched squealing sounds. She was so startled she almost lost her footing. Cursing the fog under her breath, she wished it would lift, reasoning that at least she would then be able to see what was making the bloody noise.

The idea had barely entered her head, when suddenly the swirling mist parted.

Gasping in astonishment, she had to rub her eyes to make sure she wasn't seeing things. Looking more closely she realised it was no mistake, her eyes weren't deceiving her.

There blocking her way was the largest black rat she'd ever seen. As big as any household cat, it stood perfectly still, staring at her in hatred from behind a pair of strange red eyes. Too late she was reminded of an early childhood saying, 'Be careful what you wish for, as it might just come true.' Now she was sorry she hadn't kept her thoughts to herself.

Pulling herself together, she began to rationalise the situation. So what, it was only a bloody rat! Admittedly it was the biggest one she'd ever seen, but as she'd never been particularly afraid of rats it didn't really bother her. In fact, she felt better now that she had something on which to focus her anger.

Stepping forward with the intention of kicking the thing clean off the bridge, she was suddenly taken aback, as without warning it arched its back, barred its long sharp teeth and hissed aggressively. Stopping dead in her tracks, Mrs Penrose felt the first pangs of unease.

It suddenly dawned on her the thing blocking her way was no ordinary rat; in fact, it was unlike anything she'd ever seen before. Backtracking slowly, inch by inch, she'd come to the conclusion that in this instance, discretion might be the better part of valour. She was barely three feet from safety when she heard the loathsome hissing again, but this time it was coming from behind. Turning slowly, her worst fears were confirmed, as in wide-eyed terror she saw several other rats blocking her retreat.

Unable to either advance or retreat, she was trapped!

The icy tentacles of unease she'd felt a few moments ago were back, but this time they were threatening to give way to full-blown terror. Fighting down her mounting panic, she saw that the rats behind were not as big as the giant facing her, so she came to a decision. She decided if she ran at them, showed no fear, they'd scatter. After all, the main road and safety was a mere twenty yards away, wasn't it?

About to put her theory to the test, something dropped lightly onto her shoulder from a branch directly above her head. It had been waiting patiently, watching for an opportunity to pounce. Turning her head slowly, her heart sank. Deep down she knew what it was even before she actually saw the hideous thing. In despair, she looked sideways to see the vile rodent gazing at her with malevolent glee. Looking into its yellow feral eyes, she could smell its fetid breath in her face, and it was at that moment Mrs Penrose knew she was doomed.

Within seconds, several more had landed on her, tangling in her hair and covering her face. In blind panic, she lost her footing and fell into the water some two feet below. The force of the fall temporarily winded her, until, realising she was fighting for her life, she made one last determined effort to get to her feet.

Rolling to one side, she put one hand in the water and suddenly froze, there looking down at her from the centre of the bridge was the giant rat. Gazing at her with something like contempt, she could have sworn it was grinning. Suddenly a strange thought popped into her mind; she wondered if it could be orchestrating events, displaying an innate cunning, an intelligence she'd never seen in any other animal.

She was in no doubt it was the driving force behind the others. While she'd been concentrating on that particular rat, she'd never noticed how the others had become motionless.

It was to be a brief respite.

Tired of the game, the super-rat lifted its head and gave one high-pitched squeal. The response was instantaneous, and within seconds they were all over her. As Mrs Penrose opened her mouth to scream, one of the smaller ones saw its opportunity and somehow managed to gain access to her throat. Lodged there, it cut off any attempt at a cry for help. Gagging from the stinking ball of fur that was forcing its way ever deeper into her throat, the old woman's life suddenly flashed before her. She didn't have long to ponder on it, though, as in seconds the others were all over her.

Biting and squealing they ripped open any unexposed flesh. In desperation, she tried to tear the squirming creatures from her face, but it seemed that for every one she dislodged, several others took its place. Agonising pain was shooting through her, as parts of her face were being ripped away in large chunks, leaving behind gaping wounds that showed the milky white bones beneath. Suddenly without warning, one rat more aggressive than the others tore her left eyeball from its socket in a split second of intense agony. The blood and fluid spurting from the gaping wound only seemed to heighten the rats' frenzy. In a short time several of them had burrowed under her clothes and were gnawing away at her exposed stomach, intent on eating their way through the lining in order to gain access to the more tasty pieces of offal buried deep inside. With her strength fading fast, old Mrs Penrose knew further resistance was futile, and she accepted the inevitable.

In the few moments before she slipped away, something struck her as puzzling. Why she wondered had the black rat appeared so intelligent, so special? The answer came to her suddenly. It was special because it was one of those super-rats she'd read about somewhere, one of those bred in some secret laboratory.

For some reason, the answer still didn't fully satisfy her, it still failed to explain why this particular one had strange red eyes, eyes that seemed to penetrate her very soul, eyes that afforded her a glimpse of hell itself…

Those were her final thoughts before she slipped quietly into the abyss.

It was three days before anyone found Mrs Penrose's remains, and then it was by accident. By then, the mist which had appeared so suddenly had just as suddenly lifted. One minute it was there, the next it was gone.

Bernard Daniels, a member of the local fire brigade on a flying visit to his aunt, had decided to take the short cut. What he saw baffled him.

Lying in the water, partially submerged, was what appeared to be a skeleton. At first glance he took it to be a plastic model, a display stolen from one of the local hospitals and placed there for a prank. He was within ten yards when the smell told him otherwise. This was no plastic skeleton. Realising what it was, he rushed back down the narrow path and headed straight for the police station to report his macabre find.

Within the hour, the area was cordoned off in preparation for the visit of the forensic pathologist from Swansea. When he and his team eventually arrived, they discovered the rats had done their gruesome work exceptionally well. Stripping every square inch of flesh from the woman's body, nothing had been wasted. So little did the pathologist have to go on, that it took him a great deal longer than anticipated to announce that the remains were those of an elderly lady.

The locals recounting the story afterwards were amazed at just how long it had taken to come to such a startling conclusion, claiming sarcastically they could have solved the puzzle in a fraction of the time.

Mrs Powell opposite was heard to say it shouldn't have needed a Sherlock Holmes to work out that, as poor old Mrs Penrose hadn't been seen for several days, it could leave you with only one conclusion.

Chapter Eleven

THE OLD HERCULES, RENOWNED WORKHORSE OF THE ROYAL AIR Force transport command, landed with the slightest of bumps on the runway of Brize Norton, before cruising smoothly towards the series of hangars situated at the outer edge of the airfield. Getting up from his canvas seat, the lone passenger picked up his kit from the floor where he'd wedged it between his feet and headed for the door. Walking quickly down the ramp at the back of the aircraft, he turned sideways and after a few moments stopped for a second to lift his hand in a silent thank you to the pilot, who was gazing down at him from the cockpit.

It had been a stroke of good fortune, he had to admit. A friend of a friend had managed to get him on this flight, ensuring he'd arrive home a day earlier than anticipated. Standing on the concrete walkway, which was cracked and pitted with weeds in several places, he took in his surroundings before breathing in a deep lungful of the damp cold air. Not usually prone to nostalgia, he suddenly realised it had been several years since he'd been in Britain, and he was surprised to see just how much he'd missed the old place. In a moment of wild abandon, he lifted his head so that the rain, heavy by now, could wash over him in waves. Shaking his head vigorously, he watched as the water cascaded downwards in large droplets, noticing in amusement how they slipped gracefully down his cheeks before sliding silently into his open mouth. Throwing his hands towards the sky, he uttered a silent prayer for his safe homecoming. He guessed that to an onlooker he must appear mad. However, only someone who had spent what now seemed like a lifetime in places that hadn't seen a drop of rain for years would appreciate how precious water was. Allowing himself a brief smile, he was pragmatic enough to foresee that after a few weeks living at home again, he might very well feel differently. For a brief while, however, he was content to savour the moment.

Making his way towards the terminal, he was struck by another thought: it was the last time he would ever make a journey overseas as a member of Her Majesty's Forces. From 1300 hours tomorrow, he was finished with the army. From then on he would no longer be a captain, but simply plain old Jared Hunter. Although he'd signed on for nine years, he'd obtained his discharge by purchase after six. And despite strenuous efforts by several of his superiors to persuade him to remain, he'd stubbornly refused. To a man, they'd warned him he was throwing away a glittering career; but deep in his heart he knew he was ready for another kind of challenge.

Six years, he thought to himself, and in all honesty he'd loved almost every minute of it. He'd found hidden skills he never knew existed. His martial arts instructor had dubbed him one of the most natural talents he'd ever come across, or to put it in his own words, 'Son, you're a natural killer!' On many occasions since he'd proven his instructor right, but it sometimes bothered him to think he felt no remorse. He often wondered what his family would have thought of him had they still been alive, especially his young brother. Would they have been proud, or horrified, at what he'd become? Of one thing he was certain: he was a far different animal to that which had left the little village of Raven's Hill all those years ago.

With a sudden pang he wondered what had become of his friends, especially Emma.

She was probably married with kids now, he mused, perhaps even to that boy he'd caught her with on that traumatic day before he'd run away. Still, that was all over now, he told himself sternly.

Walking through customs, he was subjected to the same scrutiny as a civilian, except that when they understood you were a member of the armed forces, they tended to be less rigorous. Not that it mattered, as he'd brought nothing back that couldn't be declared. The things he'd acquired of a more delicate nature – for want of a better phrase – would eventually be smuggled into Britain through very different channels. He had no inkling as to what he was going to do next, no thought of an occupation. Spending most of his time performing things such as 'Black Ops' in such remote areas as Afghanistan, Lebanon and Iraq, he'd needed little money, and so that wasn't an issue. Besides, he had no idea how much his grandmother had put by for him after the sale of his parents' house. Thinking about his grandmother brought about a pang of guilt.

Over the six years since he'd been out of circulation, he'd hardly ever been in contact with her or Edwin. They'd understand, he reasoned, once they appreciated the delicate nature of his work. Without warning, despite what he told himself earlier about Emma, his mind returned to her, and he wondered ruefully about the kind of reception that might be in store for him.

Well, Hunter, he thought to himself, you've got to face the music sometime.

Once through customs, he picked up a hire car, dumped his belongings in the boot and headed towards the M4 motorway and home. Cruising along in the middle lane, keeping a wary eye on his speed he was sure of one thing, there were a good many more cars on the road than there had been six years ago. Thankful for small mercies, he realised the traffic would have been a good deal worse, but for the fact it was early evening. Traditionally, it had always been a more quiet time for travelling.

Two hours later, he stopped for a break at a small roadside café that seemed reasonably quiet and ordered a full breakfast. He allowed himself the briefest of chuckles when he sensed that he must have looked pretty stupid ordering such a thing at this time in the evening. Looking around, he was relieved to see that he wasn't the only one. Sipping bottled water with his meal, he noticed a copy of the *Western Mail* lying discarded on the table opposite. With a wry smile he leaned over and picked it up, noticing with pleasure that it was a fairly recent edition. Without thinking he fell into the same ritual as he'd done when he was a teenager. Starting with the sports page, he made his way to the front, noting with amusement how it was often the small things you missed the most. As it was a weekday, there appeared to be nothing of great interest in the sports column. The remainder of the stuff, especially the items dealing with politics, he ignored. Since joining the forces, such things left him cold. With that, he came across the daily crossword. Allowing himself a brief smile, he noted that it had been completed except for one empty space. Knowing he would never be able to leave until he had filled in the missing word, he read the clue. 'Unavoidable task, something one is commanded by birth to complete.' It was a seven-letter word ending with a Y. He had it instantly – destiny. Filling it in with a biro which he took from his jacket pocket, he wondered if it would turn out to be prophetic.

Folding it up neatly, he was about to put the paper back when suddenly something caught his eye. Tucked away at the bottom right-hand corner of the first page was a small piece on the little village of Raven's Hill. Thinking about the odds of such a thing happening on his first day back, he began reading the article with interest. His initial excitement quickly turned to horror, however, when he studied its contents.

No, he screamed silently, *it can't be!* But it was…

The report was fairly detailed, explaining how last Wednesday workmen bulldozing the remains of an old chapel in the village had accidentally broken through its foundations. Suspending operations while they investigated the reason for the collapse, they found to their astonishment a room hidden directly in front of the old altar table of the chapel. Its origins were a mystery, but excavations revealed an exquisite black urn and the skeletal remains of an old man. Further investigation by local archaeologists unearthed a ring. Strangely, it displayed the same symbol as that uncovered on a flat tombstone in a remote corner of the chapel's cemetery some six years earlier. The reporter had gone on to underline one other point of interest: buried in each of the four walls were large brass crosses. To date, local historians were baffled as to their purpose.

The article concluded by saying that the objects were regarded as something of a national treasure and that eventually they would be transported to the Museum of Antiquities in Cardiff. Until then they would be put on public display, albeit under lock and key, in Raven's Hill Welfare Hall.

Checking the dates, he found nearly a week had passed since the incident had taken place, and he secretly hoped that if nothing untoward had happened, the chalice might have been undamaged. On a more realistic note, he admitted to himself that even if that were the case, it might still be of no use. Without the protection of the chapel walls, it would still be capable of exerting a huge potential for evil.

It was dark by the time he reached his grandmother's, and in many ways he was grateful. He didn't want to see anyone until he was ready. Lifting his kitbag from the boot, he looked up at the old house with fond memories. Suddenly, without warning, he panicked. Unable to move he was frozen to the spot, knowing with certainty the reason was cowardice. He'd faced and killed many people during his time in the army, had been cited for bravery on several occasions, but this was different.

Finally, his breathing under control, he made his way up the steps towards the front door. It was then he discovered with a start he no longer had his own key.

Standing outside, he took a few moments to calm himself and then, before his courage failed, pressed the bell. He was rewarded almost immediately by the deep sonorous tone with which he was so familiar. When at last his grandmother opened the door he didn't know what reaction to expect, but it certainly wasn't the one he got.

Looking up at him, she exclaimed, 'My God, but look how brown you are!' before putting her arms around his neck and bursting into tears. When she'd recovered they made straight for the kitchen and the inevitable cup of tea. Following closely behind, he noted with some alarm how much she'd aged in the six years since he'd been away, in particular how much flesh she'd lost from her face, and the sight shocked him. With a twinge of guilt, he wondered just how much his sudden disappearance had contributed.

Out of the blue, Jared said, 'Where's Grandad, isn't he home?'

Carrying on putting tea in the pot, his grandmother said, without turning around, 'I'm afraid I don't see much of him these days, love. Since his last promotion he seems to spend most of his time on the move.'

Jared didn't like the sound of that, but decided not to press the matter.

The remainder of the evening was spent telling his grandmother as much as he could about what he'd been doing during the last six years. Listening intently, she was wise enough to understand that, all things considered, he'd told her as much as he was allowed. He could hardly believe his ears when he learned how much his parents' house had been sold for, and because he was the only remaining child it was all his. Showing her wisdom, his grandmother had immediately contacted Edwin for advice, knowing full well he knew far more than her about financial matters.

With a twinkle in her eye she said, 'Knowing Edwin, I've no doubt the cheque I sent him was invested wisely. So you can bet the figure I mentioned earlier is probably worth a lot more now.' Then, in a serious tone she added, 'All things considered, you're quite well off for a young man of your age.'

The following morning Jared awoke at 6 sharp. Conditioned by his training, he needed no alarm clock. All that was required was to set a time in his head and he would wake within seconds of his allotted deadline. Beside this little trick, he'd picked up another skill, one that had saved his life on more than one occasion. On coming around he'd lie perfectly still, allowing only his eyes to open before coming instantly alert.

His daily routine, time permitting, never varied. A punishing six-mile run, the last of which was around four minutes, was followed by a gruelling routine of sit-ups and push-ups.

Heading towards the mountains at the back of his grandmother's garden, Jared unlocked the gate before taking a right turn and making for the short cut which led through the heart of the forest. At this time of the morning the ground was covered by a thin layer of mist, and although the grass was damp, the air was crisp and cold. Pushing hard, he'd forced his pulse up to the required rate within the first few hundred yards, and from there on settled into a loping gait that seemed to eat up the miles effortlessly. Some twenty minutes later he crested the summit of the mountain, stopping for a brief moment in order to take in the familiar surroundings. Acutely aware of the stillness and solitude, he'd forgotten just how green everything was, and he suddenly realised with a start how much he'd missed such things. The stark topography of such places as Afghanistan and Iraq were achingly beautiful in their own way. The austere environment and bleak barren mountains were unique, especially at night, but this was different. This was his homeland. This was where he'd been born and he thrilled in the feeling of being back where he belonged.

It was then the disturbing thoughts crowded in.

Without warning the images flashed into his mind.

Dragged up from somewhere deep in his subconscious he saw the bodies, the gaping mouths, the open staring eyes. Those who had never experienced such things would never realise that the horrors, the fears, remained even after death. The memories were indelibly burned into his brain, etched into his soul. Trying to rationalise things, he sensed there was no point in going down this alley, taking this line of reasoning. He had to remember he'd simply fulfilled a role. To reflect on what he'd done in any other way was to invite disaster. There was no point in breaking things down into what could or couldn't have been. Unfortunately, he knew life wasn't like that; instead it was a cruel world that allowed for no such luxuries. Making a huge effort, he blocked the disturbing imagery his brain had suddenly decided to conjure up, and forced his mind to think of something else.

Unexpectedly, the wailing of seagulls overhead helped dispel his mood of doom and despondency, and with that, he was reminded of the old saying that gulls this far up the valley meant a storm was brewing. Without warning, two swooped down onto the grass several yards in front of him, fighting over something he couldn't see.

About to make his way back, he stood still and listened. He was sure he'd heard something. Within seconds he knew he'd been right, his exceptional hearing had picked up the flap of wings moments before he saw the huge silver white owl. Swooping over his head from where it had been hiding in the trees, it passed so low that for a moment he thought he could reach out and touch it. It surprised Jared, as he'd always thought that, like him, white owls were normally creatures of the night. Perhaps it might be a good omen, he thought to himself. For several moments he watched transfixed by the beauty of the majestic bird, until all he could make out was a blurred distant shape.

Within the hour he was back at the house, showered and changed; he was now ready to face the world.

Over breakfast he decided to ask his grandmother about the things found under old Carmel chapel, hoping to soften his line of questioning so that it didn't sound too much like an interrogation. He needn't have worried, as she was only too glad to give him a full account. Disappointingly, her version seemed to differ very little from that of the reporters, including the fact that the objects would be on display locally for a few weeks.

Trying to sound as causal as he could, Jared took it a step further. 'Anything unusual happen lately, Gran? You know, since old Carmel was knocked down, I mean?'

'It's only been a week, love, but funny you should ask, there have been one or two odd incidents. First there was the death of old Mrs Penrose – you know, the one who lived a few doors up from you.'

'Number thirty-five, you mean – the house next door to the short cut?'

'Yes, that's the one. Well, they found her – or what was left of her, anyway – in the little stream near the wooden bridge. Stripped bare, she was; no, not only her clothes, the flesh too. It seems something had eaten her alive. Picked her bones clean as a whistle. Rumour was she'd been eaten by rats.' Wracking her brain to remember the other thing, she suddenly said, 'Of course, silly me, it was during the time of the fog.'

'What fog?' asked Jared in alarm.

'Well, it was the strangest thing,' his gran replied. 'It was a Saturday morning, I remember it well. Anyway, one moment everything was normal, the air clean as a whistle, then blow me down seconds later you couldn't see a thing! Had the weathermen really puzzled. They said it was as if someone had dropped a wall of fog around the entire village.'

Mulling over the story later, Jared was forced to the conclusion that the chalice might well have been damaged after all. With that, an icy tentacle of fear started to spread down his spine.

It was while he was thinking about the problem that he quite literally ran into Roger.

Christ, thought Roger, picking himself up from the floor, it had been like running into a brick wall. 'Watch where you're going, mate!' he said belligerently, before suddenly noticing who he'd bumped into. In astonishment he added sarcastically, 'Well, well, what have we here, then? The prodigal son's returned, has he? Been pumping iron, or something? The old Jared would never have put me on my arse so quickly. Haven't heard from you since that night you upped and disappeared.' Trying to keep the hurt out of his voice, he said, 'How long has it been?'

Before he could continue, Jared said, 'Late 1999 – six years, in fact!'

'Of course,' said Roger, 'just a few days after we found that bloody chalice thing, wasn't it?'

'A week exactly,' replied Jared. 'It was the night I came home from Edwin's. I arrived home a day earlier to surprise Emma…' Suddenly his voice failed and he couldn't continue.

'Of course,' said Roger, 'it was a Tuesday, and by the following morning you'd gone, never to be seen until now. Not a note, a letter, or even a postcard! Didn't you think you at least owed us that, Jar, especially Emma? Jesus, don't you realise what you did to her? For all intents and purposes you two were fucking married. All but, anyway! That was cruel, mate – gutless, if you ask me.'

It was a moment before Roger noticed he'd hit a raw nerve, but when he did, what he saw in Jared's eyes caused him to back off. This was not the same boy who'd left Raven's Hill. The person who stood in front of him now was a very different character, and somehow he frightened his former friend.

When Jared replied, the words were said so quietly that Roger had trouble hearing them. 'Let's not go down that road, shall we? There are things you don't know about that night, surprising things. But as far as I'm concerned, it's water under the bridge, so let's forget it, shall we?'

Puzzled at not having a clue about what Jared was on about, Roger kept his questions to himself and decided to change the subject.

'So what have you been doing with yourself? Been abroad or something? Seeing the colour on you, I mean.'

Following that, Roger was given a potted version. Thawing a little after the explanation, he said, 'You joined the army the next day, just like that? Christ, that took some guts!'

'Signed on the dotted line that morning,' said Jared. 'The reason I didn't write was because most of my time was spent in places that were so inaccessible it was impossible. They don't have post offices where I was stationed,' he explained, with a trace of his old humour.

'But you didn't have to start at the bottom anyway, not with all those qualifications of yours? Besides, the fact you'd been accepted by Oxford University must have turned a few heads, eh? What did they have to say about that?'

'They didn't know. I didn't tell them.'

Astonishment written on his face, Roger said, 'Why, for Christ's sake? It would have made things a lot easier.'

With a wry smile, Jared countered, 'That's precisely why I didn't tell them; I wanted to do it the hard way, didn't want any special privileges. To be honest I wanted to punish myself, to purge myself of all the hurt and anger that had built up inside of me, and to do that I had to push myself to the limits. Luckily, after the first year someone in high places noticed me and decided I was good enough to join the best. As soon as I moved in with my new unit, the instructors told me quite simply that they would either make me or break me. The first few months were a living nightmare, and on a few occasions I began to wonder, but strangely I loved it. You see, I knew it was exactly what I wanted. After that things got better and better; and the rest, as they say in the movies, is history.'

'Well, it certainly worked in terms of physical appearance,' said Roger. 'But what about the mental devils? Those up here,' he added, tapping the side of his head. 'Did it help drive them out?'

'To a certain extent,' replied Jared. 'I was kept so busy just staying alive, keeping one step ahead of the grim reaper, so to speak, I didn't have time for self-pity. So in that way you could say it worked.' Then in a more serious tone he added, 'I went through hell, but came out the other side a different person.'

Before he could say anything else, Roger observed, 'I can see that, but if you don't mind me saying, you look different. I can't put my finger on it, but for the want of a better expression you look like – oh, I don't know – a hard bastard, that's all.'

Looking at his feet in embarrassment, Jared said, 'If that's the case it's because I really have changed. I've done and seen things which no normal person should want to; but more worrying from my point of view is that I enjoyed it. I could have stayed on and made a career of it, but in my mind I knew if I didn't stop now, I never would. And I didn't want that. Given time, I'm confident the old Jared will return, so I decided to give him a chance.' He looked up and smiled.

The smile seemed to transform him, and for the first time since their chance reunion, Roger had the glimpse of the original article, the one everyone knew and loved. Leaning over, he touched his friend's shoulder and said, 'If it's any consolation, mate, I think you've made the right decision. But anyway, you still haven't told me exactly what it is you did.'

'I'm afraid I can't, but I can give you a clue. I spent most of my training just up the road in the Brecon Beacons, and in my early days I was based in Hereford.'

Suddenly the truth dawned on Roger, and he blurted out, 'Oh, fuck! You're one of them, aren't you? I've read about you lot. You were in the same crowd as what's-his-name?' Thinking hard for a moment, trying to recall the character, he suddenly had it. 'Yeah, I've got it now – Chris Ryan, I think his name was. Since then there have been several books published about the SAS, but if I remember correctly, people weren't too pleased about the contents. Giving out trade secrets and all that. Saw it as a betrayal of trust, didn't they? Jesus, no wonder you've changed!' He left it at that.

'What about the others?' asked Jared, with curiosity.

'Well, I'm a plumber now, got my own business. Not earning a fortune, like the media let on, but I do all right.'

'I don't know about the media,' said Jared with a grin, 'haven't seen or heard any news for a long time, apart from one quick squint of a paper yesterday, that is, but if it's any consolation I knew you'd make out.'

'Thanks for the vote of confidence,' said Roger with genuine warmth, before carrying on. 'Aled's done quite well for himself. Remember, he was always pretty good at the old theatricals; well, he dropped in lucky. Does the odd bit for the Welsh channel S4C.'

Diplomatically he didn't mention that Emma had a child, deciding it would be better for Jared to find that out for himself.

'What about Michael, then?' asked Jared.

It was out before Roger could retract it. 'Apart from Emma, he felt your betrayal more that anyone.' Jared didn't flinch. 'He's living on his own now in a one-bedroom flat, finding it hard by all accounts. Since you left we hardly ever see him; it's as if he's gone back into his shell again. Don't know how he's going to react to seeing you again.'

'I was afraid of that,' said Jared, visibly upset. 'I'll have to go and see him, put things right somehow…'

'Seriously, though,' said Roger, breaking into Jared's reverie, 'why did you come back?'

'I was coming home anyway, Rog, but then the strangest thing happened. I was sitting in a roadside café taking a short break when I picked up an old *Western Mail* and suddenly there it was – the story of the chalice and skeleton.'

'It is bloody odd,' said Roger, 'but you needn't have worried. Nothing's happened.'

Looking him in the eye, Jared said, 'Nothing's happened, eh? So what about the death of old Mrs Penrose and the mysterious fog? Call that nothing, Rog?'

'Ah, but that was a coincidence, that's all… nothing to worry about there.'

Shaking his head, Jared said, 'Same old Roger! Don't you remember that's exactly what we quarrelled about the night before I left? You weren't prepared to take responsibility for what we'd done. Gave me some bullshit about mass hallucination or something, didn't you?'

Looking at the floor, Roger said quietly, 'Yeah, I remember, but it was the only way I could handle things. Knew deep down something was wrong, but couldn't admit it to myself, could I. But it'll be all right now you're back, won't it? Remember, it said you were special… called you the special one, didn't it?'

'Yes, I remember, but to be honest that's what worries me – I haven't a clue why.' He added, 'Somehow we've got to get a look at that bloody chalice. Any ideas?'

'It's kept under lock and key in a glass cabinet,' said Roger, 'but give me a few hours and I'll see what I can do.' Then as an afterthought he said, 'Do you think it's managed to escape? Do you really think it's behind all this? Surely, if it's managed to free itself it would have done something far worse by now. What about all that biblical crap it was spouting before it tried to take your head off?'

'I'm not sure,' was Jared's honest reply. 'If the chalice isn't damaged and it hasn't managed to get out, we're in with a chance. And then you could well be right; everything that's happened to date is nothing more than a series of unfortunate coincidences. I'm not one for coincidences, though. Call me a pessimist if you like, but I wouldn't bank on us being that lucky. No, I think we'd better prepare ourselves for the worst case scenario. That way we won't be lulled into a false sense of security and get caught with our pants down. What I'm really worried about is that all these little things are a prelude to something far more spectacular. To be honest, I think its playing with us. When it's regained its full powers, God knows what will happen! Anyway, how do the others feel about it?'

Looking sheepish, Roger said, 'We haven't spoken about it. Like me, I think they've tried to bury their heads in the sand in the hope it will all go away. Besides, since you've been away, we don't hang around with each other much anymore. It'll take me a while to round them up, but once they know you're back it will be much easier.'

Jared was beginning to feel slightly alarmed at the effect he was having on Roger, so he decided to change the subject. 'Any chance of you getting me to see the chalice this afternoon? In private, I mean, so I can check it out? Once that's done we could meet in Alec's tomorrow around eight. Will that give you enough time to round them all up?'

'Yes, I think I can manage that,' said Roger, 'but its not called Alec's any more.'

'Don't tell me old Alec sold up?' said Jared in astonishment. Seeing Roger's crestfallen expression, he groaned in dismay. 'Oh, no, not old Alec!'

''Fraid so,' said Roger. 'Died two years ago; the doctors said his heart just gave out. Hardly surprising, is it, when you think of the hours he used to put in, poor bugger.'

Chapter Twelve

OPENING THE GLASS CABINET, JARED TOOK OUT THE CHALICE carefully. At a cursory glance it looked in pristine condition, but he knew appearances could be deceptive. Holding it in his hands, he knew instinctively something was wrong. It felt different, was his first reaction; it hadn't the same aura of evil he'd noticed the last time. He was wondering how to remove the lid when he was interrupted by Roger.

'Don't be long,' he whispered, 'the old boy only gets half an hour for his dinner break.'

Nodding, Jared turned his attention back to the chalice. Holding it up to the light, he noted with alarm that the top seemed to be loose. About to transfer it to his other hand, it was then disaster struck and the lid fell off in his hand. Staring at the black residue at the bottom, he suddenly recalled Edwin's story of six years ago, the one written on the scroll. Unlike his uncle, he had no doubt the story was true. In that case, the ash he was looking at was all that remained of the brother of the man called Barabbas.

With that he was forced to an uncomfortable conclusion. Although the ashes were still in the chalice, the evil itself was probably free. So his earlier pessimism hadn't been misplaced. If that was the case, away from the protective confines of the chapel... The rest of the thought was left hanging in the air. The consequences didn't bear thinking about.

Knowing he was running out of time, he hurriedly took several photographs of the symbols before replacing everything as he'd found it. Finally, he carefully dusted down the cabinet to ensure even the closest scrutiny would reveal nothing amiss.

As they made their way from the building, Roger could see by Jared's face that something was wrong. As soon as they were out of earshot, he said, 'Well, spit it out! What happened back there?'

'We've got a problem – the chalice has been tampered with.'

'Oh, fuck!' said Roger. 'Does this mean what I think it means?'

'I'm not sure,' answered Jared, 'but if it does, then the shit's just hit the fan.' Then, seeing the look of despair that appeared on Roger's face, he added, 'Don't worry, we'll work something out.'

Secretly he felt far less confident than he sounded, so to try and lighten the mood of depression he said, 'Fancy a coffee in Alec's tonight? We can talk about it then.'

Suddenly remembering his slip of the tongue, he apologised to Roger. 'There I go again, I can't stop thinking of it as his place somehow.'

'Don't worry,' said Roger, 'for us oldies, it's still Alec's. But getting back to what you were saying, yes, about seven would be fine.'

Jared had gone a few yards when he noticed Emma walking towards him in the distance. For a moment he panicked, his only thought escape. He even considered crossing the road and pretending he hadn't seen her. Finally common sense prevailed and he realised how stupid that would be. He'd known all along they would bump into each other sometime, it was inevitable, and looking at it from that perspective, he decided that sooner might be better than later.

Concentrating on what he was going to say, he didn't notice at first the little girl walking by Emma's side. Clutching her hand tightly, she was beautiful – just like her mother, he thought ruefully, and at that moment his world seemed to grind to a halt. It was as if someone had gripped his heart and squeezed. For what seemed like an eternity he couldn't breathe, and with a sinking feeling he realised Emma was not only married, but had a daughter as well.

Quite suddenly a flush of hot anger flooded through him, directed against Roger for not warning him. It disappeared as quickly as it had developed, when he sensed just how irrationally he was behaving. After all, it wasn't something you could explain to someone who had once been your best friend. Roger had known that instinctively, and so had decided to let Jared find out for himself. He'd probably reasoned it was they way things were meant to be. With a rush, Jared knew he didn't want to examine his feelings too closely in case his anger was directed against Emma and not Roger. Perhaps subconsciously he'd hoped she'd not only been with no one else, but had waited all these years for him to return...

Struggling to keep in check feelings that had lain dormant for so long, he reminded himself that anything he'd ever felt towards Emma had disappeared the night she'd betrayed him. Nothing's changed, he told himself forcibly. Until now he'd convinced himself he could do it. Now he knew better.

Steeling himself against such thoughts, he approached her with mounting trepidation.

If only his insides would stop shaking, it might help, he told himself. It was then the irony of the situation hit him: the 'hard man', as Roger had called him – the man of steel – was scared shitless!

Making eye contact was the most difficult thing, but to his surprise she looked genuinely pleased to see him.

'Hello, Jared, I thought it was you.' Looking at his tanned face, she said, 'You've got a lovely colour – been abroad or something?'

Suddenly Jared felt a constriction deep in his chest and he had to turn away in case she saw his true feelings. Taking a few deep breaths, he made sure he was in control of his emotions again before turning around. The sound of her voice was like music to his ears and for a moment he couldn't get the words out. Finally he managed to blurt out, 'Yes.'

It was strange how, once he started talking, the old familiarity returned; her name rolling sweetly off his tongue.

'I've been in the army for the last six years, Emma, out of circulation and all that.'

'Ah, that explains it then… why you never wrote to any of us.'

Suddenly it was out in the open; no condemnation, no recriminations, the words were said so matter-of-factly they came across as more cutting than any show of anger.

Biting back his hurt, he looked down at the little girl holding her mother's hand and smiled. Shyly she pulled back, sliding behind the protection of her mother's back, until almost immediately her small face reappeared abruptly. With her head full of golden curls, he realised she was the image of her mother at that age, but the eyes were different. He supposed they were a legacy of her father, whoever he was…

As she stared up at him with intense curiosity, Jared had great difficulty in tearing his gaze away. 'She's gorgeous,' was all that he could think of to say before adding, 'the image of you at that age!'

Smiling at the compliment, Emma was surprised to see the depth of feeling the little girl engendered in him. It was only momentary, but she could see it clearly reflected in his eyes before he looked away sharply.

Flustered, she reached down to rub her daughter's head and said, 'Yes, I think so, but it's kind of you to say it. You're six now, aren't you, big girl?'

For a moment Jared thought it odd she hadn't said 'we' when taking about her daughter and not 'I'. Perhaps they're divorced, he thought, blanking the idea from his mind. Before he could stop himself he said, 'Will I have the pleasure of meeting your husband sometime? Is he anyone I know?'

The warmth that had been in her eyes moments before was replaced in an instant by an icy flintiness. It only lasted for a second before she said, 'No, it isn't anyone you know.'

Without thinking, Jared said, 'What happened?'

As soon as the words had left his mouth he knew instinctively he was treading on thin ice. Realising too late the subject was private, none of his business, he'd have given anything to take them back.

To his surprise she didn't react angrily, but instead answered, 'I suppose when he'd thought about it he didn't really want a baby.' Looking wistful she smiled at her daughter and said, 'So he dumped us, didn't he, Jodie?'

In amazement, Jared said, 'Didn't he offer to marry you?' Then he broke off sheepishly.

'Not that it's any business of yours, but yes he did; but that was before I became pregnant,' said Emma.

Horrified, Jared blurted out, 'Do you mean to tell me he never got to see his child?' Looking at the little girl in amazement, he said, 'Most men would kill to have a little daughter as beautiful as this.'

'I suppose he wasn't most men, then,' Emma replied, barely above a whisper.

'How on earth have you managed on your own for so long – without a father figure, I mean?'

'Surprisingly well, believe it or not,' she said, a little annoyed. 'I had to give up my original idea about teaching, of course, but I found a job in the civil service. So I guess I'm not most women, either. Anyway, what she never knew she'll never miss will she?'

'I'm s-sorry,' said Jared, stammering, 'I didn't mean it like that. She's obviously a credit to you. It's just that I can't believe that anyone could be so stupid and heartless, that's all.' Realising how silly he sounded, he said, 'I've a knack of putting my foot in it, haven't I, Em?'

Suddenly and quite unexpectedly, Emma laughed, and for a moment it completely transformed her lovely face. Afraid his eyes might mirror his true feelings, Jared turned away quickly.

Mistaking his body language for anger, she said quietly, 'I think we should change the subject, don't you?'

His feelings under control again, he said, 'Yes, I think that's a good idea.'

Kneeling down to rub the child's head, he was gratified to see she didn't pull away. It seemed she was getting used to him. Rising to his feet, he became serious again.

'There's a meeting in Alec's tomorrow at seven... I hope you can make it, Em.'

Alerted by his tone of voice, she said, 'Sounds like it's important.'

''Fraid it is. To be honest, it's one of the reasons I felt compelled to return. I can't explain it, but it's been like a magnet dragging me back somehow. Until today I only had my suspicions; now I'm certain. You see Em; I opened the chalice and somehow it felt different, it didn't give me that feeling of evil I got the last time I handled it. The only explanation I can come up with is that the bloody thing has managed to free itself!'

'Oh, Christ!' said Emma. 'I've been dreading this for years! When it was only me it wasn't so bad, but now I've got Jodie...' She broke off and was unable to finish. After a moment's hesitation she said, 'Dear God, if it is free it means it will be able to carry out all those threats it made before it tried to kill you with the pointer!'

Leaning over she touched Jared lightly on the hand before saying, 'Be careful! You underestimated it once. Besides, don't forget, for some reason it regards you as special. If that's the case, you'll be in more danger than any of us.'

Taken by surprise, Jared said with a levity he didn't feel, 'Lighten up, Em! Nothing's going to happen to me. Anyway, I didn't know you cared...'

Suddenly the coldness was back.

'I don't, but I do care about her,' she said, pointing at Jodie. With that, she turned on her heels and walked away, leaving him standing forlornly on the pavement.

He watched for several moments, until just before turning the corner, the little girl turned back and quite unexpectedly waved.

Later that afternoon, Jared decided to get away from it all. On the spur of the moment, he made his way towards the small wooded area behind his old home. He knew from past experience the view would help him make sense of his conflicting emotions. He made his way over to where the small mountain path cut back towards the village, before clambering carefully over a fence of rusted wire that sagged dangerously.

Sitting on a small grassy knoll among the thick green ferns, he gazed with fondness at the stream and thick reed beds. Turning his head he was gratified to see that the old withered oak, dripping with ivy, was still there. Yes, he reflected wistfully, he was home, and it felt good. With that he felt a deep peace settle over him.

Gathering his thoughts, he tried to come to terms with all that had happened since he'd returned. It was all so simple back then, he reminded himself; his parents were alive and he and Emma were very much in love. So where had it all gone wrong? With a sudden burst of understanding he sensed that everything that had happened had been his fault. He could even pinpoint the beginning of the demise.

With a twinge of bitterness he remembered it had all started with Thomas and the bloody Ouija board. On reflection, he saw he was being unfair; it was he who'd made the fateful decision to go ahead with the seance. No one had forced him into anything. If that was the case, it was his responsibility to make up for things. Just how he was going to do it he didn't know, but do it he must.

The sound of persistent shotgun blasts suddenly startled him out of his reverie. Knowing exactly where they were coming from, he made his way over to Arthur Morgan's farm. His immediate thought was that it would be good to see old Arthur again, remembering fondly how it had been the old man who'd first taught him how to use a gun.

The old farmer's eyes were as good as ever, and he spotted Jared more than a hundred yards away, waving vigorously once he'd recognised who it was. Shaking his hand warmly, he slapped Jared on the back. 'Good to see you, lad! It's been a long time – five or six years, if I'm not mistaken.'

'Your memory's as good as your eyesight, Mr Morgan; it's been six years.'

'*Arthur*, boy… Call me Arthur, you're a grown man now. But enough of that. What you been up to, then? Whatever it is, it seems to have agreed with you,' he noted, appreciating how Jared looked in the peak of physical shape. 'You're certainly a far different person than the slip of a lad that left here six years ago!'

'I joined the army,' said Jared with a smile.

'Ah, that explains it,' said Arthur, as if no other explanation was required. 'Sorry about the noise, but the buggers are playing hell with the livestock today.'

Seeing the puzzled expression on Jared's face, he hurriedly explained, 'It's the ravens,' and spat on the ground for emphasis, while at the same time opening his shotgun and slipping out the spent cartridges. Reloading the gun, he set it under the crook of his arm, barrel pointing downwards, before carrying on. 'Forty years I've been farming here, and I've never known them to behave like this. True, I normally get trouble during the lambing season, but that's long gone. Can't understand what the hell's the matter with them – it en't normal, I tell you. Problem is, it's not only the sheep they're going for. Seems to be anything that bloody moves!'

As if to make a point, two huge ravens suddenly landed on the back of a fully grown cow. Despite the presence of the two adults and the shotgun, neither showed an ounce of fear.

Suddenly the first began digging its beak into the animal's neck, while the other attempted to peck out its eyes.

Moving forward, Arthur shouted in dismay, 'See what I mean!' before breaking into a run. 'It's not bloody natural!'

While all this was going on, Jared was becoming increasingly uneasy. Catching up with Arthur, he was in time to see the blast of the shotgun momentarily frighten the ravens away. Taking off in a blur of motion, they didn't fly very far. Instead they nestled in the branches of a nearby tree, looking down with disdain at the two figures below.

'It's uncanny,' said the old man in amazement, 'it's almost as if they know what they're doing – but that's impossible, isn't it?'

'Impossible or not,' said Jared, 'we just saw it with our own eyes. Did you notice what they did, though? One distracted the cow, while the other went for its eyes. That's coordinated action, Arthur. It's almost as if something is directing them.'

Just then Sandra, Arthur's daughter, shouted down, 'Is that you, Jared?' Waving she said, 'Thought it was! Come on up. I've just made a pot of tea, and there's fresh bread and Welsh cakes if you want them.'

Turning to Arthur, Jared said, 'Now that's an offer I can't refuse.'

Laughing, they made their way up the steep slope towards the house.

When they arrived, Sandra was holding her baby in her arms, and suddenly with a sly smile she handed the child over to Jared. 'Here, look after him while I pour the tea, will you?'

She was rewarded with a look of pure horror as Jared clung stiffly to the baby. Seeing his expression, she burst out laughing and said, 'He won't break, you know! Here, give him back.'

Handing him over, Jared began to relax again, while Sandra tucked the baby safely into his pram just outside the back door.

When she returned she placed the cup and saucer in Jared's hand and said wickedly, 'I don't know why you looked so worried, Hunter; the worst he could have done is to pee over you... or perhaps on second thoughts, maybe not,' she chuckled.

About to join in the fun, Jared saw the colour drain from her face, before the cup dropped from her hand. Hitting the hard flagstone floor, it bounced once before smashing into dozens of tiny pieces that scattered everywhere.

Jared was on his feet and running before either Arthur or Sandra had moved a muscle. He too had seen the two ravens landing on the pram, through the glass in the kitchen window. It was almost as if they'd been waiting for them to go inside before deciding to make their move. As quick as Jared's reflexes were, he was only just in time, as the baby had already been scratched in several places. What saved his eyes was the bonnet which had been pulled down in order to protect him from the sun; but for that he'd have been blinded. Even worse, had one of the beaks entered an eye socket, it could have penetrated the brain, killing the infant instantly.

Seeing Jared, one of the ravens managed to escape, but the other was too slow. In a blinding burst of speed, almost too quick for the human eye to follow, Jared's right hand shot out and grabbed the bird around the throat. Then in one fluid motion he broke its neck before hurling it as far away as possible.

Moments later, Sandra arrived.

Sobbing hysterically, she picked her baby up and, hugging him fiercely, said, 'Thank God you were here, Jared, otherwise the bastards would have killed him for sure! What the hell's going on?'

Putting his arms around her, he said softly, 'Don't worry, we got there in time, that's what matters.'

While all this was taking place, old Arthur hadn't said a word. Finally he walked over to Jared and, looking at him with something like awe, said, 'I've never seen anyone move so quickly in my life, lad, it was unbelievable! Thank the Lord you did, though, otherwise the little one would have been a goner for sure. We're grateful to you, lad, you saved the young 'un's life, make no bones about it.'

Putting his arm around his daughter, he said, 'It's something we'll never forget, never. If ever you need anything at anytime, you've only to ask, remember that.'

Clearly embarrassed, Jared was turning to walk away when he was halted by a hand on his shoulder. 'Not so fast, Hunter,' said Sandra, 'you haven't had your tea and Welsh cakes yet!'

As Jared turned at the door, old Arthur said something that stopped him in his tracks. 'It's the strangest thing, but they've all gone now. Perhaps you're a lucky omen or something.'

Looking behind him, Jared saw that Arthur was right; there was no sign of the ravens. However, the comment about him being a lucky omen worried him. Rather than a lucky omen, he thought to himself, he seemed to be the catalyst for an evil force which appeared to be gaining in strength daily.

Chapter Thirteen

IT WAS A SATURDAY MORNING, TRADITIONALLY THE BUSIEST DAY OF the week for the Brewster family business. Determined to do things properly, Ruth had decided to open the shop early in order to organise the displays. Normally, her husband took care of that side of things, but at the moment he was in bed with the flu. Anyway, it was nothing she couldn't handle.

Looking at it realistically, there was no point in moaning so she just got on with it. Inserting the key into the lock, she opened the door before reaching inside and switching on the lights. There was a faint buzzing from the neon tubes and then, with a sharp crackle, they burst into life.

Suddenly the room was awash with light.

Stepping inside, her husband's words were ringing in Ruth's ears. 'Remember, love, if you get the window display right the meat will sell itself.'

Moving into the main body of the room, she was still ticking off mentally what had to be done when she stopped in her tracks. To her amazement several carcasses of meat, which should have been safely stored away in the large walk-in refrigerator at the far side of the shop, were hanging from hooks in the ceiling above her. Shaking her head in incredulity, she took a few more faltering steps before she had the distinct feeling that something wasn't right. Unable to put her finger on it, she knew beyond a doubt that something was definitely wrong.

A few moments later she knew what it was. Staring in incomprehension, she saw that what she'd mistaken for fresh meat was the butchered remains of five or six animals, cats and dogs by the look of them. Decapitated and skilfully disembowelled, the entrails had been allowed to hang from the open stomachs like large pink and purple sausages. With mounting horror, Ruth realised that until a short while ago these had been household pets – and not just any pets, but the pride and joy of some of her neighbours. As the shock of what she was looking at began to wear off, the smell hit her. Holding her apron in front of her mouth, she bit back on the bile which was threatening to explode into her throat. Having been a butcher's wife all her life, she was used to the sight and smell of blood, but this was something entirely different.

Unfortunately the horror wasn't over.

Peering closely at the window, which she'd expected to be empty, she suddenly jumped back in surprise. It was then she noticed in astonishment that the window display had already been done – and extremely professionally too, she thought, before telling herself that such a thing was impossible. The only keys to the shop were in her hand, so how could it be? she asked herself in amazement. Moving towards the spectacle in a daze, it was then she saw the heads. Six in all, they were neatly arranged, each one facing outwards. Incredibly, whoever had committed the atrocity had, in order to make the display more presentable, laid them out on beds of fresh green parsley...

Despite her revulsion, for some strange reason Ruth was unable to tear her eyes away from the gruesome scene. It was almost hypnotic. While these thoughts were coursing through her brain, the heads appeared to grin at her in a gesture of silent mockery.

Anyone of a less formidable constitution would have probably fainted clean away, but Ruth Brewster was made of sterner stuff. Although terrified, her overriding emotion was one of anger, especially when she realised she recognised two of the pets. The first was Ginger, next door's cat, while she was almost sure the biggest one belonged to Scott Sutherland; it was his Alsatian, Tiger. Instead of going into a fit of hysterics, she turned on her heel and rushed away to report the incident. About to leave, she suddenly noticed the words, written in blood, she thought, smeared on the wall next to the large freezer.

Just beginning!

It was ten minutes or so before an out of breath Sergeant Hawkins arrived, closely followed by a hopping mad Mrs Brewster.

On the way over, Ralph Hawkins had been filled in on what had happened. By now he was convinced she'd either been drinking or was quite mad. On the other hand, he had to admit that he'd been unable to smell alcohol on her breath. Either way, it had to be complete nonsense, he told himself. Things like this simply didn't happen in Raven's Hill.

Then he stopped in mid thought and revised his conclusion. After all the horrors that had gone on during the last week, he was almost ready to believe anything. Just as he was about to voice an opinion, the words died on his lips. Taking in the scene, he rushed out of the shop before promptly throwing up all over next door's hedge.

When he'd mustered the courage to go back inside he couldn't believe his eyes.

Mentally apologising to Mrs Brewster for doubting her word, he was forced to admit that, if anything, it was even worse than she'd described. She'd been wrong in one of her observations, though: the Alsatian was his own police dog, Prince.

Jesus Christ! he said to himself, at the same time fighting down another bout of nausea. What kind of sick bastard could have dreamed up a scenario such as this?

With that, Ruth Brewster leaned across and tugging at his uniformed sleeve, pointed to the message written on the wall behind his head. Craning his neck in order to read it properly, Ralph Hawkins felt the first tiny tentacles of fear. This was no sick prank, he realised; this was something far more serious. Forcing down his fear before it had the opportunity to overwhelm him, he turned to her, and with a confidence he hardly felt said, 'I wouldn't take too much notice of things like that, if I were you. The sick buggers who did this are long gone by now. Just to be on the safe side, though, I'll phone the office as soon as I get back. They'll cordon off the area for you.'

'Thank you, Sergeant,' said Ruth. 'Considering the mess the place is in, that will be a great help.'

'Mind if I make a suggestion?' he enquired.

'No, be my guest,' said Ruth, by now ready to listen to anything constructive.

'If I were you I'd cover the window of the display cabinet. You don't want anyone looking in, do you?'

'Good idea,' said Ruth, 'I should have thought of it myself. Tell you what, I'll do it right away, before the first of the nosey buggers arrive.'

Within the hour, news of what had happened swept through the small community like wildfire. Shortly afterwards, Colin Brewster's shop found itself the focal point of the village.

Peeking from behind the curtains of her bedroom window, Ruth Brewster looked down in dismay as the crowds jostled and pushed each other in the vain hope of catching a glimpse of the gory spectacle, which of course by now was no longer visible.

'I don't know who's the sickest,' she said, turning to her husband, 'those who killed the poor animals or the stupid buggers falling over themselves to catch a glimpse of something no sane person should want to see.'

Lifting his head from the pillow, he said with savage irony, 'If that many turned up on a normal Saturday, we'd be millionaires in a month.' Then in a more sombre tone he added, 'I'm afraid it will be a long time before we sell any meat from that display cabinet again, love.'

The crowds seemed to be growing by the minute, and it was true: even those who'd never bought anything in his shop suddenly found his window compulsive viewing. The fact that nothing could be seen was neither here nor there, if anything it only added to the mystique, to fuel their imaginations. Such was the impact, even the local newspapers decided to get in on the act.

When it was discovered the rumours were true, one enterprising young journalist managed to bribe her way into the shop. The photographs she took were sensational and graced the front page of the local *Echo* the following morning. The shots were so graphic, so vivid, that all available copies were sold out within the hour. Such was the demand that a second edition had to be rushed out shortly afterwards.

Several days later the police called for a meeting in the Welfare Hall in an attempt to clear matters up. It was short and sweet, and at the end the locals were no wiser than when they'd started. The senior officer present declared that after two days of intensive investigation they'd found no evidence of the perpetrators. Amazingly, despite all their best efforts, which had included dusting the inside of the shop for fingerprints, no shred of evidence had been found. The police admitted they were baffled. The senior police spokesman ended lamely by saying that the villagers were not to worry because he was sure it was a one-off incident. Disturbing as it had been, especially for the Brewsters, he was confident that everyone could now put the matter behind them.

Ralph Hawkins had the last word.

Getting to his feet, he thanked the Swansea force for all the hard work and effort they'd put in over the last two days. Like them he felt it was a one-off, giving his assurance that nothing of this nature would happen again. He did add one point of interest, saying that a collection was being arranged as he spoke, in order to compensate the Brewsters for their loss of earnings. A gesture on behalf of the village, he elaborated, before adding that it was least they could do.

At the back of the hall, Jared was listening to it all. He couldn't help but think they'd conveniently brushed some very important points under the carpet. For instance, no one had commented on how, in a crime scene showing so much blood, the culprit had failed to leave one single footprint. Apart from that, no mention had been made of the fact that the attack had been carried out with such precision and cold-blooded expertise it could hardly have been a sick prank.

Inadvertently, the headline story in the local paper the following morning was far nearer the truth than the fabrications thought up by the totally inept police report. As a follow-up to the photographs that had shown the sadistic slaughter of the poor animals in brutal detail, the reporter, Jessica Ryder, had linked the killings to the occult. She theorised that the animals might have been sacrificed either to appease, or invoke, the appearance of some demon or evil spirit.

Of one thing Jared was certain; this had the creature's stamp written all over it.

The hub of life in Raven's Hill was centred on a single street less than a hundred yards long. Within such a small area were to be found several commercial buildings, including an undertaker, a pharmacist, a post office, a paper shop… and Alec's café.

Strangely, the local St John's Ambulance Hall, nestling between the paper shop and the café, was some way below street level. On the other side of the road, were the Cooperative and Margo's sewing and altering unit, while fifty yards further on was the Miners' Welfare Hall. A large building, it housed a picture house, two bars and the inevitable bingo hall.

Surprisingly, catching a bus to and from the village was easy. The stop, which nestled snugly near the top of a small hill, was never more than a five minute walk from anywhere in the village. Sitting proudly next to it was a large wooden bench. This had been erected by the council, who in their wisdom decided the locals needed a resting place. Oddly, despite everything, the bench had turned out to be something of a focal point. The older members of the village saw it as a meeting place, as somewhere to sit and watch the world go by, while at weekends the younger element of the village commandeered it, especially late in the evening.

Sardis was one of several small chapels in the village, and despite all the odds it had managed to retain a decent-sized congregation. With morning and evening services on a Sunday, it was the former that Mr and Mrs Hopkins were hurrying to attend when their thoughts turned to the strange goings-on that had seemed to plague the village during the last week or so. Such incidents were made all the more remarkable, since apart from the odd burglary, nothing sinister like this had ever happened before.

Turning to her husband, Dorothy Hopkins said, 'I'm not one to complain, as you know, Joe.'

'No, dear, of course not,' he replied, while silently thinking, If only that were true...

'But don't you think it's odd?' she carried on.

The only thing that's odd around here is you, he thought, but at the same time kept such ideas to himself. Instead he said, 'What, dear?'

'The weird goings-on in the village this last week or so.'

Thinking about it, he was forced to admit that for once she was right. For once, it seemed that she might just have a point.

'I blame it on all those things we've been sending into space,' said Joe, 'it's bound to mess up everything. Tampering with things that are none of our business, we are.'

Appearing to think about it, Dorothy suddenly turned to Joe and said, 'Yes, you're right, Joe. Now why didn't I think of that?'

Amazed, Joe looked over at his wife. That's got to be a first, he chuckled to himself silently. You admitting that I thought of something before you... But the simple answer is you didn't think of it first, because you're too bloody stupid, you old cow.

'And another thing,' she said, prattling on without taking a breath, as if the idea had been hers in the first place, 'I'm sure God will have something to say about it all in the end.'

'That's a good point, dear,' said Joe with infinite patience.

'How far do you think he'll let us go before stepping in and doing something about it, then?' asked Dorothy.

Secretly, Joe thought, If God's past record is anything to go by, then he doesn't give a shit. He said instead, 'I don't really know, dear; when he's had enough, I suppose. But when the time comes, we'll have our just reward, that's for sure.'

Looking at her from out of the corner of his eye, he wondered now what he'd ever seen in her. She'd been a good shag at one time, there was no doubt about that, but all that was a distant memory now. All he could see these days was a wrinkled old peahen, the self-satisfied smirk on her face a constant irritation. Mutton dressed up as lamb, he thought to himself. He'd have to lump it now, though, wouldn't he? After all, he was hardly likely to find anything better at seventy-two years of age. He was brought out of his reverie by a sudden flash of inspiration from his wife.

'Perhaps that's what's happening!' she exclaimed in excitement. 'Perhaps all these strange goings-on are God's way of punishing us, telling us he's finally had enough.'

'I don't think so, dear,' said Joe. 'It's more likely to be the work of a bunch of devil worshippers or something. It's in all the papers. The youngsters these days like dabbling in all kinds of things. They say some of them are even trying to conjure up spirits of the dead. You mark my words, that's the root of the problem, and if they're not careful they'll come a cropper.'

He'd just finished his little speech when Dorothy screamed. 'Oh, my God!' she said, putting her hands over her face and pretending not to look.

Joe noticed that although she'd covered her eyes, she'd craftily left a gap in her fingers to make sure she'd miss nothing. Bloody typical, thought Joe, what a hypocritical old bitch. He said, 'What the hell's the matter?'

'Look at them, Joe, just look at them! The dirty pigs are doing it.'

'Doing what, Dorothy? For Christ's sake, what are you on about, woman?'

'That,' she said pointing at the bench. 'They're having it off!'

'Where, exactly?' said Joe in exasperation, hoping to catch a glimpse before they'd finished. Following his wife's accusing finger, he stopped dead in his tracks. Christ, she's bloody right, was his immediate reaction, they *are* bloody doing it! Looking more closely, he could see that while the man was lying on his back gazing up at his partner, she was straddling him. As they were both naked he could see everything.

Turning to his wife, he said, 'But that's funny, love.'

'What is, Joe?' she asked.

'Well, they're not moving,' he said, at the same time thinking that if his wife's recent efforts at lovemaking were anything to go by, it might just be the norm.

Grabbing his arm, she said, 'Don't go over, Joe, just in case they get nasty.'

'But it's odd, Dorothy, something doesn't seem right.'

Adjusting his glasses to get a better look, he crossed the road in order to approach the bench.

Dorothy noticed he was within a few feet of the mating couple when he suddenly stopped. Then, bending over at the waist, he threw up all over the pavement.

'What's the matter?' she shouted.

Thinking he'd had some kind of funny turn, she rushed to his aid, only to come face to face with the sight that had made her husband violently sick.

She couldn't believe her eyes.

What she thought were a mating couple were in fact two dead bodies. Stolen from their graves earlier, they'd been dug up and laid out carefully in a sick parody of the sex act.

To make matters worse, they were relatively fresh corpses, because although fragments of skin were hanging from their faces, other parts of their bodies were virtually intact. Despite the horror of what Dorothy was seeing, she clung to one small consolation: at least she didn't recognise them. It was a truly horrific sight, as they lay there like two bloated maggots in silent copulation. Whoever was responsible had taken a lot of trouble in positioning the corpses. They'd been placed so they were looking into each other's empty eye sockets. The male was positioned so that his arms were around his partner's buttocks, while she clung tightly to his shoulders. Fortunately for Dorothy, she was unconscious before the foul stench hit her nostrils.

Joe wasn't as lucky. Before he could help his wife, the female corpse turned her head through a 180° arc and said to Joe with glowing red eyes, 'Don't go, Joe! Don't you want me to fuck you too? I bet it's been a long time since your shrivelled old cock has seen any action.' With that the figure uttered an insane cackle.

Joe's heart wasn't designed for such things and he was dead before he'd even hit the ground.

The coroner's verdict was that he'd died of fright, but the autopsy showed an anomaly. The report stated that by itself, disturbing as the sight may have been, it shouldn't have been enough to kill. As a matter of fact it went on to say that for a man of Joe's age his heart had been in remarkably good condition. The burning question was, what had he seen that was so terrifying it had literally caused his heart to stop functioning?

Not surprisingly, the local journalists had a field day.

Convinced by now there was something badly wrong with the village, they pounced on the idea of attributing every strange event to the work of a coven of witches. The local reporter who'd initially come up with the brainwave wrote the following article:

I'm now convinced the strange goings-on in the little village of Raven's Hill can be attributed to a group of sick, deranged people who have unwittingly unleashed a force so powerful they can no longer control it. Might it be that under the guise of the occult, these incidents were originally nothing more than a series of harmless pranks? If so, then those responsible have badly miscalculated. The latest incident ended in the death of Mr Joe Hopkins, a seventy-two-year-old man who suffered a fatal heart attack while on his way to a Sunday morning service at Sardis chapel. If part of the group's twisted agenda was to terrorise a small village community, then it has certainly achieved its objective. Many villagers are now afraid to set foot out of doors, especially the older ones. Let us hope in the cold light of day the perpetrators have come to realise the situation is rapidly getting out of hand. If so perhaps they might just have learned their lesson.

There is a more worrying scenario to consider, however. What if we are faced with real evil? Despite what we see in films and read in books, pure evil is rare, even in today's climate of greed and materialism. However, the desecration of graves and the use of freshly dug corpses indicate a level of sophistication that transcends sick and twisted games. If we are indeed up against such a force, it seems we are faced with two questions.

The first is: from where might it have originated?

While the second is even more worrying: how can it be stopped?

As a result of the latest horror, the police have finally been forced to take matters seriously. After the macabre incident that took place in the village butcher's shop recently, we were assured that things like this would never again take place in Raven's Hill. A one-off event, they claimed. It is my fervent hope that, over the course of time, the police are proven correct in their assumption. If so, this might well be the end of things. Unfortunately this reporter has a strange feeling that far from being the end of the matter, it could be just the beginning.

Keeping you ahead of the rest.

Jessica Ryder

Chapter Fourteen

DAVID NAAMI, HEAD OF CHAMELEON ENTERPRISES, GAZED DOWN from his lofty perch overlooking Cardiff Bay. From the safety of the bullet-proof glass that ran the length of the entire penthouse suite, the view was breathtaking. A monument to modern engineering, the building was yet another stunning addition to an area of Cardiff that was becoming increasingly popular with big business. In essence the structure was no different to any of the others in the vicinity, except for one anomaly; it hid a dark and deadly secret. In fact, no one who had ever seen the original blueprints had lived to tell the tale. Doubling as a boardroom and sanctuary, only those elected to the inner cadre of the Brotherhood ever knew of its existence.

Tearing his eyes away from the panoramic spectacle, David moved languidly around the table, savouring the trappings that only wealth and power provide. The smell of leather was strong in his nostrils as he lovingly stroked the arms of the antique furniture. Like all people born into poverty, David Naami took great delight in material possessions. Always clothed in the best, the veneer of civility he displayed in public was a facade. Hidden beneath layers of carefully constructed illusion, his real self was very different.

In reality he was a cold-blooded psychopath.

A loud rapping on the door brought him out of his reverie.

'Come in,' he called.

Waiting until his visitors were seated he carried on, 'I've called this meeting at short notice, because...' he smiled suddenly, 'we've managed to track down another guardian.'

At just under six feet, David Naami wasn't a big man, but his wide shoulders and trim waist bellied the fact he was nearing sixty years of age. Handsome in an unconventional way, his most striking feature was his nose. Strong and aquiline, it stood out proudly beneath a pair of piercing dark eyes that at times appeared almost black. The overall impression was of a magnificent bird of prey. An exceptionally vain man, he'd have appreciated the comparison, as he prided himself in being cruel, focused and totally without mercy.

The story of how he'd come to power was an intriguing one.

Already a legend at the tender age of twenty, he took part in a daring raid on a Paris household in March 1967, and against all the odds pulled it off. Within weeks he was promoted to the inner circle, and five years later achieved the impossible: he was elected leader of the Brotherhood. It was an incredible achievement. At twenty-five years of age he became the youngest ever Grand Master by some twenty years.

Staring at each of the seven unerringly, David Naami exuded an aura of power that belongs only to those who are born to lead.

Usually the inner cadre consisted of nine, but six years earlier one of the elite assassins broke with protocol and brought unwanted attention to the organisation. So incensed was David Naami that he dealt with the matter personally. Since that day, no one had dared to step out of line. Oddly, no one had been elected from the ranks to take the man's place.

The security measures around the building were exceptionally tight. In what some said was an excessive measure, a hint of paranoia, it included a rule that ensured no names were ever spoken. To streamline matters, a system of code names was used, except in the case of its leader, who was simply referred to as Number One.

It was the youngest, the assassin code-named Serpent, who spoke up.

'According to the records, Number One, there can't be many left.'

'I wouldn't be too sure of that; it never pays to underestimate them,' came the reply, 'but there's no doubt his head will make a welcome addition to our collection.' Then he added, 'Right, if you'd like to follow me.'

Exiting the door at the back of his private office, they headed towards the double doors which guarded the hidden entrance to the inner sanctuary. In order to gain access, they had to negotiate a security system made up of pressure pads, infra-red beams and hidden CCTV cameras. A system, according to the claims of its designers, that was foolproof. A hollow claim, as it turned out, when six years earlier it had proven to be singularly inadequate. In what had proved to be a catastrophe, the vault had been broken into and most of its precious documents photographed. David allowed himself a small smile when he remembered the punishment he'd meted out to the fools who'd installed their so-called foolproof system. True, the thief had been caught several weeks later;

but disappointingly he'd known very little of value, least of all anything about the client who'd hired him.

Although he would have been the last to admit it, the audacity of such an attack had shaken him. Until then he'd thought the Brotherhood immune to such things. For months he'd puzzled over the identity of the perpetrators, coming to the conclusion there were very few who had the financial backing to carry out such a daring raid. More worryingly, fear of retribution should have been enough to deter most; unless of course the suicide mission, as he liked to think of it, had been carried out by someone who was either without fear, or by someone who had nothing to lose. Little did he know it, but the second conjecture was very near the mark.

He had his suspicions, of course. The guardians had both the wealth and motive, but if that was the case, why hadn't the information been used against them? Surely they'd have recognised the immense importance of the documents. No, he was missing something, he was sure of it. Such thoughts were buzzing around his head when he stepped up to the control panel and switched off the alarms.

Once through the outer double doors, they made their way along a narrow corridor at the end of which stood a much smaller single door. On the outside at shoulder height was a small infra-red screen. As part of the sweeping changes made after the last debacle, access was now gained by means of a palm scanner. Only the prints of the most senior members of the Brotherhood were stored on the computer, so the organisation was confident that this time there would be no mishaps. Placing his hand onto the screen, David Naami waited for a second before a digitally mixed female voiced informed him he was cleared to enter.

With a soft hiss, the door opened automatically and they entered soundlessly. The audacity of the design of the inner sanctum was breathtaking. In reality, it was an exact replica of the sacred Temple in Jerusalem. David Naami always found it a source of great amusement to think that most Christians were blissfully ignorant of the debt they owed Judaism. They were completely unaware that Jewish synagogues were based largely on the design of the ancient Temple, which in turn had become the blueprint for the latter-day chapels of the Welsh valleys.

A short walk took them into the most sacred part, the holy of holies. In Jewish folk lore, this room had housed the Ark of the Covenant, last seen depicted on the triumphal arch in Rome. After the sacking of Jerusalem by Titus, it had disappeared never to be seen again. To the Brotherhood, this was an irrelevance. They had long since ceased to worry about the Ark. Since that time, the real object of their veneration had been kept a closely guarded secret. Kneeling, they looked up at their founder in adulation. Encased in a glass pyramid it looked down at them with lofty distain. Remarkably preserved, the bearded head was in almost pristine condition, kept that way by a secret process handed down within the order and then further refined by modern technology. It was now hermetically sealed, air having been pumped out and argon gas pumped in. By use of cleverly placed spotlights it seemed to hover majestically some twelve feet in the air, while beneath in a large semicircle, each in its own miniature glass case, stood several dozen shrunken heads. The look of horror caught on the face of each of the guardians bore testimony to the skill of the native tribesmen that had performed the delicate operation.

One of the many rituals of the Brotherhood involved recounting a short history of the origins of their movement before starting any serious business. What might have been a laborious chore for others was seen in a different light by this group of fanatics. They saw it as an opportunity to glorify their bloody past, an opportunity to boast about their nefarious origins.

Stepping onto the podium beneath the head, David Naami pressed a hidden switch.

With a low hum, the embossed design of the Brotherhood began to rise from the floor, along with nine cleverly camouflaged leather chairs.

By now, the eight had changed into their ritual attire of pure white mantles, symbolically decorated with a splayed red cross. A casual observer might have been mistaken in thinking the order was emphasising pride in its Christian heritage; the truth however was much more bizarre. In fact the garments were meant as an act of deliberate blasphemy.

Ready to begin, their leader smiled. It seemed to indicate extreme pleasure, but to the more discerning they would have noticed it never reached his eyes.

'Gentlemen,' he began. 'The foundation we represent is an ancient one, one that traces its history back more than 2,000 years. Starting life as a minority party among the Jews, as a protest against the greed and senseless cruelty of the Romans, we became known as the Zealots, or *Kannaim* in our Hebrew tongue. Already an explosive mixture, there arose among us a hard core splinter group called the Sicarii, or dagger men.'

He stopped suddenly, a pause for dramatic effect, before carrying on.

'By the year AD 70 the Romans were terrified of us,' he boasted proudly. Speaking more quietly he said, 'Not only were we utterly fearless and without mercy, but over the centuries we developed new and more subtle traits – in particular, cunning, subterfuge and infinite patience!

'The history books tell us that most of our brothers, those trapped inside the Temple walls when Jerusalem was turned into a charnel house, were eventually slaughtered to a man. Other scholars tell a different story. They would have us believe a small band escaped and made their way to Masada, where they held out for three years before taking their own lives. One thing they are all in agreement on, however; from that time on the Sicarii passed out of existence.'

Chuckling to himself, he said, 'But how wrong they were! The fools – did they think we could be wiped out so easily? Little did they realise that a small group survived Masada. More bloodthirsty and more savage than any that had gone before, they escaped, and like shadows melted into the night.'

'*To give birth to us!*' the seven chorused proudly.

'But that was not the end, my brothers; in fact it was only the beginning.

'From there we used those characteristics to infiltrate several other organisations. In the Languedoc, some of our brothers joined one of the more extreme and influential sects within Catharism, while at the same time the more aggressive of us became known as the soldier arm of the Knights Templar.' Lifting his head and laughing out loud, he said, 'An extreme Jewish sect masquerading as the saviours of Christendom… what divine blasphemy. Little did the fools understand the true source of our great wealth, and in particular the reason why we spat and repudiated the cross.'

Holding his arms to the sky, eyes blazing with the inner glow of the true fanatic, David said, 'And we, my brothers, are the direct descendants of those brave men, the elite of the elite, worshippers of the head!'

As one, the seven stood to applaud their leader, gazing at him in rapt devotion.

Turning to them, he said, 'A little earlier one of you proffered a view that by now there might be very few guardians left. We now have an opportunity to put that theory to the test.'

Two rooms lay on either side of the heavy drapes that formed the backdrop to the head.

One was a state-of-the-art laboratory, while the other housed a refined torture chamber. With startling speed, David Naami suddenly disappeared, only to re-emerge seconds later with something the others looked at in bewilderment. As it appeared from out of the gloom, they gazed in astonishment at what looked suspiciously like a wheelchair, but this seemed to be no ordinary one. Looking closely, they saw it was holding the body of a man. In his early or mid-seventies, it appeared he'd just woken from a drug-induced sleep, which indeed he had.

Returning to some semblance of consciousness, the old man looked around in confusion, unable to fathom what was happening, until suddenly it hit him. Forcing himself to remain calm, the thought came unbidden. So this was it, the moment had finally arrived. For 2,000 years every guardian had accepted the mantle, fully aware of the implications of the sacred role. Each one in turn had been ruthlessly hunted down, tortured and killed in order to find the location of the chalice.

As he studied his macabre surroundings, the heads took on a new significance. Until now, the instructions given by their founder had seemed a little melodramatic, the utilisation of cells a little excessive. In hindsight he now saw the wisdom. Knowing that he would be unable to withstand the kind of pain his captors would inflict, he uttered a silent prayer of gratitude.

Looking down at the old man, David Naami remembered with bitter regret how so far each of those tortured had seemed to know little of importance. His most ardent hope was that this time things might be different. To date he'd rejected the use of drugs, for the simple reason he enjoyed inflicting pain. Savouring the moment, knowing that anticipation was often better than the act, he never stopped to think that the information he was after didn't exist.

As a past master in inflicting pain, he knew the importance of theatrics. Regarding what he did as a work of art, he planned everything meticulously. Preparing for his latest performance, he reflected in amusement that just as great surgeons took pleasure in saving people's lives, he took pleasure in taking them. Opening a large black case, he turned towards his victim and said, 'I appreciate that some of these instruments might be new to you, so I thought we might start with something familiar. I often find the old ones the best.'

Stripped naked, his hands, feet and head secured by means of clamps, the unfortunate guardian was unable to do anything but watch, as one by one each of his fingernails were systematically pulled out by the roots. The agonising screams which accompanied the first few extractions seemed to go on for ever, but in fact within minutes he'd lapsed into merciful unconsciousness. The respite was brief, however, as he was immediately revived by the use of buckets of cold water. And then David Naami started on his feet.

Once he'd recovered somewhat, the versatility of the chair was displayed in all its grisly detail, when suddenly, without warning, the old man found himself tilted backwards, legs spread wide, backside in full view.

Making the first incision just above the anus, his torturer proceeded with great skill to peel a strip of skin about an inch wide upwards, only stopping when he'd reached the head of the penis. Surprisingly, despite the copious spillage of blood, the wound was not life-threatening. David's only concern was whether the old man's heart would hold out. He remembered ruefully that the first time he'd tried it, the recipient had gone into shock and never recovered. His fervent hope was that this victim would be made of sterner stuff. Moments later his hopes were dashed, as he looked down with scorn at the sobbing remains of what had once been a proud man. And for what? he asked himself silently; for despite his best efforts, he'd again learned nothing.

Turning to the others, David screamed, 'What is it about these stubborn bastards? To endure such pain and still say nothing, they must be fanatics!'

It never occurred to him to see the irony in his choice of words.

Struggling to regain his lost composure, he turned again to the old man and said, 'I was going to take out your eyes, but that would have spoiled my final surprise.' With a malicious grin, he explained, 'You see, I want you awake for this, I want you to see exactly what's going to happen.'

The room the old man was wheeled into would have shamed many of the top operating theatres in the country. Releasing the clamps, two of the Brotherhood stepped forward and lifted him from the wheelchair.

148

Placing him onto what looked like a stainless steel table, they made sure he was once again safely strapped down. Approaching slowly, David Naami placed the object of his latest sick game onto the chest of the old guardian. It was a transparent bowl made of specially toughened glass, flanked by two broad leather straps.

In a parody of sick humour, he said, 'I must apologise if this is cold, but I can ensure you it won't inconvenience you for long. I doubt you'll recognise the modus operandi, but I'm sure if I give you a clue you can figure the rest out for yourself. Edgar Alan Poe ring any bells?'

He'd never ceased to be amazed just how much pain the human body could endure; but psychological torture, now, that was a whole different ball game, and the moment he'd mentioned Poe he knew he'd hit the jackpot. He could see the fear reflected in the eyes of the old man. Suddenly the silence was shattered by an inhuman scream. Thrashing about wildly, the old guardian tried to escape from his bindings, knowing of course it was all in vain.

Then, as if realising the futility of his gesture, he went completely still. Like sand in an egg timer, his courage and defiance seemed to drain away, leaving behind once again a whimpering wreck.

'*Please*,' he sobbed, 'please – anything but that! I'll tell you everything you want to know.' He frantically wracked his mind for something with which to trade. Grasping at straws, he suddenly remembered a remark he'd overheard quite by accident. 'Wait! I know something,' he said, 'please… if you promise to end it quickly, I'll give you the information I have.'

During all this, David Naami, his back turned, had appeared to ignore the frantic pleading. Now, in a deceptively mild tone of voice, he said, 'That seems fair to me,' before turning in triumph and walking towards his victim.

Momentarily lulled into a false sense of security, it took a while before the old man registered what it was that David Naami was holding in his right hand. There, hanging by its tail, was a huge black rat. Staring directly at him, its deep red eyes glowed with an inner malevolence. For the old man, his worst nightmare had just come true.

Dangling the rodent before his eyes, but far enough away so it couldn't reach him, David Naami said, 'I believe we were about to come to some kind of agreement, were we not?' He paused. 'If my understanding serves me correctly, you are prepared to impart some information, and in return I promise to dispatch you quickly, am I correct?'

'Yes, yes!' said the old man, by now only too eager to help.

'I'm waiting,' said David Naami.

'Only one guardian remains,' the old man blurted out.

'Good, good, now we're getting somewhere... but are you sure?'

'Positive,' said the old man. 'As the office is hereditary, only the senior guardian is left. Ironic as it seems, had you let me alone, he would have eventually had to contact me and then you would have caught us both.'

Trembling with barely suppressed rage, David Naami perceived his mistake. Once again it seemed that fate had conspired against him. Fighting to regain his lost composure, he carried on his questioning.

'We know the original guardians were made up of only four people, two men and two women; so tell me, why so few?'

'Out of necessity,' replied the old man. 'It seems the founder was guarding a secret so explosive, he chose to entrust it to only those he knew would die to keep it.'

'*Secret!*' said David Naami, laughing. 'But we know all about *Le Serpent Rouge*, we have from day one!'

Hearing the old man's sharp inhalation of breath, he carried on.

'The cave containing your secret documents was exceptionally well hidden, I must admit. According to my sources, the little group you referred to earlier – four, according to you – had been under surveillance for weeks. It appears we would never have found it, but for the fact that one of the group, one more careless that the rest, led us right to it. Ah, yes, blackmail, such a crude word,' he observed, pursing his lips as if savouring its taste, 'but so wonderfully effective all the same. For it to work, however, there must be a powerful lever, and your little "secret" certainly provided that. Over the centuries, the Catholic Church has been only too willing to pay to ensure our silence, if you know what I mean.'

Almost incoherent by now, and drooling at the mouth, the old man gestured David Naami to come closer. 'Then you know about Project Lazarus and the prophecy,' he said, 'the ones spoken about in the codex...'

Turning away to hide his surprise, David said, as casually as he could, 'Of course, we know all your little secrets.'

Something like triumph suddenly flashed in the old guardian's eyes, and for a moment he rallied somewhat. 'You're a liar!' he snarled. 'You may have known about the prophecy, but you certainly knew nothing about the codex or "Project Lazarus". Your body language betrays you! The original founder entrusted the secret to no one. Apparently the only mention of it comes in the final chapter of the codex, where it is outlined in detail.'

By now David Naami was white-faced, the muscles of his neck taught, his fists clenched. Fighting hard to regain his lost composure, he suddenly waved his hand in a dismissive gesture. 'None of that matters any more, our raison d'être is to find the chalice and reunite its spirit with the head.'

'In that case,' said the old man, 'you are doomed to failure. From my understanding, both the chalice and codex were lost at sea.' Seeing a chance to save his skin, he carried on. 'According to our sacred tradition, our leader left the Holy Land carrying the objects in a large bag. Made of oiled animal skins, it was waterproof. Unfortunately, somewhere en route to this country, the ship encountered a storm of epic proportions and was sunk without trace. If it were not for a few survivors, we might have given up hope; but it seems they remembered the old man and his mysterious package.'

'I know all this, you fool! It was the reason I moved the bulk of my empire to this part of the world.'

The use of the word 'I' and not 'we' when talking about Chameleon Enterprises was not lost on the old man. He was convinced that apart from everything else, David Naami was a raging megalomaniac.

'Our technical experts, using the most advanced computer research engines, discovered only one such storm in the last 2,000 years, and it matched the one described by the survivors. Using the charts at their disposal, both modern and ancient, they plotted winds and currents and came up with what they considered to be the most likely location, an area some five nautical miles off the Bay of Swansea. And so began years of fruitless search. There was one moment of hope,' said David Naami wistfully, 'when a tombstone bearing our insignia was found in a small graveyard in South Wales, but nothing came of it.' Realising he was becoming sidetracked, he snapped back to the present and said, 'But why should this codex be of such importance?'

'The answer is simple,' said the old man. 'It contains a history of the chalice and how the spirit was contained. The evil is so powerful it will never be defeated, we have always known that, but whoever has the codex has the means of imprisoning it.'

'So let me get this straight, apart from knowing both the chalice and this codex thing survived the storm, you have no more knowledge than I?'

'None,' said the old man. 'For all these centuries you have hunted and murdered us for nothing. Like you, we never knew its location!' With that he burst out laughing.

Disappointment etched clearly on his face, David Naami said off-handedly, 'If that's the case, then I'm afraid you really aren't much use to me any more, are you?' Turning to the others, he barked out instructions, 'Gag him and set things up. Be careful with the rat, this one's a particularly vicious bastard.'

Unable to move, the old man could only watch in horror as the bowl was lifted and the loathsome creature placed on his bare stomach. Seconds later the bowl was replaced and fastened securely.

Watching the trapped rat scurrying frantically around, David Naami felt proud of his little adaptation. Turning to the others he said, 'A transparent bowl makes it much more interesting, don't you think? It's a big improvement on the old copper one. You couldn't see a thing with that. Now we won't have to miss any of the little drama.'

The onlookers watched with relish as the bowl was heated. Within moments the rat went berserk. It wasn't long before it sensed that unable to break through the hardened glass, the only means of escape was through the body of the man. At first tentatively and then with greater relish, it began gnawing at the unprotected flesh. Blood pouring from the open wounds served only to drive it into a more frantic feeding frenzy. To the dismay of those watching, the spectacle didn't last very long. Gradually, the old man's struggles grew weaker and weaker until with one last groaning shudder they stopped altogether. His heart had finally given out.

Leaving the room early, the group missed the final drama. Having devoured the intestines, including such tasty morsels as the heart, liver and kidneys, the rat suddenly appeared from a gaping hole in the old man's side. Dripping with blood and gore, it leapt from the table and landed with athletic grace on the cold marble floor beneath. Seemingly at ease in its surroundings, it lifted its paws and nonchalantly washed the remains of its meal from its whiskers. Satisfied, it gave one last lingering look around before twitching its nose in the air and disappearing.

Chapter Fifteen

LOOKING AT THE OTHERS FIRST, JARED'S GAZE FINALLY CAME TO REST on Roger. 'Do you want to tell them, or shall I?'

'Rather you than me!... more your cup of tea than mine.'

Never one to mince his words, Jared dived in at the deep end. 'It seems we've got a big problem.' Then he brought them up to date concerning the empty chalice.

'So what do we do about it?' said Aled, voicing the inevitable question.

'What we can't afford to do is what we did six years ago – bury our heads in the sand and pretend it will go away. The worst case scenario's already happened. Somehow the thing's managed to escape, so no amount of self-recriminations will alter that. Fortunately for us, I believe that at the moment the thing's power is limited. The strange incidents in and around the village seem to point to such a conclusion.'

'So you reckon it's building itself up slowly, flexing its muscles until its ready,' said Roger.

'I think that's a fair analogy, yes.'

'I suppose the big question is, what happens when it decides it's strong enough,' said Aled.

'Exactly, I couldn't have put it better myself.'

'It gave us a clue as to what it intended to do with all that biblical stuff it spouted, about bringing the Church to its knees and all that. The emphasis was on something about targeting figureheads within the Church, if my memory serves me right,' said Emma.

'Time will tell, Em,' said Jared in reply, 'but if you want a personal opinion, I think it's already pretty powerful.' Making sure he made eye contact with each of them, he paused for dramatic effect, feeling the tension build before saying, 'I take it this time we're all in agreement that the thing is to blame for the strange goings-on?'

A disconcerting silence descended on those present as they mulled over the implications of what he'd said. Several seconds later, he was gratified to see nods of approval from all of them. With that, he marshalled his thoughts before deciding to jump straight into the firing line.

'Now that little matter is out of the way, let's recap and see what's happened so far. First we had the death of old Mrs Penrose, and then there was the fog.'

'Those two are probably interrelated incidents,' said Roger.

'I agree,' said Jared, before continuing. 'Then we had the problem with the ravens on old Arthur's farm, followed shortly afterwards by what happened in Colin Brewster's shop. Finally we had the death of Mr Hopkins on his way to chapel. So what do we make of it all?'

'It tells me one thing for certain,' said Emma. 'The thing's powers are wide ranging.' She went on to explain, 'It can control animals, birds, people's minds and even fog. I'd say that's pretty powerful, wouldn't you?'

Seeing a mood of dejection beginning to settle on the meeting, Roger took the initiative. 'Any of you heard of Praying Mantis? No? Well, they're in Swansea this weekend, in that new nightclub that's just opened – Smokestack, I think it's called. Anyone want to see them?'

'Who the hell are Praying Mantis?' said Emma.

With that a distant memory stirred in Jared. 'Didn't they used to be big in the eighties? Wasn't that the group all the fuss was about at one time?'

Glad that someone else besides him remembered them, Roger said, 'Don't you recall their gimmick? They claimed that if you sung the words of certain of their songs backwards, you could invoke the devil.'

Looking at the others, Emma said, 'Are you sure that's a wise move, going to see someone like that, considering the mess we're in already?'

'Come on, Em,' said Aled, 'it's only a bit of fun. Anyway, you'll enjoy it. How long has it been since you had a night out?'

'It's been that long I can't even remember,' she said with an exasperated sigh. 'All right, count me in – if I can persuade my mother to look after Jodie, that is.'

'I'll drive,' offered Jared. 'I don't drink much anyway. It won't bother me so I can ferry you lot. Save on the price of a minibus.'

That settled, they split up.

The following morning, Roger was running to catch up with Jared.

'Haven't got much time, between jobs and all that, but I've got the tickets,' he said, holding them up in triumph.

'Great!' said Jared. 'But do me a favour, let me pay. It'll be my treat, OK?'

'Fine by me, and I'm sure the others won't protest too much either. Anyway, got to go,' said Roger, before handing the tickets to Jared and disappearing.

Looking at them, Jared suddenly realised it was the first time since his return that the five of them had been out together. Just like old times, he thought to himself, then with a twinge of nostalgia added, *almost*. The following day went by quickly, and as if by some miracle, nothing untoward happened in the village.

Piling into the Rover, they'd decided that the most sensible option was for Roger to drive to Swansea, seeing as it was his car anyway, and for Jared, who wasn't drinking that night, to drive home. The seating arrangements meant that Jared would sit in the front passenger seat, while Emma, Aled and Michael would sit in the back. The Rover was a fairly roomy car and so they managed to fit in with no problem.

'This is the first time I've seen this car, Rog, where do you keep it?' said Jared.

'Hired garage on the council estate nearby,' came the reply. 'Need a car when I'm on the pull, don't I? Can hardly take the old van; doesn't give off the right kind of vibes, does it?'

'I suppose not,' was Jared's measured response.

For the next few miles, no one said a word, each lost in their own thoughts. Looking out of the window, Jared spotted the eighteenth green of the local golf course through a gap in the trees. Being a rugby player, Jared had never thought much about the sport, but had often wondered at the popularity of the game. In a twenty-mile radius of where they were driving, there were no fewer than a dozen courses. How they all managed to sustain a viable membership was beyond him. Perhaps Mark Twain's description of its spoiling a good walk was wrong. At the very least, his philosophy seemed to be completely at odds with the number of people who actually played it. He'd once read that apart from fishing, in terms of numbers participating, that is, it was the most popular sport in the world. Turning to Roger, he said, 'Do you play golf these days?'

'Funny you should mention that. I took it up several years ago and since then I've never looked back. It's the best thing I've done.' Holding up his hand to ward off any argument, he said, 'I know what you're thinking: that it's either a rich man's sport or for bloody snobs. Not a bit of it, mate, believe me. Admittedly, it used to be, there's no doubt about that. Recently, though, it's all changed – open to every Tom, Dick and Harry. Take our local course, the Boar's Head. Most of the members are either old miners or ex-rugby players. And the social life is great. Sadly, a few years ago we went bust, so it's no longer a members' club. It's been taken over by a consortium from England. It's not as bad as it sounds. The four guys, rather than turning it into a little England in Wales, did the opposite. They embraced the Welsh culture with open arms and, because of that, the locals took to them. Spent a good deal of money already and, when they get the drainage right, I think the old place will take off. Fancy a knock some time?'

'I'll think about it,' was Jared's non-committal comment.

Ten minutes later they passed a building Jared was unfamiliar with, although it didn't take him long to work out what it was. 'Swansea City's new ground, I take it?' he said, pointing to the impressive white system.

'Yes,' came Roger's reply, before adding, 'and the Ospreys, of course.'

Taking a left turn at the roundabout ahead, they headed up the hill and then shortly afterwards took a right turn, which took them across the river towards the city itself. Passing Morgan's Hotel on the left, Roger said, 'Catherine Zeta Jones and old Michael Douglas have stayed there,' thinking that Jared would be impressed. In fact, it had the opposite effect – Jared couldn't care less about celebrities. His philosophy was that he never thought anyone was better than him, but on the other hand he never thought he was better than anyone else either. Shortly afterwards, they turned into the entrance to the NCP building. Alighting from the car, Roger made his way over to the ticket machine and paid an all-night parking fee. Displaying the stub on the dashboard, he clicked on the alarm before pointing the way towards the exit.

'Let's take a stroll along Wind Street first, shall we?' suggested Roger. 'Show the maestro here,' he said, pointing to Jared, 'just how much things have changed since he's been away.'

Jared was stunned. The whole place had altered so much; it was nothing like he remembered it. Either side of the road were pubs and clubs of every shape and size, but from where he was standing they all had one thing in common – access was denied to anyone the bouncers didn't like the look of.

'Fancy a pint in Walkabout?' asked Roger, turning to the others. Seeing the nods of approval, they crossed the road. A cursory look was all the five merited and they were inside.

'I'll get the first round,' said Roger, watching in amusement the astonished look that appeared on the faces of the others. 'Don't think I'm going soft or anything, but I just so happen to have had a good week,' he said, looking over at Michael and winking. 'Right, what we having then? It's a pint of lager for me, but what about the rest of you?'

'Could I have a pint of bitter, please, Roger?' said Michael.

'Any one in particular? Worthy Best? Brains?'

Spotting Old Speckled Hen on one of the pumps, he asked for that, which drew a few quizzical looks from one or two of the others.

'I'll have the same as you, Rog,' said Aled.

Turning to Emma, Jared said, 'Gin and tonic?' Seeing her nod, he added, 'and bottled water for me, please.'

Finding room to sit was impossible and Jared couldn't help commenting that it seemed busy for a Thursday night.

'Ah, yes,' was Roger's amused comment. 'Students' night, you see. They pile in from the university and the training college on a Thursday, so it's always packed.' Smiling at Jared he said, 'But if you think it's busy now, then imagine what it's like at weekends. Sometimes you can't even walk down the main street, never mind find room to order drinks in the clubs. Sardines have an easy life compared to this place on weekends, take my word for it. See that one over there,' he said, pointing through the window. 'Now that's the place to be on a Saturday, believe me. The girls dress up in all kinds of sexy costumes and dance on top of the bar while you're being served. But you'd better get there early if you want to get in.'

Not wanting to dampen Roger's obvious enthusiasm, all Jared said was, 'Think I'll give that a miss, if you don't mind.'

Sipping her drink and listening to the conversation, Emma smiled to herself, knowing full well that Jared would hate it.

'By the way, how far is this nightclub we're going to from here, Rog?' asked Jared, suddenly.

'Just round the corner. That's why I suggested a drink here first.' Glancing at his watch, he said, 'I think we'd better drink up. I know we've got tickets, but to get a good view of the band it might be a good idea to get there early.'

'Especially if it's a sell-out,' added Emma.

In fact, the club was less than a five-minute walk away and in no time they were approaching the flashing neon sign declaring the grand opening of Smokestack. Roped-off areas ensured an orderly approach to the double doors. As they were early, it took only moments of queuing before their turn arrived. Handing over the tickets to the two thugs on the door masquerading as bouncers, Jared found it amusing that in order to look intimidating shaven heads, gold earrings and a gaudy array of tattoos seemed to be the order of the day. Making their way downstairs, the whole place not only looked new, but smelt new. Knowing the volume of customers that would pass through these doors over the next year or so, Jared knew that wouldn't last. The nice fresh smell of wild flowers and pine disinfectant would very shortly be replaced by stale beer and good old-fashioned body odour.

Moving through the fake-oak double doors, the first thing that struck Jared was that the place was smaller than he'd expected. The second was the decor of the room. One thing was blatantly obvious: for this grand opening, no expense had been spared. The pièce de résistance was a series of reinforced glass pillars which, on closer inspection, turned out to be aquariums. An original touch, he thought.

Standing around the stage, Jared asked the question that had been nagging him all week. 'How did you manage to get the tickets, Rog?'

'Ah,' said Roger, 'trade secret. No, it was simple, really; friend of a friend and all that. Makes the world go round, doesn't it?'

Laughing, Aled said, 'You're getting to be quite a little Del Boy, Rog!'

'I know it wasn't meant to be, but I'll take that as a compliment,' he said smiling.

Speaking for the first time since they'd arrived, Emma looked at Jared and said, 'On behalf of us all, thank you for the tickets. It was a nice gesture.'

'Oh, that's all right,' said Jared. 'But to be honest I was worried I'd offend you by offering.' Immediately changing the subject to hide his embarrassment, he said, 'Do you know, it's been over six years since I've seen a live group?'

Becoming serious, he observed, 'There must be two or three hundred packed in here – it'll make dancing difficult later, won't it?'

Emma's reply was razor sharp. 'That's all right then, because you never were much of a dancer, were you?' She smiled to show it was meant in fun.

By now the atmosphere was bubbling, the bar doing a roaring trade. Bottles once again seemed to be the order of the day. Seeing several people with their thumbs over the top of the bottles, Jarrod was intrigued and asked Roger about it. Explaining Roger replied, 'It helps to stop spiking.'

Totally bemused Jared said, 'What the hell's that?'

Looking at him in amazement, Roger saw he was genuine. He really had no idea, so he explained. 'Some sick bastards drop little tablets into your drink. Get a kick out of seeing the mess the drug makes of you. For the girls it's even more of a problem, though. It's not called the rape drug for nothing. I won't bore you with the technical term, but it originated as a tranquiliser for horses. Yes, that's right, it's that powerful. One little tablet, and the girl wakes up the next morning and doesn't remember a bloody thing.'

'Jesus,' said Jared, 'that's frightening!'

Some even take their drink into the bogs, they're so afraid of leaving it unattended.'

About to make a comment, his words were drowned out by the roar that greeted the appearance of the band on stage. They were dressed from head to foot in black, complete with long flowing cowls, and Jared's initial impression was that they certainly looked the part. The voice of the lead singer, booming over the mike, silenced the crowd.

By the time the first song was over, Jared knew the hype surrounding their pre-ticket sales had been no idle boast. Within ten minutes they had the crowd eating out of their hands.

The change, when it came, was barely perceptible. The first Jared noticed was a sudden dramatic drop in room temperature. One minute he was perspiring freely under the glare of the spotlights and the heat emanating from the writhing bodies around him, the next he felt decidedly cold. Looking at Emma, he could see she too had noticed. Although it was becoming more unpleasant by the moment, everyone else seemed oblivious to the fact. Suddenly without warning the tone of the lead singer's voice changed dramatically, and in a low sibilant hiss he chanted, '*Are we enjoying ourselves?*'

The reply was a deafening, '*Yes!*'

'*Then let your true selves out!*'

Stunned, Jared realised that, apart from them, the audience seemed to be in the grip of some kind of hypnotic trance. Looking frighteningly like zombies, they kept staring at the singer with glazed, vacant eyes. Again the voice spoke.

'*Who am I?*'

Once more the reply was instantaneous. '*You are the master!*'

Then, deliberately staring down at the five, he said, '*Watch!*'

With that, the singer suddenly turned his head around in a 360° sweep before staring at the screen behind him.

Looking at the others, Jared said, 'But that's impossible! It must be some kind of trick, surely.'

Unable to take his eyes from the hideous sight, it was then he noticed that something was happening directly behind the band. Slowly at first, then more quickly, blood started to seep out of the thin transparent surface of the screen. Within moments it had formed the words:

GETTING STRONGER – NEARLY READY NOW!

Acting almost as a catalyst, the atmosphere, which had been so happy moments before, turned decidedly ugly. In horror, Jared watched as several people began to tear at their clothes, while others began to have sex openly, heaving and rutting like wild animals.

As the music got louder, the violence grew in intensity. Several youngsters Jared vaguely recognised began butting walls. One opened a deep jagged wound on his forehead from which blood spouted copiously.

Worried for the safety of the others, Jared was about to suggest they leave when he saw several people smashing bottles on the side of the stage and lashing out at anyone in range. It was a sickening sight, the damage to life and limb made more problematic by the fact the nightclub was packed to capacity. While all this was taking place, the singer suddenly produced a sword which he'd kept hidden under his long flowing robe. Originally meant as part of the act, it was now put to far grislier use. Lifting the weapon high above his head, he moved in a leisurely fashion towards the bass guitarist, who by now had stopped playing. His hands were above his head and he was clapping like a madman in an attempt to incite the crowd into even more lewd acts of depravity. Giving no hint at what was to come, the singer suddenly severed the hand of the bassist in one single movement.

The whole thing was so unexpected that only Jared's lightning quick reflexes saw it. Seconds later, the others caught on and watched in horror as the severed hand flew into the air with the grace of a bird taking flight. Looping in a high arc over the top of the heads of the crowd, it was a while before anyone noticed the droplets of blood which began landing on the heads of the audience like freshly falling snow.

To the five friends, it was as if they were trapped in a nightmare, watching everything through a haze. With that, the hand suddenly reached the zenith of its arc before dropping to the floor with a sickening thump. It landed at the feet of a couple having sex, but they took no notice of the thing, which lay twitching at their feet. Amazingly, the bass guitarist showed no surprise as he looked down blankly at his severed wrist. Although the blood was pumping fiercely from his ravaged stump, he seemed oblivious to it.

About to shepherd the others to safety, to get them away from the carnage, Jared was stopped in his tracks by the sound of the singer's voice.

'Don't go, Jared – the fun's just beginning!'

It was Emma who saved the day. Screaming so she could be heard above the background noise, she said, 'Jared – it's the music! The thing's controlling them through the music!'

Shouting back, Jared said, 'Then why isn't it affecting us?'

'I don't know, perhaps it's got something else in mind for us. That's probably why it wants us to stay.'

Realising she was right, Jared swung into action. Jumping onto the stage, he pushed his way past the drummer and began ripping out every electrical cable in sight. For a moment or two nothing seemed to happen, until suddenly, with a loud explosion and a shower of sparks, everything seemed to die. Eventually all that remained was a faint hum accompanied by a buzzing and crackling from dozens of different sets of cables. After all the noise, the silence which followed was almost deafening in intensity.

Emma's guess had been right. Once the music stopped, everyone gradually snapped out of their trances. Eyes became focused again and people eventually seemed to return to normal. But many wished they hadn't, as the sight that greeted them was mind-blowing.

The hall was reminiscent of a slaughterhouse. Everything seemed to be covered in blood.

It was everywhere – the walls, floor, even the ceiling – though how that had come about was anyone's guess. People stared at each in stunned disbelief, unable to accept the bloodshed and violence they'd inflicted on each other.

The girls were a pitiful sight as they tried in vain to smooth down non-existent skirts and trousers, or replace the tattered remains of panties. In total confusion they wondered why on earth they were in such a state. Those who could remember were deeply ashamed of their behaviour, of how they'd acted like animals – in some cases with boys they'd never even seen before. For many, it was too much and they collapsed to the floor in hysterical heaps.

Looking on in astonishment, Jared reflected that the demon's words had been only too prophetic. The audience had certainly revealed their true selves. Despite this he couldn't help thinking that if this was what was hidden inside of us, then God help mankind!

Glancing at the stage, he noticed the cloak, worn to such dramatic effect by the singer, was now lying on the floor, crumpled and empty.

Taking control of the situation, he said, 'Al, use your mobile and call the ambulance and police in that order. Try and impress on them the urgency of the situation. If they seem a little sceptical, give them a few details, that'll shake them up.'

Turning to Emma, he said, 'Do you mind staying with me? Between us I thought we'd see what we could do to help some of these poor buggers.' He gestured around him. 'We'll have to prioritise, of course, pick the ones you think are in the worst shape… What the hell, you're a woman, you know more about these things than me!'

Emma was still smiling at the backhanded compliment when Jared leapt onto the stage. Swivelling his head, he shouted, 'My first priority is the poor sod who's just realised his guitar-playing days are over.' By the time he reached the guitarist, he could see the man was going into shock. Lifting him into a sitting position, Jared grabbed the empty cloak lying at his feet and wrapped it tightly around the wounded man's shoulders. That should keep him warm until I manage to stop the bleeding, he thought. Looking at the stump, he saw with relief it had been a clean cut. So, taking off his belt, he said, 'You're going to be OK, mate, I've just got to put this tourniquet on to stop the bleeding.'

Attaching it to the guitarist's right bicep, he pulled tightly and was relieved to see that in a few moments the flow of blood had turned into a mere trickle. 'One last tug should do it,' he muttered.

The immediate danger over, he shouted to the drummer, 'Hold on to this belt, pal, and make sure you keep it tight until the paramedics get here. If you can manage that I'm sure he'll be OK.'

'Thanks, mate,' said the drummer, taking over from Jared, 'but tell me, what the fuck happened here?'

Moving away, Jared looked over his shoulder and shouted, 'You don't want to know, believe me, you really don't want to know!' before jumping off the stage and disappearing into the crowd.

Looking at the mess, unwanted visions of his time in Iraq returned but he dismissed them immediately. That was an avenue he really didn't want to explore at the present moment. Incredibly, despite all the blood, the more he looked, the more he was convinced there were no fatalities. True, several looked in a bad way, but nothing a few stitches or a stint in hospital couldn't cure, he reasoned.

One man in particular looked worse than the others. Glassed in the face by a broken bottle, his left eye was literally hanging by a thread from its socket. Sensing that there was nothing he could do, that the man needed specialist attention, Jared moved on. Everywhere he looked he saw the same look of bewilderment on people's faces. It was obvious most of them hadn't a clue about what had happened. Unfortunately, thought Jared, it wouldn't be long before the sickening truth hit them...

Catching up with Emma, he saw she was very pale; the sight of so much blood had finally started to take its toll. Putting his arm around her shoulder, he said, 'Remember one thing, Em: if it wasn't for you, things would have been a hell of a lot worse.'

With that her resolve finally broke and, bursting into tears, she buried her head into his chest. Startled, Jared held her tightly until moments later she realised what she'd done and pulled away hurriedly. Eyes blazing, she said stiffly, 'I'm sorry, I didn't mean that to happen!'

Trying to hide his hurt, he said, 'I think you've been wonderful, Em, but what you need now is a brandy.' He dragged her over to the bar. Then, pouring her a double, he said, 'I know you hate the stuff, but believe me it will do you good.' Forcing the glass into her hands, he noticed how she was trembling badly. However, after a few splutters she managed to drink it all, and moments later Jared was relieved to see a semblance of colour return to her cheeks.

Returning the empty glass to the bar, Emma was suddenly startled by the sound of the double doors being thrown open, followed seconds later by the ambulance crew rushing into the club. They'd covered a few yards when they stopped dead in their tracks, their faces a picture of stunned disbelief. The leader, a big man in his mid-forties, took in the scene in one glance and exclaimed, 'Christ almighty, what the hell happened?'

Making his way over, Jared introduced himself quickly before explaining the most serious case was propped up against one of the chairs on stage. 'His hand's been severed at the wrist, but the cut looks clean enough. I've managed to stem the flow of blood and I don't think he's in any immediate danger now, but the sooner you can look at him the better.' Suddenly remembering the man whose eye was hanging out he said, 'Shit, I almost forgot! There's another one over there who needs your attention. Surprisingly, the rest are mostly cuts and bruises.'

Looking at Jared with respect, the ambulance chief said, 'If you've managed to do all that, mate, you might just have saved the first guy's life.'

It took the stunned paramedics something like three hours to sort out the mess, patching up those with superficial wounds, while shipping the rest off to hospital.

Jared had been right; there were no fatalities.

About to leave, he was struck by a sudden thought: so far, no one had managed to find either the lead singer or the drummer's hand.

Inevitably, the following morning was taken up with police interviews. As the five had already decided to keep the details to a minimum, there were no discrepancies in their stories.

The meeting in Alec's that night was subdued, reminding Jared of the last time they'd been together before he'd disappeared. Glancing around, he saw the same drawn, haggard faces looking at him for answers – answers he knew he didn't have.

Suddenly, out of the blue, Aled stood up. 'I've had enough. I think we should tell the cops everything, make a clean breast of it.'

Raising his eyebrows in surprise, Jared said, 'And tell them what, Al? What would we say? That we conjured up some demon six years ago and now it's on the rampage? That over the last few weeks it's been getting stronger, flexing its muscles… until last night, that is, when it really went to town?'

Indignantly, Aled replied, 'But they've got a right to know what they're up against.'

'I agree,' said Jared patiently. 'But what then? Say they were in receipt of all the facts, what would they do? At least this way they're blissfully unaware of the true nature of the horror that's out there. Think of the panic it would create it they knew exactly what they were up against.'

'I know, I know,' said Aled sullenly, 'but I feel so helpless somehow.'

Putting his arm around his friend's shoulder, Jared said, 'Believe me, we're all going through the same thing, but when the time comes we'll tell them. At the moment I think it's better to let sleeping dogs lie.'

Seeing the sense in Jared's argument he reluctantly agreed, before adding, 'But why come back, Jar? If you'd never returned, you'd have been safe.'

'I don't think it's as easy as that, Al. Deep down I think that whatever happens, one way or another, I was meant to be part of it.'

'What about last night? said Emma. 'Can't we tell them the truth about that?'

Lifting his eyebrows in a quizzical expression, Jared replied, 'I'm afraid we daren't, Em. You see, no one apart from us saw anything. Go to them with a story like that and they're quite likely to lock us up. How much do you want to bet they'll come up with some bullshit to try and explain it away? Blame it on drugs, or something.'

'But surely no one is going to believe that! I've never taken a drug in my life,' added Emma furiously.

'Neither have I,' said Jared, 'but a mass orgy involving drugs is far more believable than the truth in this case, isn't it?' Grudgingly, he added, 'Can't you see how clever the bloody thing is? It's toying with us! It knows no one would ever believe our story.'

'Then why doesn't it kill us?' asked a clearly terrified Michael. 'Because I don't know how much more of this I can take.'

Looking at Michael with concern, Jared realised that of all of them, it would be he who would be the least likely to cope with the situation. Trying to find a way of reassuring him, he said, 'Don't you see that's what it wants? It wants you feel like that – it thrives on fear…'

'So what are you saying, Jared?' said Roger, interrupting. 'That we're safe for now?'

'I'm not absolutely sure, but yes, I think it's having too much fun to harm any of us at the moment.'

'But what happens if it tires of its little game? What then?' said Emma.

'Ah, now, that's the problem, isn't it? I've no answer to that, but I think it's time I had a word with Uncle Edwin.'

The headlines in the paper a day later made interesting reading. It explained in graphic detail how the lead singer of a group called Praying Mantis had been found bound, gagged and tied to a tombstone in the graveyard of a small chapel in the village of Raven's Hill. Tied with barbed wire, a severed hand had been fastened around his neck.

It was fortunate that a local man walking his dog had stumbled across him, otherwise he would have died. Hypothermia had already set in. Had he been there for an hour or two more, it would have been too late. Presently the man was being treated in Morriston General Hospital, but strangely he remembered nothing of the events leading up to his discovery in the graveyard.

When Jared read the story it solved one puzzle but left him facing another.

He now knew what had happened to both the singer and the severed hand. What the report failed to explain however was how the hell the bloke had managed to get from Swansea to Raven's Hill without being noticed. Especially since he'd been stark naked!

Chapter Sixteen

DRIVING ALONG THE MOTORWAY IN ROGER'S VAN ON THE OUTSKIRTS
of Ross-on-Wye, Jared realised that sooner or later he'd have to think
about getting his own transport. Staying in the middle lane, he was
amazed to see just how many cars were blatantly overtaking on the
inside. Without warning a huge juggernaut overtook him. Unable to
believe what he was seeing, he glanced at his speedometer and noticed
with astonishment that he was doing seventy miles an hour himself.
Roaring by, the driver was oblivious to it all, as diesel fumes tinged with
rubber wafted through Jared's open window. As it sped past, Jared's van
shook as if an earthquake had suddenly struck. In moments the lorry
was nothing but a speck on the distant horizon.

The journey provided Jared with ample opportunity to prepare his little
speech. He was therefore hopeful that when he met his uncle he would be
able to put his case over with confidence. One thought bothered him: the
fact he'd not made contact beforehand to announce his arrival. Instead he'd
decided to take a chance, knowing full well the real reason he hadn't
phoned was guilt – guilt at not having kept in touch.

It took him just over two hours to reach Mendel Hall. It would have
been considerably less, but for the fact he'd had to stop several times in
order to ask for directions. Cruising up the drive, he noticed an old man
taking a brief respite from collecting what he guessed where the first
instalment of autumn leaves. The man touched his flat cap at Jared
before getting back to work. Using a fan rake, he carefully collected the
leaves into mounds before shovelling them into a battered wheelbarrow
that to Jared seemed to be already full.

Arriving, he was relieved to see Edwin's Jaguar parked outside, noting
with surprise it seemed to be the same one. Stepping out of the van, he
walked across the pebbled courtyard, which was dotted here and there
with small pools of water, the legacy of the morning's heavy downpour.

Standing at the bottom of the steps, he took several moments to still
his breathing, before finally plucking up courage and running up the

short flight of steps to press the bell. Within moments the door was opened by someone he'd never seen before.

Introducing himself as Jared Hunter, he was met with a blank stare; the man had never heard of him. Turning on his heels, the man disappeared and Jared was left standing on the step for several moments, before he noticed Edwin hurrying to the door.

'My God, it's really you! I thought Max had got his wires mixed up somehow.' Hugging Jared spontaneously, Edwin finally released him and held him at arm's length, staring in silent appraisal. 'Time has been good to you, my lad.' Looking at him more closely, he said, 'But there's something different about you somehow.'

Not again, thought Jared in silent exasperation, by now tired of the reaction.

'I can't put my finger on it,' said Edwin, 'but you've changed, something about the eyes, a coldness – no, that's not the right word at all, no, it's more a kind of self-assurance. Yes, that's it,' said Edwin, slapping his thigh in triumph, 'you've grown up!'

No recriminations, no stinging rebuke; typical Uncle Edwin, Jared thought.

'I owe you a big apology, Uncle, but if it's any consolation I couldn't contact anyone where I was.'

With that he gave him a potted version of where he'd been and what he'd been doing over the past six years.

When he'd finished, he saw the astonished look on Edwin's face before he said, 'But that's some story, lad.' Then, realising they were still standing in the doorway, he said, 'Come in, come in! Where the devil are my manners!'

They'd gone no more than a dozen paces when Edwin stopped and said, 'But this is no social call, is it? I can tell by your face. There's something on your mind, isn't there?'

Not waiting for an answer, he carried on walking before suddenly shouting, 'Mrs Daniels, Mrs Daniels! Look after Jared for a minute while I get changed, will you? While you're at it, can you rustle up a cup of tea or something?'

As if by magic Mrs Daniels appeared from the kitchen, and it was clear from her reaction that unlike Edwin, she hadn't forgiven him. With a reproachful look she said, 'You're home, then,' and without further comment led him into the kitchen.

Edwin was as true as his word, and was back in the time it had taken Jared to take the first sip of his tea. Sensing the hostility in the atmosphere, he turned to Jared and said, 'Take no notice of Mrs Daniels, it's just that she looks after me like a mother hen.'

'Too good-natured for your own good, you are, Mr Hunter,' was her reply before hurrying from the room.

'This isn't the place to talk, so let's go into the study,' said Edwin.

Making sure they were both comfortable, he said, 'Well, out with it, lad! There's something you're dying to tell me.'

Despite the time he'd spent rehearsing his story, when Jared started he got into a terrible tangle. Sensing his trepidation, Edwin could tell that his nephew was wary of expressing what he really felt.

Stopping him in mid-sentence, Edwin said, 'Wait there a minute... now go back to the beginning and take it slowly.'

More relaxed now, Jared told him what had happened all those years ago. Leaving nothing out, he eventually brought Edwin up to date with what had taken place in the village over the last few weeks. When he'd finished, he looked at his uncle with a mixture of fear and apprehension. During the course of the story he hadn't once interrupted, or shown any sign of scepticism. Furthermore, to his eternal credit he hadn't burst out laughing, either, something Jared wasn't sure he'd have been able to stop himself doing had the boot been on the other foot. Instead, his reaction was astonishing.

Leaning over in order to get his pipe, he said, 'One thing seems to stand out a mile about all this...'

Jared exclaimed in amazement, 'You believe me, then?'

'Of course I believe you – you're not in the habit of making things up, are you? No, what I was about to say was, there seems to be a definite link between what you youngsters unleashed and the incredible story I discovered in the scroll all those years ago.' Stopping suddenly, he said, 'Ah, it all fits now! That's why you were so interested in the occult back then, you were hoping that between us we might have come up with some answers. Don't look so guilty! Even if you had told me everything, it would have been highly unlikely. I'm afraid what you've just described is something far beyond my experience.'

'I'm glad you didn't notice my reaction when you told me the story originally,' said Jared, 'it would have left the cat out of the bag.'

'Don't worry about that now, let's get back to basics. The first thing to do is to try and analyse what the scroll says, before jumping to conclusions.'

Mentally ticking off the list of things he thought important, Edwin said, 'Right, from what I remember, the most outrageous of its claims was that there existed a group or secret society able to bring people back from the dead.'

'But it also claimed that someone named Barabbas paid a substantial sum of money in order to resurrect his brother,' said Jared. 'Does the name sound familiar?'

'The only one I can think of is Jesus Barabbas, the leader of the Sicarii at the time of Christ. I hardly think it would have had anything to do with him though, because after the trials he's never heard of again. Besides, as far as I'm aware, the Bible doesn't even mention he had a brother.' Changing tack slightly, Edwin said, 'What about the Sicarii, what do you know about them?'

'As a matter of fact, rather a lot, they're one of my pet subjects. Regarded as the elite assassins of their day, they became known as the dagger men, for the simple reason they took their name from the weapon of their choice – the sica or dagger. In Palestine, the Romans were terrified of them. They used to hide the knives under their cloaks, slit the throat of every Roman they could get their hands on, and then disappear like phantoms.'

Warming to his task, Jared carried on, 'After the sacking of Jerusalem by Titus, they fled to Masada; there, rather than be taken alive, they committed mass suicide. According to the story they drew lots to decide the order in which they should die. The last person left alive was expected to take his own life. Archaeologists have even uncovered the potsherds they used for their gruesome task, complete with names. But from that time on they're said to have disappeared from the stage of history.'

Getting up from the chair, Edwin went over to the open fireplace and, tapping his pipe against the mantelpiece, emptied it before having his say. 'So, as far as we're concerned then, it couldn't have been these Sicarii characters. A pity, because they were beginning to look like promising suspects.'

Smiling, Jared said, 'But what if the experts were wrong? You see, I've long had my own theory about what happened at Masada.' Seeing the astonishment on his uncle's face, he said, 'Remember, although the potsherds have been used as evidence for the idea of mass suicide, no one knows exactly how many people were involved. Those pieces of broken pottery have always been touted as definitive evidence for a certain number of people, and no more. But there might be another scenario...'

Fascinated by now, Edwin said, 'Go on.'

'What if a select few managed to hide somewhere on Masada until it was all over? When the Romans found X number of corpses, they would have been satisfied. They had no reason to suspect there were others.'

'That's all very well,' said Edwin. 'Correct me if I'm wrong, but surely there was nowhere to hide on Masada?'

'That's what everyone was led to believe, but you see Masada was a bigger complex than most people realise. Put it this way, it's an accepted fact that Herod was paranoid, am I correct?'

'Yes,' said Edwin, 'he was certainly that.'

'Remember paranoid people are always concerned for their safety – the fact that Herod built Masada in the first place is confirmation of that – but do you think it would have been his only escape route? His palace was quite lavish, and deliberately made so. He wanted the best of everything, even in exile. The complex included such things as huge sunken baths, and we can deduce from this that he even had his own water storage tanks. In that case, isn't it possible he deliberately had a hidden room built? A place he and a select few could disappear to, on the off chance someone might eventually find a way around his defences?'

'I see what you're getting at,' said Edwin. 'Put like that it's certainly plausible.'

'Let's take the speculation a little further. Let's say there was such a secret room, and that a group of specially chosen survivors hid themselves there. All they had to do was wait the Romans out. Remember, they weren't looking for survivors, they thought everyone had killed themselves. Once the Romans had gone, all they had to do was to make their way down the ramps and disappear. No one would have been any the wiser.'

'It's an incredible theory,' said Edwin, 'but you're forgetting – according to the records they were never heard of again.'

'That's exactly my point,' said Jared. 'Think about the ramifications for a moment.'

Edwin tried to visualise the scene, play it through his mind before saying, 'Let me get this straight. You're suggesting that somehow this group escaped and over the centuries not only survived, but became stronger and more deadly than their predecessors. But more than that, they exist in some shape or form today.'

'That's precisely what I'm suggesting. You hear a great deal about conspiracy theories these days, and most are absolute nonsense. But think for a moment. If what I'm suggesting is true, this select group of killers not only survived, but developed into something far more extreme. They could have infiltrated other organisations without them ever being aware of it. It was the perfect cover, because as you said yourself, according to the history books they no longer exist.'

Sitting there and looking stunned, Edwin said, 'But if that's true, the implications could be enormous!'

Allowing Edwin time to take it all in, Jared decided to return to the subject of the thing in the chalice. 'I've wracked my brains trying to think of something I've missed – something that might help explain whose ashes are in the chalice – but apart from what I've already told you...' his voice trailed off.

'In that case, let's recap,' said Edwin. 'You distinctly remember it saying it was 2,000 years old, and that fits the timescale we allowed ourselves. Then there was the name, "Man of Kerioth", and for some reason you said the name was familiar.' Scrunching up his face in concentration, he pointed his pipe at Jared and said, 'Wasn't it a village somewhere near Jerusalem at one time?'

'Of course!' said Jared, thumping his fist against his thigh. 'You're right – that's why I thought it sounded so familiar.' After a few moments' speculation, he added, 'But it's more than that; something at the back of my mind is niggling at me.'

'Don't force it,' said Edwin, 'it'll come in its own time.'

'There was one other thing though, it spouted a lot of stuff I thought was from Revelations at the time, but although they're close the words aren't exactly the same.'

'What kind of stuff?' asked Edwin.

Concentrating hard in an effort to remember, Jared said, 'Strange things. "The time is coming when I shall receive retribution. Those

172

charlatans who stand as symbols of power in their pathetic sanctuaries will learn the truth. The houses of their God shall be brought crumbling down, their faith exposed as a worthless sham." Things like that, but it finished up by saying something really weird, hinting that somehow I was special. I couldn't make head or tail of that.'

'That does seem odd,' said Edwin, 'but did any of you come up with any suggestions?'

Pensive for a moment, Jared answered, 'Emma thought the part about symbols of power, pathetic sanctuaries and houses of their God being brought crumbling down, might refer to an attack on church buildings, but in particular on its leaders.'

'It could be,' said Edwin. 'If that's the case, perhaps the houses coming crumbling down might be suggestive of the demise of religion in Raven's Hill. Might it have been prophesying the closure of several of the chapels in the area? If that's the case, it seems to have been particularly accurate. It seems too much of a coincidence to me somehow, coming as it does at the end of the old millennium.'

Looking in surprise, Jared said, 'But that was the year 2,000 surely?'

Laughing Edwin said, 'You're not the first to make that mistake. Actually the error came about because of a Roman abbot. Called Dionysius Exegius, he forgot to add a minor emperor's name to the list and so he came up seven years short.'

In a hushed tone, Jared said, 'Christ, that makes it even worse; if the new millennium is actually this year, no wonder it's lining up something special.'

Taking over again, Edwin said, 'It's been puzzling me why these incidents in Raven's Hill are recent occurrences. From what you say it's only since the bulldozer accidentally uncovered the secret room that anything untoward has taken place, so to me the answer is obvious. Those archaeologists weren't the first on the scene. If I'm not missing my guess, someone beat them to it and tampered with the chalice while the dig was unattended. Now, if I'm adding two and two together and not getting five, and the chalice is the object mentioned in the scroll, the thing is free.'

'Exactly my thinking,' said Jared. 'Now the chalice has been opened, the sacrifice has lost its potency, and if that's the case we're in big trouble. Add to that the fact it no longer remains under the protection of the chapel, and bingo! But what makes you think someone else opened the chalice first?'

'Simple, they wanted what was inside.'

'Of course,' said Jared, 'that's it! I knew something was bugging me. When I first handled the chalice, it made a strange noise, so it was obvious it contained something. However, the other day when Roger and I looked inside, there was nothing but ashes. What the hell could have been inside?'

'It doesn't really matter,' said Edwin. 'Besides providing a clue about who the ashes belong to, it doesn't help explain how the evil was imprisoned, unless... I wonder if *blood* might be the answer? Yes,' he said excitedly, 'that's it, I'm sure of it! Pointing the stem of his pipe towards Jared, he said, 'Let me run this scenario by you, see how it sounds. From everything we've learned recently it seems the most effective way of exorcising evil was through sacrifice. However, our research showed that in order to destroy a more powerful demon it required the willing sacrifice of someone very special, someone like a saint.' Looking up he said, 'With me so far?'

Seeing Jared's nod of affirmation, he carried on.

'So what if the person mentioned in the scroll worked it out. Not only that, but managed to find such a sacrifice? In that case, it's possible the blood of this person was the method used to bind the evil to the chalice.'

'Yes,' said Jared in excitement, 'that's how the thing was imprisoned in the first place. It has to be the explanation.'

'Hold on – not so fast, it's just an educated guess – but it does make some kind of sense. Strange, isn't it, that years ago we touched on the very same subject. We even suggested the best sacrifice would be either a person who had lived a life of extraordinary purity...'

'...or a sacrifice performed out of pure love,' said Jared, completing the sentence for him.

'Exactly, and if that's the case and my little theory is correct, they must have found one or the other.'

'Go on,' said Jared, 'you might as well tell me the name of the sacrifice while you're at it, you're doing so well.'

Laughing, Edwin said, 'Speculation I can manage; miracles, they take a little longer.'

After a few moments of silence, Jared suddenly blinked in surprise before saying, 'If what you say is true, that someone got to the chalice before the archaeologists arrived, I know just the person to ask.'

Looking at Jared quizzically, Edwin suddenly burst out laughing, 'How stupid of me, why didn't I think of it? You're talking about old Eric Roberts, aren't you? Living next door to Carmel as he does, he's bound to have seen something.'

Surprised, Jared said, 'I didn't realise you two knew each other, you not being a chapel-goer and all that. How did you meet?'

'That's an interesting story, but I dare say he'll tell you about it when the time's right.'

Somewhat guiltily, Jared declared, 'It gives me an excuse to call on him. After all I owe him an explanation for my disappearance too. Along with my parents, Gran and yourself, he had a good deal of influence on shaping my formative years.'

Taking a pull from his pipe, Edwin blew out the smoke before saying, 'Thinking along those lines, I remember reading an article somewhere that made that very point. It asked you to try and remember who had left the most lasting impression on you as a teenager. As expected most answered their favourite teacher, but in your case it seems it was old Eric Roberts.'

'I suppose it was,' said Jared. 'What I liked most about him was his honesty.'

Seeing the puzzled look on Edwin's face Jared explained. 'You see, he never attempted to force his opinions on us, simply read the stories and left us to come to our own conclusion. He knew how brainwashing at a young age could be so easy, I suppose.'

'And dangerous,' said Edwin. 'Remember the old fundamentalist credo – "Give me a child before the age of ten and I'll give you a terrorist" – or something like that. Anyway, you know what I mean.'

'Unfortunately I do,' said Jared. 'I've seen it in the flesh.'

'Of course, I completely forgot, how remiss of me.'

'Besides he never talked down to us, never treated us like kids.'

'Ever thought it was because you weren't? Like all good teachers he probably recognised your ability and treated you accordingly. That way he got the best out of you.'

'There was that, I suppose,' said Jared, 'but he treated everyone like that, not just me. Then of course he was always so wickedly radical.'

Looking up in surprise, Edwin said, 'What's that supposed to mean?'

Laughing, Jared explained. 'He was always keeping us up to date with the most bizarre theories. The trouble was you never knew when he was being serious or not.' Looking contrite, Jared finished by adding, 'That's one of the reasons I felt so guilty about not keeping in touch.'

'He was in good company, then, wasn't he?' said Edwin, smiling to take the sting out of the comment. 'More seriously, though, I suppose those feelings only fuelled your guilt when you carried out the seance?'

'God, yes,' said Jared. 'At the time the thought almost made me call it off, but by then we'd come too far to back off. In hindsight I wish I'd listened to my instincts, then none of this would have happened.'

After a few moments of silence, his uncle's soft words of comfort broke into his thoughts. 'I wouldn't be too sure of that. If it hadn't been you youngsters, it would have been someone else. This was a disaster waiting to happen. Destiny, some might call it. Remember after all is said and done, you at least had the common sense to heed the warning and leave well alone. But for a complete accident, something totally beyond your control, the foul thing would still be imprisoned in the chalice.'

Attempting to change the subject, Jared said, 'Aren't you going to give me a little clue as to how you and Eric know each other?'

Grinning, Edwin replied, 'I suppose I'd better otherwise I'm never going to get any peace. It's no great mystery, it's just that down the years I've been able to help him out with some research.' Looking thoughtful for a moment, he carried on. 'I'd better qualify the term "research". In fact Eric is probably one of the foremost authorities on the Knights Templar in the country. Rather well qualified too, with a BD, MA and PhD. Want me to carry on? At one time it seems he was regarded as one of the most gifted students of his era. Destined for big things, by all accounts.'

Stunned by his uncle's revelations, Jared asked, 'So what went wrong?'

'Ah, that's the real question, isn't it! I'm afraid you'll have to ask him that. Reading between the lines, it seems shortly after beginning his research into the Knights Templar, he seems to have veered from the straight and narrow somewhat.'

His curiosity piqued, Jared said, 'If that's the case, he must have been aware of their links to the myth of the Holy Grail and all that.'

'As a matter of fact he was; that's one of the pieces of work he asked me to help him with. Fascinating stuff, I must admit, even got me hooked for a while.'

'What do you mean, exactly, when you said he veered from the straight and narrow?'

'Sorry to disappoint you, but there the mystery deepens. I honestly can't give you an answer. All I know is that from that time on his career seems to have hit a brick wall.' He added, 'No, that's perhaps the wrong choice of words; *nosedive* might be a more apt description. I'll leave you with a little thought, though. What do you think a person as highly qualified as old Eric was doing tucked away in the outbacks of South Wales?' Suddenly glancing at his watch, he said, 'Before we have a spot of lunch, do you mind me asking you a question?'

'Not at all, fire away.'

'How did you get mixed up in all this in the first place?'

'That's the strangest thing,' said Jared, before going on to relate the story of old Thomas, his grandad and the Ouija board.

'But how did he know about that?' said Edwin. 'I lived in Raven's Hill for many years – knew your grandmother well, obviously – but I never heard any of it.'

'I suppose it might have had something to do with the fact he was a local historian.'

'I wouldn't have thought he'd have lived in the locality long enough to qualify for such a title. I mean, he was only married to your gran just over a year before you up and went,' he added thoughtfully.

After a quick lunch they moved into the library. Stepping inside, Jared was immediately overwhelmed by the familiar ambience of leather and ancient books.

Carrying on as if they'd never stopped to eat, Edwin said, 'There's another thing in favour of a biblical setting for the chalice. It's a matter of record that Samaria in those days was a hotbed of demonology and witchcraft. Under the leadership of Simon Magus, all kinds of evil enterprises were carried out. Apparently, attempts at raising spirits from the dead were commonplace. If the dates fit, he might even conceivably have been the leader of the sect mentioned in the scroll.'

Walking towards the far end of the library, Edwin pointed upwards. 'That's the shelf I was telling you about. I'm sure with a bit of patience we should be able to find something in the middle of that lot to help us. My tired old limbs will only put up with so much exercise, so I'm afraid it's your turn to climb the ladder.'

Reaching the top, Jared ran his fingers along the spines before shouting down to Edwin, 'Some of the larger city libraries would pay a fortune for a few of these.'

In reply, Edwin said, 'If you look closely you'll find a good many of them seem to be of Jewish origin. It makes me wonder whether the original owner had Jewish connections. Try the final volume on the last shelf. That's it, the one with the red spine. It deals with mysticism and things like that. If we're going to get any pointers on what we were discussing earlier, I'll wager we'll find it in there.'

Making his way down, Jared was careful not to drop the book, and he breathed a sigh of relief when he his feet hit terra firma. Placing the volume on the desk, it wasn't long before they found what they were looking for.

'Here's something!' shouted Jared excitedly. 'It seems the type of information we're after is linked to something called the Cabala. In Hebrew it means "what is received".' He paused.

'Now get this! It says here it was originally an esoteric and mystic doctrine, purely oral and put together by the Jews of the ancient past. Like all mysticism it was designed for a limited group of people, a secret cadre if you like, made up of those professing to be "in the know". Over time it seems to have changed, to have become written instead of oral, but in the process, it was transformed into a multiplicity of complex ideas and intricate symbolism. According to this account, it eventually became meaningless… unless of course…' Jared turned to Edwin with a sly smile, 'it just so happens that you had the key to unlock the secrets.' Pausing for a moment, he said, 'Hang on, it gets really interesting here. It seems that over the centuries it gradually became more and more linked to magic, demonology and even cosmology.'

'That's more like it,' said Edwin.

'Anyway, eventually this select group – or secret society, whichever you prefer – became known as Cabalists. The account goes on to say that over time they became involved in all kind of weird stuff, including the casting of spells, necrophilia, devil worshiping, and… oh, you're going to love this bit, and I quote, "they claimed to be able to influence demons by calling them back from the dead". Ring any bells?' said Jared in triumph.

Realising it was getting late, he turned to Edwin, 'I'll have to go. Roger wants his van for work tomorrow, and I promised I'd get it back to him tonight.'

Hiding his disappointment, Edwin said, 'I know it's none of my business, and you can tell me to bugger off if you like, but what happened between you and Emma?'

'I was wondering when you were going to get around to that. No, I don't mind telling you, it's in the past now.' From the tone of his voice he knew he sounded far from convincing. 'It's simple, really. I got home from visiting you a day early, went to find her, and to cut a long story short, caught her in the arms of another bloke.'

'I find that hard to believe, somehow. The two of you were so much in love. Are you sure you didn't make some mistake?' asked Edwin.

'I wish to God I had, but no, there was no mistake, I can assure you.'

'But did you ever think there might have been a misunderstanding? That there might have been an innocent explanation for it?'

Looking at Edwin from under lowered eyelids, Jared said, 'When you catch your future wife in a clinch with another bloke, you don't find it easy to believe there might have been an innocent explanation, do you, Uncle?'

'No, lad, I suppose not,' was Edwin's dejected reply, before he saw his nephew to the van.

Chapter Seventeen

HURRYING THROUGH THE DOOR, SCORPION REALISED IN HIS excitement he'd forgotten to knock. As luck would have it, David Naami was currently preoccupied. Back to the door, phone to his ear, he was staring through the window at the wide sweep of the bay. At this time of day the tide was out, leaving the small boats stranded in the mud, their hulls tilted at all kinds of odd angles.

Breathing a sigh of relief, Scorpion made his way over to the desk and waited.

Aware of a presence behind him, David's suspicion was confirmed when he caught the reflection in the glass, before turning round and mouthing, 'Be with you in a minute.'

'Sorry, Gregor, I lost my train of thought there for a minute; someone just walked into the room. Now where were we? Ah, yes, the latest shipment.' Although he knew exactly how the consignment was brought into the UK, he also knew how his friend's mind worked. With that, he decided to stroke his feathers somewhat. 'Listen, Gregor, how the hell do you manage to get the merchandise from A to B? The process must be amazingly complicated. You certainly know your stuff, that's for sure. Run me through it quickly, will you. That way I might be able to appreciate better just how much time and effort your side of the organisation is putting into this operation.' For a moment he wondered if he'd gone over the top, laid on the compliments a little too thickly. However, he needn't have worried, he'd guessed correctly about the kind of personality he was dealing with.

Preening himself, the Mafia boss was only to glad to explain.

'The actual journey can take up to eighteen months from start to finish, but it all begins in and around the foothills of northern Afghanistan. Starting life as a humble poppy seed, the merchandise is transported from the mountains either by lorry, camel, or more often than not by donkeys. Believe me when I tell you that the poor old donkeys have to negotiate mountain trails that are often so steep they have to drop into third gear to make the ascent!' Gregor chuckled at his own little joke.

Carrying on, he said, 'Once the stuff hits the valley floor our problems start, because customs, feudal warlords and crooked politicians start vying with each other for a share of the profits. The end result for us of course is that they force the fucking price up.' Waiting for a moment to let the implications of what he'd just said sink in, Gregor carried on. 'Once it reaches Turkey, the laboratories take over and the opium is rendered into raw heroin. But you have to remember that Turkey is only a staging post. By the time it gets shipped on from there, yet more palms have to be greased before it reaches its ultimate destination, the United Kingdom. Unfortunately, even then it's not the end of things, as once it reaches here the merry-go-round begins all over again. At each new stop along the way, the price is forced ever higher... why? It's simple, because everyone wants a slice of the fucking cake! I'm not complaining, of course, but every year the customs and police are using ever more sophisticated surveillance techniques to try and catch us. So far we've been lucky, but who knows...' He trailed off in mid-sentence.

'Yes,' said David Naami, breaking in. 'The risks are great, but so are the rewards. With the street value presently at £60,000 a kilo, it provides us both with a nice little profit.'

Secretly worried that Gregor's spiel about ever increasing risks might be a prelude to raising the prices, he was pleasantly surprised when the subject wasn't even mentioned.

For Scorpion, it seemed that he'd been waiting for hours, but finally his patience was rewarded. Replacing the phone in its cradle, David Naami looked up and said, 'Right, what can I do for you?'

The look on his face and the courteous way in which he'd addressed him told Scorpion he must have received good news. Normally he wasn't this polite. Grinning to himself, he thought his day was only going to get better when he received the lightning bolt he was bringing him. Moving forward he could hardly contain his excitement as he placed the folded newspaper on his desk.

Impatient now, the facade of joviality slipping away quickly, David Naami said, 'Help me out here, Scorpion. What am I supposed to be looking at?'

'Right-hand side, near the bottom of the page number one; I've ringed the relevant article in red.'

A few terse seconds latter David Naami exploded. 'Jesus fucking Christ! I don't believe it!' He added menacingly, 'This had better not be a wind-up otherwise heads will roll, believe me!'

Startled, Scorpion suddenly blurted out, 'Oh, no, Number One, it's genuine, I can assure you. I checked.'

Seeing the look of terror on Scorpion's face, David Naami was mollified, and chuckling, said, 'All right, all right, I believe you, it's just that after nearly 2,000 years of searching it suddenly turns up on our doorstep. Sounds too good to be fucking true, that's all.'

'That's what I thought when I read it, Number One, it's the reason I checked its authenticity.'

Reading it again, this time more slowly, David savoured the moment. It was a graphic description of how the objects had been discovered, quite by accident, in a small village called Raven's Hill. The article went on to explain an oddity. A ring found on the skeleton of the old man displayed a symbol identical to one on a tombstone uncovered in the graveyard of the same chapel, some six years earlier. Shaking his head in amazement, David kept staring at the photographs. No, there was no mistake; the symbols were definitely the same. Bitterness washed over him in waves as he thought about how much time and money had been spent, convinced that once the tombstone had been discovered it would provide the secret to unlocking the whereabouts of the elusive chalice. Modern technology allied to old rumours and innuendos had proved to be correct after all, he mused; it had survived the storm. Grudgingly he had to admit the founder of the guardians had done a remarkable job, considering the condition the old man must have been in after the shipwreck. True, he hadn't realised he wasn't the only survivor, but he had probably been half dead at the time. David wondered how long he'd lasted and just how he'd died. Ironically, had he been given a dozen guesses, a heart attack would probably have been the last thing he would have chosen.

Reading on, he saw that everything was to go on display for a month in the local Miners' Welfare Hall. After this period they would be afforded a permanent home in the National Museum of Antiquities in Cardiff. He noted in amusement how to date archaeologists were baffled about the origins of the exhibits.

Suddenly giving vent to his feelings, he laughed out loud. 'My dear Scorpion, it seems our so called experts are baffled as to the nature of the chalice. If only they would ask, we could tell them exactly what it is, couldn't we? And more importantly, what it contains…'

Infected by his master's good humour, Scorpion decided to get in on the act. 'All those guardians we tortured – and it was for nothing! They had no more clue concerning the whereabouts of the bloody thing than we did. If it wasn't for you breaking down the final one, we would never have known.'

'Penultimate one,' said David Naami. 'Remember, according to him the most important one is still alive. As the senior guardian, he is in receipt of all their little secrets. What I wouldn't give to get my hands on him.'

Suddenly a new idea struck him. 'He mentioned something about a codex, remember?' The question was rhetorical, requiring no answer, and so he carried on.

'If he was telling the truth – and I'm inclined to think he was – its contents worry me. According to him, it was a detailed history of our organisation from the moment of its inception. It would provide incontrovertible proof of how we obtained all our little secrets and survived Masada.'

'Along with the truth about how we've managed to blackmail the Catholic Church all these years,' said Scorpion with a smirk.

'Yes, and that too,' said David Naami, 'but strangely there was no mention of the codex in the article. So if it wasn't with the other objects, where the hell is it? I'm sure he told us everything he knew, which as it turned out was precious little, but…' At this point he suddenly stopped. For a moment he said nothing, appearing to be deep in thought. Then he had it, the thing that had been nagging at him until now. Looking at Scorpion, he said, 'Besides the codex, he mentioned something else. I remember he pulled me close and mumbled in my ear. By now he was almost incoherent and probably insane, but he mentioned something about a secret called "Project Lazarus". I must admit the puzzle is intriguing.'

'At least we know there's only one left, Number One. When we find him, we'll have rid ourselves of all the bastards.'

'Unfortunately, that's what I'm worried about.'

'I don't follow,' said Scorpion, 'how can he possibly pose a threat to us? He must be almost decrepit by now.'

Thoughtful once again, David Naami said, 'Do you remember some six years ago when our security was breached?'

'Of course, I had the honour of helping you dispatch the fools who'd designed the system.' It was blatantly obvious the memory of the incident still brought pleasure to Scorpion.

'Be that as it may, the simple fact is our innermost secrets were stolen, and quite frankly I'm at a loss to explain why the information has never been used against us.'

'I see what you're getting at; the information on those files was explosive, worth a fortune to the right people,' said Scorpion. 'So why have they never been used? It doesn't make sense.'

'Exactly, but let's try a little hypothesis. What if the information was stolen for someone who already knew about the contents? Or, to take it to its logical conclusion, what if the files were stolen for an organisation that not only knew what was on the files, but that most of the secrets it contained originated with them?'

'Of course – the guardians!' shouted Scorpion in triumph. 'It would explain everything, wouldn't it? Although they never knew for certain we'd discovered their precious scrolls, they must have guessed. So, knowing he was the last, the old bugger must have decided to go on the offensive. And by now he knows as much as we do.'

'Unfortunately, he knows more. Remember, we didn't manage to capture everything. It seems the real treasure was contained in this codex. I'd give my right arm to know what Project Lazarus is. It's all pie in the sky of course, because unless we can find him it will remain a mystery.'

'Yes, Number One, and unfortunately, if he is as old as we think, the secret will die with him.'

'Maybe not,' said David Naami thoughtfully. 'If we can somehow manage to track him down, he might just lead us to his little secrets. As in all organisations, the information must be hidden somewhere. Find his house and our experts will do the rest. Anyway, at the moment that's not our first priority; the first thing we have to do is to bring the chalice back to its rightful home.'

Seeing the look of pain that crossed Scorpion's face, David Naami felt the first twinge of apprehension. 'Well, what is it?' he bellowed. 'What's the matter?'

'It's the date, Number One, have you seen it?'

Looking hurriedly at the page, his face darkened as he instantly understood the problem. The article had been penned weeks ago. Exploding into a string of curses, he ranted on for a full two minutes until suddenly he ran out of steam. Within moments he was in full control of his emotions again.

Fully rational now, he knew he had to act quickly. Stealing the chalice while it was in the village of Raven's Hill would be simple, but should it ever reach the museum in Cardiff, that might be an entirely different matter.

Seeing the smile on Scorpion's face, he snapped, 'It's obvious you've worked something out, so spit it out!'

Anxious to defuse the situation, to redeem himself in the eyes of the master, he said, 'It's all taken care of. The moment I noticed the date and saw that we were working to a tight schedule, I set the wheels in motion. Pretending to be a journalist doing an article for an historical magazine, I got all the information I needed.'

He stiffened suddenly when he saw David Naami's face.

'Did you give the name of this fictitious magazine?'

'Yes, I had to, the person on the phone asked for it, so I made something up on the spur of the moment. I thought on my feet, if you like, Number One.'

Passing his hand over his face in despair, David Naami let the silence hang in the air for several seconds before saying, 'Now let me get this straight. You telephoned the curator of the Hall in Raven's Hill pretending to be a journalist on behalf of a fictitious historical magazine?'

Gulping down his Adam's apple, which all of a sudden seemed to have become stuck in his throat, Scorpion knew instantly he'd made a serious mistake.

'The question too difficult, Scorpion?'

Before he could reply, David Naami went on. 'Guessing and pretending are not words with which I'm familiar. Now listen to me very carefully. If you have any aspirations as to inheriting the mantle of leadership after my days, and don't bother denying it, I know only too well you have, then in future I suggest you take a more professional approach to your affairs. Am I making myself perfectly clear?'

When he was finally able to answer, Scorpion managed to utter a hurried 'yes'. Thanks to his fear, what came out was little more than a squeak. Listening to it he was ashamed of himself and felt humiliated, realising of course it was exactly the reaction David Naami had been aiming for.

'Good! Now that we have cleared that little matter up, please continue with what you were saying about the preparations you've made.'

Recovering a little of his poise, Scorpion hurried on. 'The person who gave me the information seemed to be the caretaker of the exhibition. From the little I gleaned he appeared to be of limited intelligence; in fact he sounded like a boring old fart.'

Lifting his hand and stopping him before he could say another word, David Naami said, 'There you go again, "seemed to be", and "appeared to be"… These are not expressions I want associated with my empire. For the sake of argument, let's just say this boring old fart, as you like to describe him, is not as simple as your suppose. Remember, academics rarely are. If he isn't, then as soon as you got off the phone he would have been making discreet enquiries to make sure your credentials were bona fide. Then what? I'll tell you what; he would smell a rat and double or even triple security arrangements, making it next to impossible for even us to steal the chalice. If that's the case, we are, I'm sorry I'll correct that, *you* are in shit creek.' Mirthlessly, he smiled the grin of a predatory animal before adding, 'Let's hope for your sake you're correct in your assumption about the caretaker.'

'Hello, Ian, Jared Hunter here.'

'Hunter, you old bastard! How are you finding things since you left us? Bored shitless by now, I shouldn't wonder. Anything going down at the moment?' Then he chuckled and said, 'Of course there is, that's why you're phoning, isn't it?'

'I'm afraid so, mate, I need a favour.'

'Anything, just ask and it's yours.'

When he read out the list, the voice on the other end said, 'Bloody hell, what are you going to do with that little lot? You thinking of breaking into Fort Knox or something? Or perhaps, knowing you, start a one-man war? Not that it matters; either way you'll have too much stuff.'

Chuckling, Jared said, 'Actually, Ian, it's a bit of both.'

Formal, now he could sense Jared was in trouble, Ian said, 'In that case you might need a little help, sir. What I mean is, I could rustle up a few of the boys if you wanted.'

'Not that I'm not grateful for the offer, Ian, normally I'd jump at it, but I'm afraid this job is personal.'

'Ah,' came back the voice, 'get your drift. If that's the case then all I can say is God help whoever's upset you. Wouldn't be in their shoes for love or money. Excuse my saying so, sir, but you can be a ruthless bastard when you put your mind to it. Incidentally, are you all right for firepower?'

'Fine, Ian, thanks, it's all taken care of. I brought my own stuff with me when I finished; but the other specialist equipment, well, that could only be acquired, for want of a better word, through other channels… and that's when you came to mind.'

'What about your little pets? Still as sharp as ever, I suppose?'

'Like a razor,' came the reply, 'both of them, and if things work out the way I envisage, their due to see some action in the near future.'

The way it was said made even a battle hardened veteran like Ian Cranfield's skin crawl. 'How soon do you want the consignment, sir? It's just that as most of it is specialist stuff, difficult to get hold of, it might take a bit of time. How does two or three months sound?'

'That would be fine, Ian. I guessed there would be a delay, so I made sure to contact you early. Where and when do you suggest we make the drop?'

'The transport café outside Newport, but I'll phone you a day or two before to confirm the time. I'll leave the boot of the old car unlocked; by the way it's still the same one, the red Honda. The stuff will be in a black Adidas training bag, a big bugger to accommodate your little shopping list. You can keep an eye open for me through the restaurant window. As soon as I know you've seen me, I'll nip to the bogs, freshen up and all that, so you'll have plenty of time to help yourself.'

'Thanks, Ian, I appreciate it… I owe you one.'

'You owe me nothing, sir. Remember, if it wasn't for you, I wouldn't be here now, nor a few of the other lads,' he added with feeling. 'We haven't forgotten that and never will.'

'As the officer in charge it was my duty,' said Jared, clearly embarrassed.

'Come off it, sir, it was far more than that! You risked your life for us. That was way beyond the call of duty, believe me.' And with that the phone went dead.

The placards were professionally done, each one displaying in graphic detail the kind of evil transactions Chameleon Enterprises dealt in. The largest, however, was dedicated to proclaiming David Naami as the Antichrist.

Easing his way through the crowds at the extremity of the small park, the old guardian couldn't help but feel it was an oasis of green in what was otherwise a built-up area of high-rise buildings. Glancing around him in curiosity, he saw several groups of students either standing around aimlessly or conversely, he thought, deep in discussion about how to get the country back on its feet. Apart from the students, there was the odd jogger. Resplendent in their brightly coloured tracksuits, complete with advertising logos, they were declaring to the world the fact that they were serious athletes and not simply out for a gentle stroll. He noted in amusement how each of them had the obligatory Ipods, complete with earphones growing from the side of their heads. They looked remarkably like they had some strange kind of physical deformity, he thought. The volume, no doubt turned up to maximum, was intended to alleviate the tedium of straight-line running. These, he could tolerate; what really irritated him were the people walking their dogs. Despite the signs displayed prominently at either end of the park – the ones which warned of large fines for animals fouling the pathways – almost every owner he had come across either ignored them completely or pretended the signs were invisible.

Within several hundred yards more, he moved into a complex of alleys leading towards the area of the Bay itself. During the last few years, this area of Cardiff had become very popular, due to a mixture of modern architecture and the popularity of television series such as Torchwood and Doctor Who. As a result, the Bay – in an attempt to move with the times and cater for tourism – had set out to promote a continental flavour to proceedings. And in the old guardian's mind, they had succeeded. Chrome tables dotted everywhere, adorned with brightly coloured tablecloths, only added to the effect, he thought.

On either side of the street was an array of small shops, interspersed here and there by cafés and restaurants. The street itself was fairly narrow – wide enough for a single vehicle to traverse, it made it difficult for cars, but infinitely easier for pedestrians, which he supposed was what the designer had in mind. To add to the Mediterranean flavour, the wide pavements on either side were cobbled, while at intervals stood wooden boxes displaying a wide variety of flowers, several startling in their diversity. Occasionally a bicycle could be seen propped up against steel railings painted black and topped by gold. 'Resting' was the old guardian's immediate thought, until closer inspection revealed the truth: each one was padlocked to the railings by means of heavy-duty chains.

With that, he suddenly felt like a cup of coffee. Making his way towards a specific café, he decided against sitting outside. So, opening the glass-fronted door, he made his way inside and headed immediately for a small table near the large window.

Ordering a cappuccino from the waiter, who'd appeared from nowhere, the shrill tone of a mobile phone cut through the gentle hum of noise in the café. Not owning one, the old guardian watched in amusement as everyone dived into handbags or jacket pockets, looking for theirs. It was a comical moment, which ended when the owner held up the offending object in triumph. Moments later, the guardian's coffee arrived and he began to relax. The hard work put in over the last few weeks was about to pay off.

Watching from the safety of the café overlooking the entrance to the building, the old man was pleased. The two huge lawns that fronted the building were by now covered with hundreds of waving and shouting protestors. Surprising what a little money spread in the right place can do, he thought to himself. He was particularly pleased with the ones which quoted relevant passages from the Book of Revelation, but in particular the one proclaiming David Naami as the head of the beast. On second thoughts, knowing how arrogant the bastard was, the protests he'd been organising lately might have had the opposite effect. He might well have seen them as a compliment. In that case they would have helped fuel his megalomania even more.

As it happened he couldn't have been more wrong.

Looking down from the safety of his vantage point on the fifth floor, David Naami pounded his fist against the wall in frustration. Scowling at Scorpion, who'd made him aware of the fiasco taking place below, he said, 'That's the third fucking time this month! And before you say anything, I know who's behind it all. The old bastard may be over seventy, but he's becoming a royal pain in the arse. Apart from organising that fucking lot down there,' he said, pointing through the window, 'his tip-offs have cost us dearly in America. Two shipments of arms in the last two years might not sound a lot, and in monetary terms it isn't, in fact for us it's a drop in the ocean. No, what I'm concerned about is the loss of face. We can't be seen to have any weaknesses; otherwise…' the rest of the sentence was unfinished.

Turning to Scorpion, he said, 'You of all people know how important it is that we be seen to be strong, better than our competitors, especially in this day and age. There are so many waiting in the wings, even Gregor. At the moment he's a friend and ally, but as you know, in this business that could change in an instant.'

Lost in thought for a moment, he suddenly came to a decision. 'Take some of the hired help and find out who the ringleaders are. Once you're sure, get rid of them discreetly.' Holding his finger in the air to emphasise his point, he said, 'Take note the use of the term *discreetly*. The last thing we want is to draw attention to ourselves; it seems we're in the habit of doing that far too easily these days, and it's got to stop. I hope I make my meaning clear?'

'Perfectly, Number One, it will be taken care off immediately.' About to walk away, Scorpion suddenly stopped, and turning his head said, 'I've just had an idea about how it could be done.'

Rubbing his hand over his face, David Naami said, 'Why does that expression suddenly fill with me trepidation?' He added, 'I don't want to know the details, just sort it out, and the quicker the better.'

For once Scorpion was true to his word, and a week later three of those who had organised the rally were found dead. One had fallen from the roof of a multi-storey car park; one had been the victim of a mysterious hit-and-run, while the third had died of a heart attack.

Had the pathologist bothered to check properly, he would have found the heart attack had been chemically induced. Although the police had their suspicions, no incriminating evidence was ever found, and so that was the end of things.

The strategy seemed to work. Shortly afterwards, the demonstrations stopped as abruptly as they'd begun.

David Naami's life was about sending messages, about making statements, and according to his way of thinking he'd just made another.

Chapter Eighteen

SEVERAL DAYS LATER, JARED FOUND HIMSELF WALKING UP THE STEEP hill between his grandmother's home to the small house in which old Eric Roberts lived. Unlike the leaders of churches in the area, who tended to live in large purpose-built vicarages funded by their diocese, the ministers of small chapels usually had to make do with much less lavish accommodation. This was certainly the case as far as Carmel was concerned.

Knocking on the door, Jared experienced a moment of panic. What if the old minister had moved? Silently cursing his stupidity, he realised he should have checked first. With that a more worrying thought crossed his mind: was he even still alive? Before such a disastrous idea had time to germinate, a shadow appeared through the glass panel which formed the central part of the old wooden front door.

With that it creaked open slowly.

Knowing by now that his primary fear was probably groundless, another crept into his subconscious. Would the man opening the door be small and frail, a shadow of his former self? Instantly he was reassured. Not only was old Eric still very much alive, but apparently fighting fit. In the few seconds before he was recognised, Jared's hurried appraisal of his old mentor showed that apart from the fact his hair was now almost totally white, he hadn't seemed to have aged a day.

While Jared had been studying Eric, he'd been aware he too had been given the once-over. The old minister's clear intelligent eyes held the sparkle and piercing gaze of a much younger man. The old spirit still burnt as brightly as ever, was Jared's immediate reaction, a thought that brought him a great deal of pleasure. Until that moment he hadn't appreciated just how much he'd missed the old man.

As they stood there staring at each other, it was Eric who broke the silence. 'Well, well, what have we here, then? Young Master Hunter, if I'm not mistaken,' he said, before breaking into a huge grin.

'Mr Roberts,' replied Jared, 'without your dog collar you look more like a university professor than a clergyman. But then, considering your qualifications, you're eminently more suited to that kind of role, aren't you?'

'Ah, been talking to someone, have we? If I was allowed three guesses, the first, second and third would be that it was your Uncle Edwin.' Then he began laughing out loud.

The pleasure of seeing Jared after all this time was only too evident in the old minister's eyes; they seemed to glow with some inner strength. Then in a quite unexpected show of affection he caught hold of Jared and hugged him.

Suddenly embarrassed, he stepped back and held Jared at arm's length, at the same time looking deeply into his eyes. Yes, by God, but it was good to see him again. For several moments more he studied Jared then, suddenly remembering where they were, he beckoned him inside and closed the door.

Leading Jared through the narrow hallway and into the small living room, he waved him over to a battered armchair perched in one corner of the room. 'Just throw those files onto the floor,' he said, 'while I make us both cup of tea.'

Not taking his instructions at face value, Jared carefully removed the offending articles and placed them on the floor before sitting down. The armchair although well worn, was surprisingly comfortable.

Before Eric had reached the door he suddenly stopped and exclaimed, 'Late 1999 – yes, that's it, that's the last time I clapped eyes on you. A few days after the funeral,' he added in a more serious tone.

Seeing the astonishment on Jared's face, he said, 'Don't look so surprised! I may be old but I'm not bloody senile – not yet, anyway,' he chuckled. 'Besides it's not every day your favourite student, and brightest pupil I may add, drops off the face of the earth. Bit harsh on Emma, mind you.' He was about to say something else when he saw the dark cloud pass over Jared's eyes and immediately decided to change the subject. 'Anyway, where was I? Oh, yes, just about to make us a cup of tea. Like anything with it?' Holding his hand up he said, 'I know, it's early in the day, but humour an old man. Keeps me going, you see. My grandfather once told me only a fool drinks the old amber nectar before the age of sixty, and it's a fool who doesn't afterwards. Thins the blood, apparently. It's supposed to help the old arteries clogged by all those years of eating fatty foods. Cholesterol, they call it now. Bullshit if you ask me. Look at all the fat our ancestors ate – everything was dripping with it. What's more, they didn't have fridges and freezers or any of those kind of fancy things. No sell-by dates either, remember. All they had were cold rooms or pantries, as we called them.'

It was at times like this that Eric's North Walian accent came to the fore, and Jared was impressed how it had altered very little, despite the fact he'd been living in the South for over thirty years.

Not done yet, he said, 'Nature told the old folk when food had gone bad. If it had maggots it was ready to be thrown out, but even then if you were poor enough you tried to recover the best bits. Nothing was left to waste. I'm more inclined to believe the problem with our present diet is caused by all the bloody additives the manufacturers are putting in.'

Thinking about it, Jared found it very difficult to fault the logic behind Eric's comments.

Walking over to the old mahogany cabinet in the corner, Eric opened the top and lifted out a decanter of what appeared to be malt whisky. Jared's suspicions were confirmed when, holding it up, he said, 'Isle of Jura, fifteen years old,' before taking out the stopper and pouring a generous measure into his cup of tea.

Looking up he said, 'I should buy Welsh whisky, really, shouldn't I? Keep the local economy ticking over, and all that. But you can't beat the Scotch or Scottish as they like to be referred to when it comes to this stuff. Had a real telling-off from a Scotsman years ago when I referred to him as "Scotch" – said quite curtly that Scotch was the name of a drink.'

Replacing the stopper, Eric put the decanter back in the cabinet and closed the lid before picking up Jared's cup and carrying it over to his guest. When they were both comfortable, he took a sip of the tea and sighed in pleasure as he savoured the flavour. Within a few moments he felt the liquid trickling down his throat, before the warm glow spread slowly through his body.

When he was ready he looked over at Jared before saying, 'True whisky drinkers would say that adding it to a cup of tea was blasphemy, especially something as good as single malt. To them the only thing you add to a malt is either water or ice.' Smiling wickedly, he added, 'That's the way I like it, of course, but only after nine in the evening. 'Now then, my boy, don't think I'm not grateful to see you. You've no idea how much pleasure it gives me; but something tells me this isn't just a social call, is it?'

Jared's startled expression told him immediately his guess had been right.

Holding his hand up, he said, 'There I go, being rude again! Why don't you just tell me what you've been up to since you've been away, and then we'll take it from there,' before adding, 'and it had better be good, considering I haven't heard a thing from you during all that time.'

Seeing he was having difficulty in beginning, he reached over, put his hand over Jared's and said, 'Listen, lad, it's obvious something's bothering you. Remember I've had a little experience in such things, being a minister and all.' Carrying on, he said, 'There's something weighing heavily on your conscience, isn't there? Take my advice and get it off your chest or it will fester like a boil and then God knows what damage it might do in the long term. It's a psychological thing, you see. Besides, I'm not here to judge, just to listen and offer some advice if I can.'

With that Jared unburdened himself.

He told the old minister everything, but in particular how he'd become a professional assassin.

'The problem is I feel no remorse, and as a human being I should. Otherwise, Eric, I'm no better than an animal. So why don't I feel ashamed of what I've done, what I've become? Surely to God I should feel sorry for those I've killed, but I don't, and that can't be right. It's almost as if I've been dehumanised in some way.'

Thoughtful for a moment, the old man said, 'Jared, there are many types of evil in this world and sometimes it needs people like you, people with your brand of expertise, to clean up. Put it another way, those you terminated deserved it; besides, if you hadn't they would probably have taken many more innocent lives. Remember, lad, it's a cruel world, and looking at it from that point of view, someone has to do the dirty work. At the time, that person just happened to be you.'

Thinking about it from that perspective, Jared knew the old minister was right, he'd done what was necessary. Suddenly he felt a great weight lift from his shoulders and he felt better than he had for some considerable time. Encouraged by Eric's wisdom and understanding he went on to describe what had happened in the chapel that fateful Sunday evening and the part he'd played in it. Finally he explained how, because of a complete accident, his worst fears had been confirmed.

When he'd finished Eric didn't say a word for several moments. When he finally spoke, what he said was the last words on earth Jared thought he'd hear.

'So there was a room after all.'

The astonishment on Jared's face was transparent, and seeing it, Eric went on to explain what had happened to him all those years ago.

'It was incredible,' said Eric. 'I was minding my own business in the vestry of the chapel when suddenly there he was. Dressed from head to foot in black, he appeared from nowhere. It was like being attacked by a ghost.'

'So what happened?'

'He tied me to one of the chairs and before I knew it I was being grilled about some secret room. Told me there was no point in lying, as the tombstone proved the chalice was nearby. To be honest I thought he was crazy, but at the time I was so terrified I would have said anything to keep him happy. The interrogation seemed to go on for ages, and all the while he held this razor sharp dagger to my throat. Every time he touched me it drew blood. It didn't cause any real damage, except psychologically, which was probably what the bugger wanted, of course. In the end I must have convinced him I knew nothing, because eventually he cut me loose – but not before warning me that should I utter a word of what had taken place to anyone, especially the police, he would return and finish the job. The way he said it sent a chill down my spine. He never raised his voice, no cheap dramatics or anything like that, just the warning. I'm not one to frighten easily, but I can tell you one thing, he bloody meant it. And with that he disappeared. The strange thing was I could have sworn I knew him. There was something about the eyes. To this day I've never told anyone about the experience – until now, that is, and of course now it doesn't really matter, does it?'

'That's why it was never reported in the newspapers, then?' said Jared.

'Precisely,' said Eric. 'They would have had a field day with a story like that. Funnily enough, I searched every inch of the old building afterwards, convinced by now there really was something to the man's story. But I didn't find a trace of any secret room.'

'I'm not surprised,' said Jared. 'Even though we knew where to look, it still took us ten minutes to find it.'

'What puzzles me,' said Eric, 'is just how the evil spirit you conjured up knew of its existence. Remember, until the accident, besides you lot, no one had any idea the room was there.' After a brief pause he said, 'Have you told anyone else about this?'

'Edwin and I discussed it a few days ago, but apart from the others who were there at the time of course, no. The amazing thing is, just like you, Edwin believed me. In all honesty, if the boot had been on the other foot, I'm not sure what my reaction would have been. I would probably have thought you both mad.'

'Did either of you come up with any answers?'

'We talked over the problem for ages. In fact Edwin came up with a few plausible ideas, one of which was that the chalice had been tampered with it. He was convinced something had been removed before the archaeologists had arrived. Incidentally, I've since managed to take a look at it. Roger and I managed to acquire – I think that might be the most delicate way of putting it – the key to the cabinet, and take a few photographs. As soon as I picked it up I knew something was wrong. Apart from the fact it had obviously been opened, it hadn't the same aura of evil it had originally. I'm surmising that's because although the ashes are still intact, the actual evil has long since gone. If my guess is right, then at this very moment it might be busy searching for a suitable host.'

'I agree,' said Eric, 'but what puzzles me is why it hasn't started on its promised killing spree. Might be it isn't ready yet. Perhaps it needs to build its strength up after being imprisoned for so long.'

'That would be my guess too,' said Jared. 'Like a battery needing to recharge itself after a long period of inactivity. If we consider the cryptic messages it seems to be leaving, things like "Getting stronger", everything seems to indicate the entity seems to be working to some kind of timescale. If I'm correct, then we can expect to see some kind of escalation of its demonic powers in the very near future.'

'About the biblical stuff it was quoting,' said Eric, 'you're right, it sounds very much as if it was choosing sections from the Book of Revelation. However, if that's the case, the quotations are curiously inexact. Anyway, to get back to our original point, I take it you were unable to come up with any suggestions as to what the entity might be?'

'I'm afraid you're right. The only possible connection we could see between any of it was Palestine and Christ. They seemed to be like threads running through everything.'

'I can see how you came to that conclusion. The names Barabbas and Kerioth are further pointers that whatever it is originated in or around Palestine. The thing that's bugging me is why it hates the Church so much. It must have a very good reason, that's for sure. If only we knew what it was,' said Eric.

'And its powers are frightening,' was Jared's dejected comment.

'True, but we shouldn't lose sight of the fact they were nullified once, and if that's the case there must be a way of stopping it. We have to cling to the hope, however slim, that if it was defeated once, it can be again.'

'I never looked at it like that,' said Jared, starting to feel more positive about things.

'What about the others, what do they make of it all?'

'They've had enough; they're all for going to the police, telling them the whole story and hoping for the best.'

'What did you say to that?'

'I was brutally honest. I told them exactly what the police would say if we trotted out our little story: that we were either mad, or we were taking something. Either way, we'd have been the laughing stock of the village, our credibility rating zero. What I can't understand is that when it happened the others were as terrified as I was, but the following day they all reacted in different ways. The consensus of opinion was one of disbelief. Denial, if you like. Amazingly they came up with all kinds of stupid theories to convince themselves it had never happened. Mass hypnosis and that kind of thing. They were like bloody ostriches trying to bury their heads in the sand, pretending it had never happened. All except Emma, that is,' Jared added as an afterthought.

'You shouldn't be too hard on them. It's not an unfamiliar response you know. The technical term is called – "Collective Delusion". In layman's language, it means that when you get a group of terrified people together in one place, the mind begins to play tricks on them. They soon begin to doubt the evidence of their own eyes. It's a form of self-denial if you like, and it seems that's what happened to the others.'

'What do you think about the idea of going to the police?' asked Jared 'Do you think we should make a clean breast of things?'

For several moments Eric said nothing. Deep in thought, he seemed to ponder the question carefully before saying, 'No, I'm with you, you've outlined the scenario perfectly. You should hold back until something concrete happens. Then perhaps they'll be forced to take you seriously.'

'Until the thing chooses its first victim and all hell breaks loose, you mean!' said Jared.

'You could put it that way, but I'm not really sure they'll believe you even then. It might take several murders before they're forced to face facts, to accept that what we are up against is something beyond the normal range of human experience.'

For a few moments neither spoke.

Suddenly Eric broke the silence. 'I suppose you want to know if I saw anything when the dozer broke through the floor of the chapel,' he said with a sly grin. 'I dare say among other things it was the real reason for your visit.'

No longer surprised by the depth of the old minister's perception, Jared said sheepishly, 'As a matter of fact, you're absolutely right.'

'To put you out of your misery, I did. I was pottering about in the garden when it happened. Hidden behind the hedge as I was, no one noticed me. But when I heard the deep rumble of the foundations giving way, I was startled, to say the least. Didn't have a clue as to what had actually happened, so I stuck my head over the back gate. It was then I saw them.'

'Saw who?'

'Charlie and Albert.' Chuckling to himself he said, 'But I have to admit I admire the way they set the dozer driver up. It was a work of art.' Still laughing, he carried on.

'The bulldozer was halfway into the hole, hanging there by a thread, when suddenly out comes the driver. He popped out of the cab like a jack-in-the-box. Not that I blame him, mind. Anyway, obviously badly shaken by his narrow escape, he wanders over to Charlie and Albert. I didn't hear what was said, but a few seconds later the driver suddenly jumps over the fence, dives into his works van and disappears down the road in a cloud of dust. I bet I know what happened. I'll wager anything the buggers told the workman to report the accident as quickly as he could because of the insurance and safety implications. Of course, once he'd disappeared, the coast was clear to do a bit of illegal investigation, wasn't it? All this is conjecture on my part, but one thing I am sure of, they found something. Less than ten minutes later they both scampered out of the hole looking decidedly furtive. They weren't carrying anything that I could see; but if what you say is true, whatever they found must have been small enough to carry in their pockets. If you want to find out what was inside the chalice, look no further, they're your men.'

'Might it be possible to take a look at the site? Nip into the hole and look around?' asked Jared.

After thinking for a moment before answering Eric said, 'It's all cordoned off, of course, and from what I hear no one is going to be working there for the foreseeable future. But yes, I suppose you could sneak down after dark. Mind you, I shouldn't have thought there would be much to see after those archaeologists had finished pottering around.'

'I appreciate that, but you never know, they might have missed something,' said Jared thoughtfully, before adding, 'it's just we seem to have so little to go on.'

'True,' said Eric, 'but don't despair, between us we should be able to come up with something.' With that he had an idea. 'Could the three of us to get together sometime? You, me and Edwin, I mean... pool our resources?'

'I'm sure it can be arranged, and from where I'm standing the sooner the better,' said Jared. 'Incidentally, Edwin tells me you might have something that could shed some light on our problem.'

Seeing his puzzled expression, Jared said, 'The Knights Templar and the Cathar heresy, I mean.'

Realisation flooded in, and Eric replied, 'Of course,' annoyed he hadn't thought of it sooner. 'From what's cropped up so far, there does seem to be a kind of tentative link between the two, but I'm afraid I'm too close to the problem. What it needs is a new perspective, a fresh pair of eyes, if you like.' Looking up and smiling, he said, 'Just like yours. How much do you know about the topic, anyway?'

'Very little, really,' admitted Jared, 'besides the fact that they're supposed to be guardians of the Holy Grail and all that.'

'Ah, the romantic idea of Indiana Jones and the last crusade, you mean. I'm afraid the truth is very different to that. Never mind, I'll soon put you on the right track.' Getting up from the armchair, he said,

'Follow me. Knowing your appetite for mysteries and puzzles, I can safely say you're in for a treat.'

Moving into the parlour, Jared was amazed to see how it had been converted into a library which, in its own little way, was equally as impressive as Edwin's. Three of the four walls were covered from floor to ceiling with books, magazines, old newspapers and the like, while the remaining one boasted several large steel filing cabinets. In the centre of the room, seated on a battered old desk, stood the obligatory computer. What impressed Jared the most was that, despite the amount of material squeezed into such a small space, it still looked neat and tidy. He had no doubt Eric's filing system was immaculate, and that should he need to, he would be able to put his hand on anything he wanted at a moment's notice.

'Sit down,' said Eric, 'while I run something by you. It was the mention of the head that suddenly brought it back to me. I should have made the connection sooner,' he muttered to himself in annoyance.

All business now, he turned abruptly and, facing Jared, said, 'You're sure your uncle said that in order to bring the body back to life the head of Barabbas' brother was decapitated and preserved, while the remainder was burnt? I only ask, because you see the Jews never allowed cremation, they always buried their dead. If what the scroll says is true, it appears we might be dealing with a totally unknown sect within Judaism. Or perhaps a radically new one,' he added as an afterthought. 'From what you mention about this society called the "Sect of the Dead", it would seem the latter may be the case. Anyway it's of no consequence at the moment, so let's move on. Apart from the usual romantic image handed down about the Knights Templar, you say you know very little about them. It's hardly surprising, really; the origins both of them and the Cathars are shrouded in mystery. It took me a lifetime to uncover what I have. To make matters worse, what information I have been able to discover seems to be contradictory. It would take ages to explain, so it's best if I give you what I've found, and then you can read it in your own time.'

A few moments later he broached a subject he was obviously reluctant to talk about.

'I suppose Edwin told you about my fall from grace, about my theories that were a little too left of centre for the Establishment.'

'All he said was your career had taken something of a nosedive since you'd started your research, but that was it.'

Chuckling, Eric said, 'I'm afraid my hypothesis won't make much sense until you're thoroughly acquainted with the background of both the Templars and Cathars, but in particular the role the Albigensian crusade played in shaping both histories.' Choosing a spring-loaded folder from one of the shelves behind him, he placed it in Jared's lap. 'Here's the bedtime reading I promised. After going through that little lot you'll be better able to give an opinion on whether there is a connection, or whether it's simply my imagination. Take note of what it says about a mysterious bearded head called Baphomet. Like your uncle, I'm sure you'll come to the conclusion there's a definite link between that and the one mentioned in the scroll.'

Holding his hand up to forestall any further discussion, he said, 'I know you want to talk about it now – there's a germ of an idea forming, I can see it in your eyes. But I want you to be perfectly au fait with the notes before we carry the idea any further. Besides which,' he said, smiling, 'it's way past my bedtime. What say we meet back here in two or three days' time? That should give you enough time to read and inwardly digest, as the academics say.'

'That suits me fine, Eric, and I'll try my best to get Edwin to join us. He could stay at Gran's, there's plenty of room. Besides, I know she'd love to see him.'

'A splendid idea; I'll leave you to make the arrangements, then.'

Chapter Nineteen

SHORTLY AFTER LEAVING ERIC'S, JARED WAS WALKING THROUGH THE door of his grandmother's. Seeing the light in the hallway, he guessed she'd waited up for him. His suspicions were confirmed when her voice drifted in from the kitchen, 'There's some cold ham in the fridge, love, bought it this morning. I could make you a sandwich or something if you like.' Then as an afterthought she added, 'Not too late for you, is it?'

Walking into the room, he saw her face light up and he was reminded forcibly of just how much pain he'd inflicted on her, disappearing as he had without a trace.

'By the way, where's Grandad? I know he works long hours, spends a lot of time on the road and all that, but I haven't seen him since I've been back. He's not deliberately avoiding me, is he? Not still mad at me? It's only that…'

Before he could finish his grandmother broke in. 'Sit down, love, there's something I've been meaning to tell you for a while, but until now I haven't really found the right moment.' The look on her face told him it was serious, so he found a chair without another word.

Staring at her across the kitchen table, he could see tears forming in her eyes. Getting up quickly, he moved over to her side, placed his arm protectively around her shoulder and said, 'What's up?'

Resting her head against his chest, the story came out in a rush.

'Your grandad up and left me years ago. As a matter of fact, it wasn't long after you disappeared.'

Stunned by what he'd just heard, the guilt he'd been carrying around returned in waves. Until now he'd convinced himself the blow of his departure had been cushioned somewhat by the fact she had Grandad to look after her. Now he hadn't even that crumb of comfort to cling to. In shame, he realised he'd been so preoccupied with his own problems he'd been oblivious to his grandmother's. No wonder she's aged so much, he thought. Suddenly lost for words, all he could think of to say was, 'But why?'

Now the truth was in the open, she felt calmer. Regaining some of her composure, she leaned over and, stroking Jared's hand said, 'Who knows, love? I certainly don't. Mind you, things hadn't been right for a while.'

Waving her hand in the air she said, 'Oh, it was more than just the fact he was hardly ever here; that I could put up with. No, it was something more.'

'You think there was another woman, then?'

'Strange as it seems, I don't think there was. Call it intuition if you like, but I'm sure that wasn't the problem. I can't put my finger on it, but it was something else.

'Don't take this the wrong way, love, but you see your real grandad and me were married young. Oh, I loved the old bugger, still do even after all this time, but even before the accident, the old magic – if you want to call it that – had gone out of our marriage. We were like an ancient couple who had grown old gracefully.'

Looking pensive for a moment, she said, 'Towards the end we were more like friends than anything else, and we shouldn't have been really; after all, we weren't that old.

'Anyway, when he died along came your present grandad, and in a short while he'd swept me off my feet. Made me feel young again. One minute I was contemplating life as a lonely widow and the next, well, it just happened. Thinking back, I'm ashamed now. Your grandad had only been gone a short while… hardly turned cold, some remarked.'

Seeing Jared's shocked expression, she said, 'Oh, it's all right, love, I know what people were saying; it's a small village. The more refined among the gossipers described it as a "whirlwind romance", while the jungle drums were sending out a very different message. "Indecent haste" was the tune they were playing to.'

'So where did it all go wrong?'

'Oh, that's easy to answer. You see there's a big difference between love and infatuation. He was a charmer all right, but as I found to my cost, that doesn't always make the world go round. To be honest,' she added in reflection, 'it might have been the same for him.'

Lost in her own little world for a moment, to Jared she appeared troubled and strangely vulnerable. Deep in thought, she suddenly jerked herself out of her mood of despondency and, blinking in surprise said, 'Where was I? Oh, yes, I remember now, I woke up one morning a few months after you'd left, and he'd gone. He didn't even bother to leave a note. The funny thing is he didn't take a damn thing with him. For a while I left everything as it was, thinking perhaps he'd eventually return for them, but he never did. Finally I dumped everything into a few black bags and took them down to the charity shop.'

Interrupting briefly, Jared said, 'You don't think something might have happened to him, do you? Perhaps he was involved in a fatal accident or something.'

'It did cross my mind, love, but there was never a report of any such thing, either on the local or national news, so after a while I dismissed the theory. What struck me as even more strange was that he never came back to claim half the house. He'd have been entitled to, you know. Anyway, let's forget about it. I've finally managed to get it off my chest, so as far as I'm concerned it's water under the bridge.'

Seeing she really did look as if telling him had lifted a weight off her shoulders, he stood up.

'If you don't mind, Gran, I'm going to climb the wooden hill; I've got some bedtime reading to get through.' He indicated the ring folder he'd picked up from the coffee table on which he'd placed it earlier. 'I wouldn't mind a few ham sandwiches and a cup of coffee, if you're still offering, though. Between you and me, I think it's going to be a long night.'

About to turn away, his grandmother put her hand on his arm and said quietly, 'I want you to know, if it wasn't for Emma, I wouldn't have made it. She called to see me almost every day for the first year, and even now she still calls in several times a week to check up.'

'That's odd,' said Jared, 'since I've been home she's never once called.'

Looking at the floor, his grandmother said, 'It's no coincidence, love; since your return she's stopped coming.'

The silence seemed to drag on for an eternity until suddenly she seemed to perk up.

'By the way, have you seen little Jodie? She's a real little beauty.'

'Yes, she's gorgeous,' said Jared. 'The spitting image of Emma at that age,' he added, before realising what he'd said and tapering off lamely.

'Ah, so you're at least on talking terms again.' She was unable to hide the relief in her voice. 'You know, love, when she phoned that night she was almost hysterical. It was ages before I could get any sense out of her. Said there had been a terrible misunderstanding, that you'd got hold of the wrong end of the stick. And then of course we all know what happened after that. Don't you think it was cruel, love? For a while I was worried about her. She's such a sensitive girl, you see, always puts everyone else's needs before her own. Sees the best in everyone too.' She paused before adding, 'do you know I've never heard her say a bad word about anyone, and that's a rare thing in Raven's Hill, believe me. Bringing Jodie up on her own has been very hard, but despite everything life has thrown at her, nothing's too much trouble. Yes,' she said with feeling, 'she's an incredible girl. You know she had to give up her teaching post, don't you? She flatly refused to throw the burden of bringing up a small child onto her parents. She said Jodie was her responsibility and no one else's.' Suddenly she noticed the look on Jared's face and fell silent.

The words were out before Jared could do anything about it. 'Didn't take her long to find someone else, though, did it?'

The bitterness in Jared's voice took his grandmother by surprise.

Ashamed of his outburst, he went suddenly quiet, before adding. 'Would you like to know the truth about what happened that night? Apart from Edwin, I've told no one else.'

A silent nod was all his grandmother could muster.

For the next few moments she listened intently without interrupting as he related the story.

When he'd finished she was so shocked all she could say was, 'Are you sure, love? Couldn't you have got your wires crossed somehow?'

Looking at his grandmother quizzically, he said, 'Strangely, that's what Uncle Edwin said. You two haven't been talking about this, have you?'

Despite the seriousness of the situation, she suddenly burst out laughing. 'No, love, I can assure you it's nothing like that; it's just that old fogies like us are wise enough to know that things aren't always what they seem.'

'Take it from me, Gran, there was no misunderstanding,' said Jared in a mildly deceptive tone that brooked no argument. It was clear the matter was at an end. Desperate to change the subject, he said, 'What about Jodie's father, then? What do you know about him?'

'It's funny you should mention that; no one seems to know. To the best of my knowledge no one ever saw the bugger. As soon as the baby was born, he seems to have jumped ship, so to speak.' Sensing Jared wanted to leave matters there, that old wounds were too close to the surface for comfort, she said, 'Away with you, and I'll bring your coffee and sandwiches up as soon as I've made them.'

Propped up in bed some time later, the file held in two hands, Jared began reading.

He was immediately impressed by the welter of research material Eric had managed to produce. The amount of time and effort which had gone into the project was phenomenal. From the outset it was obvious that Eric was an intuitive and methodical researcher.

Looking at the tomes of literature before him he had a sudden thought. Sifting through such a welter of material might prove to be a laborious and gruelling task. Within moments his fears were allayed as he saw that for ease of reference Eric had cleverly used a system of bullet points. Not only that, but every so often he'd evaluated the facts by adding a comment or two of his own.

Before starting to read, Jared reminded himself exactly what he was hoping to achieve. The first thing he was looking for was evidence of a link between the spirit, the chalice and the mysterious head mentioned in the scroll.

Secondly, he was looking for a plausible connection between it and some of the things Eric had unearthed in his research; a link that both Edwin and Eric were convinced existed. As a consequence, Jared knew that once he'd studied the notes properly, he would be in a better position to deliver an honest verdict.

Settling down, the first thing that caught his attention was how Eric had divided the information into two specific categories:

(a) The Knights Templar
(b) The Cathars

Afterwards, he'd cleverly interwoven the background to the Albigensian crusade into the history of both.

The first surprise came in the first paragraph. It appeared that there was another side to the Templars, one which was very different to the side the public had come to know and love.

Eric had painstakingly delved beneath the age-old veneer of the romantic tradition, which portrayed them as honourable and brave defenders of Christendom, and uncovered something extremely unsettling. If it were true, they appeared to have dabbled in all kinds of esoteric practices. Claiming to be recipients of deep mystical knowledge, one aspect in particular caught Jared's attention. Riveted, he noted how they were described as being exceptionally skilful adepts of the Cabala. The recent conversation he'd had with Edwin suddenly sprang to mind. With mounting excitement, he realised he'd hardly scratched the surface of the files, yet he'd already uncovered one link.

Reading further, he saw how they were described as an ultra-secret society. Then he came across something he couldn't quite believe. If he hadn't known Eric was so meticulous, he would have sworn that what he was reading was a mistake. It defied logic, was Jared's initial response, too bizarre to be true. But there it was, according to the notes, the Knights Templar had been accused of not only repudiating Christ, but of trampling and spitting on the cross.

The further he read, the more amazed he became.

At one time they'd not only been necromancers, but had been accused of being both satanists and devil worshippers. Stunned, Jared learnt they'd dabbled in all kinds of obscene and heretical rituals.

The next few snippets of information were basically historical. In the main they dealt with names and dates with which Jared was totally unfamiliar. As usual however, Eric had followed each with a comment of his own.

- Guillame De Tyre, first known authority on the Knights Templar. Compiled information between 1175 and 1185.

  Comment: Written at peak of crusades, but oddly the Templars had been in existence for more that fifty years already. Why such a gap?

  Problem: He was writing about events from a second or even third-hand perspective. As such the information should be treated with caution at the very best. More disturbingly, it appeared that recently some of his accounts had proven to be incorrect.

According to De Tyre, the order was founded in 1118, but astonishingly they were only nine in number.

Comment: How could so few have possibly kept the roads and highways safe for pilgrims visiting the Holy Land? Especially considering it was supposed to be the justification for their existence!

- Once established they'd been awarded an entire wing of the Royal Palace in Jerusalem as their living quarters. Curiously, the dormitories had been built over the foundations of the ancient Temple of Solomon. The ground beneath the wing had eventually been used as the stables for the order.

  Comment: Lavish accommodation for an order that purported to the vow of poverty?

  Problem: Although there was mention of an established historian at this particular time, he seems to have written nothing about the order during these early years. If so why?

Thoughtful now, Jared wondered if the reason might be the Templars were not as noble as historians would have us believe. If so, might the other side of the Templar myth be nearer the truth?

Reading on, he saw that whichever of the scenarios was the most likely, one thing was sure: within ten years the Templars were famous throughout the length and breadth of Christendom.

- By 1127 most of the original nine had returned home in triumph, apparently to a hero's welcome.
- January 1128, a year later, and the Church had officially recognised the organisation. It was described as a military order. Hugues de Payen was officially nominated as the original founder and given the title Grand Master.

  Comment: Soldier mystics, martial zeal tantamount to fanaticism. Storm troopers for Christ, where was all this heading?

At this point Jared suddenly noticed an innocuous remark, one which was later to provide the soil for a germ of an idea. For some reason the Templars were forbidden to cut their beards. It caught Jared's eye for the simple reason it went against all the known fashion trends of the time.

Why, thought Jared, half guessing at the answer, should they conform to such a strange rule, knowing almost everyone else in those days was clean shaven?

- 1139, and a Papal decree was issued declaring that from now on the Templars would owe allegiance to no one but the Pope!

Jared didn't need Eric's comments to appreciate just how dangerous a situation was emerging. Effectively, it meant the order was now a law unto itself. As a result the next piece of information didn't come as much of a surprise. Within a very short time the order had expanded beyond belief and in the process become extremely wealthy.

- 1146. The splayed cross (Cross Pâté) was added to the mantle to become their by now famous symbol.
- 1146–1246. The order spread beyond the boundaries of Christendom and established links with the Muslim world. It struck up secret connections with the Muslim Hashishim or Assassins, Islam's equivalent of the Templars themselves. Odd?

  Comment: Increasing power and wealth led to complacency, and to cries of arrogance, bullying and corruption – not surprising!

Well, well, thought Jared, as yet another piece of the jigsaw fell into place.

- Shortly afterwards the situation in the Holy Land becomes untenable as almost the whole of Palestine comes under Muslim control. Templars move out and set up their headquarters in Cyprus.
- 1306. Things begin to turn sour for the Templars in Europe, but particularly in France, where the reigning monarch was becoming increasingly afraid of them. Strangely, he found an ally in the Pope, who by now had grown tired of the order's power and arrogance. Between them they plotted as to how they could rid themselves of the problem.
- 1307. 13 October, and the plot is hatched. It involved the seizing and confiscation of the Templars' immense wealth. The plot was a success and most of the order was wiped out. However, the treasure disappeared and was never seen again.

  Comment: Sources record how the plot was never a complete success, that for various reasons some of the Templars managed to escape. Interestingly, under torture, several confessed to worshipping a devil called Baphomet.

Suddenly Jared sat bolt upright.

This was it – the link hinted at by both Edwin and Eric.

It seemed that worship of Baphomet involved prostrating themselves before a bearded male head while dressed in ritual attire. When asked why they resorted to such sacrilege, the knights claimed the head gave them strange occult powers. At last, thought Jared, it was all beginning to make some kind of perverse sense.

Ploughing on feverishly, he hit upon another incidence of the strange comment he'd noticed earlier. Supposedly, during the ritual worship of the head, the Templars denied Christ and symbolically trampled and spat on the cross.

It made no more sense now than the first time he'd read it.

The realisation, when it came was sudden and bright, as if a firework had gone off in his head. Stunned, he knew now why the order displayed such a distinctive symbol on their ritual attire, knew too why they spat on the cross. As it happened he was only half correct. It would be several months before he would eventually discover the whole horrifying truth, a truth which in his wildest dreams he could never have imagined.

- By 1312 the order of the Knights Templar was officially dissolved. Later, in 1314, Jacques de Molay, Grand Master, and Geoffrey de Charnay were roasted to death and according to official records the order ceased to exist.

Smiling, Jared thought, how the mighty fall, before realising it was exactly what they wanted everyone to believe. Both de Molay and de Charnay had served their purpose.

By the time of their deaths the organisation had outgrown its usefulness. It was time for the chameleon to change colour again, thought Jared ruefully, to don the cloak of invisibility once more.

By now he was convinced of one thing: somewhere amid Eric's notes he would find the evidence he'd been searching for; the proof that behind both the traditional and more esoteric facade of the Templars lay a third, even more secretive, arm. More radical than either of those presented by traditional historians, it had been spawned by the survivors of Masada.

There was far more on the Templars in the file, but for now Jared decided he'd seen enough. If he needed further details on any of the points he'd filed away mentally, he knew he could easily retrace his steps. So, turning to the information on the Cathars, he read on. Almost immediately one thing became apparent. Like the Templars, documentary evidence about their origin was extremely vague; their beginnings were shrouded in mystery and intrigue. Interestingly, both groups seemed to have stepped onto the stage of history at roughly the same time.

- The Cathars established themselves in the north-eastern foothills of southern France in a mountainous area north of the Pyrenees in the Languedoc. An ancient organisation, they seemed to have arrived on the scene at the advent of Christianity. Strangely, at the beginning of the thirteenth century, the area in which they'd put down roots was not officially part of France, in fact it was an independent principality. In terms of language, culture and political organisation it had more in common with Spain than France, being ruled by a handful of noble families.

  Comment: Learning was highly prized. Philosophy and other intellectual activities flourished. Greek, Arabic and in particular Hebrew was highly prized. The Cabala was studied along with other esoteric Jewish traditions.

There it was again thought Jared, this mysterious link to Judaism and the Cabala.

Quite unexpectedly, it appeared there was not only a link with the Templars, but with the Cathars as well. Eric had underlined the last few sentences in red, so, like Jared, had obviously thought the comments important.

- During this time the Church in Rome was notorious for corruption and held in low esteem by the ordinary people. They saw their religious leaders as intent only on feathering their own nests. After centuries of complacency and abuse, alarm bells began ringing when the people in the area of the Languedoc began to turn their backs on the Church. In droves they suddenly pledged their allegiance to a strange new false teaching sweeping the country. By the twelfth century this heresy, called Catharism, had taken hold so strongly that it threatened to completely overrun the Roman Catholic Church.
- The followers of this mysterious sect were given several different names, but in the main were referred to as either Cathars or Albigensians.

- They were not a single cohesive unit, but instead were made up of several different sects, many under the influence of a single and charismatic leader.
- Through the centuries, persistent rumours kept surfacing about certain strange rituals. A cryptic reference to the head again?
- The Cathars were reputed to be extremely wealthy. Much appears to have come from legitimate sources.

The next point made Jared's pulse quicken. During the Albigensian crusade there were strong rumours of a mythical treasure, one that seemed to go beyond mere material wealth, one that was reputedly kept in the fortress of Montségur.

The more Jared read, the more he was struck by how much the Templars and Cathars had in common. Eric's research showed clearly that underneath the surface there were definite points of contact. At times a single thread could be seen running through both organisations. However, at the heart of the matter was the fact that both groups seemed to have possessed an ultra-radical or zealot arm, which was the repository of its deepest secrets.

Was it possible? Jared thought to himself, knowing that if it was, it would help explain everything. What if the Cathars were not only linked to the Templars but had originated from the same initial source as them during or around the time of Christ? What if there was a common denominator? If so, then Jared knew exactly what it was.

Looking at his watch, he was amazed to see it was nearly 2 a.m. He'd been reading for the best part of two hours. After what he'd discovered, his head was spinning. If he was correct he knew for certain that his long held hypothesis was right. The Sicarii had not only survived Masada, but over the centuries had adapted and evolved several times… until, against all the odds, they'd become Chameleon Enterprises.

Chapter Twenty

AT ROUGHLY THE SAME TIME AS JARED HAD STARTED ON ERIC'S FILES, Emma was putting Jodie to bed. Normally, after listening to one of her favourite stories from the Welsh version of *Fireman Sam*, she'd be exhausted enough to drop off quickly. Tonight for some reason she was restless. Knowing instinctively something was bothering her, Emma said, 'OK, young lady, spit it out, what's troubling you?'

Sitting upright in bed, her teddy bear tucked under one arm, Jodie said suddenly, 'Why haven't I got a daddy like all the others in my class, Mammy? Is he dead? Is that why we never see him?'

Emma went cold. She knew one day she'd have to confront the problem, but hadn't dreamt the situation would come to a head this early.

'What on earth makes you say that, princess?'

'Well, the other girls have been teasing me. They say everyone has a father. If they all have, why haven't I? The only thing I could think of, was that perhaps my daddy was dead, gone to heaven or something. Oh, you know,' she said in exasperation, 'that place where everyone goes when they die.'

If the situation hadn't been so serious, Emma would have burst out laughing. She was having a conversation about death with a little girl who had only just turned six years of age. Wondering how to put it, she decided to throw caution to the wind. 'Well, young lady, you can tell those silly little girls in your class your daddy isn't dead. He just doesn't live with us any more, that's all.'

'But if he's not dead, then why doesn't he live with us? Doesn't he love us any more?'

Realising this was going to be far more difficult than she'd first thought, Emma wracked her brain furiously. 'It's because he doesn't live in this country anymore, princess. He had to move overseas. It was his job, you see, he had to go. It wasn't that he didn't love us or anything.'

In a flash Jodie chirped up, 'Why didn't he take us with him, then?'

By now Emma could see the way her little daughter's mind was working, and so she had her answer ready.

'It was too dangerous, baby. You see, where he was going they were fighting all the time. He didn't think it would be a safe place to take us... didn't want us hurt, you see.'

'There was a war going on, you mean?'

'Yes, that's it exactly,' said Emma.

'So it wasn't because he didn't love us, then?'

'Of course not, he loved us very much, especially you. He was just thinking about our safety, that's all.' She hated lying to her daughter, but it was infinitely less dangerous than telling her the truth. Jodie was a remarkable young girl, mature and incredibly intelligent considering how young she was. 'Wise beyond her age' was how her teachers described her.

Then suddenly, completely out of the blue, she changed the subject. It was as if she'd accepted the lie and decided to move on.

'Who was that nice man we spoke to the other day, Mammy? I know you like him because I was watching you. He liked you too, I could tell.' She paused. 'Are you good friends?'

For the second time in as many minutes Emma went suddenly cold. This too was dangerous ground, she realised. Feelings she'd managed to keep firmly under control, that she'd kept securely under lock and key all these years, were threatening to break to the surface.

Overcoming her surprise at the question, she managed to retain her smile before answering, 'I did like him a long time ago, young lady. Jared, that's his name. But to answer your question, yes, in the early days your mammy and Jared were very good friends.'

'Are you still friends?'

This time the smile when it came wasn't forced.

Almost wistfully, Emma said, 'Not in the way we used to be, but yes, I suppose you could say we're still friends. Why do you ask, love?'

'I'm glad you're friends because I like him, Mammy. He looks a kind man.' It was all she said before suddenly giving in to her tiredness. She rolled over onto her side and fell instantly asleep.

Jared knew that after everything he'd just discovered he was too excited to sleep. Slipping out of bed quietly, he rummaged through his wardrobe until he found his dark running clothes and dressed quickly.

Making his way silently across the landing, he was careful not to disturb his grandmother. With relief he saw the lights were out in her room. Guessing she was asleep, he breathed more easily. Had she seen him, it would have been awkward explaining why he'd decided to go running at this time of the morning. Within moments he'd made his way downstairs, and seconds later was heading down the narrow deserted street towards the main road.

The street at this time of the morning was misted and grey, and the diffused lighting from the lamp posts overhead struggled manfully to penetrate the gloom. In places it filtered through like ghostly fingers. Jared knew that in a few short hours the first rays of the morning sun would burn away the last vestiges of the mist, but at the moment it swirled around his ankles like wraiths.

By the time he'd reached the top of the hill, the smell of ozone was heavy in his nostrils. Added to the almost stifling humidity, he knew from past experience it prefaced a storm. In an area of Wales that boasted such high rainfall, he knew with a certainty that all the signs were there. Thunder was in the air, which meant that rain was imminent. Halfway down the hill, he eased back on his pace a little as he passed the entrance to the Welfare Hall. His trainers made little sound as he seemed to glide effortlessly over the tarmac.

Suddenly he stopped in mid stride, his senses alert to the fact something wasn't quite right. Whatever it had been, he'd picked up on it. Slowing his breathing, he pricked his ears and listened intently for any foreign sound, for something that might give him a clue as to what had triggered his senses.

After several moments he shook his head in annoyance, convinced now he must have imagined things. As he was about to start running again, it suddenly dawned on him. It was nothing that he'd heard that was out of place, but something he'd *seen*. Being blessed with peripheral vision, he'd spotted a faint glow coming from a window at the back of the Hall.

It had only been for an instant, but it had been enough.

Fully alert now, he realised with concern that the light had come from the exhibit room, the one in which the chalice and skeleton were being kept. Puzzled, he reflected that at this time of night there should be no one there, unless of course it was old Tom making an unscheduled check-up.

He'd almost convinced himself that was the answer, when it registered. If that were the case, the light would have been on for longer. No, whoever had switched it on had done so sparingly. It was almost as if it had been a guilty or furtive gesture. If so, it was suspicious.

Making an instant decision he decided that as he was here, it merited checking out.

His senses on full alert, he made his way carefully towards the back of the building. He knew that something was badly wrong when he saw the Mercedes sports saloon hidden in the back of the car park. Tucked away in deep shadow, it was almost impossible to spot. Someone had obviously gone to a great deal of trouble to hide it, and that for Jared spelt trouble. It meant just one thing: he was dealing with professionals. Touching the bonnet, it felt warm, a sure indication that whoever was in there hadn't been there long.

Keeping to the shadows he moved slowly towards the back door. About to touch the handle, he noticed it was open a few inches. Convinced he was dealing with two people, he was suddenly struck by the fact he was weaponless. Despite this, he wasn't in the least bothered, knowing with certainty that he was more than a match for any two people. With that a burst of adrenaline flooded his system and he smiled mirthlessly in anticipation of what lay in store.

Easing open the door an inch at a time, he was eventually able to make a gap large enough to peer through. What he saw encouraged him. Although the corridor was dark and gloomy it seemed to be deserted.

Moving forward slowly, he knew that despite being outnumbered he had one big advantage. Unlike the intruders, he knew every inch of the building. Without further mishap, he was able to make his way soundlessly towards the exhibit room at the end of the long corridor. He was halfway there when a narrow beam of light began to flicker its way towards him. It was all the warning he had before suddenly a figure stepped through the door of the small medical room to his left-hand side. Flattening himself against the wall, he kept perfectly still, safe in the knowledge that unless the man looked directly at him, it was highly unlikely he would be spotted. And he was right!

Leaving the door open, the man simply turned on his heels and made directly for the exhibit room. Slipping through the gap left by the open door, Jared saw a sliver of light coming from inside the room. What he'd seen earlier must have been the result of a small chink in the curtain, one that had allowed the merest hint of light to escape. Sloppy, was Jared's initial reaction. Then he had a more sobering thought. If the burglars were moving about freely, it meant they had nothing to fear. So where was old Tom?

The first flicker of fear began to crawl up his spine, and with a feeling of dread he realised he already knew the answer. He knew old Tom well, and knew that at seventy years of age he would be no match for professional thieves. Turning in apprehension, his worst fears were confirmed as he suddenly noticed a body slumped in the swivel chair behind the desk. Hidden in shadow, he hadn't noticed it at first. With mounting horror he stepped quickly around the desk until he was confronted by a sight that made his blood turn cold.

If he hadn't known Tom as well as he did, he would never have been able to identify him. His face had been beaten to a bloody pulp, his features unrecognisable. It was obvious whoever had done it had systematically kicked and beaten the caretaker to death. With a tired sigh, he knew he'd been correct in his assumption: they were professionals. What he hadn't legislated for was the fact that they were also sadistic killers, no more than animals. It was beyond him why someone would want to inflict such damage on an old man, someone who'd obviously offered no physical threat.

If he'd been allowed to, Scorpion would have told him. He'd done it for the most basic of all reasons – damaged pride. David Naami had humiliated him, and the cause of that humiliation had been the old caretaker. As such, being a psychopath, it was all the justification he'd needed.

Bending down and picking up the body, Jared carried it in his arms towards an old leather sofa situated in the corner of the room. Laying him down gently, it was only then, by the light of the small lamp, that he was able to see the full extent of old Tom's horrific injuries. Feeling the anger turn the blood in his veins to ice, he was charged by a deep need for revenge.

Glancing away, he collected his thoughts; he let his inner turmoil settle a little before turning back. With that, his instincts kicked into overdrive and his training took over.

The first thing he did was open the drawer of the steel cabinet at the other end of the room, the one he knew housed cheap disposable surgical gloves. With that he slipped them over his hands. The second thing he did was retrace his steps, making sure to remove any finger-prints. Satisfied, he made his way back to the medical room. After dusting down all traces of his presence there too, he was about to step through the door when he froze; he could hear voices approaching. His immediate reaction was that his guess had been right, there were two of them.

As they neared his hiding place the voices rose in intensity.

'A good night's work, eh, Cobra?' said one. 'After 2,000 years of fucking searching the thing is finally ours. And we had a little fun into the bargain, didn't we?' The speaker suddenly burst out laughing.

'Yes, Scorpion, Number One will be well pleased. I'm not so sure we should have dealt with the old caretaker in the way we did, though. It will only bring added attention to the robbery. Why the hell did you lose it like that? You were bloody uncontrollable!'

'It was personal. Because of that old bastard I was humiliated. So as far as I'm concerned he had it coming. But don't worry about it, David Naami will be so ecstatic when he sees the chalice, he won't give a fuck about anything else.'

'I hope you're right. I don't know about you, but I still have night-mares about what he did to Wolf. To use his own words, he brought unnecessary attention to the Brotherhood. And boy, did he make a fucking example of him!'

Suddenly feeling cold, Scorpion said, 'Yes, but in this case I'm sure he'll feel the killing was justified.' He sounded far more confident than he actually felt.

'How the hell do you justify beating an old man to pulp, though?'

He never heard the answer, as the conversation was suddenly inter-rupted by Jared, who stepped silently through the door.

'May I help you two gentlemen?'

Turning on their heels they looked at him in astonishment, before yelling, in almost perfect unison, *'What the fuck?'*

Although Jared had taken them completely off guard, the element of surprise didn't last long. With one glance, Cobra summed up Jared in an instant. A fresh-faced kid hardly out of school. A pushover. Dismissing him out of hand, he turned to Scorpion and with a sneer said, 'You've had your fun – now I'm going to have mine. Take the chalice and leave the kid to me, I shan't be long.'

The sneer returned as he made his way forward.

Strangely, in their excitement at seeing Jared, neither realised they'd made a bad mistake. That inadvertently they'd disclosed the name of the Grand Master.

Summing up the situation, Jared decided to play the percentage game. Planning his strategy carefully, he watched as Scorpion turned and moved towards the exit.

Backing away from Cobra slowly, he pretended fear. Then, judging the moment was right, he turned and ran. Heading for the exhibit room, he was gambling that Cobra believed he was backing himself into a situation from which there was no escape. Rushing through the door, he slammed it shut, hoping it would reinforce the impression that he was terrified. Within seconds the door crashed open, and standing before him was a supremely confident Cobra, flipping his dagger from one hand to the other. It suddenly came to rest in his right hand. Jared noted with satisfaction how the blade faced upwards; a sure indication the man was a professional. Inwardly, Jared was relieved. In his experience, he knew more damage could be inflicted by someone who had no idea of what they were doing than a professional who thought he was the best.

As Cobra came towards him balanced on the balls of his feet, Jared thought, Yes, professionals were far more predictable – especially ones as overconfident as this.

Smiling, Cobra carried on tossing the blade from one hand to the other while at the same time never taking his eyes off his victim.

It was a trick Jared recognised. It was an attempt to mesmerise.

He knew that magicians did much the same thing. The art of misdirection, they called it. Jared knew that when the thrust came, it would be with the speed of lightning, that it would need all of his considerable reflexes to counter it.

What Cobra didn't know was that, far from facing a frightened kid caught in the wrong place at the wrong time, he was looking at a killer even more skilful than he was, and unfortunately for him one infinitely more deadly. While strutting his stuff with the knife, Cobra failed to see that he'd advertised the fact he was right-handed. That made Jared's task a good deal easier. In fact, it cut down the time he would need to react by half.

Lowering his breath into an area just below the navel called the *dan jun*, he stood perfectly still. Like all adepts of the martial arts, he knew it was not called the seat of power for nothing. When Jared was ready to make his move, it was from here the power would come. As the repository of the mysterious force called ki, it could be brought into focus in a millisecond. It was an extremely difficult skill to master, requiring years of special deep breathing techniques to control, to hone to perfection. Once mastered, however, it could be devastatingly effective.

Ready now, Jared planted his feet firmly on the floor and waited until Cobra was near enough to make his move. There was only the merest flicker of the eyes, but it was enough. It signified the game was over, signified his intent to strike. The blade was not even halfway towards Jared's throat when he suddenly moved. Like a tightly coiled spring, he exploded into action. Stepping aside, Jared moved his body in one fluid motion until suddenly, to Cobra's astonishment, he was thrusting at thin air.

Unknown to the assassin, he'd been deliberately manoeuvred towards the empty case which until a short time ago had housed the chalice. Like a man moving through wet sand, Cobra suddenly sensed what was happening, but by then it was too late. While Cobra was off balance, Jared elbowed his assailant in the kidney. Doubled over in agony, Cobra was now helpless. Completely defenceless, he could only stare in horror as the full implications of what was about to happen sunk in.

With chilling precision, Jared took hold of Cobra's hair and smashed his face into the glass of the cabinet, which suddenly exploded into fragments of all sizes. By the time he'd repeated the process several times, Cobra's face was nothing but a bloody red mask.

Not content, Jared grabbed the limp figure by the throat and lifted him onto his toes.

Looking into his eyes, he was rewarded with the faintest flicker of life. With that, he reached behind him and prised a large sliver of glass from among the debris at the bottom of the ruined cabinet. 'This is for old Tom,' he said, before slitting Cobra's throat from ear to ear. Letting him drop to the floor, he didn't even bother to watch the man's final death throes.

His task complete, Jared made his way towards the exit, making sure once again to remove any evidence of his having been there. He knew the assassin whom Cobra referred to as Scorpion would be long gone, along with the chalice. It didn't matter though, as now Jared knew the name of their leader. It shouldn't be too difficult to find this character called David Naami, he told himself. Find him, and then he would be able to find the chalice and the organisation that was the driving force behind it. Finally, he'd find Scorpion.

And then of course he had a score to settle…

His last thought before exiting the building and disappearing into the night was that he hoped Scorpion would be more of a challenge than his colleague.

Within ten minutes he was home; but before he retired to bed, he made sure he put his bloodied clothes, along with the rubber gloves, into a black bag. He'd get rid of them tomorrow.

Before falling asleep he carefully analysed the situation. He was sure no one had seen him, so he'd never be suspected of anything. Should the local police come calling, however, there was always his grandmother to vouch for him. After all, he'd been up most of the night reading, hadn't he?

Chapter Twenty-one

JARED CAME INSTANTLY AWAKE. DESPITE WHAT HAD TAKEN PLACE A few short hours ago, within seconds he was fully functional. About to get out of bed, he sat back, deciding a lie-in would add credence to the story he'd stayed up reading until the early hours. Sitting up, his hands behind his head, he wondered how long it would be before the shit hit the fan. As it happened, it was sooner than expected. Within moments he heard frantic footsteps running up the stairs. Seconds later, his grandmother's head appeared around the door and she was gasping for breath. It was obvious she was excited about something, and he knew exactly what it was.

'Something terrible has happened in the Welfare Hall, love! Bodies all over the place, apparently, and from what I gather one of them is old Tom.'

When he remembered what the bastards had done to the old care-taker, it wasn't difficult to pretend shock and horror. Jumping up, he said, 'What the hell happened then, Gran?' Then, 'Hang on, I'll be down in a minute.'

Over a hurried breakfast, his grandmother outlined what she'd learned on the village grapevine. Looking up from a mouthful of bacon and eggs in order to gauge his reaction, she said, 'You look tired, love. Up all night reading, I suppose? Missed your early morning jog, then?'

Jared hated deceiving his grandmother, but knew it was for the best and so the lie tripped easily off his tongue. 'You're right, I'm a bit bushed this morning, must admit.'

'I thought so, I got up to go to the toilet during the night and saw the light still on in your room. So I guessed what had happened.'

Breathing a sigh of relief, he was glad his ruse had worked.

An hour later, he was strolling down the hill towards the Hall when he saw the area had been cordoned off. People in white suits were buzzing about the scene like flies.

By now the crowds were so large that Jared wondered if anyone had bothered going to work. Probably not, was his immediate reaction. It was too good an opportunity to turn down the chance to see so much blood and guts, he realised.

Studying the faces, he was relieved to see Emma's was not among the ghouls, and he was particularly glad not to see little Jodie. This was no place for someone as young and impressionable as her.

At that moment he felt a tap on his shoulder. Turning, he saw Roger standing behind him.

'Hell of a mess in there, mate – not a pretty sight. Two bodies, apparently, one's old Tom, the caretaker, who seems to have been kicked and beaten to death, while the other one's a stranger. From what I can make out, though, he's in even more of a mess.'

Astonishment written all over his face, Jared said, 'How the hell do you know all this, Rog? I don't suppose the police have had time to issue a report yet. Are you psychic or something?'

Grinning, Roger pointed his finger to a young woman standing near the entrance to the Hall. 'See that girl over there, the pretty blonde one?'

'The one in the white suit, you mean,' said Jared, 'part of the forensic team?'

'Yeah, that's her… Well, let's just say that she and I are on rather intimate terms. Met her in Swansea one Friday, and – bingo!'

'Does she wear glasses?' asked Jared innocently.

'Don't think so, why?'

'Well, if she doesn't, she'd better get her eyes tested, seeing as she's going out with a nerd like you!'

'You bastard!' said Roger, laughing. 'Got me there!'

Jared's next remark was said under his breath so Roger missed it. 'Doesn't take much, take it from me.' As he said it, the girl suddenly lifted her head and looking over smiled shyly.

Serious again, Jared said, 'Doesn't she realise leaking that kind of information could get her into serious trouble.'

'I suppose she does,' said Roger, 'but it's the charm, you see, it gets them all in the end. Anyway, you know what Raven's Hill is like – give it a few hours and every bugger in the village will know.' He went suddenly quiet before adding, 'But who the fuck would want to do that to an old man? He was over seventy, for God's sake.'

It was difficult to answer that, so Jared said nothing.

'Mind you, from what Karen said, whoever did for old Tom got what was coming to him in a big way. Said she's never seen anything like it. The flesh had been deliberately ripped from his face. To date, it's the most horrific injury she's ever seen.'

'I hope it was,' said Jared with feeling.

The words were out before he could stop them and Roger looked up sharply, fully aware of the implications of what he'd just heard.

'Oh, Christ!' was all Roger could think of saying. Then as an afterthought added, 'Then it wasn't the thing from the chalice that did it?'

Glancing over his shoulder to see if anyone was within earshot, Jared said, 'No, Rog, but unfortunately there is a connection. The reason for the break-in was to steal the bloody thing. Karen won't have realised it yet, she's been too busy with the forensic side of things, but when the dust settles it won't be long before someone spots the chalice is gone.'

'But it doesn't make sense!' said Roger, shaking his head in consternation. 'Who would want the bloody thing?'

'Good question, but thanks to a stroke of good luck, I know where it is. You see, the bastards didn't know I was hiding in the medical room, so they let slip a few crucial points. The name of the organisation is Chameleon Enterprises, and their leader or Grand Master as they called him, is a guy called David Naami. Ever heard of him?'

Shaking his head, Roger replied, 'Can't say I have.'

'Well, it doesn't matter, because I promise you one thing: whoever he is, I'll find him. And when I do, I've a score to settle.'

'Wait a minute,' said Roger suddenly snapping his fingers, 'I've got it now! It didn't register when you first mentioned the name, but I remember now. He's the guy who runs that huge multinational complex in Cardiff Bay, the one that relocated from London all those years ago. I was watching a documentary about it the other evening. The focus of the investigation was centred on this chap you mentioned, David Naami, and said he was something of a mystery man. One of the most powerful men in the world, supposedly, and he's hardly ever seen. Something of a recluse, by all accounts. The programme made one thing perfectly clear: the organisation is mixed up in all kinds of illegalities. They hinted at links with factions such as Hezbollah and Al-Qaeda. Through their dealings with the Russian Mafia, it suggested they were able to supply them with all kinds of unpleasant things. One reporter hinted they were even supplying nuclear warheads to the highest bidder.'

Suddenly, Jared remembered where he'd heard the name Chameleon Enterprises, and in what context. With grudging admiration, he admitted it was the perfect name for an organisation that had prided itself on secrecy down through the centuries.

'Let's get away from here, Rog,' were Jared's next words. 'The media are already in a feeding frenzy over the rash of strange incidents in the village. In another hour or two it's going to be bloody bedlam. Fancy a cup of coffee? Don't worry, I'll pay – I always do!' That was his final comment as they threaded their way through the milling crowd towards Alec's café.

It had been a long hard day, so it was nearly 7 p.m. before Jared settled down into the comfortable armchair in the living room, conscious of the fact it had been the favourite of both his grandfathers.

Taking up from where he'd finished off last night he read on.

- The Cathars believed in reincarnation and the prominence of women in their version of Christianity.

That's odd, thought Jared. Reincarnation was an Eastern, not a Christian belief, and so according to that premise, heresy! He knew the reason the Catholic Church had made its stand against women was on the grounds that Jesus had chosen only male disciples. Jared had always believed the principle to be flawed. Through the centuries the Catholic Church had conveniently ignored the fact that although Jesus had chosen no female Apostles, he'd had many female companions. It had always been Jared's belief that Jesus deliberately chose not to accept women as disciples for two simple reasons.

The first was that he was thinking of their safety. Discipleship was a very dangerous occupation, as later events proved. The second reason was even more fundamental.

Whereas the male of the household might suddenly decide to drop everything in order to follow Jesus, the female was allowed no such luxury. In Judaism it was the mother who had the more important role. It was her duty to ensure the continuity of the religion. Ruefully, Jared was once again reminded of the fact that although Christianity had portrayed Jesus as their founder, he along with all the Apostles had been Jewish by birth. Furthermore, until the day he was crucified he claimed allegiance to no religion but Judaism.

Re-grouping his thoughts, Jared noticed the next bullet point had been underlined for emphasis.

- The Cathars denied the validity of all clerical hierarchy. They were adamant that no ordained intermediaries were needed between the people and God. They also denied the need for faith on the grounds that the Church's interpretation of it was based on second-hand knowledge and as such was open to all kinds of mistakes and fallacies.

The more Jared read about Cathar philosophy, the more he found he was in sympathy with their ideas. It had always worried him that once Jesus had been crucified, Christianity had based its system of belief on the words of one man – Paul of Tarsus. As things turned out it was Paul, not Jesus or the disciples – the natural successors – who had taken over the reins of leadership. More worryingly, his claims were based on something only he had seen – the vision on the road to Damascus. Jared wondered if this was what the Cathars were alluding to when they mentioned that the Church's idea of faith had been based on second-hand knowledge. However well meaning Paul had been, he had still only been a human being, and as such was open to human error.

- The Cathars were dualists, which meant they believed in a constant battle between good and evil. Unlike other dualists, the Cathars were prepared to take it a good deal further. Amazingly, they claimed that there were two gods, both of whom were more or less comparable in status. The first, the god of good, was seen as pure spirit, and because he wasn't tainted by materialism was regarded as the god of love. On the other hand the other god, the god of evil, was the god of all material things. Now it followed that because the universe was made of material, it bore all the hallmarks of this second or usurper god. *Rex Mundi* – the king of the world as they called him.

Jared could see where this was going.

What the Cathars were implying was that if Jesus was truly God's son and pure spirit, he couldn't be incarnate. In other words, he couldn't have come to earth in the guise of a human being. If he had, he would have had to have taken a physical form. But, if Jesus was pure spirit, without a material body, then how could he possibly have been crucified? Explosive stuff, thought Jared; no wonder they became known as heretics. The next few sentences confirmed his thinking.

- By 1200, the Roman Catholic Church had decided to stamp out the heresy.

- In 1208 they had formulated a strategy. A year later, under the direction of Pope Innocent the Third, a crusade was launched to rectify the situation.

- By 1243, apart from a small handful of isolated incidents, in particular the one at Montségur, the Cathars were systematically and ruthlessly wiped out.

- The citadel held out for months, eventually falling in March 1244.

At this point, Jared couldn't help but notice the similarities between this incident and what had happened at Masada. With increasing excitement he began to wonder if there might be a similar conclusion, that despite the odds a chosen few had managed to escape. Suddenly he'd come to the end of Eric's notes. He wasn't sure whether he'd picked up on everything he was supposed to, but if he hadn't missed his guess, then what had happened at Montségur was crucial to their understanding of the background to the chalice.

By now he was tired. The excitement of last night's savage encounter and the implications of what he'd found were beginning to take their toll. He knew however that before he gave in to exhaustion, he had one more thing to do. It couldn't wait, so he picked up the phone, hoping to arrange a meeting for the three of them in Eric's house the following day.

Glancing at his watch, he saw it was nearly 11 p.m., and he wondered if his uncle might have decided on an early night. His fears were put to rest when almost immediately he heard his voice at the other end of the telephone. Relieved, Jared's excitement was infectious. Within moments his uncle was won over, as enthusiastic about the possibilities he'd unearthed as he was. Fortunately it seemed that Edwin was due a few days' holiday from the university, and so getting time off would be no problem.

'Try and be there by mid-afternoon,' was Jared's parting comment.

He'd rung off before he realised he'd forgotten to tell his uncle where Eric lived. With that, he remembered that Edwin already knew.

The following morning, Jared's thoughts about the media turned out to be only too prophetic. The tabloids had gone to town. He had to admit the journalist who'd produced the local rag had been very thorough in her research. Somehow she'd managed to link the incident to something which had taken place shortly before Jared's disappearance from Raven's Hill. He remembered it vividly, because at the time it had caused something of a sensation. It involved a young mother and her infant daughter, and the mother had been killed in an exceptionally gruesome manner. But what had caught the attention of the public was that two days later, when the police had finished their investigation and had come up with absolutely nothing, they'd suddenly been handed the killer on a plate. It appeared whoever was behind the kidnapping had meted out their own punishment. Hanging from the lamp post which guarded the entrance to the tunnel in which the woman had been slaughtered, they found the body of a man. Why he'd been killed in such a manner was beyond the police. However, later DNA testing proved conclusively that he was the culprit.

Two curious items of interest also came to light.

The body had a symbol of a wolf tattooed on the left shoulder, but what was really unusual was that the man's tongue had been surgically altered.

In an instant it came to him: that's what the two assassins had been alluding to last night. David Naami must have made and example of this Wolf, and if the fear in the voices of the two killers was anything to go by, he had certainly achieved his purpose. After all this time it was obvious both had been badly rattled.

Suddenly Jared saw how the reporter had put two and two together. The knife that had been used to try and kill him had been decorated with the symbol of a cobra, and no doubt if he'd bothered to look, he would have seen the telltale tattoo etched into his left shoulder. Smart work, young lady, he thought, mentally congratulating her on her powers of deduction. Like all good journalists she'd been somewhat sparing with the truth, but what she had managed to elicit from her source – presumably in the local police force – had been used extremely skilfully. Hazarding a guess that the two were members of the same organisation, she'd given the story a more sensationalist slant by inventing the phrase – The Brotherhood of Assassins!

Yes, Jared admitted, you really are quite good.

The article finished by posing a question. 'If such an elite assassin had been taken out with such ruthless efficiency by a man who managed to disappear without leaving a single trace, then how good was he?'

Strangely, from Jared's point of view, very little mention was made of the disappearance of the chalice. He supposed when faced with two gruesome murders, the theft of an unknown object was of little consequence. His last thought before putting the paper down was that by dismissing the chalice so lightly, she had made the biggest mistake of her career. Unfortunately, he had the distinct feeling that in the coming months she would have ample opportunity to rectify it.

In hindsight, he wondered why he hadn't taken the knife. That and the identical one he'd carried in a leather sheath at the nape of his neck. He had to admit they had certainly been works of art. Made of the finest steel, they had been razor sharp, the craftsmanship exquisite.

'But surely, Number One, no news is good news,' said Scorpion, smiling at the cleverness of his cliché. The stare from the piercing black eyes almost cut the assassin in two.

'That, Scorpion, is a proverb that only serves to highlight your ignorance.' Carrying on in a mildly deceptive voice, he added, 'Furthermore, it is as dangerous as you are stupid. Not only that, let me assure you it is an attitude that has killed many who were far more competent than *you*.'

Contrite, Scorpion allowed his eyes to fall to the floor before adding in a conciliatory tone, 'Yes, Number One.'

'What worries me is that from the way you describe this *youngster*, as you so eloquently put it, he acted like a frightened kid. Yet it's been how long now – and there's still no sign of Cobra. I'm afraid it doesn't take an Einstein to work out that if he hasn't turned up by now, he isn't coming back.' As an afterthought he said, 'Was the man armed?'

'Not that I could see, Number One, but one thing appeared strange, he was dressed completely in black.'

Looking up with renewed interest, David Naami said, 'And yet moments ago you said he appeared to be no threat.'

'True, Number One, but once Cobra failed to return as quickly as he'd promised, I thought it prudent to get the chalice to you as quickly as possible. It was my first priority. I hope I did the right thing?'

'Surprisingly, it was the only thing you did properly. From where I'm standing I believe you were played for a sucker.' He added dryly, 'Unfortunately, that seems to be the norm for you these days.'

Having dismissed Scorpion in disgust, David Naami held the chalice in his hands. Studying it carefully, he was almost overcome with emotion. He had to admit it was even more beautiful than he'd imagined. It was then the enormity of the occasion hit him.

For nearly 2,000 years the Brotherhood had searched for the sacred relic, and now he possessed it. Apart from anything else, it would ensure his name would for ever be synonymous with its acquisition. From this moment on, whenever the Brotherhood met, his name would be mentioned with reverential awe.

He was now a legend.

His megalomania rapidly rising to the surface, he suddenly realised he would now be the most famous, most powerful Grand Master of all time.

Scorpion's gamble had paid off. His life had been spared because he'd guessed correctly. Possession of the chalice triumphed over every other feeling. It had been a close thing, though; the killing had been reckless, a flagrant breach of discipline. Worse: as Cobra had warned, it had brought more unwarranted attention to the order. Unfortunately for David Naami, that had not been the end of things. By now it was blatantly obvious that, despite all the odds, Cobra had been taken out by a slip of youth.

Then of course the problem had been compounded when an enterprising young journalist had done her homework and linked the killing to that of Wolf six years ago. Still, it was no good crying over spilt milk. It had been done and that was that.

Holding the chalice to the light, David studied the nine symbols carved into the solid block of obsidian. It was a source of amusement to him that the archaeologists who'd discovered it had no idea as to the purpose of the chalice.

Thinking out loud he said, 'You stupid fuckers! The symbols are all the clues you need to fathom its origin.'

With that he had a disturbing thought. Why hadn't the evil returned to the head? Shrugging his shoulders in a gesture of resignation, he reflected that it was not for him to know the intention of the master. He was sure of one thing, however, by now it had not only chosen its host, but had also plotted the outcome of its first victim carefully.

As a psychopath himself, he knew his bloodlust paled into insignificance compared to that of the master. Inadvertently he suppressed a shudder at the thought of the fate awaiting the intended victims.

His most fervent hope was that when the creature had accomplished what it had set out to achieve, it would return to instigate a new reign of terror and bloodshed for the Brotherhood.

Chapter Twenty-two

DEINIOL SYMONDS, THE AGEING RECTOR OF ST DAVID'S, WAS SO engrossed in his task that he never noticed a tall slim figure slide stealthily into one of the wooden pews at the back of the church. For a while the young man hidden in deep dark shadow made no move, he simply sat there watching. Suddenly, he shook his head and blinked in surprise. In total confusion he muttered to himself, 'What the hell am I doing here?' For a moment he'd felt sure he'd been sleepwalking, knowing immediately it was extremely unlikely as it was too early in the evening for that. Besides, as far as he could recall, he had no history of such a thing. Despite this, he couldn't rid himself of the feeling he'd suddenly woken from some kind of trance. With that his thoughts emerged as if from a fog.

Rubbing his eyes vigorously, he slowly began to return to some kind of normality. It was while mustering his scattered thoughts that he realised in astonishment where he was.

But it made no sense, was his initial reaction.

With that he fell prey to a host of misgivings, until suddenly apprehension like a crawling maggot began to burrow its way out from somewhere deep inside. True, he'd often in passing looked across the road at the beautiful little church, and in all honesty been tempted to call in several times. On a balmy summer's day it was so striking it needed little imagination to believe that somehow you'd managed to step into a picture postcard world of make-believe. Its prime location and pristine condition had done its architect proud. Interdenominational prejudices aside, it was probably one of, if not the most picturesque place of worship in the valley. If you were into that kind of thing, he told himself hastily.

Anyone with an ounce of appreciation for anything of aesthetic beauty couldn't fail to be impressed by its large square tower, or the superb condition of its dressed stone. The craftsmanship was truly remarkable. Yet as impressive as the old church was, the grounds were equally magnificent. Whether it was summer or winter, it seemed to make no difference. The grass, in particular the area around the graves, so scruffy in some places of worship, was always immaculate. It was obvious that whoever looked after the grounds took great pride in their work.

Dragging himself back into the present, he realised that daydreaming would get him nowhere, least of all answer the question which was nagging at him: what the hell was he doing here? Shit, he said to himself, he didn't even consider himself to be a religious person. Not any more, anyway.

So, the alarm bells were ringing loud and clear. They were trying to tell him something was definitely wrong, but for the life of him he couldn't figure out what.

For a good many years he'd been a member of a local Methodist chapel. But after that period of brainwashing, which he'd now come to see it as, he'd suddenly woken up one morning, decided God had done very little for him, and that was that.

Gazing around the interior, he grudgingly admitted that what he saw was far more impressive than the dour, austere environment he'd been used to. As his eyes took in every nuance of his alien surroundings, his first impression was at least it looked like a place of worship.

Despite his confusion, he had the distinct feeling someone or something had brought him here. If that were the case, he reasoned, there must be a purpose to this charade.

It was then he remembered the rector. Peering at him through the gloom, he was surprised to see he was changing the altar cloth. His initial reaction was surprise.

Why on earth would he be doing that, he thought, especially as the other one wasn't even dirty...

Suddenly, as if surfacing from a long way off, a hidden memory began to stir. And then he had it. It had been part of a Sunday school lesson a long time ago, a lesson in which the old minister had explained to them how the church calendar revolved around the person of Christ, around the most important aspects of his life. He remembered too how each of those events was given extra prominence by having a festival attached to it.

And then it came to him.

Of course – how could he have been so stupid? Each festival was symbolised by a different colour, wasn't it? If so, the answer was simple.

The rector was changing the cloth because some kind of special event was about to take place. The one in the old man's hand was white, and if his memory served him correctly, that was the symbol of purity. So this had to be a very important occasion.

Looking more closely, he noticed the cloth was not just any old white, but strikingly white. With that, a mental image burst into his mind. It was a commercial in which a particularly irritating man – he couldn't remember his name now – knocked on the door of housewives asking if they would like to try his brand of washing powder. Stupidly he wondered if the old rector used the same brand, as from where he was sitting, the result was spectacular. He'd never been a lover of commercials, in fact he'd found them to be a bloody nuisance, especially when they interrupted the flow of a good film. That was until one of his colleagues had explained to him just how effective they could be. Apparently they were a subtle form of brainwashing. He'd then gone on to prove his point by means of a graphic illustration. Since then he'd looked at them in a different light, appreciating just why so much money was spent each year by the big companies on their campaigns. If he wasn't mistaken, in America the figure had reached a staggering $185 billion annually.

It was his final thought before suddenly, without any warning, his mind was wiped clean. Although he didn't know it, he was no longer in control of himself. The demon had reclaimed its host. The physical shell the creature now occupied was nothing more than an empty husk, but it served his purpose admirably.

Without warning it started walking towards the altar.

Like an automaton, it made its way down the central isle of the church, oblivious to anything but the rector. It got to within six feet of him before it spoke, 'Hello, Mr Symonds!'

Startled, the old man turned quickly, fear and apprehension written on his face.

Peering closely at the young man standing in front of him, he suddenly recognised who it was and gave an audible sigh of relief. 'Oh, hello, you startled me! Gave me a bit of a fright, you did... didn't know anyone was there, you see.' Pointing behind him to the altar, he went on, 'I'm getting things ready for tomorrow evening's service. As you can tell, it's an important one, so I thought I'd make sure everything was shipshape. You know how it is; everything has to be just right. Can't leave anything to chance, can you?'

'That's why you're changing the cloth, then. I must say it looks spotless, almost dazzling in a way; but it has to be, hasn't it, being a symbol of purity.'

Pleased at the young man's insightful comment, the rector said, 'Yes, you're right, but if I may be so bold, you're slightly off the beaten track. Weren't you a member of the little chapel down the road, the one that closed not so long ago? It's a shame what happened to it, but I'm afraid it's a sign of the times. It's not the first, and I don't suppose it will be the last. As a man of the cloth I can assure you I take no pleasure in such things.'

As if he'd done his duty, been seen to be suitably contrite, his mood changed abruptly. Brightening up and radiating sincerity, he said, 'But where are my manners? Let me assure you, should you be looking for another avenue to God, you would be most welcome to join my little flock.' Then as an afterthought he added, 'Why not pop around tomorrow evening, see what we're all about – can't hurt, can it? Besides, you never know–' he put on his professional smile again – 'you might be pleasantly surprised. Speaking on God's behalf, it would be a pleasure to see you.'

'Oh, believe me, Rector,' said the demon, 'I can assure you the pleasure would be all mine. While we're on the subject, I was wondering if you could clear up a little matter for me. It's something that's been bothering me for a while.'

'Certainly,' said the old rector, by now pleased and curious at the same time.

'It's obvious you believe in the hereafter, but tell me, why are you so convinced there is one? Correct me if I'm wrong, but there seems to be no hard evidence for life after death. To me that has always been the fundamental flaw in the Church's argument; after all no one has ever come back to prove the case one way or the other, have they? Unless of course I've missed something... have I?'

Slightly indignant at the question and what he perceived as a slur on his own integrity, the old rector said, 'You're perfectly correct, my son, I do believe in eternal life.' By now he was beginning to feel a little uneasy at the way the conversation was heading. There was more to it, though. He couldn't be sure, it might have been his imagination, but he could swear in the last few seconds that the young man's whole bearing had altered. Not only that, his voice seemed different too; it was eerie.

'You see, looking at it from my point of view,' the demon went on, 'it seems we're living in an age which demands proof of everything, and so I find it difficult to accept such an outlandish hypothesis. Now, if you lot had proof,' he said, suddenly smiling, 'then it would be different, wouldn't it? It would change everything. So what I want to know is, how come you're so sure there is such a thing as heaven?'

Clearly angry now, the old man blurted out, 'The only proof I need is my faith in Christ Jesus! Take heed of what the Scriptures say. They explain how for our sins, the Lord Jesus died on the cross, only to be redeemed by the Father three days later. The physical resurrection is all the proof I need.' With that, a self-satisfied smirk appeared on his face.

Before the old rector had time to realise that something was dreadfully wrong, the appearance of the demon altered yet again. Then, in the blink of an eye, it was standing before him in all its malignant glory.

Opening its mouth it said, 'Good, good, I'm pleased you're so confident, because I'm going to give you the chance to test your little theory about heaven.' Then it added with an insane chuckle, 'The only problem is, your opportunity is going to arrive a little sooner than you expected.'

Like a magician, it suddenly produced a large hook, the kind used by big game fishermen, and with lightning speed, barb first, thrust it into the rector's mouth.

Then in a display of inhuman strength, it proceeded to lift the man's body from the floor while at the same time pushing the barb deeper and deeper into the roof of his mouth. The attack was so swift, so unexpected, the old rector had no time to react.

The pain was so excruciating that even if he'd wanted, he couldn't have shouted for help. Dangling from the end of the hook, his feet twitching several inches above the floor, it appeared to the demon in a flash of cruel humour that he reminded him of a bloated frog, one trying in vain to pedal an invisible bicycle. Taunting him, it said, 'Where's your faith now, old man? Surely if your beloved leader is all he's cracked up to be, he could intercede on your behalf?' Adding in a mocking tone, 'After all, you are a man of the cloth. I would have thought for such an eminent figure the least he could have done is to put in an appearance.'

Looking around the confines of the cold gloomy church, it shook his head before saying, 'So disappointing! On the other hand, might it be there's another explanation? What if you're not such a devout figure as you would have your congregation believe? Now there's a thought... a few skeletons in the cupboard perhaps?'

Barely pausing for breath, the demon pressed on relentlessly. 'One can never really tell with you lot. After all, hardly a day goes by without one or another of your sordid little secrets being exposed by the media.' Stopping in mid-sentence, he suddenly chuckled at his own joke. 'In your case, *exposed* might be the wrong choice of word, don't you think?' Seeing the astonishment on the rector's face, the demon said, 'Oh, don't worry, I know everything, believe me.

'I must say, however, I do find it rather baffling, considering what it is you lot do for a living, that you're not very convincing salesmen. Look at the state of the modern Church. Not a very pretty sight, is it? Falling rolls and all that, I mean. If you were in another profession you would have been sacked by now, every last one of you.'

Pausing a second to let the implications of what he'd just said sink in, it carried on. 'Nothing to say in your defence? But where are my manners? You can't at the moment, can you? What if I make you a little more comfortable?'

With that it proceeded to lower the rector until his feet touched the cold flagstones.

Looking directly into his eyes, it said, 'Like a puppet on a string,' and giggled like a little child. 'Can't you see the irony of the situation? ...No? Then let me spell it out for you: you're dancing to *my* tune now, Rector, not your fucking God's.'

Unable to utter a sound, the old man's eyes mirrored the agony he was going through. Reading his thoughts, the demon knew that far from catching a glimpse of this wonderful place called heaven, the one he'd moments before been eulogising about, he was now facing a reality check. With brutal clarity he'd been forced to discover he was standing on the threshold of somewhere very different. In fact he was standing at the entrance to the other place, the one commonly referred to as hell!

Despite his pain and suffering, Deiniol Symonds had a sudden flash of insight. There had to be a reason why all this was happening to him, and suddenly he had it: Christ was testing his faith. Hadn't Christ himself come through something similar? he reminded himself. If that was the case, all he had to do was remember that Jesus had died and suffered for him. Not only that, but he'd come back three days later to prove it.

Yes, that was it; all he had to do was believe.

It was, he reasoned, the supreme test of his faith.

Bursting with new-found conviction, he knew now what he had to do. He had to inform this spawn of Satan he'd made peace with himself. He was ready to meet his Maker, safe in the knowledge his reward would come in the hereafter. In one last glorious act of defiance he opened his mouth ready to spit on the devil. Unfortunately, instead of words, all that came out was a jet of bright red blood.

Seeing the light begin to dim in the old man's eyes, the demon pounced. It had one last cruel trick up its sleeve, something it had deliberately kept back until the very end.

Leaning over the old man, the demon whispered into his ear.

The effect was instantaneous.

The horror mirrored in the rector's eyes told the demon its words had struck home with venom.

Nodding excitedly, it said, 'Yes, yes, but don't take my word for it – you'll find out for yourself soon enough.' Then it exploded into another bout of maniacal laughter.

Fortunately for the rector, he didn't last much longer. Seconds later he passed into merciful oblivion.

Had he lived long enough, he would have witnessed the demon cut his throat and crucify him upside down. Not content even then, it used the copious amount of blood produced by the corpse to outline a strange symbol on the wall behind the body.

Standing back, hands on hips, the demon experienced a deep feeling of satisfaction as it looked at its handiwork.

Yes, it thought, all in all it had been a job well done.

Turning smartly on its heels, it made its way leisurely to the vestry at the back of the church. Going to the hot water tap, it picked up a bar of soap and calmly washed the blood from its hands. It would do no good, it reasoned, for the host to know what he'd done before he'd completed the whole of its agenda. Of course, when it was all over it would be different. Then it would allow the poor fool to see what he'd done, to see the horrors he'd perpetrated on its behalf.

With a deep throated chuckle, it thought that if it was lucky, it might tip him over the edge into insanity. Now that would be a bonus, it thought, before opening the back door and stepping out into the gathering gloom.

Listening to the sound of 'Communication Breakdown' by Led Zeppelin blasting through the stereo, Jared was dragged into the present by his grandmother shaking him vigorously. Taking off his earphones, he looked up in time to hear her say, 'Can you answer the door, love, the bell's ringing and I'm in the middle of preparing food.'

Jumping from the armchair, Jared placed the earphones on the coffee table and moved to the door. Opening it, he had a pleasant surprise, as looking up at him was Emma. Smiling, he said, 'To what do I owe this honour?' Then, inspecting her face, his former good humour evaporated, to be replaced instantly by one of concern. Looking at her he knew immediately something had shaken her badly.

Putting a protective arm around her shoulder, he ushered her into the house before asking, 'What's up?'

'Have you heard the news?'

'No, I've been listening to music all morning. Hang on a minute while I switch the stereo off.'

Returning almost immediately, he said, 'That's better. Now then, what's all this about the news? Anything important?'

Jared saw a range of conflicting emotions playing in her eyes, a plethora of fear and anxiety. 'You could say that,' was all Emma managed to get out before bursting into tears. Jared was stunned, but after the way she'd reacted the last time he'd put his arms around her, he was unsure of what to do. After several half-hearted attempts he finally took the plunge. Suddenly she was in his arms, clinging to him fiercely.

It was almost like old times, thought Jared wistfully, instantly cursing himself for his weakness. Lifting her head gently, he said, 'What's the matter, love?'

Between sobs, Emma managed to relate the story about how the rector of St David's had been found brutally murdered inside his own church.

'Christ!' was all Jared could find to say before adding, 'did they say how it had happened?'

'No, they were rather vague, almost as if they were hiding something.'

Suddenly his grandmother's voice broke into the conversation. Shouting from the kitchen, and only having heard part of what Emma had said to Jared, she said, 'Perhaps it was a heart attack or something; he was getting on a bit after all.'

'I don't think so, Gran,' was Jared's reply. Realising she had grasped the wrong end of the stick, that she hadn't appreciated the seriousness of the situation, he desperately thought of something to placate her. 'No, it can't be as simple as that, Gran, take it from me. They normally double- and even treble-check the facts before declaring it a murder. Have to, really, just in case it turns out to be something different later on. Imagine the reaction from the family if the police made a mistake by being too hasty. No, you can be sure that if they announced it was a murder, then a murder it was.'

Turning back to Emma, he said, 'There's something else, isn't there?'

'Yes,' she added, 'they stressed it had been a particularly gruesome murder.'

'If that's the case it must be bad,' said Jared. 'It'll be the reason they were reluctant to give out any details. Jesus, the body must be in hell of mess.' He suddenly stopping in mid-sentence, realising the implications of what he'd just said. Looking at Emma, he could see she'd put two and two together – and far more quickly than he had. That's what had been troubling her, why she'd been so upset over the incident. 'Oh, shit,' he said quietly so that his grandmother wouldn't hear, 'so it's finally made its move…'

In a resigned tone of voice, he went on, 'But it's not much of a surprise really, is it? It was always going to be a case of when, rather than if. We can't say it didn't give us enough warning, either. Still, at least the waiting is finally over.' Holding Emma tightly, he whispered, 'And you were right.'

Seeing she didn't understand, he explained.

'I know it isn't going to make you feel any better, but you were the one to theorise about who it would target.'

Finally, when details of the murder were released, it rocked the village. Jared's idea that it would be a particularly gruesome killing proved correct. If anything, he'd underestimated the horrific details. After all, it wasn't every day you found a local clergyman slaughtered and crucified upside down in his own church.

When everything had been taken into account, there was no doubt it had been blasphemy of the worst kind. The killer had displayed a complete disregard for a man of the cloth and his elevated position in the community. Of course, not being in possession of the full facts, the media were not to know that desecrating the church and humiliating the old rector was exactly what the demon had intended. According to official reports the sight had been appalling. The once pure white altar cloth had been stained a deep red by the blood of the unfortunate victim. It was obvious to everyone concerned the man had died in agony, but curiously the look on his face was more of horror than pain. It was almost as if just before he died he'd seen or heard something which had shaken him to the core. Another curiosity was that directly behind the body the killer had left his calling card, a strange looking motif. To date no one had been able to fathom its meaning.

The drawing, outlined in blood, was made up of a crude image of a fish and something which looked like an ankh, the Egyptian symbol of eternity. However, the ankh had been inverted through the body of the actual fish.

The next day the local newspaper reporting on the grisly death said that strangely, despite the fact the murder had been committed less than fifty yards from a busy main road, no one had seen or heard anything. The final comment was that it was almost as if the killing had been carried out by a phantom.

Afterwards the local and national divisional police forces went over the crime scene with a fine-tooth comb. Dozens of people were interviewed, but the result was always the same, no one had seen or heard a single thing. Despite the amount of blood found inside the small church, not a single piece of evidence of any kind was found. It was hardly credible, said the police chief. Perhaps the journalist, who'd dubbed the perpetrator the 'phantom killer' had been nearer the mark than she'd thought, was his tongue-in-cheek comment.

In the end the police did the only thing they could and admit they were baffled. It seemed whoever had committed the atrocity had simply disappeared. Whatever had taken place inside the little church that night was beyond their comprehension, beyond their limited experience. As a result they were reluctantly admitting defeat, knowing exactly what such an admission would mean. From that moment on, the case would cease to be their concern; it would be passed on to a higher authority.

Chapter Twenty-three

EDWIN WAS TRUE TO HIS WORD. BY 2 P.M. THE FOLLOWING DAY HE WAS sitting with Eric in his library, along with Jared and a generous helping of malt whisky. Jared made do with a glass of water. It seemed the fates had conspired to ensure Edwin arrived in the middle of the media circus surrounding the death of old Deiniol Symonds. As a result, any complacency regarding the seriousness of the situation was quickly dispelled. Deciding for the moment there was nothing they could do on that score, the three voted to move on to the discussion of more important things.

'Well,' said Eric, turning to Jared, 'what did you make of the notes?'

'Fascinating, and I found the clues you hinted at.'

'I knew you would,' said a smiling Eric, 'but you can see why I wanted you to be familiar with the background material before taking the next step.'

'Montségur, you mean. I was wondering why there was such a paucity of detail about something so obviously important. You kept those notes back, didn't you?'

Laughing, Eric replied, 'Come now, you didn't think I was going to give you the whole thing on a plate, surely? Of course I held something back. I wanted you intrigued, and it looks as if it worked.'

Smiling broadly, Jared said, 'Fine, but when you've finished I might just have a little surprise in store for you too.'

'Well, well,' said Eric, impressed, 'upstaged by the young pretender, eh?' Then he began his tale.

'The first thing you need to know is why the story of Montségur is so popular, and the answer's simple: hidden treasure! Nothing's geared to get the old pulse racing more than stories about treasure, unless of course it's a story about even more treasure. Anyway, according to persistent rumours the citadel of Montségur was supposed to be the repository of mythical riches. Not any old riches, mind; reliable sources suggest this was something far more important, one described as being "far beyond material wealth". An interesting concept, isn't it? I don't know about you two, but to me this suggests something other than monetary value, gold, jewels and the like. If so, what? That's the intriguing question. Unfortunately, after that big build-up the ending's disappointing,' he said with the hint of a sly smile, 'because when the fortress fell in 1244, nothing was ever found.'

'Nothing at all?' asked Edwin incredulously.

'Nothing whatsoever,' said Eric. 'Strange, isn't it? However, I have been able to uncover something that might help explain why. It seems that some three months before, two *parfaits* or "perfected ones", as their leaders were called, managed to escape. So it might be that the bulk of whatever it was, was smuggled away at that time. Even so, it still begs the question: if the treasure was that vast, how could only two people have managed to transport it all? Unless of course they had donkeys or the like, waiting to carry the booty away at the bottom of the hill.'

A moment later he had an idea. 'There might be a more simple explanation. What if the vast majority of the treasure was precious stones, pearls and the like, and not simply bullion? If that was the case, two men would have been able to filter away vast amounts.'

'What about the rest, then?' asked Jared. 'A moment ago you said "bulk"; if that's the case, then unless I'm mistaken, you're implying that something was left behind. And the way your eyes are gleaming, I think this might be the mysterious item "beyond material wealth" the accounts mention.'

'Very astute,' said Eric, smiling. 'You're correct. Unfortunately, what this wealth is I haven't a clue. It may be precious scrolls, documents, the inner secrets of the order, who knows,' he said, holding his hands up in exasperation.

'Come on, Eric,' said Edwin, chuckling to himself, 'you've got more than that. Spit it out!'

Before he could reply Jared stepped in. 'Sorry to interrupt, but it seems to me we have a problem. Aren't we overlooking the fact that Montségur was completely hemmed in? Soldiers ringed the entire base of the fortress, so it was impossible to smuggle anything substantial out, surely?'

'Ah, so you did read the notes! And to answer your question, yes, you're correct; but on the other hand, no one mentioned anything about impossible. As a matter of fact, escaping turned out to be quite simple.' Seeing the puzzled look on Jared's face, he said, 'This is where it gets interesting. According to documentary records the Cathars had many sympathisers, both in the ranks of the opposition soldiers and Templars. As such the ring was far from impregnable. Besides, it seems Montségur was so large the attackers simply didn't have the number of soldiers to make it so.'

'So the plot thickens,' said Jared.

'That's not all,' said, Eric grinning like a schoolboy. 'When the citadel fell on 1 March some three months later, the survivors were offered exceptionally lenient terms. Incredible as it seems, instead of accepting them unreservedly, as you or I would have done, they asked for a fortnight's truce to think it over.'

'You're joking!' said Edwin in astonishment. 'Surely the powers that be didn't stand for that? They were bloody lucky to be given such generous terms in the first place.'

Shaking his head, Eric said, 'I agree with you completely, but as daft as it sounds, they were actually granted the fortnight's grace.'

'But it doesn't make sense.'

'My thoughts exactly, until I looked into the archives a little further, and came up with what I thought might be a plausible explanation. It seems thirteen days into the truce, with a single day remaining, four *parfaits* escaped. At this point you have to remember that one of the conditions of the truce was that if any single person attempted to escape, all 400 survivors would be executed. Yet amazingly, according to official records, four of their leaders blatantly defied the order and did just that.'

'What a selfish bloody thing to do!' exclaimed Jared. 'However good a reason they had, putting all those lives in jeopardy just so they could escape was not only foolhardy, but stupid.'

'You're right,' said Eric, 'but as I said, despite everything, they took the gamble. At the dead of night when visibility was almost zero, they went down the sheer face of the western side of the mountain using only ropes.'

Giving the others time to digest the enormity of the undertaking, he carried on. 'So why on earth were they prepared to take such a risk? Effectively, if they'd waited until the following morning, they could have walked out free men anyway...'

'Unless of course,' said Jared, breaking in excitedly, 'we're missing something. Could it be we're looking at this thing the wrong way round? What if the breakout wasn't about making a dash for freedom, but instead, the whole thing was staged in order to smuggle something out?'

'Great minds think alike,' said Eric smiling. 'That's exactly the conclusion I came to. But let's take a stab in the dark for a moment. We know whatever they smuggled out must have been extraordinarily important, so might it have been this mysterious treasure "beyond material wealth" we keep reading about?'

'If you're right,' said Jared, 'then why keep it back? After all, the bulk of the treasure had already been spirited away months before.'

'Humour me for a moment,' said Eric. 'What if this mysterious thing was an object? Not just any object, but something so incredibly important it was needed as the focal point for a sacred ritual.'

'Ah, I see where you're going with this now,' said Jared. 'You mean the artefact was looked on as being so powerful, so sacred, that without it there could be no ritual. Yes, it makes perfect sense.' He paused before adding, 'And then, once the ritual was over, it could be safely smuggled out. Am I on the right track?'

Eric said nothing. He simply stared at Jared waiting for the penny to drop. When it did, it was like an explosion in his head. The look on Jared's face told Eric the truth had finally dawned.

With that he burst out laughing.

'Of course!' he exclaimed in astonishment. 'It was the head, wasn't it? How could I have been so bloody stupid?'

'Give the man first prize,' said Eric, still laughing, 'but there's more; the date is highly significant. Want to take a stab at why?'

'The spring equinox,' Jared blurted out. It was just one more brushstroke added to what he felt was a rapidly emerging picture. 'Isn't that the date on which the followers of that bastard David Naami kidnap young children?'

'Spot on! Now you know why they have to be taken on those specific dates – they were used as child sacrifices.' Looking from Jared to Edwin, Eric said, 'You were both on the right track when you talked about young children making the most potent offerings. Being without sin, they were ideal sacrifices.'

'But why sacrifice to the head?' asked Edwin puzzled.

'I'm coming to that. If I'm correct, then blood offerings at that precise time of year were supposed to provide the head with power. Feed it, if you like. By this time it had become an essential component of the ritual. According to witnesses, it was believed that as long as the sacrifice was done properly – by that I mean the correct ritual was carried out – then the head reciprocated by providing its worshippers with strange occult powers.'

'Sorry to interrupt,' said Jared, 'but while we're on the subject, what you've just said might just help explain something else.' Seeing their puzzled expressions, he explained.

'Down through the ages a mysterious head has featured strongly in Welsh folklore. For instance, we have Bran the Blessed in Celtic mythology; and then of course, it pops up again in the stories found in the *Mabinogion*. I wonder if the magical properties associated with it might have given rise to stories like that. It's just a thought, that's all.'

'That's an interesting idea,' said Eric. 'It just might be that you've hit on something there. Anyway, where was I... oh, yes, unfortunately this is where my little theory resorts to educated guesswork. Here goes; see what you think.

'My research indicates that all the pieces of the jigsaw can be traced back to our old friends, the Templars and Cathars. The notes show clearly that the origins of both are shrouded in mystery, and so it's my conviction both groups can be traced back to a common heritage – to an extreme or radical sect that gave birth to both. From where I'm standing, it's the only way the similarities can be explained. Until Edwin's scroll arrived on the scene, all I had to go on was a working hypothesis, but the evidence of the scroll clinches it. I'm convinced somehow this elite cadre, whoever they were, managed to obtain the innermost secrets of the Sect of the Dead, that strange and enigmatic group mentioned in the scroll.'

Pausing to see if they were still with him, he carried on.

'Now for the interesting bit. It's my considered opinion this select group was also in possession of a secret so explosive that it gave them the ability to blackmail the Roman Catholic Church. That's why they became so powerful and wealthy.'

Holding his hand up, he said, 'The problem is, I don't have a clue as to what the secret was. But I can see by your faces you're wondering how all this fits in with the head. For an explanation of that, we now have to turn our attention to the Templars.

'The information available points to the fact they too began life as a small elite group. However, unlike my conjecture regarding the Cathars, there is indisputable evidence to support the fact that the Knights Templar worshipped a strange bearded head. They even gave it a name – *Baphomet.* Down through the centuries there has been a good deal of speculation about exactly what this head was. Some have suggested it was that of Hugues de Payen, the order's founder and Grand Master, who by the way seems originally to have been a Cathar.'

A sharp intake of breath from Jared brought a huge grin to Eric's face.

'Yes, that's something else I held back. I wanted to see your reaction. Apparently his family tree has been traced back to the Languedoc, so it seems pretty conclusive.'

Carrying on, he said, 'Others have put forward the theory it might have been the one which appeared on the shroud of Turin. Strangely, that's not as far out as it sounds, because we know it was in the possession of the Templars between 1204 and 1307. When folded, it would have appeared as nothing more than a bearded head. An even wilder theory was that it was the head of John the Baptist.'

Waving his hand in a gesture of dismissal, he said, 'But as I mentioned earlier, what clinches it for me is the information given on the scroll. The only problem is that none of this conjecture answers the real question – who the hell's head is it?'

Catching his breath for a few seconds, he was off again.

'What we do know is both sets of worshippers believed the head endowed them with occult powers. Documentary evidence states quite clearly that when tortured, several knights admitted openly to worshipping it. It appears they prostrated themselves before it...'

'But I thought,' said Edwin, breaking in, 'that in 1307 they were all arrested and imprisoned, and then by 1314 they ceased to exist.'

'Like many you've been misled,' said Eric. 'In fact for a variety of reasons many survived the cull.'

'So why did they fall from grace?' asked Edwin. 'What did they do which was so bad the Church wanted them hunted out of existence?'

'Arrogant bullies, too powerful for their own good, a law unto themselves, heretics capable of vile blasphemy... Any of those phrases ring a bell?'

'Right, I'll accept that, but if that's the case, just how did they manage to become so powerful and wealthy?' asked Edwin again.

'It's an extremely complicated story, and once again there seems to be a definite link to the Cathars, but I'll try and make it simple. The actual moment when something concrete came to light was shortly after the Templars made a discovery of great value in a network of caves under the old Temple in Jerusalem. To me there was nothing accidental about the find; I believe they were sent deliberately, sent there by someone with prior knowledge of its existence. Anyway, shortly afterwards they had their wealth.'

At that point, Jared who had been quiet until now spoke up.

'May I hazard a little theory of my own, Eric?'

Seeing Eric nod his head, he carried on.

'According to your hypothesis, even though both the Cathars and Templars were separate entities, they began life as one, correct? Now in order for your idea to work, there would have to be a point of commonality. To put it another way, there would have to be a common denominator, an elite group that came before either, but in reality gave birth to both. From where I'm standing, it seems the stumbling block was in finding this common denominator.' Smiling now, Jared continued, 'I might just have the answer to your problem.

'Edwin has heard my little story once, so I'll keep it short. I know you're both familiar with a group of assassins known as the Sicarii – they're the ones who burst onto the scene during the time of Christ. The history books inform us that after Masada they ceased to exist. Unlike conventional historians, however, I believe a select few survived. Not only that, but over a period of time, they gradually filtered back into society.'

Listening while Jared described in detail his pet theory about the Sicarii, old Eric became more and more agitated, until suddenly he could curb his impatience no longer.

'My boy,' he said excitedly, 'you might have found the answer I've been searching over thirty years for! It could well be you've unearthed the missing link.'

Realising he'd interrupted Jared in full flow, he quickly said, 'But how rude of me. Please carry on. I can assure you, that you have my full and undivided attention.'

Smiling at the old man's enthusiasm, Jared pressed on.

'For a while this small group remained dormant, because as extreme zealots they were now an anachronism. The last thing they wanted to do was to draw attention to themselves, for the simple reason that to all intents and purposes they no longer existed. It was the perfect cover, wasn't it? Now let's take the argument to its next logical step. You see, I believe in the very beginning, around about the time the old man brought the chalice and codex from the Holy Land, the organisation had already discovered the cave and its treasures. Don't ask me how they managed it, but they did. It's my conviction they understood the implications of their discovery immediately, but were faced with a dilemma. The material wealth they could dispose of easily. The real problem was this thing they'd found and described as "beyond material wealth". How was this to be used?

'Due to a combination of circumstances, they were unable to utilise it at that particular time, and so I believe they left it where it was. They were shrewd enough to realise they could always come back for it when the time was deemed to be right.'

Turning to Eric again, Jared said, 'You mentioned you thought the finding of the wealth by the Templars was no accident, that they'd been deliberately given the location. I agree. The answer's simple: the Sicarii, by now acting in the guise of the Templars, saw that the time had finally arrived. It was time to produce their little gem from its hiding place. Experts have puzzled for years over the fact the Templars were originally only nine, arguing such a ridiculously low number could never have kept the highways of the Holy Land free for pilgrims. "Guardians of the highways" was a puerile facade; the real reason for the small number was to ensure silence. With such a small group, the chances of the secret leaking out would be minimised. Besides, each of the nine were the sons of the original families that had been handed the secret down through the centuries. It was their birthright.'

Suddenly Jared changed tack. 'Put yourselves in their shoes. This elite group of families saw empires come and go, the balance of power change between continents like shifting sand in the desert, until suddenly an opportunity presented itself. And they pounced.'

'What opportunity?' asked Eric in surprise.

'Bear with me for a moment,' said Jared, 'but meanwhile keep one thing in mind. At the time we're talking about, the Church in Rome was on its knees, under attack from all quarters. In particular, though,' and he paused for emphasis, 'especially from the area of Languedoc. Dismissed out of hand for so long, the threat suddenly developed into such a serious problem that the Church could no longer afford to ignore it. So what did it do? It realised desperate measures were called for. Belatedly, it decided nothing short of the total annihilation of every Cathar would do. While all this was going on, the Sicarii, Templars, Brotherhood, whatever you want to call them, made its move. Virtually everything was in their favour – heresy was rife, ordinary people were deserting the Church in droves – so what better time to act, to blackmail Rome? First however they needed proof, and of course they knew exactly where to find it. That's why the Brotherhood, now disguised as the Knights Templar, was sent to Jerusalem. The time had come to claim their birthright!'

Jumping up Eric said, 'It also explains why the Templars became wealthy almost overnight.'

Both Jared and Eric were startled when suddenly Edwin burst out laughing. He laughed so much that the tears were rolling down his cheeks. When he finally finished, he said, 'But it's brilliant.' Seeing the bewildered looks on their faces he said, 'You don't get it, do you? Don't you see the irony of it? The most extreme of all Jewish sects were pretending to be the saviours of Christianity. Jewish zealots masquerading as soldiers of Christ!' he said slapping his thigh with his hand. 'You've got to hand it to them, it was a stroke of bloody genius!'

'It was more than a stroke of genius,' said Eric in awed tones, 'it was inspired; but don't you see what else it means? It provides the explanation for not only their choice of clothes, but why they repudiated Christ. It's something that has puzzled researchers for years. By choosing the white mantle of purity and emblazoning it with the bloodied cross of Christ, they were taking the piss!'

Later when they'd all stopped laughing, and the full implications of what they'd discovered dawned on them, they were left with a problem that Jared voiced.

'Unfortunately, it still doesn't explain who Baphomet is, or what the secret they discovered in the cave complex was.'

Despite all they'd uncovered, Jared was still unhappy. He was convinced somewhere along the line he'd missed something – something that was right under his nose, if only he could see it. Past experience had taught him, however, that to chase the memory would do no good; that when it was ready, it would find its own way to the surface.

Chapter Twenty-four

JOHNNY DODDS WAS AN ENGLISHMAN LIVING IN WALES, AND HAD done for over thirty years. That in itself was far from unusual, but the story behind it was. Standing several inches over six feet and weighing in at nineteen stones, he was a giant of a man. Strangers tended to give him a wide berth, gazing at his size in apprehension. Starting out as a London policeman, he'd risen through the ranks quickly until by the age of forty he'd become a Chief Inspector. Then disaster struck. At the tender age of forty-two he suffered a nervous breakdown, brought about, according to the specialist who'd treated him, by spending too much time inside the heads of psychopaths and child killers.

Putting yourself in the minds of killers was all very well, the psychologist had explained patiently. It was a brilliant and innovative way of catching criminals. However, it had a down side. Ninety per cent of policemen he'd dealt with over the years had admitted openly that when they'd achieved it, when they were there actually sitting inside the heads of the sick bastards, they'd enjoyed it. Worse, it was often difficult for them to drag themselves back to reality, to escape the clutches of the dark side, as he'd coined it. Johnny knew exactly what these coppers were talking about and had no difficulty empathising with their sentiments. For him, it had been even worse as on each occasion he'd felt tainted, corrupted by the experience. Deep down, Johnny was left in no doubt it was what had finally tipped him over the edge and had led to his breakdown.

While recuperating at a small hospital in South Wales, he met Anne. According to him, it was love at first sight, and within a year they were married. Jared spent his first twelve years living next door to the amiable Johnny and his wife, and although they were totally unrelated, according to a time honoured valley custom, they soon became Uncle Johnny and Auntie Anne.

From day one he found Johnny fascinating, and until he'd left to join the forces he'd visited on a regular basis. Although Johnny rarely spoke about his past, on the odd occasion he did, Jared realised there was very little he didn't know about police work, especially the seedier and more unpleasant side of it. It needed little imagination to work out that although officially retired, Johnny was often called in to help out in an 'unofficial' role, or in an 'advisory capacity' as he liked to put it. Not a religious man, he'd long ago come to the conclusion that a God who would allow such evil and cruelty to flourish really wasn't worth knowing.

His healthy scepticism and pragmatism were exactly the qualities Jared was relying on for an honest appraisal of things. It was more important than ever now, especially since the short meeting he'd had with the others had produced a unanimous response.

After the old rector's brutal murder, it was time for the police to be brought in. It had taken him almost an hour to get the group to hold off until Jared had the opportunity to put his case to Johnny. When they'd managed to obtain his unbiased opinion, he argued, they would be in a better position to judge whether it would be prudent to approach the local police or not.

Sitting in the living room of the small terraced cottage, Jared couldn't help the rush of fond memories the old place invoked, and it was with great difficulty he dragged himself back into the present. Looking at Johnny's face closely, Jared compared it with a road map. Each little wrinkle had a tale to tell, and knowing Johnny as he did, the overall picture was a face which reflected a lifetime's experience. The conversation was only minutes old when Jared knew instinctively where the discussion was heading. Like most policemen, Johnny clung to the philosophy of believing in things only if they could be proven. No evidence, no case!

Talk of evil spirits and demons went completely over his head, although in fairness, he did hear Jared out.

Allowing an appropriate amount of time to elapse before answering, Johnny gave his opinion. What the six of them had seen and heard that night was nothing that couldn't be explained away rationally.

'I'm sure it all seemed real to you at the time, but if you want my opinion, it was simply a case of your minds playing tricks on you. Either that or mass hypnosis,' he added as an afterthought. 'The atmosphere of the surroundings and the fact you were all nervous contributed too. Remember, you knew what you were doing was wrong, so it's little wonder to me you convinced yourselves you saw or heard something. It would have seemed very real at the time, but I'm sure that's all it was.' Johnny was convinced it had been a prank that had somehow gone wrong, but no more than that.

Groaning inwardly, Jared knew the others had their answer.

In a last ditch attempt to convince Johnny otherwise, he said, 'What about the murder of the old rector, then? Surely you can see a link between that and the spirit of the chalice?'

Serious now, Johnny replied, 'Well, it's a bad one, I'll grant you that. In fact it's so unusual that the local boys have finally had to admit defeat. Within the hour a special unit from London will arrive to handle the case.'

Smiling, as if suddenly thinking of a fond memory, Johnny said, 'The chap in charge is an old friend of mine, Danny Harris. When I say "friend", I mean that when I was in charge of the unit he was a young lad. Sharp as a razor, even then. From day one I knew he had a bright future, and as things turned out he didn't let me down. Welsh too,' he said, looking at Jared. 'And yes, before you ask, he does play rugby.' Then he suddenly corrected himself. 'Or he used to, anyway; he's too bloody old now, of course. So, coming back to the murder, it's a strange one all right. Who in their right mind would want to do that to an old man – particularly a rector, for Christ's sake? Stuck a bloody great fish hook into his mouth, crucified the poor bugger upside down, and then slit his throat for good measure.'

After a suitable period of silence, Jared said, 'Apart from the horrific injuries, was there anything else you can think of that stood out as being unusual?'

'Funny you should ask, but there was one odd thing, now you come to mention it. Behind the head, the killer had drawn some kind of weird symbol – in blood, mind you; the old man's, probably. Really weird, it was. Leaning over the side of his chair, he picked up a small notebook from the coffee table and began drawing. 'There,' he said, holding it up to show Jared. 'What do you make of it?'

Studying it, Jared could see it was made up of two seemingly separate motifs. Although both of them were familiar, he decided to keep his thoughts to himself.

Subtly attempting to change the subject, he said, 'All this, and you're still not convinced there's anything supernatural to any of what's going on? To prove a point, though, I'm willing to bet that your experts won't find any evidence at the scene of the crime. There won't be any, for the simple reason this thing leaves no trail!'

For a moment Jared appeared to lose his concentration. It was as if he was in a daze. Then suddenly his eyes regained their focus and his expression hardened. Serious now, he said, 'Let me tell you something about evil, Johnny. When people talk about it, they usually associate it with comic books and cheap B movies. Real evil is far more subtle. The real terror is the one you can't see. Take this thing from the chalice: it takes over people and controls them; ordinary people, remember, not complete strangers. Someone you might know or love suddenly turns into a killing machine. If that wasn't bad enough, the real horror of the situation is the poor buggers haven't a clue what's going on.'

Finished, Jared suddenly got up and, shaking hands with Johnny, made for the door. About to let himself out, he turned on his heels. 'I'm so confident of winning my first little bet I'm going to stick my neck out and make another. Within the next month or so *another* local clergyman is going to be slaughtered, and in an equally brutal and bizarre fashion. When it does, remember you were warned!'

Clearly shaken, Johnny still clung tenaciously to his conviction that there would be a simple explanation for what had happened to old Deiniol Symonds. 'What we have here is the product of a deranged mind, and nothing more,' were his parting words.

Jared's last thought as he trudged wearily down the narrow path towards to the front gate was, I hope to God you're right, Johnny, I just hope to God you're right…

Early that afternoon, Danny Harris and his team arrived in an unofficial black BMW, 'privilege of rank', as he put it. Although he could have requisitioned a driver from the pool, he drove himself for the simple reason he liked driving. Pulling up outside the wrought iron gates which guarded the entrance to the church, they were stopped by a fresh-faced constable who didn't look a day over sixteen. Danny's immediate thought was that the lad hadn't started shaving yet.

Bending down in order to peer through the side window of the car, the young officer tried to identify who was sitting inside. He wasn't sure of the occupants, because in truth he'd never seen a police car that looked remotely like this.

Making it easier for him, Danny lowered the electronic window and produced his warrant card. Taking it from his hand, the young policemen studied it briefly before handing it back. 'Sorry, sir, I had to make sure, because we've had all kind of crackpots trying to get inside. Makes me wonder sometimes what kind of a world we're living in. Why on earth would someone go to so much trouble just to get a look at that little lot? Bloody sickos, if you ask me.'

'What about the media?' asked Danny.

'They're the worst, sir. Since very early this morning they've been like bloody ghouls. The thing that puzzles me is how they managed to cotton on. I mean, we were only called in ourselves at 9 a.m. Beats me how they found out so quickly. They've even been trying to jump over the railings. Seems they're prepared to do anything for an exclusive. So far they've been out of luck; the boys stationed around the perimeter have caught them. We threatened to lock them up if they gave us any more trouble, but even that didn't work. I suppose they've got a job to do, same as the rest of us, but there's got be a line drawn somewhere, hasn't there? Me, I only took one look and then it was straight outside to get rid of my breakfast.' Suddenly worried that they might have been too hard on the press, he added, 'Hope we did the right thing, sir?'

'Don't worry, son,' said Danny, 'you did exactly the right thing. I'm just glad to see you doing your job properly.' He paused before adding, 'But it's as bad as that, is it? Inside, I mean?'

''Fraid so, sir. You see, we're not used to seeing things like that. A few burglaries or the occasional domestic is as exciting as it gets around here. I suppose you're hardened to it in your line of work, though?'

'We get our moments,' said Danny, 'I must admit. But don't believe what they say, lad; you never get conditioned to that kind of thing.' As an afterthought he said, 'Anyway, if it's as bad as you say, then I doubt even we've seen anything like it.' With that he retrieved his warrant card and closed the electric window.

Stopping outside the front door of the church, Danny exited and stepped to the back of the car to open the door for DC Tina Reynolds. Getting out, she gave a polite smile before curtseying and saying, 'Thank you, kind sir! Contrary to popular belief the age of chivalry is alive and well.' They all laughed, before Tina looked up at the tower said, 'What a quaint little church! It's quite beautiful, isn't it?'

Answering, Danny said, 'Yes. I'm not overly religious, but I must admit you have a point.'

The third member of the group, DI Gareth Evans, suddenly spoke up. 'If what's in there is as bad as that young copper on the gate says, I'm glad I only had a light breakfast.'

'There's only one way to find out,' said Danny, reaching over and lifting up the bright yellow tape used to cordon off the area. Ducking underneath, he made his way towards the impressive porch which decorated the front of the building. Waiting for the others to catch up, he opened one of the two iron studded doors before tentatively stepping inside. The church was simply decorated, the wooden pews worn and smooth in places. At the far end of the nave three very impressive stained glass windows watched the approach of Danny and his two companions with lofty disdain, while the large brass crucifix which stood over the altar appeared to be standing guard.

Making his way down the central aisle, he'd gone no more than six feet when the smell hit him. 'Christ almighty!' he exclaimed. 'It's like a bloody slaughterhouse in here!' He fumbled in his pocket for his handkerchief. Once his mouth and nose was safely covered, he moved further into the main body of the church. Normally dark and forbidding, this morning it was anything but. All the lights were on in order to help the forensic team, who by now were working on the body.

Turning to the others, Danny said, 'Well, the lad was right – it looks like a cross between something from Dante's Inferno and a painting by Hieronymus Bosch.'

'Bloody hell, guv!' said Gareth Evans, directly behind him. 'There's a classical education hidden beneath that Savile Row suit. But I thought you were a secondary school boy?'

'I was, you cheeky sod, but I like reading, and music and art are hobbies of mine. No harm in that, is there?'

'Not at all, guv, it's just I'm impressed, that's all.' And he meant it.

'And by the way,' added Danny, 'the suit's from Burtons.'

The nearer they got to the altar the worse things appeared. By now Tina Reynolds had paled visibly.

Fighting back his breakfast, which in his case had been anything but small, Danny made his way towards the imposing figure of Ralf Edwards, the forensic pathologist, who was busy conducting affairs with his usual quiet efficiency. It never ceased to amaze Danny that, however much blood and gore might be involved in a crime scene, Ralf always turned up for work in a suit and tie. He was the consummate professional. Or might it be that he was just old-fashioned? he thought, chuckling to himself.

Unaware he was being watched, Ralf suddenly stepped into his white suit and, zipping it up, declared that he was ready.

Approaching from behind, Danny said, 'Anything to report?'

Looking up, Professor Edwards smiled. 'Wondered how long it would take you to get here! You of all people should know better, though; it's too early to tell, but I should have something concrete for you in a few hours or so.'

As it turned out his confidence was not only misplaced, but hopelessly optimistic.

Having worked together on many occasions, he and Danny knew each other well.

'Now how did I know you were going to say that, Ralf?' said Danny with a chuckle. Turning to the others, he made the introductions before adding, 'Old Ralf and I go back a long way... Don't take any notice of the way we talk to each other, he's really a good bloke when you get to know him – for a pathologist, that is.'

Ralf Edwards was an exceptionally thin man, but what made it worse was that he was also very tall. His emaciated looks and permanent grey pallor had earned him the nickname 'Lurch'. Even some of his closest friends had been heard to comment that the bodies he spent so much time studying often looked a good deal healthier than he did.

'I know exactly what you mean, though, Ralf. You're going to have to be one hundred per cent sure on this one, aren't you? One mistake and heads will roll.' Looking over at the state of the corpse he added hastily, 'I'm not so sure I should have said that.'

Pleased Danny had grasped the gravity of the case, Ralf said, 'Yes, I'm afraid all of us are going to have to be extra vigilant on this one. Normally the body is removed once the photographs have been taken, but in this instance I'm breaking with protocol. I'm going to examine it here before shipping it off to the lab. In case you're wondering, that's why the body is still here; by now it should have been long gone. Incidentally, have you found anywhere to stay?'

'No, we've only just arrived... any suggestions?'

'You could do worse than the Beech Tree down the road.'

'Thanks, Ralf, appreciate the tip. I'll have a quick nose around and then I'll nip down and book the three of us in. Convenient, is it?'

'Matter of fact, it's within walking distance,' he replied. 'Now bugger off and let me get on with my work.'

After Danny had left, Ralf moved carefully around the church dressed in the white protective suit that shielded him from the UV light he was using. To all intents and purposes he looked like a ghost. The latest equipment he was using was supposed to detect the smallest amount of body fluid; but strangely, apart from that of the old rector, which he knew would be present, there was nothing. For the first time in his life he admitted he was completely baffled.

For the next two days the area around St David's was a hive of activity. Cordoned off since that first morning, no one other than those essential to the investigation had been allowed access.

From day one, a search team had been drafted in to take care of the everyday tasks such as looking for any signs of evidence. They covered every inch of the church and its surrounding area, and everything, however innocuous, was bagged and labelled, so thorough was the search. With that side of things taken care of, the way was open for Danny and his team to concentrate on the broader aspects of the investigation.

At the end of the first week, Danny, Gareth and Tina had to admit they were at their wits' end. Equally baffling, from Danny's point of view, was the fact that even Professor Edward's expertise had failed to come up with anything. It was the first time he'd ever known him to turn up empty-handed. Despite this, the team refused to give up, going over everything for a second and even third time in the vain hope they'd missed something.

Finally, a week later, even they had to admit defeat.

Reporting to the press that morning, Danny's team conceded that despite the enormous amount of time, effort and money poured into the investigation – £30,000 a day by now – they'd been unable to come up with anything. Silently, he admitted they were pissing in the wind on this one, and unfortunately each member of the team knew it.

Not a single shred of evidence of any kind had been found; not even a fingerprint. The killer it seemed had either been invisible, or had simply vanished off the face of the earth.

Turning out of the drive the following morning, the three glanced over their shoulders at the spectacular tree from which the hotel took its name.

Suddenly Gareth Evans broke the silence. 'You know, despite everything, I've got to admit I enjoyed the last fortnight.'

'Good food, good beer and…'

Before he could finish, Tina Reynolds broke in. 'And good local girls too, from what I hear.'

'Anyway,' continued Gareth, completely nonplussed, 'what I was about to say was, good company too. But seeing as I was so rudely interrupted, I withdraw the last remark.' He paused. 'In all seriousness, though, I don't suppose any of us will ever see this little place again.'

Little did he realise just how wrong his wistful comment would turn out to be.

When Gareth had commented on the hospitality shown to the team under such trying circumstances, he hadn't realised just how near the mark he was. For battle-hardened veterans like him, the horror of the past fortnight was nothing exceptional. For the locals it was very different. They had never witnessed anything like the recent goings-on, especially now that everything seemed to have come to a head with the death of old Deiniol Symonds. By the time everyone had left, the little church was in such a state it was feared it might be another fortnight before things returned to anything like normality. Many of the parishioners were of the opinion they never wanted to set foot inside the building again.

Sarah Thomas, speaking to her friend Greta Philpot, was heard to say, 'Well, I for one won't be coming back, even if it means I have to find another church.'

'Nor me,' said Greta, 'I couldn't think of it.'

'Just imagine, every time you walked in you'd be bound to look at the altar, wouldn't you? It would give me nightmares.'

'Especially if it was as bad as everyone says,' said her friend, with unabashed enthusiasm. 'Poor old Mr Symonds, his soul will never rest in peace now.'

'In that case,' said Greta, quick as a flash, 'do you think his spirit might still be in there, tied to the earth or something?'

'I hadn't thought of that,' answered Sarah, 'but if it is we might have our very own ghost.' Thinking furiously she added, 'In that case perhaps our little church will be famous!'

'Aren't you forgetting something?' Greta chipped in. 'A short while ago you vowed never to set foot in it again.'

'Yes, well,' Sarah answered, 'perhaps I was a bit hasty. If it means we're going to be on TV, I might just reconsider. I'd like to see myself on TV, wouldn't you?'

After thinking about it for a moment, Greta said, 'Of course I would, silly! I agree with you, just for the moment I think we should forget the past and make an effort to attend. Just for the time being, mind you; see how things turn out, like.'

It hardly came as a surprise that several of the local newspapers decided to make the story their lead feature. As much as they attempted to dress it up, though, the honest truth was that like the police they were completely at a loss to explain what had happened.

Quotes and ideas abounded.

They ranged from the inventive to the downright silly. 'Gruesome slaughter of biblical proportions strikes rural Welsh church' was one of the more predictable ones.

Strangely, once you were able to get past the trite headlines, some insightful comments were made. Two in particular caught Jared's eye.

The first was that the killer seemed to be following a hidden agenda, evidenced by the fact he'd left his calling card, a symbol daubed in blood. It had prompted the same journalist to suggest the police might be dealing with a serial killer. Perhaps, he theorised, the murderer has only just started his killing spree.

The second observation was equally astute. This journalist had suggested that whatever had killed the old rector had displayed almost demonic strength.

Smiling to himself, Jared thought that had the two pooled their ideas, they would have been very near to explaining what it was the police were up against.

Chapter Twenty-five

As expected, Jared's report to his friends the following evening was greeted with groans of dismay. Word for word, making sure he left nothing out, Jared repeated exactly what Johnny had said.

After a few moments of contemplative silence, Roger asked the question which was on all of their lips. 'So where do we go from here?'

Opening his hands outwards in a gesture of uncertainty, Jared said, 'I hate to say I told you so, but I'm afraid it's how police mentality works. If Johnny didn't believe us, think what the local lot would have said. I'm convinced there'll be at least another murder before anyone's going to take us seriously.'

'And then what?' asked Aled.

'That's the big question, isn't it? But I've got an idea. If I can persuade Johnny to see what's really going on, I'm hopeful he might introduce us to this chap called Danny Harris. He thinks very highly of him, so if we can get him on our side we may have half a chance.'

'But what can he do that we can't?' said Emma in exasperation.

'For a start, he's got access to resources we can only dream about. If we can combine our knowledge, his equipment and expertise, so to speak, it's got to be a step in the right direction, hasn't it?'

'Any progress with Eric and Edwin?' asked Roger.

'Sorry,' said Jared, 'I should have mentioned that earlier. Edwin's here in Raven's Hill staying with Gran and me for a few days. He's helping us try and come up with some answers. As far as progress is concerned we've started to make inroads. For instance we know the answer to the mystery of the head. We know where it came from originally and why the organisation we've dubbed the Brotherhood wanted it so badly.'

'Shit, you've done well!' was Roger's comment.

'A compliment, Roger,' he said, raising an eyebrow quizzically. 'I'm honoured, but that's only the half of it.' He then described in detail everything they'd discovered.

For the first time since the whole affair started, Jared sensed a lightening of the mood in the camp, so it was with reluctance he delivered the next crushing blow. 'Unfortunately, despite everything, we're still no nearer to answering the really important questions.'

'Such as?' said Roger.

'Who the head belongs to, and why it's so obsessed with revenge. But even more importantly,' he carried on, 'how to stop the thing.'

'If only we could get hold of the codex,' said Roger wistfully. 'I'm sure if we could get our hands on that, it would solve all our problems.'

They were so preoccupied with their own thoughts that none of them noticed the expression of guilt that crossed Jared's face. He was only too well aware of the fact that it was a moment of madness on his behalf that had put them in this invidious position, but he knew enough to keep that particular opinion to himself.

In an inquisitive mood, Roger said, 'Wait a minute, about this codex thing. I know we haven't got it, but what the hell is a bloody codex when it's at home anyway?'

Grateful for a chance to shrug off his mood of depression, Jared started to explain. 'In short, Rog, it's supposed to be the earliest form of book. You see in the beginning, people wrote on anything they could lay their hands on. Things like broken bits of pottery, even pieces of wood. The problem with things like that was that they were only suitable for short notes, or in some cases even single words. Very little information could be stored on them. Eventually someone came up with the idea of animal skins, the best of which was called vellum. Much more could be written on this, but it still wasn't the answer because it tended to rot, however well preserved. The solution finally arrived in the form of the daddy of them all – papyrus!'

'But papyrus is a reed!' said Roger. 'How the hell did they write on that?'

Laughing, Jared replied, 'No, you daft bugger, they didn't write on reeds, they used the reeds to make paper.'

'Ah,' was all Roger could think of to say. He was afraid to look at the others in case they saw how embarrassed he was.

'Anyway,' said Jared, 'they collected all these bloody great reeds, some of which grew to a height of thirty feet, and cut them into strips. The next step was to place the strips across each other in much the same way you do when making straw mats, before putting a heavy weight on top. The weight squeezed the moisture out of the lumpy reed so that you were left with a rough square of something that looked like paper.'

'Then what did they do?' asked Aled, intrigued.

'The finishing touches were added after the sticky mess had dried out, by rubbing it down with pumice stone, you know the rock they get from volcanoes. In the end what they had was the precursor to our modern day paper.'

'What did they use as ink, then?' was Roger's next question.

'The first real ink was a simple mixture of soot and gum, and although it's hard to believe it worked, it lasted for ages. Before you ask, they made their own pens too. Again it was easy; they simply cut a short length of reed, cut one end, pointed it and bingo – you had a pen. Of course, down through the ages people improved on that.'

'A quill,' said Emma, smiling.

'Yes,' said Jared, 'you're right.'

'I'm not completely thick, you know,' she retorted in mock indignation, before Roger chipped in with, 'You could have fooled me.'

Continuing the explanation, Jared said, 'The trouble with papyrus was it was quite brittle. By that I mean you couldn't bend it. In order to transport it you had to roll it up, and you needed quite a lot of it. That's why papyrus and vellum were made into scrolls. Now the codex, when it arrived, changed all this. Suddenly, someone had the bright idea of cutting the papyrus into small squares and sewing them together. Now you could write on both sides; but even better, the pages could be folded – voila, the first book! Rumour has it the earliest Christians invented the codex so that all the Gospels could be written under one cover. It certainly would have made it easier to carry around, especially considering all the travelling the early followers of Jesus did in spreading the word. It's only a rumour, though; no one knows for certain.'

Several moments later Aled looked up. 'That's all very well, but we don't even have the chalice any more, never mind the codex, do we?'

Startled, Roger looked across at Jared, who, with an almost imperceptible shake of the head, indicated he should say nothing for the moment.

'What do we do then?' asked Emma.

'It seems we have little choice. We keep plugging away until we get a break.'

'What if even the three of you don't manage to come up with something? Before the bastard strikes again, I mean,' asked Aled.

'You'd better hope we do,' was all Jared could think of saying.

The following evening, sitting alongside Eric in his living room, Jared said, 'It's a shame Edwin had to return home so quickly, we were just starting to get somewhere. Not to worry, it's not as if we can't manage without him; besides, anything of interest we come up with can be passed on at a later date.'

'Before we start,' said Eric, 'tell me what you know about this big corporation in Cardiff Bay, the one called Chameleon Enterprises.' Seeing the surprise on Jared's face, he explained, 'It came up during some research I was doing the other week, and after our little chat the other day, I put two and two together, that's all. The question is, did I get my maths right? Is there a connection between them and the chalice?'

'Oh, there's a connection all right,' said Jared, 'it's where the chalice is sitting right now. At this very moment it's in the possession of David Naami and the Brotherhood.'

The old man was too polite to ask just how Jared had come up with this priceless piece of information.

'Chameleon Enterprises is the "missing link", so to speak, the repository of power. They are the common thread running through everything – the descendants of the original Sicarii.'

'I guessed as much,' said Eric, 'so in effect they are the original founders of both the radical arm of the Cathars and Templars. Neat, and I must say I love the name; it sums up the Brotherhood perfectly. Although I detest them and everything they stand for, part of me admires what they've accomplished.'

'I agree with you, Eric, what they achieved is incredible. For the moment, though, let's refresh our memories as to what we know about them.'

Using his fingers, he began ticking off the points. 'First we have the Sicarii, who according to official records no longer exist. As we now know, however, they not only survived, but managed to infiltrate a much larger group known as the Cathars. Gradually over time, they become an extreme sect within the set-up. It must have been relatively simple, really, because the poor old Cathars were totally unaware of what was going on. Although there's no documentary evidence, I'm willing to bet they were originally nine in number.'

'Point two. In 1104, the Sicarii, now a group of noble families residing in Languedoc, come out of the woodwork and set themselves up as the Knights Templar. This time we don't have to guess, we know they were nine in number. That's as far as I go,' said Jared. 'How they managed to develop and set up Chameleon Enterprises is beyond me.'

'But not me,' said Eric quietly. 'Everything is detailed meticulously in the notes I didn't show you. Sit back for a while; I think you're going to enjoy the next half-hour or so. By the time my research had taken me into the nineteenth century I was faced with a problem. I knew that on the same date every year, as far back as documentary evidence allowed, a young child went missing. It took me years to discover why, but of course by now you know the reason. It was so difficult to find anything concrete on the Brotherhood, but of course that's the beauty of secret societies, isn't it? – the paucity of information others have on them. The last thing a secret society wants is to draw attention to itself.'

'That's why Wolf was made an example of, wasn't it?' said Jared. 'He'd needlessly put the identity of the Brotherhood in jeopardy, hadn't he?'

'Precisely,' said Eric. 'The anonymity of the organisation had to be preserved at all costs. As you're aware, a secret is only as good as the people who know about it, so it goes without saying the fewer who know the less likely it is to be disclosed. That's why the number nine figures so prominently in the background of the Sicarii, Cathars and Templars. It was small enough to be manageable. However, human nature being what it is, it stands to reason unless you're incredibly lucky, or rule by absolute fear, as this character David Naami does, then somewhere along the line it will leak out.

'Bear with me, but I want to change tack here for a moment and talk about conspiracy theories. It seems that for one reason or another they have always been with us, but by the 1960s they had become extremely fashionable. At present they seem to be cropping up at the rate of one a month. You know the kind of thing I'm on about: Kennedy was assassinated by the CIA; the world is being run by a secret cadre of bankers; Elvis is still alive, all that kind of thing. Leaving all that aside, I believe I may have uncovered a genuine one. If I'm right, it could turn out to be the mother and daddy of them all. Not only that, it's sitting right here on our doorstep.

'Anyway to get back to basics, by the end of the nineteenth century this radical or extreme arm of the Templars had developed into a sinister new order, known as – wait for it – "Worshippers of the Head". Among its many claims was that it was in possession of ancient secrets, the Cabala, necromancy, even the ability to bring the dead to life. Ring any bells?' Eric paused before going on.

'A disturbing feature of this sect was that over the course of a year or two their motif underwent a subtle change. Whereas it had been the Star of David and the chalice, it now incorporated the swastika as well. If you know anything about the history of the Second World War, then you know that towards the end, when Hitler was losing, he became desperate. According to persistent rumours he was ready to grasp at straws, and it was during this time he became obsessed with the occult. It seems he was interested in it before, but now he saw it as his 'Holy Grail', so to speak. As far-fetched as it sounds, the story is not without some credence. You see, ultimately Hitler and the Brotherhood wanted similar things. Hitler had the kind of political power the Brotherhood craved, while the Brotherhood had in their possession something Hitler believed would turn the tide of the war. Between them they were convinced if they could only find the chalice and reunite it with the head, total world domination would be within their grasp. Of course, as we now know, Hitler didn't last much longer.'

In reflective mood, Jared said, 'Do you think the course of history might have been altered, perhaps... if Hitler had managed to get his hands on the chalice, I mean?'

'That we will never know,' said the old man, before suddenly exploding into laughter.

'But there's one thing I am sure about, they had the last word once again.' Realising that Jared had no clue as to what he was on about, he said, 'I'm sorry, Jared, but don't you see what they were doing? Hitler's regime was dedicated to anti-Semitism. He hated the Jews, regarded them as subhuman; that's why he tried to wipe them off the face of the earth. The bloody fool didn't realise that by falling in with the Brotherhood, he was consorting with the very people he despised – Jews!'

'Of course!' said Jared. 'They'd already done something similar to the Templars, hadn't they? In public they pretended to be soldiers of Christ, while secretly they not only repudiated him, but spat on the cross as well.'

'You've go to admire the cheeky bastards, haven't you?' said Eric.

It was the first time Jared had ever heard the old minister use a bad swear word, and for some reason it made him seem more human somehow. Because of this, what Jared was about to tell him was made a little easier. The problem was he didn't know how to begin, so instead of beating about the bush he came straight to the point.

'I was there the night the chalice was taken,' was all he said before sitting back and waiting for the old man's reaction.

When it came it was not what Jared had expected.

'So old Tom has you to thank for avenging his death then?'

Shocked yet encouraged by Eric's reaction, Jared found that within minutes he'd told him the whole story.

'Have you told Edwin any of this?' was Eric's first question.

'No, I've been putting it off... trying to find the right time, I suppose.'

'It has nothing to do with the fact your uncle might be horrified by your actions, then?'

'A shrewd guess, and the answer's yes! Don't get me wrong, Edwin's no prude, but when I tell him, I'm not sure how he's going to react. To be honest it took me ages to pluck up enough courage to tell you, being a man of the cloth and all that.'

Smiling, Eric said, 'You seem to have forgotten the conversation we had about necessary evil, as I like to put it. Knowing you, it was the only course of action left open. Did the man intend to kill you? Of course he did! Then all I can say is you did the only thing you could. Besides, after what he did to old Tom, he had it coming. But what's important from my point of view is that we don't look back. What's done is done, so there's no use crying over spilt milk. No, my boy, we have to look forward. So how do you intend getting the chalice back?'

'I've already worked that out. It's not just a case of retaining the chalice, though; there are other things to consider as well.' Smiling, he said, 'I've got the Brotherhood and its august leader David Naami to deal with too.'

Serious again, he said, 'I made a vow to old Tom, and believe me I intend honouring it.'

'That's what worries me,' said the old minister, before adding in a more subdued tone, 'don't take them lightly, Jared, they're a formidable combination. They must be in order to have survived this long.'

'Believe me, Eric, it's the last thing in the world I'd do. It's just that however good they are, I'm better. It's as simple as that.'

Coming from anyone else, old Eric would have said the words were nothing but arrogant nonsense. Looking into Jared's eyes, however, all he could think of was, God help David Naami.

Chapter Twenty-six

26 AUGUST DAWNED, AND IT TURNED OUT TO BE A GLORIOUS summer's day. As usual the forecast was hopelessly wrong; it was anything but overcast and cloudy. Having completed his early morning run, Jared was at a loose end, when suddenly he was disturbed by the chimes of the front door. Not expecting anyone, he was slightly puzzled. Opening it, he was astonished to see Emma standing there. Dressed in a simple summer frock, she looked incredible. It had always amazed him how anything, however simple, could always look stunning on her.

Conscious of the fact he was staring, he hid his embarrassment by saying, 'Hey, didn't expect to see you today! Nothing wrong, is there?' By now he was a little worried that something was amiss.

'No,' she said, 'it's a lovely day, that's all, so we decided to go for a walk, and madam here wondered whether you'd like to join us…'

Jared's confusion at the use of the term 'we' was resolved when suddenly, as if by magic, Jodie appeared. He felt his breath catch in his throat as he saw once again just how much alike they were.

Recovering quickly, he said, 'My mother always told me never to turn down an offer from a young lady, especially as one as pretty as this,' he said, bending down and tousling Jodie's golden curls. Beaming at the compliment, she immediately retreated behind her mother's back, suddenly shy again.

'Give me a minute and I'll be with you, unless of course you'd rather come in?'

'How long is a minute?' asked Emma.

'Just that,' said 'Jared, 'I've only got to slip on a pair of trainers, that's all.'

'In that case we'll wait here for you,' she said, before adding, 'incidentally, how is your grandmother today?'

'Fine!' shouted Jared, as he ran up the stairs to his room, taking two steps at a time. He was true to his word; within moments the three were making their way down the steep stone steps leading to the main road.

Looking directly at Jodie, he said, 'Oh, and by the way my mother had another saying: never keep a beautiful woman waiting. In this case though, she must have got it wrong; she must have meant women, because from where I'm standing there's two of you.'

After several moments of walking, Jared realised he had no idea where they were going so he said, 'Where to, then, ladies?'

'I thought we might visit our old place, you know the one behind my mother's house. The view on a morning like this will be wonderful.'

'If you're sure,' said Jared, suddenly serious.

'Don't look so worried,' said Emma, seeing his expression, 'I'm not going to eat you, if that's what your afraid of.'

Without thinking he blurted out, 'I wish you would.' The words were spoken before he could stop them.

Seeing both Jared and her mother blush deeply, Jodie squealed in delight.

When they'd both regained their composure, Emma said, 'In hind-sight I wish I hadn't told her about the place. Ever since I mentioned it this morning she's been pestering me non-stop to see it! To be honest, if we don't take her I'm afraid I'll never get any peace.'

Making their way up the shallow gradient leading past the fire station, Jared couldn't help but notice how the combination of warm sunshine and a lazy Sunday morning seemed to have brought everyone out. At the same time, he hoped they didn't all have the same destination in mind. Peace and quiet was what he was after, a chance for the first time since he'd come back to be alone with Emma and Jodie. His fears were groundless, as by the time they'd reached the small wicket gate guarding the entrance to the steep mountain path they were alone.

The small chapel of Mount Sinai, barely a stone's throw from Carmel, was nothing remarkable to look at. It was however noted for one strange feature. Right in the centre of a series of steep steps leading up from the main road was an iron walking barrier. Originally placed there to help the elderly, it had failed to take into account the problems that would occur should a member of the congregation need to be buried. Whoever had decided to put it there had either forgotten or been ignorant of the fact that once the coffin had been removed from the back of the hearse, it would then have to be lifted not shoulder high, but above the heads of the bearers, in order to traverse the railing. Even on a good a day, with young strong bearers, the clearance between the coffin and the rail was mere inches.

A few hours before, not long after midnight, and Reg Davies, the minister of the little chapel, was busy arranging the bread and wine in preparation for the communion service which was due to take place at 10 a.m. the same day. Getting on a bit, Reg would normally have been safely tucked up in bed by now. As it was, by the time he'd finished, he reflected ruefully, he'd be lucky if he managed five or six hours' sleep.

By now tired, his patience wearing thin, he felt that at such a late hour this was the last thing he wanted to do. In fact he'd only arrived home a short while ago from visiting his sister in hospital. It had been a stroke, the doctor had said. 'Hardly surprising,' was his comment; after all she was eighty-three. Until then she'd been like a top. He didn't see the irony in the fact that he was in his late seventies himself.

Sporting a full head of silvery white hair, Reg appeared a good deal younger. Worn fashionably long, it had brought many an amused comment from his congregation.

He didn't own a car, never had, so he'd had to rely on the generosity of one of his neighbours. In all fairness his driver had waited with him at the hospital and had even brought him home afterwards. In hindsight, he didn't know how he would have managed without him.

Even though it was the early hours of the morning, he was surprised to find he wasn't cold. Yesterday had been a day of glorious sunshine and some of the residual heat still remained. As a result the stone walls of the old chapel were not as cold as they would normally have been.

Busying himself, he was convinced if he put his mind to the task he would be finished in no time. Communion in chapel, unlike a church, uses ordinary bread, broken into separate pieces. Again, in a church, both the bread and wine are given at the same time. In a time-honoured tradition, the congregation moves in single file, approaches the minister and kneels before the altar rail. Everyone drinks from the same cup, normally a silver chalice, and then after every sip, it is wiped clean with a white linen cloth.

In chapels, however, the red wine – although symbolising the same thing, that Christ shed his blood for the sins of mankind – is brought around in individual glasses carried on a circular wooden platter.

As there is no such thing as an altar in a chapel, the preparation is carried out on the altar 'table' instead. When deemed ready, everything is normally covered by a silk or satin cloth. It was this that the old minister was in the process of sorting out when he was interrupted by a noise from the back of the chapel.

'Mr Davies, is that you?' said a youthful voice that reverberated off the bare stone walls.

'Yes,' said the minister in a chirpy voice, until he remembered what time of the morning it was. Pushing his glasses onto his thin beak-like nose, he peered into the gloom, trying manfully to identify who the voice belonged to. Suddenly he recognised who it was.

'Hello, lad! Taken a wrong turning, have we?'

'No,' came the reply, it's just I was passing, that's all. Saw the lights on and thought it might be burglars or something. Can't be too careful these days, can you? Anyway I popped in to make sure everything was all right.' He added, 'By the way, do you know what time it is?'

Amused, the old minister said, 'I do, lad, I do, but it can't be helped. I've only just come from the hospital, you see, and everything has to be ready by 10 a.m. at the latest. Besides,' he declared in a tone of mock severity, 'can't keep God waiting, can we?'

Changing the subject, he carried on as if nothing had happened. 'It'll be a full house tomorrow, just mark my words, it being communion and all that. There'll be members I haven't seen for ages. Somehow the morning service always attracts more people. I suppose the reason the evening service is less popular is because people just want to put their feet up and watch television at that time of night. Mind you, communion is always popular; everyone wants to be saved, you see, stands to reason doesn't it?'

'I must say you show commendable courage, Mr Davies,' said the youngster, 'being here at such a late hour and all. Aren't you afraid? You know – after the murder last month, I mean?'

'Typical of you, lad, always thinking of others. Don't think I'm not grateful, but I'll be fine, honestly. Anyway I've almost finished. All that's left to do is to put the cover over everything, fill the decanter with red wine, and then Bob's your uncle.'

As an afterthought he suddenly added, 'But on second thoughts, if you hold on a minute, I'll walk home with you.' It was then he noticed the long coat and said, 'Bit warm for that, isn't it?'

'Not really, Mr Davies, it's gone chilly outside.' At the same time the visitor admitted to himself secretly that the old man was right. Why the hell was he wearing it? And why did he have a machete and glass jar on his person? It was baffling.

Finally finished, the old minister turned and said, 'Besides, anyone wanting to murder us had better watch out; we make a formidable pair.'

'I'm not sure I'd be any good, Mr Davies, but in your case you've got your faith to protect you, haven't you?'

'Of course, lad, of course; but don't forget, you're equally protected. As long as you believe, your faith will sustain you too.'

'I wonder,' came the muted reply. 'You see I've been giving the whole thing a lot of thought lately, especially communion. Now take the Catholics, they believe that when the bread and wine have been blessed they magically turn into the body and blood of Christ, right?'

Thoughtful now, the old minister replied, 'I'm not too sure about the magical bit, but you're right about the rest. The process is called transubstantiation.'

'Don't you think it sounds a bit like cannibalism? I wonder what people would say if they were asked to eat actual flesh, drink real blood?' Smiling now, he said, 'Don't you think it would make communion more effective, somehow?'

About to burst out laughing, the minister stopped in his tracks. Suddenly a chill began to creep into his old bones. It was something about the way the comment was made, something about the tone in which it had been delivered that set him thinking. All at once Reg was afraid, and with that his forehead flashed with beads of sweat that looked remarkably like silvery pearls in the flickering light of the candles. In an unconscious gesture he looked towards the door for help. By then, however, it was already too late.

With a flourish the thing pulled out a machete from beneath its long coat. That it was razor sharp was in no doubt. The blade seemed to dance in the narrow shaft of light reflected by the largest of the stained glass windows. It was almost as if it was imbued with a life of its own, one that was evil beyond comprehension.

Numb with terror, the old minister finally managed to find his voice. Pointing at him with a finger that trembled badly, he said, 'Weapons have no place in a house of God, my son. Why on earth should you want to carry such a thing?'

Mockingly, the creature said, 'No ideas, old man – none at all? In that case, allow me to explain. You see, I thought I might give your flock an opportunity to take part in a *real* communion. Give them a chance to make up their own minds about things. I have to be careful about whose flesh and blood I choose though. I mean, it can't be just anyone, can it? It has to be someone your little congregation has come to know and love, otherwise it wouldn't be fair, would it? You see my point, don't you?'

Seeing the old man nod he carried on.

'Good, good, I thought you'd agree. Now, I don't want you to think I made the choice lightly. In fact it took me... now, let me see,' he said, putting one finger on his chin, before adding with a demented laugh, 'all of ten seconds.'

When it had stopped laughing, it made a dismissive gesture with its right hand and said, 'Still, I'm sure I've made the right choice, and that's all that matters.'

Pretending to have forgotten who he'd chosen in order to prolong the old man's agony, it continued its little charade.

'Now, let me see, who did I choose?' Clapping its hands like a little child the creature said, 'Yes, that's it, I remember now. Silly me, it's – wait for it, wait for it – *you!*'

Before the old minister could register any surprise the thing decapitated him in one single fluid motion. Falling from its shoulders with a look of stunned disbelief, the head hit the floor and rolled a few yards before coming to rest at the creature's feet. A freshly severed head takes several seconds, sometimes a lot longer before it becomes aware of the fact it is no longer alive. Apparently, it's all to do with nerve endings and messages to the brain. If the head receives no message to the contrary, then it believes it is still alive. The guillotine provided several graphic examples of this during the French Revolution, and in the case of the old minister, it was a similar scenario.

Once his head had come to rest against the feet of the demon, it stared up at it with an expression of pure horror. In the meantime the old man's headless torso carried on pumping out its life force, spraying everything within a radius of six feet with jets of bright red arterial blood. Using the glass jar, the creature captured a good deal of the blood knowing it would need it for what he had in mind later. As soon as he had completed the task, he placed the jar of blood on the pew opposite and reacted in a manner similar to that of a child who has suddenly glimpsed all its Christmas presents at once. Rubbing its hands together excitedly, it bent down and, picking the head up by its hair, straightened the old minister's spectacles. Although damaged, they'd somehow miraculously managed to cling to his face. In that instant of supreme triumph, the eyes of the creature momentarily flashed a deep crimson. For the poor old minister it was all academic. By now his nerve endings had finally managed to convince his brain he was dead.

The thing's work was far from complete, however, and putting the head down it moved over to the torso. Lifting it effortlessly in one hand, it carried it to the pulpit, wanting it to be the last thing the police found. Removing the old man's shirt, it deftly cut several strips of flesh from the body before transporting them back to the altar table. It left no mess, as by now there was very little blood left in the corpse.

Removing the communion bread from the basket, it replaced it with raw flesh. Suddenly on impulse, it popped one of the pieces of bread into its mouth, immediately spitting it out. *Stale*, it thought in disgust, before replacing it with a strip of raw meat.

With an expression of profound ecstasy, the demon chewed slowly, savouring the taste of the minister's bloody flesh.

Having taken care of that, it took the bread and the decanter containing the red wine and made its way into the vestry. Moving to the washbasin, it tipped out the wine and filled it with blood from the jar, blood the old minister had so thoughtfully provided. Meticulous as ever, it made sure there were no smears around the rim.

With that it returned to the main body of the chapel and recovered the head. With almost reverential care, it placed it on the silver salver next to the decanter and the basket containing the flesh. Once everything was to its satisfaction, it replaced the cover so that it looked exactly as the old minister had left it.

The most time-consuming part was cleaning up. Fortunately, none of the blood had landed on a surface that couldn't be wiped down easily. For anyone but the creature, the task would have been an appalling one, but it revelled in the gore, pausing every so often to lick the blood from its hands.

Its final task was to daub the wall near the pulpit with its calling card.

Making its way down the steps for the final time, it took time to stand back and gaze at its handiwork. Anyone knowing what to look for would have noticed the glowing red eyes, the telltale signs of satisfaction. Taking one last lingering look, it suddenly turned on its heels and, whistling a happy tune, headed for the exit.

Holding the gate open for little Jodie following closely behind, Emma and Jared made their way leisurely along the narrow path that eased its way gently towards the mountains in the far distance. Gazing at the largest peak, they never failed to be impressed by its majesty, how it seemed to tower over the little village and the surrounding countryside.

At this time of year mother nature could be seen in all her glory. Trees of all shapes and sizes combined to create a harmony of composition that even the most skilful of artists would have found difficult to match. The flowers on either side of the steep grassy bank, although a riot of colour, were fighting a losing battle with the brambles that were constantly threatening to overrun them. In the middle of such surroundings, Jared realised it was good just to be alive.

Suddenly a red squirrel darted across the path in front of them, and by the expression on Emma and Jodie's faces he wasn't sure who had been given the biggest fright, the squirrel or them. Red squirrels had become an extremely rare sight in these parts. From what Jared could gather, it was because the grey variety, originally brought over from Canada by accident, were wiping them out with ruthless efficiency. Part of the problem was that that unlike the reds, they never hibernated. An unfair advantage, Jared thought ruefully; on the other hand, a case of survival of the fittest perhaps, was his next pragmatic thought.

Jodie was mesmerised, unable to take her eyes off the little creature. She could only stare in rapt fascination as the squirrel darted up the steep grassy bank on the other side of the path.

Suddenly, as if aware it was being scrutinised by the little girl, it stopped, and turning began studying her too. By now it was no longer frightened but curious. Cocking its head to one side, it looked around before coming to a decision. Within moments, it made its way slowly back down the bank towards her.

Astonished, Jared could only stare in amazement as, foot by foot, the little creature moved closer. When it got to within a few inches, Jodie suddenly knelt down and extended her hand. Sensing she meant no harm, the squirrel allowed the little girl to stroke its glossy fur. After several moments the animal was completely unafraid, and so Jodie lifted it gently into her arms and hugged it tightly to her chest. As if by instinct, she judged the exact moment when both had satisfied their curiosity. As carefully as she had picked it up, she placed the little animal down again. Even then it didn't run away. Instead it simply sat there on its tiny haunches looking up at the little girl. Finally, as if deciding it was time to go, the squirrel raised its paws to its mouth, twitched its whiskers, and in a single blur of motion disappeared into the forest.

For a while no one spoke, afraid to spoil the magical moment.

Jared and Emma, unable to believe what they'd just seen did the only thing possible: they both burst out laughing.

Seconds later, when they'd calmed down somewhat, Jared voiced what they both felt. 'I've never seen anything like that in my life, Em, it was quite extraordinary.'

'Neither have I,' was all that Emma could say in reply.

Looking at the both of them, Jodie gave a little knowing smile before letting go of her mother's hand and skipping up the path in a flurry of movement.

Emma and Jared were still laughing moments later, when they made a sharp detour left. Pushing aside a seemingly dense thicket of ferns, they burrowed through until they found the secret entrance to what had once been their private little haven.

Sitting down among the undergrowth that grew to a height of several feet in places, Jared realised with a start that nothing had changed. It looked as if no one else had ever found the little spot.

It always amazed Jared that although the village was no more than a few hundred yards away, it was almost as if they were worlds apart – two different worlds thrown together in sharp relief. Smiling, the analogy of parallel universes popped into his mind. Here, away from the hustle and bustle of this other world, Jared knew there was a deep peace, a peace that seemed to settle over everything like a mantle. This was the realm of the creatures of the forest, he knew – a secret place, a place where time stood still.

Lying on his back in the middle of the small clearing, with Emma on one side and Jodie on the other, he gazed upwards into an almost clear blue sky. The few clouds that had dared to mar such a perfect day were nothing more than the tips of cotton buds drifting aimlessly across the open expanse of nothingness, resolutely heading towards infinity. Thinking back to happier times, when it seemed that nothing on earth mattered but he and Emma, her description drifted back to him. Yes, he remembered it now, an eggshell blue sky, she'd called it.

The fresh clean scent of grass and the pungent aroma of wild flowers brought back memories he'd convinced himself he'd buried for ever.

Pushing aside such thoughts he reminded himself of the promise he'd made when Emma had betrayed him. 'Live for today' was the motto that had kept him going through the bad years. Rolling onto his side, about to make a fuss of Jodie, he'd been unaware that his every move had been under scrutiny.

Emma was lying with one hand under her chin, nibbling on a piece of grass, an old habit she'd never abandoned it seemed. She said, 'A penny for them?'

Afraid to admit what he was really feeling, Jared replied, 'I was just thinking that kids in inner city environments would kill for what we take for granted.' Gesturing with his arm, he said, 'Panoramic views, clean mountain air, and yet somehow we fail to appreciate what we've got. It doesn't seem right somehow.' Seeing the amused smile on Emma's face, he was sure she hadn't been taken in so easily.

With that they both turned in time to see Jodie jumping to her feet. Within seconds she was enthusiastically chasing after a brightly coloured butterfly, which despite her most strenuous efforts managed to dance tantalisingly just out of reach.

For ages they played childish games, aware of the fact that although they were enjoying each other's company, it was really Jodie's day. Afterwards, smiling and out of breath, they simply talked. Jared was astonished to find there were no awkward silences, neither of them feeling the need to make polite conversation.

He was still in contemplative mood when suddenly he thought he heard the distinctive sound of a police siren drifting on the breeze. Getting to his feet, he shaded his eyes with a cupped hand and looked down the valley. One glance was enough. Turning to Emma, he said, 'I thought as much, it's the police; but it looks like a convoy. There seems to be a car in front, one behind and an ambulance in between. Must be serious if there are three of them,' he added as an afterthought.

Suddenly, as if she'd read Jared's mind, Emma's face was drained of colour. 'Oh, Christ, you don't think...?' She didn't have to complete the sentence, because her own fear was mirrored in Jared's eyes.

The old minister had been right about one thing. He'd guessed the service would bring everyone out of the woodwork, and he was correct.

Over the years most of the congregation had mastered the art of suffering in silence. On the rare occasion the rustle of a sweet paper broke the golden rule, the offender was greeted with a cold stare guaranteed to kill at twenty paces. Everyone knew this morning's service was special. It was an opportunity for individuals to be forgiven of their sins, shake hands with the minister and then carry on exactly as they had before.

There was a feeling of expectancy in the air, true, yet this morning something didn't seem quite right. It was nothing anyone could put their finger on, but the atmosphere was decidedly odd. Besides, the old minister was by now ten minutes late, something that had never happened before.

Turning to her neighbour, Gladys Wainwright said in a voice barely above a whisper, 'It's not like old Reg to be late, he's normally a stickler about timekeeping. I hope he's not ill.' She added, 'Can't see it somehow, can you? He would have let us know otherwise, being communion and all.'

By now even the deacons were starting to get restless. One of them, Samuel Bowen, got up and made his way over to the table, saying, 'Might as well give things the once-over, seeing as we're waiting.'

Lifting the corner of the cover used to screen the communion objects from the eyes of the congregation, he suddenly froze. Talking quietly among themselves, the others gave Mr Bowen no further thought, until suddenly they heard a sickening thud. Startled, they looked up in time to see his lifeless body hit the floor.

Rushing forward to help, convinced he'd suffered a stroke or something, the remaining deacons searched frantically for something with which to stem the flow of blood spurting from a deep gash in the side of his head. Thinking quickly, Cerith Thomas snatched at the communion cloth, reasoning it would do until they could find something better. Lifting it, he'd taken took two steps when he suddenly turned back.

It couldn't be, he thought.

Blinking rapidly several times, he tried to convince himself he was dreaming, that given a few minutes he'd wake and find it had all been a nightmare. It took only seconds however to realise it was no mistake, that what he was looking at was a flesh-and-blood reality.

Perched serenely alongside the decanter of red wine was the severed head of the late minister. At that moment, quite incongruously what came to Cerith's mind was the story of John the Baptist. Moments later, the reality of what he was looking at finally registered in his shell-shocked brain.

It seemed as if the head was gazing directly at him, its bloodless eyes boring deep into his soul. As he stared in horror, the cloth he was holding began to slip from nerveless fingers. With agonising slowness, it fluttered like a feather slowly to the floor. Although the whole incident took mere seconds, for him it seemed to last a good deal longer. It was as if time stood still.

By now everyone's attention was focused on the silver salver and its gruesome contents. The head of the old minister seemed to cast a spell over everyone. So shocking was the spectacle that for what seemed like ages no one was able to move a muscle.

It didn't last, however, as suddenly one by one the congregation began snapping out of their trances. One high-pitched scream was followed by another, until eventually the noise was deafening.

Suddenly there was a new sound – that of rushing feet, as the congregation made a mad dash for the exit.

While all this was going on, the head of the old minister stared down at proceedings in mute appreciation.

In seconds the rush had become a stampede.

The problem was it was physically impossible for more than two people at a time to navigate the narrow corridor leading to the front door. The first few dozen, those who had reacted more quickly than the others, or those who had been sitting nearest to the door, managed to escape. But it wasn't long before the inevitable happened.

At ninety years of age, old Mrs Harrison could only move about with extreme difficulty, and then by using both her walking sticks. She'd made it as far as the door leading to the corridor when a violent push from behind threw her against one of the wooden pews. Amazingly, despite all the odds she managed to stay on her feet. The respite was to be brief, however, as within moments the combined weight of those coming behind proved too much. Soon the frail old lady toppled sideways. Landing on her back, she found herself jammed into an opening between two pews. For a moment it seemed she'd been lucky. Cushioned from the worst of the mad scramble, only her legs were visible. Unfortunately they were sticking out into the main isle, and as innocuous as it appeared at the time, the incident proved to be the catalyst for the litany of horrors that occurred immediately afterwards.

Seconds later, by now unstoppable, the heaving mass was in full flow. They made for the door like a herd of wild animals.

And then disaster struck.

A burly figure, elbowing his way through the crowd in a fit of blind panic, tripped over the old lady's outstretched legs. Falling on his face, he was powerless to save himself, as like a stack of human dominoes those coming behind were suddenly catapulted forward, landing on him as they fell.

For an independent observer the whole scenario might have appeared faintly amusing. In fact a witness speaking later was heard to say, 'It was like watching a game of tenpin bowling,' before adding sombrely, 'except it was human bodies that were being toppled and smashed, not wooden pegs.' As it turned out it was an apt description.

Within moments of the first person falling, the whole of the ground floor was filled with a mass of writhing humanity. All thoughts of women and children first had long since disappeared. Instead of stopping to help those badly injured, those coming behind either conveniently chose to ignore the cries for help or simply trampled over the fallen in their haste to flee what had rapidly become a charnel house. Some simply sat on the floor, their eyes mirroring the horrors of what they'd just witnessed. Others, the more seriously injured, screamed in agony while trying vainly to protect limbs that were hanging at obscene angles.

It was discovered later that old Mrs Harrison had not been as lucky as it had at first appeared. Only seconds after falling, a man scrambling to his feet in sheer terror stepped on her head. The weight bearing down on her unprotected face smashed her spectacles and drove the broken shards into her eyes. The screams of the old lady went unnoticed however, as her voice was only one among many. Seconds later all that was left of her eyes were two empty sockets, dripping and streaming with viscous fluid.

By the time a semblance of order had been restored it was found that the injury toll was less than expected. Out of a total of eighteen casualties, five were seriously injured, although expected to recover. Another nine were found to be suffering from ailments such as concussion, cuts and bruises or broken limbs.

Amazingly, there were only four fatalities, one of which had been old Mrs Harrison.

Chapter Twenty-seven

DURING THE LAST FEW MONTHS, IT SEEMED THE FIVE HAD GONE through the range of every possible human emotion, from terror to total dejection; or so they had thought at the time, but they were wrong. At this precise moment, they were experiencing yet another – utter despair!

Holding his hands up in defeat, Jared said, 'I know, I know what I promised, and this time I have to agree with you. It's obviously time to go to the police. Fortunately we won't have to go to the local cops, because Johnny Dodds phoned earlier and he wants to see me tomorrow. This might be the opportunity I've been waiting for.'

The following morning, bright and early, Jared made his way towards Johnny's home, some two miles away. It was a glorious morning. After the previous night's sudden storm, which had appeared from nowhere, the dark, angry clouds, almost purple at times, had disappeared, leaving behind a brilliant clear sky. Not a single cloud dared mar the horizon. Everything seemed brighter today, as if cleansed by nature's tantrum of the previous evening. Storms had a way of doing that in this part of Wales. Correcting himself, Jared mentally added, no, especially in this part of Wales! No wonder it was named 'Piss-pot alley' he thought, wryly.

For the first mile, he used the main road until, reaching the small bridge which crossed the river to the Red Lion pub, he stopped. Looking over the safety railings, he peered into the river, trying to spot some trout. Although late in the year, he was still hopeful and, within moments, his patience was rewarded. Half hidden by the shadow of the bridge, he saw one swimming lazily against the current. As if sensing Jared's presence, it suddenly gave a flick of its powerful tail and disappeared under the protection of the far bank. Buoyed by his discovery, Jared pressed forward.

Fifty yards further on, he was about to cross the main road when he was stopped by a couple of young backpackers. Rucksacks bulging with all kinds of worldly goods, the obligatory water bottle placed into the string harnesses at the side of the huge bags, they were poring over a map. Seeing Jared, they had hastily decided to give up on the map, coming to the conclusion that asking for directions was the lesser of the two evils.

Smiling, Jared, pre-empting their question, said, 'The Youth Hostel is about two miles further on. No, you don't need to turn off anywhere; it's straight, as the crow flies. Stick to the main road and you can't miss it.'

With broad grins and an obvious sense of relief, the couple beamed their gratitude and, with courteous thank yous, replaced the map in one of the rucksacks. Waving, they were on their way in no time. Watching as they disappeared into the distance, Jared's immediate reaction was that if they kept up that pace, they would be there in about a quarter of an hour.

Crossing the road, he made his way up the small hill and headed for the narrow pathway which he knew would lead him to his intended destination – the tiny village of Swn-y-Nant. At the top of the hill, Jared took a sharp right and pushed aside the tendrils of thick ivy that hung down from the tall trees on either side of the tiny path. The air was redolent with leaf mould, moss and a variety of other of detritus. Once free of the clinging ivy, he pushed forward.

Looking around him, he savoured his surroundings. Since a boy, he'd been enthralled by the brilliance of nature, but in particular the ingenuity of the seasons as they melded seamlessly into their pre-ordained cycle. Spring slipped slowly into the blazing furnace of summer, before the golden leaves of autumn took over. Eventually, it too disappeared, like early morning mist. Finally, with one last defiant stand, it stood aside to allow the harsh, austere whiteness of winter to reign supreme once more.

He remembered watching a documentary recently which had shown this cycle in startling clarity. Speeding the process up through a process of fast motion filming it was possible to see the changing seasons in a matter of seconds. The array of changing colours – from green to brown, red and yellow – was astonishing. He was sure that the camera crew had won some award for such brilliant innovation. Of course, at this time of year, the sights and sounds of spring were nothing but a distant memory. All that remained was the promise of better things to come.

With such thoughts buzzing around in his head, he came in sight of the waterfall. Tumbling down from the mountain above, clouds of spray from the cascading flow of water rose into the air, and where it caught the sunlight it turned into a small rainbow that arched across the stream.

Stopping for a moment to take in the scene, Jared suddenly cupped his hands into the cool, clear mountain stream and splashed some water onto his face. It was freezing cold and he laughed out loud at the invigorating experience.

The rustle of animal presence made him turn around, hoping to catch a glimpse of what had made the sound. Whatever it was, however, was invisible, hidden behind a thicket of dense hawthorn that skirted the opposite side of the stream. It had chosen its hiding place well, thought Jared, the spiky edges of the bush providing a formidable defence. Disappointed, he made his way forward once more.

Ten minutes later, he stepped from the confines of the hidden path onto the small B-class road that cut a swathe through the centre of the village. Standing on the brow of the hill, he looked down at his place of birth. Ravens Hill was small but Swn-y-Nant was tiny. In all, there were little more than fifty houses, each one nestling snugly at the foot of the mountain range, which stretched gently towards the road. Despite its miniscule size, the village boasted a chapel – Bethlehem. As Jared had been born in the cottage next door to the chapel, he had come in for the inevitable jokes about a star in the East, the three wise men and the like.

At this time of the morning, the village was still and lifeless. As quiet as the grave, he thought, while making his way down the hill toward Johnny's house. The door was opened on the second knock and a familiar voice said, 'Come in, come in, thanks for coming,' before escorting him to one of the two comfortable armchairs in front of the fireplace. It didn't take a brain surgeon to work out that Anne had conveniently been sent on some errand. As it was, the two of them were alone.

Once Jared had made himself comfortable, Johnny began.

'First of all, it seems I owe you lot an apology. I might have been wrong, a little hasty in dismissing your story the last time you and I met. By now it's obvious that what were dealing with is more than just a case of a local maniac on the loose.'

'Or,' said Jared, 'that's it's a group of drug-crazed satanists, as one enterprising young journalist would have us believe.'

'Ah, that,' said Johnny, a thoughtful expression on his face. 'Yes, well, she's a bright kid. I suppose she views this as her big opportunity to get out of Raven's Hill. Hit the bright lights of Fleet Street or whatever they call it these days.'

'And from where I'm standing,' said Jared, 'it appears she's going the right way about it. Sold lots of papers, from what I gather. The funny thing is, if you delve behind the drivel and the sensationalist crap, she's nearer the truth than she realises.' With a dismissive gesture of his hand, he said, 'Anyway, what changed your mind about us?'

'To be honest, it was the bets; they got me thinking, you see.'

Looking up and smiling, he added, 'Which, incidentally, you won.'

Getting back to business, he said, 'When you've been in the game as long as I have, then you know it's bloody near impossible to commit the perfect crime. In this instance, two horrific murders have been committed and the perpetrators haven't left a single clue. Now in my book that's more than a coincidence.'

Pointing at Jared, he carried on, 'Let's look at the logistics of things for a moment. Take searching the crime scene, for instance; it's a thankless task, but it's done meticulously. The lads go over everything with a fine-tooth comb. Believe me, everything, and I mean *everything*, is picked up, bagged and labelled. However insignificant something might appear at the time, it is still regarded as potential evidence. It's surprising how many times it's the little things that end up providing us coppers with the vital breakthrough. Attention to detail is of paramount importance, lad; nothing is left to chance, believe me. That's what good police work is all about. Oh,' he said with a wave of his hand, 'I'm not denying that the odd case or two isn't solved by brilliant deduction, the odd flash of inspiration and all that, but in the main it's hard graft that usually cracks cases. As far as these two go though, I've got to admit I'm totally baffled. Despite everything I mentioned earlier, nothing seems to have worked. Danny Harris and his team double, and in some instances triple-checked things, but still they came up with nowt. Apart from everything else, their reputations are on the line and it hurts. Even old Professor Edwards failed to come up with anything. That was all the proof I needed to convince me that we were up against something that, for want of a better word, simply isn't human. That journalist you were on about earlier, that Jessica Ryder, she coined the phrase "phantom killer", and by Christ she's nearer the mark than she knows. Do you realise we didn't even find a single fingerprint, for God's sake? Apart from those of the cleaners and several others who had good reasons for being there, that is. As much as I hate to admit it, your story about releasing something evil into the community seems to be the only thing that makes any kind of sense.'

Shaking off his mood of lethargy, he looked up and said, 'Anyway, that's enough of that, what's important now is that we pull together on this. Pool our knowledge and expertise. I've started the ball rolling already. I've arranged for you to meet that mate of mine, the one in charge of the elite squad from London. They've set up their headquarters in the old St John's Ambulance Hall. Can you and the others be there tomorrow afternoon? About 2 p.m. suit you?'

Nodding, Jared said, 'Good choice of venue: small, compact and private. The only fly in the ointment could be Roger, but I'm sure he can take an hour or two off, seeing as he's got his own business.'

Jared was about to step through the door when Johnny said, 'Oh, and by the way I've told Danny you came to see me weeks ago, that you warned me then what was going to happen. He knows it was my fault he didn't get to hear about your story earlier.'

Smiling, Jared said, 'Don't worry, Johnny, one of the reasons I came to see you first was to assess your reaction. I'm sure if I'd gone to the local police, or even your mate Danny, they would have told me exactly what you did.' He added with a smile, 'But in considerably more colourful language. As you said earlier, the important thing now is that we pull together, because if we don't, we won't have a snowball's chance in hell of beating this bloody thing!'

Stepping inside the Ambulance Hall the following afternoon, Jared and the others were amazed to see the transformation that had taken place. The cold bare hall, unused for so long, had been turned into a hive of bustling activity. Everywhere he looked he could see stacks of high-tech equipment, some of which even he had never seen before. His initial reaction was that in terms of money and equipment nothing had been spared. That in itself was encouraging, he thought to himself.

Apart from everything else, there seemed to be enough cardboard boxes to fill a battleship, each seemingly filled to capacity with paperwork. On two walls there were rows of steel filling cabinets that almost touched the roof. Despite the clutter, it was obvious that expert hands had been at work, as the whole thing had the look of organised chaos.

None of this really interested Jared. It was the back wall that caught his attention. Covered with glossy photographs of the two murder scenes, they displayed in graphic detail what had taken place. Although the newspapers had fallen over themselves in a vain attempt to portray what had actually happened, even filling in the odd bit here and there when they thought it needed spicing up, none had come remotely near to guessing the extent of the horrific injuries both clergymen had sustained. It was so bad that Jared's first impression was that they had been attacked by a wild animal. The sight brought back unwanted memories, reminding him vividly of instances in which he'd been forced to commit such atrocities himself. But that was war, he told himself – necessary evil, as old Eric had explained. On reflection, he wondered if the situation he found himself in now was really any different. Considering the present circumstances, this too was war!

Making their way over to the far side of the Hall, Johnny began the introductions. 'Everyone, this is DCI Harris, or better known to his friends as Danny. This is the man who is going to be in charge of affairs.'

Nodding to the others in acknowledgement, Danny Harris approached Jared directly. Shaking hands, the two appraised each other silently. Danny was surprised how youthful Jared looked; according to the files he was twenty-four, but he looked a good deal younger. He knew very little about Jared, and most of that was either hearsay or simple guesswork. He'd been unable to find anything concrete on his service record, and that in itself was extremely unusual. With his influence, he was normally provided with anything he required, and in double quick time. But in this case he'd come up against a brick wall.

To all intents and purposes, it was as if Jared had fallen off the face of the earth for the last five years of his service career. By chance he'd met an old friend several weeks ago and explained the situation. Having spent time in special operations himself, he was hoping he might know a thing or two. Unfortunately, like Danny, he too had been unable to come up with anything. His only comment had been that if there was nothing on Jared anywhere, he must have been something very special indeed, and left it at that.

Looking Jared squarely in the eye, Danny immediately knew one thing: that whatever else he may have been, Jared had been a killer. Of that he was certain.

Danny Harris was a bull of a man, short and stocky with steel grey hair. He looked exactly what he used to be, a prop forward of the old school. By now, however, his once muscular frame had started to develop a layer of fat. Despite this there was no disguising the fact he was still a powerful man. What Jared saw in the eyes of Danny Harris was reassuring. He sensed at once that beneath the bluff exterior lay a real copper. He wasn't surprised, really, as anyone who could earn the respect of someone like Johnny must be good. His progress up the ladder had been nothing short of meteoric and then suddenly it had come to a sudden stop. Looking at him now he knew why. He wasn't a pen-pusher. It was obvious the chap standing in front of him was a man of action. He was certainly not afraid to get his hands dirty. No wonder he'd won the respect of friends and colleagues alike. His raison d'être was catching criminals. Jared could see instinctively that he loved it. As a man used to success, failure was out of the question. Now he realised why the last two unsolved cases, even though he and his team had not been directly involved, had hurt.

Yes, thought Jared, this is a man I can work with.

Letting go of each other's hands simultaneously, both noted each other's grip had been firm and respectful. Both were grateful that neither had attempted an adolescent display of male posturing that sometimes occurred between two men conscious of each other's reputations.

For the next few moments the other introductions were made. For Jared, three were of significant import. DC Tina Reynolds was a real looker, but he wasn't fooled by her beauty. He knew that if she was a member of such an elite outfit, then she'd been chosen for more than her looks. He wondered just what her specialty was. Finally he was introduced to DI Gareth Evans.

The main introductions over with, there was still one person that Danny wanted the others to meet, and so, herding them over to one of the computer terminals at the other side of the room, he said, 'And this old rogue, ladies and gents, is Professor Edwards; surprisingly, despite the name, there's not a drop of Welsh blood in him!'

Shaking hands with Jared, he looked over at Danny, 'Make your mind up, will you? One minute I'm an old rogue, and then when you want something, I'm a top boy, an expert. You can't have it both ways,' he said, suddenly laughing.

It was obvious to everyone the two went back a long way.

The others had been informed of Professor Edward's nickname beforehand, and now having met him they not only realised how he'd earned it, but that it was extremely apt.

That Danny Harris was a no-nonsense kind of bloke was obvious from the start.

'Right then, let's cut through the bullshit, shall we? What have you youngsters got for us?'

It took almost half an hour to explain everything that had happened, and at the end Jared was sure they'd left nothing out.

Danny's comment when it came surprised the listeners.

'Shame about the codex thing, it might have told us everything we wanted to know,' he said, before dismissing the subject and getting once more down to business.

All of them, Jared included, were impressed by Danny's handling of affairs. From the outset it was obvious he was treating them as equals and not talking down to them. His next comment bore out his observation perfectly.

'Let's get one thing straight. What's happened is not your fault. What you did was stupid and irresponsible, yes, but no more than that. Afterwards… well, that was fate. As much as we would like to, we can't alter that, so remember it. Between us we'll come up with an answer somehow. I must admit though, that coming from the old school as I do, I still find it hard to believe all this stuff about evil spirits and demons.'

Holding up his hand to ward off the flood of anticipated criticism, he defused the situation by adding, 'I said *difficult* to believe, not *didn't* believe. After the second murder, I have to agree with you; it's the only thing that makes any sense. You see, as much as I'd like to refute your story, I can't.' Shaking his head in a gesture of bewilderment, he carried on.

'Believe me, all of us in this room have seen some really weird shit over the years.' He suddenly realised what he'd said and apologised to the ladies present for swearing. 'But I can tell you one thing, we've seen nothing remotely like this. No clues, no fingerprints, nothing left behind at the scene of the crime: it's beyond comprehension. Not even our resident expert over there,' he said, pointing to Professor Edwards, 'has managed to find anything. No, as much as I hate to admit it, your story about the creature in the chalice is the only thing we have to go on. So,' he looked at them and smiled, 'however bloody weird it sounds, I'm backing you all the way.'

Changing the subject abruptly, he declared, 'you know one thing still puzzles me about all this. What has the poor old Church done to upset the creature so much? Revenge is one thing, but in my book this is something entirely different.'

Jared put the feelings of the others into words by adding, 'It's all to do with the biblical stuff it was spouting; there's a clue there some-where, if only I could put my finger on it. At times I think I've almost got it, and then suddenly it disappears into thin air again.'

An hour later they trudged out wearily, having to admit reluctantly they were no wiser than they'd been before.

Hanging back, Jared said, 'DCI Harris, could I have a word?'

'It's Danny, if we're going to be working together, lad! Now, what's on your mind?'

'Two things, but the first concerns the media. How the hell are we going to keep them off our backs? You know what they're like; some of them are really sharp. They say a shark can smell blood from a mile away, but let me tell you, compared to some of these bastards, they're beginners. To make matters worse, they're convinced they've stumbled onto the biggest story since Jack the Ripper.'

'I agree,' said Danny, 'but over the years I've learned to tolerate them – just! Don't worry about things like that, it's not your problem; we have a female officer who takes charge of that kind of thing. Now, what was the second thing?'

With that, Jared told him about the involvement of Eric the old min-ister of Carmel and his Uncle Edwin.

Danny's final comment as they walked through the door was, 'Let's just hope that between you, you manage to come up with something.'

Later that afternoon Jared did something he'd been meaning to do for a while. Hearing the knock on the front door, Charlie Tucker rose from his leather armchair and made his way slowly to answer it. Who the hell could that be? he thought to himself, while at the same time hoping whoever it was would bugger off quickly. He was in the middle of watching and old Western, for Christ's sake.

Looking down at his brand new three-piece suite as he made his way towards the door, he stifled a chuckle. As far as he was concerned, the coins had been put to good use. Surprisingly they'd fetched far more than he and Albert had expected. The jeweller had explained they were silver denarii, coins used during the Roman occupation of Palestine.

He'd said it as if he and Albert were bloody thick, but he'd put the bugger right, he had, and said he knew. Of course it was a pack of bloody lies, but he couldn't let the jeweller know that, otherwise he might have tried to rip them off. So he'd acted as if he knew quite a bit about them. In truth he still wasn't sure if he'd managed to pull it off, to con the old jeweller. Thinking about it, perhaps it was they who'd been ripped off after all. Anyway it didn't matter, as old Albert had been happy with the price.

£2,000 they'd got – more that either of them had ever seen in one go. And he'd paid in cash too, no bloody cheques and all that. Slapped the money on the counter in £50 notes, just like that. Until then neither of them had ever seen a £50 note.

He still smiled when he recalled old Albert's expression. He'd nearly had a stroke when he saw the money.

He had to admit there had been an unpleasant downside, however. Yes, it had been the easiest money they'd ever made, but it had caused a lot of grief since. Hardly a day had gone by when he hadn't worried about what would happen if the police caught up with them. One of these days, he thought, there's going to be a knock on the door and that will be it.

He went suddenly cold.

Could this be the day? he thought to himself nervously.

Pulling himself together, he stiffened his shoulders and in a sudden show of defiance marched to the door. If it's the money they're after, he thought, then they're too bloody late, it's long gone.

Opening the door he stood there for a second, puzzled.

Standing in front of him was a tall dark youngster, yet something about him was familiar. While he was racking his brains trying to place him, the visitor put out his hand and introduced himself.

'Jared Hunter, Mr Tucker, I live around here.'

Relief and understanding flooded through old Charlie in equal measure.

Once he'd recovered, he blurted out, 'Yes, I remember you now, lad, I was at the funeral. Six years now, if my memory serves me right. Tragic, it was.'

After a few moments of awkward silence, Jared said, 'Thank you, it's nice to know they were appreciated.'

'What can I do for you, lad?' Charlie was suddenly wary again.

'I was wondering if you could help me out with a little matter, that's all. It's to do with the old chapel next door.'

Looking into Jared's eyes, Charlie knew instinctively this was the moment he'd been dreading. With that, his shoulders slumped and in a resigned voice he said, 'In that case, you'd better come in.'

Immediately he sat down, Jared said, 'You can relax, Charlie, I'm not here about the money – just a little information, that's all.'

Startled, old Charlie looked up. 'What money?'

'The money you got for selling the coins.'

It had been a stab in the dark, but Jared could be see by the old man's expression he'd guessed correctly.

'How did you know about that? You're not the police, are you?'

Amused, Jared said, 'No, it's nothing like that; I'm not a mind-reader, either. Old Eric Roberts, the minister, saw you scrambling out of the hole, that's all; he guessed you'd been up to something. I meant what I said, though, I don't give a damn about the money. It's information I'm after.'

'You promise you won't let on to the police or anything?'

Even more amused now, Jared said, 'I promise.' Then in a more serious tone of voice, one that left Charlie in no doubt that he meant what he said, he finished the sentence. 'As long as you tell me exactly what happened!' Anyway, what would be the point of telling the coppers? The money has been spent, hasn't it, Charlie?' Jared rubbed the arm of the leather chair and smiled.

By now old Charlie was laughing.

'If you're not a copper, then you should be! You're sharper than a barrel full of monkeys. Right, what do you want to know, lad?'

For a while Jared said nothing, intent on trying to work out in his mind exactly what had taken place that day. Suddenly he said, 'You couldn't tell me what the coins looked like, could you?'

'I'll do better than that lad; I'll draw one for you.'

Charlie was gone for the briefest of moments, and when he returned he brought with him a piece of paper and a pencil. 'They looked something like this,' said Charlie. 'Oh, and by the way, the jeweller explained what they were. Sorry, I should have told you earlier.'

'It doesn't matter, Charlie. Carry on, please, this could turn out to be important.'

'He said they were Roman denarii or something, said they were from the time of the Emperor Tiberius.'

Yet another link to Jesus and Palestine, thought Jared, and then another piece of the puzzle fell into place.

'You probably know what I'm talking about,' said Charlie, 'being an educated lad and that.'

'As a matter of fact I do,' said Jared. 'They were in common usage in Palestine during Jesus' time.'

'Yes, that's it, that's what the jeweller said, said they were quite rare.'

'As a matter of curiosity,' said Jared, 'how much did you get for them?'

'£1,000,' said Charlie, glancing at his feet, before suddenly looking up and saying, 'No, sorry, I can't lie to you; it was £2,000. Do you think he ripped us of?'

'Probably, but all three of you were happy, weren't you? And that's what matters really. In the end each of you got something out of it, didn't you? If you'd pushed him for more, he might have turned the screw a little, asked you where you'd got them from, and that might have caused a problem...' He left the remainder of the sentence unfinished, the threat implicit.

Looking at Jared with a tinge of respect, Charlie said, 'Do you know something, lad? For someone of your age you've got a wise old head on your shoulders. You're sure you're not a copper?'

'They couldn't afford me,' was Jared's reply, and with that they both smiled.

'How many coins were there?' asked Jared.

'Twenty-nine, we counted them exactly.'

'An odd number,' said Jared, more to himself than Charlie.

'Bloody awkward too,' said Charlie. 'As it turned out, though, I had fifteen seeing as it was me who found the thing, and then Albert had the other fourteen.'

'What about the smell?'

Startled, Charlie exclaimed, 'How the hell did you know about that?'

'Simple,' lied Jared, 'it was a funeral urn.'

'So we were right,' muttered Charlie to himself. 'Old Albert and I thought it might have been something along those lines. Give us the bloody shivers, it did, thinking that the coins were mixed up with some poor bugger's ashes.'

If you only knew the truth, thought Jared, you wouldn't have touched it for £20,000, never mind £2,000.

'Anyway, the smell,' said Charlie, 'never experienced anything like it in my life... and don't want to again,' he added hastily. 'It was as if something had crawled into the bloody thing and died. Revolting, it was. Oh, and I nearly forgot, just before the lid dropped off the temperature dropped like a stone. One minute it was normal and then in a blink of an eye it was like a bloody fridge. We could even see freezing fog in front of our faces. Bloody weird, it was. By now we were shitting ourselves, I can tell you!'

'So you left the chalice exactly as you found it and got out of there as quickly as you could?' Suddenly Jared remembered something. 'But the place was covered in dust, so you must have left footprints behind. And yet the archaeologists who came after you found nothing. As far as they were concerned it was a virgin site, untouched for God knows how long.'

'Ah, that's were old Albert had a brainwave. He took his cardigan off and brushed everything... like this,' he said, acting out exactly what Albert had done. 'Said he saw it on television once. A murder thing he said it was. He reckoned it fooled the police completely; mind you, it was a film.'

'Film or not, it must have worked, because apart from old Eric, no one had a clue anyone had been down there. I reckon you two earned your money, if it was only for that little trick,' said Jared with grudging admiration.

Chapter Twenty-eight

IT WAS NEARLY 10.30 IN THE EVENING WHEN HE STEPPED CAUTIOUSLY off the bus. Avoiding the deep pools of water left by the heavy showers, it was a while before he realised that finally the rain had stopped. Getting chilly too, he thought to himself, while at the same time raising the collar of his coat to afford some kind of protection to the back of his neck.

Stepping off the pavement, his legs suddenly felt as if they belonged to someone else.

It was a strange feeling.

With that, something struck him: how the hell was he going to get home? There were no buses to Raven's Hill at this time of night. He could walk, of course, but it was a four-mile trek... and for what? So what the hell was he doing here?

It was a fleeting thought – there one moment, gone the next.

With that the creature was back in control.

As the bus stop was directly opposite the entrance to the church grounds, it required only the briefest of walks to reach the front gates. At this time of night it would be locked, an unfortunate necessity due to the rash of vandalism that had swept the area recently. Not that it mattered, on this occasion the church was not its intended destination. No, tonight the thing had much more important things on its mind.

Keeping a leisurely pace, as if it hadn't a care in the world, it was surprised to see that even though it was a Friday evening there was no one about.

Making its way through the small car park that fronted the grounds of St Martin's, light suddenly gave way to darkness. That's better, it thought, as it made its way along the narrow gravel path that wound its way through the graveyard. In the gloom of the evening, the huge conifers on either side of the path seemed to stand to attention like sentinels guarding the gates to hell.

How deliciously appropriate, reasoned the creature, it's almost as if they recognise their lord and master.

As if on cue, the wind rose in intensity. Howling like a banshee, it sounded like a demon that had been too long cheated of its quota of souls.

The rain, which only a short time ago had been so heavy, had disappeared as quickly as it had begun, allowing the moon to peek out from behind its hiding place. Suddenly, tiny fingers of weak diffused light filtered through the branches of the low-lying willows.

Pushing its hands deeper into the pockets of its hooded jacket, it smiled. Even during the day the old graveyard had an eerie quality about it, but at night it was truly atmospheric. With little imagination one could conjure up all kinds of denizens of the night.

Suddenly it had a flashback, something its host had been taught in Sunday school. Apparently, evergreen trees were planted in graveyards to remind the congregation of life after death, so that through the centuries they'd come to symbolise the hope of the faithful.

They were a living reminder that as long as they believed in Christ's resurrection, they too would inherit eternal life.

A wonderfully trite sentiment; shame about the reality, thought the creature.

Turning its back on the church, it made its way towards the manse.

The creature knew that as a confirmed bachelor, the old vicar, David Sutherland, would be alone at this time of night, and that suited its purpose admirably. Moving stealthily through the shadows cast by the trees, it was confident it had not been seen. Seeing light in the kitchen window, it knew it was in luck. It appeared the old man was still up, and so, checking the scalpel in its pocket, it approached the back door. Stealing the blade from one of the local hospitals had been easier than anticipated; it had just walked in and taken it. Such was the lack of security it hadn't even been challenged. It was a pity it couldn't have obtained the real thing, it thought wistfully, but in this day and age it supposed that flaying knives existed in history books only. Not that it mattered, it told itself, this would do almost as well, perhaps even better seeing it was so much sharper.

Knocking on the door, it wasn't long before the creature heard a voice.

'Just a minute, I'll be right there.'

With that, the door opened to reveal the old man standing in front of him, his silhouette outlined by the bright fluorescent light of the kitchen. Complete with spectacles, dressing gown and slippers, the vicar gave the creature the immediate impression that he certainly looked his age.

Squinting in the dark, the man of God adjusted his glasses and said, 'Hello, how may I help you?'

'No, Vicar, you have your wires crossed. It's not a case of what you can do for me, but rather what I can do for you.'

Then, without warning, it struck the old man viciously on the side of the head. Taken completely by surprise, David Sutherland stumbled before falling awkwardly and hitting his head on the hard flagstone floor with a sickening crack.

For a moment the creature worried he might be dead, realising if that were the case it would spoil everything. It wanted him to be very much alive for what it had in mind. It wanted to be able to look into the man's eyes, to see the expression of pain and terror while it carried out its gruesome task. Bending down quickly, it searched frantically for a pulse.

Finding one, it smiled, muttering to himself, 'Thank God for that,' before chuckling at its own little joke. Although bleeding, the cut wasn't deep. The vicar would live long enough to glimpse hell, it thought with grim satisfaction.

When David Sutherland came around, he was still groggy. Shaking his head in bewilderment, he looked around the room, struggling to make sense of what was happening. It was difficult to make out anything concrete. All he could see was a cloud of foggy mist in front of his eyes, and he suddenly wondered if he might have suffered a concussion.

Gradually the mist began to clear, and in astonishment he suddenly noticed a young man standing over him. He didn't recognise him, he was sure he'd never seen him before... so what was he doing in his bedroom?

With that it all came back, and he remembered exactly what had happened.

Glancing down in panic he saw he was tied to the bed, naked except for his underpants. His hands and feet had been bound securely by rope, each to one of the four corners of the old-fashioned bed which was his pride and joy. Despite the pain, the old man showed commendable courage. Instead of allowing his fear to rise to the surface, he blurted out, 'What do you want, young man? What kind of madness is this?'

'Wrong choice of words, Vicar,' came the reply. 'Revenge is the noun you're looking for, not madness.'

'Revenge!' said David in astonishment. 'But why? I don't even know you. Why would you feel it necessary to seek retribution against me? It doesn't make any sense.'

'You misunderstand me. I've nothing against you personally,' replied the creature, 'it's what you represent I detest. You and others like you, perverting the truth and peddling your lies. I despise the lot of you.'

Suddenly the realisation of what he was up against flooded in to David's mind. At that moment, the old vicar knew exactly what he was looking at. Standing before him, masquerading as a human being, was Satan incarnate.

He'd often wondered what the devil was really like. Seeing this creature smiling down at him, he knew now that it was nothing like the images portrayed in the Bible. There were no winged creatures, no goat-headed gods or the like. No, the beast was far more subtle, and at this precise moment it was standing at the foot of his bed.

Despite his faith, David was suddenly very afraid.

He knew with certainty he was staring death in the face.

In itself, death didn't worry him unduly. He'd lived a long and fulfilling life; in fact he had no reason to regret anything he'd done. So, focusing on his faith, he looked directly into the things eyes and with as much dignity as he could muster, shouted, 'Do what you will, foul creature, but in the end the victory you crave will be a hollow one! My faith will sustain me in this the hour of my greatest need!'

Lifting its head and bellowing out loud, the creature said, 'Brave words, old man, but I wonder how strong your faith will turn out to be when it's put to the ultimate test!'

'Strong enough, believe me. I'm resigned to meeting my Maker in the sure knowledge that like the Apostles I too will not be found wanting. They died as martyrs for what they believed, so if it means I'm to join them, I do so willingly.'

Still laughing, the creature said, 'You poor fool, I shall be only too glad to accommodate you! But which of the Apostles do you wish to follow? Do you remember how each of them died?'

'Don't insult my intelligence. As a man of the cloth I'm familiar with the Scriptures.'

'In that case,' said the demon, 'let me tell you which of them you're about to emulate.'

Suddenly it stopped. 'No, wait; better still, as you're so fond of spouting the Bible, so well versed in the affairs of your beloved Apostles, let's play a little game. Oh, it's going to be so much fun! Tell me, how did Bartholomew die? Or perhaps you know him better as Nathaniel? How did he go to meet his glorious Maker?'

The fear that suddenly sparked in the old mans eyes, told the creature it had hit the mark.

'I see your words were no empty boast after all. You know he was flayed alive, and so according to your wishes, you shall meet the same fate.'

Suddenly, as if from nowhere the scalpel appeared in the creature's hand, and with agonising deliberation it proceeded to make a long shallow incision into the old man's emaciated stomach.

Screaming in agony, the vicar shouted, 'Oh, no, God in heaven help me!' And with that his bowels involuntarily voided.

'Now that's interesting,' said the creature, 'calling on God to help you. But will he listen? That's the question. I'm afraid to be so negative, but in the case of the other two, he seemed to be deaf. In all fairness, it might have been that he was simply too busy... or could it have been he just couldn't care? Either way, it doesn't bode well for you, does it?'

Then it added in a tone dripping with sarcasm, 'But you see my point, don't you?'

Mustering the last remnants of his fading dignity, David Sutherland said, 'I'm curious about one thing. The disguise you've chosen is that of a young man, but your vocabulary is of that of someone far older. Am I correct?'

With a weary sigh the creature said, 'An astute observation. Yes, in truth I am very old – ancient, some might say – but that's another story, and I'm afraid I haven't the time to explain things to you at the moment.'

Without further warning, it stuffed a sock it had found in one of the drawers in the bedroom into the old man's mouth, before getting down to work. The vicar was still alive, even when half his skin had been peeled from his body. Although the pain seemed to go on for an eternity, in reality it lasted far less. Drifting in and out of consciousness, all he remembered was the creature's eyes, how they seemed on occasion to glow a deep fiery red.

Once again, the thing timed the delivery of its message to perfection.

Its reward was a look of pure horror and incredulity.

By the time the creature had finished, the room looked and smelt like a slaughterhouse, which, considering the mess it was in, it was! Blood was everywhere, not only on the bed, floor and walls, but the ceiling as well.

The skin peeled from the old man's body was of no use to the creature, and so it was thrown like a stinking pile of offal into one corner of the room.

As usual, it had been very careful to leave no trace of its presence. In truth, it was beginning to enjoy its little game with the police immensely, coming to view it as a battle of wits – one which so far, it reflected, it was winning easily.

After wiping everything down carefully, it removed its surgical gloves and put them into an old Tesco bag it had brought. Looking around the bedroom slowly, it mentally congratulated itself on the method of execution it had chosen for the old vicar. About to make its way downstairs, it suddenly remembered it had forgotten to leave its calling card. Moments later, it rectified its mistake.

The following morning, Edna Stapelton arrived at the manse an hour early, hoping to finish her work in time to catch the early afternoon bus to town. It had all been arranged a week ago. A nice meal followed by a look around the shops in Swansea, and then who knows, she thought to herself in anticipation. At seventy years of age, time had been kind to her, she was still in remarkably good health.

About to insert the key into the back door, she paused; it was open already. Her first reaction was the old vicar had forgotten to lock it before going to bed, but she discarded the thought immediately when she remembered just how careful he was about such things. Especially since the spate of murders a few months ago.

Stepping through the door, she had another thought. As he was an early riser, he might already be in the church, pottering about. Yes, she told herself, that was the most probable explanation. She'd been cleaning the manse for over ten years and was quite fond of the old man, grateful for the job in an area of so much unemployment. Although the pay wasn't much, it did keep the wolf from the door, and more importantly, it kept her active. A frugal person, she'd always managed to put something by for little treats, just like the one she'd planned for this afternoon.

Edna took her work seriously, however menial the task. A good day's work for a good day's pay, was her credo. Wherever she'd worked, she had always given her employer full value for money, and now she was working for God, as she liked to look on it, her principles had remained exactly the same.

The only sounds in the kitchen were the monotonous ticking of the huge grandfather clock and the soft purring hum of the refrigerator. It was while dusting the grandfather clock she first became aware of the strange smell. It was coppery in nature, and she realised she had never encountered anything like it. The further towards the stairs she got, the stronger the smell became. Glancing upwards, she sensed with a start it was coming from the old vicar's bedroom.

Setting out to investigate, she'd almost reached it when the stench became too much to bear. Lifting her work apron in front of her nose, she struggled valiantly to stem the flow of bile which was rapidly rising in her throat.

Stepping into the room, she got no further than a few yards when the sight took her breath away. There on the bed was a writhing, seething mass of black. Unable to work out what it was, she bravely took a step forward. It was at that precise moment the flies decided to rise from the bed. Lifting into the air as one, they suddenly afforded Edna a clear view of what, until a few seconds ago, they'd been feasting on. She barely had time to register the horrific spectacle before she hit the floor in an unconscious heap.

When Edna still hadn't arrived by 1 p.m., Lucy Matthews began to wonder if something had gone wrong. After all, she reasoned, it had been Edna not her who'd suggested the trip in the first place. Putting on her thin summer coat, she made her way over to the manse, belatedly realising that at this rate they'd never catch the bus.

On arrival the first thing she noticed was that the door was open.

Making her way into the kitchen, she shouted, 'Edna, Edna! Are you there?' Getting no reply, she moved to the bottom of the stairs. It was then she noticed the funny smell.

Turning her head to one side, she was sure she could hear something strange as well, a kind of weird buzzing. The more she listened the more she was convinced it was coming from upstairs. By now a sense of unease was beginning to creep over her, and instinctively she knew that something was terribly wrong.

Swallowing her fear, she made her way up the stairs.

After every step the smell and buzzing were getting stronger and louder.

She was almost at the top when she suddenly noticed a pair of legs sticking out of the door leading into the old man's bedroom. In an instant she recognised whose legs they were, and despite the stench, which by now was overpowering, Lucy flew up the last step and rushed to the aid of her friend. Bending down to check if she'd had a heart attack or something, it was then she noticed the flies. Instead of fainting as Edna had done, she sprinted down the stairs, ran the fifty yards or so to the main road and began screaming at the top of her voice.

Within moments she had an attentive audience.

Shortly afterwards the police arrived.

Chapter Twenty-nine

IT WAS ALREADY MID-AFTERNOON BY THE TIME JARED, EMMA AND Michael arrived at the emergency meeting called by Danny. Aled and Roger were unable to take time off work, but it caused no problems; both were shrewd enough to realise that by now their presence was purely decorative. Walking into the hall, Jared saw Professor Edwards deep in conversation with someone he'd never seen before. Spotting him, Edwards waved and gestured for him to join them.

'Before you disappear, I'd like you to meet Stephen Boxer, he's what we call in the profession an odontologist, or in plain language a forensic dentist. In this instance I've had to call on his services to help me out. To be blunt, if it wasn't for him the lump of raw flesh I examined this morning might never have been officially identified as the late David Sutherland.'

Coming up behind Jared, Danny Harris put a hand on his shoulder and, guiding him towards the board in the corner, said, 'I don't know whether you've noticed, but we added the third victim's photographs to our growing collage this morning.'

Examining them closely, the true horror of what had been done to the old vicar suddenly hit him. Looking over his shoulder, he risked a furtive glance at Emma, silently praying that her stomach was up to it.

Allowing the others time to adjust to the photographs, Danny became businesslike again. 'If you follow me next door, I've set up a few things ready for the meeting.'

It was Professor Edwards who got the ball rolling.

'The bottom line, ladies and gents, is that the poor chap was literally skinned alive.' Turning to his companion, he said, 'I have to tell you that neither of us has ever come across anything like this before. However, despite the problems, I can make an educated guess as to what happened to the poor devil. In my opinion David Sutherland was flayed alive. Had flaying knives still been in use, I'm sure the murderer would have used one, but seeing such things are a rarity these days, he used the next best thing – a scalpel.'

Seeing the look of astonishment on their faces, he went on to explain.

'A flaying knife is, or should I say *was*, used for tanning. In other words it was used to remove the skin of an animal by peeling it from its body. The actual knife was nothing but a long razor sharp blade flanked by two wooden handles. And make no bones about it, it was extremely efficient. In this case however, it wasn't used to skin an animal but a human being. Oh, and I nearly forgot, the animals were always killed before hand. In this case however, the old vicar was allowed no such luxury. I'm afraid he was very much alive when it was done to him.'

The stunned silence seemed to go on for ever until Jared's voice brought everyone back into the present. 'Yet another link to biblical times,' he said, before explaining exactly what he meant.

When he'd finished he asked a question of Professor Edwards. 'Would that fit in with what happened to David Sutherland?'

'Almost exactly,' was the reply.

'Sorry to interrupt again,' said Jared immediately, 'but did he leave his usual calling card?'

This time it was Danny who answered. 'Yes, that's what's getting to me. It's obvious by now that the bugger's toying with us. And before you ask, no, there were no clues, not a single bloody one.' Changing tack, he said, 'Follow me, I think its time I showed you little lot how we coppers earn our living.'

Arriving in the Hall, the three were immediately struck by how quickly it had been completely refigured.

'Right, let's get the ball rolling,' said Danny, at the same time slapping three glossy photographs on the magnetic board behind him.

'Take a long hard look, everyone.' He paused. 'Over the years I've seen some unpleasant sights, for want of a better word, but these are very different. Committed in the space of three months, the ferocity and sheer brutality of the killings is unlike anything either I or any member of my team has ever come across.

'After the first two, my gut feeling, even though I led you lot to believe I was completely sold on your story about the chalice, was that we were looking for a serial killer. A particularly unique and sadistic one I admit, but a serial killer none the less. However, the more I looked at the murders, the more I seemed to come across anomalies.

'Point one, serial killers work on a decreasing timescale; by that I mean they get a taste for their work, bloodlust they call it, and so their propensity for violence usually increases the longer they go uncaught. That's not the case with our killer, though. He seems to have spread the murders out evenly, with a month between each. As a matter of fact, up till now he seems to have made a big thing of it.

'Point two. Serial murderers are predators who look out for windows of opportunity. Despite that, there is always an underlying pattern to the selection of the victims, and in the case of the three behind me,' he said, pointing to the board again, 'that seems to fit the profile. There is a definite pattern to all three – but finding it, well, that's a whole new ball game.

'Point three. Although it may not be immediately apparent at the time, most serial murders are sexual murders. The bottom line is the killer will always have some serious sexual maladjustment in his make-up. Normally this can be traced back to his formative years, and so the criteria for selecting his victims stems from this. Very often you may not see or understand the link, but believe me it's always there. Incidentally, in case you get the impression I'm sexist or anything, serial killers are not only male. As a matter of fact one of the most deadly was a woman. Does the name Aileen Wournos ring a bell?' He looked around at the others. 'Thought not... Anyway, she was America's first known female serial killer.'

Turning once again to the photographs, he said, 'In this case we have a totally different scenario; there's no hint at anything sexual. Instead, what we have is random violence on an incredible scale.'

Silent for a moment, he carried on, 'The only possible link between what we're up against and the way a serial killer operates is the staging, the attempt to mislead the investigation by altering the crime scene. Unfortunately, I'm pretty sure our killer doesn't give a shit about misleading the investigation. In fact to me it seems to be doing just the opposite. What our boy seems to want to do is to create an impression, to show us how brilliant he is. Hence the reason why each of its victims is killed, or should I say slaughtered, in a specifically gruesome manner. There's no doubt the creature is working to a specific plan, one that according to Jared is biblically orientated. Further, it seems to think we should know who it is and what it's doing. Remember, it keeps taunting Jared, suggesting how with his background expertise he should have worked out who he is by now. I'm sorry I keep referring to it as "he" one moment and then "it" the next. The problem is, I don't really know what to call the bloody thing!'

Looking at Jared, Michael and Emma, he concluded, 'Anyway, after that little speech I have to say that that's the way my mind was working – until you lot finally convinced me otherwise.' Holding up his hand in mock surrender he added, 'And this time I really mean it. Thanks to you, I now know precisely what we're up against.'

Apologies out of the way, Danny said, 'Let's try and summarise exactly what it is we're facing, shall we?'

As it was meant as a statement and not a question he carried on. Ticking off points on his fingers, he said, 'First and foremost, for some reason it hates the Church and everything it represents. Hence its little crusade against what it perceives to be its leaders.

'Secondly, we have the innovative ways in which it kills. It sets up its victims and executes them in an almost theatrical fashion. As I said earlier, it's almost as if it's trying to make a point.

'Thirdly, we have the calling card, which I may add has us all baffled. To put if bluntly, we haven't a clue what the hell it's getting at, yet it thinks we should.

'Then point four: the creature isn't able to exist as a physical entity by itself. In other words, it needs a body in which to operate. A *host body*, if you like, one which it takes over and controls. To make matters worse, when the creature vacates the body, the host has no knowledge of what has happened. I'm not sure if it's able to endow the person with superhuman powers, but from the evidence of the photographs behind me, it seems it can.' He paused. 'Anyone want to say anything before I carry on?'

Tina Reynolds put her hand up.

'I wonder, guv, have we been so focused on the murders we've lost sight of the fact this all began long before the actual killings started. I think you and Jared are right when you say the thing is playing with us. It could be the reason why, although it could kill far more frequently, it doesn't. Instead it likes to drag things out, to prolong the agony of its victims. I know one thing: if I were a local clergyman I would be looking over my shoulder by now, and I think this is exactly what it wants. It's like a parasite feeding on people's fear.'

'Excellent analysis, Tina,' said Danny, 'I agree with you entirely.'

Looking around the room he could see the others were in agreement too.

'I've already spoken to Jared about this, so he's had time to think about his presentation. As he's the biblical expert among us, I thought he might take over at this point.'

With that he sat down.

Getting to his feet, Jared moved over to the whiteboard.

'Before I begin I want to make it clear the information I have is the combined product of three people: Eric Roberts, the old vicar of Carmel, Uncle Edwin and me. Over the course of the last few weeks we've spent ages running through all kinds of scenarios in an attempt to come up with answers. As a result, I make no apologies for condensing the information. In short, what I'm about to deliver is a synopsis of what we've discovered so far.

'The story begins in Palestine some 2,000 years ago with a group of assassins called the Sicarii. After the brutal murder of his brother, their leader, called Barabbas, enlists the aid of a powerful cadre of necromancers called the "Sect of the Dead". Why? Simple – so that he can bring his brother back to life. Using dark forces, but in particular the words of power contained in the Cabala, the sect succeed. Before they do however, they issue Barabbas a warning: once resurrected, his brother may be uncontrollable. Returning in spirit form, the thing has the ability to enter the minds of anyone it chooses and take complete control. Once it has chosen its victim, the creature simply uses the host's physical body for its own purposes. In this case we know the motive was revenge, revenge against those who had originally murdered it. As predicted however, once the creature had acquired a taste for killing, it found it couldn't stop. Belatedly, Barabbas realised he'd made a terrible mistake and with only one course of action open to him he took it. Enlisting the aid of a strange new group of people known as Christians, they managed between them to imprison the evil in a chalice.

'Unfortunately, the danger was far from over, and Barabbas and this small group of early Christians found to their cost that the evil could never be defeated, only contained. From that moment on, the group became the target of the remnants of the Sicarii. These cold-blooded psychopaths hunted them down ruthlessly, frantically searching for the ashes of their master.'

Pausing a moment to get his breath, he carried on.

'You know the details of the bearded head from my uncle's scroll, so I won't bore you with its origins. The important thing is that from the beginning it was regarded with religious awe by those who worshipped it. All kinds of abominations were performed on its behalf, and very soon it acquired both cult and mythical status. Unfortunately, 2,000 years on nothing seems to have changed. They still believe drinking the blood of a young infant in the presence of the head will provide them with occult powers. The ritual takes place on the eve of the spring equinox, when a child no more than eighteen months old is sacrificed.'

Seeing their bemused expressions, Jared explained.

'At that age it is regarded as being without sin. Too young to have a conscience, it is unable to understand the difference between right and wrong, and so according to their credo, perfect for their needs. The procedure itself is quite simple, but the inner circle are dressed in full ritual attire, the white smock and the red splayed cross pâté of the old Knights Templar.'

Holding his hand up to stave off any questions, he said, 'It would take too long to explain, but take it from me there is a reason for the charade.'

Looking over at Danny, he said, 'If you care to check you'll see that since 1953, an infant has been abducted every single year on the eve of the spring equinox. Before that time the Brotherhood had their head-quarters in Paris, so I presume the same thing happened over there.'

'But how the hell do you know all this?' asked Danny in astonishment.

'You can thank Eric Roberts for that,' Jared replied. 'Anyway, where was I? Oh, yes, there was one problem with the ritual. Even by itself the head was extremely potent, but its followers believed that should it and the spirit ever be reunited, then it would provide them with power beyond their wildest dreams. The creature may have its own little agenda, its unholy crusade if you like; but make no mistake, what the Brotherhood are really after is nothing short of complete world domination.'

Glancing over at Tina, he said, 'Let's look at your idea for a minute, that it's playing with us, shall we? I couldn't agree more. It's because of that it's leaving us clues. So far, everything – and I mean *everything* – seems to point to a biblical origin: the names, the methods of execution chosen for the victims, the vocabulary, the coins, they all fit.'

'Coins… what coins?' asked Danny, looking up in surprise.

'Ah, a slip of the tongue,' Jared said sheepishly. 'I hoped I wouldn't have to mention that.' He went on to relate his little conversation with Charlie.

'The crafty buggers,' was Danny's initial reaction, to be followed immediately with, 'I should slap both of them in the cells!'

Smiling, Jared said, 'That's exactly why I never mentioned it. You see, I promised old Charlie if he told me everything the police would never be involved. Besides, it would have made no difference to the inquiry.'

'What's so bloody special about these coins, then? These denarii things?' asked Danny, puzzled.

'Nothing, really,' said Jared. 'Like all coins, they were used simply as a means of currency. During New Testament times, money was derived from three different sources. For starters, you had the imperial money, or official Roman standard coinage, as it was called. Secondly, you had the Greek standard currency, or provincial money, which was produced at Antioch and Tyre. Finally, you had the local Jewish coinage minted at Caesarea. The coins were produced from a variety of different metals, but in terms of value the sliding scale went something like this – gold, silver, copper, bronze and brass. The most common silver coin found during the time of Jesus was the Greek Tetradrachma, or the Roman denarius, the one we're talking about now,' said Jared. 'Either of them was equivalent to a day's wage for a working man. But remember, early coins were nothing more than pieces of metal impressed with a seal. And don't forget they didn't appear much before the seventh century BC.

'Anyway, the point I'm making is that the coins, Roman denarii, were in common usage during the time of Jesus, backing up my theory that whatever took place to piss the creature off so badly, had to have happened at or very near the time of Jesus' death and resurrection. On top of what I've already given you, we also have another source of information, one which might turn out to be more important than all the others put together. It's the scroll Aled found hidden in the room under the altar in Carmel. Let's itemise the points for ease of reference.

'The chalice was transported from the Holy Land to Britain, to be more precise Wales, by sea, somewhere around the year AD 76. So it begs the question, why?'

'Presumably, because by now the Brotherhood were closing in on it, I suspect,' said Emma.

'Exactly my reasoning,' said Jared, 'but according to some sources, it was not only the chalice that was brought over by an old man, but a mysterious codex as well. Purporting to outline the history of the chalice, it was meant to be a warning for anyone – like us,' he said looking directly at Emma and Michael, 'that should it ever be found, it was to be left well alone. I'm only guessing here, but I believe the old man must have had prior connections to this part of the world, because his intention was obvious, to find a hiding place so safe the objects would remain hidden for ever. And it nearly worked, remember. Until,' he said, holding up one finger, 'two small boys discovered the package and delivered it to the old monastery which now lies beneath Carmel. Shortly after, strange things began to happen, unpleasant things that ultimately culminated in the catastrophic suicide of the old father in charge.'

'But,' said Emma in barely a whisper, 'not before he'd left instructions that the foul object should remain untouched... that instead of being opened, it should be buried in a specially commissioned room underneath the altar in the monastery,'

'Precisely,' said Jared. 'If it wasn't for the timely warning given in the scroll, we would have opened the bloody thing there and then! Not that it mattered, as it turned out,' he finished dejectedly. Throwing off his mood of pessimism, he carried on.

'Coming back to the old father, if my memory serves me right it was after translating the final chapter he took his own life.'

'The one prefaced by the funny little symbol, you mean?' said Emma again.

As if he'd seen a ghost, Jared suddenly froze, within moments a look of pure anguish creased his face. 'Oh, you bloody idiot, Hunter,' he muttered.

Danny was the first to react. 'What is it, lad?'

'How could I have been so stupid!' he said holding his head in his hands. 'I knew I'd seen its calling card somewhere, and thanks to Emma, I now know where. It's the same as the one described in the scroll – the same symbol that adorned the final chapter of the codex.'

'The one the old father drew on the wall before hanging himself, you mean?' said Danny.

'The very same; but more than that, I now know why the creature's using it. He's mocking Christianity.'

'Hold it a second,' said Danny again, 'you've lost me all of a sudden. Explain it to me again, and this time in simple terms.'

'I can't tell you why it's mocking Christianity, only the creature knows that, and at the moment it's his little secret. I can tell you what it means, though.' With that he picked up a black marker pen before stepping purposefully towards the whiteboard.

'As with all codes and puzzles it's simple when you know how.'

First he drew the outline of the fish. Pointing to it, he said, 'To you or me it's merely a simple outline of a fish, so crude even a child could draw it. In fact, it comes from the Greek word *ichthus* meaning fish. Each letter of this word is the first letter of the words, "Jesus Christ, Son of God, and Saviour". It's popular even today. I'll bet you've seen it hundreds of times and not realised what it was. Car stickers ring any bells?'

Seeing that Emma had it, he said, 'That's right, Em, the symbol of the fish on car boots and the like. "Members of the twisted fish brigade", they're called these days, I think. All they're doing is declaring they are Christians.

'However its original purpose was very different. You see, in the beginning it was a secret code. Used during the early years of persecution, it was drawn on the walls of the catacombs beneath Rome to indicate the presence of fellow Christians. Later Christians refined it somewhat and by putting in the eye like this,' he said, adding in on the board. 'It meant danger, or keep away, there are Romans soldiers in the vicinity. Like all codes, the simpler the better, and it must have been effective, because apparently the Romans never cottoned on.'

While he allowed them a moment or two to digest the information, he drew something else. Turning back he pointed at the board again and said with a chuckle, 'And that, believe it or not, is supposed to be an ankh, which in Egyptian theology stood for life and eternity. With me so far? Good, but what do you think it signifies when you turn it upside down like this?'

Emma who Jared knew had always been good at puzzles was the first to see it.

'It's the opposite!' she shouted in triumph. 'So it symbolises death and not life.'

'Go on,' said Jared patiently. 'Now take it to its next logical conclusion.'

'Of course,' said Emma,' the truth suddenly dawning, 'it symbolises the death of Christianity. That's why it prefaced the final chapter of the codex, isn't it? It symbolised the fact that it contained a secret regarded as so explosive, that should it ever become common knowledge it would signal the death of Christianity.' Not finished yet, she said, 'And that's precisely why the old father killed himself, wasn't it? He discovered the secret.'

'And I burnt the bloody scroll!' was all that Jared could think of saying. 'But for my stupidity, we might have been able to decipher the clues and find the damn thing. I've done some daft things in my time, but on reflection, that probably takes the biscuit.'

'No use brooding over it, lad, what's done is done,' said Danny.

'What about the photographs of the chalice then?' asked Tina.

'The ones you took illegally,' said Danny Harris in amusement. 'Still, it's lucky for us you did. After that fiasco in the Welfare Hall, I doubt we'll ever see it again now.'

Leaning over to withdraw the snapshots from a large Manila envelope, Jared was careful to keep the secret of what had happened that night to himself, particularly the part concerning his own involvement. Handing several of the high definition photographs around, he said, 'Now these are interesting. If you look carefully you can just make out the outline of several symbols etched into the face of the obsidian. There seem to be nine in all, and the detail is exquisite.'

Silent for a second or two, he suddenly said, 'For some reason they appear familiar, but for the life of me I can't place them at the moment.' Looking up, he said, 'Anyone else have any ideas?'

When there was no response, he carried on, 'By now we know the purpose of the chalice. It was designed to hold the ashes, but the 60 million dollar question is, whose bloody ashes are they?'

'I know one thing for sure,' said Emma in awed tones, 'whoever gave their life to imprison the creature must have been someone very special.'

'From my point of view,' said Danny, 'the only ones good enough to qualify were the saints, and there were so many of them we might never find out who it was. Anyway, does it really matter? The important thing is it worked.'

After several minutes' thoughtful silence, it was obvious no one had anything else to say.

Getting to his feet, Danny moved over to Jared, and after thanking him for his contribution declared the meeting closed.

Jared came instantly awake. Sensing something was wrong, he lay perfectly still. The only sound in the room was the beating of his heart and the faint ticking of his wristwatch. Instinctively he knew the creature had finally made its long overdue visit. He'd made no mention of the fact to the others, but once he'd been singled out as special, it was only a matter of time before the creature's curiosity would get the better of it.

And he'd been right.

Suddenly he had a thought. If that were the case, it meant he was one of the fortunate, one of those immune to the creature's power.

The smell and sudden drop in temperature dispelled any doubts that his instincts had been wrong, and so he lifted himself slowly into a sitting position. There was no need for pretence any longer; the thing knew he was awake. Jared's night vision was exceptional, and so even though most of the room was bathed in deep shadow, he noticed the creature immediately. It was standing near the window overlooking the dense forest that formed the backdrop to his grandmother's garden. Completely motionless, it seemed to be gazing down at something. One of its nocturnal friends, was Jared's guess.

'Ah,' it said without turning around, 'awake at last, are we? I didn't want to frighten you, so I let you sleep,' it continued, chuckling at its own little joke.

'No problem,' said Jared quite nonchalantly. 'I've been awake for some time now. The fact is I've been studying you while you were staring out of window.'

'So you can see in the dark, can you?' it said in a mocking tone.

'As a matter of fact I can; my night vision is quite exceptional.'

'Not as good as mine,' said the creature petulantly, before turning around to face Jared. If it expected fear and horror it got neither, and quite unexpectedly the creature displayed a very human trait – anger!

Looking at the thing's face, Jared could see it was ashen – almost white, in fact. If he hadn't known better, he could have sworn he was looking at a corpse. Then it suddenly hit him, that's exactly what it was – a freshly dug corpse. That takes care of the smell, anyway, he thought flippantly, before realising he should be flattered. It was obvious the thing had chosen a dead host in order to impress him.

Disappointed at the lack of reaction from Jared, it looked into his eyes. There didn't appear to be the slightest sign of fear, not even a flicker, and it was at that moment the creature knew it was dealing with someone out of the ordinary. For the first time since its release from the chalice, it felt a slight twinge of self-doubt.

Interestingly, for Jared it was the other way around, as he saw something in the creature's eyes that gave him hope. At the precise moment it had expressed anger and disappointment, its host's eyes had glowed a deep fiery red. It lasted only for an instant and then it was gone, but it had been there.

It suddenly gave Jared the germ of an idea. What if it was a completely involuntary occurrence, something that happened at moments of stress – greed, anger, or even satisfaction? If so, it might be something they could use against it. A way of recognising it, at the very least.

'I hope you didn't go to all that trouble of borrowing a corpse for me.'

'But of course,' came the reply. 'After all, you are special…' With that it curtsied. 'It's obvious I was expected, so it explains the lack of fear, I suppose. You are afraid, though, aren't you?'

'Of course I'm afraid,' said Jared. 'Anyone who doesn't feel fear is a fool. The trick is learning to control it, and during the last six years I've had plenty of practice, believe me.'

'Ah!' said the creature. 'I understand now. No need to worry, though, it's just a fleeting visit. I just stopped by to let you know I'm disappointed, that's all. By now I would have thought you would have been much further down the line with your investigation. God knows, I've left you enough hints.' Then it added, 'Sorry about the blasphemy.' It paused. 'You haven't a clue who I am, yet you know who my brother was.'

'What about the symbols on the chalice?'

'For someone of your background, I would have thought they would have been obvious.'

After a few moments of awkward silence, Jared said, 'There is one thing I've finally managed to work out, and that's the meaning of your calling card.'

Looking up in surprise, the creature said, 'Good! Some progress at least. So I take it you know all about the codex, then?'

'Yes,' replied Jared, 'but as you're well aware, we don't know where to find it.'

'Come now, Jared, whose fault is that? Correct me if I'm wrong, but wasn't it you who burnt it? Rather silly, that – and all because you thought you were getting back at me! It really is a shame about the codex, because it could have answered so many questions. Take the final chapter for instance, the death of Christianity and all that. Still, if you had discovered the secret of "Project Lazarus", as the old fool called it, then the game really would be all over. Apart from killing the other six, there would be no fun left. No, believe me, the codex is best left where it is… Look where it got the old father. I must say the faces of the old clergymen when they learned the truth were a picture. Oh, they didn't want to believe, but by then neither of us had anything to lose, so they knew I was telling the truth.'

'One thing still puzzles me,' said Jared. 'Why do you hate the Church so much?'

'But that's the question, isn't it?'

'But surely nothing justifies bearing such hatred?'

'Time's a great healer, they say,' said the creature, 'but you and I know differently, don't we? After all it's been, what – over six years now, and yet part of you still hates Emma for what she did. Oh, yes, you still love her with every fibre of your being, but that's with your good side. However, like me you have a darker side, and that one will never forgive. So from that perspective we're not so very different, are we?'

Looking at the creature with barely concealed contempt, Jared said, 'No! You and I are nothing alike. Yes, I've killed and even enjoyed it, and don't get me wrong, I'll do it again if needs be. But you, no, you kill for fun. You're nothing but pure evil!'

'Brave words for someone who has learned to hate only fairly recently; but take a bit of advice from an expert, my friend. I've had 2,000 years of practice. And do you want to know something? Each passing year serves only to fuel my hatred. It's all about betrayal, you see… something you and I have in common,' it said with a smirk.

Suddenly the creature's voice altered and it took on an almost pining quality. 'I believed in him, you see, in his promises! We had a deal, and then when it was all over he said he would find a place for me; but there was no place. He was a *fraud*.' It paused.

'They didn't know I was listening, but I heard them planning it all. Said it was for the best, that it was the only way it would prove he was special, but if he was special, then why did he have to resort to deception?' With a sigh that seemed to encompass centuries, it said, 'Someone had to pay for it all, and so I became the scapegoat.'

With that its demeanour altered once again. Turning on Jared, it said, 'And you ask me why I hate?'

Moments later, its emotions once more under control, it carried on.

'But you are clever and resourceful, one of the chosen, so it would never do to underestimate you. There, quite unwittingly I've furnished you with another clue.'

Smiling now, in complete control once more, it said, 'I bet Professor Edwards has been puzzling his little balls off about the expression on the faces of the clergymen! A mixture of horror and dismay... now what could have produced such a combination?

'Yes, I'm right,' it said, clapping its hand in delight. 'I can see it in your eyes. Well, it's been good chatting like this, but I really must be off. Time flies, doesn't it? Especially when, like you and your friends, you have so little of it.'

Then without further preamble, the creature opened the bedroom window and disappeared into the night.

Chapter Thirty

SEVERAL DAYS LATER JARED HAD AN IDEA. STROLLING DOWN THE MAIN street of Raven's Hill he inwardly breathed a sigh of relief, for the moment the coast was clear. Since the latest murder the media had been uncontrollable. Even though Danny had tried every trick in the book, he'd failed to shake them off. The one place that afforded any privacy was the Ambulance Hall, the reason being that access was restricted to only those with the code, the correct five-figure combination. Despite this, he knew it was only a matter of time before someone bribed their way in.

Glancing in both directions, Jared vaulted the gate at the top of the steps and was punching in the code in seconds. Walking through the narrow corridor leading to the main hall, he noticed the doors were closed and so he reasoned all the activity must be taking place elsewhere.

Stepping into the main body of the Hall, he saw his guess had been correct.

Greeting the others with a wave, he made his way over to Danny, who he saw was having trouble with the computer. Standing directly behind him, so he was unaware of his presence, Jared chuckled to himself. It was immediately obvious that computers didn't seem to be Danny's forte. His suspicions were confirmed when all of a sudden he ran out of patience. Thumping the screen with the flat of his hand, he shouted, 'Tina, what's the matter with this bloody thing again? It's dead!'

Winking at Jared, she made her way over. Placing her hand on Danny's shoulder, she said, 'Patience, guv, it's probably something very simple.'

'*Simple?*' he shouted. 'There's nothing bloody simple about computers, let me tell you! I've pressed "enter" five times now and nothing's happened; give me the old paper and pencil any day.'

Leaning over, Tina saw he was right; the screen did appear to be blank. Momentarily puzzled, she thought for a moment before suddenly realising what the problem was.

Not about to let an opportunity like this pass, she said, loud enough for everyone to hear, 'You did switch it on, didn't you, guv?' Pause. 'Oh, you plonker! It'll never work unless you turn it on at the mains!'

With that everyone stopped what they were doing and looked over.

By now Danny's face was red with embarrassment. Before he could think of a reply, Tina pushed him out of the way. Bending down, she turned the computer on at the mains, and with a single flick of the button the screen blinked into life.

Holding up her hands, she said in mock exasperation, 'Let me find the program for you, it'll save time in the long run.' Within moments she'd found the one he wanted, and standing back in triumph said, 'Now press "enter".'

He did as he was told and suddenly the correct program appeared on the screen. Unfortunately for Danny, it was followed immediately by a chorus of, 'Way to go, guv!' and, 'You're the man!' Experienced enough to know he'd backed himself into a corner over this one, and seeing it was a good-natured confrontation he knew he couldn't win, he stayed quiet.

When the noise had died down, he leaned over to Jared, who by now he'd spotted, and out of the corner of his mouth said, 'She's shit-hot on computers, you know.'

The words were barely out of his mouth when Gareth Evans chirped up, 'It's not that she's so good, guv, it's just that you're bloody hopeless!'

With that the laughter started again.

Turning around, Danny said, 'It's all right for you youngsters with your accelerated promotion or fast-tracking as you call it, you lot are computer-literate from day one. Spare a thought for coppers like me; we've had to start from scratch.'

'Guv,' said Gareth Evans again, 'that's a load of bollocks, and you know it. The truth is you're frightened of the bloody things. You can't break them, you know.'

'All right, all right, Gareth,' shouted Danny. 'Point taken!' Then he turned to Jared and said, 'Don't you bloody laugh! I suppose you're a whiz-kid on the damn things as well...'

'As a matter of fact,' said Jared with a big smile, 'I'm not. Like you, I'm hopeless.'

'Thank God for that, anyway,' retorted Danny, 'at least I've got one friend in the camp.'

Turning back, he looked hard at Jared, realising from his expression he had something on his mind. Before he could ask him what it was, Jared beat him to it.

'I had a visitor last night.'

Looking at him slyly, Danny said, 'No sex, please, I'm far too old for all that!'

Laughing, Jared said, 'No, you daft bugger, it was nothing like that. This little visitor arrived at two in the morning, having just borrowed a freshly dug corpse to use as its host.'

'Jesus Christ!' said Danny.

'No, not him, the creature,' said Jared, deadpan.

'You're really something, you know,' said Danny. 'A real cool customer... but seriously, weren't you afraid?'

'Of course I was, but I wasn't going to show that bastard, was I? Besides, as I told it, the way to handle fear is first to admit to it, and then learn to control it.'

'So what happened?'

'Not a lot, really. It tried to psyche me out, but I was prepared for that and it didn't work. No, I was more interested in what it said. First it called me special – something it's done before – and then it kept goading me about how I should have worked out who it was by now. The problem is, Danny, it's right. I can't really put it into words; the only way to explain it is to compare it to a bad dream. You know, the one where you're running as hard as you can but seem to be getting nowhere. It feels like I'm wading through quicksand. Sometimes what I'm trying to remember is almost there, it's almost as if I can reach out and grasp it, then just as suddenly it retreats into my subconscious.'

After a few second's pause Jared continued.

'There was one thing, though, something that might just turn out to be important.' And with that, he told Danny about it.

'By God,' exclaimed Danny, 'it might be we've just had our first real break! And you think the bastard doesn't even know it's doing it?'

'I'm sure of it,' was Jared's reply.

'But there's more, isn't there? I can tell by your face.'

'It's just that I've had an idea. I'd like to run it by you first though, get your take on it, that's all.' Without waiting for a reply, Jared continued. 'At the moment we're all in agreement we can't kill the thing, right? So, if that's the case, why don't we stop it getting at its victims? In other words, why don't we put them all into one place and protect them?'

For a moment Danny said nothing, until suddenly he exploded into life. 'But that's a bloody brilliant suggestion,' he said, before realising the logistics involved and going quiet.

'I know what you're thinking,' said Jared, 'the practicalities would make the idea untenable; but there are a few things you should think about before dismissing it out of hand. First we have to work out the radius of the killing ground. It's only an educated guess, but I'm convinced the creature will select its victims from the locality. In particular, with the odd exception, they will all come from Raven's Hill.'

'Why?' was the obvious question from Danny.

'If you take a minute to think about it, it's simple. You have to remember that our little village, like it or not, is where the creature's been imprisoned down through the ages. For that reason it's making it personal. So yes, I'd say five miles is plenty.

'Now that problem is taken care of, we come to another, mainly the number of religious buildings involved. Ten or fifteen years ago we would have been faced with a serious situation. We might have been looking at perhaps fifty or even more. Fortunately, there are now only eight viable propositions, hence eight clergymen. The other places of worship have closed, remember. To me the problem here is not one of logistics, but something far more mundane. Will they be prepared to accept our protection? And by the way, none are married, so it makes things a lot easier, if you see what I mean.'

Smiling, Danny said, 'It's obvious you've given this a great deal of thought, and for what it's worth I think it could work. The financial side of the equation is no real stumbling block. I'm sure the powers that be will foot the bill; but out of curiosity what kind of timescale had you in mind?'

'Thinking about Tina's point the other day,' said Jared, 'that the thing seems to be toying with us, I'd say a week tops. If you look at the three murders so far, there's been almost exactly a month between them. If the creature sticks to the same timetable it should make its move sometime in the next few days.'

'Fine,' said Danny, 'but what if it decides to change tactics? Even worse, what if it gets pissed off, thinking we've outwitted it?'

'I've already thought of that; but we've nothing to lose, and even if the worst comes to the worst it will buy us some time.'

320

'So where do you suggest we put them?'

'The Beech Tree might be as good a place as any. It's compact and easy to defend.' Taking a sheet of plain A4 paper from his pocket, Jared unfolded it. Borrowing a pencil from Danny's top pocket, he placed the paper on the desk and began to outline his plan.

'First and foremost it's a three-storey building, right? Now, on the ground floor we have a large bar, a kitchen and dining room, a pool room and a lounge. The bedrooms are on the first and second floors respectively; but this is important, they can only be accessed by one of two ways. Either by using the stairs situated next to the bar – which incidentally means it's always in plain view – or by means of an external fire escape at the back of the hotel.'

'Besides,' said Danny getting in to the swing of things, 'There are no lifts, which is a big bonus, isn't it?'

'Precisely,' said Jared, before carrying on with his plan.

'The twenty bedrooms are divided into blocks, ten on the first and ten on the second.' Using his finger, Jared indicated what he had in mind. 'Starting with the first floor, I thought we might house the clergymen here, and here. In other words, put two on this side of the corridor and two on the other side. We could then repeat the exercise on the second floor. What's important is that we have spare rooms on either side, but in particular we have a gap between the last bedroom and the fire escape. Oh, and one other thing, I would seriously think about taking one other precaution.'

'Go on,' said Danny in encouragement.

'The weak point of the plan is the fire escape, so I'd have a permanent armed guard stationed a few feet from the door on both floors. When I say "armed", I don't mean skilled or proficient in the use of firearms. What I mean is that they should be prepared to use their weapons if the need arises.'

Looking Danny in the eye, he said, 'I've seen too many good men killed simply because they didn't have the animal instinct to pull the trigger when it really mattered. They were brilliant in training exercises, but...' He left the remainder of the sentence unfinished.

In an attempt to lighten the mood, Danny said, 'What do you mean, if I were in charge? Judging by the way you've thought it all out, it looks as if you've already taken over!' He smiled to show there was no malice intended. 'Anyway, if you want my opinion, it's an excellent plan. The only thing that puzzles me is how the hell you managed to come up with it at such short notice.'

Modestly, Jared said, 'I've had plenty of practice.'

It was then Danny remembered Jared's former life. All he could think of in reply was, 'Sorry, I forgot about that.'

'Incidentally,' said Jared, 'how soon can you set things up?'

'If I get cracking right away, I should think two days might do it. If we book the hotel en bloc – it means were paying for all the rooms – but it solves the problem of underoccupancy. Just in case they make a fuss, I mean.'

'Good,' said Jared, 'but what about the clergymen? What if they give us some grief?'

'In that case we do it the hard way,' said Danny. Smiling, he added, 'And that's something I've had plenty of practice with. Give me the list of their names and addresses, the ones you've got in your pocket.'

'And how do you know they're ready?' asked Jared.

Looking Jared in the eye, Danny said, 'I know you well enough by now. Hand them over.'

Glancing at the names, he was about to say he'd see to it right away, when there was a shout from Tina Reynolds.

'Guv, there's a phone call for Jared!'

'Use one of the small rooms,' Danny called over his shoulder, 'at least you'll have some privacy there.'

Picking up the phone, Jared was pleasantly surprised to hear Edwin's voice. Then he suddenly had a thought: his uncle didn't usually phone at this time of day. Was something wrong perhaps? Instantly his senses went into overdrive.

'What's the problem?' he asked.

'No problem,' said Edwin, smiling to himself at the obvious concern in Jared's voice, 'it's nothing like that, I assure you. I've had something of shock, that's all. A rather big one, I might add.'

'Pleasant or otherwise?' asked Jared.

'It depends on how you look at it,' said Edwin enigmatically. 'At the moment I can't really believe it. Let's just say as shocks go, this one registered at about 8.9 on the Richter scale!'

'Christ,' said Jared, 'that's some shock!' Realising it must be important, he said, 'Do you want me to pop up? At the moment I'm at a loose end while Danny puts an idea of mine into practice, so it would be no problem.'

'I was hoping you might say that,' said Edwin. 'What time can I expect you?'

Looking at his watch he saw that it was twelve thirty.

'If I grab something in Alec's, I could be with you by three. Would that be OK?'

'Fine,' said Edwin, 'see you then.'

Putting down the phone, Jared was mildly alarmed. His uncle's voice had sounded strange. If he'd been asked to describe it, a mixture of somewhere between amazement and euphoria might have summed it up.

Ten minutes after eating his hurried sandwich he was on the road. The evening traffic was still surprisingly busy as he guided the Fiesta cautiously into the inside lane. Most of the journey was spent trying desperately to make some kind of sense of the strange telephone conversation. He was so engrossed in his own thoughts that looking up he found to his surprise that he was less than ten miles away from his destination.

Twenty minutes should do it, he thought to himself. In fact it took him less.

Sitting down in his uncle's comfortable leather armchair, a cup of tea in hand, he was ready.

'I don't really know where to start,' said Edwin. 'To be honest, if I didn't know better I would have said the old man was stark raving mad.' Putting his hand up to stave off any questions, he carried on, 'Anyway, he knew too much about me to be a fake.'

Jumping up from his chair, he said, 'Perhaps the best thing to do would be to show you.'

Escorting Jared to the library, he made a beeline for the back wall. Bending down, he removed several books from the bottom right-hand shelf before pressing a hidden button.

For a second nothing seemed to happen, then suddenly, without warning, a large portion of the shelving swung outwards with a loud click.

Gazing in amazement, Jared realised the whole section had been nothing but a facade, that it had been designed to conceal a hidden door. Looking more closely, he saw the door was guarded by a state-of-the-art digital combination pad.

Seeing Jared's astonishment, his uncle said, 'Believe me, you haven't seen anything yet!' With that he punched in the correct code and with a barely audible hum the door swung open. Directly behind the first door was another. Made of bulletproof glass, it was transparent, and Jared could see that beyond it again was a large room which contained what at first appeared to be scrolls and documents.

'Right,' said Edwin, 'I need to close the outer door first before opening this one; you'll see why in just a moment.' Once he'd accomplished that, he turned back to the other door and pushed it open gently. The sound of escaping air told Jared they were about to enter an area which had been hermetically sealed.

As soon as he stepped inside, he knew his guess had been correct. What he'd glimpsed from the outside were priceless documents. Turning to his uncle, he said, 'What the hell have you got in here – the Crown jewels?'

The answer astounded him, as without a trace of sarcasm his uncle said, 'Something far more important, I can assure you.'

The room was amazing.

Apart from the shelves, which seemed to be full of spring-loaded files, there were also several glass cabinets. These he saw in astonishment contained what looked like papyrus scrolls, the ages of which he could only guess at. No wonder the room had been hermetically sealed, he thought, some of them might be thousands of years old.

Pointing to the ceiling, Edwin said, 'It even has its own CCTV cameras.'

'But this little lot must have cost you a fortune,' observed Jared. 'Where did you get the money from?'

'Oh, no,' said Edwin, 'I didn't pay for all this, you misunderstand. That's part of the story I have to tell you.'

Looking at a point somewhere in the far corner of the room he began. 'It all started yesterday evening when quite out of the blue I had a visitor. I'd sent Mrs Edwards home, so I was on my own, but he knew that of course. He must have been watching for weeks, and knew exactly when Mrs Edwards had her night off. Anyway, the next thing I know the doorbell is ringing. Now, you know how far it is from the living room to the front door, and in that time he'd rung twice more.

'Impatient bugger, I thought, until I opened the door and saw him. The poor devil looked dead on his feet – no, not tired, but death, as in death can be fatal.' He chuckled at his own little joke. 'Looking at him, I realised he must be in the final stages of some kind of terminal illness, cancer perhaps. Seeing the look on him I didn't even bother to ask his name. I took him straight into the living room and offered him a drink.'

'You took a chance, didn't you?' Jared said in amazement. 'The chap might have been a lunatic or something.'

'In hindsight, I realise that now, but he looked so ill... Anyway, where was I? Oh, yes, I asked him if he wanted a brandy, and he told me he'd only have the one as he was driving. As soon as I'd poured the drinks he came straight to the point, and asked me how I'd enjoyed the little presents he'd sent me. Seeing how puzzled I was, he explained he meant the photocopy of the scroll and this house.' Edwin paused.

'Suddenly it hit me, Jared. I'd had a feeling all along the house had been too good to be true, so I asked him if he'd set me up for something, some kind of scam. Now, from here on in, I want you to imagine you're sitting in on the conversation. It will be more effective if I do it like that.'

'Ready? Right, here we go...'

' "Oh, yes, but not in the way you think," was his enigmatic reply. By now I was starting to feel distinctly uneasy, I can tell you. But what could I do? I'd let him in and so I had to grin and bear it.

'Then he carried on, "As you rightly guessed, the story about the house being a favour from the father was a pack of lies."

'Annoyed by now, I asked him if he'd been in on the scam as well. If so, what had they hoped to achieve? Then the truth finally started to emerge.

' "Oh, dear," he said, "I'm not going about this at all well, am I? I can see where you're going with this, you think the young student and I were in league in order to exhort or blackmail you. If so, you've got the wrong end of the stick completely. Rather than enlist the young man's aid to try and steal something from you, I did it so you might inherit something – this house!"

'He saw immediately that I didn't believe him – it was written all over my face. I couldn't help it, I'm afraid, but it didn't faze him in the least.

' "There's no catch, Mr Hunter. You see, after my days it would have been yours anyway. Unfortunately, due to my illness I had to make sure you got it sooner rather than later. Cancer, you see... the doctor tells me I've a few months at the most."

'As you can imagine,' said Edwin, 'by now all sorts of weird things were going through my mind. But I had to curb my impatience, let the old man tell the story in his own way.

'Looking at him I guessed he was well into his seventies, and even though it was obvious he was dying, he wasn't going to give in without a fight. His dark penetrating eyes seemed to radiate some kind of inner belief. His next remark took me completely by surprise.

' "How much do you know about your early childhood, Mr Hunter?"

'Well, Jared, as you know, your father and I were abandoned as children, so we knew next to nothing, and I told him so.

' "Then prepare yourself for a shock," was his reply, "because I'm afraid everything you've been told was a lie. In reality you were never an orphan; in fact both your parents loved you very much. Do you know who the guardians are? Ah, I see by your expression you do. I'm glad, it will make telling the story so much easier, because you see your mother was a guardian."

'Sensing I was about to bombard him with questions, he begged me to bear with him for a moment, and then I would be free to ask all the questions I liked.

' "Your mother was a quite brilliant woman, that's where you get your intellectual ability from. She knew instinctively that with so few guardians remaining, the 'Brotherhood', or perhaps you know them better as 'Worshippers of the Head', were closing in on her. As is turned out, her instincts proved to be uncannily correct, because shortly after they caught and eliminated both her and your father. By then, however, it was too late. Her scheme worked so brilliantly no one ever knew of your existence, except me as the senior guardian, of course. You see, you were our little *sleeper*... From the moment you were born you were special.

' "Once again it was your mother who noticed the mark and immediately remembered the prophecy. No one but a select few ever knew of the prophecy, and once the codex disappeared, it was left to the senior guardian in every generation to ensure it was passed on before death. And that, Edwin," he said, using my Christian name for the first time, "is why I'm here. For almost 2,000 years the prophecy was regarded as nothing but a myth, a sacred tale with no real substance. But when you were born everything changed. You see, you bear the mark. That's why your mother was determined that whatever happened to her, you were to be saved at all costs. Unfortunately, for the prophecy to be fulfilled you would have to bear a son, and that son would have to produce a child. That's the way it works, I'm afraid. Having followed your life closely, it seems the prophecy is destined never to reach fruition."

'You know, Jared, he looked so frail and dejected that I had to tell him.'

'Tell him what?' asked Jared, puzzled.

'A long time ago I had a son, but it wasn't meant to be. As it turned out, he never knew – still doesn't – and as much as I love him, I still believe what I did was for the best. When I told the old man he suddenly seemed to look ten years younger. I suppose it was because there was still hope for the prophecy after all. Anyway, from what he told me three different members of the family must bear the mark. The first would be known as the bringer of life, the second would be the destroyer, while the third would be the chosen one. It didn't make a blind bit of sense to me, of course, but after he'd showed me the secret room and what it contained, I knew the old man was right. You see, what you Eric and I discussed about the Cathars, the Templars, the Brotherhood, our educated guesses were correct; it's all there in the files, believe me.'

Smiling at the look of amazement on Jared's face, he said, 'Oh, there was one thing we didn't legislate for. As soon as the 'Sect of the Dead' brought Barabbas' brother back to life, the Sicarii slaughtered them and stole their secrets. But they badly miscalculated. Although they managed to obtain all the inner secrets, so to speak, the thing they were really after, the Cabalistic words of power, died with them. From that time on there was no hope of ever resurrecting anyone else. Consequently, the ritual became nothing more than a meaningless gesture. And still is of course,' he added.

Suddenly breaking in, Jared said, 'But you see it didn't really matter, did it? Apart from the nine who made up the original inner cadre, no one else was any the wiser, and so as far as the ordinary worshippers were concerned, the head still wielded enormous occult power.'

'Precisely,' said Edwin. 'Incidentally, we were right about how the chalice came into the possession of the guardians as well. The old man told me how just over six years ago he hired a man to break into the vaults of Chameleon Enterprises. Everything is here,' said Edwin, gesturing in a 360° arc, 'almost every last one of their grisly little secrets, albeit most of them are photocopies rather than the real things. Incredible as it seems, it appears that originally most of what the Brotherhood now own was stolen from the guardians. Somehow – and don't ask me how – they managed to find the cave which housed their secrets, things like documents, scrolls and the like, and if my guess is correct, a good deal of material wealth. The problem was the thing they were really after, the chalice, well, that had disappeared. What the old guardian sent me was a photocopy of one of the original scrolls by the way – a taster, if you like.

'Oh, and you were right, David Naami is the Grand Master, and apparently he rules the Brotherhood with an iron fist. Originally nine in number, they're now down to eight.'

'Seven,' said Jared. Seeing the surprise on Edwin's face, he added, 'Take my word for it.'

Wise enough to keep his thoughts to himself, Edwin merely said, 'Yes, well, apart from that it seems we managed to work out most everything else. Everything that is but the question of the identity of the head. It appears that was never committed to paper.'

Thinking that Edwin had finished his explanation, Jared was about to ask a question when his uncle suddenly started up again.

'Do you know, during all the time I was listening to him there was one thing that struck me as odd. Not once did the old man mention your father. And so I asked him. After all, we were brothers, for God's sake. In hindsight I wished I hadn't, because the answer wasn't the one I expected. It turns out your father was merely part of the deception. He really was an orphan, chosen for the express purpose of throwing the pursuers off the scent.

'I know what you're thinking, the birth certificates, but they were clever forgeries. In our case there never was a childhood. Everything we remembered was nothing but a cleverly constructed charade.'

After a moment of pensive silence when he seemed to drift off into a world of his own, Edwin suddenly perked up and said, 'I have to admit the old guardian was right about one thing. It seems my mother was a brilliant woman. As far as the rest of the world is concerned, I simply don't exist.'

'That's why unlike the others, those that were hunted into extinction,' said Jared, 'you survived. But you know what this means, don't you? When the old man dies, you become the final guardian.'

'No, Jared, I'm the penultimate one. After my death, my son will inherit the mantle. Come over here,' he said, 'there's something I want you to see.' Gesturing with his hand, he said, 'What we have here is photographic evidence for all our educated guesses.'

Amazingly, there before Jared's very eyes was the bearded male head. In almost pristine condition, it was kept inside a glass case designed in the shape of a pyramid.

'But why the pyramidal case?' asked Jared. 'Why not a conventional one?'

'That puzzled me for a while too,' said Edwin, 'until I suddenly remembered something I'd read years ago. It's all to do with the power of the pyramids.'

Seeing Jared still didn't understand, he said, 'According to the theory, anything placed precisely in the centre of a pyramid would be the recipient of some strange power. For example, food was said to last almost indefinitely, while knives remained constantly sharp. Don't laugh – the head dates back to the age of the pharaohs, so I suppose there must be something to it.'

Pointing with his finger, Jared said, 'This is interesting, look, on the floor beneath the head you can see the outline of the nine chairs, and in the centre there's the motif of the Brotherhood, the Star of David and a tiny chalice in the middle.'

All at once he exclaimed, 'Bloody hell, old Eric was right after all!'

'In what way?' asked Edwin.

'Look carefully at the chalice... see there right in the middle. What do you think that is?'

Pushing his spectacles more firmly onto his nose, Edwin squinted hard before saying, 'Well, bless my soul, you're right, it's a swastika! I must admit his theory sounded a little far-fetched when he proposed it, but he was right after all. And there,' he said pointing to another photograph excitedly, 'you can see the ritual costumes, complete with white mantles and splayed white crosses.'

Some time later, after they had finished browsing through the room Jared suddenly said, 'I don't suppose you found out anything about what it was the Brotherhood discovered under the old Temple in Jerusalem?'

'Relating to what they've been blackmailing the Catholic Church with? No,' Edwin said, 'I've only managed to scratch the surface of all this.' He indicated with his arm the enormous amount of material housed on shelves in every conceivable corner of the room. 'But there was one thing the old man said that might give us a clue. After talking about the prophecy, he said something to the effect the secret was a two-part thing. The first was never committed to writing, until it seems the old man did the unthinkable: he broke the golden rule and described it in the final chapter of the codex.'

'If that's the case, if the Brotherhood had no knowledge of it,' said Jared, 'it can't be what they've been using to blackmail the Church.'

'Exactly,' said Edwin, 'it means that when the Sicarii found the documents belonging to the guardians, "Project Lazarus" as it became known, was never part of the haul.'

'What about the second part, then, the one the Brotherhood did find? I take it this was what was used as leverage against the Church?'

'It must have been,' replied Edwin, 'but the old man refused to give me details. When I pressed him, he simply clammed up. However, he promised he would return the following week. The problem was he'd had his suspicions that he'd been under surveillance for some time now, so he was adamant that he was only going to make the journey when he was sure the coast was clear. According to him, he'd had the feeling he was being watched for a while. It was nothing he could put his finger on, he said, just a feeling, but the kind that he'd come to trust, for the simple reason it had kept him alive all these years. When he was convinced it was safe enough to return, it was then he would give me the details of Red Serpent.'

Chuckling to himself, Edwin said, 'There was one other thing. When I saw him to the door, I happened to see his car. You'll never guess what he was driving – a bright red Mini Cooper "S".'

'You're joking!' said Jared. 'I thought you said he was well into his seventies?'

'He is, but in his own way he's quite a character. He saw by my face I was astonished. His explanation was that it was a fulfilment of a boyhood dream. He said, if he only had a few months to live, he was bloody well going to enjoy them!'

When they'd both stopped laughing, Edwin said, 'Are you going to stop overnight? There hardly seems any point driving all the way home at this hour. Give your grandmother a tinkle first, otherwise she'll only worry. You know what people of that age are like.' He then remembered sheepishly that he wasn't much younger himself. Trying to cover his embarrassment, he added hurriedly, 'While you're doing that, I'll sort things out with Mrs Edwards.'

Terrified, both assassins were debating fiercely which of them should report back to David Naami, only too aware of the consequences of failure.

'But it's impossible!' said the younger of the two.

'Impossible or not, the old bastard has outwitted us, that's for sure.'

'How the hell could we have lost him? A car that colour stands out a mile, for God's sake.'

'And that's exactly what David Naami is going to say when you report our little failure to him,' responded the other.

'What do you mean, when I report back to him? What's wrong with you doing it?'

'Privilege of rank, old bean; as the oldest, I'm delegating the honour to you. Anyway, remember that shit always flows downwards.'

'Thanks a bundle!' was the retort, but seeing that further argument was pointless, he capitulated with as much bad grace as he could muster. A few moments later he said with a grunt, 'Give me that bloody mobile before I lose my bottle.'

Suddenly the other assassin had a thought. 'I bet the old bastard took a back road, one we didn't know about.'

'Fat lot of help that is now! If that's what really happened, you can bet Number One will tell us we should have thought of it sooner and staked the place out properly.' Thinking about it for a moment, he said, 'No, I'm not going to say anything like that – we're in enough shit as it is.'

Holding up his hand to silence any further discussion, he punched in the code and waited. In seconds it was all over. Switching off the mobile he said, 'Now, that was too bloody easy. Didn't blow his top or anything, was as calm and collected as you like.'

'Oh, shit' said the other. 'That's when he's most dangerous. What's the score, anyway?'

'It seems Number One's convinced the old man's in contact with someone around here, so we're to stay put until we pick up his trail again.'

'But, Christ, that could take weeks!'

'Do you want to phone him back and tell him that?'

Suitably chastised, his colleague answered, 'See your point. Think I'll pass on the phone call. Besides, sitting on our arses keeping tabs on a bright red Cooper "S" is better than some of the other shitty jobs he's been dishing our lately.'

As it turned out, they only had a week to wait.

Chapter Thirty-one

By 10 P.M. BOTH GUARDS HAD COMPLETED THEIR ROUNDS AND WERE reporting in. Everything was quiet. Receiving the all clear, Danny turned to Gareth and Tina and gave the thumbs up. He was about to say, 'Quiet as the grave,' before thinking better of it.

Not the time or place, he realised.

Sitting around the bar, propped up on a tall wooden stool, Danny allowed his gaze to wander over the dazzling array of drinks on display. As a self-confessed beer drinker, he couldn't stand either lager or cider, so that first morning when he'd walked in and seen the selection on offer, he had felt like a small boy in a sweetshop. From day one, he had made himself a promise: he would work himself through all of them until he'd found his favourites. Starting with what he called 'the keg beers' he'd decided to finish off with the bottles. As it turned out, he did it the other way round. Of the dozen or so bottles he'd tried, two in particular – the Fursty Ferret and Cwrw Haf had stood out. With their well-balanced malty palate and distinctive hoppy aroma, they had suited his particular taste extremely well. Of those 'on the pull', as he phrased it, he had enjoyed three – The Reverend James, Dog's Bollocks and Felinfoel Double Dragon. Commenting on the Double Dragon to the landlord, he had been amazed to find that the small Welsh brewery had been the first company in the world to come up with the revolutionary idea of canned beer. He had been further surprised to learn that a good deal of it was distributed to large pubs in London, especially the inner-city areas. 'Seems they can't get enough of it,' was his concluding remark.

The food wasn't half bad, either. As a lover of fish, the choice was extensive. It seemed that both trout and salmon were on the menu daily. Referring to the freshness of the salmon to Tina one afternoon, he had been overheard by a local who, with a straight face, had informed him that 'fresh' in this neck of the woods meant that it had been poached the night before. 'It's a flourishing trade in these parts, along with other things,' was his parting shot.

Knowing that Danny and Tina were police and that poaching was a crime hadn't fazed the old gent in the least. Not that the locals were hostile to Danny's little group – far from it, they genuinely seemed to enjoy their company. No, the message that came across was loud and clear – people around here, when it came to authority, simply couldn't give a shit. The 'other things' he had hinted at didn't bear thinking about.

Thursday was curry night and again the selection was wide-ranging. Being a lover of the stronger, more full-flavoured ones, Danny tended to keep away from the yoghurt-based curries, such as tikka massala. Instead, he'd opted for a lamb and mushroom madras, which he had to admit had been surprisingly good. The lamb, which could be stringy and tough in some curries, was delicious, prompting Danny to wonder which of the local butchers the chef used. With that, the old man's comment about poaching came back to him and all of a sudden he decided that he really didn't want to know.

The minister of Bethlehem, Aaron Gower, was in bedroom number two, the second on the left at the top of the stairs. Besides all the other precautions that had been made to ensure the safety of the clergymen, Danny had added one of his own. As an afterthought, a spyhole had been drilled into each of the doors.

It was the second night of the vigil and by now everyone had relaxed somewhat – everyone, that is, but Danny.

Seeing the worried look on his face, Tina said, 'Guv, no one is going to get anywhere near those guys, the hotel's like a fortress. Take it from me, nothing can go wrong.'

'Correct me if I'm wrong, Tina love, but didn't they say something similar about the *Titanic*?'

Looking at his watch the creature saw it was 10.05 p.m. precisely.

Walking briskly up the stairs and turning into the corridor on the first floor, it noticed the armed guard standing at the far end of the corridor. Nodding in greeting, it gestured to the tray, 'Sandwiches and coffee, do you want to check them out?'

'No need,' was the gruff reply. 'As long as I'm standing here, there'll be no problem.'

Knowing it was on a tight schedule, that there was little room for error, the creature was in no mood for its usual little games, and so it had taken control of the boy early. This was a different host to the one it normally used, but it had no choice. The other was known, and had it used him; it was sure it wouldn't have taken the police long to put two and two together and come up with four. Besides it would take the gloss off its little game. Time enough to reveal the identity of its favourite host when it had completed his unholy crusade, as it had come to think of it. No, it could return to the other when the dust had settled.

Tonight was all about making a point, about showing these arrogant bastards exactly how ineffectual all their elaborate precautions were. There would be time for enjoyment later, after it had killed the man of God.

When it knocked at the door, an eye suddenly appeared at the hole and a gruff voice shouted, 'What do you want?'

'Room service, sir,' was the reply, 'it's coffee and sandwiches.'

Suspicious now, the voice came back, 'No one here ordered anything.'

'No, sir,' the creature said patiently, 'compliments of the management. Seeing as it's been a long, hard evening, I'm delivering to everyone, but your room just happens to be the first on my list.'

Allowing himself a smile, Sergeant Glover thought that in reality it had been anything but a hard evening. In fact it had been easy, too bloody easy. The job was so bloody boring that the most difficult part was staying awake. Still, he was getting paid handsomely for it, so he wasn't complaining; besides he was due to be relieved at twelve midnight anyway. Looking at his watch, he told himself, 'And that's in less than two hours time.'

Without him knowing it, the inactivity had already got to him, his focus not what it should have been; otherwise, he would have noticed the waiter was wearing surgical gloves. True, they were flesh-coloured and difficult to spot, but that was no excuse, especially in the light of what was to follow shortly afterwards.

Taking another look, all Ray Glover saw was a tall, skinny kid. No danger there, he thought, and so turning to the minister he said, 'I know it's against the rules and we shouldn't, but fancy a cup of coffee and some sandwiches?'

'I'd love some,' was the reply, 'my throat is parched.'

'My sentiments exactly,' said the sergeant, and with that he opened the door.

Realising he couldn't take hold of the tray because he was holding his hand gun, Ray Glover walked over to the small table near the bed and placed the gun there, just as the creature knew he would. It was in that split second when the sergeant's guard was down that it struck.

Removing a short length of metal pipe from under the white cloth that covered the food, it felled the police sergeant with one well-placed blow. He was unconscious before he hit the floor.

Watching in horror, the minister was so stunned he was unable to move.

Like a rabbit caught in the oncoming lights of a car, Aaron knew what was coming but was powerless to do anything about it. He was still in a state of shock when the creature withdrew a garrotte from its back pocket and in one lightning movement looped it over the head of the helpless minister. By the time his numbed brain had registered what was happening, it was too late for the old man to do anything to save himself.

Pulling tightly on the wooden handles, the creature forced the minister onto his knees before digging its own knee into Aaron's back and pushing him face forward onto the bed. Forcing his head into the duvet so he was unable to utter a sound, the by now desperate minister was wriggling and kicking in a frantic attempt to ease the pressure on his throat. The more he struggled, however, the tighter the garrotte pulled.

The wire the creature had selected was the best money could buy. It was so fine it cut through the muscles and tendons of the minister's neck like cheese wire. Almost immediately, blood spurted into the air from the gaping wound.

In seconds it was all over.

Taking both cushions from the bed, he punched them lightly into shape before turning them over and propping them neatly against the headboard. Lifting the body carefully, he arranged it so it was in a semi-reclining position.

Extracting a handful of silver coins from its pocket, it stuffed the Roman denarii into the minister's mouth.

From now on, its calling card would be superfluous, it realised, thanks to the efforts of that cocky young bastard, Jared. Still, it had a few other tricks up its sleeve; the game was far from over.

Standing back, it looked around the room with a self-satisfied smirk. It had been a difficult task well executed, it thought, suddenly giggling at the choice of words. It was then it remembered the police sergeant. What to do with him was the problem. The thought of him recovering and spending the rest of his career in disgrace appealed enormously, but what was even more appealing was to bludgeon him to death... and so without further delay it did just that. The noise made by the pipe hitting Ray Glover's unprotected head was unlike anything the creature had ever heard before. 'Hitting an overripe melon with a hammer' was the analogy that sprang to mind, and with that it proceeded to beat him into a bloody pulp.

From the time it had walked into the room until the time it had completed his task, less than five minutes had passed. Any noise would have been masked by the sound of the television, so it had no worries on that score. Realising that any further delay might arouse the armed guard's suspicions, it moved quickly into the bathroom. Washing the blood from the surgical gloves, it stuffed them into its pocket, while the metal pipe and garrotte were hidden underneath the white cloth on the tray.

With a last lingering look it walked out of the door.

Adding what he thought was a nice touch, it shouted, 'Glad to be of service, sir!' before closing the door. Finally, with a nod to the guard, who was oblivious of anything untoward, the creature walked slowly down the stairs and into a packed bar.

Heading for the kitchen, it glanced casually over its shoulder to see if anyone was watching, but of course they weren't. After all, it thought, who would look twice at someone carrying a tray and wearing the clothes of a humble waiter? And it was right – no one even gave it a second glance. Within moments it had taken the side door leading to the car park and safety.

Suddenly realising it was hungry, it grabbed a handful of sandwiches before throwing the reminder, along with the tray and flask of coffee, into the hedge.

At 10.55 p.m. both guards started their rounds. Within moments the guard on the top floor reported all was in order.

'Rooms twelve, thirteen, seventeen and eighteen have all checked in, so the top floor is all clear,' said Danny, turning to the others.

It was then Tina noticed a little frown appear on his face. 'What's up, guv?'

Placing one hand over his mobile phone, he turned towards her, 'I'm not sure… It's the first floor, there seems to be a slight problem. Rooms seven, eight and three are all fine, but for some reason the guard can't get an answer from room two. Says he can hear the television clearly, but they're not responding. If Glover has fallen asleep I'll have his bloody badge!'

'Hardly likely, guv,' said Gareth Evans, springing to the sergeant's defence. 'What would be the point? He's off duty in another hour anyway. But even if he has dropped off, the old man should be awake. You know what old people are like. Most of them tend to stay up late. Watch telly all night, some of the buggers. No, it doesn't make sense; one of them should be answering.'

Suddenly Danny held his hand up for silence, concentrating hard on the message coming from the other end of the phone. That the news was bad was obvious, the look on his face clearly betraying his emotions. When the words came, they were delivered in a barely audible whisper. 'Oh, Jesus,' Danny said, turning to the others, 'the old minister's dead, and from what the guard says the place is in a hell of a mess.'

Recovering some semblance of composure, he switched off the mobile before ordering a large brandy for each of them. Handing them around, he said, 'If it's as bad as the description the guard gave, I think we're going to need these,' before downing his in a single gulp. Lowering his empty glass onto the bar he got up and trudged wearily towards the stairs. Finishing their drinks, the others were too stunned to do much else but follow closely behind.

They were at the bottom of the stairs before Gareth Evans finally found his voice and said, 'But it's bloody impossible! No one could have got anywhere near the rooms with all the precautions we took. I know what were dealing with isn't human, but it's not fucking invisible, for God's sake!' It was then he remembered Danny's quip about the *Titanic*.

'We sat at the bloody bar all evening. We even made sure that when one of us went to the toilet the others were watching, for Christ's sake. And apart from the brandy just now, we haven't touched a drop of alcohol, so how could it have happened?'

'Our surveillance was watertight,' added Tina. 'No one could have slipped past. The only person we saw going up those stairs was a young kid carrying a tray.'

Suddenly they both looked at each other.

With a cry of anguish, she said, 'Shit! Of course, it was the creature in the kid's body – how could we have been so bloody stupid? It was nothing to do with supernatural powers, the thing used simple logic. Unfortunately, we were daft enough to fall for one of the oldest tricks in the book. I wonder if the guv has managed to work it out yet.'

He had, but not by the same method as them.

Rather than getting there by a process of deduction, the guard had remembered the tray being taken into the room at around 10.05. As the waiter had been the only person he'd seen all evening, it was obvious what had happened and he was devastated. He admitted freely he hadn't checked the tray, and that was after the clever bastard had invited him to do so. It was to be years before he forgave himself for what he saw as gross negligence, something that had led to the death of two people entrusted to his care – one of whom had been a good friend.

Arriving home around midnight from Edwin's, Jared was passing the Beech Tree when he noticed the familiar yellow tape cordoning off the area. Parking his car, he got out and made his way over to the duty policeman. He'd opened his mouth to ask what was going on when suddenly a large white van arrived at a rate of knots, before coming to an abrupt stop several feet from where he was standing. The back doors suddenly opened and two men and a woman appeared, one of whom was Professor Edwards. He was carrying an aluminium case full of the tools of his trade: gloves, bags, tweezers, cameras and a myriad other things an ordinary person would have no clue about.

Slipping on a pair of latex gloves which he'd taken from the pocket of his standard white overalls, Jared caught his eye. Waving Jared over, he said, 'Want to see what's left of the poor buggers?'

Nodding in the affirmative, Jared followed him through the bar and up the steep stairs to the first floor. On the way the professor turned back and said, 'At least there's one good aspect to all this. The media are usually safely tucked up in bed at this time of night, so it means we can get on with our work without any bloody interference.'

'Yes,' said Jared, 'but the sharks will be in a feeding frenzy as soon as they find out about this one. By tomorrow it will be like a bloody circus around here!'

'Not to worry,' said Ralf in reply, 'by then you and I will be long gone.'

Looking over his shoulder, Jared was pleased to see that Roger's attractive girlfriend, Karen, was nowhere to be seen. The woman who had taken her place looked nothing like her. It still rankled that the information she'd given Roger and the details she'd disclosed had shown a total disregard for the seriousness of the case; but more than that, it had been highly unprofessional. In a case as delicate as this, it was the last thing they needed. Loose lips were a complication they could do without.

The door was already open and, seeing the policeman standing guard, Ralf Edwards was about to ask the inevitable, when his question was pre-empted.

'No, sir, I haven't touched a thing! Everything's exactly as it was when DCI Harris and the team arrived.'

'What about the armed guard who found the bodies – did he touch anything?'

'No, sir, he did exactly the same as me. The crime scene is in pristine condition. I can assure you it hasn't been compromised in the slightest.'

'Well done, young man,' he said, before adding with a tired sigh, 'not that it will do us much good. If the previous killings are anything to go by, the bastard will have left nothing for us to find.'

Taking one look at the carnage, Jared knew two things immediately. First, his idea about keeping the clergymen away from the creature hadn't worked; and second, there was no doubt at all that what he was looking at was the work of the creature. There was so much blood it was difficult to believe it had all come from two men.

That's sixteen pints more or less, depending on their size, of course, thought Ralf Edwards ruefully, remembering his early days as a young medical doctor. All the normal smells he associated with death were present, in particular blood, the coppery tang of which was unmistakable. Other telltale signs such as urine and faeces were also in evidence. But he'd been expecting them, knowing as he did the body involuntarily voids itself of such things in the case of a violent death – or in this case *two* violent deaths.

Attempting to kill time while assessing the situation around him, Ralf said to Jared, 'Blood has an extremely interesting history, you know.' Seeing Jared's puzzled expression, he explained, 'It's categorised into several separate stages for forensic purposes. For instance, you have classification, identification and then differentiation. You know the kind of thing I'm on about: A, B, AB positive and the like. Once we've decided on the blood group, then the next stage is to individualise it or, to put it into simpler language, to begin to trace it back to its owner.'

'Like a fingerprint, you mean?' said Jared.

'Yes, that's right. It may not sound such a big deal these days, but remember in the beginning it was a quantum leap forward in eliminating suspects. Not the complete answer, of course, for the simple reason that so many of us belong to the same blood type. Then along came DNA,' he added with a huge grin, 'and transformed the picture once again.'

Walking around the room slowly, he looked for a murder weapon, while at the same time being careful not to touch anything. Exactly what had made such horrific injuries to the police sergeant's head was anyone's guess.

What had killed the minister was obvious.

Bending over the body on the bed, he suddenly noticed there was something in the old minister's mouth. Opening the aluminium case he took out a pair of tweezers. If he wasn't mistaken... but by Christ, he'd been right, they were coins. He didn't even try to guess why they'd been placed there. Only the demented bastard who had killed the old man would know the answer to that, he reasoned. Unless of course Jared might have a clue...

Turning, he said, 'Any idea why these have been placed in the victim's mouth?' Picking one coin up carefully with the tweezers, he showed it to Jared, along with strict instructions not to touch.

Studying it carefully, Jared immediately recognised it for what it was, and if he wasn't mistaken he knew where the creature had got them from.

With that, everything slotted into place.

The thing had been right. He should have been able to put two and two together – and far earlier than now. The clues had been staring him in the face from day one, and had he but seen them he'd have known the answer all along. The problem was that for some reason his subconscious had buried the knowledge. He knew from past experience that with suppressed knowledge no amount of forcing would bring it to the surface; patience was the key, and now that patience had finally been rewarded.

It was the coins in the mouth that had been the final piece of the jigsaw, and now he knew who the bastard was. As Jared rushed out of the room without a by your leave, Professor Edwards' witty response was, 'Something I said?' Then he turned back and got on with the task in hand. He knew immediately that the two bodies had gone to meet their Maker, but following protocol he checked the necks for pulses. Finding none, he pronounced both men dead.

In this instance the time of death was unimportant, as Danny and the team could pinpoint it almost exactly. That said, the photographer could now move in, and once he'd finished, the bodies could be shipped down to the morgue where Professor Edwards would be able to conduct an autopsy.

Running up the stairs taking two steps at a time, Jared went straight to his room and booted up the computer. Clicking onto the website, he realised that not only did he know who the creature was, but if he hadn't missed his guess, he knew who the clergymen represented. If the information he was looking for was on the Internet, then he would soon know if the third part of his theory was right.

Initially what had thrown him was the number of symbols on the chalice. Again, the number of the silver coins found by Charlie and Albert had been an odd number, and that too had thrown him off the scent for a while. Scrolling his way through the mass of information, he suddenly found what he was looking for. There, staring him in the face, was confirmation of his theory. Now he could take what he had to the others without fear of making himself look a fool. And as far as he was concerned, the sooner he did it the better.

Stooped almost double, the old man shuffled painfully across the main road, turning his head constantly to check on the traffic, which seemed to be hurtling past at breakneck speed. Several people on the other side of the road, some elderly themselves, let out audible sighs of relief when he made it safely across. Totally unaware of his audience, the old man looked straight ahead. He then adjusted his walking stick, and without a second's thought made his way between two impressive expanses of lawn that guarded the entrance to the building.

The edges of the lawns which touched the extremities of the road were immaculately tended and the lush green grass contrasted sharply with the yellow sandstone path that zigzagged its way towards the imposing sign proclaiming the headquarters of Chameleon Enterprises. The reception entrance was impressive: a few steps led him to a huge set of glass doors, which opened automatically, the logo of the company displayed prominently on either side.

Eying the old man suspiciously, the armed guard, against his better instincts, ushered him in, soundlessly. Stepping inside, the old gent was greeted by a lobby of gigantic proportions that was covered in plush carpets coloured in red and gold. Either side of the reception area were rows of black leather armchairs, while the walls appeared to be made of solid marble.

Watching the old man carefully as he made his way towards the desk, the guard relaxed only when he was within touching distance of the solid oak counter. Behind the desk was an extremely attractive girl. Long blonde hair, stylishly cut, hung down to her shoulders and her eyes were a striking shade of green. The name of Chameleon Enterprises was stitched into the right-hand side of her pale-blue shirt, while on the other side hung a small white name tag, proclaiming in black letters that she was Samantha Deakon.

The request took the girl completely by surprise.

'I'd like to see David Naami, please.'

Stifling the laugh that rose to her throat, she suddenly sensed that the man was serious.

'I'm very sorry, sir, but Mr Naami doesn't see anyone, especially without a prior appointment – unless of course you have one, that is.'

'But he'll see me, I can assure you,' was his enigmatic reply.

Something about the way he said it sent shivers down the girl's spine. She was about to call one of the guards when the old man suddenly caught her eye. He was smiling, and it was as if he could see right through her.

'I wouldn't do that if I were you, young lady; there really isn't any need. Just tell David I'm here.'

Startled, she suddenly realised he'd just read her mind.

Unsure what to do now, she went with her instincts.

She knew there was something very unusual about this man, something strange and powerful. Despite his fragile demeanour there was a kind of aura about him, and it radiated from every pore. 'If you'll bear with me a moment, sir, I'll just enquire if Mr Naami will see you.'

Picking up the red phone, the one which was linked directly to her boss's private office, she was rewarded with an almost instant reply – a first in the time she'd been working here.

It seemed her good luck was about to continue, as he was in one of his rare good moods. Radiating charm, he said, 'Yes, and what can I do for you this morning, Samantha?' He instantly picked up on the girl's nervousness. Listening to what she had to say, he had to admit that on any other occasion he would have been highly suspicious, but today for some reason he was intrigued.

'You're sure he's old?'

Getting an affirmative reply, he carried on, 'Give me a short description.'

When she'd finished, he said, 'Sounds innocuous enough... but what makes you feel it would be worth my while seeing him? You know my rules, and they expressly forbid me seeing anyone without a prior appointment.'

'I appreciate that, sir, but there's something about him, something in the eyes; he's not what he seems, I can assure you.'

Making an instant decision, David said, 'Get one of the guards to give him the once-over, and then ask him to accompany the old man to my private office.'

Checking the old man over, the guard did it professionally and thoroughly. He was too afraid of the consequences should anything go wrong to do otherwise. Satisfied, he smiled down at the stooped figure before leading him over to David Naami's private lift.

Entering in the correct coding sequence, they both alighted and within what seemed no time, they were stepping out onto the top floor. Knocking, the guard waited patiently, and within moments the door swung open to reveal his boss standing there.

'Shall I wait with you while you talk to the gentleman, sir?'

'No, thank you, Conrad. I'll call when the interview is over – you can go now.'

Closing the door, he led the old man over to a pair of sumptuously covered leather armchairs. Watching the old gent collapse into one of them, he lowered himself effortlessly into the other, studying the man carefully without appearing to do so. At first glance there seemed to be nothing unusual about him, but he remembered the girl had expressly mentioned something about the eyes.

As if sensing what he was thinking, the old man suddenly raised his head and looked deeply into David Naami's own eyes, and with that the stranger flashed a deep crimson.

Startled, David wasn't sure what he'd seen, but by the time he'd got over his initial surprise, whatever he'd thought he'd seen had now gone. Baffled, he was about to open his mouth, but the visitor beat him to it.

'So you are the current Grand Master, David... I hope you've kept my shrine in pristine condition.' With that the flash of red appeared again.

Swallowing hard to fight down his growing excitement, David thought, it couldn't be, not in the body of an old man... until suddenly it struck him, the disguise was perfect. Finding his voice he said, 'Master, is it really you?'

Smiling at him, the creature said, 'But of course, my dear David, who else did you expect? Do you like my little disguise? Perfect, don't you think? Well, for the time being anyway.' With that it rose from the chair and gave a perfect pirouette, all trace of the arthritic old man gone in an instant.

Recovering quickly, David said, 'To what do I owe this honour?'

'I'm glad you asked me that, because although I've had so much fun of late, I begin to tire of the game. Therefore, on 28 October I intend to serve up a *double treat* for the residents of Raven's Hill.' Seeing the puzzled look on David's face, he explained, 'It was the date the Church decided to honour both Jude and Simon as martyrs, and so I intend choosing two clergymen from the locality and slaughtering them both on that particular day. Deliciously appropriate, don't you think? However, when I've successfully completed that little task, I want to do something far more outrageous.' Rubbing its hands together it said, 'As long as you are able to procure what I need, I shall be able to rid myself of the whole village in one fell swoop!'

In a voice dripping with sarcasm, it added, 'Not that I'm vindictive, mind you, but by doing that I will be keeping a promise I made to someone just over six years ago.'

Losing its train of thought for a moment, the visitor shook its head before saying, 'But where was I? Oh, yes, if you would be so kind and listen up for a few moments, I'll outline how I intend going about things. And then perhaps you could tell me what you think.'

After the old man had finished, David Naami was stunned. It took him several seconds to find his voice, but when he did he realised that what had been suggested was so breathtaking it was a stroke of genius, and he told him so.

Like a child, the creature thrived on compliments, and so its reaction was equally infantile. Hugging its shoulders with undisguised glee, it said, 'Yes, yes – it is brilliant, isn't it? I thought so too, but do you think you can make it work? By that I mean, are you able to deliver the means by which my plan might be expedited?'

Thinking furiously, David Naami was by now as excited as the creature, and said, 'I know we haven't the means within the organisation itself at present. Strangely, we can lay our hands on virtually anything else but that.' Suddenly he beamed, 'Not to worry! I know who I can rely on to get it. As it happens, I'm delivering a consignment of weapons to my old friend, Gregor, next week. We were to be paid in money, but I'm sure if I suggest a trade he would be amenable.'

'Good, good, so I can leave the planning to you.' Getting to its feet, it said, 'And now I'd appreciate a conducted tour of my shrine – and it had better be good, David.'

About to be shown through the hidden door at the back of the office, the old man suddenly stopped in mid stride. Placing a hand on David Naami's sleeve it said, 'Incidentally, the young girl at the desk, she's very bright; she recognised something different about me immediately.'

'As a matter of fact, she's one of our most promising. The daughter of one of our assassins, as it happens,' said David Naami. 'Why?'

'Get rid of her.' Without a trace of emotion it added, 'I want her eliminated as soon as possible.'

Stunned by the speed in which the personality of the creature could change, David was about to say something when he remembered who he was dealing with and instead said, 'Of course, Master, it will be taken care of immediately.'

An hour later the tour was complete, and David watched in relief as the guard on the entrance helped what he thought was a frail old man to the edge of the pavement. Shrugging off the proffered help, the visitor deliberately stepped off the kerb and into the path of an oncoming lorry. Bouncing off the bonnet, the body flew several feet into the air before landing on its back. A fraction of a second later the back wheels of the juggernaut ran over it, turning what was already a fragile body into a bloody pulp.

The guard could only watch in stunned amazement before the first of many screams brought him out of his stupor. Reacting as quickly as his numb reflexes would allow, he ran up the path to the front desk in order to phone an ambulance, although in his own mind he thought a shovel and black bag might be more appropriate.

Watching it all from the comfort of his top floor eyrie, David Naami chuckled to himself. The Master had taken care of one little problem very neatly. Now he realised it was time to honour his promise and take care of another.

Chapter Thirty-two

Holding up his hand to attract the attention of the others, Danny said, 'Before we start, let's be clear on one point: no one individual is responsible for what happened last night. It seems to me everyone is blaming themselves, and I won't have that. Besides, it's self-defeating, bad for morale.'

'As far as I'm concerned the plan was a good one. Don't get me wrong. Anyone who believes anything is foolproof is either stupid or naive, but if the three of us,' he pointed to himself, Gareth and Tina, 'had done our job properly, it might well have been. Instead we were completely outwitted. We fell for one of the oldest tricks in the book. Anyway, what I'm trying to say is, if anyone's to blame then it's the three of us.' Despite his brave words, the others knew only too well that Danny blamed himself for the disaster. The tone of his voice alerted them to the fact that he was shouldering the blame for the two deaths personally.

After a short period of silence, Jared spoke up. 'How about the guard, how has he taken it?'

'Badly, I'm afraid,' said Danny. 'Keeps on saying if he'd only checked the tray none of this would have happened. Not that it matters, because I'm convinced if he had, he'd have been killed along with the other two – and I told him so. It didn't help, though; seems he and Ray Glover were old school friends.

'Now we've got that out of the way, it's obvious Jared has something for us. Let's just hope it's good news for a change.' Then, making eye contact with each of them, he said, 'Because by God we need it!'

'I know who the killer is,' said Jared, 'and what the symbols on the chalice mean – but even better, when it's going to strike next!'

The announcement was met by a stunned silence. Too astonished to say anything, they simply stared. Encouraged by the response, Jared said, 'Before I carry on, let me apologise; I've been far too slow in putting this all together. After the creature's little visit the other night—'

He broke off as Emma suddenly shouted, '*Visit* – what visit?'

'I'm sorry, Em, I didn't tell anyone but Danny in case the rest of you became alarmed.'

Tina, looking straight at Emma, couldn't help but notice how her face had suddenly drained of all colour.

'That's no excuse, you might have been killed!' was all she could think of to say before running out of steam.

'The clues were in front of my nose all along,' said Jared, carrying on. 'It's just that I was too bloody stupid to work them out. As a result several people have died needlessly.'

Looking at Danny, he said, 'You can tell the guard if anyone's to blame for what happened last night it was me, and, like him, I'm afraid it's going to take me a long time to forget it.'

Trying to lift the guilt from Jared's shoulders, Danny stepped in.

'It's obvious something must have bothered you about your theory, otherwise you would have mentioned it to us before… so what was the problem?'

'Yes, Danny! You're right, it was the numbers, you see; the numbers simply didn't add up. From day one I've had this feeling that the Apostles held the key to what's been happening. Everything seemed to revolve around them.

'Anyway, let's start with the chalice. How many symbols are engraved on it? Anyone notice?'

Tina's answer was instantaneous, 'Nine – I counted them.'

'Right, that was the first problem. For my theory to be plausible, there should have been twelve. There were twelve Apostles, so there should have been twelve symbols, one for each. With me so far?'

Seeing the nods from the others, he was about to carry on when Danny broke in. 'So what changed your mind?'

'That's easy, Danny, it was the moment I realised who the killer was. Once I'd worked that out, everything else fell into place.'

Before the inevitable question could be raised, Jared gave them the answer. 'You see, the thing that's doing the killing is Judas Iscariot – or rather his spirit, anyway.'

'But it can't be!' said Emma in confusion. 'Judas hanged himself in remorse for betraying Jesus.'

'Or so the record books would have us believe; but what if they're wrong? I never told any of you about it, but when I first touched the chalice I had a distinct flashback. None of you noticed anything amiss, so I kept it to myself. Until this morning I've never been able to work out what it meant, but know I understand. You see, I actually saw Judas' death.'

Before anyone had an opportunity to interrupt, he carried on, 'Without Jesus' knowledge the Apostles dragged him from his home and hanged him.'

'But why?' asked Danny. 'It doesn't make sense.'

'It does when you look at it from their point of view. In their opinion he'd betrayed Jesus during the Last Supper. According to them, if it wasn't for Judas, Jesus might never have been crucified. In my flashback I saw their leader throw something at the feet of the dead man. If my guess is right it was thirty pieces of silver – Judas' blood money!'

'Of course!' said Emma. 'That's what was in the chalice with his ashes, wasn't it, that's what the old men found. But according to their story there were only twenty-nine...'

'Another thing which threw me until I realised the obvious solution: one of the coins must have fallen on the floor while they were tipping the money out; it probably rolled into a corner somewhere. It must still be there now,' he added as an afterthought.

'OK,' said Tina, 'if Judas is the one who is doing all the killing, that would make the number of Apostles eleven, but there are only nine on the chalice. According to my reckoning, that still leaves two unaccounted for.'

Looking at Tina, Jared smiled. 'Until this morning, it had me stumped too, but with the aid of the Internet I managed to solve the problem.'

'John – referred to in the Gospels as the "beloved of Jesus" – was never killed by Judas; in fact he lived to a ripe old age. The reason he survived was probably because he was banished to a remote island called Patmos, where, according to some sources, he wrote the Book of Revelation. That's speculation, of course, but what seems beyond dispute is that he also wrote the Gospel which bears his name.'

'That makes ten; so who else is missing?' asked Danny.

'That was the difficult one to account for, but in the end by a process of elimination it turned out to be Thomas – better known in the Gospels as "doubting Thomas". The fact he initially refused to believe Jesus had come back from the dead seems to have endeared him to Judas. And that,' Jared concluded triumphantly, 'leaves us with nine!'

'So let me see if I get this,' said a still stunned Danny, 'the symbols on the chalice are those of the Apostles he murdered? Right, I get that bit, but it still doesn't explain why Judas is being eaten alive by hatred for the Church and everything it stands for.'

'To understand that, Danny, you have to understand the story of the Messiah and the role it has played in Jewish hopes down through the centuries. Have you time to listen to a little story?'

'If it helps explain what's happening here and now, I'll make time,' said Danny, 'but make it simple, please.'

Without a trace of arrogance, Jared said, 'It is simple, Danny. I'd be surprised if you didn't know most of it already. The original idea of the Messiah was a person who would save the Hebrews from their sins. In fact the word Messiah literally means – *Saviour*! However, over the years that idea changed.

'All the problems started with the reign of King David. He was so successful the tiny nation of Israel became the most powerful in the world, and of course the population became used to splendour and riches. It lasted for fifty years, and as suddenly as it had begun it stopped. The "Golden Age", as it became known in later years, came to an abrupt end. When the empire came crashing down, it left the way open for every Tom, Dick and Harry to exact their revenge, and over the centuries things went from bad to worse. The final nail in the coffin arrived in the shape of Rome. From the Jewish point of view, they'd now hit rock bottom. They reasoned that as things couldn't possibly get any worse, this must be the age prophesied in the Scriptures, the age when the Messiah would arrive to save them.'

'Enter Jesus!' said Emma quietly.

'Yes, Em, you're right. Here was a man who possessed all the right qualities, and suddenly as if from nowhere he stepped onto the stage of history with perfect timing in order to help the beleaguered Jews.'

'So you're saying he was in the right place at the right time,' said Danny.

'That's one way of putting it; but let me put it another way. Had he arrived fifty years either side of his actual birth date, I don't think he would have stood a chance of being successful.'

'Why on earth not?' said Danny.

'Simple,' said Jared, 'the conditions wouldn't have been right. The most important thing to remember about Jesus is that from the very beginning he was convinced he was going to fulfil the messianic hopes of his people. He was an extremely charismatic and intelligent man, but his real genius lay in knowing the Scriptures inside out. In other words, by understanding them as well as he did, he knew exactly what the people expected of the Messiah.' He added, with a little smile, 'But more importantly, he knew just what to do in order to fulfil those expectations. People often pose the question that if Jesus was so convinced he was the Messiah, then why was it that he didn't allow his followers to speak about it openly? The answer's blindingly simple: if he had, it would have brought him to the attention of the authorities and that would have got him arrested. Effectively, his mission would have been over before it had started. To cut a long story short, because he didn't, he was left alone. By the last week of his life, when people were openly declaring him as the chosen one, it didn't matter. By then the first part of his mission was complete.'

'What about the bit where he rode into Jerusalem on the back of a donkey?' asked Danny. 'Why a bloody donkey? From my point of view that's never made any sense. Surely he could have chosen something a little more regal?'

Smiling, Jared answered, 'But Danny, riding into Jerusalem on the back of an ass, a humble beast of burden – not a donkey, by the way – was hugely symbolic. You see, he was saying to those looking for a warrior Messiah, that if that's the kind of bloke they wanted, then he was sorry. Sorry, because in that case they were backing the wrong guy. There's no doubt he lost a great many of his supporters by doing that, in particular the Sicarii. They'd pinned their hopes on him, and even though Judas had warned them, they still believed that when the crunch came he would turn out to be the warrior Messiah they were looking for. Knowing this, Jesus had an ace up his sleeve. He knew there was one way in which he could prove to everyone that although he wasn't the kind they wanted, he was still the genuine article. You have to remember that Jesus hated bloodshed of any kind, and he was wise enough to realise if he became the warrior leader most people wanted, thousands of his countrymen would die. So instead he set himself up to be a totally different kind of Saviour. It was a stroke of brilliance, really, because by becoming the sacrificial lamb, by delivering his people from their sins, he was fulfilling the original interpretation of the Scriptures.' Jared paused.

'At this point I'd like to bring in a little idea of my own, if you don't mind. It's conjecture on my part, but I believe it's crucial to understanding what happened afterwards. You see, for me the timing of Jesus' arrest was all important. If he was arrested during the day it would have caused serious problems for the authorities. His supporters would have fought to the death, and that would have led to possible riots in the streets. That had to be avoided at all costs. On the other hand, at night he was nowhere to be found, so Jesus came up with the perfect answer. Enlisting the aid of Judas, he engineered his own arrest at a time and place which suited him.'

'The Garden of Gethsemane,' said Emma in a whisper.

'Perfectly true, Em. A quiet and secluded place, it would have ensured any bloodshed would have been kept to a minimum. As far as I'm concerned, Judas' role in all this was pivotal; it was his task to lead the soldiers to Jesus. Let's face it, Jesus had to be betrayed; it was the whole point of the exercise, otherwise he could never have become the sacrificial lamb. Unfortunately, little did Judas realise, he was simply part of the greater plan Jesus had created for himself, and from that moment on he became reviled and vilified by countless millions of Jews and Christians alike.'

Suddenly, Danny shot from his seat. 'That's it!' he said excitedly. 'That's why Judas hates the Church so much – including Jesus.'

'Now all that biblical mumbo-jumbo makes sense too,' said Emma.

'Yes,' said Jared, 'no wonder the creature told me it had been betrayed, because in its eyes everything Jesus had promised turned out to be a lie.'

'Even worse,' said Emma, 'according to his reasoning, he thought Jesus had turned a blind eye to the mob hanging. Sadly, he never knew Jesus had nothing at all to do with it, that it was Peter who'd instigated it all.'

'My God,' said Danny, 'this explains so much! I'm almost ready to feel sorry for the thing. Is there any documentary proof for this theory of yours, or is it an educated guess?'

Smiling now, Jared replied, 'All the clues are in the Gospels if you look for them. Why do you think that when Jesus decided the moment was right, he turned to Judas and said, "Go, do what you have to"? It was the prearranged signal between them.

'However,' added Jared, 'as we now know, it backfired on Judas, didn't it? The disciples were completely fooled, and so that's why he was ultimately murdered. The irony of the situation was that in many ways, Judas, not Jesus, became the sacrificial lamb – or at the very least a scapegoat, anyway.'

Leaving a second or two pass for them to recover from their initial shock he said, 'Oh, and I nearly forgot. I know when he's going to strike next.'

'How the hell can you possibly know that?' asked Tina in astonishment, 'unless of course you've added mind-reading to your list of accomplishments!' The look of undisguised admiration on her face wasn't lost on Emma.

Handing around a series of computer printouts, Jared said, 'The Internet is a marvellous source of information, did all the hard graft for me. I've outlined the relevant information in four columns. If you run your finger along them, I'll explain what it is you're looking at. The first column gives the name of the Apostle, the second the symbol associated with him, the third the way in which each of them were martyred, and finally column four sets out the dates on which each of them are commemorated.'

'Before we go any further I want you to look at the dates of the first four. Ring any bells?'

Once again it was Tina who responded the quickest. 'Of course, he's killing them according to the dates which the Christian calendar has set out to commemorate them. Now we know what we're looking for, it's so simple.'

'My thoughts entirely, Tina,' said Jared bitterly. 'Anyway, let's work our way through them.'

'Number one took place on 29 June, and it recalls the death of Simon Peter. Regarded as the natural leader of the Apostles, he had a reputation for being something of a hothead. Supposedly in charge of the keys to the kingdom of heaven, they subsequently became his symbol, and according to rumours he was crucified upside down.'

'The next took place on 25 July, and our victim was beheaded in exactly the same way as the disciple James. His symbol was the staff and wallet of a humble pilgrim.'

'The third to die was Bartholomew, sometimes called Nathaniel, and he was flayed alive. His symbol was the skinning knife of a tanner.'

Stopping for a moment in order to pose a question, Jared said, 'When does the Church commemorate his martyrdom?' Without waiting for a reply he ploughed on, 'Yes, you've got it, 24 August.

'Finally we come to last night. 21 September is the date chosen to remember Matthew or Levi, the tax collector. That's why Judas stuffed the money into the old minister's throat; but for that I might never have put two and two together. Matthew, like Judas, was a controversial choice from the start. Tax collectors were regarded as the lowest of the low – traitors – and for a good reason. You had to bid for the post and the person who bid the most was the successful applicant. In order to get their money back on the deal, they then charged the people way over the odds, and believe me, they ended up making a handsome profit. The sad thing about it all was that it was Jews who became tax collectors. The Romans themselves never lowered themselves to perform such a menial task.'

'But surely,' said Emma, 'they could complain, couldn't they?'

'Oh, they did, Em,' said Jared with a rueful smile, 'but it made no difference. These traitor Jews, as they were called, hired Roman soldiers to take care of those who caused any problems. According to the Gospels, Jesus is said to have deliberately chosen Matthew to show the kingdom was open to all kinds. It didn't matter what you had done in the past, as long as you were genuinely sorry for your past mistakes, or repented as they called it, you would be forgiven for anything.'

'Anything seems a little excessive to me,' said Gareth Evans. 'What about murderers?'

'Good point, Gareth, but yes, according to the Christian philosophy even that was forgivable. Once you'd said sorry and turned over a new leaf, that's it – you were in.'

'Seems nonsense to me,' said Tina. 'Like Gareth, I see that as grossly unfair.'

'Of course it's unfair, that's why it's so controversial,' said Jared. 'Anyway, enough of that; I'm afraid it's back to the bad news again.'

'Bad news? What bloody bad news?' asked Danny.

Pointing to the printouts, Jared said, 'Look at Apostles five and six, Jude and Simon.'

'Found them.'

'Right, now run your finger along the column.'

Hearing a gasp from Emma, he knew he'd made his point.

'Yes, that's right; on 28 October, which is less than a month from now, Judas is going for a double kill. And at present we haven't a clue how to stop him.'

Trying to lift their spirits, Jared said, 'After being the bearer of bad tidings yet again, would you like another story, or are you bored with them by now?'

'It's not that your little tales are boring,' said Danny, 'they're fine; it's the implications that frighten me. Anyway, what's this one about?'

'An old man and a codex,' said Jared grinning.

'But that's not new,' said Tina lamely.

'Oh, no? Well, this one is, believe me,' replied Jared. 'You see, the old man in the story is Joseph.' Seeing the penny hadn't dropped, he explained, 'Joseph of Arimathea!'

'You're joking!' said Emma. 'Not *the* Joseph?'

'One and the same, Em, it all fits. It's my guess that he brought both objects over to Britain by sea. Don't look so surprised, scholars have known for a while it was a route he was familiar with. That he had connections to the tin mining industry in Cornwall is well documented. Add that to the rumours about how often he visited Glastonbury, you know, the story of the Holy Grail and all that, and we seem to have a firm basis on which to work.'

'Are you talking about the Holy Grail that Jesus used at the Last Supper?' asked Emma.

'I don't know about that, Em, I'm more inclined to believe the Grail is a mythical thing. As a matter of fact the correct translation doesn't mean a cup at all but a bloodline – a royal bloodline – but that's another story.' He paused.

'Where was I? Oh, yes… Unfortunately for Joseph, his ship was wrecked in a violent storm somewhere off the coast of south-west Wales. How do I know this? Simple: Chameleon Enterprises, using some of the vast resources at their disposal, managed to narrow their search pattern down to an area somewhere off the Gower coast. And it turns out they were right.'

'How can you possibly know that?' asked Emma in surprise.

'The old tombstone in Carmel chapel,' was Jared's amused reply.

'Of course,' she said, 'I'd forgotten about that.'

'Mind you, it was never confirmed until we five started messing about with that bloody Ouija board in the seance. One thing has always struck me about the hiding place of the codex, that wherever it is it can't be far away.' Pre-empting the next question, Jared said, 'No more than a day's walk from Carmel, anyway; otherwise those two youngsters would never have been able to find it in the first place.'

'That's a point,' said Danny, 'I never thought of that.'

'Be that as it may, it still won't do us any good, because I destroyed our only hope of finding it, didn't I?' said Jared, crestfallen.

Suddenly it was Danny's turn to shock them. 'It just so happens I might have an idea about that. How does hypnosis sound to you, Jared?'

Pensive for a while, Jared suddenly saw the potential of the suggestion before saying, 'You know something, Danny, it might just work.'

Coming out of the trance, he suddenly felt uneasy. How far had he been regressed?

It was nothing to do with ordinary fear. What he was worried about was that he might have inadvertently said something about the night he and Emma had first made love, before realising it had not only been the first, but the last time. Oh, no, please, he thought, anything but that...

Opening his eyes, he saw immediately his fears had been groundless. The faces staring down at him were smiling, but not at something embarrassing he'd revealed about himself. No, this was different, they were flushed with success.

So they'd done it!

Handing him a piece of paper, Danny said, 'Recognise any of that?'

Studying it for a moment Jared said, 'Yes, that's it, I'm sure of it.' Then he said, 'I don't want to put a damper on things during our moment of triumph, but we have to remember that we're only halfway there. We still have to work out the clues.'

'Why do you think we're all smiling, you daft bugger? Emma's already cracked it. Believe it or not, it only took her a few minutes.' Turning around, he said, 'But I think I'll let her explain.'

Stepping towards the whiteboard with the piece of paper in her hand, Emma said, 'It was quite simple, really. Take the first line – "Beneath the grave of the sleeping giant". Now, everyone around here knows it's a well-known landmark, and so it didn't take a lot of imagination to realise that an old man nearing the point of exhaustion would have immediately spotted it. In his mind, lying down as it was, indicated it was dead, and so to him it was logical to link it to the word "grave". Taking my cue from that, I reasoned the haunted forest must be close by.

'The giveaway were the words, "passageway to the gods and mountains that reach to the sky". To me they were describing a narrow gorge with steep sides; but the real clincher was, "waterfall that tumbles from the heavens".'

'Of course!' said Jared in excitement. 'It's the steep gorge leading to Dan-y-Mynydd caves. The original route, that is, not the one that's open to the public.'

Turning to the others, he said in explanation, 'In the old days that whole area must have been nothing but wild rugged forest. No wonder Joseph described it as haunted! Coming back to the waterfall, those few who have been allowed access to the cave complex say it burrows deep into the mountain for over twenty-odd miles.'

'But it's been blocked by huge steel railings for years now,' said Emma, 'there's no way in. It was for safety reasons, you see,' she explained to the others, 'as several of the caves are underwater these days.'

Breaking in again, Jared said, 'During the time Joseph hid the objects the cave system must have been dry, though, otherwise he would never have been able to get through.'

'That brings me to the final part,' said Emma. ' "With crooked fangs and ocean wide." That's fairly obvious too. If we accept that somewhere along the line Joseph must have come to a dead end, then to my way of thinking the dead end was a huge subterranean lake, hence the phrase "ocean wide"! Remember, by now Joseph must have been in a semi-delirious state, and so the "fangs" he alluded to were simply stalagmites and stalactites. The thing is, if he could go no further, it stands to reason he must have found a hiding place for the things nearby.'

'Christ, Em, that's bloody brilliant,' said Jared, while at the same time leaning over and planting a kiss on her forehead.

It was a spontaneous action, but Emma reacted as if she'd been stung by a wasp. Jerking her head away in embarrassment, she immediately made excuses and headed directly for the toilet.

Although mortified by Emma's reaction, Jared recovered quickly. 'At least we know where to look for the damn thing now,' he said.

Taking charge, Danny broke in. 'I'll contact London right away. Ask them to send me a diver and some equipment by tomorrow.'

'There's no need for the diver,' said Jared. 'All you need is the equipment. I'll take care of the rest.' Scribbling quickly on a piece of paper, he handed it to Danny, 'That's a list of what I'll need.'

'I'm not even going to ask where you learned to dive!' was Danny's reply. 'Nothing about you surprises me any more.'

'I wish the same could be said about Emma,' was Tina's catty reply.

Picking up the phone, Danny said, 'Anything else, while I'm at it – a rubber dinghy or something?'

'No,' was Jared's reply. 'Hang on, though, I almost forgot, we're going to need a Land Rover to take us and the equipment to the site.' He hadn't seen Emma return, so when she spoke it startled him.

'You'll need a key to open the gate to the railings, and rust remover as well. Remember that lock has been under the waterfall all these years, covered by spray constantly, so it's not going to give up its little secret easily. And there's another thing: you're going to need permission to open it from whoever owns it, the water board, the caves, I don't know.'

Looking at Emma, Danny had come to appreciate lately that beneath the exterior of an extremely pretty girl lay a razor sharp mind, and his respect for her had grown with every passing day. It was obvious she and Jared had once had something special going, and as far as he could see he was still very much in love with her. The interesting thing from his point of view was that to anyone but Emma, it was blatantly obvious she felt the same way. For some strange reason however, she was refusing to accept the truth, trying hard to disguise the fact. The way she'd reacted to Jared's spontaneous show of affection earlier had been astonishing. Something very serious must have happened between them in the past, and Danny was wise enough to know that whatever it was, it was none of his business.

Instead he said, 'You just leave that to me, Emma love. If I can't find out who owns it, I'll cut the bloody thing open with an oxyacetylene torch if needs be.'

Chapter Thirty-three

A LOUD BLAST ON THE HORN WARNED JARED THAT DANNY AND THE crew were waiting. Grabbing his duffel bag from the chair, he gave his grandmother a peck on the cheek before heading for the door. Breakfast in the Hunter household was always early, to accommodate Jared's strict training regime. At this hour it had come and gone ages ago, and so he was ready to face the rigours of what he fully expected to be a difficult day.

Bounding down the steps two at a time, he saw Danny had managed to commandeer a police Land Rover complete with jam sandwich markings, as the locals liked to refer to them. Subtle the vehicle was not; as for being practical, now that was a different matter.

Jumping into the back, he moved some of the equipment to the side in order to make room for himself and the bag.

Turning around, Danny said, 'I managed to get everything on the list so it should be all there.'

'It doesn't really matter, I'll give them the once over when we get there,' Jared replied.

Their destination was less than a ten-minute drive away, and soon they were turning off the main road. Danny was impressed with the surroundings of the Dan-y-Mynydd cave complex, except for the dry ski slope which looked as if it was in need of urgent repair. 'Sad and forlorn' was the expression that came to mind, especially considering the small holiday cottages which dotted the hillside on either side seemed so charming. Laid out in small self-contained units, they looked extremely inviting. A mental image suddenly popped into his mind, that of the same complex during the winter months, when the mountains would be covered in a blanket of deep fluffy snow. At times like that it must possess a fairy-tale quality, Danny thought, almost as if a tiny piece of Austria or Switzerland had been magically lifted from its original destination and transplanted into this little area of Wales. A tribute to its designers, was his next thought, as no doubt that's exactly what they had in mind when they'd built the complex.

Turning around in his seat once again, he pointed to the ski slope through the back window and voiced his opinion to Jared. 'Shame about that; used to do a bit myself when I was younger, you know,' clarifying his statement by adding, 'skiing, that is. Not that I was much good, mind, spent most of my time on the blue slopes, though I did manage the occasional red. "Snowplough Harris" they called me because I was so bloody slow. Still, it didn't stop me enjoying myself, let me tell you.'

Bet it didn't, Jared mouthed silently before asking, 'What about the après-skiing? I bet you were up to black standard as far as that was concerned, eh, Danny?' He smiled to himself as he said it.

'Well, there was that, I must admit,' was Danny's tongue-in-cheek reply, before getting back to more important matters. Danny had insisted, quite sensibly in Jared's opinion, that Emma and Tina remain behind. To say that the girls were far from happy with the decision was an understatement.

The powerful three-litre engine of the Land Rover made short work of the steep hill leading up to the caves. Parking near the main entrance, Danny got out first, followed closely by Gareth Evans, who'd been driving.

Closing the door, Danny said, 'Forgot to tell you, we've got the place to ourselves this morning, I've managed to close the place down for a few hours.'

Hefting the heavy equipment from the back, Jared mentally ticked off each item before placing them gently on the grass verge near the tarmacadam path, before noticing Danny's reaction to the dinosaur theme park.

'Pretty impressive, eh, Danny?'

'True, bloody true,' was Danny's comment. 'A brilliant idea, if you ask me. Apart from all the other benefits, the kids must love it,' he said, gazing at the life-size display of the gigantic Tyrannosaurus Rex in wonder.

'Not only the kids, either, if the look on your face is anything to go by,' was Jared's amused comment before declaring himself satisfied with the equipment. With that he shouted to Danny, 'Be right back,' as he made his way over to the gents' toilet in order to change.

When he returned several moments later, Danny thought he looked every inch the professional. After a moment's reflection he suddenly realised that's exactly what he was. Jared looked so young it was easy to forget that behind such a cherubic countenance lay years of experience. Reaching out to touch Jared's tight-fitting neoprene suit, he said, 'What do these things do, anyway? Can't see how they keep all the water out, some is bound to trickle in somewhere.'

'Strange as it may seem, Danny, but that's a popular misconception. The suit isn't meant to keep water out, but in. In fact it forms a layer between the skin and the suit. Now, in climates such as ours, where the water is relatively warm, it's ideal, because your body temperature does the rest. Mind you, it doesn't work well in colder conditions. In those extreme temperatures you're facing a whole new ball game, believe me.'

'What about those guys on the oil rigs – the ones in the North Sea; they earn fantastic money, don't they?'

'The conditions are atrocious, that's why. Take it from me, Danny, they earn every penny.'

Picking up a length of nylon rope, Jared threw it over his right shoulder, before picking up his fins and mask and carrying them in his right hand. Changing into his trainers, he hefted the tank from the grass verge and placed it on his left shoulder.

Danny carried a small rucksack, while Gareth Evans, having drawn the short straw, remained behind to protect the vehicle. By the look on his face it was something he wasn't best pleased about.

With Jared in the lead and Danny bringing up the rear, they made their way carefully one step at a time down the treacherous path leading to the bottom of the ravine. Even though the equipment was heavy, Jared seemed to make light work of his burden.

Halfway down, Danny exclaimed, 'You can see what the old man meant by describing this place as the haunted forest! It certainly has an eerie quality about it. Imagine what it must have been like when all of this,' he said, gesturing with an outstretched arm, 'was nothing but virgin forest.'

'Wait till you hit the ravine,' said Jared, 'the sight will take your breath away.'

He had a sudden thought. Turning to Danny, he said, 'When Joseph made his way along here, this valley would have been virtually invisible. If I were to guess, I'd say he found it by accident.'

Several hundreds yards further down, Danny saw just what Jared was getting at. Gazing upwards in astonishment, all he could think of saying was, 'It's exactly as the old man described.'

'Sorry to be the bearer of bad tidings,' said Jared, breaking into Danny's thoughts, 'but from here on in the going gets really difficult. Just around that bend we hit some serious shit.'

All he heard in reply was, 'So you reckon the first part was easy.'

Muttering away, Danny thought, What the hell have I let myself in for? Several minutes later he said, 'I take it you've been here before, then, seeing as you know so much about the place.'

'Yes. As kids, a few of us tried our luck with this ravine at one time or another,' said Jared. 'The waterfall was as far as we got, mind you. The iron grille was there even then. In hindsight I realise it was for our own safety, although at that age we didn't see it that way. In our eyes, all it did was spoil our fun.'

Seconds later he shouted, 'Watch your step here, Danny! It gets very steep once we get around this corner.'

Grateful for the warning, Danny found it was every bit as treacherous as Jared had warned, and then some. Each step he took only increased his admiration for Joseph. And he had been over eighty years of age, for goodness' sake, he reminded himself. Voicing his opinion to Jared, he added, 'He must have been a tough old bastard!'

'I couldn't agree more,' was Jared's honest opinion, 'and don't forget he'd been shipwrecked, half-drowned perhaps even injured. On top of that, he'd been without food and water for at least two days, and all the while carrying the chalice and codex. That speaks volumes for the mental strength of the man.'

Minutes later they turned left sharply, and there was the waterfall.

It hung in the hot summer's air like a mirage, the old man had some-how managed to capture its essence perfectly. From this angle the iron grille was invisible.

Jared's voice suddenly broke into Danny's thoughts once more. 'I don't want to sound dramatic, but one false step and… I think it's better to show you,' he added. 'Look down… No, don't stare, one quick glance, otherwise you might panic.'

One glance was enough to confirm that Jared was not exaggerating.

Never one for heights, Danny was literally terrified.

'It's not so much the drop as the green algae that's the problem. It covers the stones and tends to make them very slippery,' said Jared. 'It's the fine mist that does it, constantly covering everything with spray. You'll be all right if you follow me. Just be careful to step in exactly the same places I do, and you should be OK.'

Swallowing his fear, Danny shouted in a voice that was barely above a croak. 'Why do I find myself not totally convinced by your remarks? Especially by the use of the word "should" and not "will"!' By now he was breathing in short ragged gasps, his face and clothing covered in sweat.

Suddenly they were there.

Stepping under the curtain of water, they came face-to-face with the iron grille that covered the opening completely. The coating of paint that had originally been used to protect the metal had been tarnished a sickly brown, punctuated here and there with deep red patches of rust. In places there seemed to be very little metal left, while the obligatory warning sign – 'Danger, keep out' – looked in no better shape.

At first glance, the whole thing looked far from safe to Danny.

Stretching his hand behind him, Jared shouted, 'Give me the key!'

'Now that's what I was just about to explain,' came the reply, 'the buggers couldn't find it so I brought my own.' With that he placed the small hacksaw in the palm of Jared's outstretched hand. 'That should do the trick,' he said, with a huge grin on his face.

Unable to stop himself, Jared burst out laughing. 'I guess it will,' he replied.

They were right; in seconds they were gazing down at the remains of the rusty old lock. Opening the gate at the right-hand side of the grille, Jared hefted his tank onto his shoulder from the small ledge where he'd placed it moments before. Handing the other equipment to Danny, he eased his way through the small gap. In a short space of time both were safely inside. After walking about fifty yards, Danny suddenly stopped and delving into his rucksack produced two torches.

'Heavy duty,' he said gesturing to them, 'just in case.'

Switching his on, he said, 'You know, what puzzles me is how the hell the old man managed to negotiate such difficult conditions without any modern equipment.'

'Good point,' said Jared in reply. 'All I can say is I'm bloody glad we've got all this kit.'

For a moment Jared imagined the weight of the mountain pressing down from above, felt the closeness of the countless tons of rocks pressing in, before realising with a start that it was for such moments as these he lived. It was the only time he felt truly alive.

The beam of light produced by his torch was sufficient to cut a narrow swathe through the almost impenetrable darkness which surrounded them. The deep subterranean complex seemed to go on for ever, and on several occasions he noticed what appeared to be narrow openings branching off at odd angles. He cursed himself for forgetting to bring something with which to mark their passage, reflecting that it was too late to do anything about it now. His only consolation was considering the state of Joseph's health, he would have had little option but to carry on going in a straight line.

Several times they came across deep pools of dark water that stretched from one side of the cavern to the next. One or two came up to their waists, and it was only with great difficulty Danny was able to get through.

As they went on, they were able to see some of the caves were huge, but more importantly several seemed to possess a light source of their own. Turning his neck, Jared said, 'Well, that partially explains how the old man was able to get this far.'

Ten minutes later they reached an impasse; it was what Jared had been expecting, but hoping to avoid. The expanse of water stretching into the distance wasn't the problem; they could have swum across if they had to. No, the real problem was the roof. Over the ages it must have sagged, so that at the moment there was only a few inches of headroom between it and the surface of the water.

Turning to Danny, he said, 'The level of water was nowhere near this high when the codex was brought through, on both occasions, otherwise they would never have managed to get past this point.'

'Unless of course this is the cave described in the scroll,' ventured Danny.

'No way!' said Jared. 'It's nowhere near large enough; besides, there aren't any stalagmites. The problem is I haven't a clue how deep the water is, or how far back it goes. I'm afraid there's only one answer, I'm going to have to use my gear.'

'What if you get into trouble?' asked Danny. That he was genuinely concerned was obvious; the note of alarm was clearly audible in his voice. 'I'm sure I read somewhere you should always have someone with you, buddy breathing and all that.'

'Very true, Danny,' said Jared. He was serious now, especially given the murky water. 'But let me worry about that. This is where I earn my keep, old son.'

Lowering the rope from his shoulder he said, 'It's my contingency plan,' while handing one end to Danny, and tying the other to his waist.

'So that's what it's for!' quipped Danny. 'I wondered about that.'

'Hopefully, it should be long enough for my needs,' said Jared, 'but just in case, if you should feel two sharp tugs like this...' he demonstrated, 'then start pulling like hell! Two pulls means I'm in trouble.'

'That's all very well,' said Danny, 'but what if you hit another pool like this on the other side?'

'You catch on quickly! To be honest, that's what worries me. In that case I'm afraid we're up the creek without a paddle.' Seeing Danny's worried expression, he said, 'But I'm sure it won't come to that. Look, from a practical point of view, we've been walking for bloody hours, so I don't think the old man would have been able to go much further, especially in his state. No, I'm sure what were looking for is at the other side of this little lot.' Then he added, 'I hope so, anyway.'

Seeing that arguing with Jared was futile, Danny grudgingly gave his consent to the plan. Sitting on the ground, Jared put on his fins and then lifted the hood over his head, before putting on the white helmet and built-in torch. Getting to his feet, he asked Danny to place the tank on his back while he adjusted the straps.

About to spit on the inside of his mask before rubbing it in and placing it over his face, Danny decided to ask another question. 'Won't you be affected by the bends?'

Laughing aloud, Jared said, 'No, that only applies when you're diving deep, say ninety feet or so, and I'm sure this pool is nowhere near that depth!' Humouring Danny, he went on, 'Do you know why it's called that?'

'Not a clue,' came the reply.

'It was given the name because if you don't decompress properly at those kinds of depths, the nitrogen in the compressed air mixture you're breathing from the tank doesn't get expelled completely from your lungs. Instead, it starts going into solution in your bloodstream.'

'Christ, that sounds dangerous!' Danny spluttered.

Seeing Danny's alarmed expression, he said, 'Don't worry, you daft bugger, I'll be all right.'

Placing the helmet on his head, Jared shifted his mask from side to side until it was sitting comfortably on his face. Finally he inhaled several times on his air supply to check everything was in order. Declaring himself satisfied, he gave the time-honoured signal, making a circle between thumb and forefinger, before walking slowly into the pool.

With the water lapping around his waist, he gasped slightly. The temperature had taken him by surprise. Suddenly he realised why. These were waters that never saw the light of day, had never had the opportunity to warm up. It brought back memories of a childhood holiday in Spain, at Guadalest, to be precise. Jumping into a small stream that fed the gigantic reservoir had taken his breath away. He remembered vividly how only after a few minutes' immersion he'd literally turned blue with cold. This was a far different situation, however. Thanks to the protection of his wetsuit, all he would experience would be a few moments of unpleasantness, and then, as he'd explained to Danny earlier, his own body temperature would do the rest.

For the first few feet the going was easy, but the further he descended, the more he realised just how deep the pool was. It was as if the whole floor had dropped away at some remote time in the past. Descending into the depths, Jared felt the familiar tingling sensation in his body, the familiar rush of adrenaline kicking into the bloodstream. He had no doubt it was the sense of uncertainty that did it. It was the reason he'd survived during those times of deep despair, when all around him there seemed to be nothing but death and destruction. He was unable to explain the feeling, but his senses became so heightened he felt as if he was standing outside his body. To him, danger was like a drug, and he knew with a rush of certainty he missed it. Adding to the buzz was the feeling that he was exploring waters which few if any had ever been in before.

The depth of the lake confirmed his earlier suspicion. No way would it have been possible for either Joseph or the emissary from the monastery to have negotiated such an expanse of water without the aid of modern diving equipment. The only sensible answer was that the water hadn't been there in those days. Somewhere in the last 600 years or so, a whole section of the cave complex must have collapsed, leaving as its legacy this almost inaccessible expanse of cold, murky water. It was the only rational explanation.

Pensive for a moment, Jared was experienced enough to acknowledge that although the clues given in the scroll had led them directly here, there was always the chance, however remote, that something could still go wrong.

What if they'd missed something?

Had Emma misinterpreted the clues?

If the codex was here, would it still be in one piece?

After all, if this section of the labyrinth, originally dry, had become flooded, there was no guarantee the same thing might not have occurred elsewhere. Should that be the case, he knew it might already too late, the codex destroyed, or at the very least by now be totally illegible.

Negative thoughts began to crowd his mind as he watched the bubbles of air make their deliberate but leisurely way towards the surface. Pushing his thoughts aside, he told himself this was no time for doubts. Mentally, he was determined that so much time and effort would not be wasted, especially when they were so near to achieving their goal.

Approaching twenty feet, he hoped he was somewhere near the bottom. Although the water was relatively clear, the fact no sunlight penetrated the surface meant the going was extremely difficult. Despite its high intensity discharge, the light attached to his helmet had very little impact on the stygian darkness which seemed to coil around him like a burial shroud. At times it gave the distinct impression it was trying to suck the breath from his body.

The sensation of knowing he was totally alone, in what was best described as an alien landscape, only added to what was already an unsettling experience. He suddenly realised that in all his other dives he'd never felt like this. Here, he was completely alone. For him this was a new experience. The almost total blackness produced a high degree of disorientation, especially as there were no points of reference.

Just then the bottom came into view a few feet below.

Several large boulders dislodged from the ceiling of the cave were all he could make out, before the silt disturbed by the movement of his fins made anything smaller invisible. Now he'd orientated himself, he started his way to the surface, hoping to see something that might suggest the lake was coming to an end, and several moments later he was rewarded with the faintest glimmer of light.

Jared glanced at his watch. He had been diving for a little under five minutes. The trailing rope was no problem; he could have gone double the distance if needs be. So, checking to see that it was still safely attached to his waist, he made his way to the surface.

His initial guess had been correct. The slightly lighter patch of water above his head was the indication he'd reached the lake's extremity. Fortunately, the bottom seemed to shelve upwards at a fairly gentle angle, and so he was able to make his way to the surface without much difficulty. Within moments his head broke the surface of the water, and he saw he was in a large cavern.

Lifting his mask and taking out his regulator, his first suspicions were confirmed: this was certainly not the one he was looking for. Fighting back his disappointment, he eased the tank from his back and lowered it gently to the cold stone floor, before removing his other equipment. Finally he untied the rope from around his waist, knowing if he had to walk any kind of distance it would be a hindrance.

The way ahead was considerably narrower than anything he'd yet encountered, and he hoped it wasn't a prelude of what was to come. No sooner had the thought entered his head when his sprits suddenly lifted. The rock formations on both sides of the narrow passageway were of a different type to anything he and Danny had come across on the other side. There were even the odd stalagmite and stalactite, although nothing of the size he was looking for.

Placing his feet gingerly on the floor he made his forward with re-newed vigour. Having already removed his fins, he cursed himself for not bringing his trainers, it would have made things so much easier. Adjusting the light on his helmet he made his way forward a few feet at a time. By the time he'd gone a few hundred yards, he was getting worried.

The passageway was becoming increasingly narrow, forcing him to the conclusion that perhaps he'd taken a wrong turning along the way.

It was then he hit the jackpot.

Turning a sharp left hand corner he stumbled into a cave of gigantic proportions. Like Joseph centuries before, he was dumbstruck. Unable to move, he was entranced by the sheer size and majesty of the sight before him. That it was the one described in the scroll was beyond doubt; all the clues were there. An inland ocean was certainly what he was gazing at, while the stalagmites and stalactites were huge. No amount of words could ever adequately describe the scene. The colours alone were beyond belief, incredible, and immediately a thought came to mind: 'a picture is worth a thousand words'. Until now, he'd never really appreciated the implications of the saying, now he did.

Several minutes later, when he'd managed to drag his eyes from the beauty of his surroundings, he realised that finding the codex – if indeed it was still here – might prove to be more difficult than he'd first expected. One quick glance confirmed his suspicion; there were literally dozens of suitable hiding places. Fortunately, Jared's instincts were good, and when he eventually stumbled across it, it was a case of third time lucky.

Mentally congratulating the old man for his choice of hiding place, Jared sensed that unless he knew exactly what he was looking for, he might never have found it. No one would ever have stumbled across it by accident, that was for sure. The skeleton had provided the marker for the youngsters, but without it... He left the thought unfinished.

Placed on a narrow shelf several feet from the floor, it was almost invisible, despite the light thrown by the beam of his helmet torch. Lifting it down with almost reverential care, he saw that considering its age is was in remarkably good condition. Wrapped carefully in an oiled leather bag, it had been protected from the worst of the elements.

Seeing it was sealed, Jared left it that way. The honour of opening such a sacred relic should be a joint venture he reasoned. With a sigh of relief, he reflected that his stupidity in burning the only clue to the codex had not proved irrevocable after all.

Placing the treasure in a special waterproof bag that he'd brought with him, he was surprised at how heavy it was. Even though he knew it would be a fairly large book, he hadn't expected this. Running his fingers along the outline beneath the leather, it felt more like a ledger than a small codex. At that moment his admiration for Joseph went up yet another notch.

Hurrying back to where he'd left his equipment, Jared was ready to dive in a very short space of time. Checking the rope was securely attached to his waist, he stepped into the water. The return journey was far easier. All he had to do was follow the rope, and so it seemed as if in no time at all he was standing on the other side. His broad smile said it all; there was no need for Danny to ask whether he'd been successful.

Chapter Thirty-four

THE SILENCE WAS ALMOST DEAFENING, THE ARMED POLICE READY AND in position, when the radio O'Neil was carrying burst into life.

'Anything your end?' came the voice of Eddie Carmellini above the crackle of static.

'Quiet as the grave,' O'Neil replied. 'Too fucking quiet if you ask me,' before cutting short the conversation. In a short while he was kneeling besides Carmellini on the roof of the building, breathing heavily from the exertion of climbing the steep steps on the outside of the warehouse. Looking at his partner in the gloom he voiced his concerns. 'I hope your buddy didn't get the dates mixed up, because if he did…' The remainder of the sentence was left unsaid, the threat only too implicit.

'Don't remind me!' muttered Carmellini. 'If anything goes wrong, heads will roll, and mine will be the first,' he added in a subdued tone. But hey, what the hell, he came through the last twice, didn't he?

'Yeah, but the last one was almost a year ago,' said a subdued O'Neil. 'Since then you haven't heard a dickey bird. Care to take a stab at why?'

Unsure of what to say, Carmellini said the first thing that came into his head. 'It must be something to do with the guy who runs the organisation we're staking out at the moment. Keeps prattling on about him all the time. Hates his guts for some reason – that much is obvious.'

'Know anything about the guy?' asked O'Neil.

'Plenty. He's the leader of a group of assassins known as the Brotherhood. From what I gather, they seem to be the driving force behind a huge multibillion-dollar organisation called Chameleon Enterprises. If there's anything dirty going down anywhere in the world, but in particular those countries we regard as flashpoint areas, then you can bet your bottom dollar they're behind it. We've had our eyes on them for years, but their security is so tight we can't get anywhere near them. Even with our resources,' Carmellini added, with grudging admiration.

Holding his hand up to stave off the inevitable question, he said, 'And before you ask, the answer's in the affirmative. We've tried all ways to infiltrate them, but on both occasions our undercover agents were terminated within days. How the fuck this guy manages to get such information is beyond me. But what the hell, if he keeps coming up with the goods who gives a shit.'

After a few moments' pause, Carmellini carried on, 'You can bet your sweet arse about one thing: the number one man, the real brains behind the organisation won't be here. We nearly nabbed the bastard last time, but for a case of sheer dumb bad luck...' His voice trailed off lamely, betraying the fact that he was still sore about how he'd managed to let the man get away. 'Anyway, I can tell by your voice you've never heard of Chameleon Enterprises? What if I threw in the name David Naami?' asked Carmellini.

'Ah, now that does ring a bell,' said O'Neil. 'But I see what you mean about him not being here in person. As you said, we nearly nailed the bastard last time, didn't we? Didn't know this was the same organisation, though. Still, the devil looks after his own, they say.'

Carrying on from where he'd left off, Carmellini said, 'My informant calls himself "the guardian". I know it's a bit dramatic, but you know the Brits and their little theatrics. Anyway, he seems obsessed with this son of a bitch Naami. Anything he can do to hurt the bastard, like this bust for instance, he does. Suits me fine, though. As you know, he's delivered the goods on the last two occasions, and that's a fact.'

Chuckling to himself, he lowered his voice further and whispered, 'Anyway, you should be so lucky! You've been living off the feel-good factor ever since. If this one goes down as well as the others, it'll probably see you through to your pension. You can retire as a departmental legend.'

Not seeing the funny side, O'Neil said, 'It's my pension I'm worried about. If this goes tits up, there won't be any pension. It will be "sayonara", big brother. Instead of a legend, I'll be the departmental laughing stock!' Suddenly a thought struck him. 'Sure it's the same guy?'

'Positive,' said Carmellini, 'It's an educated Brit voice, but with a hint of something else. Old too, and if I'm not missing my guess, he's ill. Could hardly catch his breath over the phone, sounded to me as if he was on his last legs.'

Pensive now, O'Neil said, 'If he really is as ill as you seem to think, it's hardly the time to make fools of us. He probably wants to go out in a blaze of glory, so maybe the tip-off is kosher after all.' With that O'Neil disappeared.

The truck arrived at the docks led by what looked like a BMW 7-series; he wasn't really sure, as cars weren't his forte.

Through the night scope vision of his Zeiss binoculars, Carmellini watched the procession wind its way carefully through the streets leading to the front gates. Even from his vantage point high above the road, he was still unable to see inside the car. Not that it mattered; the infrared thermal imaging of his night scope showed clearly the heat imprints of four people, two in the front and two in the back.

As the BMW approached the gates cautiously, the passenger window wound its way down slowly and a cursory wave to the guard took care of the rest. With that the convoy sped through the gap heading for docking area eight, a secluded section of the pier where everything was already in place for the exchange.

At one time, Carmellini had toyed with the idea of placing one of his own people on the gate, but at the last minute had decided against it. Apart from the fact there might have been some prearranged signal, he wanted the whole thing to remain as natural as possible. That way, it was less likely something would go wrong.

Once the gates had been negotiated, they were immediately closed.

With four in the car and two in the lorry, it made a total of six people.

It didn't seem as if they were expecting any trouble, otherwise they would have brought a good many more hired guns, he reasoned. The problem was he didn't have a clue how many others were on board the ship.

In a moment of self-doubt he thought perhaps he should have brought extra firepower.

The mood passed quickly. Backup was ready and waiting should the need arise, including a chopper less than two minutes away.

Switching on his small two-way radio once more, Carmellini checked the others were in position.

The reply was instantaneous. 'Affirmative!'

Each of his snipers had been placed in strategic positions around the dock so that between them they traversed a 360° arc. Unlike the heads of other specialist FBI units, Eddie Carmellini allowed his people to use the weapons of their choice. The only thing they had in common were the standard night scopes attached to their rifles, and of course the silencers, without which a mission as delicate as this would have been impossible.

Even though most of the area was bathed in bright light, there were still pools of dark shadow dotted at random around the dock, providing ample cover for anyone who didn't want to be seen. Carmellini was too experienced to ignore such an obvious threat and he proceeded with extreme caution. It was one of the reasons he'd been so successful over the years, had lost fewer men than any other commander in the division.

Once he'd received the OK, he moved cautiously down the steps of the fire escape. Reaching the bottom, he stood perfectly still for a few seconds until satisfied he'd not been observed. Then he set off in a low loping run towards the ship. Keeping as near to the ground as possible, utilising every bit of shadow, he reached the series of crates he'd pinpointed earlier.

He was still amazed at how quickly the whole area had been turned into a hive of bustling activity. They were certainly well organised, but then they had to be. The Russian Mafia had learned from bitter experience that to take on the triads in their own back yard they had to be constantly one step ahead. During the last few years they seemed to be getting the upper hand, and that spoke volumes for their ruthless efficiency.

Studying the ship at close quarters, Carmellini saw they'd chosen well.

Nothing ostentatious, the boat looked exactly what it was supposed to be – a working vessel. The rust patches, clearly visible through what had once been the pristine white of the hull, gave the *Morning Star* an air of respectability. No one would look twice at such a ship, especially tucked away in an isolated area of the quay such as this.

Following the wooden walkway upwards, he saw the line of lights used to illuminate the deep shadows of the deck immediately below the wheelhouse. Strung out in a single file like soldiers in a shooting gallery, the old tin shades protecting the bulbs from the worst of the elements were badly in need of repair, while here and there several of the lights were out. Watching them sway gently in the evening breeze, he wasn't sure whether this was deliberate or not.

For some five minutes Carmellini stood stock-still, his eyes straining the darkness in an attempt to spot any hidden guards. About to give up, his patience was rewarded when he saw the glowing end of a lit cigarette. Despite the fact that the smoker had cupped it with his hands, it had been a dead giveaway. But for that moment of carelessness, Carmellini might never have seen the man, positioned as he was beneath two unlit bulbs. Sloppy work, he thought. With that he made a mental note to take the guard out early. Even though he was fairly sure there were no others, he stayed where he was for several more minutes just in case. But there was no one.

By now the winches were in operation, and as he looked, one large crate was already being brought up from the depths of the hold, swaying gently from side to side in its rope cradle. So intent was he on what was going on, the first he knew of O'Neil's presence was a light touch on his shoulder.

'Getting old, buddy,' he said in tones barely above a whisper. 'A few years ago you would have made me from a long way off!'

Although the darkness hid his embarrassment, Carmellini knew his partner was right. Despite the fact it was said in jest, the stark reality was he'd been caught off guard. Maybe he was getting too old for this, he thought ruefully.

Holding his hand up for silence, he suddenly pointed to the car as it made its way slowly towards the ship.

It was O'Neil, looking not at the car but at the ship, who noticed the two figures suddenly appear at the top of the wooden walkway.

Leaning over and whispering in Carmellini's ear, he indicated their presence with an outstretched hand. Hidden by the overhang of the wheelhouse, they'd been invisible, waiting patiently for the arrival of the car. At that moment the taller of the two appeared to lift his hand in greeting.

Turning his attention back to the car, Carmellini was in time to see the headlights appear on full beam, two long flashes were followed by two short bursts, in what was obviously a predetermined signal. Suddenly, the smoke which had been billowing from the exhaust stopped. The driver had switched off the engine.

'Looks like a go,' said O'Neil.

No sooner were the words out of his mouth than the doors of the car opened. Three of the four passengers exited the car immediately, while the fourth remained inside. When the bodyguards were convinced it was safe, that there were no hidden dangers, they motioned to the other man to exit.

Stepping out gracefully, Scorpion made his way casually towards the figures waiting at the foot of the walkway, his long black coat billowing behind in the light breeze. At the same time the others closed ranks around him in what was obviously a protective gesture.

As they reached the bottom of the gangplank, one of the figures from the ship, the shorter of the two, broke off and approached Scorpion with what looked like some kind of small case. Patting it affectionately, he handed it over with one hand, while with the other he shook Scorpion's vigorously. After the cautionary greetings, there was a good deal of hugging and back-slapping, before they turned around and made their way up the wooden walkway.

'Must be the money,' whispered Carmellini.

Satisfied, the bodyguards who'd been watching turned on their heels and headed back to the truck.

As O'Neil watched, they rapped on the back of the doors, which swung open instantly to reveal two more armed guards. Jumping from the back of the vehicle, they placed their weapons at the side of the doors and hurried over to the first crate, which by now had been placed on the side of the quay several feet from where they'd alighted. Prising it open with crowbars, they formed a chain of five, and working with military precision swiftly began loading them into the back of the lorry.

O'Neil was surprised at how laid-back the whole operation seemed to be. The fact the guards had placed their weapons at the side of the lorry, and how few of them there were, spoke volumes for their arrogance. Still, he supposed it had been a long time since anything had gone wrong for them. And so they'd been lulled into a false sense of security.

'Naughty, naughty,' he muttered to himself. *Always expect the unexpected*, was his motto, and it had saved his hide on more than one occasion. Watching the weapons being unloaded, he again wondered at the love–hate relationship his fellow countrymen had with firearms. This was a side of New York the tourists never saw. If only, he thought.

By now, a second crate had been lowered onto the side of the dock. It was nearly time to make their move, so Carmellini, taking one last look around, gave the signal.

The first five snipers found their mark, and those who were handling the crates fell silently within a few feet of each other. It was almost surreal, almost as if they'd fallen instantly asleep, their inert bodies making little sound as they hit the hard concrete surface of the pier.

The element of surprise was crucial to the success of the operation.

Carmellini was only too aware any noise might have fatal consequences.

In that respect, it was make or break time. It only needed one of his snipers to miss either of the guards at the head of the walkway, and all hell would break loose. Even though he knew they had sufficient firepower to overwhelm the smugglers in the long run, in the short term he could lose several of his men. He needn't have worried; seconds later both the other snipers found their mark, the results being equally spectacular.

One problem remained however: the guard whom he'd spotted earlier. And with that a worm of self-doubt started to burrow its way to the surface. He tried to visualise the scene, to think of some reason why the guard hadn't reacted by now. As a realist, Carmellini knew that however well the snipers had done their work, no guard however slovenly could have failed to notice the almost comical demise of the five on the dock. Even more so the two who'd been standing barely twenty feet from him. The words 'had been' instead of the word 'was' suddenly flashed into his mind.

Surely not, he chuckled, he couldn't be that lucky... but he was.

The guard, seeing everything was running smoothly, had decided to take a piss.

Taking advantage of this unexpected bonus, Carmellini gestured to O'Neil to follow as he sped up the walkway, gun in hand. According to his calculations the only people left to worry about were the two leaders, who unless he missed his guess were by now sharing a bottle of vodka in the wheelhouse. As a precaution, both of them had firearms fitted with silencers and it turned out to be a good thing, for as soon as they made the deck the missing guard reappeared. The smile of deep satisfaction was instantly replaced by one of horror, as he belatedly realised what had happened.

In fairness he reacted well, his gun clearing his waist in a blur of speed. But by then it was already too late. It was still several inches from the horizontal when the bullet from Carmellini's SIG Sauer took him in the middle of the forehead. The look of astonishment lasted less than a fraction of a second, before the soft-nosed bullet exploded in his brain, his features instantly turning into a pulpy mash. Brain tissue and blood covered the steel wall behind him as he slid like a drunken man down the wall, finally coming to rest in a crumpled heap on the floor.

So professional were Carmellini and O'Neil that neither broke stride, knowing full well the guard was dead before he'd even hit the floor. Their black Nike training shoes made no sound as they made for the stairway leading to the bridge. Once again, O'Neil's sense of danger, some sixth sense, warned him it was all too easy, and he was right.

Suddenly, from behind one of the bulkheads two armed guards appeared.

Fortunately, neither of them was aware of what was happening, and so their Uzi sub-machine guns were hanging from their shoulders. By the time they'd recovered enough to bring their weapons to bear, both were dead. One shot took the first guard through his left eye, while the other was hit in the throat. Once again, the soft-nosed bullets did exactly what was required. The horrific damage ensured neither made the slightest sound. Stepping over the bodies carefully, the two made their way tentatively towards the bottom of the steel stairway.

Taking the lead position, Carmellini eased his way up gently a few inches at a time, while several feet behind, O'Neil in the classic position of a professional, gun held straight in front of him, brought up the rear. Reaching the top, Carmellini risked a quick glance.

He needn't have worried because his earlier guess had been right. Standing at the far end of the wheelhouse, with the door wide open, were the two top dogs. Flushed with success, neither had the slightest idea of what had just taken place.

'Here's to you, Gregor,' said Scorpion holding up his glass and swallowing the contents in one.

The gesture was repeated several seconds later by Borrochev, who actually looked as if he was enjoying the fucking stuff, thought Carmellini.

While the glasses were being refilled, Scorpion lifted a small cylindrical object from the small aluminium case on the table and held it fondly to his chest. Cradling it in his arms like a child, he said, 'You have no idea how much death and destruction we can create with this.'

Something in the way he said it warned Carmellini to hold back for a minute, and so he gestured to O'Neil to remain still.

'Tell me, my friend,' said Borrochev, 'may I be permitted to ask what it is you specifically intend doing with these little beauties?'

'Of course, Gregor, there are no secrets between us. As a matter of fact they will be used to wipe out a shitload of people, in essence an entire village,' he said with a deep-throated chuckle. 'Something like this has been a dream of ours for years, but even with our connections we've never been able to get our hands on the right stuff. Until now that is,' he said, laughing once more.

'It's a fair trade, old friend,' said Borrochev in reply. 'The guns you supplied will be used to good effect, I can assure you. Once again it's been a pleasure doing business with the Brotherhood. But if I may be permitted another question, why has David decided to wipe out an entire village? More to the point, why this one in particular? In all honesty I have not heard of such a thing since the troubles in Bosnia. What has this little community done to offend him so? Don't misunderstand me, the idea appeals to me enormously. A whole village wiped out in one fell swoop, it's breathtaking. But why? I'm curious, you see.'

'Strangely, as brilliant as the scheme is, it wasn't his brainchild. The genius behind it is someone who stands head and shoulders above even David in terms of cruelty,' said Scorpion, smiling inwardly at his own little joke.

Looking up in surprise, Borrochev said, 'Someone more of a psychopath than David? Somehow I find that hard to believe. It's a shame he could not have been here tonight, I've grown quite fond of him over the years. His bloodlust surpasses even my own, and for that I respect him... So this other one, he must be something very special?'

'Oh, yes, you can safely say that. But coming back to David, you can see why he couldn't be here tonight, after the last time...'

'Of course, of course, caution is something I also respect; but I assure you nothing will go wrong tonight. You see, those failures have made me even more sensitive. Two failures out of a hundred or so is nothing, trifling even. Still it leaves a – how do you say in your language? – *sour taste in the mouth*, no?' He was teasing Scorpion as in reality his English was excellent, almost faultless, in fact. Hurrying on, he said, 'More worrying is how those failures came about. There must be a leak somewhere, in one of our organisations, is it not so?'

'You can rest easy on that score, Gregor. David believes the leak is from our end, not yours.'

The look of relief on the face of the Russian was not lost on Scorpion. Carrying on, he said, 'There's no doubt the last of the guardians, the one I mentioned before, is behind everything. Even though the old bastard must be well into his seventies, he's a thorn in our side – one soon to be taken care of, I might add.' Slamming his fist onto the table he said, 'We nearly had the bastard a short while ago, but the fucking idiots lost him somehow! No matter, we'll get him eventually, I guarantee it.'

Picking up the canister from where he'd placed it on the table, Scorpion was about to replace it in its foam slot inside the case, when Carmellini decided it was time to make his move.

Diving into the room, handgun outstretched, he suddenly saw that he'd miscalculated. Until then he hadn't realised there was room for only one of them at a time, so instead of O'Neil being tight to his arse, he was several seconds behind.

To give Scorpion credit, he didn't panic.

Summing up the situation in a split second, he used Borrochev's body as a barrier to take the bullet he knew was meant for him. It was a calculated gamble at best, but one that worked.

He was halfway through the door when the bullet hit his companion. Turning for a split second, he saw the Russian's head explode in a spray of blood and gore. Increasing his speed, he ran through the open door and in a blur of motion lifted himself onto the railings. A moment later he launched himself into open space. He hit the water in what was less than a perfect dive – in terms of technical merit it would have recorded a very low rating – but it was effective. More importantly, he hit the water an instant before the first bullet zipped alongside him. Forcing himself deeper into the depths, Scorpion noticed in alarm that the first bullet was soon accompanied by several others, which whipped past his head like a hive of angry hornets. He'd read somewhere a bullet was far less effective in water because of the decrease in speed and the deflecting effect of the surrounding water. Not about to put the theory to the test, he strived for even greater depth.

Having filled his lungs to capacity before he'd dived, he knew he had sufficient air to last him nearly two minutes, after which he would be forced to come up for more. His speed was hampered by the aluminium cylinder he was clutching tightly in his left hand, but he was not about to abandon that, as he knew only too well it was his only hope of redemption. True, the mission had turned into a disaster, but as long as he still had the canister, it was not entirely irredeemable.

The fact he'd been sent on such a prestigious mission was not lost on him. In his mind he'd been earmarked for the number one spot after David Naami's days. He'd made the odd mistake along the way, he readily admitted, but this was different. If he could come out of this with some credit, it might turn out to be his salvation.

Kicking his legs furiously to increase his speed, he made for the wooden pier he'd glimpsed briefly before he'd launched himself overboard. By his calculations he was almost there, but before he could take his bearings, his head struck something solid. Dazed and about to open his mouth to scream, he suddenly came to his senses, telling himself such an action might well prove fatal. Instead he fought back the pain and made his way as quickly as possible to the surface. As it happened, lady luck was with him and his head broke water immediately below the pier itself. The wooden slats directly above his head made the perfect cover. He was invisible to anything but the closest scrutiny.

He touched his head with his fingers and they came away with blood. For a moment he panicked, until further probing revealed it was nothing more than a graze. It was then he realised what he'd collided with, the cut he'd sustained had been from one of the myriads of barnacles which festooned several large wooden posts holding up the pier.

Although safe for a moment, he knew his respite would be brief, reasoning it was one of the first places they would think to look. About to submerge again, to put as much space between himself and the ship as possible, he had a sudden flash of inspiration.

That was exactly what they would expect him to do, so what if he did the exact opposite? If he made his way back towards the ship, it might be the last thing they expected.

Taking a few shallow breaths and then one deep lungful of air, he slid beneath the waters. In less than two minutes he'd made the relative safety of the pier directly alongside the ship, and although beginning to shiver from the cold filthy water, he knew for the moment he was safe.

Suddenly he froze, straining his ears until he was sure... Yes, there was no mistaking it now, it was what he'd been secretly dreading. The unmistakable sound of the helicopter's rotor blades, *thwump*, *thwump*, *thwump*, carried clearly across the stillness of the night. In seconds, it was almost overhead, the area around the ship thrown into bright relief by the powerful beam of the chopper's searchlight. Built into the nose of the helicopter, it was equivalent to some 30 million candles. In dismay, Scorpion knew that with that kind of power it was capable of illuminating virtually anything. With that, he sunk lower into the water.

From his vantage point beneath the pier, Scorpion could see clearly a huge circle of water directly beneath the helicopter's fuselage boiling like a cauldron, the surface thrown into turmoil as the downdraught churned the waters into a mini-maelstrom. Hovering a few feet above, hemmed in by ships of all shapes and sizes, it was an extremely dangerous manoeuvre, one born of desperation. Apart from the danger to the pilot, it was also putting at risk a hugely expensive piece of Uncle Sam's merchandise.

It was at that moment Scorpion knew they wanted him badly.

From the very beginning his choice of hiding place had been a gamble, but suddenly, with a burst of elation, he knew it was going to pay off. For the next twenty minutes or so, heart in mouth, he watched in trepidation. He expected any minute a beam of light to pinpoint his hiding place, to capture him like a moth in a flame, but it never happened.

Instead he watched in amazement as the beam of the chopper, cutting a swathe through the inky blackness of the docks, made its way inexorably towards the entrance of the dock complex. He still couldn't believe they hadn't searched around the ship; even a cursory examination would have revealed his hiding place.

When he realised they weren't coming back, he allowed himself a self-congratulatory smile. He'd done it – he'd outwitted the bastards!

For another hour he stayed in the freezing water, his only company several dead dogs, stinking refuse all shapes and sizes, and one particularly large used condom. By now the cold had seeped into his bones and he knew with certainty he couldn't stay there much longer.

He was faced with a choice: move or die.

Swimming the fifty yards or so towards the ladder that ran down the edge of the concrete causeway was more difficult than he'd anticipated. It was only then he found just how much the freezing water had taken out of him. Hauling himself onto the first step took almost all of his remaining energy, his arms taking most of the strain, for by now he had very little feeling below the waist. Knowing it might be his one and only chance of escape seemed to fuel his determination, and he made one last desperate effort. With a grunt he made it.

Approaching the top step, he grew more cautious. Taking a chance, he lifted his head and with a quick glance took in the situation, before immediately ducking down again.

Confident there were no guards, he slid over the top on all fours. Like a predatory animal he remained motionless for several moments while checking out the lie of the land. A narrow gap between two huge cargo containers suddenly caught his eye. Covered in deep shadow, it didn't look particularly inviting, but he realised it would afford some modicum of safety.

Rising to his feet like an arthritic old man, he shuffled forward painfully. In a matter of moments he'd reached the narrow gap. Feeling he was now relatively safe, he let out an audible sigh of relief. The most difficult part was now behind him. Slapping his hands against his sides and rubbing them over his body, he was able to restore some vestige of feeling and warmth to a torso that had become numb. Fortunately, he was in the peak of physical condition, and within a reasonably short space of time he was sufficiently recovered to make his move.

Keeping to the shadows and taking advantage of every possible hiding place, it took him twenty minutes to reach the outskirts of the dock, and a further few minutes or so to scale the high metal fence which guarded the perimeter. Thankfully it wasn't electrified.

Scorpion knew that making for the front entrance would have been suicidal. Although the search had thrown up nothing, he knew they would have left a guard, just in case. No, he'd come too far, suffered too much to get caught that way.

Looking down from his lofty perch at the top of the fence, he some-how managed to scramble his way down the other side. Several feet from the bottom, he became exhausted again, and in desperation he allowed himself to drop the remainder of the distance to the ground. There, crumpled like a rag doll, feet splayed, he knew he must have looked like some lady of the night. Several moments later when he'd allowed his bruised and battered body sufficient time to recover, he picked himself up, dusted himself down and pushed on.

Finding a taxi was easier than he'd expected, and surprisingly his dishevelled appearance brought no comment, until he recalled where he was. Working in a district such as this, the driver must have seen far worse, he reasoned.

It was a fairly long ride to the small airport on the outskirts of the city, but the worst was now behind him. To be caught at such a late hour would be sheer bad luck, and after the way things had panned out tonight, he was sure the dice were loaded in his favour.

Paying off the driver he was careful not to overtip. To do so might have drawn excessive attention to his shabby and sodden appearance. To start flashing sodden $100 bills around would have done just that.

An hour later, thanks to the far-reaching tentacles of the Brotherhood and the private facilities of Chameleon Enterprises, he was unrecognisable as the filthy creature that had rolled up at the gate some time earlier. Frustratingly, it had taken him ten minutes to convince the people in charge of the facility that he was not only a member of the Brotherhood, but an extremely important one. Even then, it had needed a phone call to Number One to sort it out. As expected, he'd been almost apoplectic on hearing of the demise of the operation, only calming down when Scorpion had told him about his little present.

Making his way up the steps of the Gulfstream, cradling his precious cargo under his arm, he made a quick mental calculation – he'd be in Britain in about ten hours. As it turned out, he underestimated the speed of the jet, and he was there earlier.

'How the fuck did they miss him? I saw the son of a bitch hit the water! Even if I didn't wing him, he couldn't have got far. We had a small fucking army out there, for Christ's sake – and that's without the bloody chopper!' Carmellini raged, before venting his frustration on the bulkhead. Slamming his fist hard against the steel, he winced in pain, bringing his tirade to a sudden stop. Much of the anger he vented on those around him was also directed inwards, against what he saw as his own ineptitude; after all, he admitted privately he'd had the son of a bitch in his sights. What really hurt however was that it was the second time he'd allowed a key figure of the organisation to escape his clutches. To his way of thinking, a single failure could be attributed to sheer bad luck; but two failures in a row, especially to a perfectionist like him, smacked of ineptitude of the highest order. No, it was more than that – it was bloody inexcusable. Calming down somewhat, he realised it wasn't entirely his fault. The clever bastard had used his so-called Russian buddy, to take the bullet meant for him, and then got clean away. In grudging admiration, he had to admit the bastard had been as quick as a striking cobra – or should that be a scorpion? He chuckled to himself, slowly regaining some of his former good humour.

'Anyway,' said O'Neil, breaking into his thoughts, 'it wasn't a complete disaster. We managed to take out all their guys, except Scorpion of course, plus all those we rounded up on the ship. Not to mention the guns and the money. Don't know about you, but in my book that's a good day at the office, buddy.'

'Son of a bitch!' said Carmellini, the colour draining from his face. 'In all the excitement I'd forgotten about the money.' And with that he was off like a frightened quarterback.

Diving through the door of the wheelhouse, as if the hounds of hell were after him, he let out a huge sigh of relief when he saw that the aluminium case was exactly where he'd left it, top open, facing away from him.

Hurrying over, he turned it round.

The look on his partner's face told O'Neil something was wrong, badly wrong. Thinking someone had beaten them to the money he said, 'No way, there's no way anyone could have taken it.'

'It's not the money,' was the stunned reply.

Sliding the case towards his partner, Carmellini said, 'Take a look.'

Glancing down, O'Neil's face scrunched up in puzzlement. There was no money. From where he was standing, it looked as if there was never meant to be. No, the case looked as if it had been designed with an entirely different purpose in mind. Extremely well padded, it looked as if was meant to hold something fragile. Staring at him were spaces for two small cylindrical objects, one of which was obviously missing. Something was tugging at the back of his mind; he'd seen something like this before, but for the life of him he couldn't recall where or for what purpose.

'I don't get it,' was all he could think of saying, before the buried memory of exactly what he was looking at rushed to the surface and exploded into his brain. '*Oh, shit!* I hope this isn't what I think it is!' Picking up the remaining cylinder with infinite care, he turned it over in his hand. Grinning at him like a death mask, the biohazard warning gloatingly confirmed that his worst nightmare had suddenly come true.

'I meant to tell you,' said Carmellini, 'but in the middle of everything…' He broke off. 'It's a bacteriological container, as you know, but

384

what's in it, is anyone's guess. Anyway, at the moment that's the least of our worries. Our real problem is that Scorpion, or whatever his fucking name is, has the other. What I do know is that the son of a bitch was planning on using both to wipe out some town or village in the UK. He was rambling on about this David Naami, the guy we were talking about earlier. Said he was getting it for someone very special, said the whole thing was his brainchild.'

'Very fucking nuts if you ask me, not special,' said O'Neil, breaking in. 'He must be insane if he thinks he can use this stuff to wipe out an entire village. What if something goes wrong? What happens if it's airborne? One change of wind direction and God knows how many will be killed.'

Stunned by the implication, Carmellini said, 'All I know is he seemed to be in awe of the guy, said he made David Naami look like a fairy, or words to that effect.'

'But we've got to warn the Brits,' said O'Neil. 'Any way you can get hold of this guardian, the guy who gave you the tip off?'

Thinking hard for moment, he said, 'There is one way… I just hope to God it works,' was Carmellini's reply.

'You and me both, brother,' said O'Neill. 'Otherwise we might just be looking at the start of World War Three.'

Chapter Thirty-five

'SO WHAT DOES IT LOOK LIKE?' EDWIN SAID BREATHLESSLY. THAT HE was excited was beyond doubt. 'Does the papyrus and ink look genuine? Is the language Aramaic?'

'Slow down, Uncle Edwin! said Jared in amusement. 'I haven't opened it yet.'

The disappointment was almost tangible, even over the phone.

Suddenly the silence was broken by another excited outburst. 'But why not? By now I would have been tearing my hair out in frustration, my professional curiosity wouldn't have been able to stand the strain.'

'Simple,' said Jared, 'from my point of view I didn't think it fair, so I thought I'd wait until we were all together. After all, it is a joint venture.'

'Hmm, yes,' came the reply, 'I see what you mean. Still, you were the one to risk life and limb to find it, so to speak. You might have taken that into consideration when making your decision. But yes, I see your point; very magnanimous of you all the same.'

'Come off it, Uncle, you would have made exactly the same decision had you been in my shoes, and you know it.'

'Ah, well, yes,' said Edwin a little flustered, not at all sure whether he would have.

Despite that, he felt it more prudent to agree and said, 'I suppose you're right, but God I wish I was there. I'd give anything to be with you when you finally open the damn thing.'

'I was thinking of holding back for a day or two,' said Jared, 'to give you an opportunity to get here, until I remembered you promised to stay at home this week in case the old guardian turned up.'

A tired sigh came over the air. 'You're quite correct; as a matter of fact I'm expecting him any day. He did say a week at the most, and it's been, let's see now, ah, yes...' he paused while trawling through his memory… 'that's it, five days now. It's Thursday today, so technically Saturday would be the deadline. And you're right, he was most insistent, said it was imperative I be here. So I suppose I must respect his wishes. Still, if he hasn't arrived by Sunday morning, I could jump in the car and be there in a few hours. How does that sound?'

'Brilliant! Besides, knowing my limitations in Aramaic, I don't suppose I'll have got very far in two days.'

Brightening up considerably at Jared's comments, Edwin carried on, 'What time have you called the meeting for?'

Glancing at his watch, Jared said, 'About half an hour's time. And before you ask, yes, Eric will be here. After all the hard work he put in he's now officially part of the investigation.'

Changing tack, Edwin said, 'You realise Eric won't be able to help with the translation, don't you? It's not his area of expertise.'

'If it's anything more abstruse than Aramaic,' was Jared's modest reply, 'then I'm going to struggle myself.'

There was a pause for a moment before Edwin broke in again.

'If the document is the genuine article, then I can't see how it could be anything else but Aramaic. Still,' he carried on, 'see what you can do until I get there on Sunday.' As if suddenly remembering something else, he jumped in again quickly. 'Incidentally, how big is it? I know you haven't opened it yet, but you should have a good idea from handling the package.'

Smiling at Edwin's shrewd question, Jared said, 'Big – and heavy too. As a matter of fact, it's more like a ledger than the simple codex I envisaged primarily. Still, in hindsight I suppose it would have had to be fairly large in order for it to outline in detail the whole history of the chalice, the rise of the guardians and of course the secret of Project Lazarus.' After a brief pause he said, 'Oh, and I nearly forgot, there's also that enigmatic prophecy the old man hinted at, something to do with the Red Serpent. Add all that together, and then the whole thing would of necessity have to be quite substantial, wouldn't it? In all honesty, how Joseph managed to carry it in his condition is beyond me.'

'*Joseph?*' exclaimed Edwin. 'What Joseph?'

'Of course,' said Jared guiltily, 'there are a few things you've missed out on during the last few days, but between everything, I really haven't had time to buzz you.'

With that he began to fill Edwin in on what he'd come up with. Leaving nothing out, he ran through the visit from the creature, the name of the killer, how he was choosing his victims, to eventually, the final part of the puzzle, the dates on which he was going to strike next. Right at the end he said, 'Of course we haven't much time, because the early Church set aside 28 October for the martyrdom of both Jude and Simon. As a result of that, Judas is planning a little treat for us – a double killing. Whatever we decide to do will have to be done quickly, or I'm going to have another two innocent lives on my hands.'

The implications of the use of the singular 'I' was not lost on Edwin, who could find nothing to say.

'What the hell made you say a stupid thing like that? We already have enough problems with the bloody media without you adding to it. Jesus Christ,' said Danny, 'what the hell am I going to do now?' Rubbing his hands over his eyes in exasperation, he carried on wearily, 'We haven't seen you for nearly a month, and now this! You certainly know how to stir things up, that's for sure.'

Seeing how upset he was, Roger attempted to explain his actions.

'It happened so quickly, I said the first thing that came to my head.'

'But why that? Surely you could have come up with something better?'

With a huge grin, Roger said, 'You didn't hear the last bit, because if you had you'd have seen how I threw them off the scent completely. Go and see for yourself – as from a few moments ago they've backed off.'

Totally confused now, Danny said, 'But I thought… Oh, never mind, finish the bloody story, maybe then I can have some peace of mind.'

Whistling in a deliberate attempt to further rile Danny, Roger said, 'It was like this. I was approaching the gate at the top of the steps. The one leading directly here from the main road, and the coast was clear. Believe me, I checked, when all of a sudden they were there, like flies around the proverbial. Don't ask me where they came from, I haven't a clue, but suddenly there they were. Thinking on my feet, as you do,' he said, winking at Jared at the same time, 'I thought I'd stitch them up.'

'Oh, Christ,' said Danny, 'this is going to take longer than the saga of *The Fugitive*.'

In an attempt to avoid the inevitable, he raised his hand and said, 'Don't even bother, it was way before your time. It's dating myself, I know, but anything to cut a long story short.'

'I'm only mentioning Hebrew at this juncture because it's so closely related to Aramaic. By the year 705 BC, Aramaic had become the language of diplomacy and shortly after was used for business and commercial transactions. More importantly, though, in New Testament times it was the one spoken by the ordinary people of Palestine, including Jesus himself, of course.'

Looking at the attentive faces surrounding him, he said, 'It might appear strange to us, but what's even weirder is that it's read from right to left, not the other way round.'

'But that would mean you would have to read it backwards,' exclaimed an astonished Emma.

'Yes,' said Jared, amused at her facial expression.

'But why on earth would anyone want to read and write backwards?' asked an equally bemused Roger.

'An interesting question, Rog, but don't forget to these people it is we who are doing things backwards and not them. Anyway, in answer to your question, I don't know. According to one group of scholars, it was because it was easier to chisel words into rock by starting from the right.' With an expansive shrug of the shoulders, he said, 'But it's only a theory; the truth is, no one really knows.'

Pointing once more to the open codex, Emma said, 'So what you're saying is that in order to translate this, you will have to start from the right-hand side of the margin?'

'That's right, Em.'

Suddenly, Emma's question reminded him of something he had meant to do earlier. Turning to the codex, he leafed through the pages until he found what he was looking for. There, staring out at him from the top of the page was the strange symbol they'd managed to decipher weeks before. As far as he was concerned it was the final clincher. It was genuine.

With that, a feeling of dread began to descend on him, one that had started with the brainstorming sessions he'd had with Edwin and Eric. As the weeks had passed, the feeling had grown stronger, so much so that by now he was almost certain he knew the secret of the final chapter – the one code-named 'Project Lazarus', the one the old father had died in order to protect. He'd kept his idea to himself, of course, as without conclusive proof such an explosive and heretical idea would have left him open to ridicule. If he hadn't missed his guess, Eric had already worked it out as well and probably long before he had.

Now he'd come this far, he wasn't so sure he wanted confirmation of his theory, to know the secret. There were some things better left undiscovered, some things best left unsaid, and he couldn't help the feeling burrowing deep inside that this might just be one of them.

In all honesty, if his guess was right, then he didn't feel the world was ready for such a revelation. Amid all the jumble of confusing thoughts, he shook his head vigorously in an attempt to drag himself back into the present, before making an announcement.

'I think I should head home and make a start on the translation. I want to get as much done as I can before Edwin arrives on Sunday. I know you lot will be running up the walls waiting for the details, but if I shut myself in until Saturday morning, I can make a full report then. It goes without saying, anything earth-shattering and I'll get back to you right away. That's a promise. Its hardly likely, though, because, reading between the lines, the first part of the codex deals with things we've managed to work out for ourselves, the founding of the Brotherhood, Judas being brought back to life, the killing of the Apostles, that kind of thing.'

As there were no signs of disagreement, he picked up the codex, wrapped it carefully in its original packaging, and made for the exit.

No sooner had he stepped through the door of his grandmother's than she was shouting, 'Phone call for you, love… he's phoned twice already, seems quite important.'

'Hello,' said Jared picking up the phone, 'how can I help you?'

'You've got that the wrong way round, sir; it's how I can help you that matters.'

Laughing, Jared said, 'Sorry, Ian, my grandmother said she thought the call sounded important… if only she knew!'

The deep-throated chuckle at the other end said it all; there was no need for words.

'Your toys have arrived and you'll find everything in order. Oh, and by the way, I've added a few other items that might just come in handy… you never know. Friday, 1100 hours. Same arrangements as we discussed last time, red car boot unlatched.' Before ringing off, he added. 'Remember, the offer is still open; me and the boys are always ready. I know you don't like to hear it, being a gentleman and all that, of a kind anyway,' he said, chuckling again, 'but we still owe you big time.'

The sincerity in the voice was only too apparent, and Jared wasn't foolish enough to think that at some time in the distant future he mightn't be in need of that help, but not on this occasion. So he said, 'I'll keep that in mind, Ian, but right now I'm going to have to decline the offer. As I mentioned last time, this particular job is personal. And by the way, thanks once again.' With that he killed the call.

Knowing how much time and effort he would be spending on working on the codex, he saw the journey to pick up his little toys, as his old friend had so delicately described the consignment, as a welcome break.

The first section of the codex took Jared by surprise. Instead of being an integral part of the ledger, it contained a handwritten account of a confession by Barabbas, faithfully preserved by Joseph. As it unfolded it became apparent why:

I am writing this in fear of my life, should they ever find my hiding place I am done for. May Yahweh have mercy on me, for I know with certainty my soul is doomed to the everlasting flames of Gehenna. There is no redemption for such a sin.

It began when I persuaded my brother Judas to become my eyes and ears in the company of the Galilean called Jesus. The aim was to find out whether the rumours were true, to establish whether or not he was the long awaited Messiah. I held little hope, so many had come and gone, each one destroyed by the might of Rome, each one ultimately proven false. All the gossip in the Temple precinct however seemed to indicate that this time things might just be different, that this Nazarene might well turn out to be the one prophesied in the Scriptures.

At first the reports from Judas were encouraging. He'd been witness to many wondrous deeds. And his words seemed to enchant the people. Could it be, I asked myself, that finally the Sicarii had a leader?

Slowly at first, so as not to arouse suspicion, my brother began to question him. How long would it be before this New Kingdom he taught about would arrive?

Think of our amazement when we found out that the Kingdom he was talking about was not of this world, but of the next. The man spoke in riddles.

But worse was to follow, much worse.

Imagine our horror when he declared himself a king of peace, preaching love for all mankind and not war.

Initially Judas thought he'd been mistaken. Very soon however he came to realise the imbecile was serious. All the patient negotiations had been for nothing. The man was nothing more than a poor deluded fool.

Then he added blasphemy to his list of other crimes by claiming he was about to die for us. According to him, his body would become the Passover lamb, the physical sacrifice spoken about in the Scriptures. As leader of the Sicarii, I realised should people begin to believe in such philosophies we would be doomed. The idiot didn't seem to grasp that driving the hated Romans out of Palestine was the answer. The people wanted freedom, a return to the golden days of David, not some foolish notion of being forgiven of their sins.

But I underestimated him.

He was dangerously persuasive, so much so that even my own brother began to succumb to his charms, to his promises of a place in this strange Kingdom.

Something had to be done before it was too late, and that something could be no less than his removal from the scene – permanently!

Strangely, it was easier than expected, as to our surprise the priests had come to the same conclusion. Therefore the solution when it came was simple. Judas had to be persuaded to lead us to his hiding place, somewhere he went at night, somewhere he could be arrested with little outside interference. Through my brother we learned such an opportunity would present itself in a few days' time. It seemed this Jesus wanted all the Apostles to be near him for a special meal. The Last Supper, he called it.

When he was finally taken, it was the oddest thing. Eyewitness reports stated that the Nazarene made no move to resist, indeed if anything he seemed to be expecting it. There was only one moment of violence. That fool Peter, he cut off someone's ear, but the problem was resolved quickly.

When he was crucified we all thought it would be the end of things, but horror of horrors, several nights later, my brother was dragged out of his home and hanged. The one called Peter spat at him during his death throes, and added insult to injury by throwing thirty pieces of silver at his feet. Blood money for the betrayal, he called it.

When information of this reached my ears I was so enraged I vowed vengeance. The hatred burnt inside me like boiling pus. It festered until I could stand it no longer. Finally I knew what I must do and so I set off in search of the Sect of the Dead, a group of necromancers with strange mystical powers I'd heard of several years previously.

Taking my life in my hands, I eventually managed to track down their hiding place.

Blindfolded and led through what I can only guess was a labyrinth of caves, I was paraded in front of their leader, a strange man to say the least.

The audience was conducted in a huge cave lit only by several black candles. The only thing visible was a large stone altar, well used by the look of it.

The signs and symbols decorating the sides were of a type I'd never seen before. The smell was overpowering, like the inside of a freshly dug grave. It was as much as I could do not to choke on the vomit I felt rising to my throat. However, I knew should I do that it would seal my fate. They were looking for any sign of weakness, and so I was determined not to show either the slightest indication of discomfiture or fear.

Apart from the leader, who had a beard and long black hair falling to his shoulders, the others were covered with vestments which included hoods to hide their faces.

Only the leader spoke, but his voice was truly terrifying.

Within moments I made it clear what I was after, and to my surprise it seemed to delight the figures. The deep throaty chuckles which followed my request left me with the distinct impression that they enjoyed bringing people back from the other side of the grave.

The ritual they outlined was extremely detailed, and for it to be effective they gave me a list of things I would have to retrieve. They made it clear the head would be severed from the body and preserved by some secret formula derived from Egypt. In the final part of the process, the body would be burnt and pounded into ashes, which were then to be kept safely, as they were the real seat of power.

When I asked what would happen once the ritual had been performed, they once again gave their throaty chuckles. At this point the leader said something strange, 'What would you like to happen?'

I explained I wanted revenge for my brother, revenge on the murdering bastards who had dragged him out and killed him. 'Would Judas have the power to do that?' I enquired.

This seemed to please them no end.

The answer, delivered in a mocking tone said, 'Oh, have no fear, it will have the power to do that – and much more besides.'

I didn't have time to comment on the odd use of 'it' rather than 'he' before the speaker carried on.

'Whether you will be able to control the power is another thing.' Laughing, he said, 'so I must warn you against what you are about to do.'

Foolishly, I turned my back on the risks and went ahead.

It was months later when things started to go wrong; by then of course I knew what their leader had been hinting at. Whatever had come back from the other side, disguised as my brother, was an animal. Unwittingly I had awakened a thirst for blood no amount of savagery could satisfy.

In the end I did the only thing I could. I went to a man called Joseph, who was the leader of a devout band of people who called themselves Christians, and explained the situation to him. Of course, Joseph was only too glad to see me, for it was the followers of Jesus – a good friend of his before he'd been taken up to heaven as they liked to brag – whom the creature was targeting. Between us, we managed to stop the evil which had once been my brother.

I must make one thing perfectly clear: the evil can never be defeated, only imprisoned.

For my part in the creature's demise, I am now a hunted man. Human nature being what it is, I have gone from being the leader of the Sicarii to being a traitor. In one of life's little ironies the head of the thing – I refuse to accept it as my brother – has now become a figure of worship, a bringer of occult power. While the chalice and the ashes of the creature remain separate, there is hope for us all, but should my fellow brothers ever find it and manage to reunite them, then God help us all!

Chapter Thirty-six

'EXCUSE ME, MR HUNTER, THERE'S SOMEONE AT THE DOOR FOR YOU, an old gent by the look of him.'

For a moment Edwin was slightly perplexed until it suddenly struck him who it was. Jumping up from the armchair, he hurried to the door. Once he'd confirmed the identity of his visitor, he turned to Mrs Daniels and said, 'If you would be so kind as to get us both a cup of tea and some biscuits, please. Oh, and once you've done that, you can take the rest of the day off.'

'I know when I'm not wanted,' she said huffily, 'but are you sure you're going to be all right? It's just he looks a bit strange to me.'

'Don't you worry,' said Edwin, slightly amused at her concern. 'Of course I'll be all right. I've told you before you fuss too much about me.' At the same time he smiled in order to show the comment wasn't meant as a rebuke. 'Anyway, he's not well, that's why he looks the way he does.'

'Ah,' she said, 'that explains it then,' before turning on her heels.

When they were sitting comfortably in the living room, Edwin decided to start the conversation. 'Your looking better than the last time we spoke,' he observed, at the same time trying hard to hide his true feelings. What he really thought was that the old man looked like death warmed up.

Taking a sip of his tea from the bone china cup, the old guardian savoured the flavour before looking up and saying, 'Well, Edwin, since my last visit it appears you seem to have added diplomacy to your long list of qualities.' Looking him straight in the eye he said, 'I look like shit and you know it.'

Waving his hand in the air as if the matter of his health was of no consequence, he suddenly broke into a smile and said, 'It's the strangest thing, but surprisingly for the last few days I've felt better. But the quack told me that would happen, said it would get better before I started to go downhill fast.' More serious now, he added, 'He also told me once the signs were there it would be a matter of days only.'

Edwin could only admire the bravery of the man; he'd obviously come to terms with all of it and was ready to meet his Maker.

Putting his cup down, the old guardian said, 'You wouldn't have a drop of whisky – the same brand I had last time – hanging around, would you? The condemned man and his last request and all that.'

'Of course,' said Edwin, how remiss of me. 'I should have asked,' he added, making his way towards the bureau. Bringing the decanter over, he poured a generous measure into the old man's cup. On the spur of the moment he declared, 'I think I'll join you,' and with that added a small measure to his own.

Rolling the liquid around his mouth first, the old man savoured the peaty tang of the whisky before swallowing. In seconds the amber liquid trickled down his throat before hitting his bloodstream and warming his body from head to toe. Within moments the fiery liquor began to weave its magic and he felt his old bones easing somewhat. Suddenly he was all business again and said, 'Right, let's get down to it, shall we?'

Sifting through his mind trying to work out how he was going to broach the subject, he said, 'It's difficult to know where to start. By now you know about the secret cave, the hidden documents and about our leader, Joseph of Arimathea. Perhaps what you're not aware of was the fact that apart from a good deal of wealth which Joseph had accumulated over the years, the cave contained something far more precious, the secret knowledge that Jesus was not only married to Mary Magdalene, but had fathered a male child. In essence that is the secret of *Le Serpent Rouge* or *The Red Serpent* as it came to be known. After Jesus' death and resurrection, the fledgling religion spread like wildfire, and eventually they were given a nickname – Christians – literally meaning followers of Christ! In a very short space of time, the Romans became horrified at the speed with which Christianity spread, not only through Palestine, but further afield as well. Driven by the need to stop it in its tracks, they instigated a wave of persecution, intent of course on wiping out every single one of them. It was against such a background that Joseph, intent on keeping the child of Jesus safe, arranged for Mary and the baby to be smuggled to Glastonbury in England. Already familiar with the area through ongoing business ventures, Joseph knew it was the ideal place in which to hide the pair. Incidentally, he made frequent visits afterwards in order to make sure they wanted for nothing.'

Wistful for a moment, he finally added, 'I believe that's where the myth of the Holy Grail started. Unfortunately for the followers of Indiana Jones, there never was any Grail. The translation of *San Graal* or *Sang Real* is Bloodline, not chalice – the bloodline being the offspring of Jesus. By now you will have probably guessed that the choice of phrase, *Le Serpent Rouge*, or *The Red Serpent*, was deliberately symbolic, and when you think of it like that everything suddenly falls into place. The serpent uncoiling across the centuries is describing the family of Jesus, and of course the colour red signifies blood.'

Holding his hand up to ward off Edwin's questions, the old man said, 'At the time such knowledge was explosive; the mere hint of such blasphemy would have brought the Church crashing to its knees. After all, if Jesus was divine, how could it be possible to father a child?'

'So,' said Edwin, 'that's what the Brotherhood was blackmailing the Catholic Church with all these years.'

'Precisely,' said the old man. 'Oh, I know it's not such a big deal these days, in fact it's been the subject of a great deal of debate, even made some authors famous. But the truth is the clues have been there all along.'

Changing tack, he said, 'How much do you know about the secret or hidden gospels?'

'Surprisingly, a fair bit,' said Edwin, 'but I'm sure you know a lot more, so please go ahead and enlighten me.'

Gathering his thoughts before he spoke, the old man was soon ready. 'The story of the Christian canon begins in the fourth century AD, when a bishop called Athanasius decided to make a stand against all those books and letters he regarded as being heretical. It's thanks to him the New Testament now contains twenty-seven books and no more.

'The reason for making a closed list was simple. There were so many different ideas about Jesus doing the rounds that Athanasius realised one definitive philosophy regarding his life and works had to be agreed on. Otherwise,' said the old man with an expansive gesture of his arms, 'the whole of Christianity would have been nothing but a sorry mess.

'Now, there was nothing wrong with the idea in principle, but what it meant was that all other documents produced at the time, those which fell outside his idea of orthodoxy, or correctness, if you like, were labelled false. He knew as long as other variant forms of gospels survived, ones that painted a different picture of Jesus to the one the early

Church wanted us to see, trouble would always lurk around the corner. To him the answer to the solution was simple – everything outside the twenty-seven "correct" books had to be destroyed. And so they disappeared almost overnight. Or so we thought, anyway.

'Then in 1945 a discovery was made in Nag Hammadi, a small village some 300 miles south of Cairo that forced scholars to question the validity of the traditional Jesus, the one painted for us by Matthew, Mark, Luke and John. You see, it seemed not everyone had listened to the edict. In fact some had deliberately smuggled out what they clearly regarded as precious documents from a nearby monastery – which incidentally now lies in ruins – and then buried them. In all there was a collection of fifty individual works. Known in antiquity, but lost for nearly 1,500 years, they painted not only a different picture to the Jesus handed down to us by the early Church, but even a different picture of God. That they had been regarded as very valuable by their owners was obvious – they'd been written on the very best papyrus.

'I won't bore you with a complete survey of their findings, but the worrying thing from the point of view of the Church was that the Jesus portrayed in these writings was unrecognisable. One of the scrolls in particular is pertinent to *Le Serpent Rouge* and helps give credence to the secret. The hidden Gospel of Philip is the most important, because it says Jesus loved Mary more than any of the other disciples. The implication is obvious, not only was she a disciple – a female, mind – but she also played a key role. One passage hints strongly that the relationship between Mary and Jesus was more than spiritual. In fact, it claims he kissed her on the mouth. Not once, mind you, but several times. At the moment this point of view is controversial, as there appears to be a hole in the papyrus at the very point where they say it reads mouth. However, experts have suggested "mouth" seems to be the only word that fits.'

Seeing the startled expression on Edwin's face, he carried on quickly, 'Hold on to your hat, there might even be a Gospel of Mary Magdalene. I know it sounds far-fetched, but it seems it's true. A fragment of it was found, in a rubbish dump of all places, along with lots of other scraps. Apparently it had been found years before, but had been lying among hundreds of other similar pieces of papyrus, until someone suddenly realised its importance. So you see, as difficult as it is to believe, all the evidence points to the fact that Mary had enormous influence among the early disciples. If that is the case, the intriguing question is, why did she disappear from the scene so soon after the death of Jesus? Why is it from that time on we hear nothing of her?'

By now it was clear the old man was very tired, but drawing on reserves of energy which Edwin found amazing, he carried on.

'As for "Project Lazarus", only God and Joseph know what that is. However, should the codex ever be found, all will be revealed. Finally, before I take my leave, remember the prophecy: the first shall be the bringer of life, and that is you. The second shall be the destroyer of enemies, and although he doesn't yet know it, that's your son, whoever and wherever he is. The final part of the prophecy is that the third shall be the chosen one. Born in the year of the old millennium, the child will begin to display powers beyond human understanding by the dawn of the new.'

Smiling, Edwin said, 'That's something you don't have to explain, I know about the Roman abbot and how he messed up our calendar; but one thing still baffles me, what is the purpose of this special child?'

'Why, to defeat the Antichrist and restore a semblance of world order again, of course!'

Then in a more sombre tone, he said, 'The problem is in order to bring that about, both David Naami and the creature must be destroyed... and soon, before a new year begins; otherwise the potency of the child saviour will be lost, or at the very least diluted.'

'Have you ever read Revelations? Properly, I mean?'

'Well, yes and no,' said Edwin, honestly. 'Yes to reading it, but no to taking it all in. But surely most scholars are in agreement that it's nothing but symbolism.'

'True,' said the old man, 'but let's look at it from another point of view for a moment. For instance, the book talks of an Antichrist. Now, many suggest the great Satan or Antichrist was Rome; but what if the book was talking about a real evil, an actual person?'

'I don't follow,' said Edwin.

'Put it this way: might John have been writing about the Antichrist from first-hand experience?'

After a moment's deliberation, Edwin suddenly realised what the old man was getting at and shouted excitedly, 'Of course! For him the great Satan was Judas or the demon, whichever way you look at it. He saw what it had done to the Apostles and so he was a witness to the horror.'

'Correct,' said the old man. 'John himself escaped only because he was banished to Patmos, from where scholars suggest he wrote the book. It's an extremely remote island, so its isolation provided the perfect hiding place.

'Right, let's move on to the second point, and take a brief look at the contents. At one stage it specifically mentions seven years of destruction leading directly to a final showdown, a final battle between good versus evil, or Armageddon as the media like to label it dramatically. Interestingly, some of the descriptions once laughed at as being nothing more than the product of a delusional mind are now being looked at more seriously... self-propelling chariots belching flame, birds producing sounds that are literally able to drown out everything else. Until the advent of modern technology, no one would have been able to recognise that perhaps John was alluding to tanks or aeroplanes. Again, it speaks of plagues with the ability to wipe out half the population of the world. In this day and age, with some of the germ warfare left over from the cold war and the biohazardous material we are engineering, it might well be that estimate could turn out to be on the low side. Many scientists are convinced that unless we stop now, it won't be long before someone produces the doomsday virus.'

Waving his hand in the air, the old man carried on, 'Whether you believe that Revelations is nothing more than one man's flight of fancy or simply a book full of irrational symbolism, there's one thing that even the most ardent sceptic can't deny: the signs are all eerily topical. There's no doubt that what John warned of all those years ago is happening here and now. Forget the weapons of mass destruction we mentioned earlier and let's look at a few examples from good old mother nature, shall we?'

Ticking them off on his fingers he said, 'Tsunamis and earthquakes – ring any bells? True, it can't be said that they're a new phenomena, but in the last few years they seem to be taking place on an unprecedented scale. Then we have comets, and asteroids threatening to destroy our world completely, or at the very least plunge us into another ice age. What about the ozone layer breaking down, and all the problems that entails? No one is sure of just how much damage has been caused already, but more worryingly, is there even a solution to the problem? Some scientists suggest that whatever answers they can come up with in the near future, it may well be a case of too little too late. On top of that we have the latest scare, the threat of global warming leading to the melting of the polar ice caps. So far we haven't even scratched the surface of what happens if the meltdown carries on at its present rate. The consequences don't bear thinking about. Might this be what John was describing when he talked about the Apocalypse?'

With his eyes seeming to look deep into Edwin's soul, the old man asked the inevitable question, 'What more portents does mankind need?'

After a few moments' silent contemplation, he said, 'Finally I come to my last point, the world in which we live in. Look at it, wallowing in greed and materialism! Its hedonistic qualities seem to be the antithesis of Jesus' teachings. Far from following what he advocated – by that I mean his philosophy of "Do unto others as you would have done unto you" – it seems to be that modern man has decided to write its own credo, "Do unto others before they get an opportunity to do it to you". You don't have to be a rocket scientist to see that if we carry on in this vein we're hell bent on a roller-coaster ride to destruction. True, you could make a case for other eras being as destructive. I'm the first to admit that other ages have been equally as savage; but you see they lacked the weapons of mass destruction that are helping us on our inexorable slide to total annihilation.'

With that the old man seemed to run out of steam. Bone-weary, he slumped into his seat in exhaustion.

Stunned at the implications of the old man's words, it was several minutes before Edwin could find his voice. When he did he said, 'And you see the child as being the instrument of our salvation, then? Yes, I can see that, but how will you recognise him?'

'Simple, like you and your son, he will have the birthmark, the one that looks remarkably like a coiled serpent.'

'There's one problem,' said Edwin. 'Apart from the fact that my son doesn't even know I'm his father, he isn't even married, let alone being the father of a child,' he added despondently.

'Then let's hope God will see to that side of things,' was the old man's enigmatic reply.

It had been almost a week and there was still no sign of the old bastard, and then suddenly there he was. It had been pure luck. Out of sheer boredom, David Naami's henchmen had decided to trawl the lanes around where they'd lost him last time. Turning out of the gates of some big mansion, he would have gone unnoticed but for the colour and make of the car he was driving.

Reaching the far end of the small country road, the assassins did a handbrake turn. They took no notice of the damage caused to the hedge directly behind. That was the least of their worries; if they should lose him this time… The thought didn't bear thinking about. Suddenly the man in the passenger seat had an idea, a way to get back into David Naami's good books. Punching in the number on his mobile phone, he was rewarded with an answer on the seventh ring.

'Number One, is that you?'

'Of course it is, you idiot! Who did you expect – it's my private number, isn't it? Anyway, what is it? And it had better be good, disturbing me at this time of day.'

On imparting the news, he could almost see the beam of pleasure on David Naami's face, and he was sure a little white lie at this late stage of the game couldn't hurt. After all, the old man was almost in their clutches, wasn't he…

It was as he was about to switch off he remembered. 'Number One, there's more.'

With that, he explained how they'd spotted the old man coming out of a drive leading to a large mansion. Guessing it was the place he'd been visiting last time, he suggested to the Grand Master that perhaps the owner was important, someone the old man knew well.

Listening intently, David Naami grew more and more excited. Could it be, he thought, that finally he'd managed to uncover the hiding place of the guardian's long held secrets? With that he shouted down the phone, 'The name, you fool! What was the *name* of the mansion?'

'Oh, yes, that… I've got it written down here somewhere, Number One, hold on.' Flipping open his notebook he said, 'Mendel Hall.' A sudden thought crossed his mind and he voiced it. 'Do you want directions, just in case you need to send some of the others to check the place out?'

'Yes, yes,' said David Naami, by now barely able to contain his agitation. Fumbling wildly in the top drawer of his desk, it was as if his hands belonged to someone else, such was his excitement. Several moments later he eventually found his notebook and shouted, 'OK, fire away.'

Stealth was no longer a priority, and so they sped after the Mini as fast as they could.

406

Leaving behind a trail of burning rubber, the Land Cruiser accelerated smoothly through the gears in attempt to catch the old man as quickly as possible.

He'd gone about a mile when, glancing in his mirror, the guardian spotted them. Amazingly, he felt no fear. Instead what coursed through his veins was elation. Now he'd carried out his sacred task, his life meant nothing. Suddenly a germ of an idea began to blossom: if he was to die then at least he would take some of the bastards with him. That way he could bow out with dignity, he reasoned.

Having lived in the area for years, he knew the country lanes well, so he knew that less than a hundred yards ahead was a series of tight s-bends. Unmarked, they had proven lethal to those unsuspecting motorists who had attempted to take them too quickly. Several people had been killed recently and the locals had waged a losing battle with the local authorities to have the accident black spot signposted. To date, the protests had proved singularly unsuccessful, and for that he was now eternally grateful.

The more he considered it, the more he thought he had a chance of pulling it off.

Nearing the approach to the first of the bends, he dropped the Mini into third and accelerated. Ever since he'd bought the Mini Cooper 'S' he'd felt a perverse pleasure, knowing for a man of his age he looked ridiculous. Now he was grateful for his show of ostentatiousness.

The Mini took the tight left-hand corner effortlessly, the tyres merely kissing the tarmac of the small country road. Glancing in the mirror, he was rewarded with the sight of the pursuing Land Cruiser doing exactly the same thing; if anything it had gained a few yards on him. Lulled into a false sense of security, they'd seen the gap narrowing and increased their pace.

The old man hit the next bend, a right-hander, at seventy miles an hour and this time there was a squeal of protest from the low-profile tires. When he looked in the mirror he was gratified to see the SUV was showing the first signs of distress. A slight fishtailing bore testimony to the fact that, unlike the Mini, it hadn't been built for such things as this.

Exactly the same thought was going through the minds of the two assassins, but by now they were on an adrenaline surge. Besides which, an honest appraisal of their motives would have shown that their egos would simply not allow an old man to put one over on them. Such arrogance proved their downfall, as they failed to see the Mini accelerate into the third and final left-hand bend. This time it was doing ninety miles an hour.

The assassins were halfway around the same corner when they realised they'd never make it. There was a squeal as the driver of the SUV stood on the brakes in a vain attempt to cut down its momentum. At such a suicidal speed, however, it was impossible, and the inevitable occurred. Almost imperceptibly at first, but then more rapidly as it gained ever more impetus, the heavy vehicle started to slew sideways – a slide that, once begun, was impossible to stop.

Meanwhile, up ahead the old man was resigned to the fact his last moment on earth would be a roller-coaster ride far greater than any he'd experienced as a youngster. With that thought coursing through his brain, the little Mini clipped the grass verge at the side of the lane and ploughed through a hedge guarding the side of the road. Such was its momentum that the little car cut through the hedge as if it didn't exist, before coming to rest on its roof in a mass of tangled wreckage and steam. Seconds later the driver was unconscious. Before he'd lost control of the car however, the old man had the satisfaction of seeing the assassin's vehicle take the final bend twenty yards behind – but almost side on. Although it took mere seconds, it was for the old man as if time stood still and he found to his astonishment that he was watching everything in slow motion. Through his rear mirror, he saw the Cruiser hit the steel barrier on the opposite side to his before flipping into the air at almost eighty miles an hour. The force of the impact sent the passenger, who had not been wearing a seat belt, exploding through the windshield in a spray of blood and tissue. Although the driver had been wearing his, it did him little good, as when the heavy vehicle finally came to rest at the bottom of the steep embankment, the impact broke his neck like a twig.

Moments later the old man regained consciousness. Amazed he was still alive, he looked down. The sight was so appalling it nearly made him pass out again. From the knees down, there was nothing left of his legs, only ragged stumps, and as he watched they began to spray the inside of the wrecked Mini with blood.

Unable to take the slightest risk that one of the assassins had survived, he decided to take his own life. Slipping the cyanide capsule from a hidden cavity inside a false tooth, he bit into it before his courage failed.

His last thought was, What the hell... I only had a few weeks to live anyway.

Chapter Thirty-seven

ENGROSSED IN TRANSLATING A PARTICULARLY INTERESTING PART OF the codex, Jared nearly missed the newsflash. Glancing at the screen, he was just in time to hear the report of a fatal accident on a notorious black spot near Ross-on-Wye. Hitting a steel barrier, the SUV had flipped into the air and tumbled down a thirty-foot drop before coming to rest in a drainage ditch. Both the driver and passenger had been killed instantly. Oddly enough, it hadn't been the end of the story, as it appeared that twenty yards further on the police had come across another car, this time upside down in a field on the opposite side of the road. The driver, an old man, seemingly in his late seventies and driving a bright red Mini Cooper 'S', had been killed almost outright, both legs having been severed below the knees. At the moment the police were baffled, as there was no evidence that the vehicles had come into contact with each other. As such, the cause of the accident had yet to be determined.

Sitting bolt upright, Jared suddenly remembered.

A bright read Mini Cooper 'S' and an old man in his seventies were too much of a coincidence, he realised, which meant the other two had been members of the Brotherhood. By now, several scenarios were running around his head, none of which were pleasant. The one that made the most sense was that the old man had known they were on to him, and if that was the case it stood to reason that with only a short time to live, he had deliberately sacrificed himself. The question was, had he passed on the secret to Edwin before they'd traced him?

With that he dived for the phone.

After the twentieth ring went unanswered, Jared knew something was seriously amiss.

It meant one thing. The old guardian had been wrong. Somehow the Brotherhood had managed to track him down and so, despite the fact he'd taken the two assassins with him, it wouldn't be long before they found Edwin.

It might take days, but there was one thing sure: find him they would.

Suddenly he had a more disturbing thought.

If he was in the assassins' shoes, he would have informed David Naami immediately in order to give him the good news, before just as quickly filling him in on the location of the mansion. And if that were the case, they might already have traced him.

Running up the stairs in panic, Jared burst into his bedroom. Taking out the false bottom of his wardrobe, he pulled out two oilskin packages. Making sure everything was in order, he dumped them into his battered training bag, before replacing the bottom carefully.

Dressing hurriedly into a pair of black jogging bottoms and a black roll-neck sweater, he put on a pair of old trainers before throwing his combat boots into the bag along with the other equipment. Zipping it up, he was now ready.

Realising his gran was out, he let out a sigh of relief. He didn't know how he would have managed to worm his way out of this one had she been at home. As it was, a simple note saying he'd be away for twenty-four hours would keep her happy. Leaving the note on the table, he was on the road within ten minutes of seeing the newsflash.

Touching nearly eighty miles an hour for most of the way, he made sure there was always at least one car in front of him. His reasoning was that although he was over the speed limit, he knew police cameras tended to focus their attention on solo vehicles.

By the time he reached Edwin's it was already dark.

Not wanting to draw attention to himself, Jared parked the car in a gloomy lane a hundred yards or so from the mansion. Tight against the hedge, he reasoned the foliage was dense enough to make it almost invisible to anything but the closest scrutiny. Changing his trainers for black combat boots, he opened the back door and retrieved his weapons from the hidden compartment he'd cut into the underside of the back seat.

Opening the first of the oiled packages, he fitted the silencer to his SIG P226. Quickly he stripped down the weapon, rebuilt it and then, satisfied, unloaded and then reloaded the magazine, before working the action several times. It was a habit he'd got into over the years, one which had saved him on more than one occasion. His credo was, *Leave nothing to chance.*

Having already filed off the serial number, he knew the gun was untraceable. Slipping the leather harness over his shoulder, he placed the pistol into the well-worn holster. Adjusting it until he was comfortable, the weight felt good. Replacing the package, which contained several spare clips of ammunition, into the compartment, he opened the other and fitted the two razor sharp throwing knives into their individual holders sewn into the nape of his black turtleneck sweater.

Sliding the balaclava over his head he was now ready.

Locking the door, he hid the keys, wanting as few impediments as possible.

With one last lingering look, he jogged to the perimeter wall surrounding the mansion.

Knowing the wall was for decorative purposes only, that there was no razor wire or alarms, he scaled it effortlessly. Crouched at the top, he looked around cautiously before dropping soundlessly onto the other side. Although it was an eight-foot drop, any noise he might have made was cushioned by a carpet of dead leaves which covered the area directly beneath the wall.

Standing in the shadows thrown by several large oak trees, he flattened himself against the rough stone, before taking a moment or two to control his breathing. The only sound was the low sighing of the wind through the branches of the trees immediately ahead.

When he was ready, he set off towards the house.

Keeping as low as possible, he jogged the first hundred yards or so, before picking up speed and making for the thorn hedge which protected the front of the house.

Knowing he was up against professionals, he reasoned there had to be at least two, maybe even three to contend with. If it was his shout, he would have left one man guarding the front while the other two would have been used to take out Edwin.

Using every spare inch of cover available, he eased his way gradually closer until he was within ten feet of the front porch. Studying the entrance, he had the feeling something was wrong, something was out of place, and then he had it. He realised suddenly what had been bothering him for the last few moments. The light which normally illuminated the porch was out, the doors bathed in deep shadow. He wondered whether the bulb had blown, or if it had been deliberately smashed. If the latter were true, the pieces would have been left scattered over the floor as an early warning indicator.

Mouthing a silent prayer that he would be in time, every foot of ground he covered simply added to the cold feeling at the pit of his stomach, the one that said he might already be too late.

Dropping flat, Jared crawled forward, arms and legs working in unison until he sensed that he was rapidly reaching the limit of his cover, soon he would be able to go no further without betraying his presence. He forced himself to remain perfectly still.

The waiting seemed to go on indefinitely; five minutes turned into ten and still he could see nothing untoward. He knew the assassin had to be there, but where? That was the problem.

One thing was certain, however good the other man was, he was better, he knew that; but time was against him. Every moment he was forced to remain where he was meant his uncle's life was put in further danger.

Fortunately, it was the assassin who made the first mistake.

It was the slightest of sounds, but for Jared it was enough, carrying as it did to where he was hiding.

Although the sound had inadvertently betrayed the man's position, it had taken Jared by surprise. He hadn't expected the guard to be posted there. In hindsight it made perfect sense, as it afforded a view across the lawn and gravel path leading to the front door. Had he decided on a frontal approach he would have been spotted easily.

While he was thinking about his next move, lady luck decided to afford him a helping hand. When he'd started out there had been a bright, almost full, moon, peeking out occasionally from its hiding place among the fast-moving clouds. Now it had disappeared altogether. It suited Jared just fine.

Familiar with the layout of the house, he now pieced it together from memory. Several of the second floor bedrooms had access to a small balcony through individual patio doors that ran the length of the building.

The sound had alerted him to the fact the guard had taken refuge on the end balcony, and although it had been a sound choice of hiding place, it had one flaw, a flaw which Jared intended taking full advantage of. He knew if he could reach the side of the house undetected, he would be able to worm his way underneath the balustrade completely invisible to anyone from above.

Crawling forward, making sure to keep beneath the contours of the small hedge, he made his way around to the side of the house. About to get to his feet, he stopped when a large portion of the lawn was illuminated by a shaft of light piercing the inky blackness of his hiding place, the legacy of poorly drawn curtains. Just then he caught a glimpse of someone's face behind the heavy drape before it fell back into place. The light was cut off instantly, and with that the surrounding area was bathed once again in deep shadow.

Taking advantage of the situation, Jared sprang to his feet and covered the short space between him and the back of the house in record time. Looping around the side, he slid past an old barrow full of leaves ready to be added to the large mound in a corner, before stepping gingerly over several loose flower pots. About to negotiate the low wall directly in front of him, he was careful not to trip over the coil of garden hose that in the gloom looked like a huge black reptile.

Negotiating the wall cautiously, he was suddenly there, directly below the assassin's hiding place. Sliding the SIG from its holster, he held it alongside his right cheek, silencer pointing upwards, grip in both hands.

Hugging the wall tightly, he inched his way forward, stopping every few feet to control his breathing, alert for the slightest indication that he might have been heard.

Reaching the base of the steps, he altered his position.

Rolling over onto his back, he eased his way upwards, holding the gun straight in the air, prepared for any sudden movement. For several moments he lay perfectly still until suddenly he risked a look.

It was a quick glance, but it was enough.

Despite the dark shadow cast by the overhang of the balcony above, the man was clearly visible. Making a short mental calculation, he realised that for someone of his calibre it was an easy shot. Easing off the safety catch, he placed the barrel of the silencer on the top of the concrete lintel and gave a low whistle. Startled, the assassin looked up. By now Jared had stilled his breathing, and caressing the trigger as lightly as a lover's kiss, he squeezed it gently. The gun made a slight spitting sound before the assassin fell in a crumpled heap, half his head blown away by the impact of the 9 mm parabellum bullet.

One down, two to go, Jared told himself… unless of course he'd got his calculations wrong.

Although there was no way the man could have survived a direct hit from such close quarters, he made sure. Moving forwards quickly he knelt down and rolled the man over.

There was so little of the head left it was impossible to check the carotid artery, but seeing the state of the body and how it was already beginning to cool, he knew he was looking at a corpse. Satisfied, he made his way back the way he'd come.

Turning right at the bottom of the steps, he made his way cautiously towards the front door. He was within six feet when he found his guess had been right. The shattered remains of the bulb lay on the floor providing a simple but effective snare for anyone foolish enough to approach the door in an unwary fashion. Stepping on the pieces would have meant he would have alerted the guard. He would have been dead within seconds.

His senses still on high alert, Jared moved forward with grim intent.

Pausing for a moment to put on a pair of surgical gloves, he stepped over the glass and turned the handle of one of the large double doors before easing it open gently with his foot. Not expecting trouble, he still took no chances.

Sliding around the door, gun outstretched in both hands, he dropped onto one knee while, at the same time swivelling the pistol from left to right. Nothing! It was quiet.

On the balls of his feet, he made his way soundlessly along the long corridor to his uncle's study. As this was where the light had been coming from earlier, he decided to check it out first.

By now he was moving more swiftly, confident in the knowledge he knew the interior of the house far better than the intruders. The door to the study was open slightly, and hearing no sound from inside, he took a chance. Easing the door open with his foot, he went through the same procedure as with the front door, and with the same result – there was nothing.

The light had been from the table lamp near the window, he now realised, but as far as he could see nothing was amiss. Despite this, he felt a rapidly swelling unease rise to his stomach; his internal alarm was ringing loudly. Something definitely wasn't right, of that he was sure… but what? About to leave, something caught his eye.

Unsure of what to do, he decided to take a closer look.

He was within a few feet of the strange sight when he suddenly understood what it was.

At the far end corner of the room, near his uncle's collection of bows, he saw the body of a man. He'd been crucified by the use of crossbow bolts. One had been used for each of the hands and feet, while as a final touch, a fifth had been fired into the man's throat.

It was a macabre sight. Unlike in a normal crucifixion, where the head would inevitably rest on the chest, in this instance it had been forced into an upright position, the victim staring directly at Jared from cold, lifeless eyes. And in that instant Jared knew who it was. For what seemed like an eternity, he was unable to move. The killing of old Tom had brought an upwelling of anger and hatred to the surface of an already tormented soul, but it was nothing compared to what was going through his mind now.

Glancing away, he collected his thoughts, allowing his inner turmoil to settle a little before he turned back. Suddenly, he was brought to his senses by the chiming of the grandfather clock in the hallway, heralding midnight. For a brief moment he hesitated and then he heard it: the sound of objects clattering onto a wooden floor. Instantly he knew what it was, the sound of books being forcibly swept from the shelves of his uncle's library.

Despite the horror he felt at seeing Edwin's body, the wave of grief was swiftly overtaken by a sentiment which was much more fundamental, one much more dangerous. Anger and an atavistic need for revenge coursed through every fibre of Jared's being, but it was not mindless anger. This was something far more dangerous. It was calculated fury, and it sounded the death knell for those who had cold-bloodedly murdered his uncle.

Making his way silently down the hall, he saw the door to the library was fractionally ajar. Opening it a few inches at a time, the gap was soon wide enough for him to peer through.

There were two of them.

Dressed in a similar fashion to Jared, they were collecting armfuls of his uncle's books and throwing them around the floor in heaps.

That they were searching for something was obvious, and to Jared it meant one thing: his uncle had died telling them nothing. Smiling mirthlessly, he knew they could rip the library to pieces and still not find what they were looking for, so cleverly had the secret door been hidden. One thought nagged at him. Who had given them the idea there might be a hidden room? In seconds he had it. David Naami was far too intelligent not to have put two and two together and come up with four.

They were so intent on what they were doing, so confident in their invulnerability, they never noticed Jared step soundlessly into the room.

By now there was no need for caution, and so he said calmly, 'Can I help you with something?'

To their credit they showed no signs of panic.

Although taken completely by surprise, they acted in unison.

In a fast and controlled movement, the man furthest from the door threw a book at Jared's head. Lifting his arm in a purely reflex action in order to ward it off, it was all the distraction the killer nearest the door needed. In a split second he'd made his escape and was racing towards the kitchen situated at the rear of the house.

The slight distraction cost the other assassin his life. By the time the book hit the floor, Jared had steadied himself, and in a blur of motion the man was dead, a hole in his chest the size of someone's fist. Such was the impact of the bullet, he was dead before he'd hit the floor.

Spinning on his heels, Jared sped after the first killer while thinking, *Two down, one to go, and I'm going to enjoy it…*

Although his prey had several seconds' start on him, Jared knew where he was heading – the deep dark forest behind his uncle's house. Suddenly he had a thought. Stopping dead in his tracks, he replaced the pistol into its holster and returned to the study. Ignoring the body of his uncle, knowing there was nothing he could for him now, he smashed open one of the glass cases with his elbow. Carefully removed the remaining shards of glass, he selected a hunting crossbow with night scope, knowing from experience it would be ideally suited for what he had in mind. Inserting one bolt, he picked up several others and took them with him.

Heading for the kitchen at a leisurely pace, he realised the assassin was going nowhere. Once he stepped out of the door, the man was entering a killing ground with which he was totally unfamiliar. For Jared it would be different; he would be in his element. To him the darkness was his friend and ally. With that he made his uncle a promise. When he finally caught up with his killer, the bastard would die slowly.

Reaching the kitchen, he hesitated, knowing once he stepped from the door he would be a sitting target. So he killed the light. Now his silhouette would be far more difficult to pick out against the bare stone walls of the kitchen.

Placing the bow and the spare bolts on the floor, he paused for a few moments to regain his night vision after the glare of the kitchen light. He knew the longer he stayed in darkness the more his eyesight would adapt, but he didn't have time for that. If he hadn't missed his guess, the assassin would be sitting on the fringe of the forest, ready to pick him off as soon as he stepped outside. There was only one thing for it, and so, making an instant decision, he hurled himself out of the kitchen door. Tucked into a tight ball, he rolled over and over making himself as small a target as possible.

From past experience he knew a moving target was extremely difficult to hit, far more difficult than paperback novels would have you believe, especially a target moving as quickly as he was.

He'd covered less than a few yards when he heard the first of several coughing sounds as the bullets from the killer's silenced weapon hit the ground a few inches from where he'd been only milliseconds before. Whether it was skill or just plain old-fashioned luck, he never knew, but one bullet came too close for comfort. Kicking up splinters of concrete, he felt one slice into his cheek, even through the balaclava, before seconds later he crashed into the safety of the trees. Getting to his feet quickly, he was rewarded by the sound of footsteps stumbling through the undergrowth.

Smiling to himself, he knew his gamble had paid off. So, returning to the kitchen, he retrieved the bow and steel bolts before setting off in pursuit. He was in no hurry because he knew there was only one way the killer could go. The undergrowth was so dense, the only easy way through was by means of a small animal trail that wound its way up into the mountains beyond.

Breaking into a gentle jog, Jared's footsteps made no sound on the thick carpet of leaves, while the aromatic scent of pine needles filled the night air.

Within several hundred yards, the path became steep, and despite his superb physical condition his body was covered by a thin sheen of perspiration beneath his roll-neck sweater.

There was no need to track the killer, as unknown to him the trail entered a small clearing a mile further ahead; beyond that it was a dead end. Stepping off the path for a few yards was like entering an alien landscape. The tree cover was so dense, the shadows formed by the thick covering of branches so uninviting, it was almost as if civilisation had made no impact on it.

From previous training runs, Jared knew that within a few yards lay a small stream, and it was this he made for, knowing for what he had in mind it would be perfect. Within moments he found it. Kneeling at the side of the bank, he tilted his head to one side.

When he was certain he was alone, he went to work. Taking off his balaclava he checked the gash on his cheek. Fingering it gingerly, he noted that although it was small it was deep. Washing it out with cold clean water made it bleed again, but he knew it would continue to do so until he could get it stitched, and at the moment it was low on his list of priorities.

Drinking a little of the water, he replaced the balaclava over his head before keeping low to the ground and leaving the cover of the tangled undergrowth. He was within a hundred yards of the clearing before he suddenly came to a halt. Stepping quickly into the thick foliage at the side of the trail, Jared could hear his uncle's murderer moving through the woods several feet from where he stood. He was almost soundless, but not quite.

The assassin couldn't put his finger on it, it wasn't anything definitive, but suddenly he had the feeling he was being watched. He hadn't spotted anyone, but some sixth sense or other warned him he wasn't alone.

He passed so close that Jared could smell the stale sweat on his clothes. That was good; if he was sweating heavily it meant he was nervous and if he was nervous he was using up energy more swiftly than he should be. Within moments it was obvious the man was lost. He'd taken a gamble by leaving the track and was now running around in circles; his body language showed clearly he was becoming increasingly frustrated.

And Jared was right on all counts.

Led to believe he was the best, the elite of the elite, it had come as an unpleasant surprise to the assassin to find he was up against someone better than himself. For the first time in his life he felt the faint stirrings of fear, and it provoked an angry desperation in his movements.

Watching from his vantage point in the murky undergrowth, Jared knew the jaws of the trap were closing. Little by little he was moving in for the kill, but more importantly from his perspective the killer knew it. But not yet, Jared told himself, it was too early to take him out yet. For now, the bastard had to suffer, and so he melted back into the shadows. Suddenly the moon peeked out from behind the thick cover of clouds it had been hiding behind. Spreading its silvery glow over the mountain trail, it caught the assassin in full profile. With that a pang of disappointment crossed Jared's features as he realised this wasn't the man he was hoping to catch up with. This wasn't Scorpion.

This man was a stranger.

Startled, the assassin turned on his heel and headed back for the clearing.

Once he was out of sight, Jared stepped out of his hiding place and followed at a brisk trot.

After several minutes spent exploring the little clearing, the assassin understood too late he'd cornered himself, that unless he returned the way he'd come there was no way out.

The open air, which not so long ago had seemed so inviting, symbolic of freedom, now took on a more threatening aspect. Every corner became suspicious and foreboding.

Almost frantic, he was about to dive headlong into the impenetrable foliage, prepared to take his chance that way, when the silence was broken by the cry of a rabbit in its death throes. Already nervous, he was almost on the edge of losing it, when a bird, alarmed by the cry exploded from the branches above his head.

While all this was going on, Jared had wriggled to within inches of the man, stopping only to brush away from his path any small twigs which, if broken, might have accidentally disclosed his whereabouts.

Fighting down his panic, it was the age-old will to survive that forced the assassin on.

Choosing to take the second option, attempting to go back into the dense forest, he took a step forward when suddenly Jared stood up. Using the knife which miraculously appeared in his hand, he inflicted a deep wound on the man's cheek before melting back into the thick cover. Frozen into immobility, the assassin heard the mocking tones of his pursuer carried on the evening breeze. 'I'm sure you enjoyed your little game with my uncle, because of that I'm going to have some fun

seems it's linked to the birth of three people. The first would be the giver of life, which we now know was Edwin. The second would be the destroyer, and the third would be the chosen one. According to the final guardian, this chosen one would be born at the end of the old millennium, and seven years later, at the dawn of the new, would begin to display strange powers that would leave no doubt as to his claim to the title.'

Seeing the puzzlement on their faces, he carried on.

'I know it's tricky, but bear with me for a moment. The old guardian claimed the prophecy was linked to the Book of Revelation, that between them the destroyer and the special child would be strong enough to overpower what it refers to as the Antichrist.'

'Yes,' said Danny, 'but I thought Revelations was supposed to be nothing but symbolism.'

'Until I read what the old guardian told Edwin, so did I, but the clues were there all along. Cast your mind back to a few days ago, to when we spoke about the Apostle John. Didn't we say he was spared the same fate as nine of his fellow Apostles by being banished to the remote island of Patmos? But what if the Antichrist he alluded to in Revelations was a real person?'

'Of course,' said Tina suddenly clicking on. '*Judas!* As an eyewitness to what had happened to his close friends, he would have viewed Judas as the Antichrist, wouldn't he?'

'That was my way of thinking, but if we take it a step further, who would be Judas' representative on earth now? Or to put it another way, the modern version of the Antichrist?'

'The Brotherhood!' shouted Danny.

'Or to be more precise,' said Jared, 'Chameleon Enterprises – and if that's the case, the head of the beast is the Grand Master, David Naami.'

Allowing a few moments for the implications of what he suggested to sink in, he carried on.

'As fanciful as it sounds, it all fits, because you see Chameleon Enterprises is synonymous with everything that's evil in the world today.' Ticking off the points on his fingers for effect he said, 'First we have drugs, arms and prostitution,' before adding, 'and of course, its latest little scam involving illegal immigrants. That's a real money-spinner, let me tell you. Promising to bring them to places like Britain, they cram them into ships and specially adapted road vehicles, like sardines. With very little ventilation and almost no food and water, they invariably die in their thousands. But of course it's no problem, as the Brotherhood receives the money up front.' Seeing their shocked faces, Jared said, 'It's one of their most lucrative trades, believe me, I've seen it at first hand.

'Secondly, you have what I term the more hard-core crimes, and these can be divided into two sections. In the first instance you have the run-of-the-mill arms dealings with factions such as Al-Qaeda, Hezbollah and the like. Weapons like the very latest ground-to-air missiles for bringing down helicopters. Providing the price is right, of course. But think, an organisation as corrupt and ambitious as this can never be content with such things as providing arms to renegades engaged in what they consider to be nothing more than petty squabbles. Oh, no, they've set their sights much higher than that. What they are after is to provide the latest in high technology to the highest bidders, and remember, there are plenty of takers out there. How do they get their hands on such technology? Now that's the question, isn't it? That's their genius, you see. Somehow they're able to penetrate even the highest security areas and get hold of the very latest weapons, some of which are not yet off the blueprint stage. It's their area of expertise.'

By now he could see that several of the others were finding it difficult to accept what he was saying.

Suddenly Danny spoke up. 'But where on earth would they get their hands on some of the real dirty stuff? Things such as plutonium to create a nuclear bomb, I mean. Surely in this day and age with all the security measures guarding places that house things like that, it's impossible to get hold of it? The prelude to the war with Saddam was a prime example of that. After all, that's why Uncle Sam moved in and took him out of the equation. According to the media it was the knowledge that Saddam was either housing weapons of mass destruction, or that he was attempting to create facilities to produce such things, that brought about his downfall.'

'I'm hesitant to give you a lecture on military history, Danny,' said Jared, 'but listen up. For a start, hardly anyone in their right minds now is convinced the USA invaded Iraq for the reasons you just laid out. By now even the most ardent of Americans accept it was done in order to protect its interest in oil. Don't forget, America is the biggest user of petroleum in the world. You've only got to look at how many gas-guzzlers they own per head of population to see that. No, that war was about safeguarding their interest in black gold. I haven't forgotten our role in it all, either. In all honesty our motives were just as dubious, and I should know, I saw much of it at first hand. In that respect, I'm as guilty as hell. Anyway, let's move on for a minute and take a look at good old Saddam himself. Have you ever wondered why he wasn't removed the first time? Remember, he was there for the taking during the first Gulf War, but instead of getting rid of him they left him in place. Ask yourself why? No idea? Well, the answer's simple: they knew that his ruthless method of dealing with the locals, for want of a better word, was the only thing that kept the warring factions in that part of the world in line. American intelligence advised the President that in order to keep peace among the indigenous population, they would be well advised to leave Saddam in charge. To them the atrocities he committed were a small price to pay for stability in that area...'

'If that's the case,' said Danny interrupting, 'then why did they get rid of him the second time around?'

'For want of a better phrase,' said Jared, by now warming to the task, 'he'd got too big for his boots! Outgrown his usefulness, if you want to put it another way. During the first confrontation, it wasn't regarded as expedient to take him out; this time it was. And the rest, as they say, is history. Everything is easy in hindsight, but from where I'm standing it hasn't done anyone much good, has it?'

Seeing Danny didn't understand, he added, 'Look at the mess in Iraq now! In many ways it has simply proven American intelligence's point about leaving the idiot in place. Saddam ruled with the iron fist. True, he was nothing but a psychotic butcher, but at least when he was in charge there was some semblance of leadership, some semblance of order. Now all we have is chaos. At the moment it's a no-win situation for everyone – apart from the rebels, of course,' he added as an afterthought. 'As for your second question, let me turn the tables and ask you one. Were there ever any weapons of mass destruction found? Any means by which any could be produced?' Seeing Danny's blank stare, he said, 'At this point, I rest my case.'

Obviously impressed with Jared's summing up of the situation, Danny said, 'I can see your point, lad, but you still haven't answered my original query. Where the hell would even such a highly sophisticated and powerful organisation as Chameleon Enterprises find the means to produce the kind of weapons of mass destruction we alluded to earlier?'

'Believe it or not, Danny, it's quite easy. You see, since the collapse of the old Soviet Union or Mother Russia, whatever you like to call it, there are literally hundreds of thousands of redundant weapons of all kinds hanging about. Even things like plutonium and enriched uranium are up for grabs... as long as you have the connections, that is. And I have it on good authority that during the last few years David Naami has made friends with a leading figure in the Russian Mafia. From what I can gather, Gregor Borrochev – that's his name by the way – is every bit as crazy as him.'

Smiling, he added, 'By using their influential sources, they can produce nuclear warheads and missiles to order. The clever buggers are even obtaining beryllium and tritium by extracting them from old weapons such as nuclear submarines, ones which were mothballed after the end of the cold war. Apparently they use open air vats where acid burns out the plutonium, after which the sludge is reprocessed. Oh, and I nearly forgot, they've also managed to steal one of Uncle Sam's latest ideas, IM weapons.'

Seeing the blank expressions on their faces, Jared said, 'Improvised Munitions. To cut a long story short, the philosophy behind the idea is to use nature in order to create weapons. For instance, in the Arctic special rifles have been developed which use compacted snow as bullets. Even better are sand bullets. This time the rifle heats the sand into glass projectiles, and then bingo – you've got a limitless supply of ammunition right on your doorstep. All this is a revolutionary concept, of course, but it's amazing, isn't it? Unfortunately, David Naami and his cronies have somehow managed to get their hands on the original blueprints.

'It seems you're having difficulty in getting your heads around such revolutionary concepts, by the look on your faces,' said Jared, 'but believe me, everything I've told you is true, even the IM weapons. As a matter of fact I've tried them out,' he said without a trace of arrogance, 'so I can assure you they work. I could go on longer, but just take my word for it the range of their acquisitions is truly frightening.'

Wanting to get the original discussion back on track, Jared said, 'Anyway, let's get back to the role of David Naami and his relationship to the modern Antichrist. Take the signs of natural destruction

Revelations goes on about, the ones which are supposed to preface the day of Armageddon. The portents are unmistakable. Natural disasters on an unprecedented scale, tsunamis, earthquakes, global warming leading to the melting of the polar ice caps... the facts and figures are all there. You don't have to be an Einstein to work out where it's all leading. To me, however, there's something far more worrying about it all, because from where I'm standing, the Brotherhood are intent on nothing short of world domination. Until now, despite their vast resources they've had limited success. Now Judas has been released from the chalice, it's a different matter. They finally have the means to achieve they're goal.'

'So what you're saying is that if we take the prophecy to its logical conclusion,' said Danny, 'in order to achieve these global aims the Brotherhood has to make their move very soon. In that case, it stands to reason if we're going to have a hope in hell of stopping them, we've got to act quickly. The problem is, none of us have a clue how to go about it.'

'But I have,' said Jared matter-of-factly.

Seeing Danny's stunned expression, he said, 'It's simple. If you want to stop a monster you chop off its head. David Naami is the undoubted genius behind Chameleon Enterprises – correct? So stop him and you stop the Brotherhood. Without his leadership the whole thing grinds to a halt.'

'That's easier said than done,' said Danny. 'We'd never be able to get near him.'

'Not with a small army, you wouldn't,' said Jared, 'but one person might, and I know just the guy.'

'You're good,' said Danny in a serious tone, 'but you're not that good! There's no way on earth you could get anywhere near the bloke. Even if you could, what about the bodyguards he surrounds himself with?'

'What bodyguards? The man is so arrogant he only has a handful, and they're nothing better than hired help. Besides, you're forgetting that originally there were never more than nine elite assassins, his praetorian guard so to speak. The nine became eight when David Naami made an example of Wolf and never replaced him. Then over the course of the last few months, due to one reason or another,' he said smiling, 'the eight became two.'

Looking Danny in the eye, he said, 'Seems you have little confidence in me, Danny, so how about a small wager? I'll not only take out the two remaining assassins, but I'll do it in the next few days. And that's no idle boast, it's a promise!'

Something about the way Jared said it sent a chill down Danny's spine, and it was he who dropped his gaze first.

'Logically, when I take the last two out, Chameleon Enterprises will be effectively finished, for the simple reason apart from the nine, no one else knows about the vault and what it contains. One of the failings of any secret society is that in order to retain its mystique it keeps those in the know to an absolute minimum. True, it's the best way to ensure the secret remains just that, a secret, but there's a fatal flaw in that line of reasoning. Take away the inner cadre and there's no one left to run the ship. Oh, and by the way, when I've finished, I'll make sure nothing will remain of their little empire – lock, stock and smoking barrel as the title of the film famously says. Once it's gone...' He left the rest of the sentence unfinished.

It was Tina who asked the inevitable. 'But, you said the prophecy is a threefold thing, and so for it to come true there would have to be three people. The first is Edwin, but what about the other two? Where are they going to come from?'

'Yes,' said Emma, 'according to the prophecy, Edwin would have had to have fathered a male child – I say male, because a destroyer would hardly likely be a woman – and then that child would have had to have produced a male child of its own. As far as I know Edwin had no children, so there's no way the prophecy can be fulfilled.'

As the implications of what the two women had said sank in, the room fell silent.

'And another thing,' said Danny several moments later, 'the prophecy mentions two millenniums, and that makes no sense either.'

Jared explained how the Roman abbot had made a mistake which had led to the discrepancy in our calendar, and the others could hardly believe their ears.

Recovering the quickest, Emma said, 'Yes, but it still doesn't solve the problem of Edwin's son, does it?'

'But he has a son,' was all Jared said.

The astonishment on Emma's face was a picture, but as Jared related the conversation between him and his uncle, she became more and more incredulous.

Chapter Thirty-nine

TIME WAS OF THE ESSENCE. 28 OCTOBER WAS APPROACHING RAPIDLY and he still had no answers. In truth so far he'd found little that could be regarded as earth-shattering, and so he reasoned everything of value had to have been written in the final chapter.

Suddenly he was there!

Looking at the symbol which prefaced it, he traced the outline with trembling fingers. After 2,000 years the condition was remarkable. Strangely, now he was faced with the moment of truth he was reluctant to continue. Knowing he was only delaying the inevitable, he began translating.

> From the very beginning it must be made clear that Jesus had no knowledge of Project Lazarus. In fact when the truth was made known to him he was in despair, feeling he'd not only deceived everyone, but that he was a charlatan. His only crime, if indeed it can be viewed as a crime, was in believing he was the Messiah.
>
> From very early on it was apparent that he was far different to the false prophets who had gone before him. Unfortunately, his charismatic personality ensured he became a victim of his own success. Such was his popularity, that in an incredibly short space of time everyone was convinced he was the long awaited Saviour, the chosen one spoken of in the Scriptures. So convinced was he of the validity of his claim that he was prepared to die and come back three days later in order to prove it. What was I to do?
>
> Was I the only one who could see the disastrous consequences of his being wrong, of his failure to return as promised?
>
> Imagine my consternation. Sitting on the sidelines I was powerless to do anything but watch, until suddenly the idea came to me.
>
> It would have to be a closely guarded secret, the number kept to an absolute minimum. After all, there were so many people who would have to be taken in: the Roman authorities, including Pilate, and then of course

there would be the eyewitnesses crowding the cross like bloodthirsty vultures. In particular, though, the Apostles would have to be convinced. As a result I decided on only four people. Besides myself, there was to be Mary, Jesus' mother, Nicodemus and finally Mary Magdalene, who, as his wife and mother of his child, had to be included.

At first the logistics of the whole affair seemed almost insurmountable, but from my point of view there was no alternative, the consequences of failure a disaster. From what Jesus and Judas had arranged between them, it was obvious he expected the crucifixion to take place on the Friday, the eve of the Sabbath. It was here I took a gamble. I calculated roughly how long it would take for Pilate to pass sentence, how Jesus would react to the questioning, but in particular the answers he would give.

It wasn't difficult, because he wanted to die. I knew he wouldn't defend himself, and so the verdict was cut and dried: 'Treason'. After everything that had gone on before, it could be nothing less, and because of that he would be scourged and crucified. More importantly for what I had in mind, it would limit the time he would be left hanging on the cross. Following the Jewish custom, he would have to be taken down before the beginning of Sabbath, which according to my calculations would allow a maximum of four hours, and I knew full well people had survived for far longer than that.

After that the rest was relatively easy.

I already owned a property near Golgotha, the Hill of the Skull, where the crucifixion would take place, and so the tomb was ready and waiting. Private, away from prying eyes, it was perfect for the next stage of the operation.

One of the most essential parts of the plan was to make it look as if Jesus had really died on the cross, while at the same time ensuring Jesus himself knew nothing about it.

The answer when it came to me was simple; he would have to be drugged. It must be stage-managed to look as if Jesus had died prematurely, and as luck had it, the scheme worked perfectly. It wasn't unusual for a refreshing drink to be administered to a dying man and so no suspicions were aroused.

The following part of the plan was the trickiest, and as soon as he lapsed into unconsciousness, his head dropping onto his chest in the classic posture of death, I made my move.

Seeking an audience with Pilate wasn't difficult. As an important member of the Sanhedrin, that was no problem. It was the next part that worried me, and as I guessed, Pilate was suspicious when I asked for the body. He was astonished to hear Jesus had died so quickly, but I had already pre-empted that. I made a great deal of the intensity of the scourging, and then I produced my ace. As a final precaution I'd paid a soldier to drive a spear into Jesus' side. He had orders to make it look good – a flesh wound only, but one that produced plenty of blood.

Still not convinced, Pilate sent one of his soldiers to check on my story with the centurion in charge. When he returned shortly afterwards with confirmation, he grudgingly gave his consent.

From here on in the women's task was vital. The body had to be taken to the tomb as quickly as possible and Jesus patched up in readiness for moving him that night. It involved a certain amount of risk, since we might have been spotted; but more importantly from the point of view of Jesus' health, but it had to be done.

The spices and linen bandages, along with everything else that were required for a speedy recovery, were already in place. For a while I was worried that someone might notice that the spices placed in the tomb were those associated with healing rather than the normal ones for preparing the body for burial. Again I took a chance.

During the night we smuggled him away, giving credence to the idea that he'd risen from the grave. We took him to a property I owned on the outskirts of Jerusalem, where for the next few days he received the best possible care and attention. Even so it was touch and go for a while, and it was several more days before he was in a fit state to walk. The most difficult part of the whole charade from my point of view was convincing Jesus that everything had been done with his best interests in mind. Eventually, after much soul-searching and persuasion, he agreed to go along with the scheme. The final part of the operation proved to be the most troublesome. Convincing Jesus that in order to perpetuate the myth that he'd risen from the dead would involve making several personal appearances proved almost impossible, for the simple fact that his conscience was troubling him dearly. Eventually he gave in, and of course as far as I was concerned it was the final confirmation that my carefully orchestrated plan would work.

Some time later, when it appeared everyone was satisfied and the fledgling religion was going from strength to strength, I decided he should be smuggled overseas, along with Mary Magdalene and the boy child. After a short stay in France, I eventually moved them to Glastonbury, a safe place in my estimation, as no one had the slightest idea who they were.

So he'd been right after all, was Jared's stunned reaction. It was what he'd feared all along. Now he had incontrovertible proof of the fact, he was uneasy, he was unsure as to what to do with the information. One thing was sure, he had to tell Eric before doing anything else, thinking at the same time that if he hadn't missed his guess he would only be confirming what Eric already suspected.

Sitting in Eric's armchair, watching him pour himself a stiff whisky, Jared was struck by the fact that this time there was no tea.

Accepting the file from Jared's trembling fingers, Eric's first thought was that Jared looked pale and drawn, realising if that were the case, he now knew the truth about Project Lazarus.

Deciding to be cagey just in case he was wrong, he said, 'I'm sorry to hear of Edwin's death, but if it's any consolation I can give my permission for him to be buried here in Carmel next to your parents and Robert. When the old chapel was sold off, the deacons made sure there was a clause in the contract outlining the fact that as long as there were people alive who were members of Carmel then they would have a right to a burial there. I know Edwin can't really be said to have been a member, far from it,' he chuckled. 'However, I'm sure we can make out a case for him on the grounds that as a youngster he attended Sunday school on a regular basis.'

'On a regular basis?' said Jared, nearly choking. 'I'm afraid you're being a little sparing with the truth there, aren't you? From what my father – Tommy, that is,' he murmured, 'told me, it took wild horses to drag him to Sunday school, and sometimes even they weren't enough!'

Wondering why Jared should falter when he came to mentioning his father, Eric dismissed it as a slip of the tongue and forgot about it. Instead he carried on as if nothing had happened. 'Be that as it may,' said Eric, knowing the same story, 'it can be arranged. I'm sure I can persuade the powers that be to bend the rules a little for you. That is, if you want to, I mean. I could even conduct the service, if you'd like.'

With a start Jared suddenly realised he hadn't had time to tell Eric about his uncle's... there I go again, he thought... his *father's* letter. Wondering how to go about it, he finally threw caution to the wind and told him the whole story.

After listening quietly throughout, Eric didn't bat an eyelid, which made Jared suspicious he might have guessed already. Strangely, his grandmother's reaction had been something similar.

'Before you ask, no, I didn't know; but you're right, I guessed. The way you look, the way you act, your personality, but in particular your academic ability made me wonder. Don't think me insensitive, under the circumstances and all, but the offer is still open, regarding the burial, I mean.'

'I'd like that very much, Eric, but you know it's funny; despite everything I still look on Tommy as my real father. I can't do anything else. To me he was the best father you could ever wish for.' With that he had a sudden thought. 'You don't think he knew, do you?'

'I'd be surprised if he didn't,' was Eric's honest reply. 'He may not have been in your uncle's, sorry, *father's* league up here,' he said, tapping the side of his head with his forefinger. 'But take it from me, TV was a shrewd old character. I'm sure just like me he had his suspicions.'

'In that case he was even more of a wonderful person,' said Jared, stunned. 'Do you know, he never once differentiated between my brother and me, never once showed him any favours. That was the true character of the man.'

'I'm glad you can look at it like that, Jared, because believe me, many men wouldn't have been able to hide their true feelings. Every time they looked at you, they would have been reminded of their wife's infidelity, even if it was only the one time, "a moment of madness after drink", as Edwin described it. He must have truly loved your mother... and she him, might I add.'

'Funnily enough, that's what Edwin said in his letter.'

For many moments they were lost in contemplative silence, before Eric broke it.

'So you translated the final chapter of the codex? It's written all over your face... and yes, I know what's coming. And if I'm not mistaken it came as no real surprise to you, either, did it?'

Smiling, Jared said, 'You've know for some time, haven't you?'

'Known might be too strong a word; perhaps suspected might be a better description. So Joseph admits to the whole thing then, does he?'

Handing over the file, Jared said, 'It's all there, warts and all.'

Some time later when he'd finished reading, Eric said, 'Ingenious, bloody ingenious! But the clues were there all along if you could be bothered to look for them. The one thing I am pleased about is that Jesus never took part in the deception. Only towards the end, that is, and then only when he realised the alternative was infinitely more dangerous. You see, I had suspected at one time he might have been involved, and in that case...' He trailed off.

'But there's more, isn't there? There's something you're not telling me.'

'Before I go into that,' said Jared, 'what did you mean when you said the clues were there all along?'

Mentally placing the information in convenient boxes in his mind, Eric began. 'For a start, the only one capable of pulling off something like that would have been Joseph. He was the perfect man in every way, close to Jesus, his secret eyes and ears within the Jewish parliament, rich, influential and immensely powerful. Only a man with such qualities could have hoped to have been successful.

'Secondly, Joseph, being a practical man, would have been the only one level-headed enough to stand back and look at the wider picture, the only one to have realised the horrific consequences of Jesus' failure to return from the dead…'

Breaking in, Jared said, 'Strangely, that echoes Joseph's words exactly.'

'Thirdly, we have the evidence – or lack of it, whichever way you want to look at it – from the Gospels.' Pointing to Jared, he said, 'And of course we mustn't forget Judas' role in all this,' before chuckling and adding, 'he hasn't, that's a certainty. As you guessed, without his participation, none of what followed later would have been possible. I've got to admire the devious old bastard. He took several calculated risks, but as we now know, they paid off. His main worry must have been whether Jesus would survive long enough to be nursed back to health by the women. He wouldn't have known it, of course, but the odds were in his favour. The first-century historian Josephus gives us proof of just how long a person could survive crucifixion when he describes an incident in which he was an eyewitness. It involved three prisoners who it turned out were acquaintances of his. Horrified, he goes directly to Titus, the general in command of the region and asks for their release. Successful in his plea, they were taken down shortly afterwards, and upon being administered the best possible treatment, one survived. The point of the story is that contrary to popular belief, it was possible to recover after crucifixion. And that character was hanging on the cross for considerably longer than Jesus, may I add. Remember, according to John's Gospel, Jesus' ordeal lasted barely three hours.

'Then we have the man with the cane,' he said, on a roll now. 'The one who fed Jesus the drugged wine. There's never been any doubt in my mind that he was in the pay of Joseph. Note how the Gospels say that the sponge soaked in vinegar and held to Jesus' mouth was given only to him. Neither of the other two crucified with him were offered it. As such, we can discount it being an act of mercy on compassionate grounds. Incidentally, it wasn't vinegar as we know it, but vinegar wine. It was the cheapest possible wine, the dregs, or rotgut, as we call it today. Given to the soldiers to augment their pay, they used it to dip their stale bread in, to make it slightly more palatable. Interestingly, in Mark's Gospel this incident takes place just after Jesus cries, "My God, my God, why hast thou forsaken me?" As the words were given in Aramaic, "*Eloi, Eloi, lama sabachtani*", some bystanders thought he was calling for Elijah. To me, the man who'd given the drink to Jesus saw the opportunity it presented and turned the words to his own advantage. By mocking Jesus and saying, "Let's see if Elijah will come to take him down", he turned suspicion away from himself. Very clever bit of improvisation, that, I must admit. I know it's only a theory, but I believe the above scenario is the only one that adequately accounts for so much that is otherwise unexplainable.

'The fourth Gospel has some curious additions too, and if what it says is true: the two robbers on either side of Jesus had their legs broken to hasten death. A truly barbaric ritual, it involved the use of a huge wooden club, something you might see in an episode of *The Flintstones*, but it was often made even more effective by the addition of small stones embedded into the wood. Anyway, they smashed this across the shins of people who appeared stubborn. The shock and pain made sure they died almost immediately.'

Clearly enjoying himself now, Eric said, 'Incidentally, do you know how people died when they were crucified?'

Shaking his head, Jared indicated he hadn't a clue.

'Strangely, it wasn't because of the pain or the injuries they sustained by being scourged, but instead they died of suffocation.'

Seeing Jared's puzzled expression he said, 'The only way to ease the pain and suffering on your body was to lift yourself onto your toes, that way your lungs were clear. The problem was, the weaker you became the harder it was to do. In the end you gave up, and once that happened the head flopped onto the chest and the lungs collapsed, hence suffocation.

'Now, where was I before I was sidetracked? Ah, yes, seeing Jesus was already dead there was no need to smash his legs; instead a soldier thrust a spear into Jesus' side. Now that was a stroke of genius on

Joseph's part because I suspect that when he went to ask for the body of Jesus – and note he specifically asked for the 'body' and not "corpse" – in order to bury it in his private tomb, Pilate was suspicious.'

'Before reading the final chapter in the codex,' said Jared, 'I would have said that would have been defeating the object – that it would have probably finished him off.'

'No, you see that's the touch of genius I was alluding to. I'll wager Joseph was gambling that Pilate would have been thinking along the same lines as you. All he had to do to cover this eventuality was to pay one of the guards at the cross to plunge a spear into his side. Remember, these guys were professionals so it would have been easy for him to create a superficial wound, one deep enough to ensure a copious amount of blood, but nowhere near deep enough to prove fatal. Jesus was already unconscious, so he would have felt no pain or even been aware of anything untoward. From a medical point of view, the fact that blood was still flowing from Jesus' side after he was supposed to be dead, only confirms to me that in fact Jesus was still very much alive.'

'But a Roman soldier couldn't have been bribed that easily,' said Jared, 'surely?'

'Don't you believe it! A soldier's pay was a pittance. Many joined up either because they couldn't find anything else, or they'd been forced into it as a member of a defeated army. The choice was simple: join us or die. Either way, the soldier would have jumped at the opportunity to supplement what was in reality a non-existent wage. And before you say it, no, he wouldn't have spoken about it afterwards. Even sleeping on duty brought the death penalty, so taking a bribe would have been seen as much worse.'

Looking up, Eric said, 'What does the Gospel of Mark have to say about it all? And don't forget, we're talking about the first Gospel written, so theoretically it should have been the most accurate. I can see that you know as well as I do that there's no mention of Jesus rising from the dead after three days. Even as a young student, I was always suspicious about Mark's ending, convinced in my own mind he never wrote anything after chapter 16 verse 8. Suggestions by misguided scholars trying to defend Christianity, that there originally was a resurrection story, but that it had somehow been burnt in a fire, or that the original words had been lost, cut no ice with me. If you look even more closely, Mark 16, verses 19–20, the so-called "longer ending", doesn't really stand up to serious scrutiny either. They can't be found on several of the early manuscripts, including the two oldest Greek versions – Codex Sinaiticus and Vaticanus.' He paused. 'Want me to go on?'

Seeing Jared's nod, he said, 'In that case, even more worrying is the fact that some manuscripts which do contain the passages show clear signs that copyists considered the verses to be a later addition. In other words they'd been tampered with. Yet despite all the evidence to the contrary, for most Christians the physical resurrection of Jesus is the basis for their whole faith. Without it there would be no Christianity.'

Then, with a ghost of a smile he added, 'Even the august St Paul, it seems, had his doubts. In 1 Corinthians he states, and I quote:

' "And if Christ has not risen, then our preaching is in vain, and your faith is also in vain." '

'Even worse,' said Jared in a hushed tone, 'then Christianity would appear to be based on a lie.'

'Your words, not mine,' was Eric's comment.

After several moments of contemplative silence, Eric said, 'I've done my bit, so let's have it, what have you've been keeping back from me?'

It was then Jared dropped his bombshell.

'The sacrifice which imprisoned Judas in the chalice was Jesus.'

Watching the play of emotions which crossed Eric's face, he realised that for once he'd taken him completely by surprise.

'But it makes no sense,' was Eric's initial response.

Seeing that Jared was about to react to his comment, he stopped suddenly. 'But of course, how stupid of me! It makes all the sense in the world, doesn't it? Correct me if I'm wrong, but this was Jesus' chance to make amends, to atone for what he did all those years ago, or rather what he *didn't* do all those years ago. Am I right?'

'Exactly,' said Jared. 'Or put another way, he probably saw it as the perfect opportunity to rid himself of something that had been hanging over him for decades, what he regarded as "the shadow of the cross". Do you want a potted version or would you like to take a few educated guesses?'

Weary now, as if the finality of what he'd just heard had taken its toll, Eric slumped back into his chair, a tired old man. 'If it's all right with you, I'd rather listen,' was all the reply he could muster.

'It doesn't explain how they came up with the idea that sacrifice was the only way to get rid of the creature,' said Jared, 'but it seems Jesus came to the conclusion early on. From what I could glean from the codex, it seems he and Joseph argued at great length about what he saw as Jesus throwing his life away. Wasn't above a little emotional blackmail, either, was old Joseph, but I'll get to that in a moment. According to Joseph's account, if the sacrifice was accepted or deemed worthy, the evil would have no option but to be forced back into the ashes where, as long as the lid was sealed firmly, the blood would ensure it would remain imprisoned.'

Pulling a piece of paper from his pocket, Jared said, 'From here on in I'll quote Joseph's own words; it seems more appropriate that way, somehow.

'Finally I had to admit defeat. Jesus was right, his selfless sacrifice was the only way in which to put an end to the vile creature's orgy of bloodshed. Realising I'd given in, he said to me in a voice as old as time, "Don't look so sad, old friend, you know how long I have waited for a chance to redeem myself. You of all people know how I have wrestled with my conscience over the years. Don't you see, I finally have an opportunity to put things right. Rather than be sad, glorify in the fact I will soon be with my father in heaven."

'The serene look on his face as he spoke convinced me more than words ever could that his mind was made up. I'd lost the battle to persuade him otherwise. In a vain attempt, I made one last desperate plea, I asked him what was to become of David, how was he going to cope without his father? For a moment, a look of pure anguish crossed his face; it was for an instant only and then it was gone. All he said to me was, "Leave that to me, old friend; besides, David is a grown man now. He will understand. Some day he might even be proud of me, who knows. One thing is certain, he will want for nothing, I know you will see to that."

'By the following morning everything had been resolved. I never knew how he told them or what was said, and in many ways I was grateful. Coward that I am, I couldn't face it.

'The sacrifice was simple, involving a swift cut across both wrists. Holding them over the open chalice, I watched his life force drip away inexorably, and could do nothing about it.

'As he grew weaker he asked me to hold him, as he felt suddenly cold. His last words before he passed away chilled my very bones. Although by now he had only moments to live I heard them clearly:

' "Father, into thy hands I commit my spirit – finally it is over!" '

444

Chapter Forty

DANNY THOUGHT JARED LOOKED TIRED, BUT IT WAS LITTLE WONDER, he reflected, after everything he'd been through recently. There was no doubt he'd called the meeting to explain what the last chapter contained. Looking at his body language, he prepared himself for bad news. Running his eyes over those present, Jared tried to judge their mood. He was looking for excitement, curiosity – anything to suggest that they realised the enormity of what they'd been summoned for. What he saw was a mixture of several emotions but perhaps the overriding one was trepidation.

'Glad you could all make it,' were Jared's opening words. 'I've finally managed to complete the translation. Before I go any further, could I ask how many of you regard yourselves as Christians?'

A quick show of hands revealed they all were – even Danny, which came as no surprise, as he'd originally been brought up in the valleys at a time when religion was not only fashionable, but in some professions a necessity.

'In that case, I sincerely advise you to think long and hard before listening to what the last chapter says. As for the symbol which precedes it, we were right. Should whatever I'm about to reveal to you become public knowledge, it would most certainly signal the death of Christianity.'

Allowing a few moments for the message to sink in, he said, 'Then I take it you all want to know?' Double-checking, he made sure to make eye contact with everyone, looking for the slightest sign of doubt or hesitation. Seeing there was none, he said, 'In that case, on your own heads be it.'

Lifting the file from the table where he'd placed it moments before, he began reading.

It took nearly thirty minutes and he held nothing back.

First he read out Joseph's story word for word, before going on to explain Eric's comments. He made no mention of the fact both he and Eric had guessed what the final chapter contained.

Finally, he explained who it was had given his life in order to imprison the evil in the chalice.

When he'd finished, he realised that for the whole of the time he'd been speaking, no one had interrupted. No one had spoken a single word; such was the depth of feeling caused by the revelation. The silence seemed to drag on interminably before Jared decided to break it.

'I did warn you – and before anyone asks, no, there is no mistake. The only possible way the story could be wrong is if the whole thing is an elaborate hoax, the codex a brilliantly constructed fake. There is always the slim possibility of that, of course, and without detailed testing of the ink, the grammar and radiocarbon dating, we can never be sure.'

Pausing he said, 'But in the light of everything we already know, I don't think there's much chance of that.'

Suddenly a quavering voice broke into everyone's thoughts.

'As far as I'm concerned,' said Emma, 'it doesn't make any difference. If the codex is an accurate account of what really happened and Jesus' death was stage-managed, to me it's irrelevant.'

'How can you possibly say that, Em?' said Jared in a soothing voice, mindful of the fact he was broaching sacred ground, treading on eggshells.

'Simple,' she replied in a voice full of conviction. 'The codex makes it perfectly clear that Jesus knew nothing about Project Lazarus, knew nothing about Joseph's deceit. If that's the case, then he was totally innocent of any attempt at faking his own death. In fact he admits it took him years to get it out of his system, to ease his conscience. And again, as soon as he saw the opportunity to atone for Joseph's duplicity, he took it. So in the long run he made up for it, didn't he?'

'I suppose you could look at it that way,' said Jared. 'It's certainly an interesting interpretation. But to me it seems you're missing the point.'

'As a non-believer, you would think that,' countered Emma, 'but to me what Jesus did, the sacrifice he made, makes him all the more human; something which is sadly lacking in the way he's portrayed in the Gospels. Now I know that he was a genuine human being and not simply God's little clone, he appears far more approachable. And remember, in the end he suffered and died for us, that's what counts. I've never admitted to it, but like thousands of Christians the world over, I've found that the resurrection has bothered me, and not the part about coming back from the dead, the fact that if he was the son of God he cheated. According to those ideas, he never knew love, or suffered pain or despair. Oh, I know the Church came up with the idea of the Trinity to try and explain how he was three different things rolled into one, but it was so complicated even they didn't really understand what it was all about. Let's face facts; it doesn't really make any sense, does it? From my point of view, it's always been a poor attempt to explain away what is basically unexplainable. No, if Joseph's account is an accurate rendering of what really happened, then it paints an entirely new picture of Jesus. It forces us to look at him in a whole new light. Now that I know he was *married* – and to a prostitute, of all people – it proves he experienced not only love, but displayed forgiveness. It means he practised what he preached, doesn't it? More importantly, it now throws open all kinds of new possibilities. Far from being depressed, I'm elated – and for the simple reason that it makes Jesus all the more meaningful to me.'

Astonished at Emma's reasoning, Jared nevertheless had to admit she had a good point. 'I never looked at it in that way, but I suppose you're right. In that case his sacrifice was not only for his family and friends, but for everyone he felt he'd let down originally.' He added, 'And don't forget had he not done so, Judas' spirit would probably have gone on killing indefinitely. In that way he certainly made up for it, didn't he?'

Listening to all this, Roger, ever the pragmatist, couldn't hold back any longer; he'd bitten his tongue long enough. 'If he was such a wonderful person – loving caring, unselfish and all that – then how come when he regained consciousness he went along with Joseph's little plan? After all is said and done, whichever way you want to dress it up, he still deceived everyone, but in particular his closest friends, the Apostles. Instead of bringing things into the open, he went along with the charade, pretending he was the son of God brought back to life. Why didn't he just come out and tell everyone what had happened? Surely that would have been the honest thing to do? No, sorry, Em, I can't agree with your reasoning, I'm afraid.'

It was Jared who took up the challenge.

'The answer to your question is easy, Rog. By now Jesus realised things had gone too far. By owning up to the plot, it would have done far more harm than good. Remember, despite all its faults, millions believe Christianity has done more good than harm. If Jesus left behind nothing else, he left a legacy the world owes a debt of gratitude to.

Condense his teachings into one sentence and the worlds problems would be solved overnight: "Love your neighbour as yourself", or put in simple terms, "Treat other people as you would want them to treat you". Strip away all the fancy theological interpretation the Church has imposed on his teachings and his ideas are very simple. What's left is human nature at its most fundamental. Let's take a topical example: violence and aggression. It goes without saying that before you perform either, you have to think about them. Violent actions aren't conjured up from thin air. As a man of peace who hated all kinds of violence, Jesus knew that and it's why he refers to the heart as the 'seat of evil' in the Gospels. The point he was making is that aggressive acts first appear or take root in the heart. Once these ideas are allowed to germinate, they flourish and then they move from there to the brain. So what's the answer? It's simple; before you act on these thoughts, stop and count to ten. Why? There is an instant and an instant only when evil can be stopped in its tracks. And counting to ten allows the brain to interpret and then filter out such aggressive tendencies before they can take root.'

Pausing for a moment, Jared then continued, 'Take it a step further, to evil thoughts and words.' Looking from face to face, he added, 'Unless you are perfect, then each one of us knows exactly what I'm on about. In this case, Jesus' advice is even more simple. The next time any of us feels the need to say something evil about someone we know, use the safety valve – count to ten! It allows the brain to compute the fact that it would be very unhappy if those same things were said about us. It's exactly the same principle as I mentioned earlier, except that this time it's a three-way process and not two. The evil thought comes from the heart, moves to the brain and, unless you stop it, pops out of your mouth. Once that happens, it's too late, isn't it? You can't take the words back. The damage has been done!'

Letting his gaze wander over each of them individually for dramatic effect, he said, ' "Oh, I wish I hadn't said that." Ring any bells? So you know exactly the point I'm making. Anyway, that's all Jesus was trying to say. Put everything together and his philosophy was devastatingly simple. Taken to its logical conclusion, if everyone did what Jesus advocated – in other words, engaged the brain before the mouth – there would be no violence, racism, hatred, suffering or greed. In plain, simple language, there would be no wars; the need for aggression would have been eradicated. Then and only then would his vision for humanity come to fruition. Peace on earth and goodwill to all mankind would be a reality and not empty rhetoric.'

Letting a few moments for his words to sink in, Jared gave a rueful smile before adding, 'In all fairness, I'm not so sure I'm the right person to try and explain Jesus' philosophy to you. With my past record, I mean.'

The silence which followed was deafening, until finally Jared broke it.

'Anyway, now you know the facts, what are you saying? That we leave well alone? That we don't breathe a word of what's in the codex to anyone?'

Surprisingly it was Eric, silent when the debates had been raging, who decided to step into the breach. Jared had noted how he'd not once interrupted, and it suddenly dawned on him that listening was an art, one that he'd perfected. At that moment Jared appreciated that good listeners made good friends. Perhaps that's why he and Emma had been so comfortable in each other's company. Fond memories rose to the surface, and he recalled the times they'd simply held each other, neither saying a word, blissfully happy just to be in each other's company. Neither had felt the need to talk for the sake of it. The periods of silence between them had simply been another way of showing their love for each other. He'd often heard that some couples, especially when they first met, underwent long periods of silence which sometimes seemed to drag on interminably, and then in desperation they attempted to fill it in with small talk. Contrived as it was, it never worked.

With a start he remembered where he was.

Annoyed, he reminded himself this was not the time for nostalgia; there was important work to be done. Concentrating again, he was just in time to hear Eric's words.

'I agree with everything Emma said, but even more with Jared's wonderfully insightful comments. In all my years as a minister I've never heard anyone explain Jesus' attitude regarding people's responsibility to others put so simply and profoundly. However, if I may make an observation, we seem to be missing an important point. Should we decide to disclose what we know, the results could turn out to be catastrophic. You see, so far we've been giving personal opinions; but what about the bigger picture? As corrupt as many of our systems of belief are, they're all we have. Take them away and all that's left is chaos.

'Let's take an example out of context, the police. I've very little time for them myself. The last few years have shown how corrupt the system is, but that's only a few examples. Ninety per cent of the police are hard-working, honest people, trying hard against insurmountable odds to bring some level of law and order into a corrupt world. We seem fond of looking at the bad in everything and ignoring the good. Take the police away, and what have we left?'

Seeing he'd made his point, that he had their full attention, he suddenly looked directly at Jared. 'Without the police and other systems of law enforcement, the law of the jungle would prevail. God knows its bad enough in some areas now, but without them, I dread to think what would happen. The same thing might apply here. Try and imagine the scenario: in one fell swoop billions of people world wide would lose their reason for living. Leaderless, they would be almost suicidal. No, I propose we keep quiet, leave well alone. The world isn't ready for such a revelation.'

'What if we take it a step further,' said Jared, 'and burn the bloody thing? That way, no one would be any the wiser. Only we few in this room would know, and let's be fair, without the codex, we would be publicly ridiculed if we dared suggest such a thing. I'm not saying that, like Eric and me, certain people, and some in high places, might have their suspicions, but without proof it's only idle speculation.'

'Aren't you forgetting something?' said Danny, butting in. 'The Brotherhood know, and they have documentary evidence.'

'No, Danny, they don't, they know about Jesus being married. It's what they used to blackmail the Catholic Church down through the centuries, but unlike us they know nothing of the finer points about the prophecy of the Red Serpent and Project Lazarus.'

'I'm still not sure in my own mind about that,' said Danny suddenly. 'I know your late uncle – sorry, *father* – was the bringer of life, and that it follows you as his son are the destroyer. But how can you be certain about it all? Where's the proof?'

'Simple,' said Jared. 'The three mentioned in the prophecy would have a distinguishing mark. That way there could be no mistake.'

Unbuttoning his shirt and taking it off, he turned his back to them.

Swivelling his head so he could be heard, he said, 'Until all this came about, I was totally unaware of its true meaning. Like everyone else who knew about it, I imagined it was just a red birthmark.'

Turning around again, he said to Danny, 'So what did you see?'

'A red snake or rather a coiled serpent… small, but once you know what you're looking for its clearly recognisable.'

Engrossed as they were in looking at the mark, no one was aware of Emma's gasp of astonishment.

'And to answer your next question, no, I'm not married, nor do I have a child, which according to the prophecy I must have in order to bring it to fruition. So in all honesty I haven't a clue how the prophecy is going to work.'

Smiling, he said, 'I think I'm going to have to leave God sort that bit out. After all, he's better at things like that than me isn't he? What's the saying? "He works in mysterious ways…" '

Suddenly there was a knock on the door. It was opened abruptly and a uniformed PC stuck her head through. 'Sorry to interrupt, guv, but there's a phone call from New York, and incidentally he's on hold.'

Seeing the astonished look on Danny's face, she shrugged her shoulders in a gesture which indicated she didn't have a clue as to who it was.

'Be back in a minute,' said Danny, turning to the others and hurrying from the room.

As it turned out, he was gone considerably longer than a minute, which prompted a thought from Jared that he was glad he wasn't footing the bill.

When Danny returned it was apparent something was terribly wrong. His face was ashen and his shoulders had slumped in a gesture of dismay.

'Don't tell me I got the dates wrong!' exclaimed Jared. 'Has the bastard moved his deadline forward now he knows were on to him?'

'I'm afraid it's infinitely worse than that,' before going on to explain.

'That was Eddie Carmellini, a guy I met years ago on a course in New York. We got friendly and have remained on good terms ever since. In this instance it's lucky we did. He was trying to get hold of a "Brit", as he politely called him, code-named "guardian", and when he failed, he thought of me. As soon as he told me about the tip-offs he'd been receiving, how each had been designed to hurt David Naami, I knew who he was talking about. When I explained he'd been killed, he said in that case the ball was my court. He explained how he'd overheard a conversation during his latest bust which was chilling in its implications. Apparently the organisation was getting ready to wipe out an entire population, or to be more precise an entire village. Looking up the name of the village proved a nightmare; it took him ages to locate it.' Pausing for a moment, Danny said, 'Want to take a stab at the name? No? I thought not...

'Anyway, he went on to say how surprisingly it was not David Naami's brainchild, but someone far worse, who – and I use his words – "Had become tired of the game, so was going to take every single person out in one fell swoop". Incidentally the guy in charge of the operation was code-named Scorpion.'

At the mention of the name, Danny looked over at Jared and saw an instant reaction.

'The bad news is the guy managed to escape along with a small canister. Originally there were two, but thanks to Eddie's timely intervention he was forced to leave the other behind. Unfortunately, knowing what it is, one will be more than enough for what the Brotherhood have in mind.'

Pausing for effect, he carried on, 'The little package he took with him was a steel canister some ten inches high and four inches in diameter. Fairly innocuous, you would have thought, as far as weapons go, it's—'

He never completed what he was going to say, as suddenly Jared broke in, '*Sealed*, so that nothing can escape, and carries a very distinctive yellow and black motif! Dear God, the bastards intend using a biological weapon to wipe us out!'

'I'm afraid you're right,' was Danny's reply, 'and the problem is that Eddie doesn't have a clue what we're up against. Although the other aluminium container is intact, the powers that be refuse to acknowledge its existence. Not that it would do much good; there's no guarantee the same stuff was in both canisters. So you see, as from this moment, we're faced with a whole new ball game.'

'That may be the case,' said Jared, 'but I wouldn't let it worry you.'

'*Worry me!* exploded Danny. 'What the hell's got into you? We're talking about something that's going to wipe out every single person in Raven's Hill, and you say not to worry! Have you gone out of your fucking mind?'

It was the first time Jared had heard Danny swear as badly as this, especially in front of the women, and that he had done so was an indication of just how rattled he was.

'As I said,' continued Jared, totally unruffled, 'there really is nothing to worry about. At the last meeting, I promised you I'd take care of both David Naami and Chameleon Enterprises. At that time there were a few things to sort out first, a few delicate items to be procured and all that,' he added smiling.

'However the time has arrived for action. By tomorrow, the organisation will no longer pose a threat to anyone. And by the way, Danny, don't forget our little bet – £20, if my memory serves me right.'

When everyone had recovered, Danny said, 'OK, I'll take your word for that, but in case you've forgotten, we're still left with one problem. Even though you managed to translate the codex, we're still no nearer finding a way to get rid of Judas. According to my estimation, saints seem to be rather thin on the ground these days!'

Serious now Jared said, 'Looking at it from my perspective, it was me who got us into this mess in the first place, so as far as I'm concerned, it's my responsibility to get us out of it. Take it from me, I'll deal with both problems in my own way.' When it seemed that all the arguments had been exhausted and no one had anything left to say, an expectant hush fell over the gathering. It was broken by Jared. Pointing to the file on the table, he said, 'As for that, each of us has had our say on the matter, and whatever you decide to do I'll go along with. Before I go, though, I'd like to make it clear that whatever happens from here on in, it's been a pleasure working with you all. For better or for worse, this thing with David Naami and the Brotherhood finishes tonight!'

With that he spun on his heels and left the room.

Chapter Forty-one

AFTER A TENTATIVE START, JARED GRADUALLY GAINED IN CONFIDENCE until in moments he was making steady headway. Taking the aluminium staircase two steps at a time, he made his way effortlessly up the inside of the enclosed steel cage that formed the safety barrier of the fire escape. Like a phantom, he kept to the dark side, knowing that in doing so, the deep shadows would help mask his presence.

Pausing for a moment to take in a deep lungful of the clear night air, he suddenly felt he was in his element. The rush of adrenaline that coursed through his body was what he lived for; he loved being on the edge. For him there was no other feeling like it.

Despite this, he was under no illusion about the consequences should he fail in his task. Such was his confidence in his own ability, however, that he knew failure was extremely unlikely, especially when the fires of revenge burnt so brightly within him.

At the peak of his physical fitness, he was hardly out of breath when he reached the final step. Within seconds he'd picked the lock of the safety gate and was standing on the roof of the building.

Stopping for a moment to take in the panoramic view, he jerked the rucksack from his back, and placed it on the surface of the darkened roof. He was pleased to see that despite the rigours of the climb, glistening beads of sweat on his forehead were the only indication that he'd exerted himself.

Removing the crossbow from his back, he had no need to check the bolt it was already in place. Lifting the coil of thin nylon rope from his shoulder, he deftly attached it to the notch in the arrow. Gazing through the telescopic sight and pointing it at his target, he was happy. Then he made a final adjustment to his sights before declaring himself ready.

Making sure the nylon cord was looped behind him and free of any impediment, he made his way slowly forward.

He knew the shot had to be as near as horizontal as possible in order to make climbing easy. Not only was it his means of access, it was his escape route as well. And if things went according to plan, he would probably be leaving in a hurry. If things didn't go well, then that he decided was in the lap of the gods.

Because of that, he suddenly decided on a last minute change of plan. Instead of what he'd originally intended, he would angle his shot slightly upwards. Getting across would require more effort, but it would mean his return journey would be far easier.

Raising the crossbow to his shoulder, he checked once more to see there were no obstructions, before taking steady aim.

Tucking the but firmly into his shoulder, he took a deep breath and eased the trigger gently. There was the slightest hesitation before it kicked into action and the bolt leapt forward effortlessly. Closing the gaping chasm between the two buildings in fractions of a second, it struck the side of the cooling tower within inches of where he'd been aiming.

Pulling hard on the rope, making sure the explosive points of the bolt had done their work, Jared was gratified to see they held firmly. Attaching the other end of the rope to a stench pipe several feet behind him, he was now ready to cross.

Replacing the rucksack on his back, he held the rope in both hands until he was hanging precariously over the void. Then in one lithe movement he lifted his body up and placed his legs over the rope. Encircling it like a monkey, he inched his way forward slowly, a foot at a time, being careful to keep his gaze directly in front of him and not down.

In what seemed no time at all, he was standing on the opposite roof, gazing down at the sign which declared proudly the building was the headquarters of Chameleon Enterprises.

Thanks to the schematics lifted by the old guardian years ago, he knew exactly how to break into the top floor.

The alarms were the least of his worries, as he knew that while a meeting was in progress, they would be deactivated.

Unfortunately that's as far as his plan went. From here on in he would be improvising.

Undeterred, he pushed on and within a short time he was standing inside the boardroom of David Naami and his cronies. The opulence of his surroundings took him by surprise and he wasted several precious moments before he finally managed to drag his mind back to the task in hand.

Knowing exactly where he was heading, he moved soundlessly over the thick pile of the luxurious carpet, taking care not to come into contact with any of the furniture, which was barely visible in the gloom.

Making directly for the double doors, which he knew were cleverly designed dummies, his one thought was that from now on he needed a bit of luck. Almost immediately his prayers were answered, as he heard the muffled sound of approaching voices.

Flattening himself against the wall, he was only just in time, for almost immediately the door opened and a figure dressed in a white smock displayed with the distinctive motif of the Knights Templar stepped through.

Taking in the situation at a glance, Jared realised the gods must be smiling on him, as the other man had turned back.

The luckless assassin never knew what hit him. Without warning, his windpipe was crushed by a forearm that appeared to be made of steel. Despite knowing the man was dead, Jared took no chances on betraying his presence. Tightening his grip on his forearm by locking his wrist with the other, he tensed, and in one sharp twisting motion, broke the man's neck. Allowing himself a brief smile, he was about to hoist the body onto his shoulder before he realised something was wrong.

Looking carefully at the man's features, it struck him immediately.

According to his calculations there were only two of the original eight left – David Naami and Scorpion. As this body was neither of them, who the hell was it? The only answer he could come up with was that David Naami had panicked, and after all these years had decided to replace Wolf.

Suddenly a more worrying thought came to mind. If he'd decided to recruit one, then why not more? It might be he'd replaced all those which Jared had taken out over the last few months. If that was the case, he might be up against far more formidable opposition than he'd originally anticipated. Not that it made much difference, he told himself grimly. All it meant was that from here on in, he'd have to be extra vigilant.

Picking up the body, he threw it over his left shoulder and pressed on.

He knew entrance to the inner sanctuary was limited to the inner core of the Brotherhood. Only the palm prints of the elite were stored on the computer, and so the dead assassin was essential for the next part of his plan. Suddenly he chuckled to himself mirthlessly. What plan? There was no plan, he reminded himself, ever since he'd entered the building he'd been flying by the seat of his pants.

Making his way forward, he was gratified to see that the way ahead was lit brightly by means of several decorated wall brackets that lined either side of the corridor.

Reaching the door without further incident, he lifted the body into an upright position and placed its hand against the screen. He had one moment of doubt. If the character he was carrying was new, had the organisation had time to enter his specifications onto the mainframe computer? Within seconds he had his answer, as a violet light flashed from left to right and a female voice spoke, 'Your palm print has been recognised, you are now cleared for entry.'

With that, there was a gentle hiss of escaping air before the door opened smoothly inwards.

Afraid the body might be discovered if he left it where it was, Jared hefted it once more onto his shoulder, while at the same time wondering whether the sensors that cross-matched the body's palm print had built-in heat monitors. If so, he might be in trouble, he realised. Getting rid of the corpse was his next priority, and within a relatively short space of time he found the perfect spot, a broom cupboard which was fortuitously unlocked.

No longer burdened by the dead weight, he moved forward with greater speed.

Although he'd studied the old guardian's notes carefully and knew what to expect, he was still unprepared for the sight that met his eyes. To say it was breathtaking would have been an understatement. He recognised instantly that he was looking at an exact replica of the old Temple in Jerusalem, even down to the two bronze pillars, Joachim and Boaz.

Not having time to admire its beauty, knowing every moment was precious, he collected his thoughts and focused on the task in hand.

Knowing what he wanted lay beyond the holy of holies, he pushed forward.

About to step through the small door at the rear of the Temple, the one described in his notes as the chamber of horrors, he froze, sure that his acute hearing had picked up something. It was either that, he realised, or the movement of air being displaced by a body behind him. Reacting with lightning speed, he threw himself into a forward roll, and he was only just in time. The moment he moved, a sica buried itself in the wooden door inches from where he'd been standing fractions of a second before.

Completing his roll, Jared came instantly to his feet, thinking to himself it had been too close for comfort.

It was then he spotted the assassin.

Hidden in the shadows at the side of one of the pillars, he'd been invisible, and he grudgingly admitted the man was good, very good.

Hoping to catch him off guard, he called out to him softly, 'So you must be the one they call Scorpion.'

Hearing his name spoken had the desired effect, and the killer stopped in his tracks.

'Don't look so startled!' said Jared. 'There's only two of you left.' At the same time he hoped his calculations had been right.

Seeing the startled expression on Scorpion's face, he said, 'Ah, obviously you haven't heard the good news yet. Your latest recruit isn't with us any more. No, I'm afraid that as far as the Brotherhood is concerned, it's down to just you and David Naami now.'

Recovering quickly, Scorpion said, 'Unfortunately you have me at a disadvantage… I have no idea who you are.'

In a voice curiously devoid of any emotion, Jared replied, 'I'm the one who took out your fellow brothers, is all you need to know.'

Suddenly recognition dawned in Scorpion's eye. 'So you're the one our network couldn't penetrate! Your service record was buried so deeply, even our organisation couldn't find anything. I must say I'm impressed. However, as well as you've done up to now, I'm afraid it's the end of the line as far as your little killing spree is concerned. The others were good, admittedly, but not in my class. You're about to discover you've never come across anyone as good as me.'

Totally unfazed, Jared said, 'I don't think your anywhere near as good as you think you are – and by the way, the others were piss poor, not good. Considering you lot like to think of yourselves as the elite, I was singularly unimpressed. In all honesty I've had stiffer pillow fights. Not to worry, I'm keeping the best until last. Even though David Naami, or should I say your Grand Master, is much older than you, I anticipate he'll be a far superior class of opponent.'

Jared knew that members of the Brotherhood had two fatal weaknesses, arrogance and a sense of their own infallibility. The flash of anger that appeared in Scorpion's eyes at the deliberate insult informed Jared that Scorpion was no different.

Jared's eyes never left the assassin's face, knowing that although one of the twin sicas was buried in the woodwork several feet away, the other was being primed as they spoke.

Unknown to Scorpion, Jared was an expert with the knife as well, and was backing his skills against those of Scorpion, wagering that as good as Scorpion thought he was, Jared was quicker. In instances such as these, with two killers of exceptional skill facing each other, it inevitably came down to fractions of a second.

Like his adversary, Jared carried two throwing knives in a pouch behind his neck, but what Scorpion didn't know was that during the time he'd rolled away from Scorpion's surprise attack, he'd palmed one.

Scorpion's anger had made him careless, as Jared had gambled it would, and so he saw the flash of anger spark into his eyes a split second before he threw the knife.

Too late, Scorpion saw the smile appear on Jared's face, and with a sudden flash of insight he knew he'd been outsmarted.

Surprisingly he felt and saw nothing. One moment he was contemplating teaching this slip of a kid a lesson, the next he was staring in astonishment at the hilt of Jared's knife protruding from his throat.

Taking a few faltering steps forward, unable to believe he'd been beaten, he made a sudden gurgling noise before sliding to the floor amid a rapidly growing pool of his own blood.

Seeing that he was still alive, Jared knelt down by him. Lifting Scorpion's head by his hair, he whispered into his ear, 'I told you that you weren't as good as you thought you were.'

Seconds later the light died from Scorpion's eyes.

Removing the knife and wiping it on Scorpion's white mantle, he replaced it in its pouch.

Careful now, alert to the fact the most dangerous assassin of them all had yet to be faced, he moved towards the black drapes at the back of the holy of holies.

Even for someone as cold-blooded and emotionless as Jared, the sight rendered him speechless, filling him with loathing. Blocking out everything but the task ahead, he prepared himself mentally and pushed forward with new resolve.

The head was just as he'd imagined it, along with the smaller heads of the guardians.

All these things were rendered superfluous, however, when he spotted the chalice. It had been placed directly under the head on a tall plinth that looked like solid marble. Waiting for the return of its master, was Jared's immediate thought, but if I have any say in the matter, it will be one hell of a long wait...

Acting quickly, he made straight for the chalice.

About to lift it from its plinth, he was stopped in his tracks by a voice that was achingly familiar.

'Hello, Jared, what kept you?'

Without turning his head, he said, 'Hello, Grandad – or would you prefer I call you *Grand Master*?'

Stepping from behind the curtains, Jared could see the shock clearly outlined on David Naami's face. It was several seconds before he recovered properly, but by then the old confidence was back.

'I'm impressed, Jared, I must say. How long have you known about me?'

'For a while now; it was the little things that kept bothering me, the fact you married my grandmother shortly after the tombstone was found. At the time I thought it was a coincidence, but then I remembered I never believed in coincidences, and so gradually I became suspicious. Then we had the riddle of old Eric being convinced there was something familiar about his attacker. And of course we had the story about old Thomas, which was a complete fabrication. I must admit that was inspirational; you set me up treat. It took me ages to realise the dates; in particular, Aleister Crowley's didn't fit. What I still can't work out is what you hoped to gain by it?'

'I would have thought it obvious; you were just too bloody good to be true! Leader of the pack, popular with everyone, you had brains, looks... and on top of that, Emma. That gorgeous little creature was hopelessly in love with you. Oh, I know what you're thinking, as the leader of the most powerful organisation in the world, I can have everything I want. But let me explain something: it wasn't always like that. From the time I was barely able to walk, I literally had to drag myself out of the gutter. Yet for you, the boy wonder, everything was so easy. Until I intervened, that is.

'When I set you up with the Ouija board in the attic I was hoping you'd become so obsessed, all of you, it would ruin your lives. And to a sense it worked, didn't it?' he said bellowing with laughter. 'You lost Emma, didn't you? And then, like a typical coward, as soon as the going got tough, you ran away – you deserted her.

'But you have no idea of the sacrifices I made in order to find the chalice. I was married to that slag you call your grandmother for over a year. Can you imagine what would have been said had the brothers found out? A man of my influence and stature... it was degrading. And yet I was prepared to do it in order to reunite the Master with the head.'

Silent for a moment, he then said, 'And to think it was on my bloody doorstep all along. As you're about to die shortly, I suppose there's no harm in telling you how I managed to become Grand Master.'

For the next few moments Jared listened spellbound, and when he'd finished he had to admit grudgingly it was an incredible story.

Suddenly changing tack, David Naami said, 'She was certainly something in bed, your grandmother – she loved it! I bet your real grandfather never fucked her like I did.'

About to react, Jared suddenly sensed where this was heading. The crafty bastard was using the same psychological trick he'd used on Scorpion, and it had nearly worked. Getting his emotions under control, he said, 'I'm glad you mentioned my grandfather; it was the final clue. A hit-and-run that was never solved, far too convenient.'

Knowing he'd somehow lost the battle of wits, David Naami attempted to regain the initiative.

'What do you think of the chalice then, Jared?'

Never taking his eyes off his adversary, he replied, 'Oh, we're old friends. Didn't you know?'

Seeing the astonishment on his face, Jared pressed home the advantage by explaining the circumstances which had led them to its hiding place.

'You see, David, your little plan backfired. Instead of becoming obsessed with the Ouija board, it led me right to the chalice. Unwittingly, you set the wheels in motion for its discovery, and you knew nothing about it. In hindsight I often wondered why I never confided in you, but

I suppose the reason was obvious. Some sixth sense warned me even then not to trust you. You poor pathetic fool! All these years you thought you'd ruined my life. In fact you couldn't have been further from the truth.'

Despite his age, David Naami's reflexes were still razor sharp.

Fortunately Jared had anticipated the move, and his golden rule of never underestimating an opponent saved his life. The strength in the old man's hands as they closed around his throat was shocking, and so, using a street fighter's instinct, he resorted to the only thing he could. He butted him squarely in the face. Such was the force behind the blow it shattered his assailant's nose, showering Jared with blood.

Startled, David Naami eased the pressure on Jared's throat slightly, while at the same time letting out a bellow of rage.

It was all the incentive Jared needed. Clenching his fists together, he drove them upwards with all the force he could muster. It was enough, as suddenly David Naami's hands flew from his throat.

From a distance of several feet, Jared looked deeply into his former grandfather's eyes, and what he saw confirmed his belief that he was facing the most lethal opponent he'd ever come across. He knew in order to beat him he'd have to be at his very best, and even then it might not be enough.

Suddenly he remembered Edwin, and with that an icy calm settled over him.

David Naami noticed the change, and for the first time in his life felt a tingle of doubt prickle up his spine.

As Jared moved slowly forwards, the words of his instructor came filtering through his brain. 'First of all, never lose your temper; do that and you lose your coordination. Secondly, keep a clear head. Now we come to the third and final point, and it's the most important. Always, and I mean *always*, look your adversary in the eye. An instant before he makes a move, he'll telegraph it. The day you come across someone whose eyes don't react, then you're in big trouble. If that happens then watch his feet; they behave in the same way as the eyes. Before throwing a kick or punch, your opponent will invariably betray their intent by a slight movement of the feet. It might be the slightest redistribution of weight, but it will be enough for you to react accordingly.'

'What happens when you come across someone who does neither?' was Jared's puzzled response.

462

'Tell me, Mr Bentley, from what you have been able to discover so far, does the fire seem to have been caused deliberately?' Holding the microphone at arm's length to await his reply, she made sure it wasn't too near his mouth to cause distortion.

'In my opinion, there can be no doubt. You see, the resulting damage was more than even the hottest of fires could have caused. Allied to that, going over the scene with a fine-tooth comb, my fellow officers and I came across what, at first glance, appeared to be the remains of several small mechanical devices.' Smiling at the pretty reporter, he added, 'To me they looked suspiciously like detonators.' Wanting to impress the public with his knowledge, he said, 'A detonator is basically a blasting cap, which contains a core of fulminate or mercury, or a similar explosive, and wires. When heated up, an electrical charge is sent through them. These set off the primer explosive, which in turn sets off the main charge. It's really quite simple,' Bentley concluded.

'And, of course, being a veteran of some twenty-years' experience, you are obviously regarded as an authority on such matters,' said Sarah Thomas.

'Yes, you can safely say that. However, listening to eye-witness accounts from several residents living in and around the area has only confirmed my suspicions. They were unanimous in their agreement that, prior to the inferno, they heard several loud explosions. Several testified that they seemed to be like shotgun blasts, each one occurring within several seconds of each other. Such evidence leaves me with no alternative but to conclude that the fire was set deliberately.' What he wasn't about to tell the reporter was that apart from the remains of detonators, he'd found traces of something else – C4 explosive. The problem with this was that it was quite rare. Available to the military and a few other high-placed agencies, it was not used in commercial demolitions. Finding it had thrown a completely new slant on his investigation.

'What about bodies, Mr Bentley; did you find any?'

It was an inevitable question, one that an old hand like Mark Bentley had been expecting. The mere mention of fatalities would add spice to an already newsworthy story, he realised. Putting such thoughts aside, he said, 'To date, all I can tell you is that so far we have come across three.'

Turning to the scene behind him, he added, 'But, as you can see, at the moment there is so much mess it is really impossible to say with any certainty whether or not there might not be others.' Shrugging his shoulders in a gesture of resignation, he continued, 'Unfortunately, the bodies we found were nothing but charred remains – burned beyond recognition. The identity of the victims will sadly have to be determined by people with far greater skill than I.'

Stepping in before he could elaborate, Sarah Thomas said, 'What about terrorism? Do you think Cardiff has suddenly become the target of terrorist activities?'

Unable to hide his mirth, Mark Bentley burst out laughing, before saying, 'Most definitely not.' Staring into the camera as if what was taking place was a private conversation between him and his audience, he continued, 'I can assure the public that there is not the remotest chance of this being a terrorist attack, so you can all relax on that score.'

Feeling that she had been slighted somewhat, and made to feel small on air, Sarah Thomas attempted to win back some face. With an ingratiating smile, she said, 'How can you be so sure of your facts, Mr Bentley?'

Matching her smile for smile, Mark Bentley said, 'That's easy. Look around you. How many bodies do you see? Apart from this one building, how much peripheral damage was caused? It's a safe bet that had it been terrorists the body count would have been far higher than three. They would have struck at a time of day when loss of life would have been maximised.'

Turning to the interviewer, he was gratified to see her squirm in embarrassment. The only answer she could muster was, 'Ah, yes, I see your point.'

Not giving her time to recover, he added, 'On a more positive note, I can safely say that, terrorist activity aside, had the incident taken place during the day and not in the early hours of the morning, then the problems we are facing would have been compounded. Simply put, had the explosions occurred during the late morning or afternoon, then we would have been facing a nightmare scenario. People working in office blocks in and around Chameleon Enterprises would have had to be evacuated as a safety precaution. Added to that, remember, we would have had the additional problem of flying debris and the incredible heat from the flames. I don't have to fill in the rest of the picture, do I? Amazingly, none of the buildings nearby seem to have been damaged – yet another indication that the person who planted the explosive devices was someone who knew exactly what he was doing. But, more than that, was targeting only the headquarters of Chameleon Enterprises. It was almost as if he wanted no one else to get hurt. It's baffling.'

'If that is the case,' said Sarah Thomas, breaking in, 'then why is it we have three bodies on our hands.'

'Now, that's where we have a problem, isn't it? Maybe he miscalculated. Maybe it was an accident. Perhaps he didn't realise there was anyone in the building. Who knows?' Silent for a moment, he suddenly had a thought, 'What if the three victims were his intended targets all along, that his mission was to take them out and then blow up the building? And, before you ask, I honestly have no idea why the headquarters of Chameleon Enterprises seems to have been the intended target.' Holding up his hands to indicate the interview was over, he added finally, 'Questions like that will be far better directed towards the police.'

'Heard enough, guv?' asked Gareth Evans, turning his head towards Danny. Seeing the nod of the head, he switched off the television and turned back to the others.

Looking over at Jared, Tina pointed to Danny and said, 'Unlike old misery guts over there, I had no doubt whatsoever you would pull it off!'

With that, she walked over to Jared and, putting her arms around his neck, kissed him full on the mouth. Standing back, she watched as he squirmed in embarrassment, before putting him out of his misery, 'That's from all us – a token of our appreciation, if you like.'

Completely at a loss for words, Jared was grateful when Danny came to the rescue.

'OK, hero! Care to tell me how it went?'

'There's not much to tell, really – not concerning the action, anyway. To be honest, considering the fact they thought so highly of themselves, they were disappointing when it came to the crunch. But I think there are one or two items you might find interesting.'

When he came to the point about how David Naami had been his second grandfather, Danny couldn't hold back any longer. 'Jesus Christ! How the hell did you manage to figure that out?'

When he'd finished explaining, Jared added that just as in the case of the identity of Judas, he should have worked it out far more quickly.

'You're far too hard on yourself, if you ask me, lad, but you still haven't told me how the hell you managed to work out that as your grandfather, he was able to be in two places at once. In some instances he was clearly reported as being seen in his little fortress, while at exactly the same time, he was living with your grandmother in Raven's Hill.'

'That stumped me for a while too, I must admit, until I woke up one morning and remembered the body found floating in the bay six years ago...'

Seeing Danny's blank expression, he said, 'Of course, being a local thing, it probably never warranted a mention in your neck of the woods. It was a strange case. The corpse had been in the water for several days and although it had been weighted down, it had somehow managed to find its way to the surface. Probably snagged on an anchor cable from one of the small boats, or something,' he added.

'Anyway, it came in for a good deal of media attention for the simple reason the body was in such a state. The poor bugger's face had been peeled away and every single tooth extracted.'

Hearing Danny's low whistle of surprise, he said, 'And that wasn't all: his hands and feet had been hacked off for good measure...'

'...so that no one could ever establish his identity,' said Danny, breaking in. 'But why go to such extremes?'

'That's exactly the question I asked myself, Danny, until I remembered something old Eric mentioned in his notes. It was about the Brotherhood moving its headquarters from Paris to Cardiff in 1967. Interestingly, it coincided with the murder of three influential people in the space of two days. The odd thing was that each of them had been hanged. It was almost as if someone had deliberately made an example of them, in much the same way David Naami had with Wolf all those years later. We now know, of course, that hanging was the Brotherhood's way of dealing with traitors; it was a symbolic link to Judas.'

Waving his hand in a dismissive gesture, he said, 'But that's not what got me wondering. No, it was the fact that a day later, a body with exactly the same injuries to the one found in the bay all those years ago was found washed up on the banks of the Seine.'

'Coincidence?' said Danny.

'No, I wasn't buying that.'

'In order to go to so much trouble, they must have been hiding a pretty big secret. And then I had it: the clever bastards were using a double of the Grand Master. It's not uncommon; remember, it's been rumoured that Saddam Hussein selected several in the hope that if anyone ever went after him, one of the doubles would be taken out by a sniper instead. Anyway, until I disposed of my grandfather, it was pure conjecture on my part, but before I killed him he boasted about it. He wanted me to hear about his rise to fame, how he'd dragged himself from the gutter, as he put it, to become the leader of the most powerful organisation the world has ever known.'

'So why did the first corpse turn up in 1967, then?' asked Danny.

'Simple, he got too greedy. He wasn't content with what he had, he wanted even more. Old Eric's notes uncovered a complicated story, but the more I studied them the more I was convinced I had the answer. The whole thing began in 1956, when out of the blue a quantity of documents supposedly leaked from "inside sources" began appearing on the scene. Arriving in piecemeal fashion, they alluded to some "secret" of monumental importance. Alluded to is the key phrase as the secret itself was never revealed. In fact, most of the information was nothing but cryptic asides and footnotes, which eventually found their way into the Bibliothèque Nationale in Paris. To cut a long story short, what I was looking for was something that took place nearly ten years later. On 17 January, a privately produced work was deposited in the Bibliothèque Nationale called *Le Serpent Rouge* or *The Red Serpent*.'

Seeing Danny's surprise, he added, 'Yes, the one the old guardian referred to when talking about the prophecy. The bulk of the work consists of thirteen short poems. Each, roughly a paragraph long, was linked to a sign of the zodiac, but one which contained thirteen signs and not the conventional twelve. Told in the first person, the poems dealt with a type of allegorical pilgrimage. The thirteenth sign was inserted between Scorpio and Sagittarius, but the important thing as far as the prophecy is concerned, is that at one point, a red snake is mentioned, one that is uncoiling across the centuries. To me it clearly hinted at a bloodline or lineage. Now, if the prophecy the old guardian told Edwin about is true, it could be pointing the finger at Jesus.'

Pausing for a moment to let the implications sink in, he carried on.

'Even more interesting is what Eric found under the sign of Leo. The paragraph seemed to suggest that according to *Le Serpent Rouge*, the Mother Goddess of Christianity appears to be Mary Magdalene and not the Virgin Mary. If that's the case, we have the unthinkable: "Notre Dame" – the title given to all of France's great cathedrals – would seem to be dedicated to the Magdalene and not the Virgin! Explosive stuff, eh?

'Now, think back. According to traditional Church thinking, the Magdalene is a prostitute. She is only afforded a mention in the Gospels because the author saw her as a symbol of redemption. So, according to that line of thinking, she should be the last person in the world to be linked with the Christian religion. Interestingly, John's Gospel states she was the first person to see Jesus after the resurrection, and now that we know the secret of Project Lazarus, we know why. But what's more, on the strength of that incident she is hailed as a saint in France, and according to legend is said to have brought the Holy Grail to those shores. Once again, thanks to the information on the codex, we know the Grail was never a cup, but a bloodline, the bloodline of Jesus. As the wife and mother of his child, it's no wonder she's given a place of such prominence by those who knew the truth.'

'And to those who knew the truth we can add the hierarchy of the Church,' Danny chipped in. 'After all, it was this knowledge the powers that be wanted so desperately to keep from the common people. A secret they were willing to pay the Brotherhood a fortune to suppress.'

'Precisely, Danny, you've got it in one,' said Jared.

'To get back to the point I was making at the beginning, it seems that in 1967 three powerful businessmen were offered a secret of immense value by a mysterious fourth party, one who promised to provide the original documents in order to back up his claims. However, somewhere along the line, the Brotherhood managed to get wind of the transaction, and two assassins were sent to take them out.

'Apparently at the tender age of twenty, David Naami was already a legendary figure, and he not only planned the whole thing, but led it.'

'But something went wrong, I take it,' said Danny.

'No, strangely enough nothing went wrong; in fact the operation worked like a charm. No, something happened that no one could have foreseen. A mole inside the Brotherhood warned the three that they were about to be raided, with the result that the lookalike Grand Master, the one selling the secrets, realising the game was up, tried to get rid of the precious documents.

'Apparently, David Naami was just in time, as several had already been destroyed by the time he managed to get to him. Rendering the man unconscious, imagine his surprise when he recognised him as the Grand Master – or so he thought. Fortunately, he'd been given a telephone number in case of emergencies, and so, using his initiative, he explained the situation. Once it had been established the man lying at his feet was a double, he was asked to perform a rather delicate operation. After explaining what he wanted done, the genuine Grand Master left him in no doubt he would be properly rewarded... and you can guess the rest.'

Several moments passed before Danny was able to come to terms with what he had just heard, but then suddenly he said, 'While we're on the subject, there's been something I've been meaning to ask you for a while.'

'Fire away, and if I can answer your question I'll do it gladly.'

'Well, the thing that's been puzzling me is, if Judas is so intent on making a personal crusade against the local clergy, then how come Eric has been spared? Surely, looking at things from Judas' perspective he would have been the first one I would have gone for. After all, it was his little chapel that had imprisoned him down through the centuries.' After a brief pause he added, 'Unless of course he's keeping him back until the end, in order to savour the moment, I mean.'

Shaking his head in amusement, Jared said, 'A shrewd guess, but think back. If you remember the look on the faces of the first few killed it was a mixture of pure agony and horror. No, wait, that doesn't really describe such a complicated array of emotions. I'm forgetting that somewhere in the midst of that little lot there was *despair* too. What I'm trying to get at is that when Judas spoke to me in person that night in my bedroom, he gloated over the fact that Professor Edwards was tearing his hair out in an attempt to interpret it. As a matter of fact, he never worked out the reason, did he? Strangely enough, the answer is surprisingly simple. In each case, just before they died, Judas revealed to them the secret of Project Lazarus, knowing that such a revelation would destroy everything they had held dear. Their final moments on earth would have been ones of torment. I dread to think what they went through when it dawned on them that their firmly held convictions about life after death were nothing but a worthless sham. Their final moments were not only ones of physical torture but spiritual agony as well.'

'Yes, but that's exactly my point,' said Danny in exasperation. 'If that's the case, think of the buzz it would have given Judas to reveal such a truth to old Eric! After all, as you said yourself, it was Carmel that had been his prison. More than that, though,' he added as an afterthought, 'just think how much pleasure it would have given him to destroy his faith.

By now Jared was laughing. 'You still don't get it, do you?' he said. 'Don't you see, killing Eric would have been pointless. Judas was crafty enough to realise that Eric already knew or at least suspected the truth about Project Lazarus. His research into the Knights Templar had led him to the conclusion that Jesus' death and resurrection was nothing but a carefully contrived plot. That's why when I revealed to Eric what the final chapter was all about, he didn't seem surprised. To be honest, neither was I, because for months I'd been having the same doubts. All the codex did was to provide us with incontrovertible proof.'

'B-but...' stammered Danny, 'I still don't get it.'

Exasperated, Jared said, 'To put it in simple language, Judas would have derived no pleasure from revealing either the secret of Project Lazarus to Eric or by killing him, for the simple reason he would have been killing a man who had already lost his faith. As he already knew the truth, it would have been a hollow victory. It would have done nothing for Judas' ego, would it?'

'Of course,' said Danny, trailing off lamely, 'it all makes sense now.'

Chapter Forty-two

JARED COULDN'T HELP BUT FEEL A SENSE OF DÉJÀ VU. EVERYTHING WAS almost exactly the same as it had been on that fateful night six years ago, the board, the trimmings, but in particular the atmosphere of dark, brooding menace. Looking around the circle of taught faces, the fear the apprehension that too was there and in abundance.

The only major difference was the dark blue tarpaulin which covered the gaping opening where the large wooden double doors of the little chapel had once stood. And of course there was the hole in the middle of the floor which had once been the hiding place of the chalice.

It was a strange sight, almost surreal, because the bright yellow bulldozer remained in exactly the same position as it had when it had tumbled nose first into the pit all those long months ago. With its blade and serrated teeth pointing downwards, it looked remarkably like a prehistoric dinosaur foraging for food.

Jared had also brought five candles.

They were not for decorative purposes; they were a necessity, as at this time of night it was almost pitch black inside the main body of the little chapel. One to represent each of the five people present, they'd been placed at strategic points around the altar table. The chairs which had formed part of the original seance had been rescued from the vestry next door. Dusted down, they were now arranged neatly around the small table. The light from the flickering flames danced eerily across the friends' faces as they looked at each other for inspiration.

'So what's the plan?' asked Roger.

Knowing he didn't really have one, apart from the fact that he would be the willing sacrifice demanded by the chalice, Jared stalled.

'Let's join hands, close our eyes and concentrate for a moment, see what happens.'

'Reminds me of New Year's Eve,' was Roger's caustic comment, 'expect there's one thing certain: this is no bloody social occasion.'

After several moments, Aled opened one eye tentatively and said, 'What makes you think the creature is going to make an appearance?'

'Besides,' said Roger joining in, 'I'm not so sure I want it to, considering what you did to the Brotherhood. I'm sure when it finds out it's going to be rightly pissed off.'

'I don't think you need to worry about him making an appearance. An opportunity like this, one where he can show off his power, will be too much to resist, believe me.'

While he was talking, Jared fingered the razor sharp knife strapped to the inside of his wrist. For weeks he'd known it would come to this; there was no other way in which the creature could be stopped. The only nagging fear was whether his life would be regarded as a worthy sacrifice. It would be given willingly, of course, but he had hardly lived a life of purity and devotion. In his own mind the atrocities he'd committed had made a mockery of such noble sentiments. As always he blamed himself for the mess they were in, and so he regarded it as his duty to get them out of it. Anyway, in practical terms he'd nothing to live for, and no one would grieve for him when he was gone. True, his gran would for a while, but she'd get over it. And then there was old Eric; but he was sure the same could be said of him.

Looking back at his life, ever since he'd found that bloody board everyone he'd ever loved had been taken away from him, except Emma and little Jodie, of course. It was strange how he'd come to feel so attached to her. But in Emma's case, she'd made it plain that although she valued his friendship, that was as far as things went. Smiling inwardly, he realised they were completely unaware that should anything go wrong tonight, the house and all his vast wealth would revert to them. He would give anything to be a fly on the wall when the solicitor read out the will. His gran wouldn't mind; she loved Emma like a daughter. Besides, she had more than enough for her own needs, and of course there was the big house as well.

It was while such negative thoughts were running around in his head he felt a sudden chill, and suddenly a blast of cold air ripped through the centre of the chapel.

Opening his eyes, he expected to see Judas standing next to him. Instead he was taken completely by surprise when the silence was broken by a booming voice that reverberated along the walls of the old chapel.

Looking quickly from Roger to Aled, he knew instantly that neither had any more clue as to the origin of the disembodied voice than he did. Until, that is, his gaze rested on Emma. Following her horrified gaze, he was frozen into immobility when he saw Michael – or what had once been Michael – standing next to him.

Gazing up at him, everything suddenly fell into place. No wonder Judas had always seemed to be one step ahead! Strangely, Jared felt no animosity towards Michael, instead a wave of pity washed over him. Of one thing he was certain, when it was all over, his psyche, fragile at the best of times, would be unable to cope with the guilt.

Under his scrutiny, Michael's thin frame seemed to expand and grow at an astonishing rate, until moments later, covered in a dark halo that radiated pure evil, the creature towered over the group. Satisfied it had made a sufficient impression on the gathering; it opened its gaping mouth and boomed, 'Surprised, Jared?' Allowing him no time to reply it carried on, 'You shouldn't be; after all it was you who put forward the theory that in order to get near its victims the host would have to be someone either well known, or innocuous in terms of a physical threat. Now in that respect, Michael here,' he said pointing to itself, 'was the perfect choice. Mild-mannered, orphaned as a young lad, gentle, caring… I could go on, but I think you get my point. No one in their right minds would look twice at him. That was my reasoning, anyway, and if my success rate was anything to go by it certainly worked. It was easily good enough to fool you lot. And you were supposed to be the experts,' it said, chuckling away to itself.

'Not right in the head,' said the creature, tapping the side of its temple, and mimicking the tone of voice used by many of the villagers when referring to Michael behind his back. 'I wonder what they would think if they could see him now?'

While all this was going on, Jared noted with concern how this was a far different Judas from the one who'd visited him in his gran's bedroom that night. Gone was the sibilant whining, the persuasive deceit, to be replaced by a loud arrogant braying.

What stood in front of him now was something in complete control of itself.

Looking directly at Jared, it said, 'Nothing to say, special one? Fear tends to do that, but don't say I didn't warn you. Anger, hatred, revenge, those are far more powerful emotions than mere love. Compared to those, love is a poor second.'

Feeling the first stirrings of despair, Jared dropped his head onto his chest, while at the same time frantically wracking his brain for an answer. Suddenly he had an idea, one that, given a bit of good fortune, might just work. He reasoned that if he could only taunt the creature enough to make it lose control, then who knows. Anyway he didn't have much choice; it was the last throw of the dice.

Nothing ventured, nothing gained, he thought, and so he went for it.

Staring directly into the creature's enormous bloodshot eyes, Jared said, 'At least I know who you are!'

Taken by surprise, the creature said, 'Care to enlighten me how you came to your startling conclusion?'

'After the final piece of the jigsaw fell into place it was quite easy, really,' countered Jared, 'you're the celebrated – or should I say infamous – Judas Iscariot.'

Genuinely stunned for a moment, the creature recovered quickly. '*Quite easy?*' it sneered, and with that it burst out laughing. 'Correct me if I'm wrong, but what you so dismissively describe as quite easy cost four gentlemen of the cloth their lives. If it was so simple, why did it take so long for you to work it out? God knows I left you enough clues. Anyone with a modicum of intelligence would have solved the puzzle in a fraction of the time you took.'

Seeing Jared's agonised look, it knew the barb had struck home, and so it pressed home its advantage. With a sweeping gesture of its hand, Judas said, 'Be that as it may, how did you finally manage to figure it out?'

By now back in control of his emotions, Jared said, 'It was the Roman denarii – the ones you stuffed into the Reverend Gower's mouth – that did it. It reminded me of the thirty pieces of silver in the story of the Last Supper, and when I remembered that, everything else fell into place.'

'Ah, the so-called "blood money" mentioned in the hopelessly misleading Gospel accounts.'

Raising his eyebrows, Jared said, 'Why hopelessly misleading?'

'What do the archives have to say about it?'

'That you betrayed Jesus at the Last Supper for thirty pieces of silver.'

'Yes, but you're missing my point. Why do they say I betrayed Jesus for this fictitious amount of money?'

'Now that's where things get a little tricky... there are several suggestions.'

'Name them!' the creature challenged.

Mentally ticking them off, Jared said, 'First and foremost it was greed,' adding, 'which I never believed, by the way. Thirty pieces of silver was a pittance, the price of a slave; so if it had been greed, you could have demanded a great deal more.'

Pursing its lips, the creature said, 'Interesting. Perhaps I did you an injustice when I called you semi-literate, but do go on.'

'Another group of scholars came up with the idea you did it because you were disillusioned. You believed that when the time finally arrived, Jesus would rid himself of this peace-loving facade and become the warrior Messiah that the people, but in particular you, the Sicarii, craved. Yet another suggestion was that you chose that particular moment in the garden of Gethsemane deliberately, viewing it as an opportunity to force Jesus to reveal his true nature. However, when it went wrong and Jesus died on the cross in exactly the manner he'd predicted, you realised you'd made a horrible mistake, and so in a fit of remorse hanged yourself.'

Throwing back his head, Judas laughed uproariously.

When he'd recovered, he said, 'Would you like to hear what really happened – set the record straight, so to speak? Before I kill you, that is.'

Holding his hand in the air, Jared said, 'No need. So far all I've done is outline what others have said about you. Unlike them, I know the truth.'

Not allowing the creature an opportunity to interrupt, he pressed on quickly. 'Funnily enough, the truth is rather sad, because through no fault of your own you've been vilified down through the ages. Quite unfairly, you've been portrayed as a figure of ridicule by the Church – and for something you never did.'

Seeing the look of astonishment on Judas' face, he hurried on. 'What you never realised was that Jesus was on to you from day one. From the very beginning he knew you were a Sicarii plant. Why do you think, despite vigorous protests from the others, he allowed you access into the inner circle? He knew full well whatever he said would be reported back to your brother, Barabbas. But Jesus was cleverer than either you or your Sicarii brothers. In fact he played you all for suckers.

'You see, while you were mentally congratulating yourself on duping Jesus, his charisma and magnetic personality won you over. Fuelled by promises of a place in his mysterious kingdom, he enlisted your aid in bringing it about. After explaining how it would operate, you were entranced; but more than that, you wanted to be a part of it, one of the chosen. From that moment on it was easy for Jesus to manipulate you. All he did was to convince you that to usher in the kingdom, he, Jesus, would have to be arrested, crucified and brought back to life. But – and this is the essential point – at a time and place chosen by Jesus himself. When this had come to pass, it was then and only then, the kingdom would arrive in its full glory.

'Jesus was so clever, he made sure you were totally unaware of how essential you were to the success of his plan. Had you stopped to think for a moment, you might have understood that you were the ace up his sleeve. And it worked. At the prearranged signal, you led them to the privacy of Gethsemane. What no one realised, besides you and Jesus of course, was that there *never were* any thirty pieces of silver! That was a rumour circulated by Jesus to convince the others the choice of time and place for his arrest had been purely arbitrary. Unfortunately, as far as you were concerned, it was Jesus' only mistake. He never thought everyone would believe it, and so quite by accident you became the instrument of his betrayal. By spreading the story about the thirty pieces of silver, he unwittingly signed your death warrant. Looking at it from the point of view of the early Church, in particular the Apostles, it was no wonder you came to be regarded as a traitor.'

The creature's jaw was hanging open like a gutted fish, but one thing was very much apparent, it could see the ruthless reasoning behind Jared's thinking. The cold calculated logic of his words was undeniable. And deep down it knew they were true.

Pressing on resolutely, Jared said, 'For the last two millennia you've blamed Jesus for deceiving you, when in fact he knew nothing about your murder. He only found out later, and of course by then it was too late. Peter, ever the hothead, took the story about the thirty pieces of silver at face value, and dragged you screaming and pleading your innocence out of your home. Shortly afterwards you were hanged. While the others watched, he threw the blood money, as you so nicely described it, at your feet, while you wriggled like an eel above him.'

Shaking his head in a show of mock sympathy, Jared said, 'The final irony was on that particular night in question, the fates conspired against you. For some reason known only to you, there were actually thirty pieces of silver in your room. To Peter, it clinched the argument. Already looking for a scapegoat, it was conclusive proof as far as he was concerned. So you see, you poor misguided bastard, you've been blaming the wrong person all this time! Jesus had nothing to do with any of it. And before you say it, no, it wasn't Jesus you overheard plotting Project Lazarus a few hours before your murder, it was Joseph and Nicodemus. They were the instigators of the scheme. Jesus knew nothing at all about it, he was completely innocent.'

Seeing that by now Judas was about to explode, he decided to play the creature at its own game and delivered the final insult.

'Oh – and by the way, this will kill you,' he said, before chuckling and adding, 'sorry, in the overall context of our little discussion I must admit that was a bad choice of words. Anyway, I thought you might like to know it was Jesus who provided the sacrifice to imprison you. Ironic, don't you think? So you see, all this hatred of the Church has been based on a misconception from day one. And you had the audacity to question my intelligence!' Jared said with a smirk.

'Before I forget I've another little surprise for you. Your little plan about wiping out Raven's Hill with a biological weapon will have to be put on the back boiler. As from yesterday, Chameleon Enterprises no longer exists.'

Without a trace of conceit, Jared went on. 'Didn't you know? The Brotherhood, or the elite of the elite as they so arrogantly referred to themselves, have gone to meet their Maker, every last one of them. They really were disappointing, apart from my one-time grandfather, or David Naami as you knew him. Now, he was rather more of a difficult nut to crack, I must admit.'

Dragging the suspense out a little he said, 'Where was I? Oh, yes, your sanctuary and its little secrets no longer exist either. As from last night, your evil empire is nothing but a pile of smouldering rubble. But seeing as you're so bloody clever, I'm surprised you didn't already know.'

Without warning, Jared suddenly threw back his head and laughed, mimicking the creature's earlier cheap theatrics.

It was the final insult, the one which tipped Judas over the edge. The flash of red which danced in the creature's eyes betrayed its anger, but strangely, Jared missed it.

Emma, however, didn't.

Listening to the insults with mounting trepidation, she studied the creature's body language carefully. As a result, she saw what Jared missed. Each insult had pierced the beast's arrogant psyche like a dagger, until without warning it lunged.

By now Jared had finally come out of his dreamlike trance. Unfortunately, for once in his life he was far too slow in reacting.

Aiming for Jared's throat with one of its talon-like fingernails, the creature's blow never arrived. Anticipating the move, Emma threw herself in front of Jared in an attempt to save him. Although it missed her carotid artery it severed several smaller ones, and immediately blood started bubbling from the gaping wound. Holding it closed with her fingers, she was amazed to see that one artery, more severely damaged than the rest, threw out a single spurt of blood, which quite by accident dropped into the open neck of the chalice. It had an instant effect on the creature, who stepped back as if it had been slapped in the face.

It took a few moments to register, but suddenly Emma realised what was happening. Gesturing for Jared to move the chalice closer, he pushed it towards her, hardly conscious of what he was doing. The moment the second drop of Emma's blood hit the ashes, the creature screamed in agony. To Judas if felt as if someone had poured boiling acid over his face. With each fresh drop of blood, his screams grew weaker and weaker, while amazingly, in terms of stature he grew smaller. With that it was no longer the creature that was standing in front of them, but Michael.

As the others watched in horrified fascination, black tendrils of smoke began to drift from Michael's open mouth, followed closely by an appalling stench.

Surprisingly, it was Roger who reacted the most quickly.

As the final wisp of black smoke entered the open mouth of the chalice, he replaced the lid. Moments later, he'd sealed it tightly with black duct tape that Jared had brought with him for such an eventuality.

While the drama had been unfolding, Danny, Gareth and Tina had suddenly appeared. Guns drawn, they raced up the aisle. Keeping a wary eye on the hole, they bounded up on either side of the steps leading to the altar table, Danny taking the left, and Gareth and Tina the right.

Oblivious to what was taking place around him, Jared was cradling Emma in his arms. Although the flow of blood had been reduced to a small trickle, he knew she was doomed. With her lifeblood pumping away, he held her head against his chest, while rocking her back and forth on his heels.

'Don't die, Em, please don't die!' he repeated, over and over.

Lifting his head and looking towards the ceiling he shouted, 'Why Emma, God? Why her? It was me the bastard wanted, so why didn't you let him take me instead?'

Despite his fury he already knew the answer. As a sacrifice, his life would not have been deemed worthy, but Emma... now that was different. The kind of person she'd been, and the fact she'd sacrificed herself willingly for him, said it all.

Kissing her gently on the forehead, he was alarmed to feel how damp and cold it was, and in that instant he knew with sickening finality she was slipping away from him. Grief-stricken, he gazed lovingly into her eyes, while every few seconds her body convulsed with shock. Tears streaming down his face, he said, 'Why did you do such a stupid thing, my love?'

Lifting a trembling hand, she reached up and traced the outline of his jaw, murmuring, 'It wasn't stupid, my darling, it was a symbol of my love for you. Believe me, if it meant saving your life, I would do it again without a moment's hesitation.'

Through a mist of anguish and tears, he replied, 'But I thought you hated me?'

'Hate you? How could you have ever thought that, you fool? I loved you from the moment I set eyes on you; for me, there's never been anyone else. You were my whole life.'

Clearly baffled, Jared said, 'But how can you say that when...?' He was too embarrassed to complete the sentence.

'You idiot, there was nothing to it! What you saw was me comforting a school friend. We had our arms around each other because he'd just told me he'd been diagnosed with leukaemia. The only kiss you saw was a compassionate peck on the cheek. A year later he was dead.'

'Dear God – and all this time I believed...' His voice trailed off.

Knowing she was fading fast, Emma gripped Jared's sleeve tightly with one hand, while with the other, she touched her fingers to his lips.

'Shush, my darling, let me talk while I still have a little strength.'

Gasping for breath, she suddenly said, 'Promise me one thing.'

'Anything, my love,' whispered Jared, 'anything.'

'Look after Jodie.' The she added with the faintest of smiles, 'After all, she is your daughter.'

Seeing the amazement on his face, she carried on, 'Don't look so surprised! I never even looked at another man, never mind slept with one.'

'But – but...' stammered Jared helplessly.

'Ah, my *husband*, you mean. There never was a husband, it was a little white lie to ensure the other kids wouldn't make fun of Jodie.' She went on, 'Sadly, it never worked. I know she's the image of me, but the eyes – did you never notice? – they're yours.'

'Of course I n-noticed her eyes... they're beautiful,' stammered Jared, 'but I thought they were a legacy of your husband. Oh, Christ, Em, if I could only put it into words! That night when I saw, or thought I saw... Well, from that day on I lost my reason to live. I became nothing but an empty shell. All those acts of bravery I performed while fighting for my country, they were a sham. What people never realised was that I wasn't being brave, I was hoping to die. I had nothing to live for, you see?'

'But you have now,' whispered Emma, 'and she loves you. She may be only six, but to use the words of her teachers, she's wise beyond her years. I knew something bad was going to happen tonight, so I told her everything about us. She knows you're her father, and believe me, it was worth telling her just to see her little eyes light up.'

Suddenly she began coughing. When she'd recovered somewhat, she tightened her grip on his sleeve, 'Promise me you'll look after her, and remember there was never anyone else but you.'

For a moment the light in her eyes burned fiercely, but even as he watched, it grew dim, until suddenly, within seconds it was extinguished altogether. With that her hand fluttered to her side and with one final shudder she was gone.

Respecting Jared's privacy, the others left them like that for what seemed an age. Eventually it was Danny who made the decision. Touching Jared gently on the shoulder, he said, 'Come on, lad, you'll have to let her go now, she's gone.'

'No, you don't understand, Danny, she's not dead – she's only sleeping,' said Jared. 'In a minute she'll wake up and everything will be all right. You just wait and see.'

Soaked in Emma's blood and rocking her gently in his arms, he was a pitiful sight. Danny was in no doubt he would never have let her go, but for the intervention of the doctor, who injected him with a strong sleeping draught. Eventually Gareth took charge of the unconscious figure, while Danny carried Emma's body from the chapel.

It was left to Tina to take care of the chalice.

Several hours later, Michael awoke in a hospital bed, completely unaware of the drama that had taken place earlier.

The following day a bulletin was issued by the doctor in charge. He stated that in some instances a traumatic experience such as the one Michael had undergone could cause long-term memory loss, before adding as an afterthought that under the circumstances it might be a blessing in disguise.

It was a wet and miserable day. The white mist threading its way through the cemetery looked remarkably like the bony fingers of some long-lost ghost. From the point of view of the villagers, their Emma deserved better. Jared was gratified to see that it seemed as if everyone in the village had turned up to pay their last respects.

Some time earlier, there had been a short service at Emma's parents' house, which Jared did not attend for the simple reason that he was afraid how they might react to his presence. In his mind, they probably blamed him for their daughter's death and, in all honesty, he couldn't disagree with that conclusion.

Hidden in the corner of the cemetery, his face masked by a huge willow tree, he watched as the coffin was brought up the steps from the main road. Although officially retired, old Eric conducted the service as he had with Edwin. Jared was pleased about that as he knew it would have been what Emma wanted.

After a few simple hymns and a short prayer, Eric summarised briefly what had been said in the privacy of Emma's own home earlier. Deeply moved, the old minister repeated just how special a person Emma had been. He emphasised the value of her life in the small community by explaining how she had touched the lives of everyone she had come across. Her departure from this world would leave a void that would never be filled. One thing was certain, he pointed out, she would never be forgotten. She would live on in the hearts and minds of everyone who had known her. In particular, of course, her parents and her little daughter Jodie, the true love of her life. Knowing Jared was nearby, he looked directly at him for the briefest of instants as he said the words, before beckoning the bearers over.

Jared was glad to see that the four bearers were Roger, Aled, Gareth and Danny as, once again, he knew it was what Emma would have wanted. At that point, his courage nearly failed him. Wanting so desperately to be able to show his love and devotion to the whole world, he knew how ironic it was that he, of all people, should be denied the privilege of laying Emma to rest.

As the coffin was lowered into the grave, Eric spoke the words of committal. 'We have entrusted our sister Emma to God's merciful keeping, and we commit her body to the ground. Earth to earth, ashes to ashes, dust to dust. In sure and certain hope of the resurrection to eternal life through our Lord Jesus Christ who died, was buried and rose again for us. To him be glory for ever and ever.'

As everyone moved towards the grave to pay their last respects, Jared was unable to move. Burdened by guilt, he stayed where he was until the cemetery was almost deserted. Only then did he feel able to make his way forward.

Glancing about him, he noticed how at this time of year, the leaves on the trees dotted around the graveyard had turned a rich golden yellow. He was admiring their beauty when suddenly, without warning, a cold wind swept down from the mountains, driving a wedge between the heavy curtains of water.

Turning his collar up against the pouring rain, Jared looked down at the fresh grave and studied its inscription. After a few moments of silent contemplation he lifted his head to the heavens.

'Well, Judas, you boasted that anger, hate and the likes were far more powerful emotions than love. That compared to them, love came a poor second. Although I was totally unworthy of her love, she made the ultimate sacrifice for me. And it worked, didn't it? So what do you believe now?'

With such thoughts coursing through his brain, he dropped his eyes to the tombstone once more. In black and gold letters the words jumped out at him.

EMMA STEVENS
BORN 13 MARCH 1981. TAKEN 27 OCTOBER 2006.

If there is another world please wait for us.

Lost in his own private grief, it took him a while to realise someone was tugging insistently at his sleeve.

Glancing down, he suddenly saw Jodie smiling up at him. Unsure of what to say, as he hadn't seen her since Emma's death, he was about to open his mouth when she beat him to it.

'Are you my daddy?'

Not waiting for an answer, she ploughed straight on. 'Mammy says you are, and she told me to tell you she loved you very much.'

Picking her up in his arms, he hugged her tightly to his chest.

Suddenly, the tears he'd been fighting against for the last few hours flooded out, and once they started he couldn't stop them. Like a water-fall they cascaded over the golden curls of the little girl he was holding in his arms – his little girl!

Lifting her from his chest, he looked into her eyes and said, 'Yes, Jodie I'm your father, and like your mother, I love you very much.'

'I know that, silly,' she giggled, 'she told me! I knew anyway, though, I can tell these things, you see.'

Looking at her curiously, Jared said, 'When did your mother say that?'

'Just now when she spoke to me,' Jodie replied, pointing to the grave and saying, 'look, there she is now.'

Following the direction of her tiny finger, he suddenly noticed a shimmering ball of white light hovering over the freshly dug mound of earth. It was only visible for a second before it disappeared.

Blinking back his astonishment, he looked again convinced he'd made a mistake.

Clapping her hands in glee, she said, 'There, you saw it too, didn't you, Daddy? Oh, and she said to tell you the words are true, the ones on the marble headstone. There is another world, and when our time comes, she'll be there waiting for us.'

With that she buried her head into his neck and hugged him fiercely.

Fighting back another bout of tears, one which threatened to over-power him completely, Jared caressed the back of his daughter's neck, while at the same time trying to untangle the mass of golden curls which had become trapped at the back of her tiny raincoat.

It was then he saw it: the outline of the coiled red serpent was unmistakable!

Printed in the United Kingdom
by Lightning Source UK Ltd.
132563UK00002BA/101/P